From Cobb to "Catfish"

128 Illustrated Stories from *Baseball Digest*

From Cobb to "Catfish"

128 Illustrated Stories from *Baseball Digest*

edited by John Kuenster

foreword by Joe Garagiola

Rand McNally & Company
Chicago • New York • San Francisco

Permissions and Photo Credits

"Goslin vs. Manush: Face to Face for the Bat Title" by Heinie Manush, as told to John P. Carmichael; "The First Baseman Who Outpitched Walter Johnson" by George Sisler, as told to Lyall Smith; "My Greatest Thrill as a Player" by Casey Stengel, as told to John P. Carmichael; "They'll Never Forget Dizzy Dean" by John P. Carmichael; "How an .095 Hitter Won the 1924 World Series" by Muddy Ruel, as told to Lloyd Lewis; "The Day I Fanned Lajoie" by Ed Walsh, as told to Francis J. Powers; "You Could Catch Matty Sittin' in a Chair" by Roger Bresnahan, as told to John P. Carmichael; and "Ron Santo's 12-Year Secret" by Armand Schneider, reprinted with permission of the *Chicago Daily News.*

"The Humor of Casey Stengel" by Maury Allen, © 1970; "Roy Campanella Recalls Branch Rickey and the Dodgers" by Milton Gross, © 1969; and "The Night Tommie Agee Ruined the Cubs' Pennant Hopes" by Larry Merchant, © 1963, reprinted with permission of the *New York Post,* New York Post Corporation.

"Rogers Hornsby's Five Fabulous Years" condensed from *Baseball's Greatest Hitters* by Tom Meany, published by A. S. Barnes & Company, Inc.

"Connie Mack: First Citizen of Philadelphia" by John R. Tunis, reprinted with permission of the Atlantic Monthly Company, Boston, Mass., © 1943, R 1971.

"Baseball in Paris, 1918" by Heywood Broun, reprinted from *The A.E.F., with General Pershing and the American Forces,* published by D. Appleton & Co., 1918; Harcourt, Brace & Co., 1941.

"Mental Blunders Are Part of the Game" by Edward Prell, condensed from the *Chicago Tribune Magazine.*

"Baseball's Best Batters" by Billy Evans, reprinted with permission of *Esquire Magazine,* © 1942 by Esquire, Inc.

PHOTO CREDITS: *Baltimore News American,* 34; Clifton Boutelle, 33 (right), 35 (top), 42 (left), 43 (left); George Brace, 26 (center), 28 (center), 60, 95 (right), 102, 103, 107, 114 (center), 160, 166, 213 (right), 214, 215 (left), 225 (center), 251, 265 (left), 268, 269, 283; Frank Bryan, 15 (bottom), 57, 74, 80, 139 (bottom), 193 (bottom), 194 (right), 211 (top); Central Press Association, 177 (bottom); *Chicago Daily News,* 95 (left); *Chicago Sun-Times,* 123 (right), 127 (left); *Cincinnati Enquirer,* 164; *Cleveland Plain Dealer,* 233; Culver Pictures, 87, 185; Ray De Aragon, 16, 97, 285; James De Pree, 194 (top), 211 (bottom), 258 (bottom); Dorrill Photocolor, 150, 227; Michael Grossbardt, 287; Hall of Fame, 67, 75, 86, 88, 90, 98, 105, 116, 117, 147, 162, 169, 177 (top), 190, 217, 218; Ronald L. Mrowiec, 25, 33 (left), 62, 137, 138, 139 (top), 156, 210 (right), 246; *New York Post,* 230 (top); National Broadcasting Co., 132; *Philadelphia Bulletin,* 277; Louis Requena, 21 (top); James Roark, 21 (bottom); Jim Rowe, 28 (right), 36, 50 (top and left), 72, 101 (top), 108, 121, 128, 142, 215 (right), 225 (right), 276; Carl Skalak, Jr., 15 (top), 43 (right), 148; Paul Tepley, 35 (bottom); United Press International, 26 (left), 127 (right), 235; Wide World Photos, 22, 23, 24, 30, 31 (top), 37, 41, 42 (right), 52, 81, 84, 91, 92, 101 (bottom), 106, 112, 122, 123 (left), 165 (bottom), 173, 193 (top), 194 (bottom), 241, 242 (bottom), 244, 248

This book was prepared with the cooperation of the Century Publishing Company and Norman Jacobs, publisher of *Baseball Digest.*

Library of Congress Cataloging in Publication Data
Main entry under title:

From Cobb to "Catfish".

1. Baseball stories. I. Kuenster, John.
II. Baseball digest.
GV873.F73   796.357   75-15828
ISBN 0-528-81017-0

Preface

Baseball, for the vast majority of adult loyalists, might be described as a state of mind, a subjective condition in which certain players and certain games are frozen in time.

These players and these games have left an indelible imprint on the mind's eye of millions of fans who saw them firsthand, in many instances, during an age of impressionable youth.

Once witnessed in person who can forget:

The boyish exuberance and majestic swing of Babe Ruth?

The unorthodox, high kick by little Mel Ott as he batted?

The gracefulness of Joe DiMaggio running, throwing, and hitting the ball?

The volatile aggressiveness of Jackie Robinson on the base paths?

The shrill chatter of Nellie Fox in the infield?

The proud, regal mannerisms of Roberto Clemente?

And how could any observer fail to remember the setting in detail when:

Bobby Thomson hit his pennant-winning homer in 1951?

Willie Mays made his unbelievable catch in the 1954 World Series?

Bill Mazeroski won it all for the Pirates in 1960 with his shot over the left-field wall at old Forbes Field?

Henry Aaron broke Ruth's record with his 715th home run in 1974?

These are memories to be stored, to be passed on to another generation in another day.

And, in this sense, baseball remains timeless, enduring in its appeal to those who appreciate its simplicity and beauty and look upon it as a reminder, perhaps, of one of life's happier, more carefree interludes.

Nostalgia for the game will always be with us, and there is nothing wrong with that. A certain amount of reverence for the past is good, for what we have today is the product of many yesterdays.

Over the last three decades and more, *Baseball Digest,* founded in 1942 by Herb Simons, has captured in print the drama and vitality and humor and, yes, the seemingly endless trivia of the game.

With such a divergent array of subject material available, one of the most difficult tasks in pulling together this compendium of baseball was to pick and choose the articles to be used.

In the beginning, 761 titles were culled from the 34 volumes of *Baseball Digest,* dating back to August, 1942. And from these qualifiers were distilled the 128 articles reprinted in this book. Many of these appeared originally in *Baseball Digest.* Others were condensed and reprinted from various magazines, newspapers, and books.

Together, they provide a rich slice of Americana and offer a selective insight into the game as it was in the days of John McGraw and Ty Cobb and as it is in the days of Lou Brock and Catfish Hunter, making this a rather unique baseball treasury.

The purpose of this book is not to blanket the entire history of the game from the moment of its organized inception to the present. Rather, the purpose is to touch upon some of the highlights of that history and upon the great, near-great, and even obscure players who helped write it.

Our hope is that some of your favorite baseball memories will be rekindled as you read on.

JOHN KUENSTER / *Editor*

Contents

Foreword

I envy you the hours of pleasure that lie ahead as you begin reading this book. The title, *From Cobb to "Catfish," 128 Illustrated Stories from Baseball Digest,* promises a lot. And when I looked over the Table of Contents, I realized that these had to be the best stories from *Baseball Digest.*

As I read the list of titles, I found myself being snowed under with memories. There's a story here about Stan Musial getting his 3,000th hit. I remember that hit. I was in the ball park that day. But I remember Musial long before that, when he was a young outfielder on the Springfield, Missouri, farm club of the Cardinals. I was on that club, too. I was an assistant groundkeeper and clubhouse helper. I started out in baseball washing Stan Musial's socks.

There is also a story about Ted Williams. I remember very well the first time I stood next to Williams. It was in the 1946 World Series. I was catching for the Cardinals, and Williams came to bat for the Red Sox. I didn't know whether to give a sign to the pitcher or to ask Williams for his autograph. [Joe is too modest to mention that he hit .316 in the 1946 Series and Ted Williams hit .200. Ted gave his loser's share, $2,410, to the bat boy.]

What I like about the book is that it's not just about the superstars. There's a story, for example, about Dusty Rhodes. I finished the 1954 season with the New York Giants, and that was the year that Dusty made pinch-hitting look so easy. He had a super year, and an even better World Series. But my fondest memory is of Dusty playing right field one day and having a little trouble with a couple of flyballs. He called time and jogged in toward the dugout. Durocher hollered at him, "Do you want your sunglasses?" Rhodes hollered back, "No. I want my helmet."

Speaking of Durocher, there is an article about how the legend of Durocher saying, "Nice guys finish last" started. I won't spoil it for you but it all began when Leo was interviewed by the late Frank Graham, who was an outstanding writer and a very nice man.

Once, he was writing a column about a guy who had been kind of surly with everybody during most of his career, but started to be more pleasant as he was finishing up. Frank Graham summed him up by writing, "He learned to say hello, when it was time to say good-bye."

There are stories about ball parks that aren't around any more. I did a show about that on my TV series, *The Baseball World of Joe Garagiola.* I know these articles will prompt a reaction from a lot of people, because my show did. My mail proved that everybody has his own memory of his favorite park, his own reason for believing there could never be another like it.

The Table of Contents lists an article called "A Chat with Cy Young." It made me think of a friend of mine who sat next to Mr. Young at a Little League luncheon in Williamsport, Pennsylvania, about 20 years ago. One of the speakers mentioned the late Connie Mack, and his name brought applause. Cy Young turned to my friend and said, "Fair catcher, but not much of a hitter." My friend never got over it. He and I used to laugh about it, because we always figured, I guess, that Connie Mack was born 70 years old. And yes, there's a story about Connie Mack also.

There are stories about guts, too. The guts of a Jackie Robinson breaking a color barrier, and the guts of a Rip Sewell, who wouldn't quit no matter what the doctors did. In a personal way, their stories are special to me. One of my first meetings with Robinson wound up in a big argument over a call by Beans Reardon. Sewell once knocked me down with a pitch, and when I bunted for revenge, he hit me a rolling block I can still feel. Yet, I would sum up the two relationships by saying that I am proud, really proud, that both of them became my friends.

In this book you'll find winning streaks, .400 hitters, and the strategies of "inside" baseball. That's as it should be. But you'll also find slumps, and .220 hitters, and bonehead plays. That's as it should be, too.

One of the things that I feel strongly about regarding baseball is that it is, after all, fun. That doesn't mean it doesn't have its serious moments, and even its tragedies. But, by and large, it's a game, and games are supposed to bring people fun.

I know that as you leaf through this book you'll find evidence of that fun, and reading it will guarantee a lot of happy moments.

JOE GARAGIOLA

From Cobb to "Catfish"

128 Illustrated Stories from *Baseball Digest*

Editor's Note

Unless otherwise identified with a credit line, the articles in this anthology appeared originally in *Baseball Digest,* over a span of more than 30 years. The month and year in which they were published in *Baseball Digest* are printed in boldface type at the start of each story.

No attempt was made to update the articles. In most instances, this was unnecessary, since many of them describe incidents and personalities of a bygone era or were written as recently as 1975.

Up-to-date statistics, individual records, and other achievements have been included in the picture captions or added in an Editor's Note.

The Mad, Mad World of the A's

by John Kuenster

November, 1974

When baseball historians get around to summing up the strange goings-on of the Oakland A's during the 1974 season, the chronicle will probably read like something lifted from the script of *"It's A Mad, Mad, Mad, Mad World."*

In chasing after their third straight American League pennant, the A's reminded some critics of the money-crazed mob in that Hollywood flick.

The bickering began early in the season when manager Alvin Dark was learning what type of personnel he had inherited from Dick Williams.

The players he inherited were talented and spirited and had no qualms about speaking their minds. They had liked Dick Williams; they reserved judgment about Dark . . . temporarily.

Early in June after the A's lost an 11-inning game to the Red Sox, Sal Bando (who went 0-for-4 at the plate) marched into the clubhouse and angrily kicked a plastic trash can. In mid-kick, he verbally chastised Dark.

"He couldn't manage a ————— meat market!" exclaimed Bando.

Bando didn't know it at the time, but Dark was standing right behind him and overheard his remark. Dark summoned Bando to the manager's office, and a few minutes later Bando emerged, obviously embarrassed.

"I told Alvin I didn't mean it personally," he said. "I was mad because I made the last out on a good pitch to hit. It was just a fit of anger.

"Oh, well, at least I took some of the heat off North and Jackson."

The last remark was in reference to a previous, well-publicized fight between Reggie Jackson and Bill North that took place in Detroit.

In that set-to, North said something to Jackson, Jackson shouted back, and in no time the two were at each other. Catcher Ray Fosse tried to be the peacemaker and wound up with a separated cervical disk trying to hold Jackson off. Fosse later went on the disabled list.

There was a brief intermission, and Jackson and North began fighting again, this time Gene Ten-

ace and Bando pulling them apart. In the second round, Jackson fell on his right shoulder and bruised it.

When owner Charlie Finley got word of the fight, he blew his top and joined the A's in their next stop in Milwaukee, where he blasted the players in an angry clubhouse speech.

"You're world champions," he told them. "Stop acting like a bunch of kids!"

"Being on this club," reliever Rollie Fingers said later, "is like having a ringside seat for the Muhammad Ali-Joe Frazier fight."

As the season progressed, there were further fireworks in store for the A's. Third-base coach Irv Noren, who had waved home the winning runs in

Bill North

Rollie Fingers

Reggie Jackson, with little regard for decorum, douses Commissioner Bowie Kuhn with champagne as the A's celebrate their 1974 World Series victory over the Dodgers. Tony Kubek (with mike on the left) describes the proceedings, while Sal Bando (right, foreground) joins in the hilarity.

Sal Bando soars over the head of catcher Ray Fosse (No. 10) as the A's join in the traditional on-field jubilation after winning the final game of the 1974 World Series. The A's put down the Dodgers in five games to capture their third straight world championship. Four of the five games were decided by one-run margins.

two straight World Series for Oakland, was fired. So was bullpen coach Vern Hoscheit.

"If they told me that half the team had been traded—Reggie Jackson, Joe Rudi, Sal Bando, Billy North—to Mexico, I'd believe them," said pitcher Catfish Hunter. "Nothing on this club surprises me anymore." Hunter himself, accusing Finley of reneging on his contract, announced he would bring his case before an arbitration board at the end of the season and would seek to become a free agent.

The bickering and sniping continued. Sprinter Herb Washington, who had been hired by Finley this season exclusively as a pinch-runner, was the target of one griper. "Charlie [Finley] said Herb Washington would win 10 games for us," the player cracked. "He'd better win 13 between now and the end of the season because he's already minus four," an obvious reference to Washington's then mediocre record on the base paths.

Dark also fined pitchers Ken Holtzman and Vida Blue $250 for tossing the ball in the air in disgust when Dark came out to replace them with relievers.

Both Holtzman and Blue had complained earlier about Dark lifting them too soon from games.

At this juncture, Dark decided he had turned the other cheek long enough. He was ready to lower the boom. Dark called a clubhouse meeting. He laid down the law to every man on the team, with special emphasis on his pitchers. He notified Holtzman and Blue of their fines and warned them that a second offense would bring a $500 fine.

Blue was still angry about being lifted sooner than he thought he should have, but admitted he deserved the fine because he accidentally hit Dark when he tossed the ball toward him as the manager crossed the baseline on his way to the mound.

"I didn't mean to hit him," said Blue, "so I paid my fine promptly the next day."

Blue couldn't resist the opportunity to express his "don't put me down" attitude when he paid his fine.

16

Gene Tenace (left), Sal Bando, and Catfish Hunter express the uninhibited attitude of the A's as they "ham it up" in the shower room after Oakland beat the New York Mets, 2-1, in the opener of the 1973 World Series.

"I dumped $250 in pennies, nickels, dimes, and quarters on Dark's desk," he grinned. "I wanted to make it all pennies, but they're hard to come by."

These are only a few of the incidents that have been woven into the A's story this season, but they reflect the defiant spirit that bubbles beneath the surface of the team.

Until 1975 events determine otherwise, the A's are still champions of the baseball world. They reached that status through some shrewd moves by a man who can be pretty obstinate and cantankerous in his own way, Charles O. Finley.

And while we're on the subject of the A's, we think more recognition for their success should be given to shortstop Bert Campaneris and left fielder (sometimes first baseman) Joe Rudi.

Campaneris has received little attention in the press maybe because he isn't as articulate as Jackson or Bando. But he has had flashes of spirit, too— like his bat-throwing incident in the 1972 playoffs.

Rudi seems to be the forgotten man in the disturbances that have a habit of erupting in the A's clubhouse.

"He's the best left fielder in the American League," says Jackson.

"You don't win a pennant without a guy like that," says Bando. "You need me and Jackson to drive in runs. You need a guy like Catfish Hunter to pitch.

"But you need a guy to drive in runs, get on base, and do some of the big and little things before the big guys get up there. Joe not only makes the great plays in left, but he makes the routine plays consistently, too."

And what does the underrated Rudi say?

"I think when I do something I get the ink," he comments. "I get more ink about not getting any ink than about what I do."

Well, it takes all kinds to make up the A's family.

And what ever happened to Mike Andrews?

Sandy Koufax: Player of the Decade

by Jim Perry
Los Angeles Herald-Examiner

Koufax beat the Cubs, 1-0, in 1965 without allowing a runner to reach base, his fourth no-hitter. Until Nolan Ryan came along, no other pitcher in major league history accomplished this feat. In addition to his perfect game against the Cubs, Koufax pitched no-hitters against the Phillies (3-0) in 1964, the Giants (8-0) in 1963, and the Mets (5-0) in 1962.

May, 1970

When Sandy Koufax was throwing a baseball for a living, a frustrated batter looked out at the mound in agony and moaned:

"Against that guy we should all get four strikes."

Most players, however, settled for three, which Sandy blew right by them with all the ease of a boy skimming rocks.

Unfortunately, arthritis knocked him off the mound at age 30, and Sandy never got to close out the Swinging Sixties.

It didn't matter. A special Associated Press poll rejected Mickey Mantle, Willie Mays, and Henry Aaron and chose Sandy Koufax as Baseball's Athlete of the Decade.

Sandy admitted surprise over his selection.

"I'm not being modest," he said, "but I never had 10 good years in the decade. I had about five. A lot of people had 10 good ones."

Sandy's arithmetic is a little off. He had six strong seasons. From 1961 through his final year, 1966, the lean left-hander won 129 games and lost only 47 and ruled baseball with a fastball, curve, and a change-up.

The only thing that bothered him consistently was the pain in his throwing elbow and the lack of hitting support of his Dodger teammates.

"He comes closer to being unhittable than any other pitcher I ever saw," said Frank J. Shaughnessy, the late president of the International League. And Frank J. watched Christy Mathewson, Grover Cleveland Alexander, and Walter Johnson.

"This award was a very big one," Sandy said. "But there were so many great players in the decade, it had to be hard to single out one.

"I might have chosen Mays or maybe Mantle or Aaron. I'm still surprised I got it, because I haven't pitched since 1966."

The records he compiled in his 12 seasons with the Dodgers, however, reach out and grab you. Most of those were inscribed in the 1960s. The writers and sportscasters who voted in the AP poll were aware that Koufax:

Koufax warms up for his final major league appearance, the second game of the 1966 World Series which he lost to the Baltimore Orioles and Jim Palmer, 6-0. Plagued with an arthritic elbow, Sandy retired after the 1966 season at age 30. He was elected to the Hall of Fame in 1972.

—Pitched four no-hitters, more than anyone else. One was a perfect game.

—Led the National League in earned run average for five straight years (1962–66) and compiled a startling lifetime ERA of 2.76.

—Struck out 382 batters, a major league record, in 1965.

—Won the Cy Young Award three times and the Most Valuable Player Award once.

—Averaged more than one strike-out per inning, a feat never approached by any other pitcher.

—And won 27 games his last year, a modern National League record for a left-hander.

"It's hard to single out the highlights," Sandy said, "because big years are more important than single big moments. Consistency is the main thing.

"That's why I'm most proud of the great seasons, 1963, 1965, and 1966. [Sandy was 25-5, 26-8, 27-9.]

"But there are some moments that stand out in my mind.

"The perfect game against the Cubs might be the biggest, but I'll never forget my victory in the seventh game of the 1965 World Series [2-0 against Minnesota] and that win over the Yankees in New York to start the 1963 Series."

In the latter game, Koufax beat Whitey Ford, 5-2, and struck out 15 Yankees—a new Series record. New York didn't do much better two games later, when Koufax beat Ford again, 2-1, to complete a four-game sweep that stunned baseball.

"You know, I never won 30 games in a year," Sandy said, "but that doesn't gnaw at me at all. To do it, you have to be terribly good and terribly lucky.

"But you have to get the decisions, too, and if you don't get a lot of runs, you won't. Thirty is just a number. Heck, I would have liked to win 40, or all of them for that matter."

Detroit's Denny McLain, who did win 31—in 1968—finished fifth in the AP poll. Koufax in first had 225½ votes, Mantle had 154½, Mays had 106½, and Aaron was fourth with 51½.

The rest of the top ten behind McLain included Roger Maris, Frank Robinson, Ernie Banks, Roberto Clemente, and Bob Gibson.

"As the years go by, I miss baseball less," said Koufax, "but I still get the urge to pitch when spring training comes around. Or when the pennant race goes into the last week.

"But you have to face the fact that everything ends."

In 1971, Koufax was reunited with two other Dodger pitchers who earned the coveted Cy Young Award, presented annually for pitching excellence. Don Drysdale (left) won the award in 1962; Don Newcombe, in 1956. Koufax was a three-time winner of the award—in 1963, 1965, and 1966.

A Chat with Cy Young

by Burton Hawkins

Condensed from the *Washington Evening Star*

October, 1943

The 76-year-old gray-haired man puffed contentedly on an ancient, battered pipe behind the Indians' dugout in Cleveland's League Park and said softly, "I haven't kept in close touch with baseball for the last 30 years, but once or twice a year I come up from Paoli to see Cleveland play. I pitched the second game ever played in this park. It was back in 1891, and in those days you wouldn't see three home runs a year here. Shucks, they've taken too much away from the pitchers with the lively ball they're using now."

The fellow doing the talking could speak with authority on pitching. Most veteran baseball fans would rank him among the three best pitchers of all time. As a major league pitcher he won 511 games, and that record probably never will be approached. He pitched three no-hit games, one of them a perfect performance in which no man reached base. His name is Denton (Cy) Young.

"I guess the reason I was good was because I had great control and a lot of good stuff on the ball. Hans Wagner said I had two great curveballs, and he was right—one of them didn't break as wide as the other. I had a fine fastball, too, but the secret of my pitching success was being able to get all that stuff over the plate. I could throw anything with a count of three-and-two on the batter and be reasonably certain of pitching a strike.

"Bob Feller is the best pitcher I've seen among the modern boys. He was crude when he started because he had a hitch in his delivery, but he overcame that. I don't want to sound like I'm bragging about myself, but Feller wasn't as fast as Walter Johnson or myself.

"I can't talk with much authority about modern players, though, because I haven't seen too much of them. I retired 30 years ago and I haven't seen a lot of baseball since. I just like to stay down on the farm at Paoli about 100 miles from here and work just like when I was a kid there.

"I'm still in good shape. Last summer I got out on the mound here and pitched to a batter in practice. Right now I could get out there and get the ball over, but it wouldn't have anything on it.

"I still have a little money left, but it's running out. Guess I'm living too long. Some of my best

Elected to the Hall of Fame in 1937, Cy Young once claimed he was the greatest pitcher in the history of the game. And his records indicate he wasn't far off target. He pitched in 960 games, a total of 7,277 innings, and posted 511 victories, a record untouched since his retirement in 1911. Young pitched three no-hitters during his career and five times won 30 or more games in a single season. The baseball fraternity considered his achievements worthy enough to name the coveted pitcher trophy after him—the Cy Young Award.

years I never made more than $2,400—that was the salary limit then—but I'm not complaining. I saved enough to retire on, and I guess some of the modern boys don't handle their money that well.

"What kind of a pitcher was Clark Griffith? Well, he was what I'd have to call a dinky-dinky pitcher. He didn't have anything but he had a lot of nothing, if you get what I mean. He was smart, though, and he was good at mixing 'em up. I pitched against him many times.

"I pitched 874 major league games in 22 years, and I never had a sore arm until the day I quit. My arm went bad in 1912 when I was in spring training, and I guess it was about time. I was 45 years old then. I never had a trainer rub my arm the whole time I was in baseball.

"That doesn't mean pitchers make a mistake now by having their arms rubbed. The explanation in my case was that a good arm hung from my shoulder, and in my early years in the game we didn't even have trainers.

"I pitched every third day, and I remember one Eastern trip we took in which we played 18 games and I pitched every other day. The biggest thrill I ever got out of baseball was pitching that perfect game against Rube Waddell, but I never realized what a nice game I had pitched until it was over. The fellows on the bench never said anything about it when we got into the late innings, and I just never realized nobody had gotten on base. Another game I like to remember was when I pitched 20 innings against the Red Sox and didn't walk a man.

"Cobb was the greatest batter I ever pitched to. Wagner was great, too, but Cobb did a better job of outguessing the pitchers. On my all-time team I'd put Cobb, Tris Speaker, and Babe Ruth in the outfield, Pop Anson at first base, Nap Lajoie at second, Wagner at shortstop, Jimmy Collins at third, Roger Bresnahan behind the plate, and pitching would be Johnson, Waddell, Alexander, Walsh, and myself."

Young is one of the more famed members of baseball's Hall of Fame. Fifteen times he won 20 or more games a season, five times passing the 30-victory mark. After winning 21 games for the Boston Red Sox in 1908, he was sold to Cleveland for a mere $12,500, but he wasn't washed up. He won 19 games for the Indians in 1909 when he was 42 years old.

Not more than a dozen fans knew Young was on the premises as they thrilled to a pitchers' battle, but that 76-year-old `farmer in the first-base field box didn't mind the lack of attention. Cy wouldn't have wanted much attention. He had his day in baseball, and his record says he did all right. He's a happy old man, with many fond memories.

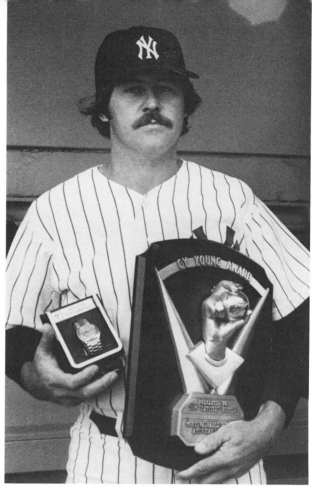

The Yankees' Catfish Hunter holds the American League's 1974 Cy Young Award he won as a member of the Oakland A's. The watch was presented to Hunter by *The Sporting News,* honoring him as the American League Pitcher of the Year; Mike Marshall was the National League winner.

Mike Marshall of the Dodgers appeared in a record-breaking 106 games as a reliever in 1974, a feat that earned him the Cy Young Award in the National League.

When Hank Aaron Was Put on "Hold"

by Frank Dolson
Philadelphia Inquirer

March, 1974

There were lines at the ticket windows. Big, long lines. And the Falcons weren't even playing. Finally, Atlanta had discovered Henry Aaron.

The date was Sunday, September 30, 1973, final day of the regular National League season, a day for history to be made; a day for 40,517 people to show up at Atlanta Stadium for a game that meant absolutely nothing between two baseball teams that were going absolutely nowhere. Except home for the winter.

Up north in the Bronx, they were closing down Yankee Stadium, the House That Ruth Built. Down in Atlanta, they were getting ready to wipe out one of the Babe's greatest records.

"The Countdown Is One; Tickets On Sale," glowed the message board outside the stadium.

What a storybook finish. On the next-to-last night of the season Aaron had rocketed No. 713. Now, on the final day, he was going for No. 714. The magic number. The Babe's number.

This was history in the making. A nation of hero-worshipers held its breath, waiting for the bulletin from the Deep South.

FLASH: Aaron hits No. 714.

Even in the Houston Astros' clubhouse, they were waiting.

Dave Roberts didn't arrive with the first wave of Astros on Sunday, which gave one of his fun-loving teammates a chance to cut the left-hander's picture out of an Atlanta paper and stick it on his locker with these words:

"Thanks for numbers 586, 599, 618, 655, 712, 714, and 715. [Signed] Hank."

Somebody tore it down by the time Roberts showed up, and maybe that was just as well. As the sacrificial lamb chosen to pitch to Henry Aaron on this day of days, chances are he wouldn't have laughed.

Sure, Babe Ruth had his Tom Zachary. Roger Maris had his Tracy Stallard. But Henry Aaron wasn't going to have his Dave Roberts. Not if the one-time Phillie farmhand could help it.

Connecting on a low pitch, Aaron delivers his 713th career homer in a game at Atlanta against the Houston Astros on September 29, 1973. Jerry Reuss was the pitcher who was victimized. The homer left Hank one short of equaling Babe Ruth's lifetime record of 714.

He had given up five homers to Aaron. He would probably give up some more before he was through. But not No. 714. "I'd rather be nobody in baseball than go down as an immortal because I served up one of the big ones," Roberts had said.

And besides, he didn't feel like giving those laugh-a-minute teammates of his a chance to have fun at his expense.

"Everybody's kidding me," Dave said. "They tell me, 'You'll be famous. You'll make the banquet tour all winter. You'll get fat by serving a fat pitch . . .'" The left-hander grimaced. There are better ways to get famous.

Still, the pranksters wouldn't let up. Maybe the phony message from Aaron had been removed from his locker, but so had the number on top of it. Instead of 15, Roberts' uniform number, some clown had changed it to 714. Ha! Ha! Get it, Dave? Pretty subtle fellas, those Astros.

No wonder Roberts wasn't in a particularly talkative mood when he entered the Astros' clubhouse less than an hour before game time and saw the crowd of writers waiting for him. Shaking his head, he turned and walked in the opposite direction, but that was only a temporary salvation. He had to put on his uniform sooner or later. Bowie Kuhn would never have stood for having the man who served up

Aaron awaits his final turn at bat in the last game of the 1973 season. In the eighth inning, with Houston's Don Wilson on the mound, Aaron bloops a weak pop fly that ended his chance of tying Ruth's mark, and he throws his bat away in disgust over his failure to "get good wood" on the ball.

No. 714 doing so in his street clothes. Trapped, Dave finally walked toward his locker, saw the big, red 714 above it for the first time, took it down as quickly as he could, and turned to face his tormentors.

"Talk to Cecil [Upshaw]," he said in a loud voice. "Talk to [Jerry] Reuss . . ."

That was the signal for manager Leo Durocher to rush to the rescue. "All you men who want to talk to my man, talk to him after the game," the Astros' manager shouted. "Not now."

There was silence for several seconds. Reuss, who served up No. 713 Saturday night broke it. "How ya doin', Dave?" he asked as he sauntered past the condemned man's locker, and then he laughed.

"I've got one question," Roberts bellowed, unable to keep still any longer. "How's Hank taking this?"

Beautifully, thank you, Dave. Just beautifully. He had been nervous the night before, but for some strange reason Aaron felt fine Sunday, as relaxed as a man could be under such difficult circumstances. If he got it, he got it. If he didn't—well, there *would* be a next year.

The people who had come to see No. 714 stood and cheered the first time he approached the plate. They were ready. So was Houston right-hander Don Wilson.

Wilson had a glove in one hand, a bat in the other as he left the right-field bullpen and took up his position in center field, behind the low fence.

"If a home run came over, I was going to catch it," Wilson explained. "That 714 would be a valuable baseball. Last night I just missed getting 713. I got to talking to [Jimmy] Wynn, and I didn't quite get back to my position in time." He snickered. "I'd like to say, 'I got 714.'"

And the bat? What in the world was that for?

Simple, to hear Wilson tell it. He planned to use it to knock down the ball, in the event it was just out of reach. "Like a lacrosse stick," he said.

Roberts, the party-pooper, had other ideas. Standing on the mound, he waved toward center field, telling Wilson to get back where he belonged.

"I was trying to collect myself, get my composure," Dave said. "I didn't want to make a stupid mistake. If he did hit it out the first time, I wanted to know he hit my best pitch. . . Waving Don Wilson back like that, that kinda relaxed me."

Maybe so, but if Aaron got one pitch all day that

23

was suitable for immortality it was Roberts' first one.

"He used reverse psychology," Henry would say later. "I was expecting a change-up. He threw a fastball right down the middle. . ."

"A slider," Roberts said. But whatever it was, Aaron took it. Two pitches later, he chopped the ball down the third-base line—and beat it out. Big deal. The crowd had come to see homers, not singles.

Next time up, as a quartet played "For He's a Jolly Good Fellow" and the people stood and clapped once more, Henry looped a soft single to center. Now he was 2-for-2 and batting .300, a fantastic achievement for a 39-year-old man who was in the low .200s at mid-season. No matter. To all those fans and writers and photographers, Aaron was 0-for-2.

His third chance came in the sixth inning as rain began to fall and lightning flashed in the distance. On the big board in center it said, "The Hammer's Got the Babe's Number. . ." Not this trip, he didn't. He ripped a one-and-two pitch through the middle for a clean single. Now—as far as the spectators were concerned—he was 0-for-3.

One more chance. Ironically, it would come against that funny man in the right-field bullpen, Don Wilson. The sky was darker now, the lightning closer, the rain harder.

Darrell Evans fanned for the second out of the eighth inning and Aaron, who had been kneeling in the on-deck circle, stood up and began his last walk to the plate of 1973. Horns blew, the applause grew. Overhead, thunder roared. As he had on Henry's previous three appearances, second-base umpire Lee Weyer took up a position in left-center field, more than 200 feet away from the plate. Just in case.

Wilson, a hard thrower, unleashed the first pitch. Aaron swung. . .

The ball hit the handle of his bat and blooped in the air near second base, the weakest, softest-looking pop fly you ever saw. "The pitch was over the inside part of the plate," Wilson said. "He dove out after the ball. I didn't jam him. He jammed himself."

Rain poured down on Henry Aaron as he trotted to left field for the ninth inning. And with the rain came applause. Loud applause. Prolonged applause. "It was great," said the man who will be searching for home run No. 714 at the start of the 1974 season.

Durocher used the same word. "A great day," he called it. "An exciting day. I admire my two pitchers for not walking him. . ."

Did Leo mean that he would have pitched to Aaron under any circumstances in this meaningless game?

"If there's two outs and let's say the score's 2-1, my favor, and first base is open, that's where Mr. Aaron goes," Durocher retorted. "They may boo the bleep out of me. They may have tarred and feathered me. I don't give a damn. He's not going to beat me. . ."

Leo lowered his voice and smiled. "I'm glad that didn't happen," he said. "I'm glad they pitched to him. He's the best right-handed hitter I've ever looked at—outside of Hornsby. Listen, there's no question he's going to break the record. It's just a question of how many he's going to break it by."

In the meantime, the countdown is at one and "holding." In April this hero-worshiping nation will start holding its breath again, waiting for the day, the pitch. . .

His long pursuit of Ruth's record ended swiftly for Aaron in 1974. On his first swing of the new season, he hit his 714th homer over the left-field fence in Cincinnati on April 4. Then, on April 8 at Atlanta, he slammed a fastball by the Dodgers' Al Downing over the left center-field fence for his 715th homer, surpassing Ruth's long-standing mark. His teammates greet him at home plate after he hit the record-breaker.

Don Wilson:
The End Came Too Soon

by Bill Christine
Pittsburgh Post-Gazette

April, 1975

When word came last January that Houston pitcher Don Wilson had been found dead, the victim of carbon monoxide poisoning, the immediate thought wasn't of the right-hander's no-hit games or of his periodic strike-out binges, but of a dugout scene at Forbes Field a few years ago.

The night before, there had been a marginal decision required of the official scorer on some ball struck by a Houston batter, and the call was an error instead of a hit.

When the scorer appeared the next day, it seemed as though the entire Astro ball club was prepared to have him for its pre-game meal. Harry Walker, then the Houston manager, and at least a dozen players harangued the scorer about his poor judgment.

One of the most vitriolic of the Astros was Jim Owens, the one-time big league right-hander who was then Houston's pitching coach.

Wilson hadn't even been pitching in the game, but he felt a responsibility to interrupt the argument. "Hey, Jim," Wilson said. "I happen to think the guy made the right call. Lay off him, will ya? Those guys in the press box have got a tough job. It doesn't make it any easier if we get all over them every time we think they've missed one."

The scorer, who didn't know Wilson that well, was startled that the pitcher would come to his defense—particularly when Wilson was contradicting Owens, his own pitching coach.

When the story was told to a man from Houston, he said: "That sounds just like Don Wilson. A guy with a lot of class."

Wilson, who died just short of his 30th birthday, could still have become the star major league pitcher which his potential always suggested, but now he will only be remembered as a short-term sensation.

In 1967, he pitched a no-hit game against the Atlanta Braves. "He's the kind of guy," Henry Aaron once said, "who makes me want to retire from the game."

In 1968, Wilson struck out 18 men, including eight in·succession, in a game against the Cincinnati Reds. Wilson always seemed especially effective against the Reds, one of the most feared lineups in baseball.

Later in 1968, Wilson struck out 16 Reds, and the following year his second no-hit game came against Cincinnati.

In 1971, Wilson would have no-hit the Reds again but for a second inning double by Tony Perez. Last September, pitching a no-hitter against the Reds through eight innings, Wilson was lifted for a pinch-hitter by his manager, Preston Gomez. The Reds got a hit off a Houston relief pitcher in the ninth, and the defeat was charged to Wilson.

Reporters covering the game expected a tirade from Wilson at the expense of his manager. On the contrary, Wilson said: "I respect Preston Gomez more than ever after tonight. We both want to win, but when people start putting personal goals ahead of team goals, you'll never have a winner."

Don Wilson never won more than 16 games in a season. His lifetime record in the big leagues was 104-92. That's not enough to get a pitcher into the Hall of Fame. But off the field he was something special—"a guy with a lot of class."

Some Other Mid-Career Tragedies in Baseball

Ed Delahanty, 35, Washington Senators first baseman, died reputedly in a fall from Niagara Falls bridge, July 2, 1903.

Addie Joss, 31, Cleveland Indians pitcher, died of tubular meningitis, April 14, 1911.

Ray Chapman, 29, Cleveland Indians shortstop, killed by pitched ball, August 17, 1920.

Ross Youngs, 30, New York Giants outfielder, died of Bright's disease, October 22, 1927.

Urban Shocker, 38, New York Yankees pitcher, died of heart disease, September 9, 1928.

Len Koenecke, 29, Brooklyn Dodgers outfielder, killed in fight on plane, September 17, 1935.

Mickey Cochrane, 34, Detroit Tigers catcher, suffered fractured skull from pitched ball, ending career, 1937.

Monty Stratton, 26, Chicago White Sox pitcher, lost leg in hunting accident, 1938.

Willard Hershberger, 29, Cincinnati Reds catcher, committed suicide, August 3, 1940.

Lou Gehrig, 37, New York Yankees first baseman, died of amyotrophic lateral sclerosis, June 2, 1941.

Harry Agganis, 25, Boston Red Sox first baseman, died of pulmonary embolism, June 27, 1955.

Herb Score, 24, Cleveland Indians pitcher, suffered eye injury when hit by batted ball, 1957.

Roy Campanella, 36, Brooklyn Dodgers catcher, suffered broken spine, paralysis, in auto accident, 1958.

Ken Hubbs, 22, Chicago Cubs second baseman, killed in plane crash at Provo, Utah, February 13, 1964.

Jim Umbricht, 33, Houston Astros pitcher, died of cancer, April 8, 1964.

Tony Conigliaro, 22, Boston Red Sox outfielder, suffered eye injury when struck by pitched ball, August 18, 1967.

Walter Bond, 29, Minnesota Twins outfielder, died of leukemia, September 14, 1967.

Minnie Rojas, 33, California Angels pitcher, suffered paralysis from auto accident, March 31, 1970.

Roberto Clemente, 38, Pittsburgh Pirates outfielder, killed in plane crash near San Juan, Puerto Rico, December 31, 1972.

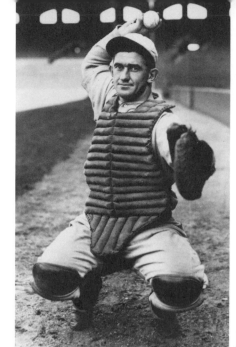

Mickey Cochrane

Roy Campanella

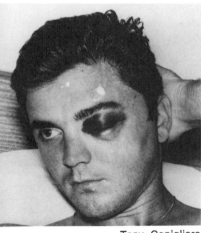

Tony Conigliaro

Monty Stratton

Len Koenecke's brief major league career came to a tragic end in 1935 when he was killed in a fight on a chartered airplane. Brooklyn manager Casey Stengel had told him he was through with the Dodgers for constantly breaking training rules. Koenecke had hit .283 in 100 games for the Dodgers that year before the irate Stengel disposed of him. After leaving the club, Koenecke boarded a commercial plane for Chicago. He was drinking heavily, and when the plane landed in Detroit he was put off. He then hired a small, private plane to take him to Buffalo where he had played previously. Inebriated, he attempted to wrest control of the plane in mid-air and sank his teeth into the pilot's arm. The pilot hit Koenecke with a fire extinguisher to subdue him, and the blow proved fatal. The incident was substantiated by a third man on the plane. Koenecke had played in 265 major league games with the Giants and Dodgers.

Seven Greatest World Series Upsets

by George Vass

October, 1974

There's cause to wonder if there really is such a thing as an upset in the World Series.

Consider this: two teams that win the individual league championships during 154 games (or 162 plus a playoff starting in 1969) already have proved they are superior. Each champion, whatever its total of victories or margin over the second-place club, has triumphed in a far more severe test than any best-of-seven World Series can provide.

Baseball's long season is a guarantee that two strong teams will face each other for the ultimate title. There never have been nor ever will be "accidental champions" in baseball. Every team that has played in the Series got there on merit.

On the other hand, in a number of instances since the first World Series in 1903, one of the rivals has been markedly favored either because of a tremendous performance during the regular season or a roster loaded with great stars.

And in a few cases these highly favored teams have been beaten in the World Series by lightly regarded underdogs. In fact, it's one of the curiosities of baseball that teams holding the records for most games won in both the American and National leagues lost the World Series.

The 1906 Chicago Cubs, winners of 116 games, were beaten by the Hitless Wonders of 1906, the Chicago White Sox. The 1954 Cleveland Indians, winners of 111 games, were sunk by the New York Giants.

And such other big winners as the 1931 Philadelphia Athletics, who won 107 games, and the 1969 Baltimore Orioles, who captured 109 victories, also fell in October.

The reason for such surprising turns of fortune is no secret and has been repeated endlessly since Cub pitcher Ed Reulbach, one of the victims of the 1906 White Sox ambush, stated it possibly for the first time.

"In a 154-game season the best club is pretty certain to win, but there is no such certainty in a World's Series," wrote Reulbach. He was saying that in a short series any team can get hot and beat a much superior aggregation.

Looking at the record of the respective teams, one would have to agree with Reulbach's statement:

"The Cubs in 1906 were in their prime. I think no person, however prejudiced, will claim the White Sox were their equal."

The Cubs had a 116-36 record for a .763 percentage and finished 20 games ahead of the second-place team. The White Sox had a 93-58 record and a percentage of .616 to finish three games in front.

Perhaps the only other teams with such disparate records to meet in a World Series were the A's and Mets in 1973. The White Sox victory was unquestionably an upset, the greatest in Series history.

The triumph of the Hitless Wonders over the Cubs in 1906 heads our list of the seven greatest Series upsets.

But before discussing the top seven, let's eliminate one Series triumph that often has been listed as an upset, the victory of the 1942 St. Louis Cardinals over the New York Yankees.

The reason this Series is considered an upset by some is that the Yankees had one of their greatest teams and many of their greatest stars. Joe DiMaggio, Charlie Keller, Bill Dickey, Joe Gordon, Frankie Crosetti, Red Ruffing, Tiny Bonham, and Spud Chandler were the heart of the team.

The Series-wise Yankees, winners in five of the previous six seasons, went into the 1942 contention almost universal favorites over the Cards. But analysis indicates that the Cardinals had the better team, if only by a hair.

The Yankees won 103 games in 1942 to finish 10 games ahead of the Boston Red Sox. The Cardinals won 106 to finish two ahead of the Brooklyn Dodgers. More significantly, they overcame a 10½-game Dodger lead in August.

If the Yankees had great stars, the Cardinals had even more of them and younger ones. They were the youngest team (average age 26) ever to play in a Series, with a roster that included Stan Musial, Country Slaughter, Terry Moore, Marty Marion, Whitey Kurowski, Walker and Mort Cooper, Johnny Beazley, Harry Walker, Max Lanier, Johnny Hopp, and Ernie White.

This was probably the finest Cardinal team of all, and it would take New York-oriented bias to rate the results of the 1942 Series as an upset.

There are some other supposed upsets in baseball legend, but let's ignore them and present our list of the greatest upsets in World Series history in chronological order.

1906—White Sox over Cubs

The first Series upset was not only the biggest, for several reasons, but also set a pattern for many others in one way: the major role played for the victors by an improbable hero.

George Rohe, a reserve infielder, filled in at third base and won two games for the Sox with his hitting, thus setting the Series upset pattern which in later years brought fame to players such as Pepper Martin, Dusty Rhodes, and Al Weis.

No more formidable foe could be faced in the Series than the 1906 Cubs, not only because they won 116 games—still a major league record—but because they were "hot" going into the Series.

An axiom has it that the team with momentum has the edge. Well, from start to finish, the Cubs never lost momentum. As they roared toward those 116 victories, their August record was 26-3 and in September they were 24-5. That's 50-8 down the stretch!

After such a showing, the gamblers installed the Cubs as 3-to-1 favorites to beat the Sox, who had batted only .228 as a team (lowest in the American League) but had fine pitching, led by Ed Walsh, Doc White, and Nick Altrock.

The equally good Cub pitching staff, headed by Mordecai Brown, Ed Reulbach, and Orval Overall, however, couldn't stem the Sox attack, led by fill-in Rohe, whose triples won the first and third games, 2-1 and 3-0. The Sox won the Series four games to two, outslugging the Cubs in the final pair, 8-6 and 8-3.

Rohe hit .333 to star as the Hitless Wonders upended the seemingly invincible Cubs to get World Series upsets and unlikely heroes off to a good start.

1914—Braves over Athletics

This upset by the Boston Braves of the Philadelphia Athletics is one you wonder about. Were the teams really disparate enough to call the Braves' sweeping triumph in four straight an upset, or was Boston just underrated?

The fact that Boston had been in last place on July 19 and had come on to win the National League pennant and the appellation of Miracle Braves had much to do with their victory over the A's being termed an upset.

But when you consider the record, there wasn't much to choose between the two clubs. The Braves won 94 games, five less than the A's, but they finished 10½ games ahead of the pack, two more than did Philadelphia.

And the Braves finished sizzling, with a 52-14 record in their last 66 games. They had good pitching. Bill James provided a total of 26 victories, winning 19 of his last 20. Dick Rudolph was 27-10.

So the Miracle Braves, with such stars as pitchers James and Rudolph, catcher Hank Gowdy, shortstop Rabbit Maranville, and second baseman Johnny Evers, weren't a club to be despised.

Their names couldn't match those of Connie Mack's famous Athletics, perennial winners and loaded with big stars such as pitchers Chief Bender, Bob Shawkey, Eddie Plank, and Joe Bush and players Stuffy McInnis, Eddie Collins, Home Run Baker, and Jack Barry. The A's were heavy favorites.

But the A's, who were in their fourth World Series in five seasons, were a team in decline and reportedly torn by dissension. They were ripe for the kill, and the Braves, led by Rudolph's two pitching victories and Gowdy's spectacular .544 hitting and Evers' .438, did them in.

This upset was a stunner not just because the Braves won but because they did it so convincingly, in four straight.

Dick Rudolph

Hank Gowdy

Pepper Martin

1926—Cardinals over Yankees

The Cardinals of 1926, winners of the first National League pennant in the history of the club, weren't exactly patsies. Such famous players as second baseman and manager Rogers Hornsby, first baseman Sunny Jim Bottomley, outfielders Chick Hafey and Billy Southworth, and pitcher Grover Cleveland (Old Pete) Alexander decorated the roster.

Statistically the teams were practically even for the season—the Yankees winning 91, three games in front of the second-place team, the Cards winning 89, two games ahead. But the Cardinals were up against a Yankee team just a season away from being what is considered the greatest club of all time. The Yanks had Babe Ruth, Lou Gehrig, Bob Meusel, Tony Lazzeri, Mark Koenig, and Earle Combs and pitchers Waite Hoyt, Herb Pennock, and Bob Shawkey.

The Cardinals battled the Yankees even in the first six games, although Ruth was Ruth, hitting three home runs in the fourth game. It's seldom recalled but Old Pete, then 39, beat the Yankees 6-2 in the second game and 10-2 in the sixth game, going all the way in both and in one inning striking out Gehrig, Lazzeri, and Joe Dugan in order.

But Alexander's great moment, perhaps the most famous in Series history, was to come in the seventh inning of the seventh game, with the Cards clinging to a 3-2 lead and the Yanks having the bases loaded with two out.

Called in as a relief pitcher, Alexander struck out Lazzeri, second only to Ruth as an RBI man that season, then went on to hold the Yanks through the eighth and ninth innings to earn a Series upset for the Cards. What made Old Pete's performance all the more remarkable was that the night before he'd been out celebrating his victory in the sixth game.

There's no question about this Series being an upset because the Yanks had the greatest talent in baseball, and the Cards just squeezed by. But they had picked up Alexander in mid-season and it proved the key for them to go all the way.

1931—Cardinals over Athletics

Seldom has there been a better team than the legendary and powerful A's of 1931, whose names are still treasured even by those who have just read about them.

The first baseman was Jimmie Foxx, Mickey Cochrane was the catcher, Al Simmons played left field, Mule Haas center field, and Bing Miller right field. Simmons hit .390 that season to lead the American League. Pitcher Lefty Grove had a phenomenal 31-4 record. The club was experienced and had won the last two World Series.

Against the powerful A's, who had won 107 games and finished 13½ games ahead of the runner-up, the Cardinals pitted a less impressive but scrappy team which had won 101 and ended in front by 13.

The Cards didn't have quite as many big names as did the A's, but they had quality, including veterans Hafey, Bottomley, and second baseman Frankie Frisch. And they had a rookie center fielder named Pepper Martin.

Martin was the Rohe, the Gowdy, the Alexander of this upset. All he did was hit .500 with 12 hits in 24 times at bat in the seven games. He had four doubles and one home run, but it was his five stolen bases that proved decisive for the Cardinals.

And as in 1926, it was an ancient, picked-up pitcher who won the seventh game for the Cards. This time it was Burleigh Grimes, 38, the former Dodger star, who with relief help from Wild Bill Hallahan in the ninth inning, beat the A's, 4-2, in the decisive game. Grimes had also gone the distance to win the third game.

This upset was also followed by Connie Mack's decision to break up his powerful Philadelphia team, as he had done in 1914. But he was never to get another team into the Series, although he managed for 19 more years.

1954—Giants over Indians

No, these weren't the Giants of the miracle finish—that was accomplished in 1951, when manager Leo Durocher's team won the pennant with Bobby Thomson's three-run homer against the Brooklyn Dodgers in the third game of the playoffs.

This time Durocher's Giants won the pennant less nerve-rackingly, with a clear five-game margin over the Dodgers. They won a respectable 97 games.

But the Indians had won 111 games, more than any other club in big league history except the 1906 Cubs, and finished in front by eight. Manager Al Lopez could count on the best pitching staff in baseball, led by starters Early Wynn, Mike Garcia, and Bob Lemon and bolstered by two super relievers, left-hander Don Mossi and right-hander Ray Narleski.

The Indians had plenty of punch to go with their pitching. Power hitters Al Rosen and Vic Wertz were the best of the sluggers, and second baseman Bobby Avila hit .341 to lead the league in batting.

The Giants weren't exactly helpless. They had Willie Mays, who batted .345 to lead the National League and also provided the major power with 41 home runs and 110 RBI. They had other good hitters like shortstop Alvin Dark, first baseman Whitey Lockman, and left fielder Monte Irvin.

The Giant pitching staff was headed by 21-game

winner Johnny Antonelli, with Sal Maglie and Ruben Gomez among the others. But it did not compare with the Indians' pitching.

Yet in the end, as in so many World Series upsets, it was an improbable hero, this time a utility outfielder named Dusty Rhodes, who was the decisive factor.

Rhodes' act started in the first game, the one in which with the score 2-2 in the eighth Mays made his celebrated over-the-head catch of Wertz' 460-foot center-field drive with two Indians on base.

With two men on and the score still 2-2 in the 10th, Durocher sent in Rhodes to pinch-hit for Irvin. Rhodes hit a 260-foot homer just on the right-field line to win the game and start the Giants toward their Series sweep.

Rhodes' hitting also helped win the second and third games. The Giants went on to become the first team, other than the Yankees, to sweep a Series since the 1914 Miracle Braves.

1960—Pirates over Yankees

The regular-season records for the Yankees and the Pirates were almost identical: New York, 97-57 and an eight-game margin over the second-place team; Pittsburgh, 95-59 and seven games ahead of the runner-up. But when the statistics for the 1960 Series were compiled after the seventh game, it was clear the Pirates had no business defeating the ever-victorious Yankees in this Series.

The Yankees battered Pirate pitching at a furious pace, hitting .338 as a team (a record) and outscoring the enemy 55 runs (another record) to 27. The Yankees hit 10 home runs, the Pirates four. Yankee second baseman Bobby Richardson batted in a record 12 runs and Mickey Mantle drove in 11.

In addition, Yankee pitching ace Whitey Ford shut out the Pirates twice in two tries. The Yankees belted out a total of 91 hits—still another record—and in the three games they won, trounced the Pirates, 16-3, 10-0, and 12-0.

But it was all in vain although the Yankees had one of their finest clubs, with such stars as Bill Skowron, Yogi Berra, Roger Maris, Elston Howard, Clete Boyer, and Gil McDougald on the field, in addition to Mantle and Richardson.

The Pirates, who had won their first pennant since 1927, had no business being in contention but somehow they managed to stay even in games with the far more powerful Yanks right to the end. That's when the improbable hero of 1960 showed up.

In the seventh game, with the score tied 9-9 in the bottom of the ninth inning at ancient Forbes Field in Pittsburgh, second baseman Bill Mazeroski led off against Yankee pitcher Ralph Terry. Mazeroski hit Terry's second pitch over the left-field wall.

This was the first time a World Series had ended with a home run.

And it was a shocker all the way. The Pirates had no business winning the Series of 1960. Just check the statistics.

1969—Mets over Orioles

The memory of this upset is still fresh, recalled almost daily in the stories of New York sportswriters, especially since the Mets almost repeated the victory of 1969 last season.

Yet this Series may not have been as much of a mismatch as it seemed at the time.

True, the Miracle Mets not long before had been a much joked-at expansion team, admitted to the National League in 1962. And some of their best players were rejects from other clubs.

But midway in the 1969 season they jelled, as the saying goes, and overtook the strong Cubs, who had looked like a shoo-in for the division title in this first season of a two-division, 12-team league.

Extraordinarily good pitching provided by starters Tom Seaver, Jerry Koosman, and Gary Gentry and a strong relief staff, was the heart of a late-season Met drive to catch and pass the Cubs.

The Mets, 100-1 underdogs at season's start, won

With Al Smith at bat, Sal Maglie of the Giants unleashes the first pitch of the 1954 World Series against the favored Cleveland Indians at the Polo Grounds. Although Maglie was not credited with the victory, the Giants won the opener, 5-2, and went on to complete a four-game sweep over the Indians. Wes Westrum is behind the plate, and Alvin Dark at shortstop. The umpire is Al Barlick.

Pirate catcher Hal Smith is given a jubilant welcome at home plate by Roberto Clemente and Dick Groat in the eighth inning of the final game of the 1960 World Series against the Yankees at Forbes Field. Smith had homered, scoring Groat and Clemente, to give Pittsburgh a 9-7 temporary lead. New York tied it up in the top of the ninth, setting the stage for Bill Mazeroski's home run that won it all for the Pirates, 10-9, despite a record 91 hits by the Yankees in the seven-game Series.

Al Weis

The fourth game of the 1969 World Series between the Miracle Mets and the formidable Baltimore Orioles was won by New York with this controversial play. With the score tied, 1-1, in the bottom of the 10th, runners on first and second, and none out, pinch-hitter J. C. Martin (No. 9) of the Mets laid down a bunt. Baltimore relief pitcher Pete Richert pounced on the ball, but his throw to first hit Martin on the wrist. The ball caromed away, enabling pinch-runner Rod Gaspar to score the winning run from second base. The Orioles later claimed Martin had run out of the base path and should have been called out for interference. The play was only one of many memorable incidents that forged an eventual World Series triumph for the Mets, whose pitchers posted an incredible earned-run average of 1.80 in the five games.

37 of their last 48 games and a total of 100 for the year, closing eight games in front of the competition, hardly the mark of an inferior team.

But after sweeping the National League playoffs in three games from the Atlanta Braves they went up against something special in the Orioles.

Baltimore won 109 games during the season and finished 19 games ahead of its nearest rival before taking three straight in the playoffs from the Minnesota Twins.

Brooks and Frank Robinson led a formidable Oriole attack, and the pitching was first class, fea-

turing a pair of 20-game winners, Mike Cuellar and Dave McNally.

Yet, after dropping the first game, the Mets took the next four, with second baseman Al Weis, who had hit only three home runs in two seasons, belting a key one in the fifth and last game as well as batting .453 to lead all Series hitters.

The writers referred to the Mets' victory as the "impossible dream" come true. It was, of course, but it was just the latest in a sequence, and perhaps the seven we've selected will be joined by an eighth this October.

1974: A Year of Oddities in the Major Leagues

by John Kuenster

January, 1975

Every major league season produces its share of oddball incidents, and 1974 was no exception. Even if you discount the antics of the champion Oakland A's, enough goofy things happened on the field and in dugouts and clubhouses to provide most of us with a welcome respite from such weightier subjects as inflation and the energy crisis.

Without setting them down in exact chronological order, here are a few of the weird and eccentric events of the season:

Last April at Fenway Park, Willie Horton of the Tigers hit a foul pop-up in the ninth inning, allegedly killing a pigeon. The bird plopped down only a few feet from home plate after Horton hit his pop-up.

"It scared the hell outa me," said Red Sox catcher Bob Montgomery. "I jumped a foot in the air—and Willie jumped even higher."

Umpire Jim Evans summoned a bat boy to remove the remains, and the game proceeded. One observer said he could not pin the crime on Horton "beyond the shadow of reasonable doubt, but circumstantial evidence pointed to him as perpetrator of the fowl deed." Whatever, the Tigers were just as dead as the bird at game's end. The Red Sox won, 7-5.

The same day, strangely enough, a swarm of bees in San Diego took over the home plate area delaying the Padres' game against San Francisco, but it must have put some sting in the Padres because they won, 6-5.

Even stranger things happened to the Padres earlier the same month when their owner Ray Kroc, the hamburger tycoon, garnished his own players with a little salt and pepper.

In their home opener against the Astros, the Padres were being thumped, 9-2, in the eighth inning when Kroc grabbed the public address system.

"Ladies and gentlemen, I suffer with you," he told a crowd of 39,083, second largest in San Diego's history.

Kroc was about to proceed when he was interrupted by the sight of a naked man who had jumped out of the stands and dashed across the field.

"Get that streaker out of here! Throw him in jail!" snapped Kroc.

Then the Padre boss resumed, and ripped his own players. "I've never seen such stupid baseball playing in my life," he complained to the stunned crowd.

The outburst spurred the Padres temporarily. They scored three runs in the eighth, but lost 9-5, then went on to finish the 1974 season with a horrendous 60-102 record (worst in the majors) and 42 games behind the first-place Dodgers.

Hourly wage earners thought Kroc's remarks were right on. The players thought the remarks were intemperate, if not a crock of mustard. Oh well, Kroc's hamburger sales kept mounting in 1974.

Also in April, Graig Nettles of the Yankees belted 11 homers, tying a major league record for most homers in a single month. Suddenly, his home-run production stopped, and later in the season when he broke his bat on a pitch, it was discovered cork had been impacted in the barrel, strictly a no-no in the rule book. Nettles finished the season with 22 homers, and the suspicious-minded can make of that what they will.

There was nothing mysterious about the blunder committed by Dick Allen of the White Sox in a game against the Indians at Cleveland in June. With the Sox leading, 4-1, and nobody out in the seventh inning, Joe Lis of the Indians walked and Oscar Gamble singled to put runners on first and second.

The next batter, Dave Duncan, rapped a routine grounder to short. The double play was completed, 6-4-3, but after getting the toss at first base, Allen, thinking he had completed the third out, tossed the ball to first-base umpire Merle Anthony.

Anthony smartly sidestepped Allen's toss, and Lis, who had broken from second on the play, romped all the way home. Allen later made up for his daydreaming by slamming a two-run homer in the ninth as the Sox won, 7-3.

There was no daydreaming during a weird play in another game in June at California between the Angels and Tigers. Only a comedy of errors that left viewers a bit bug-eyed, believing they were watching a Little League encounter instead of a major league performance.

Denny Doyle of the Angels blooped a double down the right-field line, and as he headed into second, Detroit right fielder Jim Northrup fired the ball in and it sailed into left field. Doyle cranked up again, and raced for third. Meanwhile, left fielder Ben Ogilvie retrieved the ball and threw it past third baseman Aurelio Rodriguez.

Doyle dazzedly got up, thankful for small favors, and raced home, slid in and was safe for a cheapie trip around the bases.

Dick Allen

Willie Horton

Even the mighty A's had their foul-ups on the field. Against Detroit in a game at Tiger Stadium in June, fleet-footed Bill North slammed an opposite field double off Joe Coleman in the first inning.

With Bert Campaneris at the plate, North broke for third as Campy lined sharply to Dick Sharon in right. North had already rounded third base and was heading home when he realized that Sharon was going to catch the ball. North made a speedy retreat and beat Sharon's throw to shortstop Ed Brinkman at second base, thus avoiding being doubled up.

The ball was returned to Coleman on the mound, and the Tigers called an appeal play at third base. Umpire Larry Napp ruled that North had failed to touch the bag at third in his haste to return to second base and was out.

The official scorer was riffling the rule book on that one, but finally charted the double play, Sharon-to-Brinkman-to-Coleman-to-Rodriguez.

Sometimes specific points in the rule book escape recall even by umpires and managers. Failure by Red Sox manager Darrell Johnson to recall Section 4.06 of the Official Rules may have cost Boston a game against the Twins in late May at Fenway Park.

The Twins won the game, 5-4, in 13 innings, but their winning run was tainted. With Rod Carew on third base and Jerry Terrell at bat, Boston pitcher Diego Segui was called for a balk. Segui had started his pitching motion as Terrell reached down to scoop up some dirt in the batter's box.

Segui, caught off guard, broke his hands from a set position before taking his foot off the rubber. First-base umpire Bill Haller called the balk.

Haller appeared correct, until someone later finally found rule 4.06 which reads in part: "No player shall . . . commit any act while the ball is alive and in play for the obvious purpose of trying to make the pitcher commit a balk. . . . If a balk is made, it shall be nullified."

"I knew there was a rule in there somewhere," said Johnson, "but I just didn't know it at the time."

Since Johnson did not file a protest before the next pitch was delivered, the Red Sox had to accept the call—and an eventual loss.

When the storm subsided, Terrell admitted he had once pulled the same trick as a high school player in Minnesota—and gotten away with it.

The list of snafus last season could go on and on, including the failure of the Cubs, in two separate games, to cover home plate, allowing the winning runs to score. But perhaps the roll call can be ended with the game between the Cardinals and Mets in September that lasted 25 innings and ended at 3 o'clock in the morning!

The Cardinals won, 4-3. Bake McBride finally put an end to the madness when he scored on a bizarre play in the top of the 25th inning.

With McBride on first base, Met pitcher Hank Webb threw over to keep him close. The ball sailed past first baseman John Milner. McBride raced all the way to third, but he must have decided there was no sense stopping at 3:13 a.m. and came charging home.

Milner's throw to catcher Ron Hodges was there in time, but Hodges, his equilibrium off at that late hour, dropped the throw. "I don't think he would have had me even if he held the ball," said McBride.

Maybe so. However, it was still a crazy play—first to home on an overthrow!

But that's major league baseball, folks. We think.

33

Frank Robinson — The Game I'll Never Forget

as told to George Vass

September, 1973

Naturally, there are games that stand out for me more than others, like my first major league game with the Cincinnati Reds, my first home run, games in the World Series, and All-Star games.

But the game I'll always remember for sure is one in early May of 1966. That was my first season with the Baltimore Orioles after being traded to them during the winter by the Reds.

Changing leagues didn't mean much to me. I can't say I was worried about that. I figured if I could play in the National League I could play just as well in the American League.

What concerned me was how the fans would accept me in Baltimore. Players don't talk about it much but they like to feel they belong, that they're a part of the team and also of the city in which they're playing. That means a lot to a player, don't let anybody tell you otherwise.

Of course, the players and management made me welcome right away. I still remember my first meeting with Hank Bauer, who was managing the Orioles.

"Frank, I just want to tell you you're on your own," Bauer said to me. "We know you can do the kind of job for us we expect from you. And we'd welcome any suggestions you could make to the younger hitters. Anytime you want to pull one aside and help him out I'd appreciate it."

So from the beginning of spring training I felt comfortable with the Orioles. I liked the guys and they seemed to like me. But I was not sure yet about the fans. We played most of our early schedule out of town.

That year Baltimore got off to a real good start, but the Cleveland Indians got off to an even better one. We both broke out in front of the league, and there was a lot of excitement when we opened a four-game series in early May in Baltimore.

We won the first two games and went into a doubleheader before a crowd of 40,000 or more on Sunday, May 8.

Luis Tiant was to pitch the opener for Cleveland, and he'd pitched three straight shutouts, so he was hot. I had never faced him before, and really all I knew about him was what I read in the papers.

I've learned a long time ago not to ask about a pitcher even if I haven't faced him. The reason is that it's an individual thing how a pitcher's stuff looks to you.

One guy may think a pitcher's velocity is great, by his standards. Or he might describe his breaking stuff a certain way. Besides, pitchers throw differently to different batters. What might hold true for another batter might not be the way he pitches you.

The only thing I want to know about a pitcher I haven't faced before is if he throws a freak pitch, like a forkball or a knuckler. Other than that, I don't want to know too much.

So I went up there against Tiant knowing nothing about him but what I'd seen while waiting my turn to bat in the first inning. I came up with a man on, Russ Snyder having singled.

In 1966, Frank Robinson slammed one of the longest home runs ever hit in Baltimore's Memorial Stadium. Two young fans, Michael Sparaco and Bill Wheatley, presented the ball to him after the game. One of the boys had recovered the ball, the first ever hit out of the stadium, in the parking lot beyond left field, some 540 feet away. Robinson, who went on to become the American League's Most Valuable Player, also was named MVP in the National League when he was with Cincinnati in 1961.

Tiant's first pitch was a fastball. It broke down and in on me, and I got the wood on it.

The ball carried farther than any ball I'd ever hit. You know the ball park in Baltimore, where the stands curve in and there's a tower? It carried clear past the tower and out of the park.

It was the first time a baseball ever had been hit out of Memorial Stadium.

I didn't know the ball had gone out of the park even when I rounded the bases. I could hear the cheering but didn't think it was more than what you ordinarily hear when you hit a home run.

After the inning was over and I was going back out to right field, the field announcer told the crowd that nobody ever before had hit a ball out of Memorial Stadium.

The fans in right field began to cheer again and then, all of a sudden, everybody in the ball park stood up and gave me an ovation. I'd never heard anything like it before.

The ovation started and it mounted and it was a little touching. I was a little embarrassed, though tremendously pleased. It was one of the greatest things that ever happened to me. It was so unexpected.

I can't describe the feeling that came over me. When it happened I felt that the fans of Baltimore had accepted me now, that I had become one of the members of their team, that I belonged. That's the greatest feeling you could have.

We beat the Indians twice that day to sweep the series, and I guess you could say that started us on our way to the pennant, the first Baltimore had ever won.

I remember having a good day all-around, 5-for-7. I had another home run, a triple, a double, and a single.

But that first home run and the crowd's response are what stick out in my mind. A fan recovered the ball in a parking lot 540 feet away, and the management gave him a season ticket for it. I still have the ball, in a place of honor in a trophy case.

That was the start of some great years in Baltimore. From then on, people recognized and applauded me. They weren't sitting back anymore. It's like I was a kind of Williams or Mantle or Musial or Mays, which I never felt before.

Frank Robinson, Baltimore slugger

Frank Robinson, manager and designated hitter of the Cleveland Indians

The Debut
of Walter Johnson

by Shirley Povich
Washington Post

October, 1957

It was just 50 years ago August 2 that a small headline in the *Washington Post* said "Idaho Phenom Will Pitch Today." Washington baseball fans and the Detroit Tigers finally were going to get a look at 19-year-old Walter Johnson in his major league debut.

Young Johnson wasn't coming into the major leagues unheralded exactly. For a month Washington fans had been alerted to the tall boy scout Cliff Blankenship had signed for the Senators on June 29, 1907, on a trip to Weiser, Idaho, where tales of Johnson's strike-outs in a semipro league were current.

In announcing the signing of Johnson, there was unqualified endorsement by the Washington club: "Manager Joe Cantillon has added a great young phenom to his pitching staff . . . the young man's name is Walter Johnson. Cantillon received word today from Blankenship telling of his capture! Johnson pitched 75 innings in the Idaho State League without allowing a run and had a strike-out record of 15 per game. . . . Scout Blankenship is very enthusiastic but fails to state whether the great phenom is left-handed or right-handed."

On the morning it was announced Johnson would be unveiled in the first game of a doubleheader with league-leading Detroit, the *Post* reported that Johnson the day before had pitched batting practice for both teams, as was the custom of that day. "Walter Johnson pitched from the rubber before the game yesterday," wrote sports editor Ed Grillo, "but he afforded little batting practice for the players of both teams, as his fastball seemed unhittable."

There were 5,000 fans in the stands when Johnson took the mound and their first sight of him was accompanied by gasps. This couldn't be the fastballer they'd heard about. He was pitching side-arm, almost underhand, with a long sweeping delivery and no great snap of the wrists. That's not what fastballers were made of. The Tigers soon could dispute them.

The Tigers learned that Johnson's smooth delivery was a disarming thing. The big country boy who didn't look as if he were throwing a fastball was actually unleashing a pitch that hissed with danger.

They didn't take their regular cuts, except for Sam Crawford. Ty Cobb found it expedient twice to lay down bunts.

They beat Johnson, 3-2. He left at the end of eight innings, with the score 2-1 against him. For the first six innings Johnson allowed only three hits, and two of them were bunts in succession by Cobb and Claude Rossman. Cobb streaked from first to third on Rossman's bunt. Johnson was green at fielding bunts. He lost, but the high promise he showed was not lost on the critics.

"His work proves beyond doubt he is the pitching find of the season," the *Post* reported. "His wonderful speed, perfect control, and deceptive curve were nothing short of astonishing. He has more natural ability than any pitcher seen in these parts in many a moon, and it really seems Cantillon has picked up a real live phenom."

Johnson a curve-baller? Seems that he was, and more than that, he threw a spitball, too. That last is the testimony of Wild Bill Donovan, the Detroit pitcher who told Cantillon, "If I were you, Joe, I'd tell that big kid of yours to quit fooling around with that spitter. He doesn't need it. He only needs that speed he's got. All spit-ballers except Ed Walsh are in-and-outers."

Not his strike-outs, of which there were only six in Johnson's debut, but his control was the item that drew the most praise from manager Cantillon. "His absolute control was the best part of his work," Cantillon said. "He has a great shoot to his fastball, and, to tell the truth, he's the best raw pitcher I've ever seen. If nothing happens, that fellow will be a greater pitcher in two years than Mathewson ever dared to be."

Five days later Johnson ended his one-game losing streak. In his second start he yielded two hits to Cleveland in the first inning and no others until they got two in the ninth.

He beat them, 7-2, for the first of his 414 victories. In its report of the game, the *Post* said: "His speed was so terrific that several Cleveland players acted as if they did not take particular delight in being at the plate. Once or twice Johnson shot fastballs close to the batter's head, and they usually swung at anything after that."

Stan Musial—
The Day I Got
My 3,000th Hit

as told to Bob Broeg
Condensed from the *St. Louis Post-Dispatch*

Musial holds the ball he hit in a 1959 game at Pittsburgh to tie the National League record for most lifetime doubles. Musial had hit his 651st two-bagger to equal the mark held by Honus Wagner. When he finished playing four years later, Stan had amassed 725 career doubles.

May, 1967

My greatest thrill in baseball was just putting on the uniform of a big league ballplayer, especially for every season's opening game.

I believe the joy of getting paid as a man to play a boy's game kept me going longer than many other players. Whether getting $100 a month in Class D or $100,000 a season in the majors, I never lost the feeling that I had the best way in the country to make a living, meager or plentiful.

So even though the games tend to run together in the memory when a guy has played more than 3,000 of them, a few stand out, above and beyond the satisfaction of driving in the tying or winning run.

When I came up to the Cardinals in September, 1941, the year I went from a dead-armed left-handed pitcher in the minors to a wide-eyed outfielder in the majors, I had a remarkable day on the pennant-contending Redbirds' final Sunday at home.

In the first game of a doubleheader against the Chicago Cubs, playing left field, I made two good catches and threw out a runner at the plate. I had two singles, two doubles, stole a base, and scored from second with the winning run in the ninth inning, 5-4, when the Chicago catcher, Clyde McCullough, left the plate unguarded after fielding a topped roller and throwing too late to first base.

In the second game, playing right field, I dived to my right for one low line drive and charged for another, turning a double somersault. At bat, I bunted safely and singled to cap a six-hit day of all-round delight—for me, anyway.

The Cubs' manager, Jimmie Wilson, was fit to be tied. "Nobody," he exploded, "can be that good!"

He was so right, but I was just 20 and too numb with excitement to know better. Numb and confident. I always did believe I could hit and, I'm proud to say, until age slowed me so much in the field and on the bases, I did more than swing a bat.

I regret only that I played on no pennant winners after the Cardinals won in each of my first four years in the big leagues. The World Series is baseball's greatest satisfaction, and I was too young to appreciate early what I missed later.

We came close in my last season, 1963, with that 19-of-20 surge in September before the Dodgers stopped us in a great series at St. Louis. The club won in 1964, but I couldn't have contributed as much at that stage as Lou Brock did, spectacularly, at bat and on the bases.

When I hit five home runs in a doubleheader against the Giants in St. Louis in 1954, son Dick, now my business associate, was only 13 years old. And when I came home that Sunday night, he said, gravely:

"Gee, Dad, they must have been throwing you fat pitches today."

I can remember so many big ones. . . . like winning the 1955 All-Star game with a 12th-inning homer at Milwaukee . . . getting a record-tying fifth hit for a fourth time in 1948 at Boston, taking only five swings because both wrists were injured . . . hitting four homers in succession in 1962 at the Polo Grounds . . . and finishing with base hits my last two times up off Cincinnati's Jim Maloney on September 29, 1963, the day the fans gave me the finest send-off any ballplayer ever had.

There were so many moments, and yet there was just one, the day I got my 3,000th hit—May 13, 1958.

Only seven players previously had achieved 3,000

Stan (The Man) Musial had an odd, peek-a-boo stance at the plate, but when he brought the bat around and stung the ball, it was poetry in motion. He left a monumental legacy in the record book by the time he retired after the 1963 season, including 3,630 hits and a lifetime batting average of .331. In the post-World War II era, few major-leaguers enjoyed the popularity he did no matter where the Cardinals were playing.

hits, a mark of consistency, durability, and good fortune. Between 1925, when both Tris Speaker and Eddie Collins made it, and that mid-May day at Chicago in 1958, only one player had got there—my old boyhood favorite in Pittsburgh, Paul Waner.

After suffering a hairline shoulder fracture going down the stretch in 1957, the last time I won a batting championship, I could see what injury might do to a dream. Still just punching the ball, I got 43 hits in my first 22 games in 1958, but I was still one shy the day before the Cardinals were to come off the road.

I said to coach Terry Moore, almost idly, "I hope we win tomorrow, Tee, but, you know I'd like to walk every time up—and save the big one for St. Louis."

Moore mentioned my wistful thought to manager Fred Hutchinson, who huddled over a beer with his coaches at the Knickerbocker Hotel and then phoned me upstairs to tell me that unless he needed me to win, he wouldn't use me.

I was grateful, and Hutch, forthright as usual, called in the writers traveling with us and told them the truth.

I was at Wrigley Field the next afternoon, sunning myself in the right-field bullpen when we batted in the sixth inning, trailing 3-1 with a runner on second base and one out.

"Hey, Stan," coach Boots Hollingsworth nudged me, motioning to the dugout, "Hutch wants you."

Hutch wanted me to hit for our pitcher, Sam Jones. There were fewer than 6,000 fans there, compared with a sell-out 30,000 expected at Busch Stadium the next night in St. Louis, but a ball game was at stake.

The Chicago pitcher, a young right-hander named

Moe Drabowsky, born in the land of my father, Poland, got the count to two-and-two, then fired a curveball for the outside corner.

I picked up the spin of the ball, strode into the pitch, and drove it on a deep line into left field. I knew as soon as it left my bat that it would go between the left fielder, Moose Moryn, and the foul line.

When I pulled up at second base with my 3,000th hit, which, like my first one, had been a run-scoring double, I heard a deafening roar. Frank Dascoli, the third-base umpire, hurried over to hand me the ball, and as I turned toward first, there was a sight that must have reminded spectators of an old Keystone Kop comedy.

Hutchinson lumbered toward me, followed by a swarm of photographers, who ordinarily are not permitted on the field. Hutch grinned, stuck out his hand, and said:

"Congratulations, Stan. I'm sorry. I know you wanted to do it in St. Louis, but I needed you today."

To make the day perfect, we won the game, 5-3, and had a wonderful evening's train ride back to St. Louis, complete with cake and champagne. At stops at Clinton, Illinois, and Springfield, crowds gathered for a few words and autographs.

When we pulled into St. Louis, late, nearly 1,000 persons were crammed into Union Station, where they had set up a platform.

"I never realized that batting a little ball around could cause so much commotion," I told those smiling, friendly faces below me. "I know now how Lindbergh must have felt when he returned to St. Louis."

Somebody in the crowd yelled, "What did he hit?"

Everybody laughed, and carried away, I turned to the eager small fry present and said, "No school tomorrow, kids."

The 3,000-hit occasion had pleasant postscripts, many of which are in the baseball record books. One personal gratification came the next night before the home fans in St. Louis who had expected to see the big one.

They gave me a standing ovation the first time in the first inning, and I made No. 3,001 a home run. Gee, I felt that night the way I did my last season when, after staying up late to get the good news, I celebrated the birth of my first grandson by hitting the first pitch out of the park.

(Editor's Note: Stan Musial is the only man to play 1,000 games each in the infield and outfield. He finished his career in 1963 first in National League base hits, 3,630; first in major league extra-base hits, 1,377; first in major league total bases, 6,134.)

The Night
It Rained Home Runs

by Irv Haag

March, 1972

In all likelihood it will be a long time before two teams surpass the almost unbelievable storm of home runs that had 51,400 fans limp and pop-eyed on June 23, 1950, at Detroit's Briggs Stadium. Even the usually calm and collected Harry Heilmann, Tiger broadcaster, went slightly bananas describing that one.

According to one who played a big part in the seesaw battle, Paul (Dizzy) Trout, one of Detroit's all-time great pitchers, "We had the Yankees in, and the fans were hangin' from the rafters. The game started off with a pretty good bang. The Yankees hit four home runs off lefty Ted Gray, Detroit starter, and were coasting along with a 6-0 lead.

"Tommy Byrne started for the Yankees. He was a hard man for the Tigers to beat—in fact, we couldn't score any runs off him hardly anytime. So it looked like it was gonna be a walkaway, and our fans were certainly disgruntled. Then all at once the phone rang down in the bullpen, and they said, 'Get Dizzy hot.' "

To put it mildly, the call was a surprising jolt to the big right-hander who came by his nickname Dizzy quite naturally. Trout wasn't supposed to be in the bullpen but figured that was as good a place as any to watch the ball game. And besides, he loved to swap stories and "kinda keep the boys company."

Diz couldn't find his glove, and by the time he tracked it down, the umpire was bellowing for him to get out on the mound. As Trout recalls it, "the Yankees said, 'We gotcha tonight—you haven't thrown any!' At the mound, I was met by Teddy Lyons, our coach, and he tells me there's nobody out, the score's six to nothing, Gene Woodling's the hitter, and there's a man on first. Johnny Groth, who was kind of a cutup, asked me how I wanted to play the hitter and I said, 'Deep, cut across, and don't spike anybody!'

"I got in about five pitches before facing Woodling. One, maybe, was a good one. Anyway, I got Woodling to ground out, struck out Joe DiMaggio, and got Yogi Berra to pop up."

Trout went to the dugout under a wave of thunderous cheers, and somebody asked if he wanted a jacket. He refused. "I haven't even worked up a sweat," he said. "I didn't throw a ball in the bullpen."

Meanwhile, the Tigers got something going in the bottom of the inning. Next thing Diz knew, Gerry Priddy's telling him he'd better get a bat, he was the next man up. With the bases loaded, Trout thought there was no way manager Red Rolfe would let him swing. But Rolfe handed him his second jolt of the night. "Go ahead, see what you can do," Rolfe said.

So Trout stepped in and worked the count to two-and-two. Right after Berra needled him about how he was "takin' pretty good swings at Byrne," Trout parked the ball into the left-field stands. A grandslammer!

Briggs Stadium went up for grabs. The fans were throwing coats, hats, shoes, ties—everything—onto the field, and it looked for quite a while as though they'd never get back to normal.

But the rafters rang again as Priddy homered, making it 6-5. George Kell doubled and Vic Wertz unloaded another booming shot, and it was 7-6 Tigers.

To complete the onslaught, Hoot Evers also got into the act with a towering drive into the left-field upper deck.

Eight runs in the inning, and every one as a result of a home run!

Trout shut the Yankees out until the seventh inning, when he let up on a slider and Joe DiMaggio uncorked the Yankees' fifth homer of the night to make the score Tigers 8, New York 7. Diz got into more hot water in the eighth. After a broken-bat single, Yankee manager Casey Stengel sent in left-hander Tommy Henrich. The veteran repaid Casey's confidence quickly with a two-run homer. So, after four and one-third innings, having given up three hits and three runs, Trout was through for the night. With the Yankees now back out in front, 9-8, the Bronx Bombers proceeded to get two straight hits off reliever Paul Calvert.

Rolfe had seen enough and summoned big, gutsy right-hander Fred Hutchinson, another long-time Tiger favorite. Hutch retired the next two batters on three pitches and also held them hitless in the top of the ninth.

Going into the Tiger ninth, the Yankees were nursing a one-run lead, and famed fireman Joe Page had taken the hill. With one away, Wertz pounded out his second hit of the night, a solid double that represented the tying run. In stepped Hoot Evers. The crowd, hoping for a miracle, chorused the familiar H-o-o-o-o-t battle cry. Evers, who was to enjoy his best season ever that year, with .323, 21 homers, and 103 RBI, laced into one of Page's pitches and sent it deep.

Up in the broadcast booth, Heilmann—apparently not believing what he saw—kept saying, "It's between the outfielders, it's between the outfielders!" That it was, between DiMaggio and Hank Bauer. Wertz raced around to score the tying run, and Evers just kept pumping, too. DiMaggio's relay throw to Phil Rizzuto was a little low and off the mark, and Hoot slid across home plate with an inside-the-park home run, winning it for the Tigers, 10-9.

Ironically, Diz Trout, who had triggered the Tigers' eight-run fourth inning and kept them in the ball game with his long-man relief job, didn't see the fantastic finish. Because he had thought he wasn't going to pitch, Diz had made arrangements for dinner with some friends and was hurrying to keep his reservation.

"My wife and I were goin' out of the park just as Evers scored the winning run," Trout recalled.

One of baseball's more colorful characters, Dizzy Trout spent his prime years as a major-leaguer with the Detroit Tigers. During the Tigers' stretch drive for the pennant in 1945, he pitched six games in nine days, winning four of them. After his playing career, he worked as a broadcaster and later as director of the Chicago White Sox speakers' bureau.

"We heard all kinds of whoopin' and hollerin'. I stopped and said, 'Honey, we won the game!' And just as I said it, a car pulled up on our left on Michigan Avenue. It had about seven people in it and they were yellin' 'We won the game, we won the game!' "

"Of course, they didn't know who I was," Trout added, with a little note of sadness.

So ended one of the most unforgettable games ever played in Briggs Stadium.

A game in which every one of the 19 runs scored was a result of a homer... including a grand-slammer by a pitcher, a pinch-hit homer, and one inside-the-park!

The feat still stands as an American League record: 11 home runs in all, five by the Yankees and six by the Tigers, with five homers coming in the fourth inning to tie another mark.

Trout himself had many a lustrous moment in Tiger flannels. He spent 13½ seasons with Detroit, compiling a record of 160 wins against 157 losses, and threw 28 shutouts. That record takes on a lot more glitter when you note that Dizzy won an average of 21 games a year four straight years between 1943 and 1946—including 20 shutouts.

His 27 wins in 1944 were only surpassed among all-time Tiger hurlers by George Mullin's 29 in 1909, Hal Newhouser's 29, also in 1944, and, of course, Denny McLain's 31 victories in 1968.

The big right-hander out of Sandcut, Indiana, is also in the record books for having thrown four shutouts against the same team in a season—the Philadelphia Athletics in 1944. And if nudged enough, he'll readily admit he was one of the game's top-hitting pitchers.

Few brought more color to the game than Diz.

For all the shining moments in his career, however, Trout always had special reason to recall June 23, 1950—the night it rained home runs!

The National League record for most homers by two clubs in a nine-inning game is also 11, set June 11, 1967, by the Chicago Cubs (7) and the New York Mets (4) at Wrigley Field. It was during a doubleheader swept by the Cubs. Chicago outlasted the Mets, 5-3, in the first game and outblasted them, 18-10, in the second.

Three of the Cub homers came off the bat of center fielder Adolfo Phillips, who also had one in the first game, giving him a total of eight RBI for the day. Randy Hundley belted two for the Cubs, and there were single homers by Ron Santo and Ernie Banks. The Met clouts came from Ron Swoboda, Jerry Grote, Bob Johnson, and Gerry Buchek.

Pete Rose:
They Still Call Him
"Charlie Hustle"

by Bob Hertzel
Cincinnati Enquirer

July, 1973

It is sometimes hard to believe the passage of time; so swiftly, so quickly, slipping by unnoticed.

When the baseball season opened in April, it marked the beginning of Pete Rose's second decade as a Cincinnati Red.

A decade . . . it sounds like an eternity, especially in the life of a baseball player. Ten long years; 10 memorable, exciting years. And now the brash Cincinnati kid, a few gray hairs dotting a style that is anything but the crew cut which helped make him famous, is engaged in his 11th major league season. At 32 years of age he is the veteran, the man with whom Cincinnati Reds' baseball is identified.

"It sneaks up on you," he said.

A lot of water has passed under the bridge since Peter Edward Rose scrapped his way into a starting job in 1963, hit .273, and won Rookie of the Year honors. A lot of water.

There were 1,922 hits during those years, more than anyone has ever collected wearing a Cincinnati uniform. There were two batting titles, with .335 in 1968 and .348 in 1969.

There have been eight .300-plus seasons in a row and five 200-hit seasons. There has been a lot, a whole lot. He played second base, third base, center field, right field, and left field. He won an All-Star game, starred in a playoff, played in the World Series.

The memories are great, and they are still collecting, still building.

"Although this is my 11th season, two of the last three have been the most enjoyable," said Rose, referring to the pennant-winning seasons of 1970 and 1972.

Pete Rose's mind wandered into the past, thinking back to the highlights. He smiled.

"Do you know I got the last hit at Crosley Field?" asked Rose, who spent a good part of his youth watching the Cincinnati Reds play in the old ball yard. "It was against the San Francisco Giants and I was 4-for-5."

Crosley Field, though, is no more, and the home of the Reds is shiny new Riverfront Stadium.

"I got Cincinnati's first hit in the new stadium, too," he recalled. "I went 4-for-5 again. I should have been 5-for-5. My last time up I made a perfect bunt and beat it, but I was called out. Really, I beat it. It should have been a perfect night."

Unfortunately, and Rose really does regret it, he didn't get the first hit in the new stadium . . . just the first Cincinnati hit. The first hit belonged to Atlanta's Felix Millan, who singled in the first inning.

"I got my hit in the first inning, too," Rose said almost sadly, thinking had Atlanta gone down one-two-three, the honor would have been his.

The years may have passed, the days may have gone by, but Pete Rose remains as enthusiastic as the day he broke in. Baseball, he says, is still fun.

For a spirited player like Pete Rose, defeat is always hard to accept. Here, he sits dejectedly with his son, Pete Jr., then two years old, after the Reds lost the seventh and final game of the 1972 World Series to the Oakland A's, 3-2.

"What's the most fun?" he was asked.

"Easy," he answered. "Hitting. That's what I enjoy most. It's such a challenge. Realistically, it's probably the hardest thing there is to do in all of sport. Think about it. You've got a round ball, a round bat, and the object is to hit it square."

Hitting, the thing Pete Rose does best, that's what thrills him.

"Baseball, you see, is an individual game. It's a lot like tennis. You go up to the plate, and no one can help you. There's no one blocking for you or setting up a kick. It's you against the pitcher, and that's what it's all about."

But how, Rose was asked, can anyone enjoy something he has failed at 69 percent of the time, using his .309 lifetime batting average as a guide?

"It's like winning," he answered. "You know you have to lose 65 or so games a year. But winning the pennant, that's the thing. Come to think of it, hitting comes behind winning in enjoyment."

There are other things about baseball that keep Pete Rose forever young; the Peter Pan of the sport.

He loves to race from first to third on a single, sliding head first and bringing the crowd to its feet with a roar. He loves to run full-speed to first base after drawing a walk and to race around the bases on a home run.

As it is with all entertainers—and ballplayers are entertainers—he loves the adulation of the crowd, playing before a full house and on national television, signing autographs.

He still brims with enthusiasm and confidence. There is, for example, no doubt in his mind he will hit .300 or more as long as he plays.

"I'm a believer the only way I can't hit .300 is if there is something physically wrong with me," he said. "I really get a kick out of picking up the newspaper early in the season and seeing guys with 25 or 30 more hits than me and knowing I'll catch them. I'm a slow starter, and always there's someone hitting .400 through the first month or so."

But other mortals tail off. They drop out of the lineup to rest. Pete Rose goes on and on, missing games only when they chain him to his locker.

Someday, though, Pete Rose is going to reach the end. It may come before he finishes his second decade in the game, certainly not long after. The day has to come when baseball is no longer fun for him, when hitting isn't a challenge.

Does Rose realize this, could he accept it?

"A couple of bad losing years and years of hitting .225 can mess up anyone's mind," he said.

Somehow those bad losing years and years of hitting .225 seem far off in the distance, as far off as the 1973 opener seemed when Pete Rose won over the late Fred Hutchinson's heart and started on the long road toward fame and fortune in 1963.

It has been an eventful few years since Pete and his dad sat in general admission seats far down the right-field line in Crosley Field watching Ted Kluszewski, Jim Greengrass, and Gus Bell. "The Dodgers were always my favorite because I liked Pee Wee Reese," he said.

Pete's last game as an amateur was at Dayton's Howell field in the Dayton Amateur Baseball league. Rose was a catcher and went 5-for-5 against Ed Kruer. "Old Ed Kruer, remember him?" asked Pete. Rose was astounded when he was told that the 49-year-old Kruer is still pitching.

"I doubt if I'll be playing regularly when I'm 40," Rose said. "Not the way I play the game. I'm too hard on myself to last that long. Maybe I could hang around if they put the designated-hitter rule in our league. Hell, if they had it in our league, Stan Musial still could play."

Pete started his second decade as a major-leaguer needing 78 hits to reach 2,000.

"My goal is 3,000. If I can play 150 games for the next five years, I'll reach 3,000 on July 16, 1977 —no make that 1978," said Pete.

"It would be nice to make 4,000. That would be one of two untouchable baseball records. The other will be Hank Aaron's eventual career home-run record," Rose added.

"I'm the only active guy with a legitimate chance to get 4,000 hits," Pete continued. "I'm proud of the fact most of the name guys like Ty Cobb got most of their hits in their second 10 years. I got 1,922 in my first 10 years—and if you throw out my first two seasons when I got 170 and 139, I've averaged 202 hits the last eight years and hit over .300 each time."

When "Charlie Hustle" talks of hitting goals, horizons seem unlimited.

(Editor's Note: In the first year of his second decade, Pete Rose did better than even he had expected. His 230 hits, for a .338 average, and 115 runs scored earned him the National League's Most Valuable Player Award in 1973.)

One of Cincinnati's native sons, Pete Rose earned the nickname Charlie Hustle for his aggressive style of play, which includes running to first base even when he's walked. By hard work, he has made himself into one of baseball's most successful switch-hitters. "Pete is a self-made person," says his manager Sparky Anderson. "No one jumped out of their shoes to sign him when he got out of high school. He made himself into what he is, and to do that you've got to be a competitor." Says Pete: "I keep in good shape and I take care of myself, so I don't see any reason why I can't play until I'm about 40."

That Called Homer?
It Never Happened!

by Herbert Simons

October, 1957

This is the 25th anniversary of a historic baseball event that never happened.

I know. I was there. I saw it never happen.

It was 25 years ago this World Series that Babe Ruth, standing at home plate before 50,000 hooting fans in Chicago's Wrigley Field, gestured with an upraised hand a moment before golfing a terrific line drive over the center-field fence for what has been called the most storied home run of all time.

Legend has it that the great Babe "called his shot" by finger-pointing to the precise spot he would homer to on Charlie Root's next pitch.

He didn't.

He didn't—in spite of what you may have read or heard, in spite of what you may have seen in the movies or on television.

True, the Babe did gesture with his right hand in that third game of the 1932 World Series, in which the Yankees whipped the Cubs four straight, and he gestured not only once, but twice—but he wasn't "calling his shot."

Not according to the memory and records of this eyewitness, who, as the baseball expert assigned to do the "lead" story of each game of that World Series for the *Chicago Times,* had a vantage seat in the center of the main press box, slung from under the second deck right back of home plate, less than 150 feet from the Babe.

Not according to such an authoritative observer as Warren Brown, whose columns for the *Chicago American* continually reflect his 35 years' covering of top sport assignments.

Not according to Gordon Cobbledick, able sports editor of the *Cleveland Plain Dealer* and a 30-year veteran on the big league beat.

And not according to scores of other veteran reporters to whom we have talked and whose from-the-scene writings we have researched in the task of setting the legend at rest for you and for ourselves.

Cobbledick wrote recently: "The story has no basis in truth, but that hasn't impeded its circulation. It has become part of the Babe Ruth saga. Persons who were present at Wrigley Field that afternoon and saw no such gesture have heard it and read it so many times that they are now convinced that they have witnessed the making of history. Now *they* are telling it, with embellishments limited only by their own inventiveness."

Damon Runyon was one of the truly great reporters of all time, one with an inherent flair for the dramatic. Yet you can't find a mention of the pointing incident in his story of the game in the next morning's *New York American*—and his story, starting on the front page, ran *two and one-half* columns long!

You won't find a mention of it in the story in the same issue of the *American* by Bill Slocum, another great baseball writer of the era, and his story ran one column and a half.

You can't even get Joe McCarthy, who managed the Babe and the other Yankees in that Series, to say the Babe "called his shot." I know that, too. I tried. At Cooperstown, a few weeks ago. It was the morning McCarthy was enshrined in the Hall of Fame, and we were there to help pay tribute to an old friend whom we had covered in his pre-Yankee managerial days with the Cubs.

"By the way, Joe, what is your version of that Babe Ruth 'called homer,' " we asked during what to then had been a pleasant reunion.

Old Marse Joe bristled.

"I'm not going to say he didn't do it," he snapped, obviously quite agitated by the question. "Maybe I didn't see it—maybe I was looking the other way."

"Come now," we chided, "you don't mean to say that with your team at bat in the World Series, the score tied, and nobody on base, you weren't watching the plate."

"No," said Joe, uneasily, "but maybe I was looking here or there. Anyway, I'm not going to say he didn't do it."

As Shakespeare would have phrased it, "Methinks my manager doth protest too much."

As the psychologists would phrase it, the fact that McCarthy became so emotional would indicate he wasn't revealing his true feeling, probably because he didn't want to be a party to destroying the legend.

Most significant, of course, is that McCarthy didn't say, "Sure, he did it—I saw it," or "I didn't see it myself; I happened to look away for a moment, but a lot of the fellows on the bench said they saw it."

For years now, Charlie Root has been having to answer the question, too, the last time (or probably not the last time, at that) when we saw old Chinski in New York this summer when the Milwaukee Braves, for whom Root is now the pitching coach, were at the Polo Grounds.

Having heard Root's heated denials through the years that Ruth never called the shot or anything like it, we didn't bother to ask him if it *did* happen. We merely said we were bringing up *that* subject again.

"You know," said Root, with a forced smile, "I'm better known for that—for something that never happened—than for the things that did happen."

[The "things that did happen" made Root one of the outstanding right-handers of all time. From 1926 through 1941, he won 201 games for the Cubs, including a 26-win season in 1927.]

"Did you ever talk to Babe about his version of the incident?" we asked.

"No," said Root, "because I never heard the story until years later. The only time I talked to the Babe after that game was before batting practice the next day. He was up at the plate and I walked over and was looking at the bat he was using and asked him if that was the bat he had hit it with, and he said 'yes' and handed it to me to feel.

"It was heavy—about 50 ounces I would say, and it was dark, a sort of hickory color; in fact, I think the wood was hickory.

"You know I had two strikes on him on fastballs right down the middle, belt high, in that fifth inning. Then I threw him a change-up curve, intending to waste it to get him off-stride. It wasn't a foot off the ground and it was three or four inches off the outside of the plate, certainly not a good pitch to hit, but that was the one he smacked. So I asked him how he happened to hit such a pitch.

" 'I just guessed with you,' he told me.

"And that's all that was said," Root recalled. "You know me well enough, Herb, to know that if I had thought he had tried to show me up, I'd have knocked him right on his tail."

He would have, too.

The Cub hurlers of that era, Guy Bush, Pat Malone, Jakie May, and Root in particular, weren't at all bashful about setting any batter, even a Ruth, on his ear or any other portion of his anatomy.

In fact, the Babe did get it in his first time at bat the day after he had hit the legendary homer, but not because of the homer or by Root. Guy Bush, red-necked because of the Babe's and other Yankees' reference to his dark complexion in the raucous jockeying that earmarked the Series, almost maimed the Babe with an inside fastball that caught him on his right arm in the fourth and last game of the affair.

Next day, in the *New York World-Telegram,* Dan Daniel, now national president of the Baseball Writers Association, wrote: "Had there been a fifth game today, the Babe would have been forced to the sidelines. For in the first inning yesterday Bush struck the Babe with a fastball. The arm swelled at once and the pain was terrific, the Babe explained today. But he did not even tell McCarthy and played through. When the Babe was mobbed after the game, the arm pained so much he could not sign a single ball or autograph a scorecard." [The Babe, though he threw as well as batted left-handed, wrote with his right hand.]

Since the Babe didn't "call his shot," just what was the significance of his gestures? For a better understanding, let's review the setting. The Yankees, in McCarthy's second year at their helm, won their way into the Series in a breeze—their 107 victories giving them a 13-game bulge over Connie Mack's Athletics, whom they succeeded on the American League throne. The Cubs, lagging behind Pittsburgh until Charlie Grimm replaced Rogers Hornsby as manager on August 2, came on with a furious stretch drive to win by four games.

A big factor in the Cubs' resurgence was Mark Koenig, the Yankees' own star shortstop of their 1926–27–28 champions. Salvaged from the minors in late season, he sparked the Cubs' stretch rush. He played in only 33 games, but was a spectacular figure in most of them. However, in the pre-Series meeting to divvy their share of the forthcoming players' pool, the Cubs placed the emphasis on Koenig's length of time with the club, rather than what he had accomplished in it. They voted him only a half share.

The Yankees considered this unfair treatment of an old pal. The "cheapskate" theme became a featured part of their bench jockeying. Roast riders still rode high in that era. It wasn't until quite a few years later that the yearly edict from the Commissioner's office "to be little gentlemen—or else" turned the Series into the dignified, sedate affair it now is.

Both clubs were "on" each other unmercifully as the Yankees took the first two games in New York, 12-6 and 5-2. When the Series was resumed in Chicago Saturday, a crowd of 49,986 jammed Wrigley Field and also the temporary stands built outside the park in the streets back of the left- and right-field bleachers.

"The fans simply would not believe how severely or decisively their champions had been manhandled by the mighty Yankees in the East," wrote John Drebinger, then and now an outstanding baseball writer for the *New York Times.* "The fans roared their approval of every good play made by the Cubs. They playfully tossed bright yellow lemons at Babe Ruth and booed him thoroughly, even when he homered in his first time at bat.

For years, there have been conflicting reports as to whether Babe Ruth actually "called" his home run against the Cubs in the 1932 World Series. Ruth, pictured here before the Series with Lou Gehrig and Yankee manager Joe McCarthy, was a bit ambiguous about the matter himself. However, what he and Gehrig did to the Cubs in that Series is in the record books. In leading the Yankees to a four-game sweep, Ruth hit two homers, drove in six runs, and batted .333. Gehrig collected three homers, eight RBI, and a juicy .529 batting average. It was Ruth's last World Series.

"And they howled with glee as Ruth failed in a heroic attempt to make a shoestring catch of Billy Jurges' low liner to left in the fourth inning (a double that enabled the Cubs to tie the score at 4-4). Good-naturedly the Babe doffed his cap to acknowledge the adverse plaudits."

"As the Babe moved toward the plate with one out in the fifth inning, swinging three bats over his shoulders, a concerted shout of derision broke out in the stands," wrote Richards Vidmer in the *New York Herald Tribune*. "There was a bellowing of boos, hisses, and jeers. There were cries of encouragement for the pitcher, and from the Cubs' dugout came a storm of abuse leveled at the Babe.

"But Ruth grinned in the face of the hostile greeting. He laughed back at the Cubs and took his place supremely confident. A strike whistled over the plate and joyous outcries filled the air, but the Babe held up one finger as though to say, 'That's only one, though. Just wait.'

"Another strike—and the stands rocked with delight. The Chicago players hurled their laughter at the great man, but Ruth held up two fingers and still grinned, the supershowman. On the next pitch, the Babe swung. There was a resounding report like the explosion of a gun. Straight for the fence the ball soared on a line, clearing the farthest corner of the barrier, 436 feet from home plate.

"Before Ruth left the plate and started his swing around the bases, he paused to laugh at the Chicago players, suddenly silent in their dugout. As he rounded first he flung a remark at Grimm; as he turned second he tossed a jest at Billy Herman and his shoulders shook with satisfaction as he trotted in."

Beautiful descriptive writing—but notice not one word about a "called shot."

In the *New York Times* Drebinger recounted: "Ruth signaled with his fingers after every pitch to let the spectators know exactly how the situation stood."

On the day after the Series ended, the *New York World-Telegram,* which had no Sunday edition in which to run follow-up stories on the Saturday "Ruth game," printed six full columns of World Series comment by such competent observers as Joe Williams, Tom Meany, and Dan Daniels—but in all six columns there was nary a word of a "called homer."

Warren Brown once recalled: "The Babe indicated he had one strike . . . the big one . . . left. The vituperative Cub bench knew what he meant. Cub catcher Gabby Hartnett, in the Babe's immediate vicinity, heard Ruth growl that this is what he meant. Ruth, for a long while, had no other version, nor was any other sought from him.

"Only recently, in a very authoritative volume, I read that Ruth *deliberately* took two strikes, before pointing in the direction to which he was going to hit that home run!"

The first mention in print of a "called homer" that considerable research could find was made by Bill Corum and Tom Meany simultaneously three days after the game. In a column on "Men of the Series" for the *New York Journal,* Bill Corum wrote of Ruth:

"Words fail me. When he stood up there at the bat before 50,000 persons calling the balls and strikes with gestures for the benefit of the Cubs in the dugout and then, with two strikes on him, pointed out where he was going to hit the next one and hit it there, I gave up. The fellow is not human."

On the same day Meany, in the *New York World-Telegram,* noted:

"Babe's interviewer then interrupted to point out the hole in which Babe put himself Saturday when he pointed out the spot in which he intended hitting his homer and asked the Great Man if he realized how ridiculous he would have appeared if he struck out.

" 'I never thought of it,' said the Great Man, which is the tipoff on the Babe. He simply had his mind made up to hit a home run and he did."

Fifteen years later, Meany elaborated on the incident in his book, *Babe Ruth,* calling it "the most defiant, and the most debated, gesture in World Series history."

"Root threw a called strike past the Babe and the Cub bench let the big fellow have it. Babe, holding the bat in one hand, held up the index finger of the other, to signify it was indeed a strike. Root threw another called strike. Ruth held up two fingers and the Cub bench howled in derision.

"It was then the big fellow made what many believe to be the beau geste of his entire career. He pointed in the direction of dead center field. Some say it was merely a gesture toward Root, others that he was just letting the Cub bench know that he still had the big one left. Ruth himself has changed his version a couple of times, but the reaction of most of those who saw him point his finger toward center field is that he was calling his shot.

"Late that winter, at a dinner at the New York Athletic Club, Ruth declared that calling his shot against Root was the biggest thrill he ever had in baseball. As time went on, however, there was a general move to discount the big fellow's gesture and in the general debate which followed, Babe himself grew confused and wasn't certain whether he had picked out a spot in the bleachers to park the ball, was merely pointing to the outfield or was signaling that he still had one swing to go."

Let the confusion end now. What a few romantically interpreted as "pointing" was merely a sweep of his hand as he brought it down from his "that's-only-two-strikes" gesture.

If Ruth had done the pointing act—one that was dramatic enough to have lived in legend for a quarter of a century—why didn't such top-rank observers as Damon Runyon, Warren Brown, Gordon Cobbledick, Dan Daniel, John Drebinger, Dick Vidmer, or many, many others even mention it, yet alone feature it?

Why doesn't Joe McCarthy say Ruth did it?

Why wasn't Ruth sure himself whether he did or not?

The answer is obvious.

It never happened.

I know.

I was there.

I saw it never happen.

(Editor's Note: Here's how Herbert Simons, then editor of *Baseball Digest,* telegraphed the details of Babe Ruth's legendary homer from the Wrigley Field press box to the *Chicago Times* a few minutes after it happened:

"Root pushed a strike past Ruth. The crowd roared. Good-naturedly the Babe lifted his right forefinger so that all could see. Only one strike, he indicated. Another called strike and another razzing roar from the crowd. The Babe good-naturedly stuck up two fingers. And if there was a fan in the crowd who couldn't appreciate the full significance of this 'I've got a big one left' motion, it certainly dawned on him on the next pitch. Ruth took his stance, and the ball took a 440-foot ride to the center-field flagpole, a liner unequaled in the history of Wrigley Field.")

Baseball's Unbeatable Records

by George Vass

May, 1970

As part of the celebration of the 100th anniversary of pro baseball in 1969 a poll was taken to determine the most notable individual achievement of the first century.

Ranking 1-2-3 in the voting were Joe DiMaggio's 56-game hitting streak, Babe Ruth's 60 home runs in 1927, and Johnny Vander Meer's successive no-hit games for the Cincinnati Reds in 1938.

Many of those voting for Vander Meer's feat gave as a reason for their choice that the odds against successive no-hit games are so great that it was impossible the achievement ever could be equaled.

Certainly, the odds against wiping the record completely out of the books are immense. It would take a mathematical whiz to figure out the numerical odds against throwing three no-hitters back-to-back. And even the odds against another pair back-to-back are immense.

But you can't be sure because it almost happened again just nine years after Vander Meer did it. And the only reason it didn't was that Ewell Blackwell was a trifle careless.

On June 18, 1947, Blackwell pitched a no-hitter for the Cincinnati Reds against the Boston Braves. Four days later, Blackwell was holding the Brooklyn Dodgers hitless with one out in the ninth and Eddie Stanky at bat.

"Then Stanky hit a ground ball which I should have fielded and turned into an out," said Blackwell. "I did get my glove down fast enough to get it but misjudged the speed and hop, and it passed through my legs for a single to center."

The next batter, Al Gionfriddo, hit an easy flyball to center fielder Bert Haas. If Blackwell had fielded Stanky's ground ball properly and thrown him out, Gionfriddo's fly would have been the final out of the game and Vander Meer would have had company in the record books. Blackwell, too, would have gained double no-hit fame.

Of course, Blackwell didn't quite make it, which is what makes the game of choosing "imperishable" records as compared with those that figure to fall sooner or later so much fun. You can't tell them apart, it being strictly a matter of personal opinion, based on seemingly reasonable thinking.

No better example of the pitfalls of reason when applied to individual achievement can be given than the widely held assumption of just a few years ago that Ty Cobb's record of stealing 96 bases in 1915 would stand up forever.

The arguments against wiping out Cobb's mark were sound. The art of base-stealing was at a low ebb, other stratagems for moving up a runner being more important. Few men could have as many opportunities for stealing as did Cobb, a .369 hitter in 1915. Yet along came Maury Wills, batting just .299, and he stole 104 bases in 1962.

Similar is the case of the National League earned-run-average record, set at 1.22 by Grover Cleveland Alexander in 1915. No pitcher came within half an earned run of matching that for more than five decades. Given the changes in the game it seemed impossible to match.

Yet in 1968 Bob Gibson of the St. Louis Cardinals, working 305 innings, came up with 1.12. Another impregnable mark had fallen.

Ruth's record of 60 home runs—in a 154-game season—was in a different category. As revered and as earthshaking as the record was when he set it—after all, no other *team* in the American League hit more home runs in 1927 than he did—it was under assault almost from the beginning.

The fact that it took 34 years to topple it, when Roger Maris hit 61 in 1961, doesn't change the basic assumption which existed all along—that the record could be broken (though it took a 162-game schedule to do it). Hank Greenberg and Jimmie Foxx, with 58 each, and Hack Wilson, with 56, had shown its potential vulnerability.

So when one separates records into two categories of "impregnable" and "vulnerable," it's well to take into consideration the adage that whatever one man can accomplish another can surpass.

Still, considering the odds, let's try it, choosing five records that should stand for all time and five that probably will fall.

THE IMPREGNABLES
1. Rogers Hornsby's .424 batting average of 1924.
2. Hack Wilson's 190 runs batted in, in 1930.
3. Lou Gehrig's 2,130 consecutive games played.
4. Jack Chesbro's 41 victories in 1904.
5. Joe DiMaggio's 56-game hitting streak of 1941.

THE VULNERABLES
1. Roger Maris' 61 home runs in 1961.
2. Sandy Koufax' 382 strike-outs in 1965.
3. Rube Marquard's 19 consecutive pitching victories in 1912.
4. Johnny Vander Meer's successive no-hitters in 1938.
5. Maury Wills' 104 stolen bases in 1962.

Let's analyze the "impregnables" one by one:

Hornsby's .424: Even old-timers are willing to admit that fielding techniques and gloves have improved immeasurably over the last 45 years. And there's little doubt the pitching staffs are deeper, with big, strong, hard throwers available as relief pitchers.

All this has made it likely that the peak level of batting performance, even by the best, has been reduced to around .360. Few hitters have topped this mark in the last 30 years.

The last man to hit .400 was Ted Williams, who batted .406 in 1941. Before that, Bill Terry came up with .401 in 1930, when the ball was admittedly much livelier than when Hornsby hit .424. Williams and Terry are the only two men other than Hornsby—who hit .403 in 1925—who even topped .400 since 1924.

Another aspect of this remarkable feat was that Hornsby's margin over the next batter in the league was 49 points (Zack Wheat hit .375).

The verdict: Hornsby's mark is unassailable because it is unlikely that under present conditions a hitter can reach .400 much less top it by 24 points.

Wilson's 190: Only two men have even approached this season mark of 190 runs batted in since Wilson did it in 1930. Lou Gehrig had 184 in 1931, and Hank Greenberg had 183 in 1937.

Since then the fall-off has been sharp, the maximum feasible output apparently leveling at around 150. No one in the National League has even come close to what Wilson did for the Cubs in 1930. The best since then was Joe Medwick's 154 in 1937 and Tommy Davis' 153 for the Dodgers in 1962.

Obviously, prime requirements for driving in runs are having a lot of men on in front of you and being able to hit the long ball. The Cubs of 1930 batted .309 as a team, and Wilson hit 56 home runs, batted .356, and had 423 total bases.

The verdict: Because such a combination of team and individual hitting skill is inconceivable, given today's conditions, Wilson's record is safe.

Gehrig's 2,130: It is impossible that anyone should break this record—that it was set in the first place is incredible. No record in baseball is as clear-cut as this one, Gehrig playing more than 800 games in a row *more* than his nearest rival.

The verdict: Untouchable because—unlike most records—this is one that no player today would even attempt to surpass.

Chesbro's 41: The fact that this record was set in 1904, the beginning of what is considered the modern era, doesn't make it any the less remarkable. Only Ed Walsh, with 40 victories in 1908, even came close to matching it.

Two years ago Dennis McLain won 31 games for the Detroit Tigers to debunk the argument that winning 30 games under modern conditions was impossible. But that's still 10 victories short of Chesbro's 41.

The real bar is that few pitchers, no matter how good, get more than 40 starts a season now, and many victories go to relievers.

The verdict: Chesbro's record is safe unless baseball goes to a 200-game, eight-month schedule.

DiMaggio's 56: From a mechanical standpoint this record could be broken by a superlative hitter.

Maury Wills dives headlong into the bag, a maneuver he used frequently to save wear and tear on his legs after he set a major league one-season stolen base record of 104 in 1962. His record, since broken by Lou Brock, was the best in the majors since Ty Cobb stole 96 bases in 1915. Small of stature and a switch-hitter, Wills was an artist in getting "the jump" on the pitcher when he wanted to steal a base.

Maury Wills

Johnny Vander Meer

Jack Chesbro

In 1961, Roger Maris hit 61 homers, a season record, and Yankee teammate Mickey Mantle hit 54.

A few breaks here and there could carry a great batter a long way.

The real problem would be psychological. The pressure as a hitter's streak approached the 50-game mark would be tremendous. Yankee manager Ralph Houk made this point in comparing DiMag's achievement with that of Maris.

"Even Maris wasn't under the tension that DiMaggio was because Maris could go a couple of games without his homer," explained Houk, "but DiMaggio always had to get his hit. He had to keep his health, and he had to face every kind of pitching there was, whether he liked it or not, and he knew also that the scorers would bend over backwards not to give him an advantage.

"His has to be the top achievement of them all."

The verdict: Unassailable if for no other reason than the mounting pressure that would resist any effort to break it.

And now let's analyze the "vulnerables":

Maris' 61: Reggie Jackson's assault up to mid-season of last year proved again how vulnerable the home-run record is. True, Jackson didn't come anywhere close to the mark, but he indicated the promise is there for the future.

The real weakness of this record is the fact that so many men through the years have penetrated the over-50 mark in home runs even before the increase in the schedule to 162 games (which helped Maris).

Verdict: There is certain to be a player within the next few years who'll come into the stretch close enough to make a determined drive to top this mark. It's just a matter of time.

Koufax' 382: It's hard to say whether the improvement in pitchers or the deterioration in batters imperil this mark, but certainly the free swinger is all around us.

Such hitters as Bobby Bonds, who set a major league record by striking out 187 times last season, provide increased opportunity for the strike-out artist.

Improved pitching techniques, which have seen the pitcher get the advantage over the hitter in recent years, also favor the breaking of this record.

Still, the chief threat is the rise of a young pitcher with the ability of a Koufax, a Bob Feller, or a Walter Johnson. He will have to be capable of going 350 innings a season, with a repertoire equal to the best.

Verdict: You'll know it when you see it, but it's for sure. Furthermore, a workhorse with top skills will strike out 400.

Marquard's 19: It has been 58 years since Marquard, lanky southpaw of the New York Giants, started a streak of 19 straight victories on opening day of 1912. He didn't lose until July 8.

No one has really come close to matching this, although such worthies as Christy Mathewson, Carl Hubbell, Blackwell, Walter Johnson, Joe Wood, Schoolboy Rowe, and Lefty Grove put together strings of 16.

Still, the fact that so many men have done as well as they have induced the belief that someday somebody's going to do even better.

Incidentally, Marquard always claimed he had 20 victories in a row, being robbed of a verdict credited to Jeff Tesreau.

Verdict: A tough nut to crack, but given the breaks a pitcher should be able to beat Marquard's record.

Vander Meer's No-Hitters: The odds would say no but experience says, yes, it can be tied even if it's unlikely to be topped.

The Blackwell attempt to match the consecutive no-hitters, even though it failed, shows that given a "hot" pitcher, the mark is definitely vulnerable.

Verdict: This one is sure to be tied, but that the record will ever be surpassed is unlikely.

Wills' 104: Every mark in track has fallen in recent years as superior training techniques have yielded better results from superior athletes.

This has only an indirect bearing on base stealing, yet an important one. More and more youngsters are coming out of high schools trained in the art of running. And with Wills leading the way, the base-stealing techniques have been considerably refined over the years.

Given a combination of greater speed and better technique, it's highly likely that a good hitter will emerge with the desire to steal and the knowledge of how to do it. Everything being equal, the techniques of base stealing are capable of greater improvement than the defenses against them.

Verdict: The 104 mark is a solid one, but given the effort and skill, it can be wiped out by a fast .330 hitter who must make up for a lack of power.

Now, all this is just one man's opinion, but remember: the higher the goal the greater the achievement. In other words, most records stir men to greater efforts to surpass them.

Just look at the record.

(Editor's Note: Since this article appeared in *Baseball Digest,* two of the "vulnerable records" listed by Mr. Vass have fallen by the wayside. In 1973, Nolan Ryan of the Angels struck out 383 batters, and in 1974 Lou Brock of the Cardinals stole 118 bases. All of the "impregnable records" remain standing.)

Curfew Rules
Are Made To Be Broken

by John Kuenster

September, 1970

There was a time not too many years ago when a baseball writer was sitting in a coffee shop, talking to Bo Belinsky, a celebrated nonconformist who then pitched for the Los Angeles (now California) Angels.

The dialogue revolved around two subjects: baseball and (What else?) girls.

At that juncture in his life, Belinsky had become famous as a no-hit pitcher, a sharpie at pool, and as an after-hours vagabond who liked to date Hollywood starlets.

He had just broken up his romance with Mamie VanDoren, which prompted the writer to ask a rather inane question.

"Why?" inquired the writer.

"I need her," said Bo rather haughtily, "like Custer needed more Indians."

The writer thought Belinsky was a little bereft of his senses at the time, but actually, it was a typical rejoinder for Bo, who, as Red Smith once said, "never lost the air of conscious grandeur" after pitching that no-hit game in 1962.

In subsequent years, notoriety continued to pursue Belinsky, even though he never reached his promise as a major league pitcher.

During spring training in 1968, he collected headlines again by disappearing from the Houston Astros' camp with a fetching creature named Jo Collins whose picture once adorned the center fold of *Playboy* magazine.

Bo got mad and left the Astros because general manager Spec Richardson refused him permission to stay out later than the curfew, which was 1 a.m.

Bo and Jo, evidently as close together as their names, were making plans for marriage, and who looks at the clock when such crucial matters must be discussed. You know, young love and all that.

Maybe Bo couldn't be blamed for staying out past the deadline with such a beautiful friend as Jo Collins, but rules are rules, and it will be a cold day in the middle of the Sahara before baseball management dispenses with curfew regulations.

Curfews may seem to be the evil inventions of grouchy spoilsports, but they are put into effect to maintain at least some semblance of order and discipline among the players. They are also designed to tone up a player's eyesight and reflexes, but that's open to debate.

Yet curfew rules have been and will continue to be broken. Some attempts to circumvent the law have succeeded. Some have not. An example of a classic failure comes immediately to mind.

It involves a White Sox pitcher some years ago when the club was in Baltimore. As a fitting stroke of bad luck for the miscreant, manager Marty Marion was returning to the hotel lobby at 2 a.m. after spending the evening with general manager Frank Lane and a writer traveling with the Sox. And lo and behold, he spots the pitcher tiptoeing down the stairs.

"Where," Marion demanded of the startled pitcher, "are you going at this hour?"

"Oh," said the pitcher rather weakly, "I was just coming down to check and see if I got any mail."

An authentic story about curfew violators involves a clique of White Sox players who were outfoxed by manager Jimmy Dykes years ago. The club stayed at the Kenmore Hotel in Boston then.

The hotel has a back door through which guests can enter and get on the elevators undetected by anyone sitting in the lobby.

Actress Mamie Van Doren (left) and Bo Belinsky were romantically linked during Bo's peripatetic baseball career that included stops—between 1962 and 1970—with the Angels, Phillies, Astros, Pirates, and Reds. Belinsky, no respecter of curfew rules, frequently ruffled management's sense of propriety, but there's no denying he also holds one of baseball's rare distinctions: He pitched a no-hitter—on May 5, 1962, against the Baltimore Orioles.

Dykes was aware something unlawful was afoot that night, so he stationed himself at the back door, engaging the hotel chef in a game of gin rummy.

After midnight, the wayward players, one by one, entered the back door and were nailed by Dykes. Everybody, that is, but Luke Appling. Luke went in like a man, through the front lobby, and Dykes missed him.

In later years, Appling liked to chide Dykes about his suspicions. When the story was repeated in Dykes' presence, Luke would look Jimmy in the eye and say, "Didya see me?" And the answer was always no. Dykes would merely smile, and blow vigorous puffs of smoke from his cigar.

There was one time in Detroit, though, that Dykes confronted Appling just as Luke was about to make an exit from the hotel after curfew had passed.

"You might just as well stay on this side of the door," said Dykes, "because it's gonna cost you twice as much to come back in."

Probably the most ingenious scheme to catch curfew violators was concocted by the late Rogers Hornsby, who managed the Cubs, Cardinals, and Reds in his long baseball career.

Always a stickler for detail, such as getting eight hours of sleep a night, Hornsby one year was disconcerted to find a number of his players casually ignoring curfew restrictions.

The Rajah brought a swift end to the players' brazen disregard for club regulations. One night, at the stroke of midnight, he gave the hotel's lone elevator operator a baseball.

"I want you to get the autograph of every player on this ball who comes in after I get up to my room," said Hornsby.

The operator complied with Hornsby's wishes. The curfew culprits were only too happy to sign the baseball for the nice, old elevator man. The next day, Hornsby had all the evidence he needed to slap fines on the offending players.

As managers, Jimmy Dykes (left) and Rogers Hornsby followed the usual strategies to catch players breaking their clubs' curfew regulations.

Baseball in Paris, 1918

by Heywood Broun

Condensed from the book
*The A.E.F., With General Pershing
and the American Forces*

March, 1943

The day after the Americans marched in Paris one of the French newspapers referred to the doughboys as "Roman Caesars clad in khaki." The city set itself to liking the soldiers and everything American and succeeded admirably. Even the taxicab drivers refrained from overcharging Americans very much. Schoolchildren studied the history of America and *The Star-Spangled Banner*. There were pictures of President Wilson and General Pershing in many shops and some had framed translations of the President's message to Congress. In fact, so eager were the French to take America to their hearts that they even made desperate efforts to acquire a working knowledge of baseball.

Excelsior, an illustrated French daily, carried an action picture taken during a game played between American ambulance drivers just outside of Paris. The picture was entitled: "A player goes to catch the ball, which has been missed by the catcher," and underneath ran the following explanation: "We have given in our number of yesterday the rules of baseball, the American National game, of which a game, which is perhaps the first ever played in France, took place yesterday at Colombes between the soldiers of the American ambulances. Here is an aspect of the game. The pitcher, or thrower of balls, whom one sees in the distance, has sent the ball. The catcher, or *attrapeur,* who should restrike the ball with his wooden club, has missed it, and a player placed behind him has seized it in its flight."

The next day *L'Intransigeant* undertook the even more hazardous task of explaining American baseball slang. During the parade on the Fourth of July, some Americans had greeted the doughboys with shouts of "ataboy." A French journalist heard and was puzzled. He returned to his office and looked in English dictionaries and various works of reference without enlightenment. Several English friends were unable to help him, and an American who had lived in Paris for 30 years was equally at sea.

But the reporter worked it out all by himself, and the next day he wrote: "Parisians have been puzzled by the phrase 'ataboy' which Americans are prone to employ in moments of stress and emotion. The phrase is undoubtedly a contraction of 'at her boy' and may be closely approximated by *au travail, garçon.*" The writer followed with a brief history of the friendly relations of France and America and paid a glowing tribute to the memory of Lafayette.

The high tide in the American conquest of Paris came one afternoon in July. I got out of a taxicab in front of the American headquarters in the Rue Constantine and found that a big crowd had gathered in the Esplanade des Invalides. Now and again the crowd would give ground to make room for an American soldier running at top speed. One of them stood almost at the entrance of the courtyard of "Invalides." His back was turned toward the tomb of Napoleon, and he was knocking out flies in the direction of the Seine.

Unfortunately it was a bit far to the river, and no baseball has yet been knocked into that stream. It was a new experience for Napoleon, though. He has heard rifles and machine guns and other loud reports in the streets of Paris, but for the first time there came to his ears the loud sharp crack of a bat swung against a baseball. Since he could not see from out of the tomb the noise may have worried the emperor. Perhaps he thought it was the British winning new battles on other cricket fields. But again he might not worry about that now. He might hop up on one toe as a French caricaturist pictured him and cry: *"Vive l'Angleterre!"*

One of the men in the crowd which watched the batting practice was a French soldier headed back for the front. At any rate he had his steel helmet on and his equipment was on his back. His stripes showed that he had been in the war three years, and he had the Croix de Guerre with two palms and the Medaille Militaire. His interest in the game grew so high at last that he put down his pack and his helmet and joined the outfielders. The second or third ball hit came in his direction. He ran about in a short circle under the descending ball, and at the last moment he thrust both hands in front of his face. The ball came between them and hit him in the nose, knocking him down.

His nose was a little bloody, but he was up in an instant grinning. He left the field to pick up his trench hat and his equipment. The Americans shouted to him to come back. He understood the drift of their invitation, but he shook his head. *"C'est dangereux,"* he said, and started for the station to catch his train for the front.

The Night Elroy Face Bowed Out

by John Robertson
Montreal Star

December, 1969

They came—24,336 of them—to cheer the Expos and vent their spleens upon the prodigal Maury Wills. But both the huzzahs and the hoots were to curdle into sporadic groans of frustration by the sixth inning, as the Dodgers pulled five ahead and appeared this night to be home and cooled out.

So there was scarcely a ripple of recognition as 41-year-old Elroy Face ambled in from the bullpen, rewriting the National League record book with each mincing step. It was his 819th trip into the pressure cooker, and there was more raw courage than strength in his right arm now, as it reached back but could not quite grasp the greatness that had flowed so effortlessly out of it too many yesterdays ago.

No one in the park, least of all Elroy Leon Face, suspected that this night in August, 1969, he was finally to run out of tomorrows as an active major leaguer.

He had hinted at retirement at the end of the season, but pride had convinced him he could do the job at least until then, because if your name is Elroy Face you are entitled to overdraw on tomorrow's adrenalin, coil your five-foot-seven frame into a defiant knot, and put them down with a withering look and a well-aimed memory.

And put the Dodgers down, he did, in order in the sixth. He got Willie Davis on a fly to left to open the seventh. Then Andy Kosco hit one into the seats. Face glowered into catcher Ronnie Brand's mitt, and got Wes Parker on a liner to center for the second out. Then Bill Sudakis hit another downtown. And when Elroy got Tom Haller to fly to left to end the inning, he walked off the mound amid derisive hoots from people who only saw him as another aging hand grenade thrower, who had snapped their last thread of hope in a ball game that only added up to another lead weight in the Expos' cement overshoes.

A decade ago, they had stood and cheered and wept with joy in Pittsburgh's Forbes Field as he put together a string of 22 straight victories in relief, and the papers were plastered with ecstatic pictures of Elroy mobbed by teammates; Elroy grinning under a fireman's hat; Elroy swigging champagne in October in a city gone mad with adulation for him and his fellow world champion Pirates.

But here he was, walking off the field in a funny three-colored hat, in a city still squirming with major league diaper itch; a city gone berserk with adulation for the Rusty Staubs, Coco Laboys, and Mack Joneses; a city that arrived 10 years too late to see the real Elroy Face.

When the game ended, reporters still had no inkling of the agonizing decision general manager Jim Fanning and manager Gene Mauch had just made. They flocked to seek out Maury Wills and listen to him refuse to comment on the bronx cheers which had punctuated his every move. They listened to Dodger pitcher Don Sutton bubble with enthusiasm about pitching for a team that got him some runs this year, for a change. They heard manager Mauch wax philosophically about the great years ahead of some of his younger, talented Expos.

But no one took notice of the little guy in the dark red T-shirt walking with head bowed through the tunnel from Jim Fanning's office back to the dressing room.

The lights were out, the park was empty, and there were just a few stragglers left in the press room when someone burst in and said:

55

"Hey . . . they just cut Elroy."

The news was received with infinitely more regret than surprise.

I decided, out of duty, to go look for him, to find out his reaction. But halfway to the dressing room I stopped in that same dark tunnel he had walked through and tried to put myself in Elroy's shoes. And I decided that I wouldn't feel like talking to me . . . or to anybody right now.

Anything I could say to him would be pitifully inadequate. And no mumbled regrets on his part could possibly do justice to the glowing legend of greatness he was leaving behind him. Most games, pitcher: 846. Most games, relief pitcher: 819. Most games won, relief pitcher: 96. Most games finished, pitcher: 574—all National League records.

How can a typewriter jockey possibly fathom what is churning through the windmills of the mind of a man who has just been told, after 20 years in the pressure cooker, that he's too old to do the job anymore. Odds are this very thought has been haunting him ever since he started slipping off that pedestal of super-stardom many years ago.

And in lasting until he was 41 had he indeed not beaten old age?

Jim Fanning was obviously upset when he told me how he had broken the news to Face. "Earlier this year, he was one of the best in the National League. He won four games for us . . . and saved five more. He gave us respectability, when we were really struggling. He gave us everything he had. But finally we had to make a move. We needed a fresh arm. And Elroy had to go."

This is the way it is in professional sport. No office party. No gold watch. No nostalgic speeches. Just a long walk down a long, darkened tunnel beneath an empty concrete stadium, and no one waiting at the other end rubbing up a ball, plunking it in your palm, and saying: "Go get 'em Elroy."

If it's any consolation, no one ever did it better.

Elroy Face, who weighed no more than 160 pounds in his playing days, was the Pirates' most dependable reliever in the late 1950s and early 1960s. In 1959, he posted an 18-1 won-lost record in relief and saved 10 other games. When the Pirates won the National League pennant in 1960, he had a 10-8 record with 24 saves. He is seen here pitching against the Yankees in the fifth game of the 1960 World Series. He registered three saves in the Series for the victorious Pirates. After the fifth game, Face said the powerful Yankees all looked alike to him. "I respect 'em all and fear none of 'em," he told reporters.

Al Kaline—
The Game I'll Never Forget

as told to George Vass

May, 1974

There's a game in 1955 I sometimes think about when things aren't going as well as they might.

It was the kind of day you dream about, something that happens once in a lifetime and you never forget even though some of the details may become obscure in time.

I was 20 then, in my third year with the Detroit Tigers. It was early in the season, April 17, and we were playing the Kansas City A's in Detroit, our first Sunday home game of the year.

Neither team scored the first couple of innings, and when I came to bat in the third there was a man on first base. John Gray, a right-hander, was pitching for the A's. I can't remember the count or the pitch, but I hit a home run to put us ahead, 2-0.

In the fourth inning, I got a bloop single to drive in another run, one of four we scored that inning. We were leading 6-0 by that time, but there was nothing sensational about that inning.

What happened in the sixth inning was different, though. I led off the inning with a home run, my second of the game. A pretty good day, but it wasn't over yet. We kept on batting and scoring, and I got another time at bat in the same inning.

Harvey Kuenn was on third base, and I hit another home run. My second of the inning and third of the game. Later on, they told me that's the first time anybody had hit two home runs in an inning in the American League since Joe DiMaggio did it in 1936. So that was something.

I had a chance for four home runs in a game, but I popped up my last time at bat.

Oddly enough, though I treasure that game, it's not the one I'd describe as the one I'll never forget. That came a lot later in my career, in the 1968 World Series against the St. Louis Cardinals.

Winning that American League pennant in 1968 was thrill enough. I'd waited 16 years for that, and sometimes I'd wondered if the Tigers would ever make it, if I'd end my career without ever playing in a World Series.

It was sort of funny when we had the celebration after beating the New York Yankees to clinch the

pennant. I grabbed a bottle of champagne and tried to get the cork out, but it wouldn't budge. Imagine that! I'd been waiting 16 years for this moment, and I couldn't get the damned cork out.

With the Series coming up I made one of the tougher decisions of my life. It had been a rough season for me personally, and it seemed as if I really didn't belong in the starting lineup against the Cardinals in the Series.

Willie Horton, Mickey Stanley, and Jim Northrup had played well all season in the outfield, and Norm Cash had had a good year at first base. It seemed to me that those guys would give us our strongest lineup, and I didn't want manager Mayo Smith to be on the spot, to feel he had to play me because of all the years I'd been with the Tigers.

I had a long talk with Mayo and later I told Joe Falls, the *Detroit Free Press* columnist, about what I'd said to the manager. I told Mayo I'd waited all my life to get into the Series but that he should go with the kids. They deserved the chance, they'd helped win the pennant.

Mayo listened to me, but he had figured out a way to get me in the lineup. He tried Stanley, our center fielder, at shortstop in the last few games of the regular season. When the Series against the Cardinals opened, there was Stanley at short and me in right field.

It took a lot of guts for Mayo to make that move, and he got a lot of criticism.

The Cardinals were favored to win the Series because everybody figured they had the better club.

They had Lou Brock, Curt Flood, and Roger Maris in the outfield, Orlando Cepeda at first base, and so on, and Bob Gibson at his peak as the top man on a great pitching staff.

The way things started there was no reason to suppose the experts were wrong. The Cardinals chased our 31-game winner, Denny McLain, in the first game at St. Louis, and we lost.

We won the second game to even it up, but the Cardinals won the next two games at Detroit and it looked like it was almost over. We were down three games to one, and everybody was writing us off.

The fifth game of the Series, the big game as far as I'm concerned, looked for a time like it would be the last one and the Cardinals would beat us four out of five.

The game was played on Monday, October 7, in Detroit. The Cardinals wasted no time getting in front. They got three runs in the first inning off Mickey Lolich, who'd won the second game for us. Cepeda hit a two-run homer.

We got a couple of those runs back in the fourth inning off Nelson Briles, who was pitching for the Cards, but we were still trailing, 3-2.

In the fifth inning, came what turned out to be the key, and most controversial, play of the game. Brock doubled with one out, and when Julian Javier singled to left, Lou went for the plate. But he didn't slide, and Horton's throw to Bill Freehan beat him.

A lot of people thought Brock should have slid. I'm glad he didn't.

We were still behind, 3-2, when we got our turn in the seventh inning. We loaded the bases with one out, and I came to bat with a chance to tie the game or put us ahead.

Briles was gone by this time, and the Cardinals had Joe Hoerner, a left-hander, pitching. The Cardinals had been pitching me low and away all through the Series, and I figured that Hoerner would do the same thing.

Hoerner's first pitch came in, and I swung at it but missed. The next pitch was just off the corner. The count was one-and-one.

The third pitch was low and away, but I was counting on that and I got a good cut at it. It was a line drive over the second baseman's head into right-center. Two runs came in and we were ahead, 4-3.

Cash drove in another run with a single, and we went on to win the game, 5-3. We won the last two games in St. Louis to take the World Series.

I hit two home runs in that Series, but the single was the big hit. That's what won the key game, the one I'll never forget.

Al Kaline had to wait 16 years before playing in his first—and only —World Series, but when he finally reached his goal in 1968, he made the most of the opportunity. He batted a crisp .379, hit two homers, and drove in eight runs in helping the Tigers turn back the Cardinals in seven games. Here, he is greeted at the plate by Dick McAuliffe (No. 3) and Norm Cash (No. 25) after driving a home run into the upper left-field stands in the third game. Kaline also hit a homer in the sixth game.

A Most Forgettable Moment

by Joe Falls
Detroit Free Press

July, 1964

It is not necessary to delve into the depths of the middle ages to uncover some of the most "forgettable" moments in sports history.

If your name happens to be Paul Foytack, you need think back only to the night of July 31, 1963, in Cleveland to remember something you would rather forget.

That was the night he created history of a sort by throwing not one, not two, not three—but four home run balls in a row!

"Let's see 'em top that," said Foytack. "Me and the Babe, we'll be in the record books forever. His 714 homers and my four."

It was funny now as Foytack sipped his coffee at the Detroit Press Club. And, surprisingly enough, it was pretty funny that night in Cleveland.

"I'll never forget it," said Foytack, grinning that boyish grin of his. "They were hitting them off me so fast that the poor guy in center field couldn't shoot off the fireworks quick enough. He missed a whole round."

Foytack was pitching for the Los Angeles Angels. It was the sixth inning of the second game of a twi-night doubleheader, and he had disposed of the first two batters when it happened.

Bang, bang, bang, bang—Woodie Held, Pedro Ramos, Tito Francona, and Larry Brown connected in succession.

"I still can see every pitch," said Foytack. "Held hit a low inside fastball and hit it good. Ramos hit a high curve, and he hit it down on the trademark of the bat, but it still went out. Francona reached out for a high outside fastball and pulled it down the right-field line. Brown hit a slider that was right down the middle.

"I have trouble remembering my wedding anniversary, but I'll never forget those four pitches."

A question, sir: "How could you possibly throw the ball right over the middle of the plate to Brown after you'd been rocked for three straight homers?"

"You may not believe this, but I was trying to knock him down with the pitch," said Foytack. "That shows you the kind of control I had that night."

Foytack shook his head.

"The thing that gets me," he said, "is that when you're grooving the ball in batting practice, laying it right over the plate, they never come close to hitting four in a row out of the park on you.

"And you may not believe this, either, but I had shut out the Indians on three hits the previous time I faced them."

Another question, sir: "What did Bill Rigney say when he came to the mound to take you out?"

"I think Gabe Paul [the Cleveland general manager] was the guy who took me out. I was costing him too much dough in baseballs.

"I remember I got a big hand from the crowd when I left."

Jack Spring replaced Foytack. He was greeted by two singles. "They were pooped from swinging at me," said Foytack.

Foytack, of course, is an expert on home-run pitches.

He was the one who got Roger Maris started on his 61 homers in 1961. He threw Maris the first one in Tiger Stadium.

Foytack also threw a pair of over-the-roof pitches to Mickey Mantle in Tiger Stadium.

"But one day I showed that Jim Gentile a thing or two," said Foytack. "He thought he had hit one over the roof against me, but I showed him."

Huh?

"The ball hit the light tower and bounced back on the field."

Paul Foytack

How It Became the "Lucky Seventh"

by A. H. Tarvin

A pre-1900 National League pitcher and a member of the Hall of Fame, John Clarkson is credited with originating the phrase "the lucky seventh." He won a total of 327 games before finishing his career in 1894.

November, 1944

A baseball custom as rigidly observed as is the umpire's call of "Play Ball" at the start of the game is the seventh-inning stretch. In the stands of every ball park, big league or little, all customers rise and stretch between halves of the seventh inning. The belief is general among the superstitiously inclined that such a gesture, indulged in at that time, will bring good luck to the home team. But the fact of the matter is that the "stretch" didn't start out as a bid for the favor of Lady Luck. Indeed, it started out for the most practical of reasons—relaxation.

After maintaining a sitting position through six and one-half innings of a ball game, the average mortal becomes a trifle cramped, so he stretches. The practice was begun many years ago—just what year, no one can say, but it was done at least as far back as 1860 as is attested in a letter written by Harry Wright, the captain and center fielder of the unbeaten Cincinnati Red Stockings of that year. In this letter, addressed to Howard Ferris, of the same city, Wright said, in part: "The spectators all arise between halves of the seventh, extend their legs and arms, and sometimes walk about. In so doing, they enjoy the relief afforded by relaxation from a long posture upon the hard benches."

One of baseball's best-known—and longest-lived—expressions is "the lucky seventh." It is more than 50 years old. In the late summer of 1886, the Bostons were playing an important game against Anson's Chicago White Stockings, in the Windy City. When the White Stockings came in to take their turn at bat in the last of the seventh, they were trailing, 4 to 1. Captain Anson was much disturbed and so expressed himself to several of his players.

"Now, Pop," said Chicago's ace hurler, John Clarkson, "don't go getting all fussed up about nothing. Remember, this is the lucky seventh." And in that half inning, Chicago scored three runs to tie the score and put over the winning tally in the eighth.

It so happened that Clarkson's remark concerning the lucky seventh was overheard by Tim Murnane, then a celebrated baseball writer who was traveling with the visiting team as correspondent of the *Boston Globe*. Murnane scented a story in those words, the "lucky seventh," and he determined to see just what Clarkson meant by them, especially in view of the fact that the assurance had apparently relieved Anson of his worry.

Following the game that afternoon, Murnane was given permission by the Chicago club officials to examine the files containing the score of each game played by Chicago from the day it began its National League career, on April 25, 1876, down to that time. It was a tremendous task the Boston scribe assigned himself, but after working far into that night, all the next morning, and half the second night, he discovered what he sought. He found that the Chicagoans had scored far more runs in seventh innings than in any other and that in that period, they had turned more seeming defeats into victories.

When Murnane returned to Boston, he wrote the story of the "lucky seventh" for the *Globe;* it was copied by newspapers all over the country and thus a chance remark by a star pitcher to a celebrated first baseman-captain, within the hearing of the most noted baseball writer of the time, became part of baseball's language.

Ron Santo's 12-Year Secret

by Armand Schneider
Chicago Daily News

October, 1971

Baseball fans were bound to find out sooner or later that Ron Santo is a diabetic.

He has been for 12 years, but Santo asked repeatedly that newspapermen and other media people not write or say anything about his handicap.

"I don't know why," Santo said. "Maybe it's because I never wanted people feeling sorry for me or pointing at me or maybe saying I was using diabetes as a crutch or an alibi when things were going bad."

But slowly, word trickled out, and when Santo visited the Summer Camp for Diabetic Children in Lake Geneva, Wisconsin, last August, his secret was out. The Diabetic Association of Greater Chicago, the camp's sponsor, publicized Santo's visit, and what he had kept within a circle of close associates became generally known.

"I've avoided this kind of thing," said Santo, "but I think that after 12 years in the majors I proved I can play with it, that I'm not different from anyone else, and that there is really nothing to fear.

"I've done a heck of a lot of talking about diabetes to individual kids and to small groups. Doctors have called me and said, 'Ron, we'd like to have you talk to these children because they're afraid and they're having trouble adjusting.'

"Then I'd go out and talk to these children and point to myself and say, 'Look, here I am, a big, husky-looking ballplayer. And I have diabetes, too. I have learned how to cope with it, how to control it, how to recognize the reactions, and you can, too.'

"I tell them they can do anything they want once they learn not to be afraid to give themselves that shot of insulin and how to control their diets—and sometimes their emotions.

"I understand what they're going through," Ron said, "because I went through the same thing myself. I found out I had diabetes back home in Seattle when I was 18. I'd just signed a pro contract and the first thing I asked the doctor was, 'Can I play baseball?' That was the biggest fear I had, that I wouldn't be able to play baseball.

"He assured me I could and for the first couple of years I tried taking pills to keep my diabetes under control.

"But I found that pills didn't work. I went down from 185 pounds to 169 that third year, and I was really feeling lousy.

"Then I went to a Dr. Levin in Chicago. He told me I had to take insulin. There was no other way.

"I spent five months with him. It wasn't only a question of learning how to give myself injections of insulin, but also learning how to recognize the reactions I would get from not enough sugar in my bloodstream. It was learning how to eat enough food to keep up my energy, and what kind of food.

"It was Dr. Levin who taught me how to cope, who taught me so much. Now I try to pass on some of what he taught to those kids because I think I can communicate with them.

"Why, those first few years, no one on the Cubs knew I had diabetes. I was afraid if they found out they'd think they had an invalid or something on their hands, especially if I went into a slump.

"The first one I eventually told was Dr. Jacob Suker [the Cubs' physician], so he was prepared in case anything happened. And Doc [trainer Al Scheunemann] was told, and he keeps candy bars in the dugout runway for me and can recognize when I have a reaction.

"These reactions," Ron continued, "give you some warning time. You get hungry and weak, and you get double vision, your tongue gets numb. All these things happen before you go into a reaction, and it takes 20 to 25 minutes.

"I know because Dr. Levin prepared me for all this. He made me go through all the stages of reaction so I'd recognize them. I'd go through them with a glass of orange juice and a bowl of sugar beside me so that I could snap out of it before it got to the stage where I'd lose consciousness.

"It was a process of recognizing the reactions so I could cope.

"I remember once, when we were playing against Los Angeles, I started to get a reaction while Billy Williams was at the plate.

"I started feeling weak, and got a little dizzy and that double vision, but I didn't do anything. I figured Billy would be out of there soon and I could get up and out soon enough. After all, it would take a long time for anything drastic to happen.

"Well, Billy keeps fouling pitches off and I keep getting dizzier and weaker. But I didn't want to run back to the dugout because I was afraid they might pull me.

"Anyway, after all those fouls, Billy walks, against Bill Singer, I think. The bases are loaded

In 1969, when the Cubs were challenging for the pennant, Ron Santo made a custom of running off the field, bounding in the air, and clicking his heels in joy after the club won. Santo finished his major league career with the White Sox in 1974. He was a member of the National League All-Star team 10 times, hit 342 lifetime homers, and batted in 1,331 runs.

Rated an excellent defensive third baseman, Santo charges in as the Pirates' Vic Davalillo attempts to lay down a bunt against the Cubs in a 1972 game. Santo set a major league record for third basemen for most years (seven) leading the league in assists, 1962 through 1968. In seven different seasons, he also topped National League third basemen in number of putouts.

and I could barely get up there. I just didn't care. I figured to myself, 'Just swing and get out of there.'

"So I swing and would you believe, it's a bases loaded home run," he laughed. "I really sped around those bases to get back to the dugout and those candy bars in a hurry.

"That was about as close to going into a bad reaction as I've come on the field.

"As I tell the children who have diabetes, it's a matter of learning to give yourself those insulin shots and not being afraid. Some kids just can't bring themselves around to injecting themselves. That fear is really something.

"Then they have to learn those reactions and how to avoid them. Too many kids don't have enough food in them when they go out to play, and they burn an awful lot of energy and don't replenish that sugar and they're in trouble.

"They have to learn to do it themselves because their parents aren't going to be around forever to do it for them.

"It's all control," said Ron. "On hot days, for instance, I'll take less insulin because I'll be burning up more energy. In winter, I'll take more because I'm not burning up as much.

"Even in winter, I try to get as much exercise as possible to burn up some of that sugar.

"When we play day games, I'll give myself that shot of insulin at 9 a.m. because the peak is at 4 p.m.—the midway point of its strength.

"When we play night games, I'll inject myself around noon. And I try to eat enough, like an early dinner, to have food and energy in me.

"After the game, I'll always grab a pop and a hamburger or candy or something to build up some of the energy that's been taken out of me.

"One of the biggest problems," Santo said, "is learning or trying to learn how to control emotions. For me, that's really tough because I'm a real emotional guy. I have real peaks and valleys that burn up energy fast, and this can bring on those reactions."

As Ron has told young diabetics: they, too, can become major-leaguers—or most anything they want to in life—if they learn to cope and control.

I Remember the Polo Grounds

by Jack Lang

March, 1975

It has been more than a decade since the New York Mets played their last game at the Polo Grounds in New York City, but it will be many, many more decades before the millions of fans who witnessed games there and the thousands of players who trod the lush green turf will forget the old horseshoe park that stood in the shadow of Coogan's Bluff.

The Polo Grounds, when it finally fell victim to the wreckers' iron ball in 1964, not only was the oldest major league ball park in America, it also was the most unique.

Boston's Fenway Park has its famed Green Monster for a wall in left; old Yankee Stadium had the short porch in right; Crosley Field had its terraced outfield, and Wrigley Field still maintains its ivy-covered walls.

But no other ball park ever had the Chinese Home Run (Editor's Note: Excluding the Los Angeles Coliseum, which was used temporarily by the Dodgers after they left Brooklyn). No other ball park had a right-field foul line of 259 feet and a left-field line of 280. In no other park in America was it possible to hit a routine flyball to either left or right fields and have it nick an upper grandstand that jutted out and become an automatic home run while an outfielder stood helpless under the ball. "Hit the facade," was the umpire's cry as he waved the batter around the bases.

And in no other ball park in America was a fan ever shot to death in a bizarre, real-life re-enactment of the famed Death on the Diamond movie.

That tragic event took place prior to a July 4th doubleheader between the Giants and Dodgers in the late 1940s, when baseball's greatest rivalry was at its peak.

I recall police rushing to the aid of the fan in the left-center grandstand and finding him dead on arrival. The first reaction of the gendarmes was to clear the park.

"We may have a nut in the park," said one lieutenant.

Chub Feeney, then a veep with the Giants and now the National League president, pleaded that the games go on. The Giants didn't want to lose that 50,000 gate.

"Okay," the lieutenant replied almost comically, "but if one more guy gets killed, we're clearing the park."

The shot, it later developed, came from atop an apartment house roof high on Coogan's Bluff. A young man had found a rusty rifle, fired it out over the bluff, and the bullet traveled almost a quarter of a mile before piercing the forehead of the innocent fan in the left-field seats. It was a million-to-one shot.

There was another shot a few years later. This one was forever to be known in baseball as the Shot Heard Round the World. It was, of course, Bobby Thomson's dramatic ninth-inning home run off Ralph Branca in the bottom of the ninth inning in the third and deciding playoff game that gave the Giants the victory and the 1951 National League pennant.

It was the climax of a tremendous stretch drive by the Giants that began in mid-August, when they were 13 1/2 games behind the Dodgers. They wound up tied for the pennant on the final day, and the three-game playoff series followed.

To this day old Brooklyn fans will argue that Charlie Dressen brought in the wrong relief pitcher. That Clem Labine, who had pitched a 10-0 shutout the previous day, could surely get the final outs when Don Newcombe faltered.

While it may be one of the most dramatic home runs ever hit, it was also one missed by many of the sportswriters covering the playoffs. When the Dodgers went into the bottom of the ninth with a 4-1 lead, most of us afternoon-paper writers began the long trek from the press box behind home plate to the Dodger clubhouse in left field. We were in the clubhouse getting the final inning on the radio when Thomson connected.

Ironically, the writers didn't even hear Russ Hodges' famed description of the shot . . . shouting "The Giants win the pennant! The Giants win the pennant! The Giants win the pennant!" The radio in the Dodger clubhouse was tuned into the broadcast of their own announcers, Red Barber and Connie Desmond. There was a quick sign-off by Barber that day.

I made my first trip to the Polo Grounds on Memorial Day, 1937. I was the guest of my sister and brother-in-law, and when we arrived at the park around noon, the only seats still vacant were in the far reaches of left field. I spent the afternoon talking to a fan in the bleachers, the two of us separated only by a screen. My neighbor had paid half what my brother-in-law shelled out for our "grandstand" seats.

The crowd that day was to set a record. There were 60,747 jammed into the old park for a holiday doubleheader between the Giants and Dodgers. It constituted the largest National League crowd in New York history up to that time.

And the fans—especially the loyal Brooklyn rooters—were not to be denied a thrill of thrills. In the opening game, with the great Carl Hubbell on the mound for the Giants, the Dodgers knocked King Carl out in the fourth inning and ended his 24-game, two-season winning streak. With unheralded Freddie Frankouse pitching for them, the Brooks rolled to an easy 10-3 victory.

Between games, Babe Ruth, by then retired, approached home plate and presented Hubbell with a gold watch, emblematic of his selection as the National League's Most Valuable Player the previous year.

Cheered by the fans, Hubbell accepted the watch and said: "Defeat had to come some time. A fella can't keep winning every game. I'm glad the pressure is off."

Before the day was over, it was the Dodger fans who were saddened. In the second game, Buddy Hassett, their first baseman and leading hitter, was hit on the wrist by a pitch and suffered a fracture that sidelined him for a few weeks. Thus a streak and a wrist were broken in one day.

The Polo Grounds was opened in 1889 and was built specifically for the New York Giants and for baseball. History shows that polo was never played there, but the name was given the new park because that was the name of the park the Giants had formerly occupied downtown.

Like most old parks, history permeated from every nook and corner of the Polo Grounds. But few moments have lived on in baseball lore as vividly as some of those that occurred at the odd-shaped stadium on the banks of the Harlem River.

It was at the PG, as they called it, that Fred Merkle was guilty of his famous "boner" on September 23, 1908, . . . a mistake that eventually gave the Cubs a pennant over the Giants.

Merkle was on first base for the Giants with two out in the bottom of the ninth when Al Bridwell singled to center and Moose McCormick scored from third with what Merkle thought was the winning run.

But the alert Johnny Evers of the Cubs, after seeing that Merkle didn't bother to go to second, called for the ball from the outfield and stepped on second, where umpire Hank O'Day ruled a force play that ended the inning.

The turmoil on the field when the fans ran all over it prevented continuation of the game into extra innings, and it had to be replayed in its entirety on October 8. The Cubs won that day and also won the pennant.

Perhaps the greatest individual feat in All-Star game history and one of the most electrifying strike-out streaks of all time took place at the Polo Grounds in the 1934 All-Star game when Hubbell, at his peak, struck out Babe Ruth, Lou Gehrig, and Jimmie Foxx with two men on base in the first inning and then fanned Al Simmons and Joe Cronin to open the second. Five of the American League's outstanding sluggers in succession!

One year earlier, Hubbell had pitched one of the greatest single games in history when he worked a full 18 innings to defeat Tex Carlton and Jess Haines of the Cardinals, 1-0. In the second game, Leroy Parmelee edged Dizzy Dean in another 1-0 game in regulation time.

The Polo Grounds was, of course, Willie Mays' first playpen, and how he roamed that spacious outfield. His back-to-the-plate catch on Vic Wertz in the first game of the 1954 Series, followed by his return throw to the infield, has been hailed as one of the greatest catches ever. That Series also made famous an itinerant outfielder named Dusty Rhodes, a deluxe pinch-hitter who took advantage of the short right-field foul line.

Rhodes went to the plate six times as a pinch-hitter, had four hits, including two homers, drove in seven runs, and batted .667.

Rhodes' three-run homer in the ninth won the first game and was a typical Polo Grounds homer—right down the line about 260 feet into the lower deck. These cheapie homers are what caused fans years ago to refer to them as Chinese Homers.

In the second game of the Series, Dusty drove in two runs, one with a single and the other with another PG homer—this one ticking the facade of the upper deck in right as Wally Westlake waited in vain for the ball to come down.

There are many memories of the Polo Grounds, with its strange dimensions and all those intense contests between the Dodgers and Giants. It was there that Carl Furillo won a batting championship for Brooklyn when he was unable to play the last few weeks of the 1953 season after someone stepped on his hand and broke it during a melee between the outfielder and the entire Giant bench.

It was there also that Rex Barney pitched a no-hitter in the rain in 1948. And the place where little Mel Ott, right foot cocked high, hit so many of his 511 homers.

It was also the scene where the Mets were born —still-born, people said for years—in 1962 and where they lost 115 home games in two years. It was there that banners first flourished in ball parks—only after newspapermen pleaded with club press to let the kids parade around after the brass first tried to eject them.

I attended or covered games at the Polo Grounds for more than a quarter of a century, and I will always treasure the memory of having been the official scorer for the last game ever played there. Two years after the Mets moved to brand-new Shea Stadium, a high-rise apartment stood in the old ball park's place.

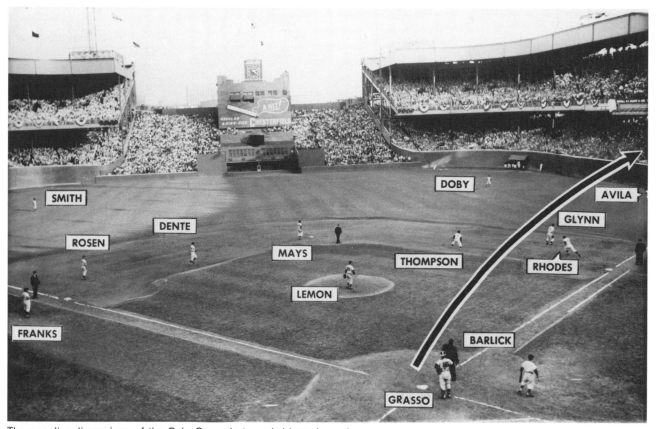

The peculiar dimensions of the Polo Grounds turned drives down the left-field and right-field lines into "cheap" home runs, while balls hit to center field had to travel some 460 feet to reach the stands. In this scene, pinch-hitter Dusty Rhodes of the Giants rounds first base after sending the ball into the lower right-field grandstands, approximately 257 feet away, for a three-run homer to win the opener of the 1954 World Series against the Cleveland Indians. Rhodes clouted his drive off Bob Lemon. Dusty, who was batting for Monte Irvin, sent Willie Mays and Hank Thompson home on the blow. Cleveland right fielder Dave Pope, not shown, made a futile attempt to catch Rhodes' drive. Second baseman Bobby Avila, partially shown, had raced out to right field to help in the event the ball came off the wall.

Roger Bresnahan — "You Could Catch Matty Sittin' in a Chair"

by John P. Carmichael

Condensed from the *Chicago Daily News*

October, 1943

When Roger Bresnahan strode to the plate at the war-bond exhibition in New York, it marked the first time he ever caught Walter Johnson. "He must have been quite a pitcher," said Bresnahan, "because he's still fast. His ball sails . . . and that side-arm delivery! Oh how hitters hate a side-arm thrower. They did in my day and they do now."

Bresnahan, naturally, always insists he handled the greatest of them all when he and Christy Mathewson were making Giant history 35 years ago. "Carl Hubbell's screwball was the nearest thing to Matty's fade-away," said the old catcher. "Nobody else ever came up with a pitch quite like it. The secret of the fade-away was due to the change in its speed.

"Matty threw it overhand . . . just like his fastball. He let it go shoulder high, with plenty on it, but just before it reached the plate the ball lost all its zip and just floated down over the plate. He was more effective against southpaw hitters than right-handers because the pitch broke away from them. It never was any effort for him to throw the fade-away, and I'd call for it 90 percent of the time when left-handers were up there."

Nobody ever hit Matty hard consistently, as Roger remembered, but eventually Joe Tinker, the old Cub shortstop, came as close to regarding Big Six as a cousin as anybody in the league. "For a few years we had no trouble with Tinker," recalled Bresnahan. "We'd even pass fellows to get at him. Finally he started hitting Matty, and we couldn't get him out. I'll always believe Joe used to be scared of being hit. When he discovered that Matty didn't hit one guy a season, on an average, he simply took a toehold on him."

It was against the Cubs in their old West Side park that Bresnahan caught Matty in a no-hitter . . . beating Mordecai Brown. "Mathewson was an easy worker," said Roger. "You could catch him sittin' in a chair. If you held up your glove he'd hit it and likely wouldn't be an inch off plumb center. He didn't have any long-winded windup, and if he was out in front he'd ease up and start lobbin' the ball over . . . but he always could put on the brakes in a pinch. He never lost his stuff or control. Well, this day he had the Cubs beaten going out for the seventh inning, and Art Devlin, our third baseman, stopped by the mound.

" 'Bear down now, Gumshoe,' said Devlin. 'They haven't got a hit off you yet.' There was a sudden roar from the Giant benches, and Devlin jumped a foot at the sound of John McGraw's voice. 'Shut your mouth, you bonehead,' screamed McGraw at Devlin, 'and play that bag.' " Artie realized shamefacedly that he'd put the jinx on Matty, but the brilliant hurler kept right on mowin' down the Cubs until he had his no-hitter. Bresnahan thinks it was the Cubs, on an occasion in the Polo Grounds, who handed Matty his worst lacing, 19-0.

"They hit him and Joe McGinnity all over town," said Roger. "Hell, it was an event when anybody beat Matty mor'n 3-2 or 4-3. But if they started touchin' Matty up at all McGraw'd yank him. He thought the world of the big fellow, but he treated him just like anybody else. I remember one spring we played an exhibition game at Memphis, and we had a morning workout beforehand. There was a bus waitin' to take us from the park to the hotel for lunch, and McGraw finally called: 'All right . . . three times around the park and into the bus.'

"I guess Matty didn't feel like running, so he went once around and slipped into the bus ahead of time. When everybody got there McGraw asked Matty: 'How many times around?' He told John J.: 'Once.' McGraw said: 'Get out there and go twice more.' Mathewson hesitated. 'We're going to stay right here until you do,' snapped the stubby Giant manager . . . and Matty knew he had no choice. We sat in the coach while he ran twice around the park and then got into the bus."

Bresnahan never will forget that day in 1905 when the Giants took the field for the first time against the Athletics in the World Series. "We wore brand-new uniforms of black broadcloth," he said, "and I mean black . . . like the ace of spades. We wore white stockings, and there was white piping around the edges of the suits and white visors on black caps. We really looked swell alongside the A's in their ordinary white outfits, and you could hear the crowd take a loud, deep breath when we showed up."

Matty shut the A's out three times in that Series. "They never came close to beating him," said his old battery mate. "Just pop-up, pop-up all day. You know 90 percent of the hitters those days were choke-hitters. They didn't swing from the end of the bat like nowadays. If Matty was pitching today he'd break their backs."

ROGER BRESNAHAN

BATTERY MATE OF CHRISTY MATHEWSON
WITH THE NEW YORK GIANTS, HE WAS
ONE OF THE GAME'S MOST NATURAL
PLAYERS AND MIGHT HAVE STARRED
AT ANY POSITION. THE "DUKE OF TRALEE"
WAS ONE OF THE FEW MAJOR LEAGUE
CATCHERS FAST ENOUGH TO BE USED
AS A LEADOFF MAN.

CHRISTY MATHEWSON

NEW YORK, N.L., 1900–1916.
CINCINNATI, N.L., 1916.
BORN FACTORYVILLE, PA., AUGUST 12, 1880
GREATEST OF ALL THE GREAT PITCHERS
IN THE 20TH CENTURY'S FIRST QUARTER
PITCHED 3 SHUTOUTS IN 1905 WORLD SERIES.
FIRST PITCHER OF THE CENTURY EVER TO
WIN 30 GAMES IN 3 SUCCESSIVE YEARS.
WON 37 GAMES IN 1908
"MATTY WAS MASTER OF THEM ALL"

For the Hall of Fame: Red Faber

by James T. Farrell

September, 1957

Living on the southwest side of Chicago there is a tall, well-preserved, gray-haired man whose record is sufficient to qualify him for the Hall of Fame. Old-time White Sox fans remember him and remember him well—Urban Charles (Red) Faber.

Red saw 20 years of service with the White Sox. He appeared in 669 league games, pitched 4,087 innings, won 254 games, and lost 214. His lifetime earned run average was 3.15, and his pitching percentage figures out at .545. He also won three games and lost one in the six-game 1917 World Series when the White Sox dumped the New York Giants, managed by John McGraw, four wins to two.

During the second game of that Series, Faber was in the box and turning back the Giants. In the Sox half of the fifth inning, he happened to be on second base while Buck Weaver was on third. Inexplicably, Faber lit out for third base and vainly "stole" the sack—for Weaver was still occupying that base. Faber's futile effort ended the inning for the White Sox.

"Where are you going?" Weaver asked.

"Right out to pitch," Faber said.

During his active career, Faber was a hard, mean, tough pitcher. Ray Schalk, old-time great catcher and a member of the Hall of Fame, caught many tough pitchers. But Ray says that Faber was probably the toughest pitcher he ever caught.

"He threw a heavy ball," Schalk remarks.

When Faber is reminded of his long-time battery mate, he smiles and says:

"Cracker [Schalk's nickname] says I forced him to put a sponge in his glove."

"When you wanted a pitcher to go in there and win, Faber was the kind of pitcher to send in," Schalk reminisces. "He was always a 60-to-40 bet to win your ball game."

Faber was born September 6, 1888, in Cascade, Iowa. As a boy, he liked to play ball. He got his start at St. Joseph's Prep School in Prairie du Chien, Wisconsin. Recalling it, he says:

"I was taking a bookkeeping course. I was told I could get a job at $40 a month."

In 1909, Faber began his professional career with Dubuque, Iowa, winning seven and losing six. His manager was an old-time White Sox infielder, Frank Isbell. Isbell played an important role in the White Sox victory over the Cubs in the 1906 World Series. Faber does not exactly recall his first minor league salary but believes it was $100 a month.

He was bought by the Pittsburgh Pirates, then managed by the left fielder, Fred Clarke, and owned by the late Barney Dreyfuss. Red tells the story of how he went to spring training broke. Needing money for incidentals and tips, he got a five dollar advance from Clarke. He nursed it along as carefully and as long as he could. Finally it was gone. When he went to Clarke again broke, he was asked what he had done with the five dollars.

"You must be gambling," he was told.

He broke into no games with the Pirates and was loaned back to Dubuque of the Three-I League. Pitching against Davenport, Red turned in a no-hit game, and in August, 1910, he was recalled by the Pirates. Again he was not used in games. He was already throwing a spitball but says:

"When I was with the Pirates, they wouldn't let me throw any spitters. I don't know why but they wouldn't let me do it."

In May, 1911, he was released by Pittsburgh to Minneapolis in the American Association and in turn shipped to Pueblo of the Western League. He spent 1912 and 1913 with Des Moines of the Western League and was then bought by the White Sox. He is not certain but thinks that his purchase price was $3,000. He recalls that his first White Sox salary, for the 1914 season, was $1,200. That year he won 10 and lost nine.

"Do you remember your first game with the Sox, Red?" I asked.

"Yes, it was against Cleveland. I won it but was relieved."

At the end of the 1913 season the late Charles A. Comiskey, owner of the White Sox, and John McGraw arranged to take their two ball teams around the world. Faber went with the Sox on the 31-game junket to the Pacific Coast. Then, at the last moment, it developed that Christy Mathewson could not embark with the Giants. Comiskey had enough pitchers, but McGraw, needing a replacement, invited Red to accompany the Giants.

"I didn't have a passport. I didn't know what one was, and I didn't have time to get one."

Facing the White Sox on the world tour, he won four games and lost one.

I asked him what batter gave him the most trouble in his career.

"A .250 hitter, Jack Barry [Philadelphia Athletics' shortstop]. Everybody else could get that son-of-a-gun out, but I couldn't. I don't know why. But the batter who was easiest for me was Duffy Lewis [of the Boston Red Sox]. He was a good hitter, too. I think he did get one hit off me one time when he was backing away from a pitch." He laughed at that. "I always could get him out."

"Did you ever pitch against Rogers Hornsby, Red?" I asked.

"I struck him out—but it was in an old-timers' game at Comiskey Park."

I asked Faber how he used to pitch to Ty Cobb.

"I did pretty good again' him. One time I struck him out on a spitter that broke in. It hit him on the hip and broke his hip."

"No, Red didn't have much trouble with left-handed hitters," Schalk said.

"Ray, remember that game in New York when Cocky [Eddie Collins] made me walk Ruth. I was mad. I didn't want to walk him. But Cocky said, 'You better do it.' So I walked Ruth, and I struck out that first baseman they had before Gehrig—who was he?"

"Wally Pipp."

"Yes, Pipp. He was a pretty fair hitter. I struck him out on three pitched balls. I won that game, 1-0."

Schalk began comparing Faber's record with those of pitchers who have been elected to the Hall of Fame. Ray was checking off those who had won less games than Faber. Among them was Ed Walsh (195).

"Walsh was a good pitcher," Faber said. "And Eddie Cicotte was a hell of a good pitcher."

"Red had a knuckler but he wouldn't use it," Schalk said.

I asked Schalk if Faber had been a difficult pitcher to handle.

"Red had one signal all the years when he didn't want to throw what I called for."

Faber gave the signal. He wiped his right hand across the left side of his breast and said that that signal had been a good enough one. Schalk and Faber had only two signals, one for a fastball and one for a curve or spitter.

"We fought a lot," Faber said, referring to himself and Schalk. "But after the game we forgot it."

Faber, as well as Schalk, thinks that Eddie Collins was probably the smartest ballplayer he ever knew. And like most ballplayers who knew him, Faber speaks with most affectionate respect for his old manager, Kid Gleason.

"He was tough. But the ballplayers loved him."

Many other players were recalled.

Urban (Red) Faber was elected to the Hall of Fame in 1964 by the Committee on Veterans. In his prime, he relied frequently on a spitball, which was then a legal pitch. "I had pretty good control of it," he recalled. "I could throw it side-arm, and it'd break like a curve, only sharper. When I threw it overhand, it would duck down, and if the batter got a piece of it, he'd usually hit it into the ground." In June, 1975, when he was approaching his 87th birthday, Faber said he still maintained an interest in baseball. "I watch the games on TV," he said. Asked to name one particular player from his time who would fit right in with the style of major league baseball today, he responded: "Buck Weaver [former White Sox third baseman]. He could run, hit, and field. He was a switch-hitter. He could do it all, and he was tough." Weaver was one of eight White Sox players banned from baseball for "throwing" the 1919 World Series to the Reds.

"That Sam Rice was a hell of a hitter," Red said. "He'd make 200 hits almost every year."

"And he was fast," Schalk said. "He'd beat out hits in the infield."

"He was a good hitter. That Sam Rice belongs in the Hall of Fame," Faber said.

And Stuffy McInnis of the old $100,000 infield of Connie Mack's Philadelphia Athletics.

"I learned never to throw 'em high to him. One day I threw him one up here above his head and he cracked it over the third baseman's head for two bases. I learned never to give him anything up high."

"Red was a low-ball pitcher," Schalk said.

"The best center fielder was Spoke [Tris Speaker]," Faber went on. "Happy Felsch was good, but as a center fielder I give it to Spoke. Johnny Mostil was good, too. But Spoke had it on them. And he had an arm."

"He'd never throw it at the plate," Schalk said. "It would curve in there, though, on the hop."

Joe DiMaggio? Faber couldn't comment. He was living outside of Chicago during DiMaggio's best years and hadn't seen enough of him in his prime in order to comment.

"But say," he said, "that Rizzuto was one hell of a shortstop—the greatest. In the World Series, I saw him on television getting balls in back of third and behind second. He was the greatest. That Peckinpaugh in our day was good, but I didn't 'see' most of the shortstops in our league. That Rizzuto was in a class by himself."

Faber liked to pitch against Walter Johnson because this was more of a challenge. He recalls how, because of an error, he lost a 1-0 game to Johnson but then got his revenge the next time they faced one another, winning by the same score. He also remembers how he beat Herb Pennock, 1-0, in New York. He always tried for a shutout no matter how many runs ahead the White Sox might be. He felt that if he pitched a shutout then he knew that he had done a good job.

Faber says that he would practically never get a sore arm. However, he went into the Navy in 1918, contracted influenza and during the 1919 season, he was about 30 pounds underweight. That season his record stood 11 won and nine lost.

"My arm was all right, but could only go four innings."

Faber did not pitch in the 1919 World Series which was thrown by some of his teammates to the Cincinnati Reds. Many say that had Red been stronger and able to serve, there might even have been no scandal. The young pitcher, Dickie Kerr, has often been described as winning two games which some of his teammates were trying to lose behind him. Had Faber then been right, he might have repeated Kerr's performance and won the Series for the Sox.

For only a few years did Faber have good teams behind him. He won the majority of his games for weak teams. In 1921 he took 25 games and in 1922, 21, with poor teams. (The White Sox won only 62 games in 1921, *including* Faber's 25.) His record would have been probably sensational had he been fortunate enough to have pitched all his years for a club like the New York Yankees of the last quarter-century.

Red's last game was a shutout performance to win the 1933 City Series from the Cubs. He didn't want to quit then and was practically forced to. However, the next season the Cubs wanted him.

"I'd have gone with them if I could have helped them."

He worked out and pitched batting practice, but decided that he had had enough. He was approaching 46.

The Divine Art of Being Superbly Awful

by Don C. Trenary
Milwaukee Journal

October, 1963

When the time came to make out his lineup, manager Burt Shotton looked reality in the eyeball and found it glaring balefully back. So as his pitching choice he wrote, "Willoughby and everybody."

A stuffy umpire made him rub it out. Came the first inning. In it, Willoughby departed. Majestically, Shotton took the lineup card again, rewrote "and everybody" with a firm hand.

"See," he said. "I told you."

Shotton's 1930 Philadelphia Phillies, gentlemen, are an example of sterling lack of worth and a lesson to us in our degenerate, money-grubbing age. The 1930 Philadelphia Phils were a classic of awfulness, and to be superbly awful requires a touch of the divine. It cannot be accomplished by mere diligence. It has to be done with a flair.

There is current a carefully nurtured fable that the New York Mets are the worst team in the history of baseball.

In a way, this is beneficial. It gives patrons of the Polo Grounds the illusion that they are seeing something outstanding in the line of horror. In a city containing as many boobs as Talltown on the Hudson, this brings a healthy glow to the ball-yard turnstiles.

And during its home stands, it likewise provides the New York sportswriters with an unending source of news stories without going out of town into barbaric hinterlands where the bartenders might put too much vermouth in the martini.

But in the true annals of baseball awfulness, the Mets, however earnest and willing, rank only as another bad baseball team.

Connoisseurs of such things discount the Mets' latest feat of losing 22 consecutive games on the road. The streak, they point out, was interrupted by the disgrace of victories at home, and is a phoney record, like most hits against left-handed pitching by a right-handed infielder with freckles. A bad club with real singleness of purpose, they say, can lose at home as well as on the road; it has no weak desire to show off in front of the wife and kiddies.

The Mets? Bah! A club cannot be exalted merely because it messes up a triple play. Anybody can mess up a triple play. There have been teams that could mess up standing safely on base.

One that did so was the Brooklyn Dodgers, beloved among their buffs as the Daffiness Boys. The accomplisher was Frenchy Bordagaray, who for some years played outfield after his own fashion, part of the time in a mustache.

When Bordagaray was called out on second base, it fetched forth the team manager, Uncle Wilbert Robinson. Uncle Wilbert had had many things happen to him in his time, including catching a grapefruit dropped from an airplane, having three men on third base, and owning a pitcher who gave a hog call after each strike-out. (Robinson eventually got shed of the hog-caller. "No man has a right to be sillier than God intended him to be," he said.)

So Uncle Wilbert approached the new matter, not in anger, but in a spirit of scientific inquiry. He found out Frenchy enthusiastically endorsed the umpire's call.

"With this batting slump I'm in," he explained, "I was so happy to hit a double that I did a tap dance on second base. They tagged me between taps."

And Bordagaray was only a minor performer. The life and soul of the Dodgers was the great Babe Herman, who kept a lighted cigar in his pocket, who fought Homeric duels with flyballs.

Herman was traded for a while, then brought back to Brooklyn in 1945. In his first time at bat, he rapped out a double. Proudly he ran down the baseline, turned first with a flourish, tripped over his own feet, and fell flat on his face.

The Mets, bah!

Back in 1899, shortly after the era of Jack the Ripper, the National League possessed the Cleveland Spiders, a product of syndicate baseball and undeniably the worst major league team of all time.

The club played 154 games and won exactly 20 of them. It had one losing streak of 24 games and others of 16, 14, and 13. Once, and once only, it had a winning streak . . . two games in a row.

It finished 80 games behind the pennant winner and, in a 12-team league, 36 games out of 11th place.

On the last day of the season, the Spiders found that the 19-year-old cigar clerk at their Cincinnati hotel had a hankering to play baseball. They let him pitch.

The Mets, phooie!

In the seven straight years from 1915 through 1921, the Philadelphia Athletics finished a rousing last. They averaged 101 losses a year.

In 1915, owner Connie Mack employed the revolving-door system and used a record 56 players,

27 of whom said they were pitchers. The club won 43 games, an average of not quite 1.6 per pitcher.

This made a nice warm-up for the really outstanding 1916 club (36 wins, 117 losses).

Tom Sheehan, later manager of Minneapolis and San Francisco, pitched for that team. He won one game, lost 17.

"I went out to pitch one day," Sheehan related years later, "and a fellow I'd never seen before came out. He carried a mask. 'Who are you?' I asked. 'I'm your catcher,' he said."

Sheehan did not have the worst pitching record on the club. Jack Nabors won one game and lost 20.

And Nabors was not a bad pitcher. One sweltering day, he pitched eight innings of shutout ball and led, 1-0. In the ninth, successive errors behind him tied the score and perched an enemy on third base. Nabors wound up and threw the next ball high over the grandstand.

"If they think I'd stand there in that sun and pitch another nine innings waiting for our bums to make another run," he confided to Sheehan, "they're crazy."

For 12 games the club used a 17-year-old St. Louis scorecard boy at first base. Happy, left-handed kid named Charlie Grimm.

The Mets? Akh!

It took them 162 games to make 210 errors. The 1930 Phillies made 239 in only 154.

That was the club that had a team batting average of .315—and a pitching staff with an earned run average of 7.02. The opposition racked up 19 runs four times, 18 runs once, and 17 runs twice. The longest game was a spectacular 13-inning struggle which ended in favor of the Pirates, 16-15.

The Mets?

No tradition. Every really bad team leaves behind it a heritage of anecdotes.

Like the Pirates in their pitiable days of rebuilding, which was known in the trade as Operation Peach Fuzz.

"We had a lot of triple threat guys," said Joe Garagiola, a team member, "—slip, fumble, and fall."

George (Catfish) Metkovich was first baseman, and one game he was having a terrible time. As balls thrown by inept infielders went over, past, and through him, he turned to the first-base umpire, August John Donatelli.

"Don't just stand there, Augie," he snapped. "Grab a glove and help me."

Even the New York Giants, who finished last only once since World War I, have a legacy of legend. On a dreary day, a fellow spotted Groucho Marx, the comedian, sitting in the illy-populated Polo Grounds. He asked, quite logically, what Marx was doing there.

"I'm here because I don't like baseball," Groucho explained. "And if you don't like baseball, the Giants are the team to watch."

There were bumblefeet in those days, gentlemen.

But the Mets? Nice boys, but after all, just a bunch of downstarts.

The 1930 Phillies' infield of (left to right) Don Hurst at first, Fresco Thompson at second, Tommy Thevenow at short, and Pinky Whitney at third committed 121 errors as the club stumbled to a last-place finish, 40 games behind the pennant-winning Cardinals. In all, the Phils committed 239 errors, most in the majors that year.

Nolan Ryan: The Pitcher Batters Hate To Face

by Jackie Lapin
Washington Post

December, 1974

Nolan Ryan has now struck out more than a thousand batters in the last three seasons, but he still cannot explain why.

The fan explains it simply on the basis of Ryan's blazing fastball. But Ryan's teammates and victims say the man who in 1974 became the major leagues' first to strike out 300 or more batters in each of three consecutive seasons has added fear and cleverness to raw speed—that he's in a class by himself.

"It's a gift. I was born with it," Ryan says. "It's probably pitching rhythm more than anything. I get into a groove like a hitter goes on a hot streak."

But others who have observed Ryan through the years, during his relatively ineffective days with the New York Mets and in his prime with the California Angels, offer a much more ominous reason.

"Pitching is the art of instilling fear," says Sandy Koufax, the man to whom Ryan is most often compared, "making a man flinch by making him look for the wrong pitch. You're trying to control his instincts. But if your control is suspect like Ryan's is, and the thought of being hit is in the batter's mind, you'll go a long way."

Since Ryan hit Boston's Doug Griffin in the head early last season, the Red Sox became exceptionally wary of him, Boston's Carlton Fisk conceded. "The intimidation factor works on your psyche," the catcher explained.

Detroit's Dick Sharon says it most succinctly. "He is baseball's exorcist. He scares the devil out of me!"

"Ryan is the only guy who puts fear in me," admits Oakland slugger Reggie Jackson. "Not because he can get you out, but because he can kill you. There are just no words to describe what it is like standing up there and seeing that ball come at you. I simply couldn't do him justice. It's like trying to drink coffee with a fork. I like fastballs, but that's like saying I like ice cream, but not a truck load of it."

If anyone had a tough time getting wood on a Nolan Ryan fastball last season, it was Boston first baseman Cecil Cooper. Ryan fanned him six times in one game in June, a major league record. In his first 16 trips to the plate against Ryan last season, Cooper struck out 11 times!

"You're not really sure where he'll throw the ball, and when a guy is throwing that hard, you just can't get out of the way of it, like you can with other guys," Cooper says.

"If he had the control of a Catfish Hunter, he would be completely unhittable. I think he could win 35 games."

Angels' coach John Roseboro, who as a Dodger caught Koufax, thinks Ryan will be at his peak when he can limit himself to one or two walks a game. He has walked at least one in every game he has ever started and had 202 for the 1974 season.

One of the reasons, Roseboro says, is that Ryan tries for strike-outs and does not want the hitter to

HARDEST THROWERS IN THE MAJOR LEAGUES

Pitcher	Club	Age	Throws	M.P.H.	Year	Site
Nolan Ryan	Angels	27	R	100.9	1974	Anaheim Stadium
Bob Feller	Indians	27	R	98.6	1946	Washington, D.C.
Steve Barber	Orioles	21	L	95.5	1960	Miami
Don Drysdale	Dodgers	24	R	95.3	1960	Miami
Atley Donald	Yankees	29	R	94.7	1939	(unavailable)
Bob Turley	Yankees	27	R	94.2	1958	(unavailable)
Joe Black	Dodgers	21	R	93.6	1953	Ebbets Field
Sandy Koufax	Dodgers	24	L	93.2	1960	Miami
Ryne Duren	Yankees	31	R	91.1	1960	Miami
Herb Score	White Sox	27	L	91.0	1960	Miami
Mickey Lolich	Tigers	33	L	90.9	1974	Anaheim Stadium
Bob Turley	Yankees	27	R	90.7	1960	Miami

The speed of each of the above pitchers was scientifically timed. Ryan, clocked by Rockwell International scientists who used an infrared radar device, was timed at 100.9 m.p.h. on August 20 against Detroit. Ryan was clocked again, on September 7 against the White Sox, and was timed at 100.8 m.p.h.

Feller was timed on August 20 at Griffith Stadium in Washington, D.C., by a U.S. Army lumi-line chronograph for five pitches after warming up for 10 minutes prior to the game.

make contact. So unlike other pitchers, he tries to fool the hitter with a curve or change-up when the count is in the hitter's favor.

It is the nearly impossible adjustment from Ryan's fastball to curve to change-up (which, according to many, is as fast as most pitchers' fastballs) that has most hitters in a quandary.

"He can get you to chase a lot of bad pitches," says Minnesota's Rod Carew, who struck out 15 times in 39 tries against Ryan over the last three seasons.

"The ball rises if a hitter is standing up straight. It looks like it's coming in at a good part of the strike zone, and the next minute it's at your eyes. If a guy crouches a bit, he wouldn't have quite as much trouble because Ryan has to keep the ball down lower. He's not as effective because he has to take a little bit off his pitches, and the ball doesn't move as much when it's low in the strike zone. Then it comes in belt-high."

Ryan's greatest success has been against home-run hitters. According to Carew, trying to meet speed with power is not the answer. He says he has counseled teammates not to try to pull the ball off Ryan, a technique that has proved successful for him.

Cooper, too, has tried to change his swing against Ryan and found out the hard way it was the wrong thing to do.

"To hit Ryan, you have to put the fear on the side of your mind—you can't forget it entirely—and you dial up your bat, be little quicker," concludes Jackson who hit about .300 against Ryan last season.

Many tough pitchers start to tire by the sixth or seventh inning, but batters have no such solace when it comes to Ryan. He starts picking up momentum at that stage.

"There is no fatigue factor with him," observes Jeff Torborg, Ryan's battery mate from 1973 and now an assistant coach at Rutgers University. "He is extremely well conditioned, and he has exceptionally strong legs that help him push off the rubber with extra velocity."

It is the strength in Ryan's legs and thighs and not in his arm that makes him the fast-baller he is, according to Tom Seaver, his former Mets teammate who says he is built much like Ryan.

Seaver says Ryan is no stronger in his arm than anyone else, but through coordination he is able to generate greater speed with the proper use of his lower body. Ryan, incidentally, runs daily, including on the team's off days.

"It's peculiar to him because of his body structure," Torborg says. "His arm is not muscular and he is not a giant of a man [six-foot-two, 195 pounds], but he is strong.

"He just has the perfect combination of factors—proper release point, balanced follow-through, and retention of weight on the rubber—that are needed to throw a baseball at extremely high velocity. He has nothing extraordinary like Sandy Koufax' large hands that made Koufax' curve drop a mile."

It would seem that Ryan has had the skill all along. Why, then, did he not show it in New York?

"He was a diamond in the rough. Our club should never have let him go," criticizes Seaver. "It was just a matter of time until we harnessed his potential. All the Angels did was simply give him the ball every fourth day."

It was only after Ryan joined the Angels, where he was forced to throw at a target until his control improved substantially and where he finally developed a curve and change-up that would complement his fastball, that he began to fulfill his promise.

Ken Henderson, who as a San Francisco Giant played against the "old" Ryan and with the White Sox has come up against the "new" Ryan, says there are two differences. The new Ryan gets the curve over consistently, and he also gets the benefit of the American League's so-called high strike, Henderson said.

(Editor's Note: In the years 1972, 1973, and 1974 respectively, Ryan's won-loss record was 19-16, 21-16, and 22-16; he struck out 329; 383, and 367; and walked 157, 162, and 202. His 383 strike-outs in 1973 shattered Koufax' record of 382, set in 1965.)

"Mel Ott?"
This Is Who He Was

by Fred Russell
Nashville Banner

July, 1966

Almost every day, it seems, something happens in sports to accentuate time's hurried flight. Like the young friend, listening to a conversation about Willie Mays breaking Mel Ott's total of 511 National League home runs, asking: "Who was Mel Ott?"

Well, when Ott was in his prime as right fielder with the New York Giants about 35 years ago and John McGraw was the manager, McGraw called him "the perfect ballplayer."

The compact five-nine, 170-pounder from Gretna, Louisiana, set all kinds of hitting records in his 22 years in the majors. Not as fully appreciated was his defensive ability.

"I never saw Otty ever look bad on a ball hit in his direction," said Clydell Castleman, a Giant pitcher from 1934 to 1940. "He was masterful in the field. And when I first joined the club, he had as great a throwing arm as I've ever seen."

Who was Mel Ott? Well, he was one of the very few athletes ever to report to a big league ball club when he was 16 years old.

In the summer of 1925, he had caught for a semi-pro team at Patterson, Louisiana, which a lumber baron, Harry Williams, ran as a hobby. Williams was impressed by his natural left-handed swing and told McGraw about the boy.

McGraw said: "Send him up when your season is over."

"So I went," Mel related, "taking my straw suitcase. I didn't even try to check into a hotel. I headed toward the Polo Grounds. But from Penn Station it must have taken me two hours, because I changed from one subway train to another trying to get there."

After watching Ott in batting practice, McGraw realized what a gem he had.

"Did you ever play in the outfield?" he asked.

"Yes, sir, a little when I was a kid," Mel replied naively.

The next season McGraw had Ott playing the Giants' outfield a little and pinch-hitting a lot. He wound up with a .383 batting average.

Ott had the odd habit of cocking his right leg when he swung. His form was unique.

McGraw declined to send him out for seasoning, saying: "I'm not gonna' let any minor league manager try experimenting with that batting swing."

When he was 20 years old, in 1929, Mel hit 42 homers and drove in 151 runs for the Giants.

In explaining his peculiar swing, Ott said: "I got my main power from my back foot. With my right foot off the ground, I wouldn't be caught flat-footed. I had a better chance to wait on the pitch."

Castleman marveled at Mel's never getting fooled on a change-of-pace. "If pitchers slowed up on him," Castleman said, "Otty would punch the ball into left field. Too, he was great protecting the plate with two strikes on him, yet he never choked up on the bat.

"Mel was a prince of a person. He never complained about anything. He rarely got mad. Fellows like Pat Malone, Guy Bush, Charlie Root, and Lon Warneke would make him hit the dirt just like anybody else, but it never seemed to bother Mel. He was one of the true greats."

On the night of November 14, 1958, driving their station wagon on to the highway from a restaurant at Bay Saint Louis, Mississippi, Ott and his wife were struck head-on by another car.

Mel lingered for a week before dying of uremia, kidney damage, and multiple fractures. His wife, seriously injured, survived.

Ott was only 49, ready to enjoy life after a stretch as the Giants' manager and later a baseball broadcaster. He had a beautiful home, no financial worries, was fond of golf, hunting, and fishing. But his No. 1 interest was his family—his wife and two daughters.

It's a pity such a fine person had to leave so soon, and in such a way.

Gene Mauch:
The Little General

by Ross Newhan
Los Angeles Times

November, 1973

They call him Napoleon and the Little General. They say he's a delight in victory and a demon in defeat.

They tell you he has ripped a clubhouse phone from the wall, overturned a buffet table, and broken down a door with a bat.

They also say he's the Bobby Fischer of major league managers, that no one knows the rules better or studies box scores more intently, that no one has a better sense of strategy or more knowledge of his players' limitations.

The name is Gene Mauch. He is manager of the Montreal Expos, formerly manager of the Philadelphia Phillies, and before that an infielder who came out of Fremont High in Los Angeles with the belief that fists and spikes were as much a part of his equipment as bat and glove.

He played for 16 years and has managed for 16, but his features and personality have not been marred by the long summers.

"In all the time I've known him," says Nina, his wife, "the one thing that hasn't changed has been his feeling for baseball.

"We all went to Puerto Rico one winter. Gene, our daughter Leanne, and me. We were there 12 days. Leanne and I went sight-seeing and sunbathing. The Winter League was on, and Gene went to the ball park. He saw over 20 games.

"There is no doubt in my mind that if Gene were single he would sleep at the park. He'd move in, in fact, and live there the year around."

"He's the thinking man's manager," says Pete Rose, the Cincinnati outfielder.

"Show me a manager who doesn't think and I'll show you a manager who's out of work," says Cincinnati manager Sparky Anderson. "It's just that Gene thinks a little more than the rest of us."

"Gene Mauch," wrote John Robertson in the *Montreal Star,* "is such a stickler for perfection that if you happen to walk past him in a hotel lobby and toss a casual 'Good morning' in his direction, you'd better be able to back up your claim with documented evidence.

"The first thing he'll do is mentally weigh the latest weather reports, the current trend of the National League standings in relation to last night's box scores, and the inside dope on tonight's opposing pitcher.

"Then, after his mind digests all the pertinent data, he will decide:

" 'Yes, it IS a good morning.'

"Or . . .

" 'Did you say good? Tell me one thing good about it.'

"One of the first things a new writer on the baseball beat learns is that there is no time in the Little General's ever-active think tank for idle conversation. If you want to talk to him, you arrive armed with direct, meaningful questions.

"Gene Mauch is not a raconteur of the Casey Stengel ilk. He does not milk the celebrity image and look upon the game as something to be exploited for his own self-aggrandizement, like Leo Durocher. He does not generate homespun informal warmth, like a Gil Hodges or a Danny Murtaugh. He is not a professional nice guy, like Sparky Anderson.

"But as I watch him run the Expos with increasing admiration, it becomes more and more evident to me why baseball people consider him possibly the most astute mind in the game.

"He is constantly prepared for every eventuality, therefore he is never taken by surprise. He is totally absorbed in the game, therefore you'll never see him hand in a wrong lineup card by mistake.

"He gambles incessantly—and you get the idea he's a notorious hunch-player—and then you find out that his 'hunch' was a piece of 10-year information from his memory bank on a certain opposing pitcher or hitter.

"Get him talking baseball, reliving game situations involving moves and countermoves during crucial ball games past, and he'll tell you what the count was, what the weather was like, and what everyone involved was thinking on that particular play."

It does not all come out of the box scores and the rule book.

He had it when he was 18 and in his first big league training camp, the one the Dodgers ran during the war years at Bear Mountain, New York.

Branch Rickey was in charge of the 1943 camp. He walked into the office one day, and Leo Durocher, the manager, was sitting there going over reports on all the kids.

"See anybody you like?" Durocher asked.

"Mauch," answered Rickey, "I like Mauch."

"Can't run," responded Durocher.

"True," said Rickey, "but I'll tell you something

important. You look at this boy and you think he's 16. You talk to him and you think he's 26. You talk baseball with him and you think he's 36."

Almost three decades later, Mauch sits in a small office off the Montreal clubhouse at Jarry Park.

"I remember the day I decided I wanted to be a manager," he said. "It was the day I met Durocher. It was 1943 and I was in Rickey's office in Brooklyn. I was there to sign my first pro contract.

"Durocher is an impressive man, and I was an impressionable young fellow. After that it struck me that while his players were there to do a job, it was more than a job to Durocher.

"It was a crusade, and that's the way I've always felt about baseball. You don't just go out to play— you go out to win.

"I thought if that's the kind of guy that becomes a manager, maybe some day I'll be a manager. It seemed to me that guys who really care ought to be managers."

Among those he played under, besides Durocher, were Billy Southworth, Frank Frisch, Charlie Grimm, Charlie Dressen, Eddie Stanky, Mike Higgins, and Billy Herman.

Frequently riding the bench, Mauch would sit beside his manager, study his tactics, and say to him, "Why the hell did you do that?"

Mauch insists that no manager resented it.

"One day with the Dodgers," he recalled, "I walked into Durocher's office and said, 'This isn't a second-guess. I'd just like to know why you hit-and-run in the third inning. With Stanky on first and Pee Wee [Reese] up, it looked to me like a bunt situation.'

"Durocher said to me, 'Kid, people talk about percentages. I got my own percentages.' "

That thought has stayed with Mauch.

"When the game starts," he said, "you throw away the book, and you make your decisions according to the situation. I'll let a certain hitter hit in one situation and tell him to bunt in another. It might depend on the hitter, on the pitcher, or on the team we're playing. But there's no cut-and-dried strategy. It varies from game to game, from situation to situation."

But it doesn't hurt to be prepared. Mauch frequently is in his office at 1 p.m., reading the box scores in preparation for the game that begins at 8 o'clock.

"There isn't any other place I'd rather be," he said. "I'll talk baseball 24 hours a day and enjoy it. The rule book and the box scores are necessities. A box score gives you the tendencies of a manager. It tells you about the hot hitters and the hot pitchers.

If you can add—such as the number of outs and the men left on base—you can tell which pitchers pitched to which batters and which were the most effective.

"I know you're supposed to lose X number of games, but I like to spend a few extra hours doing all I can to win. When you win there is nothing— nothing—that can make you feel any better. Not money, not anything."

He paused and then continued.

"Yes, I'd like to be known not just as a good manager, but as the greatest who ever lived. But the moves are there for anyone to use, and every manager is familiar with them.

"The key is in knowing the capabilities of your players. There is no substitute for material. The manager with the best material will generally win."

It is possible, insists Dave Bristol, for the manager to make the average player a better one by not asking him to do something he can't. Now a coach under Mauch and formerly a manager at Milwaukee and Cincinnati, Bristol said:

"Gene has several strengths, but most important, I think, is that he doesn't ask a player to do anything he can't do. The player may not realize it, but this maintains his confidence.

"Gene also has unbelievable concentration. When the game is on, he blocks out everything around him.

"He's also fearless. He'll never drive home from the park thinking, 'Damn, why didn't I try that?' He won't have to think it because he'll have tried it. And he has the ability, the farsightedness, to end up with his best defensive team on the field no matter how many moves he's made."

Gene Mauch quit the first managerial job he had. It came in 1953 after he had spent 10 years in the uniforms of 10 teams, jumping from the minors to the majors and back.

The owner of the Atlanta club in the Southern Association had asked John Quinn, general manager of the Boston Braves, to recommend a player-manager.

Quinn, having sized up Mauch, recommended the nomadic infielder. Mauch went to Atlanta and managed the team to within three games of the pennant, whereupon he resigned.

"I wasn't ready to manage," he said, reflecting. "I expected everybody to play with as much dedication as I had. Well, everybody doesn't. I was impatient. I ranted and raved. I fought umpires. I fought opponents. I fought my own players. I determined that my ideas were sound, but I wasn't prepared to put them into execution at the age of 27."

He spent the next five years with Los Angeles of the Pacific Coast League, the Boston Red Sox, and as a player-manager with the Minneapolis Millers.

Mauch led the Millers to third and second place finishes, successfully concluding one game with a pitcher at first and another pitcher at third.

During his second year in Minneapolis, events were taking place in Philadelphia that would bring him the managerial reins there.

Owner Bob Carpenter hired Mauch's former benefactor, John Quinn, as general manager. Early in the 1960 season manager Eddie Sawyer quit, prompting a call for Mauch.

He inherited a last-place team. The Whiz Kids had become Whiff Kids. His 1961 team lost a record 23 straight games, and it may have been a blessing.

"In all the years I thought about managing," he said, "there was one possibility I never considered. That was having a bad team. I figured if I caught a club that lacked power, we could run a lot. If we couldn't score runs, we could make it up with defense. Well, I found out a bad team is a bad team.

"With the Phillies, we brought in a lot of new players during my first two years. None liked the idea of being a Phillie. They didn't consider themselves Phillies. They were ex-Dodgers or ex-Cubs. Then we lost 23 games in a row that second year, and it was one of the luckiest things that ever happened to them. The reason is, it made the players realize they were Phillies. They were in it together. It was a back door to pride. From then on, they weren't going to let anybody push them around."

The 1960 and 1961 teams finished last. The 1962 team was last until Mauch whipped it down the stretch, winning 30 of the last 44 games to finish seventh. The 1963 team won 14 of its last 21 to finish fourth.

The stretch magic faded in 1964. With a pennant virtually clinched, the Phillies lost 10 of their last 12 to finish second.

Many reasons have been offered for that collapse. The Phils ran out of gas, they encountered some hot clubs, their pitching deteriorated. The truth would seem to be that Mauch did a marvelous job with only a modestly talented team through 150 games and a bad job over the last 12.

Philadelphia writers say he made two mistakes—both involving personalities, an area in which Mauch prides himself. The first, they say, was bringing in the late Don Hoak, a former player, as a scout. Hoak had been an intense, hard-nosed athlete whose personality created friction among his fellow players.

Mauch admired him and instructed him to scout ahead during the final weeks. He then allowed Hoak to make his reports directly to the club rather than to Mauch. The players resented the reports, which, it is said, were presented with an air of superiority.

The second mistake, according to the writers, was that Mauch did not use relief ace Jack Baldschun at the proper moments, bringing him in only to mop up. One theory was that Mauch didn't think Baldschun could do the job because his personality wasn't that of a tough brawler.

Mauch reflected on the theories and said:

"Hoak gave us hard work and all he had. I don't believe the players blamed him. As for Baldschun, you look up how many times I brought him in to help us over tight spots. He may not have pitched in the stretch as much as some people thought he should, but it's not because I lost any faith in him. I was trying to use certain types of pitchers to get certain types of hitters out. We lost the pennant and that's that."

That isn't the end of it, however. Mauch says that he is still haunted by sleepless nights, that he keeps a list of mistakes that were made then and which he will not allow to happen again.

Excluding 1973, that was as close as Mauch has

A nimble tactician and regarded by some writers as a "walking rules book," Gene Mauch has had his share of run-ins with umpires. Challenging an umpire's interpretation of a rule has an irresistible lure for Mauch. In 1975, the feisty, little Montreal skipper ranked second among active major league managers only to the Dodgers' Walt Alston for longest service as a club pilot. Jim Fanning, the Expos' general manager, once summed up Mauch's unusual grasp of detail: "Ask him to recall any situation in a game years ago, and he'll tell you the count, where the pitch was, what it was, and who hit it. And he uses it all to beat you."

been at the finish. His last four years in Philadelphia were marked by troubles with Dick Allen, which brought him into conflict with the front office and ultimately led to his firing.

Mauch refuses to knock the Phillies or say disparaging things about Allen. He normally, however, will let a player know what is on his mind. He has rules, curfews, and fines. He demands obedience.

Clay Dalrymple, now retired, recalled an incident while he was catching for Mauch in Philadelphia. Mauch had instructed Dalrymple to see that his pitcher gave Pittsburgh's Bill Mazeroski nothing in the strike zone. Dalrymple called for an outside pitch, but it was down the middle and Mazeroski doubled in two runs. Mauch angrily bawled out the catcher.

"I was embarrassed," said Dalrymple. "I was burned up at Mauch. But later I could see that he wanted to find out if I had the intestinal fortitude to come back or if I would put my tail between my legs and run. I decided that the next time a pitcher didn't put the ball where I wanted it, I'd go out to the mound and straighten him out.

"In fact, Gene told me later, 'If you want to go out and slap your pitcher's face, go slap him. I'll tell the sportswriters I told you to.' "

Once, in the process of removing a pitcher from the game, Mauch reached for the ball only to have the hurler deliberately drop it on the mound.

Mauch grabbed the pitcher by the shirt. "Pick up that damn thing and hand it to me," he roared, "or you'll be lying there with it." The pitcher picked it up, along with a $100 fine.

Mauch has been fined on numerous occasions and suspended three times by the National League presidents for arguing with umpires.

Several players have vendettas against Mauch, saying he ordered his pitchers to throw at them, which Mauch denies, while steadfastly supporting his pitchers' rights to earn their living.

What he is as a manager is what he was as a player, an intense competitor who believes that the game isn't played strictly with bat and glove.

Players have described his spring training camp as Little Iwo. One, referring to Mauch's diligent enforcement of rules, said, "He's a one-man CIA. You don't dare goof on the field or off. He's the kind of man bad news gets back to."

The flame that burns inside of Gene Mauch (he was going to be named Jack but his father had a hunch that Gene Tunney would beat Jack Dempsey) can leave him hot and all but unapproachable after a defeat.

Jacques Doucet of *LaPresse,* one of Montreal's French newspapers, tiptoed into Mauch's office after a recent loss, groped for words, and finally said: "If . . ."

"If," shouted Mauch. "If my bleeping butt. Don't come in here and throw hypothetical questions at me."

In Pittsburgh, in June of 1971, a wire-service reporter approached Mauch minutes after his relief ace, Mike Marshall, came in from the bullpen to protect an 8-4 lead and ended up losing, 9-8.

"What about Marshall?" the reporter asked.

"What do you mean?" said Mauch.

"Well," the reporter said, "this is the third time you've brought him in to protect a lead in this stadium, and this is the third time he's failed."

"So?" snarled Mauch.

"So doesn't a little red light begin to flash in your head that maybe the next time . . ."

"Out!" screamed Mauch. "Get out of this clubhouse. If there had been any damned red light flashing I wouldn't have brought in Marshall in the first place. I don't need any of your damned questions. Now get out!"

Mauch is said to react to player mistakes in the same manner. His most celebrated outburst came in Houston when he was at the helm of the Phillies, who had lost, 2-1, in the ninth on Joe Morgan's first big league hit.

The loss dropped the Phillies into fifth, three games out of third and only three ahead of seventh place.

When Mauch reached the clubhouse and spotted a buffet of barbecue spareribs and assorted relishes, he flipped the table upside down, splattering sauce over players and their clothes. Mauch bought new suits for several and later, when the season was over, said:

"Lots of things have happened to me in baseball, but that was the one thing that really hurt me. I mean, the way it was misinterpreted.

"I did it because I didn't want my team to fold up. All I had in mind was that we had six games to go. It must have worked because we won five of the six and the players got $700 each for finishing fourth. And they had pride to live with during the winter."

Mauch's pride has been tested in Montreal, where he manages players of "proven mediocrity," according to columnist Robertson.

But the owners stand solidly behind their thinking man's manager. They have extended his contract three times. The last time, Mauch stood up before the press, turned to president John McHale and said:

"If I was in your position, I'd have done exactly the same thing."

Brooks Robinson:
The Vacuum Cleaner

by Bill Braucher
Miami Herald

July, 1974

This was a muggy summer night in 1969 and Brooks Robinson was fighting a dreadful batting slump.

"He was down around .235 and swinging at bad pitches," said Earl Weaver, the declarative Baltimore manager. Put Weaver in a bowler hat and morning coat, stick a cigar in a corner of his mouth and he would emerge with the angry-baby look of Winston Churchill. Like Churchill, Weaver seems to remember everything as though it happened the day before.

"I was on Brooksie a little that year. He was too anxious to raise his average. He'd get a count of two-and-0 and reach for pitches he should have been letting alone," Weaver said.

"Naturally, Brooks didn't like me jabbing at him. He was mad at himself anyway. Well, this night the count goes to three-and-one and here comes a pitch that's maybe an inch from the ground.

"I say to myself, 'Don't do it Brooksie. Take the walk.' But he swings and grounds out. Now here he comes back to the dugout, straight to me before I can say a word.

" 'That pitch,' Brooksie snapped, 'was right on the black [over the corner].' I had to laugh," Weaver said.

Robinson laughed, too, at the memory. Weaver had to reach back four years for an instance of Robinson's congenial equanimity failing him. Displays of anger are so rare coming from No. 5 that the Orioles celebrate them by mimicry.

"Last year I hit a fly to right with one out, Tommy Davis on second, and Bobby Grich on third," Robinson said. "It's an out, but I told myself I've got a sacrifice fly and an RBI at least. Both runners tagged up, but the right fielder threw to third and got Davis before Grich could score.

"I didn't get the RBI and was charged with a time at bat. I really got angry. I threw my helmet down."

Robinson laughed. "All the guys imitated me for days, jumping around and throwing their helmets on the ground."

Brooks Calbert Robinson first wore a Baltimore uniform in September · of 1955, the month Juan Peron was deposed as dictator of Argentina, Dwight Eisenhower was in his first term as President, and the Beatles had yet to be heard. The Orioles were only a year away from being called the St. Louis Browns.

"I got $4,000 that first year, no bonus. There was a rule then that bonus players had to stay with the major league club two years, so I was better off playing in a league closer to my level," said Robinson, who spent most of 1955 in the Piedmont League at York, Pennsylvania.

"Physically, I wasn't somebody you'd give a lot of money to, anyway. At the time I had no doubt I'd be a major leaguer. Now, looking back, I wasn't that outstanding, just average speed and an average arm.

"I could field as long as I can remember. But hitting has been a struggle all my life."

He has fielded well enough to have won the Gold Glove award as the best defensive third baseman the past 14 consecutive years. The hitting struggle has produced a .271 major league lifetime average. Since 1960, when he stopped spending most of his summers at York or San Antonio or Vancouver in the

Brooks Robinson makes a diving catch of Johnny Bench's liner in the third game of the 1970 World Series against the Reds. The Series was a high point in Robinson's career. He played brilliantly on defense at third base and batted .426 to lead the Orioles to the world championship in five games.

grooming process, Robinson has averaged 18 home runs and 82 RBI a season.

The combination of superb fielding and timely if not intimidating power has worked with inflation to raise Robinson's $4,000 base to an estimated $115,-000 in his 20th season in the Baltimore organization.

"That figure is about right," confirmed Frank Cashen, executive vice-president and general manager of the Orioles. "It takes 15 or 20 minutes every year for Brooks to sign."

Baseball has rewarded Robinson's devotion to the game. Wayne Causey was the bonus kid at third in 1955. Another competitor was Chuck Diering, a combination outfielder-third baseman, before George Kell was acquired from Detroit in 1956 to give the Orioles a trace of class at the corner in the evening of his career.

"I was lucky. The timing was right," Robinson said. "Paul Richards [the manager] was also right. He advised me when I signed that the position was wide open. It was there for the taking. Fortunately, I happened to come along."

Gracious to everybody and grateful to baseball almost to a fault, Robinson tends to describe his tenure as a happy accident.

Weaver states flatly that "Brooksie's got to be the best third baseman who ever played this game. I never saw Pie Traynor, but day in and day out nobody could possibly be better than Brooksie."

Others are equally convinced. Paul Blair stood at third and Boog Powell at second as Robinson came up in the third and final game of the 1971 American League playoffs with Oakland. A's manager Dick Williams had ordered his pitcher, right-hander Diego Segui, to play percentage and walk Elrod Hendricks, a left-handed hitter. Robinson is a right-handed hitter. Besides, his glove is quicker than his feet and he hits a lot of grounders.

Still, Blair couldn't believe what he saw. The score was 1-1 in the fifth inning, and Robinson was being allowed to bat with the bases filled. Blair turned to Sal Bando, Oakland's third baseman.

"Brooks will hit a grand slam or something," Blair said.

On second, Powell turned to Oakland's Dick Green. "I wouldn't do this," Powell said. "Brooks is one hell of a hitter in a spot like this."

Robinson stroked a two-run shot over second. About an hour later the A's went home to watch the World Series on television.

"In situations like that you tend to bear down, to concentrate a little more," Robinson said. "I've al-

81

ways been able to make contact with the ball. I don't strike out much and I guess that's half the battle."

But the moments frozen in Robinson's history occurred in the 1970 World Series when the Cincinnati Reds and John Bench in particular could hit nothing past him.

The fingers of his glove scraping the ground as usual, Robinson was an octopus, stabbing shots either in the hole to his left or on the foul line to his right. He snatched a blow by Bench backhanded off the left-field chalk line, his back to the plate, then recovered to throw the runner out in a spine-chilling play.

"Hoover" the Reds labeled him, after the vacuum cleaner. But like the snake after the mongoose, they kept trying Robinson and got gloved out of the Series. Robinson won a car as the Most Valuable Player.

"If we'd have known he wanted a car that bad," said Bench, a partner with Pete Rose in a Cincinnati auto dealership, "we'd have given him one."

Robinson chose to recall the first inning of the opening game. "Nobody remembers I blew the first ball hit to me," he said. "An easy chance, a 42-hopper I call it. I made a bad throw to first that drew Powell off the bag.

"As for the rest of it, I've never had five games like that in the 20 years I've been in baseball. During the Series I thought to myself, 'I hope this gets over. It's unreal.' "

Robinson's glove went to the Hall of Fame despite the error. The Orioles say it grabs every baseball in Cooperstown.

Robinson schemed for half the flight from Kansas City to Boston in July of 1959 before stopping the blonde stewardess as she made the rounds. He relates the incident in his book, *Putting It All Together.*

"Miss," he said boldly, "could you please bring me a glass of iced tea?"

Three glasses and three trips by the stewardess later, he brought the glass back to the galley.

"Still thirsty?" she asked.

"No, just returning the glass."

"Oh. Thank you."

"Miss, have you got a moment? I want to tell you something. If any of these other guys ask you for a date, tell them you don't go out with married men. Understand? Every one of them is married. I'm the only single guy on the team."

"Well," she said. "I'm certainly grateful for that piece of information, Mr. . . . Mr. . . . ."

"Brooks Robinson. What's your name?"

"Constance Butcher."

A practical lie can be more virtuous than the truth. Most other Oriole bachelors on the plane were still bachelors when Brooks and Connie were married 15 months later.

One morning last spring at Miami Stadium, the Vacuum Cleaner was at his customary post, scooping grounders as regularly as Billy Hunter, the coach, could slap them his way. Other Orioles look like strangers at third.

Robinson's cap was tucked into a back pocket as he worked with obvious relish. "He'd stand out there all day as long as there was somebody with a bat," Weaver said. "Nobody on this club, not the youngest guy, works harder or has more enthusiasm."

Robinson turned 37 in May. His six-foot one-inch frame remains slim but is sloping at the shoulders and gathering flesh in the middle. With the cap off, half his head glared back at the sun. Viewed from the side, his skull is bisected with all the brown hair to the rear.

"A friend made me a toupee a couple years ago. We had a lot of laughs out of it," Robinson said. "But I'll tell you, it was pretty good, too. What I need is half a toupee. Where I need it is in front with this receding hair."

Toupees interest him less than hits, though. Vanity and pretense are unknown to him. "Once I was sitting having a beer with Clay Dalrymple," he said, referring to the former Baltimore catcher. "I just reached up and snatched the wig off his head. He sat there exposed, bald as a stone."

Brooks Robinson passed the legendary Traynor for hits by a third baseman (2,417) in May of 1973. In August he got his 2,500th hit, and Weaver said, "It's a shame a man has to wait five years after he retires to get in the Hall of Fame. Brooksie should be in it five days after he hangs up his glove."

Even five days after retirement will be a long time from now if Robinson has his way.

"I'll play as long as I can," he said. "I've been physically lucky. My body seems to be built for durability. I've never had a single pulled muscle in my whole career."

Robinson has been beaned seven times. "But I'm sort of loosy-goosy, though not physically strong."

He laughed. "They kid me about shots that hit my chest. The ball doesn't bounce away. It just goes 'thud' and drops down in front of me.

"I think the trouble with most players in the mid-30s is that they've had it mentally. But that's one problem I don't have."

When it comes to fielding the tough ones and the easy ones, Brooks Robinson still does it with grace.

Baseball's Best Batters

by Billy Evans

Condensed from *Esquire Magazine*

August, 1942

I shall never forget the day that I heard Wee Willie Keeler expound his now-famous batting theory: "Hit 'em where they ain't!" That was in 1906, the year I made my big league debut. We were sitting on the bench of the New York Highlanders, now better known as the Yankees, awaiting game time. Mark Roth, then a baseball writer on the *New York Globe,* had come down to the bench to interview Keeler on the art of hitting.

The day before, Keeler who was on the way out at the time, having passed his peak, had made five hits in a row. Two of them were bunts that he beat out; another was a drag bunt that the pitcher, first baseman, and second baseman chased, with the latter finally reaching the ball but finding no one covering first. The other two hits were flyballs that dropped between the shortstop and left fielder, although the outfielder seemed to be playing almost directly back of the shortstop.

"What have you to say to the kids of America on how to become a great hitter?" asked Roth.

"Hit 'em where they ain't," replied Keeler.

"I understand," said Roth, "but you must explain to the youngsters how you manage to hit 'em where they ain't."

"Just do it," was Keeler's answer.

It is questionable if the game ever produced a hitter just like Keeler. He had no power. The outfielders knew it and played in close. In reality, when Keeler came to bat there were seven infielders, all set to stop him. Yet he always batted better than .300.

Despite all the defenses set up to stop him, Keeler, with his uncanny ability to place the ball out of reach of the opposition, baffled all attempts to stop him. Hitting was a science with Keeler. He was one of the originators of so-called "place-hitting," so gauging his batting stroke, according to the pitch, that the ball would fall where no one was playing.

It is my conviction that all the great hitters past and present are born not made. Over nearly 40 years in baseball, 22 in the role of big league umpire in which I have called balls and strikes on these great hitters who made baseball history, I have reached the decision that hitting is a gift. You either have it or you don't. It is seldom, if ever, acquired. I have asked many of the great hitters to explain just how they did it, but invariably their answers were just as illuminating as the favored reply of Wee Willie Keeler to all such questions: "Hit 'em where they ain't."

Unquestionably, timing is the greatest asset of all the outstanding batsmen. Timing at the bat is a combination of a number of things. There must be perfect rhythm between the stride and the swing. If either is a trifle late, the coordination between brain, muscle, feet, and arms is lacking.

If there ever was a greater all-around baseball player than Ty Cobb, I have yet to see him. Babe Ruth had more power, Tris Speaker was a greater fielder, Joe DiMaggio has a better arm, but none possessed the all-around finesse of the Georgia Peach. Cobb did everything well.

Well do I recall a reply that Cobb made to me years ago when sitting on the bench with him. I asked how he analyzed batting slumps, which every now and then overtook even him.

"It's hard to explain why they happen," Ty replied. "It's even more difficult to offer a solution as to how to come out of a batting slump. Illness and injuries often cause a batter to fall into a slump. Illness destroys some of his physical resistance, causing him to press in an effort to make up for the lack of that little extra zip in his swing. Injuries to either arms or legs often cause a player to lose his timing, simply because in favoring the injury he throws himself off stride. When a slump is directly attributable to temporary physical defects, a return to normal invariably gets the batter back in stride.

"In a great many cases, however, worry is the start of a slump. When I went into a slump, I tried my best to keep from worrying. I tried to think of the many lucky hits I had gotten to balance a lot of the hard-hit balls that were going directly into the hands of some fielder. I always determined not to press."

Cobb had fewer batting slumps than most of them. And I have always felt the reason was that Cobb had great confidence in his ability, knew that batting slumps were merely temporary and that if he continued in the routine way he would emerge without any great handicap. Yet I also always felt that Cobb's spread grip, which he affected most of the time, was his greatest asset in keeping him out of slumps. I have never seen a great hitter who had better control of his bat at all times than Cobb.

Ty Cobb (left), Babe Ruth, and Tris Speaker were generally regarded as the greatest outfielders of their time, and are seen here in a 1941 reunion wearing the uniforms of the teams they played for in their heyday. Cobb had a lifetime batting average of .367; Ruth, .342; and Speaker, .344. All were left-handed batters.

In any discussion of the great hitters of the game, you have to come quickly to Babe Ruth, the greatest distance hitter of them all. When the sagacious Ed Barrow, who, more than any other man, made the New York Yankees what they are today, decided that Ruth would have more value every day playing in the outfield rather than taking his pitching turn every fourth day, I seriously doubted the wisdom of the move.

As the best left-handed pitcher of his pitching era, Ruth every now and then would make you gasp at the distance he would drive some pitch to his liking. However, he was often a strike-out victim, and there was a serious question in my mind whether Ruth, because of his penchant for striking out, wouldn't be a bust as an every-day hitter. However, Barrow saw possibilities in Ruth that others couldn't see. For a time he took considerable criticism as Ruth con-

tinued to strike out a couple of times in most every game—sometimes more. But Barrow never wavered in his belief in Ruth, and it wasn't long before Ruth began to definitely justify his opinion.

Babe Ruth was a do-or-don't batter—always shooting the works. He called on no tricks to get his base hits. They were manufactured through the medium of sheer power. Every now and then, more for the humor of the situation, he would lay down a bunt and beat it out, to his great satisfaction. Reaching first base he would shake with laughter, at the same time deriding the opposition.

Ruth, greatest slugger of all time, could be pitched to but there had better be no slip in the procedure.

The smart pitchers—those with a limited amount of natural stuff—caused Ruth more trouble than pitchers who had plenty. Such type pitchers worked on Ruth, seldom gave him the ball he liked best to

84

hit—the fast one—and kept trying to make him swing at the ball they wanted him to, rather than the one he liked to hit. As a result Babe often struck out; on the other hand, pitching smart to Ruth, meaning just missing the plate, caused him to get a lot of bases on balls, in addition to the many intentional passes he received.

Lou Gehrig, who followed Ruth in the Yankee batting order for many years, was in some respects as great a hitter as Ruth.

There was a rhythm to Gehrig's swing that made you feel there was no excuse for him not hitting every pitch. The start of the swing by Gehrig and Ruth was entirely different. Ruth was fidgety and seemingly nervous. His bat would move back and forth on his shoulder awaiting the pitch. His feet were close together, ready for the lunge into the ball that meant the kill. Gehrig, on the other hand, used an open stance of perhaps a foot. His bat rested quietly on his shoulder as the pitcher prepared to deliver the ball. When the delivery was started Gehrig slowly lifted the bat from his shoulder and assumed an almost defiant attitude. When the pitch neared the plate he took a short step and a rhythmic swing that made for almost as great power as Ruth, although their styles were definitely different.

Gehrig was much harder to pitch to than Ruth. He murdered the change of pace and slow curve that Ruth disliked.

Ruth, because of his lunge, was unable to control his bat as could Gehrig from his flat stance. Gehrig was never off balance and always able to adapt his swing and timing to the slow ball and speed ball.

The greatest difference between Ruth and Gehrig, however, was not so much of a mechanical nature as it was in temperament. Ruth oozed color, while Gehrig had none. Ruth's every move was that of the showman, while Gehrig was the well-oiled machine, the robot that wasted no effort but moved constantly in the same perfect groove. When Ruth hit a home run he let you know that he was just as delighted over the happening as his most loyal rooter. By the time he reached first he was in tune with everything. The crowd seemed to sense his enthusiasm and became a part of it. His every step as he circled the bases was wildly cheered. He would repeatedly doff his cap to the crowd in a manner that increased the applause.

The four batters we have discussed—Cobb, Ruth, Gehrig, and Keeler—were left-handers. So let's consider two of the greatest hitters ever produced by the National League—Hans Wagner and Rogers Hornsby, both right-handers.

Wagner did all of his hitting against the dead ball and before the abolition of trick deliveries. I believe it is conservative to say that had Wagner hit against the lively ball now in use, his average over his career of 21 years would have been closer to .350 than the .329 figure he amassed.

Honus was very bowlegged and had unusually long arms. His style at the plate was rather grotesque because of his bowlegs and long arms, but he had no weakness as far as I could judge and I never heard a pitcher argue that he had. He had a remarkable eye and seldom hit at bad balls.

Unquestionably in the field and at the bat, Wagner was the most awkward "graceful" performer in all the history of the game.

Rogers Hornsby, one of the greatest right-handed hitters of all time, on the other hand, exemplified motion. At the plate, he was the modern Adonis of the game. He had a perfect physique. His stride and swing were in keeping with his physique—models of grace and precision. In some ways the style of Hornsby was as unique as that of Wagner. Certainly it was more unorthodox, though not to Hornsby.

Hornsby stood in the extreme rear of the batter's box—at least four feet from home plate. It appeared that the smart pitcher could keep the ball low and on the outside, particularly the curveball, and make a sucker of Hornsby. A lot of smart pitchers had such a notion during the early years of Hornsby's career, but soon found their strategy a boomerang.

I once remarked to Hornsby that his style seemed definitely contrary to all mechanics of the game. He smiled and replied:

"On the contrary, Billy, my style enables me to meet all the different pitches. The toughest pitch for any batter is the 'tight' pitch—high or low and inside. My position takes the dynamite out of the tight pitch and to hit the low pitch on the outside, curve or fastball, you take a full stride in the direction of the plate as the pitch is started, which brings you pretty much on a line with the plate and enables you to either push the ball to right field or drive it for distance—depending on the power you put behind the effort. I have always felt that my style at the plate immediately created a hazard for the smart pitcher by practically eliminating his having a chance to pitch to your stance and make you hit the ball that he wants you to hit."

Tris Speaker, the last word in center-fielding, was not far behind in his activities at the plate. Speaker was another of the rhythm hitters. His stance was just about the opposite of Hornsby. He used a spread stance lined up with home plate, rather than being three or four feet back of it like Hornsby. Speaker took no devastating swing but had a perfectly timed follow-through, like a golfer. His swing stressed timing and the follow-through. Ordinarily he didn't go for distance but in a pinch, when an extra-base hit was needed, Speaker could slip his grip to the bottom of the bat and swing from the ground.

The career of Eddie Collins covers 25 years as a big league star, more than any of the other great hitters of the game. Ty Cobb, who played one year less than Eddie, ranks second. Collins was not a power hitter. He was in the same class as Keeler and George Sisler, who might be termed the brain hitters of the game.

Collins, unlike many of the other outstanding left-handed hitters, was not a pull-hitter. A great majority of Collins' hits went to left field, line drives over the shortstop's head, or sizzling grounders just between the third baseman and shortstop.

Collins was a difficult man to strike out. He had a keen eye. He was a fine bunter, got away from the plate quickly, and beat out many a bunt or dragged ball for a well-earned base hit. Next to Cobb, Collins was the best base-runner in the history of the American League. When it came to laying down a perfect sacrifice with runners on, there was no one in the game who could compare with Collins.

Of all the modern hitters, George Sisler, who over a period of 16 years in the majors turned in a .340 batting average, bore the closest resemblance to Willie Keeler. Sisler, a left-handed hitter, was faster than Keeler and used his speed to better advantage than any of the other stars with the exception of Cobb. Sisler always had his eye on the play of the rival infield. If it was playing deep, he was quick to take advantage of the bunt and the drag to get base hits. He would poke bad pitches just over the infield, to the consternation of the opposition, the pitcher in particular.

Larry Lajoie, great right-handed hitter of the old school, was the good-to-look-at hitter. There was an aloof nonchalance in the manner in which Lajoie stepped into the batter's box that ordinarily would have caused the pitcher to become careless had not Lajoie's fame as a hitter made him feared by all. Larry's theory was to hit the pitch to the field to which it should go. He was definitely a straight-away hitter whose chief thought was to get proper timing and thereby make correct contact.

To my way of thinking, there never was a greater hitter than Joe Jackson. A left-handed hitter, Joe stood well back of the plate, keeping his feet fairly close together, and as the ball approached him, took a slow, even stride, and started the swing of the bat in unison with the stride. No hitter had more per-fect coordination than Jackson. He could have hit fourth on my all-time team of great hitters of the game.

That brings us to the two great hitters of modern times, Joe DiMaggio of the Yankees and Ted Williams of the Red Sox. The styles of these two batsmen are entirely different. Of all the great hitters, past and present, DiMaggio, the greatest present-day right-hander, uses the most open stance of all. He is the only power hitter who ever swung from a flat-footed position.

Ted Williams, in contrast to DiMaggio, is a bundle of nerves. He seems to bubble over with enthusiasm for his work from the time he leaves the bench until he reaches the batter's box. Getting into the box, he goes through a dozen acrobatic maneuvers. It seems that he will never be ready for the pitch, but American League twirlers will testify to the contrary. He laughs at his own antics when he misses a healthy swing. He grins with satisfaction when he connects for the base hit. He is the big kid all over and, like Babe Ruth, wins his audience early. I have always felt that Williams, the greatest of today's left-handed hitters, is the nearest approach in every way that baseball has had to Ruth.

(Editor's Note: Billy Evans was elected to the Hall of Fame in 1973 as an umpire and front office executive. When he analyzed some of the game's greatest hitters, such excellent batters as Stan Musial, Roberto Clemente, and Hank Aaron had yet to make their impact on the major league scene. Evans died in Miami, Florida, in 1956.)

Billy Evans

Hans Wagner: "The Greatest All-Round Ballplayer"

by Francis Stann
Washington Star

February, 1956

In the course of his 50 years in baseball, which included that period from 1920 to 1945 when he made the Yankees what they are today, Edward G. Barrow developed one unshakable conviction: the late Hans Wagner was the greatest ballplayer of all time.

As he put it in his own words:

"Babe Ruth was the game's greatest personality, and its greatest home-run hitter. Ty Cobb was the greatest of all hitters . . . though I have always had a tremendous admiration for Larry Lajoie and consider him only a step behind Cobb as the greatest batsman of all.

"But there is no question that Wagner was the greatest all-round ballplayer who ever lived."

Barrow, builder of the Yankees, essentially was an American Leaguer and had been Ruth's man. It was he who converted Ruth from a great pitcher into a greater hitter. But Barrow it was who more or less discovered Wagner. That is, he talked Honus into playing ball for a living. So he had a rooting interest in each man, and if he says Wagner was the greater—and greatest—it must be assumed Barrow was speaking impartially.

Certainly John McGraw was impartial toward Wagner, Ruth, and Cobb and the late leader of the Giants had agreed with Barrow.

Hans could play all the infield positions and the outfield with equal facility, so the early historians agree. As a matter of record, Wagner was a big-leaguer for six years before manager Fred Clarke of the Pirates made him a permanent shortstop. Since he wasn't any teen-ager when he began in pro ball, Honus was about 29 at that time.

This is a late date to begin a shortstopping career so outstanding that whenever qualified baseball men pick all-time teams they arbitrarily choose Wagner at short and go on to some other position.

Back in 1939, sitting on the porch of a small inn at Cooperstown, some of the Hall of Fame old-timers were chewing the fat with some newspapermen, who were asking for their versions of all-time players. Larry Lajoie said:

"You know, except for Ruth and Cobb, there's only one other man, Wagner, who is unanimous. People quibble over the pitchers, catchers, first basemen, and so forth, but never about those three."

"I can think of a lot of other great shortstops," said a reporter, "so Wagner must have been good."

Walter Johnson was there. "You weren't born when Wagner was at his best," he said. "There wasn't anything he couldn't do—hit, run, and field. I'm glad he stayed on his side of the fence [the National League]."

The reporter, who had known Wagner slightly because of his connection with Pittsburgh as a coach, said, "I wonder how he could run so fast on those bowlegs. I never saw such bowlegs."

"Find any old catcher, infielder, or outfielder who had to throw out Wagner and ask him," Lajoie advised. "He'll tell you if he could run."

The record books tell the story—not only of how Wagner could run but do everything else—as eloquently as any human voice. During his 21-year career, Honus' feats bordered on the incredible. Seventeen straight seasons he batted .300 or better, and he was over 40 years of age before he dropped below that figure. Between 1900 and 1911, he led the National League in hitting eight times, four times in succession. Defensively his skill is so well remembered by old-timers that whenever praise is heaped upon a Travis Jackson or a Marty Marion, they merely smile and say:

"But you should have seen old Hans."

Only three players in history stole more bases than Wagner, they being Cobb, Max Carey, and Billy Hamilton, the latter excluded from "modern" baseball. Hans averaged better than 55 stolen bases per season over one stretch of five years and finished with 720.

Until a couple of years or so ago, Wagner was the oldest man in uniform. He was frankly a pensioner, although listed as a Pirate coach, but he survived many a manager and even a change of ownership.

Because he was Hans Wagner, that's why.

The Day Paul Waner Refused a Base Hit

by Herbert Bursky

August, 1971

Paul Glee Waner was one of baseball's foremost batting stars. A sharp, always dangerous hitter who struck out infrequently, he amassed 3,152 hits, including 603 doubles, 190 triples, and 112 home runs, and recorded a lifetime plate average of .333. From 1926 to 1939, his most fruitful seasons with the Pittsburgh Pirates, his average slipped under .320 only once, and then to .309, a mark many players today would gladly settle for.

Over a span of 14 years, Paul, known as **Big Poison**, and his younger brother, Lloyd, Little Poison, played together in the Pirate outfield and provided Forbes Field fans with many satisfying moments. Paul entered the Hall of Fame in 1952, and Lloyd was selected 15 years later. They are the only brothers who played in the 20th century to be so honored. (George and Harry Wright, brothers who were heroic figures in the post-Civil War baseball era, are also in the Hall.)

But there was a day when Paul Waner actually refused a base hit. It happened in 1942 when Waner, near the end of his career as a part-time performer for the Boston Braves, was striving for his historic 3,000th major league hit. At shortstop for the Cincinnati Reds was 25-year-old Eddie Joost. This is how Joost recalled the incident years later:

"Waner was trying for his 3,000th hit, something done by only a handful of players. He hit a hard shot past me. I got my glove on the ball enough to slow it up but it went through. It was surely a hit by any stretch of the imagination.

"The umpires stopped the game right there and one of them went over to Waner to present the ball to him as a souvenir. But Waner was waving his arms to the press box to indicate he wouldn't accept a hit on that ball. He wanted his 3,000th hit to be completely clean, and this one wasn't good enough because I'd gotten my glove on it.

"So they charged me with an error, strange as that may sound. I suppose it turned out all right though. Waner was a nice guy and he wanted his 3,000th hit, a lifetime ambition, to be one he could be proud of."

Waner, of course, subsequently made his 3,000th hit and became the seventh man to accomplish the feat. (Ty Cobb, Tris Speaker, Honus Wagner, Eddie Collins, Napoleon Lajoie, and Cap Anson were the six who preceded him.) Joost concluded the 1942 season with 45 errors, the most of any big league shortstop, and his .933 defensive average was the lowest among shortstops in the majors. Obviously, the "error" given Eddie on the Waner ball didn't help his record.

After World War II, Joost developed into a capable shortstop for Connie Mack's Philadelphia Athletics. Bespectacled Eddie formed an effective double-play combination with Pete Suder and showed surprising strength as a home-run hitter. Connie liked him and, in 1954, he served as the Athletics' last manager in Philadelphia before the franchise was shifted to Kansas City. But Eddie would always remember the day he was charged with an error he claimed he didn't commit.

Paul Waner (left) with his brother Lloyd when they played the outfield for the Pittsburgh Pirates. Both are in the Hall of Fame.

Bill Terry Remembers John McGraw

by Red Barber
Condensed from the *Miami Herald*

November, 1971

Bill Terry was the last man in the National League to hit .400. Terry hit .401 in 1930. The highest any National League batter has hit since then was Arky Vaughan with .385 in 1935. Then came Stan Musial with .376 in 1948. Ted Williams hit .406 in the American League in 1941. The closest to .400 in Ted's league since he did it was Ted himself with .388 in 1957 (when Ted was 39 years old).

Terry had not spoken to his manager, John J. McGraw, for two years when McGraw handed Terry the job of leading the New York Giants. That was on Friday, June 2, 1932. McGraw died a year and a half later.

McGraw managed the Giants 30 years. McGraw was "The Giants." He built them into greatness. He won 10 pennants. He dominated the National League. There is no way to talk about baseball and not speak of McGraw.

Terry turned 73 in October. He sells autos in Jacksonville, Florida. The other day I said to him, "Bill, people today don't know McGraw, don't remember him. You knew him better than any man alive today. What sort of a manager was he?"

"It's unfortunate they don't have the opportunity to know him," he began, "especially some of these ballplayers today. He wouldn't stand for some of the things the ballplayers are doing these days. He was a taskmaster, no question about that.

"But after you left the ball field, it was forgotten . . . until the next day. Then he'd remember it again when he got to the ball park."

Bill didn't waste time repeating the obvious facets of McGraw's great success. Bill and McGraw battled each other since Bill refused to sign the very first contract McGraw offered him when Terry was an unknown semipro pitcher that McGraw wanted to convert to a first baseman (at Toledo). Terry dared to face up to McGraw, always stood his ground, and finally they went separate ways without a word between them. McGraw the boss, Terry his first baseman.

"For a few years Mr. McGraw had Uncle Robbie [Wilbert Robinson who later quarreled with Mc-Graw and went to Brooklyn] handle the catching and pitching assignments. The Old Man took care of the infield and the outfield. And he was a past master at picking outfielders and infielders.

"I'm not criticizing him, but it seemed to me then he lacked knowing his pitching . . . when to take 'em out and when to leave 'em in there. Also, he was the type fellow who would call all the pitches until you got in a spot . . . then he'd leave you on your own. And if you did the wrong thing it was just too bad.

"There were times he would pitch one way and his ball club would be playing the other because they didn't know which way the pitcher was pitching. Consequently we'd get in trouble. He didn't hold the right type meetings so that the ball club could coordinate itself."

Terry switched to the positive. "He had a tremendous ball club all the time. In those days the Giants and the Yankees were the greatest ball clubs I've seen on the field. He had great players who could do the things he wanted them to do . . . hit-and-run, protecting the runner, bunting when necessary. He was a sharp man.

"I remember one time there were two outs . . . last of the ninth . . . a man on third base. I was at bat and I was considered a pretty good hitter. I looked down at the coach and he gave me the bunt sign.

"Two outs . . . the winning run on third! I liked to dropped my teeth.

"But I took another look at the coach. The bunt was on. So I bunted the ball and we won the ball game. Nobody expected that.

"This was the sort of thing that makes me remember Mr. McGraw very vividly. Yet on the other hand there were times he and I practically came to blows over the way he would put the blame on certain fellows, including me. I couldn't take it. I wasn't built that way.

"Finally we didn't speak for two years."

Rogers Hornsby hit more than .400 three times. Ty Cobb did it three times also, and once when he hit .401 in 1922 he failed to win the batting title because George Sisler had .420.

I asked Terry what had become of the .400 hitter. He began explaining.

"One thing is that the batter of today is swinging differently, using a very light bat around 31 ounces. Lou Gehrig and I used a 44-ounce bat. Babe Ruth's was 45 ounces. Even little fellows like Paul Waner were using a 42-ounce bat.

"We had a different idea about hitting. We had very few strike-outs. Look at the records and you'll find that in comparison with players of today, we didn't strike out much. I was taught by John Mc-Graw, and he himself was a fine hitter. I learned

Bill Terry and John McGraw. Terry (left) succeeded McGraw as manager of the New York Giants in June, 1932, and went on to win National League pennants in 1933, 1936, and 1937 before closing out his major league career in 1941. Although he and the fiery McGraw had their differences and hardly spoke to one another for an extended period, Terry was the man McGraw wanted as his successor when he resigned.

from fellows like Hornsby. They impressed on me that with two strikes you get up to the plate and protect it.

"Consequently you got hold of the ball more frequently. These fellows today are back in the same position with two strikes as they are with no strikes. And they're still swinging away. Therefore, they strike out 100 or 110 or 120 times. That naturally hurts a batter's average."

Terry continued. "We have some pretty good hitters today who have a chance to reach .400. At least they look good. I thought Aaron had a chance. I haven't seen him, but from what I hear Oliva could do it.

"However, they've got to protect the plate, get the base hit and not go for the long ball, especially when a pitcher has two strikes."

Terry was hitter, fielder, and manager. When he managed the New York Giants to three pennants, he also was the general manager. Young Horace Stoneham began interfering with his managing, so Terry quit with a year to go on his contract. He was smart to quit, and his success in business proved the correctness of his decision to leave baseball.

"The other day," Terry related, "I had a call from Spec Richardson, general manager at Houston, and he told me, 'Bill, we're not scoring any runs.' I asked him about his pitching, and he said, 'good.' What kind of defensive club? I wanted to know. He answered, 'A real good one.' I told him, for heavens sake, why doesn't your manager go for one run instead of a group of runs? Don't play for the big inning. You'll win more games."

Terry continued to press his point.

"The concept of baseball is changed today. They won't play for one run anymore. They complain when they don't have home-run hitters.

"I didn't have home-run hitters with the Giants except Mel Ott. I used to hit one once in a while. But we won with good pitching and good defense.

"The greatest day I ever saw was in July, 1933. We were fighting with the Cardinals . . . the Deans, Frisch, Pepper Martin, Medwick. We had a doubleheader at the Polo Grounds, and the place was packed to the rafters.

"We played 27 innings. We scored two runs and won both games. Hubbell beat them, 1-0, in 18 innings of the first game. It was getting dark for the second game and we didn't have lights. So we carefully warmed up that big Roy Parmelee for the second game. Johnny Vergez hit a home run off Dizzy Dean in the first inning and we won, 1-0."

Terry laughed. "Two runs . . . 27 innings . . . win both ball games."

Mickey Mantle—
The Game I'll Never Forget

as told to George Vass

August, 1971

When you look back on the kind of career I had, I guess you could think about a lot of games that might stir up a few memories. I know one thing... when I read what some of the sportswriters have written about me it makes me feel that it all was worthwhile.

Sure, there are a lot of World Series games out of which to pick the game I'll never forget, especially the one in which Don Larsen pitched the perfect game in 1956. Nobody's about to forget a thing like that, not if you live to be a hundred.

But the game I've thought the most about didn't come in a World Series or in any of the years I was going good. It came in a year when I had most of my troubles, in 1963, when I played just 65 games, the least in any year.

I remember how I thought it was going to be a good year. I had a good spring, and when the season opened I figured it was going to be fine all the way. But right at the start I hurt my rib cage trying to make a throw to double a runner off first. Well, I couldn't swing a bat for a few days, and I don't

know how long it was before I got back in the lineup.

I wasn't in there long, though. I was going good, hitting well and feeling strong, when we got into Baltimore in early June. I remember it was a rainy night, and I chased a ball hit by Brooks Robinson right up to the chain link fence. The ball went over the fence, but I went right into it. I broke a bone in my left foot and injured my knee.

I can tell you that when they put the cast on my left foot and I realized I'd be out six weeks, maybe more, I was about as discouraged as I'd ever been. People were writing and talking that I might retire, and I suppose the thought went through my mind that I might as well do it.

I always loved the game, but when my legs weren't hurting, it was a lot easier to love. I got as much of a kick out of playing ball late in my career as I did when I first came up—as long as I wasn't injured.

I remember sitting in the Yankee locker room after that injury in Baltimore in 1963 about as down as I could get. I was thinking that every time I'm doing well something happens. It had always been like that and now it had happened again.

I had to use crutches for a while. Somebody asked me, "Do you know how to use those things?" I think I told him, "I've lived with them." And I sure did.

About five weeks after I was hurt, I rejoined the Yankees on a road trip, although I still wasn't ready to play. But Ralph Houk, our manager, wanted me with the team. He told the writers, "Just having

Mickey Mantle being carried off the field on a stretcher after fracturing a bone in his left foot when he caught his spikes in the fence at Baltimore in a game on June 5, 1963. Mantle was injured when he tried to catch a home-run ball hit by the Orioles' Brooks Robinson. A cast was put on Mantle's leg, and he didn't return to action—but not on the field—until August.

Still recuperating from his foot injury, Mantle hit a two-run pinch-homer against the Orioles in Baltimore's Memorial Stadium on September 1, 1963. Greeting Mickey is Clete Boyer, who was on base when Mantle connected. The homer helped the Yankees down the Orioles, 5-4.

Mickey around gives the guys a lift, and I thought it might give him a lift, too. He can't play, but he makes the others play a little harder."

Ralph was always like that with me. Whenever he started bragging about me, it made me believe in myself. I could take the bad days and the boos a lot better.

There were quite a few bad days in 1963 until that leg healed. I got tired of sitting on the bench and of hearing people ask when I'd be able to play again. I didn't know.

Two months had gone by since I'd run into the fence at Baltimore, and now we were playing the Orioles again, this time at Yankee Stadium. It was a doubleheader on August 4, 1963, and they won the first game.

They were leading by a run in the ninth inning of the second game, and I don't remember who was supposed to be batting, but Ralph motioned to me to go up and pinch-hit. I picked up a bat and started to walk out of the dugout.

That's a moment I'll never forget. There were 40,000 people in the stands and when I came out of the dugout, they all stood up and gave me one of the loudest ovations I'd ever heard. It was the first time in my life I ever got goose pimples.

You can't imagine how I felt. I've heard a lot of cheers in my time, and a lot of boos, too. You try to tell yourself the boos don't make any difference, but you hear them all the same. You wouldn't be human if you didn't.

But here they were cheering me—all 40,000 people—just standing there yelling their heads off and I hadn't done a thing. Just walked out of the dugout with a bat on my shoulder.

Then I got scared. I prayed I wouldn't look foolish at bat, that I would at least pop up or ground out—anything but strike out. I don't remember how I got up to the plate. All I know is I was just hoping I wouldn't disgrace myself, that I'd make some contact with the ball.

I don't know whether it was on the first swing, the second, or what, but I hit the ball and it went for a long ride. It went all the way for a long home run and tied up the game.

I've hit a lot of balls harder, but I can't say that any of them had more behind it than that one. To come off the bench and do that, after the ovation those people had given me—well, I can't express myself well enough to tell you how it felt.

We went on to win the game in the 10th inning, but that wasn't the big thing. It was mostly the way the fans greeted me and that I was lucky enough to be able to do what I did that makes this the game I'll never forget.

When the Red Sox Scored 17 Runs in One Inning!

by Joe Falls
Detroit Free Press

Steve Gromek

April, 1972

It was like a bad dream to Steve Gromek. As he sat in the bullpen in Boston's Fenway Park, he watched in stunned silence as the Red Sox scored run after run against the Tigers, until the final score mounted to a shattering 17-1.

The date was June 17, 1953.

It was Gromek's first day in a Detroit uniform. He'd just joined the Tigers after a trade with the Cleveland Indians—he and Ray Boone and Dick Weik—and he could hardly believe what he saw.

He knew the Tigers were pretty inept—they were dead last in the American League, hopelessly out of contention even though it was only the middle of June—but he never dreamed they were this inept.

The Red Sox scored almost at will, getting seven runs in the fourth inning and winding up with 20 hits for the day.

Generally, in times like this—times of complete embarrassment—ballplayers will laugh about their plight because there isn't anything else they can do about it.

But Gromek, who was considered something of a jokester in his day ("OK, Steve, where'd you hide the typewriter?"), didn't utter a word. Not a word.

"I didn't want to say anything because I didn't know too many of the guys, and I didn't want them to think I was a pop-off," he said.

That reflected some sound thinking on Gromek's part . . . some very sound thinking.

The Tigers, by edict of the American League, were forced to show up in Fenway Park again the next day. It was Gromek's turn on the chopping block.

The Red Sox again rolled up 17 runs on the Tigers —only this time it was 17 runs in one inning, one incredible, illogical, impossible inning.

The date was June 18, 1953.

The Red Sox sent 23 men to the plate in the 48-minute carnage. They turned a routine 5-3 game into a crushing 23-3 rout.

Gromek remembers it all right. He was on the mound when that frightening seventh inning started:

"White singled to right. Stephens singled to right, White taking third. Stephens stole second. Umphlett singled to left, scoring White and Stephens . . ."

"Enough! . . . Enough!" Gromek cried as he recalled the incident not too long ago. "I was hoping I'd never hear about that inning again.

"I never saw anything like it. They got some clean hits but most of them were flukes. The ball kept bouncing just out of the reach of our infielders or falling in front of our outfielders."

Hold on, friend. Didn't Dick Gernert wallop a three-run homer in that inning?

"Yes," said Gromek, smiling now. "I also set a long distance record that day."

Gromek was charged with nine of the runs. When he trudged to the dressing room, after being lifted by manager Fred Hutchinson, he sat in front of his locker in a state of shock.

"I was wondering if this was the end, if I was going to keep right on going down to the minors," he said. "I was feeling pretty sick."

The radio was on in Hutchinson's office, and Gromek could hear the runs still pouring over the plate.

"Oh, oh," he remembered saying to himself, "when is it going to end?"

Four days later, the Tigers were in Philadelphia and Hutchinson approached Gromek in the clubhouse and said: "Steve, you're going to start today."

Gromek was flabbergasted.

"I thought he might never let me pitch again."

Gromek not only pitched against the Philadelphia A's that day—he shut 'em out.

Ed Walsh—
The Day I Fanned Lajoie

as told to Francis J. Powers
Condensed from the *Chicago Daily News*

March, 1945

Did you ever see Larry Lajoie bat? No? Then you have missed something. I want to tell you that there was one of the greatest hitters—and fielders, too—ever in baseball. There's no telling the records he would have made if he'd hit against the lively ball. To tell you about my greatest day, I'll have to go back there to October, 1908, when I fanned Larry with the bases full and the White Sox chances for the pennant hanging on my every pitch to the big Frenchman.

That was October 3, the day after I had that great game with Addie Joss, and he beat me, 1-0, with a perfect game: no runs—no hits—no man reached first. There was a great pitcher and a grand fellow, Addie. He was one of my closest friends, and he would have been one of the best pitchers of all time but for his untimely death two years later.

I didn't think there'd ever be another pennant race like there was in the American League that year. All summer four teams—the Sox, Cleveland, Detroit, and the Browns—had been fighting, and three of 'em still had a chance on October 3. When Joss beat me the day before, it left us two and one-half games behind the Tigers and two behind the Naps, as Cleveland was called in honor of their player-manager, Lajoie (whose first name was Napoleon, not Larry). And we had only four games left to play.

It was a Saturday, I remember, and the biggest crowd ever to see a game in Cleveland up to that date jammed around the park. Fielder Jones started Frank Smith for us, and we got him three runs off Glenn Liebhardt and were leading by two going into the seventh. I was down in the bullpen, ready for anything because, as I said, we had to win this one.

As I recall it, George Perring, the shortstop, was first up for Cleveland, and he went all the way to second when Patsy Dougherty muffed his fly in the sun. I began to warm up in a hurry. Nig Clarke batted for Liebhardt and fanned, and things looked better. Smith would have been out of trouble, only Tannehill fumbled Josh Clarke's grounder and couldn't make a play. When Clarke stole second,

that upset Smith and he walked Bill Bradley. So I rushed to the pitcher's box, and the first batter I faced was Bill Hinchman. Bill wasn't a champion hitter but he was a tough man in a pinch. I knew his weakness was a spitball on the inside corner so I told Sully (Billy Sullivan) we'd have to get in close on him. And I did. My spitball nearly always broke down, and I could put it about where I wanted. Bill got a piece of the ball and hit a fast grounder that Tannehill fielded with one hand, and we forced Perring at the plate.

So there were two out and Larry at bat. Now if the Frenchman had a weakness, it was a fastball, high and right through the middle. If you pitched inside to him, he'd tear a hand off the third baseman, and if you pitched outside he'd knock down the second baseman. I tried him with a spitball that broke to the inside and down. You know a spitball was heavy and traveled fast. Lajoie hit the pitch hard down the third base line, and it traveled so fast that it curved 20 feet, I'd guess, over the foul line and into the bleachers. There was strike one.

My next pitch was a spitter on the outside, and Larry swung and tipped it foul back to the stands. Sully signed for another spitter, but I just stared at him; I never shook him off with a nod or anything like that. He signed for the spitter twice more, but still I just looked at him. Then Billy walked out to the box. "What's the matter?" Bill asked me. "I'll give him a fast one," I said, but Billy was dubious. Finally, he agreed. I threw Larry an overhand fastball that raised, and he watched it come over without even an offer. "Strike three!" roared Silk O'Loughlin. Lajoie sort of grinned at me and tossed his bat toward the bench without a word. That was the high spot of my baseball days: fanning Larry in the clutch and without him swinging.

Well, we came home to finish out the season with three games against the Tigers. We still were in the race but needed three straight for the flag. We got the first two. In the opener, Doc White beat the Tigers, 3-1, and held Cobb and Claude Rossman hitless. I pitched the second and beat 'em, 6-1, and allowed only four hits. This was my 65th game and 40th win of the season. And that left us a half game out of first, and Cleveland was out of the race when it dropped the first game of a doubleheader to the Browns.

That brought it down to the final day of the season. We heard that Hughie Jennings and Harry Tuthill (Detroit trainer) had sat up to four in the morning putting hot towels on Bill Donovan's arm, trying to get it in shape to pitch. At game time we weren't sure Bill would pitch until Jennings told him to warm up.

94

Big Ed Walsh won 195 games for the Chicago White Sox, including one season (1908) when he was credited with 40 victories. Twice in his career he won two games in one day and pitched a no-hitter in 1911. He was elected to the Hall of Fame in 1946.

Considered one of baseball's all-time great second basemen, Nap Lajoie began his career in the National League, but jumped to the American League in 1901, winning the league batting championship that year with a .422 mark for the old Philadelphia A's. Lajoie played in the majors through the 1916 season, mostly with the Cleveland Indians, and won two more batting titles—in 1903 (.355) and 1904 (.381). He finished with a lifetime average of .339 and was elected to the Hall of Fame in 1937.

Most of us thought Jones would start Smith against the Tigers, for he really had them handcuffed and always could be expected to pitch his best against them. We were startled rather than surprised when Jones said Doc White would pitch.

When Jones came in, I said: "Are you going to pitch Doc?" He said "Yes." Then I said, "That's a great injustice to a fine young man. You know White needs his full rest to be effective. I'll pitch if you want me to [I'd pitched in 65 games, my arm felt great and another game wouldn't hurt me]. But the man you should pitch is Smith . . . but you're mad at him."

I couldn't argue Jones out of starting Doc, and he didn't last long. I'll never forget that first inning. Matty McIntyre singled. Donie Bush was hit by a pitched ball, but the umpires wouldn't let him take first because he hadn't tried to duck the pitch. Then Donie fanned. There was a crowd around in the outfield, and Sam Crawford hit a terrific drive into the fans for two bases. And then Cobb—Cobb the man who never could hit White—tripled, cleaning the bases.

I got down to the bullpen in time to get warmed up a bit, and after Cobb's hit, Jones sent me in. The Tigers scored two more before I could stop them, and then I pitched through the fifth. When I came to the bench, I threw my glove in the corner. "What's the matter with you?" Jones asked. "I'm through," I said. "Now you'll have to pitch Smith, the man who should have started." Smith finished but the Tigers beat us, 7-0, and there went the pennant. Donovan allowed only two hits and fanned nine, and we dropped to third place when the Naps won from St. Louis.

I like to think back to the White Sox of those days. In 1906 we won the pennant and beat the Cubs in the World Series. Next season we were in the pennant race until the last days of September, and in 1908 we fought them down to the final day of the season. There never was a fielding first baseman like Jiggs Donahue in 1908, when he set a record for assists. Sullivan was a great catcher, one of the best. It was a great team, a smart team. But the tops of all days was when I fanned Lajoie with the bases filled. Not many pitchers ever did that.

When the Real Reggie Jackson Stood Up

by Frank Dolson
Philadelphia Inquirer

January, 1974

Joe Rudi, Reggie Jackson's friend, knows what it was like. He remembers the tortured look on his buddy's face, the tears in his eyes. Imagine. His team was in the World Series in 1972, and Reggie Jackson couldn't play. Play? Why, he couldn't even walk without crutches or get dressed without help.

"He was really down," Rudi said. "A guy plays a whole career waiting for a chance to play in a World Series. Here's the chance, and he's hurt . . ."

Rudi did his best to pull his friend through those difficult times. "I went up to his room," Joe recalled. "I ate with him. I tried to take his mind off it. . . ."

"He's the best friend I have," Reggie Jackson was saying after he had powered the A's to a 3-1 victory in the sixth game of the 1973 Series. "The man came over. He fed me; he helped me put my underwear on, my pants on."

Now it was different. Now it was Reggie Jackson's turn to help Joe Rudi and all the other Oakland A's. The team was in another World Series and this time he was able to run, to play, to hit. And he couldn't wait. You could see that on his face, too. Maybe that was the trouble. Maybe Reggie Jackson was trying to jam two World Series' worth of hits into one World Series.

"This time," said Rudi, "I think he was pressing. He's a good hitter; he had a good year, and he was trying so hard to do good. Trying too hard . . ."

The big man in the Oakland lineup, the guy who led the American League in home runs and runs batted in got one hit at Shea Stadium in three games. One crummy single in 12 at-bats.

"I was thinking about last year," Jackson said. "I was thinking about being hurt, thinking about my legs . . . and I didn't produce."

Trouble was, there was so much to think about. Extra-curricular things that shouldn't have been necessary to think about during a man's first World Series. There was Charlie Finley to think about. And Mike Andrews. And Dick Williams . . .

"We didn't talk about Seaver and Harrelson and Grote . . ." Reggie said. "All those guys are great

ballplayers, but all we talked about was this crap going on off the field. It takes the little boy out of you. You want to run, slide, have fun . . ."

Instead, Reggie Jackson's first World Series was turning into a nonstop hassle.

"In New York," he said, "it was a pain in the tail to play in the World Series, a pain in the tail to go to the ball park, a pain in the tail to walk in the lobby. All you heard was 'Is Dick Williams going to quit?' 'What do you think of Mike Andrews?' 'What do you think of Finley?' "

Or, for a change of pace, "What do you think about striking out three straight times against Tom Seaver?"

It was getting Reggie Jackson down, this chance of a lifetime. People expected so much from him; in the first three games he had delivered so little.

"If I don't have 15 hits, I'm doing bad," he said smiling faintly. "Like Willie Mays. If he don't hit a five-run homer, he's a bum. . . ." The smile broadened. "I hope we win this son of a gun. Maybe I'll be a hero."

Like he was in game No. 6.

"I felt pressure the first couple of games here," Reggie said. "I thought I was a stud, but I felt the pressure. I wasn't me at the plate."

But in the sixth game, with the A's desperate for a victory—and with Seaver on the mound—the real Reggie Jackson stood up, took his cuts, and kept Joe Rudi and the boys alive for another day.

"When I faced him in New York, he had me 0-and-two my first three times up," Reggie said. "What kind of a chance have you got against Tom Seaver when you're 0-and-two?"

When Seaver is throwing his best stuff, not much. But Seaver wasn't great in game No. 6, merely good.

"He needs an extra day's rest," Jackson said. "The man's shoulder is obviously bothering him. He was Tom Seaver today only in heart and fortitude. . . . If he'd won that ball game today he'd have been the greatest athlete in the world. He went out there knowing he didn't have his greatest stuff. He didn't complain or bitch . . . and he could've won that game, 3-2."

But he didn't. Reggie rifled a pair of two-out, RBI doubles against Seaver, then singled and scored the A's third run against Tug McGraw. At last, playing in a World Series was what Jackson always thought it would be: running . . . sliding . . . having fun. For one beautiful day he all but forgot about what a hassle it was playing for Charlie Finley, what a raw deal Mike Andrews got, how much he would miss playing for Dick Williams. Reggie Jackson felt like a little boy again.

"Hey, let's not have the article say, 'Reggie Jackson wants to be traded,' " he said. "Let it say, 'Reggie Jackson got three hits.' "

His eyes were sparkling, his lips were smiling. Suddenly he was as revved up about this World Series as he used to be in the '50s, when he was a kid.

"If you were from my family you had to be a Brooklyn fan because they had black players," Reggie said. "We rooted for the Dodgers because of Jackie Robinson. If we rooted for anyone else we got the . . . beat out of us."

The smile was back, bigger than ever. Reggie Jackson was thinking about his father. Sure, it would be nice to win this World Series for Joe Rudi and the guys. But most of all, he wanted to win it for a Philadelphia tailor named Martinez Jackson.

"My old man is the greatest guy in the world," Reggie said softly. "When I was a little b——, running around stealing yo-yos, he'd close the shop and come and get me . . . I just want to make it nice for him. I think he should have an American Express card, an air-travel card. He ain't a bad guy, my old man . . ."

And he raised an exceptionally talented son.

It was nice that Reggie Jackson finally got some fun out of the 1973 World Series.

Jackson being congratulated by manager Dick Williams in the seventh game of the 1973 World Series. Jackson's homer in the third inning had given the A's a commanding 4-0 lead against the Mets, and Oakland went on to win, 5-2.

Reggie Jackson being interviewed with Oakland owner Charlie Finley following the A's triumph in the 1973 World Series against the New York Mets. Jackson was a big factor in Oakland's victory in seven games. He batted .310 against Met pitching and drove in six runs. He had been forced to sit out the 1972 Series because of an injury.

Mystery of Sam Rice's Famous Catch Resolved

by Shirley Povich
Washington Post

Sam Rice (at right)

February, 1975

Sam Rice's 49-year secret has ended, with his own testimony from beyond the grave that he did, indeed, catch that long, homer-bound drive Earl Smith hit in the 1925 World Series between the Washington Senators and Pittsburgh Pirates.

The truth about the most disputed play in the 71 years of World Series history surfaced in a newly found testament written by Rice in 1965, "to be opened after my death."

The Washington outfielder died at 84 on October 13, 1974, having steadfastly refused to say unqualifiedly that he had made the catch on October 10, 1925, in game three of the Series. He long ago, however, had hinted he would put it in writing for the archives of the Baseball Hall of Fame.

Rice's document turned up the other day, but not at Cooperstown, New York, where Hall of Fame officials had combed the files for more than two weeks and were ready to dismiss reports of a Rice letter as unconfirmed rumor.

It surfaced in downtown New York City, at 30 Wall Street, where Paul S. Kerr, president of the Hall of Fame, has his office. Kerr, to whom the letter had been committed by Rice, was unaware that a search for the letter was under way.

Kerr made a ceremony of disclosing the contents of the letter left by Rice. Before witnesses, and as though ready to read a will, he slit open the envelope and recited its contents.

On that October Saturday almost 50 years ago, President and Mrs. Calvin Coolidge and 36,493 others jam-packed Griffith Stadium. Boy-manager Bucky Harris made a defensive move that was prescient, after right fielder Joe (Moon) Harris singled home the run that gave the Senators their 4-3 lead in the seventh.

In the eighth inning, Harris replaced the slow-moving Joe Harris as his right fielder, moved Sam Rice to that spot from center, and called in Earl McNeely as his center fielder.

Rice's speed (at 35 he may have still been the fastest man on the team) paid off for the Senators.

It took him into the path of Smith's swat into deep right-center, and he got a glove on it as man and ball crashed over the three-foot fence into the seats. Rice and his trophy, or nontrophy, disappeared into the laps of the bleacher fans.

It was at least 10 seconds before Rice disengaged himself to show the umpires a baseball in his glove.

In his letter, Rice described all the circumstances in the eighth inning of the game in which catcher Smith came to bat for Pittsburgh: ". . . the ball was a line drive headed for the bleachers towards right center . . . I . . . jumped as high as I could and back handed . . . but my feet hit the barrier . . . and I toppled . . . into first row of bleachers . . . at no time did I lose possession of the ball."

Such was not the view of the Pirates, who protested loudly that Washington fans in the bleachers had replaced in Rice's glove the ball he had dropped. A score of Pittsburgh supporters in the bleachers offered affidavits that Rice did not hold the ball. The Senators won the game, 4-3, but lost the Series, four games to three.

For the remainder of his life, Rice helped to make mystery of the catch by refusing to make any comment except, "The umpire called him out, didn't he?"

For the rest of his years, Rice's was the sardonic smile across the face of the baseball world.

It was at one of the annual, private dinners of members of the Baseball Hall of Fame at Cooperstown that Rice told fellow honorees he had written his version of the catch, to be opened after his death.

Bill McKechnie, the Pirates' manager in 1925, was one of those to whom Rice confided in 1965 that he had written down his version of the catch. In a postscript, Rice wrote, "I approached McKechnie and said, 'What do you think will be in the letter.' His answer was, 'Sam, there was never any doubt in my mind but what you caught the ball.' "

McKechnie's agreement in 1965 that Rice had made the catch off Smith did not square with his opinion of the play on that October day in 1925.

According to the *Washington Post* account of the game, McKechnie was furious at the decision of umpire Cy Rigler in calling Smith out, and demanded that the other umpires overrule him. Like the other Pirates, McKechnie insisted that Rice had dropped the ball when he fell over the fence.

McKechnie, it was also reported in the *Post,* later took his protest to the box seat of Commissioner Kenesaw Mountain Landis, without success. Landis pointed out it was a judgment play that could not be appealed to him.

Rice's secret letter originally was supposed to go into his file at Cooperstown, but Hall of Fame officials have indicated that because of the public interest in it, it would have its own special display case.

The letter deposited by Rice with Kerr was actually inspired by the late Lee Allen, historian of the Hall of Fame. Allen refused to be content with Rice's evasion when questioned on the subject of the catch.

At each of Rice's visits to Cooperstown, Allen prodded Rice to make public his version of the disputed catch for the Cooperstown records. When Rice refused to tell his secret, Allen pleaded, "You could at least leave us some kind of document to be opened after your death." It was this suggestion that Rice accepted.

Allen's death preceded Rice's, leaving many officials at Cooperstown unaware of the existence of the letter and fouling the search for it.

Rice was inducted into the Hall of Fame in 1963 by the special Old-Timers' Committee, in recognition of his .322 lifetime batting average, his fame as a base-stealer, and 20 years of consistent stardom in the American League.

He was more than the fielding star of the 1925 Series. His 12 hits led both teams at bat.

Over his 20 years in the American League, 19 with Washington and one with Cleveland, Rice batted as high as .350 and .349 and was as great a threat on the bases as at bat. His 63 steals led the league in a year when Ty Cobb still was in his prime.

Rice was having a big year at bat in 1932 until late in the season, when his average slumped to a modest, for him, .323. Of course, he might have been tiring a bit near the season's end; he would be 41 on his next birthday.

Barely 5 feet 10 inches and a mere 160 pounds, Rice was no overpowering figure in the batter's box. But he was the very model of a big league hitter drawing a bead on a pitcher with malevolence aforethought.

An episode in Cleveland one year gave evidence of Rice's ability to manage his bat. A Cleveland pitcher, angered by a Washington home run, took a shot at the next batter, Rice, who was forced to hit the dirt. Dusting himself off, Rice on the next pitch aimed a line drive and got him on the knee. Cleveland needed a new pitcher.

Later in the same game, another pitcher took a shot at Rice out of team loyalty, or some such. One pitch later, he was out of the game; Rice got him on the shin.

Testimony of Sam Rice: "I had a death grip on it"

It was a cold and windy day, the right field bleachers were crowded with people in overcoats and wrapped in blankets, the ball was a line drive headed for the bleachers towards right center. I turned slightly to my right and had the ball in view all the way, going at top speed and about 15 feet from bleachers jumped as high as I could and back handed and the ball hit the center of pocket in glove (I had a death grip on it). I hit the ground about five feet from a barrier about four feet high in front of bleachers with all my brakes on but couldn't stop so I tried to jump it to land in the crowd but my feet hit the barrier about a foot from top and I toppled over on my stomach into first row of bleachers, I hit my Adam's apple on something which sort of knocked me out for a few seconds but [Earl] McNeely arrived about that time and grabbed me by the shirt and pulled me out, I remember trotting back towards the infield still carrying the ball for about halfway and then tossed it towards the pitcher's mound. (How I have wished many times I had kept it.) At no time did I lose possession of the ball.

—Sam Rice, Monday, July 26, 1965

The Spitter That Lost a World Series

by Herbert Simons

October, 1961

The legal spitter has won a lot of World Series games; an illegal spitter has lost at least one.

Using the damp delivery, Cleveland's Stan Coveleski defeated the Dodgers three times in the 1920 Series, holding them to two runs in 27 innings. In the 1917 Series the White Sox' Red Faber, also a saliva server, beat the Giants three times in four appearances.

Burleigh Grimes, last of the special spitball licensees given lifetime dispensation when the pitch was outlawed in 1920, beat the Athletics in behalf of the Cards twice in 1931. Dick Rudolph of the 1914 Braves and Phil Douglas of the 1921 Giants also won two World Series games with the wet ones.

The last spitball ever to be thrown *legally* in a World Series was to the Yankees' Frankie Crosetti in the ninth inning of the fourth game of the 1932 classic at Chicago. The one who threw it was Grimes, who had used it for a World Series win for the 1920 Dodgers as well as for his two Series triumphs for the 1931 Cardinals.

But Grimes wasn't the author of the last spitter ever to appear in a World Series, not by a good many dewdrops. Claude Passeau did a pretty good job of dishing up some moist ones in holding the Tigers to one hit, a single by Rudy York, for a 3-0 shutout in the third game of the 1945 doings at Detroit. Passeau as much as admitted it to us on the train back to Chicago that night. And Hugh Casey, also by his own admission, put the wet on one in what may have been the deciding pitch of the 1941 Series.

The Dodgers were playing the Yankees that year. The latter, regaining the American League pennant, won in their patented runaway. The Dodgers, winning their first flag in 21 years, beat out the Cardinals by two and one-half games in a furious stretch drive.

The first three games of the Series that year were bitterly contested. Each was decided by a run. The Yankees won the first and third games, the Dodgers the second. Scoring pairs of runs off Atley Donald in the fourth and fifth innings, the Dodgers overcame an early 3-0 Yankee lead in the fourth game and entered the ninth inning ahead, 4-3.

Hugh Casey, the Dodgers' ace reliever, who had pitched scoreless ball from the fifth inning when he had been rushed in to quell a Yankee uprising, easily retired the Yankees' leadoff and No. 2 batters, Johnny Sturm and Red Rolfe, to open the ninth and had a three-and-two count on Tommy Henrich.

Within one strike of victory, Casey loaded up and poured in a wet one for the kill. Henrich swung and missed for the third strike, a strike-out that apparently ended the game with a Dodger victory and the Series tied up at two games each.

But the pitch swerved erratically, and catcher Mickey Owen, who was no more expecting it than was Henrich, saw the ball skitter away from his glove and fly right by him for an error as Henrich reached first.

"They caught lightning in a bottle," was Durocher's comment on the play to us in the clubhouse afterward.

If it were lightning, the thunder certainly followed. The opening was all the Yankees needed. Joe DiMaggio whistled a single into left. Charlie Keller, on a two-strike, no-ball count, doubled off the right-field wall, scoring Henrich and DiMaggio, and the Yankees went on from there for four runs and a 7-4 victory.

All after "three outs"!

Instead of the Series being tied up, two games each, the Yankees were ahead, three games to one. Next day the disheartened Dodgers were easy 3-1 victims, and the thing was over.

Until Casey, quite a few years later, admitted moistening up the fatal pitch, Owen wore goat's horns, still does in some quarters, in fact.

But he didn't have to wait until they found horns specially suitable for such a happenstance. Old-timers recalled that Owen's failure behind the plate duplicated the performance of Detroit's Charles (Boss) Schmidt in the first game of the 1907 World Series with the Cubs when, in the ninth inning, he let the game-ending strike on Del Howard get away after Wild Bill Donovan had struck out the pinch-hitter.

On that error, Harry Steinfeldt bounded in with the tying tally, and there was no scoring in three extra frames, the game being called at the end of the 12th inning because of darkness, with the score tied, 3-3.

So in 1941 history once again was written with carbon paper—wet carbon paper, to be sure.

Hugh Casey

Mickey Owen

Ebbets Field in Brooklyn was the scene of one of baseball's most memorable "tough breaks"—a third-strike pitch by Hugh Casey eluding Dodger catcher Mickey Owen and opening the way for a decisive Yankee victory in the fourth game of the 1941 World Series. Casey, who had come on in relief, held a 4-3 lead, had already retired two Yankee batters, and had a three-and-two count on Tommy Henrich in the top of the ninth inning when disaster struck the Dodgers. Casey's pitch, which he later admitted was a spitter, flew right by Owen, and Henrich reached first base safely. The Yankees went on to score four runs and win the game, 7-4. Henrich, who had swung and missed Casey's pitch, is seen breaking for first base, as Casey comes off the mound and Owen frantically chases the ball. Note the plate umpire, Larry Goetz, signaling a strike-out.

When the Cubs Won 21 Games in a Row

by Emil Rothe

October, 1973

In all the annals of baseball, few teams have ever made a run at a pennant as dramatic and unbelievable as the 1935 Chicago Cubs. Ten and a half games behind the leading New York Giants on July 4, the Cubs suddenly began to develop winning habits. From July 5 through July 31, they won 24 games while losing only 5 and, thereby, declared themselves in the fight for the National League flag.

After spending most of August on the road, the Cubs returned to Wrigley Field for a 20-game home stand starting with a Labor Day doubleheader with Cincinnati. Manager Charlie Grimm held a clubhouse meeting before that twin bill and reminded his team, "We're home for 20 games and we either do or we don't, but we *are* going to be loose."

Even ever-optimistic Grimm did not anticipate just how "loose" his charges would really be during that September drive. After splitting the Labor Day doubleheader with the Reds September 2, winning the first but losing the second, the Cubs were in third place with a 79-52 record.

St. Louis was in first with a 79-47 mark, and New York held second with 76 wins and 48 losses.

Then began the most astonishing, pressure-packed consecutive win streak ever recorded: 21 straight wins and the National League championship. This is still the major league record for consecutive victories that culminated in a pennant. The New York Giants of 1916 won 26 in a row, all in the Polo Grounds, but that skein was interrupted by one tie game and that year the Giants finished the season in fourth place!

On Tuesday, September 4, Chicago lefty Larry French beat the Phils, 8-2, to launch a phenomenal run of superb pitching. In 19 of those 21 games the starting pitcher was still on the mound for the Cubs at the finish. In the 11th successive victory on September 14, Charlie Root needed help when, despite an early 8-0 lead and his own hitless pitching through the first four innings against the Brooklyn Dodgers, he wilted and surrendered 12 hits in the next three innings and had to be lifted. Roy Henshaw and Fabian Kowalik protected Charlie's lead as an 18-hit Chicago attack produced as many runs in an 18-14 slugfest. This sloppy game, however, was the one that vaulted the Chicago Cubs into first place as the New York Giants beat the league-leading Cardinals in St. Louis, 5-4, in 11 innings.

The only other game of the streak in which the starter had to have help from the bullpen was win No. 17 on September 21. Roy Henshaw, a persistent annoyance to Pittsburgh whom he had already beaten six times in the season, started against the Pirates and was sailing along with a 4-0 lead and a yield of only two Pittsburgh hits through seven innings. The Pirates scored one in the eighth and then four straight hits and two runs with nobody out caused

Larry French

Bill Lee

Grimm to summon one of his starters, Lon Warneke, to clamp on the lid for a 4-3 win.

The performance of the Cubs' pitching staff during September is worthy of detailed note. Larry French and Bill Lee each won five complete games. Warneke added four route-going jobs. Charlie Root contributed four wins, three of them complete. Roy Henshaw won two, one complete, and Tex Carleton had one nine-inning victory.

Each of the Big Four—French, Lee, Root, and Warneke—pitched one shutout during the string. Early in September the Cubs won two 3-2 games in extra innings, Root winning in 11 frames on September 5 and Warneke doing the job in 10 the very next day.

It seemed that each day a different member of the cast would assume the hero role. In that 11-inning win of September 5, Frank Demaree had three hits, his first single in the second driving in two runs and his third one-base blow in the 11th driving Billy Herman across with the winning tally. On September 6, it was Augie Galan's 10th-inning homer that did the job. In wins No. 11, 12, and 18, the Chicago offense produced scores of 15-3, 13-3, and 15-3.

The schedule makers for 1935 wrote a great script. They had the two final contenders meet in a showdown in Sportsman's Park, St. Louis. (The New York Giants had been mathematically eliminated a few days earlier.) A St. Louis sweep would have given the Cards the pennant. Four out of five for the Cardinals would have created a season-end tie. So the Cubs needed two wins to clinch the championship.

The first of that truly crucial series, on September 25, matched Warneke and Paul Dean, Dizzy's younger brother, in a terrific pitching duel won by Warneke, 1-0, on young Phil Cavarretta's second-inning home run onto the roof of the right-field pavilion. Phil, in his first full season in the majors, had taken over at first base from Charlie Grimm, who only saw service in two games in 1935.

Rain on September 26 forced a postponement, the game being rescheduled as part of a double-header the next day. Assured of a tie and needing only one more win to clinch the title, Grimm selected big Bill Lee to face Dizzy Dean in the first game on September 27, a cold dismal day that held attendance to 9,000 extremely hardy souls.

The Cubs donated a pair of runs in the very first inning. Pepper Martin was safe when Billy Herman fumbled his grounder. Lynn King, rookie center fielder, walked. Frank Frisch attempted to advance the runners with a bunt but was credited with a hit when Lee neglected to go after the ball. Joe Medwick slashed a ground ball to Stan Hack, who threw low to Gabby Hartnett trying to nip Martin at the plate. Herman made a good stop of Rip Collins' smash to throw out King at home. Bill Delancey rammed a single over second, scoring Frisch, and when Medwick also tried to score, a perfect throw from Fred Lindstrom in center got him for the second out. Durocher ended the inning with a fly to Augie Galan.

Lee settled down, and in the last eight innings he gave up only four more hits. The Cubs, meanwhile, launched a 15-hit attack on Diz, who was obviously worn out from a season which saw him start 36 games and relieve in 14 others.

Charlie Root

Lon Warneke

MOST CONSECUTIVE VICTORIES*

NATIONAL LEAGUE

No.	Club	Home	Away	Year
26†	New York	26	0	1916
21	Chicago	18	3	1935
18	New York	13	5	1904
17	New York	14	3	1907
	New York	0	17	1916
16	Pittsburgh	12	4	1909
	New York	11	5	1912
	New York	13	3	1951
15	Pittsburgh	11	4	1903
	Brooklyn	3	12	1924
	Chicago	11	4	1936
	New York	8	7	1936

AMERICAN LEAGUE

No.	Club	Home	Away	Year
19†	Chicago	11	8	1906
	New York	6	13	1947
18	New York	3	15	1953
17	Washington	1	16	1912
	Philadelphia	5	12	1931
16	New York	12	4	1926
15	New York	12	3	1906
	Philadelphia	13	2	1913
	Boston	11	4	1946
	New York	9	6	1960

* Since 1900   † Includes one tie

The Cubs tied the score on Galan's double and Herman's single to left, juggled by Medwick and permitting Herman to reach second. Herman scored on Lindstrom's first single. The lead and winning run was recorded in the fourth on Hack's two-base blow and a single by Lee. Single runs in the last three stanzas were just so much "frosting."

In beating Dizzy Dean the Cubs nailed down the National League championship and won their 20th straight game. For Chicago fans that game was the only one that really mattered.

Between games the Chicago locker room was a scene of wild excitement. Grimm, grinning from ear to ear, shouted to Root, "Charlie, get in there and pitch the second game and don't worry about this winning streak. We'll start another in Detroit." (Detroit had won the American League championship.)

Veteran Fred Lindstrom was one of the most exuberant of all the team, "At last I have amounted to something. After being a bum for three years, I've helped my old hometown win a pennant."

The Cardinal clubhouse, in contrast, was a gloomy place, but the St. Louis players conceded that the Cubs deserved to win. Pepper Martin summed it up, saying, "They've got what it takes plus the hustle that makes a great team."

For the Cubs and their fandom, game two was anticlimactic, but it is the game that has earned the 1935 Cubs a line in the record book: Most Consecutive Games Won, Season, No Tie Games—21.

Root started the second game and was in control until the sixth, when he walked Charlie Gelbert. Mike Ryba, his pitching opponent, sacrificed. Lyle Judy, a stand-in at second for Frisch, also walked, and when Bill Jurges failed to handle King's grounder, the bases were full. Ernie Orsatti was declared out on the infield-fly rule. Medwick topped a dribbler that got by Root for a single as Gelbert scored. A double by Rip Collins sent both Judy and King across the plate. Root survived the inning by retiring Sam Narron and Burgess Whitehead.

The Cubs tied the score in the seventh. Cavarretta and Hack singled. Jurges fanned. Johnny Gill, batting for Root, doubled to right, driving in Cavarretta. Hack and Gill rode home when Galan also doubled down the right-field line.

Roy Henshaw blanked the Cardinals the rest of the way, while the Cubs scored two more in the ninth to post consecutive win No. 21. Cavarretta lashed a triple into the right-field corner and came across as Hack also tripled to the same area. Stan scored the final run on Jurges' single over second.

On September 28, the Cubs' win streak came to an end but not until they had forced the game to go 11 innings. With St. Louis enjoying a 5-2 lead, thanks to Ducky Medwick's triple, single, and sixth-inning homer, the Cubs rallied in the top of the ninth with four straight hits—singles by Chuck Klein and Ken O'Dea, a triple by Frank Demaree, and Phil Cavarretta's single. Medwick's second home run of the game with Jack Rothrock on base decided the issue in the 11th.

His players gave Grimm full credit for that fantastic win streak and the NL pennant which crowned that feat. "He's the greatest guy I ever worked for," said Chuck Klein. "He didn't drive us," continued Klein. "He told us to be ourselves and to keep going. We did and we won the pennant." Chuck echoed the sentiments of the entire team. Grimm gave credit to the team. "You're the gamest guys that ever wore a uniform," was Charlie's appraisal.

Grimm's prediction of starting another win streak in Detroit did not materialize. The Tigers beat the Cubs four games to two in an interesting World Series that had its exciting moments, but that's another story.

Babe Ruth's Last Game

by Emil Rothe

November, 1972

During the winter following the 1934 season, the New York Yankees, suspecting that Babe Ruth had reached the end of his career as an active player, offered him an interim contract for one dollar until he could prove in spring training that he could still produce as a player.

Ruth did not accept this offer and also rejected a Yankee offer to manage the minor league Newark Club.

Judge Emil Fuchs, owner of the Boston Braves, hoping to improve that club's financial balance sheet, signed Babe as a vice-president, assistant to manager Bill McKechnie, and an occasional outfielder.

Babe opened the 1935 season in left field for the Braves in an auspicious manner with a home run and a single. Thereafter, however, he tailed off badly, and it was evident that Ruth was through. On June 2, 1935, he announced he was quitting as an active player. He wanted to stay in baseball, but no other club sought his services as player, manager, coach, or scout.

If Ruth had but known, he would have chosen May 25, 1935, as his last day as a player. On that day, in Pittsburgh, he was for the last time Babe Ruth, Slugger Supreme.

In the first inning, he powered a home run into the right-field stands off Red Lucas. The next time he came to bat, Guy Bush was on the mound for the Pirates, and the Babe propelled one of his sinkers onto the roof in right. In the fifth, he managed only a single. In the seventh, with Bush still pitching, Ruth powered the longest home run ever seen in old Forbes Field *over* the right-field wall into Schenley Park. No other player before that day had ever been able to clear that roof.

Considering Babe Ruth's prodigious home-run production, three homers in a single game might be thought to have been a relatively common occurrence for him. Not so, however. The Babe had only two such games in his 22 years in the majors. He added two more three-homer days in World Series play. It must be noted, too, that he was primarily a pitcher in his first few years with the Boston Red Sox.

Babe Ruth as he appeared in his final major league season as a member of the 1935 Boston Braves, a club destined to finish last in the National League.

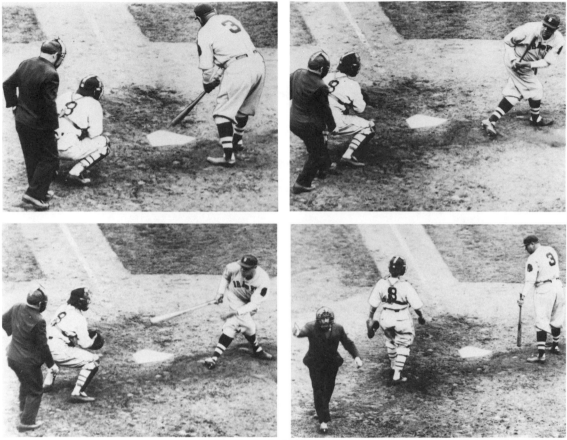

In his final playing days, Babe Ruth was a far cry from the powerful slugger who had devastated American League pitching for years. In this sequence of photos taken in April, 1935, when Ruth was closing out his career with the Boston Braves, the Babe swings mightily at one pitch (upper right) and misses; fails to connect on another (lower left); and takes a called third strike (lower right).

The Babe was at his best when the chips were down. As a pitcher he set a record for most consecutive scoreless innings pitched in World Series competition, 29⅔, compiled over two Series, 1916 and 1918. This record stayed in the books until Whitey Ford shut out National League World Series opponents for 33⅓ innings starting in 1960 and ending in the second inning of the opening game of the 1962 Series.

The two games in seasonal play in which Ruth clouted three out of the park in each represented 2,502 games played. He equaled that total in only 41 games of World Series play, in 1926 and again in 1928.

But of those four three-homer games, the one in Pittsburgh demonstrated his awesome power as well as any the Babe ever played. It was as if he had summoned his remaining strength to put on one last exhibition of the Ruthian specialty that changed the game. Three homers in one game, 4-for-4, and six runs batted in! What a final curtain that would have been for the Babe!

But Babe Ruth Days had been scheduled in other National League cities, and he was persuaded to stay with the team. His final five games were a sorrowful denouement. The next day, May 26, was Babe Ruth Day in Cincinnati with Ruth starting in left. He didn't get a hit off Si Johnson and struck out three times. On May 27, he was inserted as a pinch-hitter for Huck Betts, and Danny MacFayden walked him. Paul Derringer of the Reds held him hitless in two at-bats May 28. May 29th was designated Babe Ruth Day in Philadelphia, and while the Braves won, Ruth went without a hit again.

The last time the name of Babe Ruth appeared in a major league lineup was in the first game of a Memorial Day doubleheader, May 30, 1935. Ruth was the third man to bat in the Boston half of the first inning. He grounded out to the Phils' first baseman, Dolf Camilli, unassisted.

After limping out to left field for the bottom of the first inning, he was replaced by Hal Lee at the start of the second. The name of Babe Ruth, who had exerted the greatest individual influence on our national pastime, never again appeared in a major league box score. Three days later he retired.

Trick Pitches Aren't New

by H. G. Salsinger
Condensed from the *Detroit News*

July, 1943

Each spring comes the report that some new deliveries have been perfected by one or more of the big league pitching gentry, some new invention that will give batters nightmares.

There are three cardinal deliveries—fastball, curveball, and slow ball—and any other pitch is a variation of one of the three.

You hear of screwballs, sliders, sinkers, fadeaways, knucklers, fingernail balls, forkballs, and various other unorthodox pitches but they are all fastballs, curves, or slow balls.

Years ago the spitball was outlawed and it is still an illegal pitch, but there are few pitchers in the major leagues who never throw spitters. We know an umpire who counted 41 spitball pitches in a single game last summer. Since both pitchers were throwing spitballs whenever a run threatened, neither team complained.

Big Ed Walsh was probably the best of all spitball pitchers, at least over a stretch of three or four years.

They ruled out the emery ball along with the spitball.

"Russell Ford of the New York Highlanders was the inventor of the emery delivery, although he is rarely given credit for it," says manager Steve O'Neill of the Tigers.

"Big Ed Sweeney did the catching for the Highlanders, and Sweeney was the only man outside of Ford who knew what he was doing to the ball. Sweeney knew how it broke and was able to catch it.

"Each year Sweeney would be a holdout. He'd announce that he was the only man living who could catch Ford, and the club would have to meet his demands.

"The Highlanders would open the season with Sweeney still holding out. A rookie would be doing the catching. The first time Ford pitched, the kid would be knocked flat; he couldn't judge the emery ball.

"Cy Falkenberg got hep to the emery business some way or other, probably by experimenting. He was the second pitcher to use the delivery. The Highlanders then traded Sweeney, and he told every-body what Ford was doing to the ball. Within a month every pitcher in the league had a strip of emery sewn in his glove," says O'Neill.

Fred Blanding, who had pitched for the University of Michigan, was a member of the Cleveland staff in 1913.

"By various experiments, Blanding had developed a 'rise' ball. Thrown fast, the ball would suddenly take off, and the batter would be swinging under it," O'Neill recalls.

"We were playing Washington, and Blanding was pitching against Walter Johnson. Now Johnson didn't know that Blanding was doctoring the ball and that's what scared us; we were afraid that the same doctored ball, thrown with Johnson's speed, might easily kill one of us.

"Along about the second inning Johnson cut loose with one. Tommy Connolly was umpiring behind the plate and called the pitch a strike. Passing the plate the ball suddenly took off. It passed over the heads of the catcher and Connolly and hit the grandstand.

In the 1930s, Carl Hubbell was one of the best pitchers in baseball, relying primarily on a screwball which catapulted him to fame in 1933 when he struck out five of the game's most feared batsmen in a row in the All-Star game (Ruth, Gehrig, Foxx, Al Simmons, and Joe Cronin). Once the property of the Detroit Tigers, Hubbell was advised by manager Ty Cobb not to throw the screwball, contending it was an unnatural pitch and would ruin his arm. Hubbell paid no heed to the advice, and after joining the New York Giants, he went on to post 253 career victories, a lifetime ERA of 2.98, and five seasons (1933-37) in which he won 20 or more games. He was named the National League's Most Valuable Player in 1933 and 1936 and once ran up a string of 24 victories over two seasons. After retiring as an active player he became head of the Giants' farm system in 1943, a position he still held in 1975. He was elected to the Hall of Fame in 1947.

"That ended trick deliveries for the day. We hustled out some balls that Blanding hadn't touched."

Twenty-five years ago the White Sox had the best pitching staff in baseball.

"Every pitcher was doctoring the ball. We couldn't figure out just what they were doing. One day, when they were playing in Cleveland, we went to the park early in the morning and got into the White Sox locker room. We found nothing suspicious in the lockers. Then we examined the uniforms of the pitchers. Every pitcher had a rubber pocket in his trousers and the pockets were filled with paraffin.

"Eddie Cicotte was the trickiest of the lot. He wasn't particularly fast but he was almost unhittable. He would throw the ball with the same motion we used as kids when we'd throw sailers over the water. You know how those flat stones would take off and skip over the water? That's how the ball acted when Cicotte threw it with the same side-arm motion that he'd used as a boy.

"Look up the box scores of games that Cicotte pitched and you won't find more than three or four assists per game. The batters who faced him were retired on unassisted putouts. They kept hitting under the ball and popping it to the infield or striking out.

"Cicotte was supposed to fill the seams on one side with paraffin and then shine one side, not alone

Ed Rommel spent his entire major league career with the Philadelphia A's, from 1920 through 1932, and pioneered the art of throwing the knuckleball. He won 27 games in 1922 and 21 in 1925. He later became an American League umpire, serving in that capacity from the 1938 through the 1959 season.

creating an unusual dip and rise but making the ball extremely hard to follow. The ball would always break in the opposite direction from which he held it, making it possible for him to have full control over the delivery.

"One day when Cicotte was pitching against us Tris Speaker went to bat twice without getting a hit. After his second time up he walked to the Chicago dugout and told Kid Gleason, then the manager of the White Sox:

" 'There isn't a pitcher living who can keep throwing me fastballs without me getting a base hit and if you don't tell Cicotte to cut out his tricks, I'll cut your infield to shreds if I get on base.'

"Cicotte didn't give Speaker a chance to cut the infield to shreds. He kept him off the base."

Christy Mathewson perfected the fade-away. When delivered by Mathewson, a right-hander, it broke into right-handed batters and away from left-handers. When pitched by a left-hander, it broke into left-handed batters and away from right-handers, making the fade-away by a left-hander easier for left-handed than right-handed batters and vice versa.

The screwball and the fade-away are the same delivery. Jim Bagby, father of the present star of the Cleveland pitching staff, mastered the fade-away, and so did Hub Pruett and Garland Braxton. Carl Hubbell's screwball is the same pitch that Mathewson made famous as the fade-away.

The sinker is a sinking fastball. Wilcey Moore, the Yankee's great relief pitcher of other years, had the sinker as his stock in trade. Johnny Gorsica of Detroit has about as good a sinker as you will see pitched today.

The slider is a fastball that slides rather than sinks. Steve O'Neill says Johnny Allen had the best he ever saw.

The knuckleball is a curveball first made famous by Eddie Rommel of the Athletics, now an American League umpire. Many pitchers use the knuckler today. Some "knuckle" the ball and others grip it with their fingernails and call it the "fingernail" ball, but it is actually a knuckler and behaves the same way.

Johnny Niggeling, the St. Louis Browns' veteran, is a knuckleball pitcher who uses only one finger in gripping the ball.

Then there is the forkball, held between two fingers.

There are several other deliveries, like the butterfly ball, which is a slow ball, and the floater, which is also a slow ball, and when you analyze the freak deliveries you will discover that they are all fastballs, slow balls, or curves under fancy names.

Johnny Podres—
The Game I'll Never Forget

as told to George Vass

October, 1973

There's no doubt in the world about the game I'll never forget because it's the one they'd been waiting for in Brooklyn all the years they had a major league team.

I'm sure all the old Dodger fans will immediately remember the game I'm talking about. It has been 18 years since it was played, but every time I think about it, it still gives me a thrill.

A numb feeling took hold of me as soon as Pee Wee Reese threw the ball to Gil Hodges for the final putout. I remember being in a sort of a daze as if I couldn't believe what happened.

I guess most of the Brooklyn fans, who'd always been waiting for "next year," could hardly believe it finally had arrived—that this time the Dodgers had beaten the New York Yankees and won the World Series.

I could understand the way they felt. As a kid, growing up in Witherbee, New York, I was a Dodger fan from the start. They were my favorite team, and I rooted for them as long as I can remember.

We lived too far from Brooklyn in those days to get the day games on the radio, but when the Dodgers played night games I'd stay up with my ears glued to the set. That's the kind of fan I was when I was a kid.

That's what made it unbelievable to me when the Dodgers gave me a tryout in 1950 and signed me to a contract. Three years later, I was up with the big club and won nine games that season. I even got to start in the fifth game of the 1953 World Series and was the losing pitcher.

We lost that 1953 Series to the Yankees, as we always did, as far back as anybody could remember. The Dodgers had lost to the Yankees in 1952, in 1949, in 1947, and in 1941. They'd never won a World Series.

We didn't win the pennant in 1954, but we won in 1955, and wouldn't you know it, we were up against the Yankees once more in the World Series.

When they beat us in the first game, it looked like we were on our way to losing another World Series to them. When they beat us the second game, every-body really was writing us off—the same old story.

Manager Walt Alston picked me to start the third game, which was in Ebbets Field on Friday, September 30. It happened to be my 23rd birthday, which added to the situation.

I didn't feel a whole lot of pressure, strange as it may seem. Here I was, a young kid, and nobody expected me to beat the New York Yankees. I'd had just an 8-9 record during the season.

Using mostly change-ups, I held the Yankees pretty well. They got seven hits, including a home run by Mickey Mantle. But our batters came alive, got 11 hits, including a home run by Roy Campanella, and we beat the Yankees, 8-3, to give me a Series victory and keep us alive.

We beat them again the next day and also in the fifth game to take a three-two edge in the Series. The sixth game Whitey Ford closed the door, and the Yankees beat us, 5-1, to send the Series into a seventh game.

That's the game I'll never forget. The seventh game of the 1955 World Series on Tuesday, October 4, in Yankee Stadium.

Since I'd had good luck with my change-up in the third game, I used it the first three or four innings of the seventh. But after that, I switched to my fast-ball most of the time and didn't use the change-up more than a couple of times. One was the biggest pitch of the Series.

We didn't get a lot of hits, just five, but they were enough. In the fourth inning, Campanella doubled and Hodges drove him in with a single. Hodges also drove in our other run with a sacrifice fly in the sixth.

I was in and out of trouble through the whole game. I think I was in and out of jams at least four times.

Most people still remember the catch Sandy Amoros, our left fielder, made to save the lead in the sixth inning.

We were leading, 2-0, when Billy Martin started out the Yankee sixth with a walk. Gil McDougald beat out a bunt, and they had two men on and nobody out.

The next batter was Yogi Berra. Amoros was shifted over toward center for Berra, who was a left-handed hitter. Yogi hit a high fly to deep left toward the foul line. It looked like it was going to drop for a double. But Amoros took off after it and at the last second got his glove on it.

Martin and McDougald, figuring Berra's flyball was going to drop in, were running. Amoros threw the ball to Reese, the cutoff man, and he relayed it to first to double up McDougald.

That catch by Amoros probably saved the game.

But I got into another jam in the eighth. The Yankees had runners on first and third with one out and Berra up. He flied out and Hank Bauer then struck out.

I was throwing nothing but fastballs by this time. I got the first two batters in the ninth with them, and the third man was Elston Howard. I threw him five fastballs and he fouled 'em off.

I shook off the catcher, Campanella, on the next pitch. I wanted to throw a change-up. I did. Howard hit a grounder to Reese, and the game was over.

We'd won, 2-0. The Dodgers had won the World Series.

All of a sudden everybody was grabbing me. Somebody had my leg, somebody had my arm. I didn't know what was going on.

It was a great winter. I must've made $10,000 in appearances. Everybody wanted me.

Funny thing, so did the armed forces. I'd been 4-F until I'd won the seventh game of the Series. They reclassified me 1-A that winter and drafted me the following spring.

Johnny Podres jumps gleefully after winning the final game of the 1955 World Series against the Yankees. Don Hoak (left) runs in to join Podres, who is being hugged by catcher Roy Campanella.

The Big Green Monster at Fenway Park

by Ross Atkin
Christian Science Monitor

November, 1973

The left-field wall at Boston's Fenway Park is the most notorious landmark in major league baseball. It has helped some players, primarily right-handed hitters, and been the undoing of others, usually left-handed pitchers.

The massive green monster rises 37 feet and spans the distance between the left-field foul line and the center-field bleachers. It looms menacingly close to home plate, a mere 315 feet down the line.

Even the banjo-hitter is capable of occasionally reaching the wall. Home runs are hit almost on the hour. But they are not what really rankle the pitchers. What burns them up are the routine flyballs, sure outs in other parks, that graze the wall and wind up as extra-base hits. Many rallies have started this way.

Over the years the Red Sox have tried to take advantage of this architectural idiosyncracy, stocking their lineup with powerful right-handed batters. That strategy has paid off at home with strong won-loss records. But on the road, Boston is seldom as potent.

During the memorable 1946 season, the Red Sox turned loose the slugging quartet of Rudy York, Bobby Doerr, Mike Higgins, and Dom DiMaggio. They pounded the wall relentlessly on the way to compiling a remarkable 61-16 record in Fenway Park. The feat left an indelible impression on the club's management.

But in dictating the team's style, critics say the wall has hurt the Red Sox more than it has helped them. To fuel their argument they are fond of recalling how Boston gave up Pee Wee Reese in 1940. The promising, young shortstop was with the Louisville farm team at the time, nearly ready to move up to the parent club and solidify the Red Sox defense. But eyeing more long-ball strength, Boston traded the superb infielder away to the Brooklyn Dodgers.

In an era of gleaming, symmetrical stadiums, Fenway Park is an antique. The intimate red-brick grandstand nestles snugly and unobtrusively into the heart of Boston's Back Bay area.

Inside are an immaculately groomed grass field and a manually operated scoreboard.

When built in 1912, the left-field wall was considered a near impossible shot for the home-run hitters of the day. The official ball had almost no rabbit in it then.

When Hugh Bradley hit the park's first homer over the left-field fence, everyone shuddered in amazement. One local paper ran a cartoon depicting the event with the caption: "It doesn't seem human." Ironically, it was Bradley's only home run of the 1912 campaign, and one of only two he hit during his five-year major league career.

A famous companion to the wall during the early 1900s was the steep embankment that rose up at its base. Outfielder Duffy Lewis was so expert at catching flyballs on the incline that the embankment became known as Duffy's Cliff.

But not every fielder was as adept as Lewis. Someone once tried teaching Smead Jolley how to run sideways up the cliff and snare flyballs. Without Lewis' mountain-goat instincts, Smead kept falling down. "They taught me how to run up the cliff," Smead explained, "but they never taught me how to run down it." The cliff finally was removed before the 1933 season.

With a livelier ball, the home-run output rose. By 1934, the year in which the reconstruction of Fenway Park was completed, the home-run pace had tripled in the major leagues.

The wall was no longer merely a mammoth backdrop, it was a target. Left field had become an overgrown handball court for the fielders assigned to roam in the wall's shadow.

Boston's left fielders eventually adjust to playing the rebounds, but visiting outfielders seldom do. The slightest miscalculation can turn a single into a double or triple.

Ted Williams was a master at judging balls hit off the wall, as is Carl Yastrzemski today. Yaz plays caroms with the same intuitive feel Minnesota Fats has with a billiard cue.

Home runs don't come cheap over the wall, yet they hop out often enough to make Fenway Park a hitter's haven. During the previous decade, an average of 163 homers were hit there each season, or more than two a game.

The wall invites right-handed hitters to develop the Fenway Stroke, a swing from the heels that aims to put the ball into New Hampshire. As the preoccupation with pulling the ball with power saturates the hitter's thinking, he starts swatting mightily at thin air, a la Casey at the Bat. The ability to make consistent contact disappears.

The left-field wall at Fenway Park looms ominously close as Boston's Jim Lonborg releases his pitch and the Cardinals' Lou Brock breaks for third base during a 1967 World Series game.

Four Red Sox players have won batting titles over the last 32 years. All four were left-handed batters—Williams, Billy Goodman, Pete Runnels, and Yastrzemski.

No wall stared them in the face. Even after moving the bullpens in front of the right-field bleachers to shorten the fence for Williams in 1940, it was still 380 feet away—too far to be tempting.

While Fenway Park is an oddity today, it has had company in the past. Who will ever forget the hatbox they called Ebbets Field in Brooklyn? And right across town was the famed Polo Grounds, where hitters could bloop home runs down the foul lines or blast long outs into canyon-like power alleys.

Fenway's wall might well have come tumbling down if the Red Sox had ever secured the land rights to Lansdowne Street, which runs beyond left field. With extra room, the fence could have been moved back.

Owner Tom Yawkey once had an opportunity to secure the valuable real estate but turned it down, fearing political shenanigans.

Fortunately, Bostonians have grown to love Fenway Park and the wall, and no one more than Freddie Leathers. Freddie has seen well over a thousand games at Fenway, all right from the concrete-buttressed stomach of the wall. He is the senior member of the three-man crew operating inside the scoreboard.

The narrow walkway he calls his working home is equipped with piles of metal numerals, a phone to the press box, a refrigerator, and a very modest bathroom.

In addition to his duties supervising the activity behind the board, Freddie retrieves the home-run balls from the 23-foot screen atop the wall after each game. He takes pride in his job, but most of all relishes the moments peering out through narrow slits at the greats and not so greats.

Occasionally a player will come back to the board and ask the score of another game. Willie Horton of the Tigers sometimes asks for a drink of water, and Lou Piniella of the Kansas City Royals kicks the board in anger or just to surprise its dwellers.

Whenever anything hits the scoreboard, it makes a thundering noise inside. "It would scare anyone who hasn't been out here before," Freddie says.

But he's used to the thunder, because if you stick around Fenway Park long enough you learn one thing for sure: the Green Monster never quits rumbling.

Reprinted by permission from the Christian Science Monitor, © 1973. The Christian Science Publishing Society. All rights reserved.

112

Baseball — A Bridge Between Two Silences

by Frank L. Ryan

July, 1971

Major league baseball is in full swing again, and the game jostles my memory into sharp recall of my father.

Father-son relationships are delicate affairs, poised perpetually on the brink of small and large clashes of will and temperament. This is something which modern youth thinks it has discovered and to which it has given a solemn title, "the generation gap."

In reality, today's youth is merely reflecting, perhaps in an exceptionally conscious way, what history records as an inevitable consequence of the existence of fathers and sons.

My own relationship with my father suggested what history proves. It was a relationship which was not only delicate but painful. I spent my adolescence in the Depression years, the 1930s, and the warmth and vitality which ideally exist between father and son were thwarted both by the times and by the temperament of my father, which even in better times might have been sorely tested.

My father drank heavily in that desperate way in which some frequently unemployed men drank in those desperate days, and the drinking and the oppressive presence of idleness drove him often into deep silences which I answered with silences of my own. But there was one bridge between us during the 1930s, and I've always hoped that in the last years, when we were unable to close the gaps of our silences, he remembered our mutual love for baseball.

If my father took to drink as a grim solace for unemployment, he turned to baseball in the same spirit in which a monk turned to a cloister—for its own sake. I use the comparison in earnest. To him, attendance at a ball game was an experience detached from any local economic or civic interest. I don't think he ever cared who won a game, and it wasn't until years after we stopped going to games that I fully realized why he didn't care.

He saw baseball as a kind of synchronization of opposing forces, not a battle between the invaders and the local heroes. If a defensive player made a brilliant play, my father attributed it not only to that player's ability but also to the pressure exerted by an offensive player.

If an outfielder crashed into a wall, for example, and yet made the catch, it was because a hitter was capable of driving a ball against the fence. He saw games this way, and that's why he was indifferent to who won.

I remember being at a Giants-Braves game in Boston with him when Bill Terry, then managing the Giants and playing part-time, put himself into the game as a pinch-hitter with the bases loaded, and he tripled off some remote spot on the center-field wall. It was one of those acts of almost supreme self-confidence that you expected of Terry, and though the Braves lost, my father was tremendously pleased. What was important to him was not that the Braves lost the game but that they had forced Terry to a challenge which he had accepted and handled beautifully.

And I remember another game, this time between the Cardinals and the Braves, in which a Cardinal hitter, I think it was Frankie Frisch, batting right-handed with men on base, hit a vicious drive foul and almost out of the park. This so alarmed the Braves' manager that he brought in a right-hander to pitch, and Frisch simply switched to the left side of the plate and hit another vicious drive, this time fair and out of the park. It was another moment of tremendous pleasure for my father, another case of challenge, confrontation, and fulfillment. Years later, when I had acquired intellectual pretensions, I wondered what his response would have been had I suggested that baseball was a kind of ballet to him. He probably would have expressed amused tolerance, since part of his detachment was the conviction that baseball as a human activity was unique and invited no disturbing comparisons.

I have come to admire this detachment. In this our day of fierce competition and emphasis on champions and championships, the detached view seems to have vanished.

Some of my father's detachment got through to me. I have not yet abandoned his idea that you went to the park for an afternoon of baseball and not just for the game. The game was the big thing, of course, but it was also the culmination of an afternoon of something closely approaching ritual. We always left home early enough to be in the park, either Fenway Park or Braves' Field, about an hour before the game was to begin. I think if you love baseball you must do that. If you don't, you miss the gradual unfolding of the rituals. The first thing was the initial glimpse of the field. After the hot, summer streets and the cool, steel-smelling shade under the stands,

I was always surprised by the greenness of the grass and the sense of concentration of brightness within the enclosure of the park.

Usually, there was only a little activity on the field, perhaps an infielder getting some practice on ground balls to his left or right or a couple of players jogging around the outfield. After a while, the batting practice would get underway, and my father thought this a rare treat because you could watch different kinds of great hitters like Hack Wilson and Paul Waner take 20 or 30 cuts, sometimes calling for special pitches and hitting them off or over the fences or, in the case of Waner, spraying them all over the field.

Another pre-game ritual that had great fascination was the pitchers of the day warming up. You could lose a great deal of satisfaction in missing that.

Lefty Grove, for instance, was something to watch. It used to take Lefty quite a while to warm up. At the start, he would merely toss the ball lazily to his catcher, I think it was usually Moe Berg, the bullpen catcher. After a few minutes, Lefty had a rhythm going and you sensed that you were watching a great pitching machine getting underway. It was best to keep one eye on him from the beginning so that you had something to which you could compare the ending, when he was firing them into Berg not quickly but with great concentration as though he were already facing hitters. When he was finishing, you could see Berg pulling his glove back to take some of the force out of the pitch, and then a split second later you could hear the smack of the ball in the mitt.

My father taught me to watch all this ritual-like activity so that the beginning of the game would not be abrupt, something that gave the appearance of just having been decided upon.

As a result, I got some long looks at the great hitters and fielders of those days: Mel Ott, Babe Herman, Lou Gehrig, Bill Rogell, Chuck Klein, Charlie Gehringer, and many others. And it seemed that they had a special ease and grace in those moments, probably the reason why my father enjoyed that time so much. The grace was important to him. He never thought of baseball as a complex game and said that if the game was as complex as some writers and commentators thought it to be, there would be no grace to it.

It was the gracefully competent whom he admired most, though both of us admired Pepper Martin, who did things on the bases and at third which were tributes to his enthusiasm but alien to grace. My father had seen many of the great players who had had their peak years before 1925 or thereabouts: Ty Cobb, Joe Wood, Nap Lajoie, and Eddie Collins. But the one he admired most was a player named Hobe Ferris. Whenever he wanted to give a player the highest of praise, he compared him to Ferris. And there were only three whom he thought to be as graceful: Joe Judge, the Washington first baseman; Kiki Cuyler, the Cincinnati outfielder; and Pie Traynor, the Pittsburgh third baseman.

We saw our last game together early in July of 1938. I'm glad now that it was a fine game, a pitcher's battle between the Phillies and the Bees (formerly the Braves) which the Bees won.

It is customary in these days when reminiscing about one's father to make him sound like the one in "Life With Father," a combination of Charlie Chaplin and W. C. Fields, with a touch of God. My father was not like that. To me his life was tragic, made so by a complex combination of social events and personal temperament. Baseball did not help him find an escape from either the panic or the anxiety of the Depression, and the panacea he did turn to was worse than the ailment.

But baseball did provide a bridge, temporary and fragile to be sure, whereon we could meet for a few moments. It seems almost romantic to call those moments imperishable, and yet here I am remembering them again and speculating, with just the smallest tremor of apprehension, on whether or not the bridges which I have so carefully built between my sons and me will prove as enduring.

Heroes from a distant past (left to right): Lefty Grove, Chuck Klein, and Charlie Gehringer.

I Remember DiMaggio

by Sam Elkin

March, 1963

Back on May 23, 1948, Joe DiMaggio hit two homers off Bobby Feller and one off reliever Bob Muncrief in successive times at bat at Municipal Stadium in Cleveland. Later, in talking to reporters, Joe remarked that this was the best day he had ever had in baseball. (DiMaggio also hit three homers in a game two other times, June 13, 1937, and September 10, 1950, but not in successive times at bat.)

Now I know how much, even today, Joe must cherish the memory of those three home runs in one game. But there was a homer Joe hit one night, and not in a major or minor league park either, which he probably doesn't remember, but which I saw and haven't forgotten and won't forget—ever. Joe may not remember that particular homer, for it is not in the record books, but I'm sure he'll remember Convention Hall in Atlantic City, late in 1944.

In the late fall and winter of that year, I was stationed at Atlantic City along with a good many other G.I.'s, including a staff sergeant named Joe DiMaggio. I saw Joe for the first time, one cold November day, on the enormous floor of Convention Hall.

Convention Hall had been completely taken over by the Army, and its main floor was laid out for many different sports. There were a full-sized softball field, three basketball courts, about 18 Ping-Pong tables, several badminton courts, a regular-distance archery range, and two full-sized tennis courts. We had mass exercise at least twice a week, and the first time I showed up for it Joe DiMaggio walked out in front of us.

In appearance he was unassuming—even a bit shy. His voice was low but forceful. And he sent us through our drills quickly and easily. After the exercise everybody crowded around him until it began to look and sound like a press conference. He didn't have to answer any questions, but he did. And he didn't have to sign autographs but he did that too, though I could see that he didn't like doing it while in a G.I. uniform.

I saw Joe DiMaggio off and on after that. Often at night I would go back to Convention Hall to work —we had our offices in one section of the building— and along about 7 or 8 o'clock I'd go out on the balcony overlooking the main floor of the hall. And there would be Joe DiMaggio playing softball with one team or another that had come to play without the required number of men.

One night I got into one of the games, and DiMaggio was on my side. Against us was one of the fastest softball pitchers I had ever seen. As you probably know, softball is quite different from baseball. The playing infield is smaller, the bases are closer, the ball is larger than a baseball, and the pitcher is many feet nearer to the batter. When you get a real softball pitcher against you, I don't see how anybody manages to hit him.

Joe DiMaggio didn't see how that night, either. Twice he went to bat—and twice he struck out. He was swinging way behind the pitch. None of us was doing any better, but it was obvious that the pitcher was bearing down particularly when DiMaggio got up to bat. With the rest of us, he played cat and mouse, tossing up slow curves, fast curves, let-up pitches. But when DiMaggio got up, he concentrated on zooming that ball through there, three pitches and all strikes. When Joe struck out the second time, I looked at the pitcher and saw one of those irritating little smiles curl his lips.

I didn't like that pitcher from then on. He was medium height, but stocky and solid. He was obviously a professional softball pitcher, and when he struck out DiMaggio the second time, I could almost hear him saying: "Boy, if I only had you in my league!"

I'm sure Joe wasn't aware of this, because each time he missed the third strike he'd come back to the bench, smiling and shaking his head and shrugging his shoulders, as if to say: "That kid's really got it out there."

But I was well aware of it. For me the game had become a battle, real and significant, and I kept wishing that Joe would really tag one the next time he got to bat. I just wanted to see the pitcher's face when that happened.

In our half of the seventh I led off and walked into a slow curve. The umpire waved me on to first base, and there I stayed while the next two men struck out. Then Joe DiMaggio walked up to the plate, and I started to yell to the pitcher, trying to unnerve him.

As far as the pitcher was concerned, I could have been out in left field or up in the balcony. He never even looked at me. He just went through his full underhand motion and shot that ball past DiMaggio twice—two strikes. And Joe didn't move a muscle. He kept his eyes on the pitcher, his bat back and ready, his feet spread apart. It looked as though he

Joe DiMaggio (No. 5) had a smooth, graceful stroke as a batter, obvious in this photo which shows him during his famous 56-game hitting streak in 1941. Only twice in his 13 years with the New York Yankees did DiMaggio fail to hit .300 or better. He batted .290 in 1946 after spending three years in military service, and he batted .263 in 1951, his final season in the majors. Joltin' Joe won American League batting championships with .381 in 1939 and .352 in 1940, finishing with a lifetime mark of .325. Three times (1939, 1941, and 1947) he was named the American League's Most Valuable Player, and it is significant that in 10 of his 13 years with the Yankees, the club won pennants. DiMaggio was the heart of the Bronx Bombers, as they were called in his time.

was studying the pitcher—just standing there, watching and studying the pitcher.

I roared my lungs out as the pitcher wound up for the third pitch and laid the ball in. Joe came around with his bat, and the ball shot foul down the first-base line.

"That's it! . . . Now you got him, Joe!" I yelled. "The big one! . . . Get the big one, Joe! . . . You can do it! . . . This guy's only a bum!"

The pitcher just gave me a quick look, shook his head once, and faced Joe again. DiMaggio was standing in the box, as before, watching and waiting.

The pitcher's face was tight and set as he stepped on the mound. His right arm went up, then down and around, and I didn't see the ball go in—but brother, I saw it go out! Joe caught it full, as he had caught many a pitch before at Yankee Stadium, and the ball rocketed away from his bat, straight up into the balcony in left field.

I just stood there on first base and laughed and yelled until a voice behind me said: "You moving, or do I have to climb over you?" I looked around and laughed up at Joe. I jogged around the bases, touched home plate, turned around, and shook Joe's hand as he crossed the plate. For one quick moment I felt as though I were in a Yankee uniform, shaking Joe DiMaggio's hand in Yankee Stadium.

"The greatest homer I ever saw you hit, Joe," I said as we walked back to the bench. He smiled, and I glanced out at the mound and saw the pitcher, nervously bouncing a new ball in his glove, his chin on his chest, his eyes on the ground.

Well, a lot of years have gone by since then, and I don't suppose Joe DiMaggio remembers that home run of his. But I do. I haven't forgotten it—and I'll never forget it. In fact, it takes on a legendary luster for me as the years go by, and no matter what ball park I'm in, no matter who is hitting a ball in the stands, the one home run I inevitably bring up in comparison is the one Joe DiMaggio hit into the balcony of Convention Hall in Atlantic City on a November night in 1944.

116

The Lingering Shadow of the Iron Man

by Al Hirshberg
Pageant Magazine

An awesome hitter, Lou Gehrig had a .340 career batting average and seasons when he drove in 175, 174, 184, and 165 runs. He was elected to the Hall of Fame in 1939.

October, 1963

"Twenty-five years—is it that long?" Joe DiMaggio tugged at his cap and looked off into space. We were standing near first base at the New York Yankees' spring training camp in Fort Lauderdale, Florida, where DiMaggio was helping out as a special coach. I had just asked him about Lou Gehrig.

A legend in his lifetime, Gehrig ran up a record streak of playing in 2,130 straight games before he was stricken with amyotrophic lateral sclerosis, a rare disease that eventually killed him.

Lou Gehrig played his last full season with the Yankees in 1938, when Joe DiMaggio was baseball's brightest young star.

"It doesn't seem like 25 years," DiMaggio mused. "The time goes by so fast. I remember now—1938. They called it a bad year for Lou, but anyone else would have gladly settled for it. He was close to hitting .300 and had nearly 30 home runs, but that wasn't up to his usual pace. And he got only four singles in the World Series."

DiMaggio ducked a flying baseball and we moved out of range. Then he went on: "None of us thought there was anything seriously wrong. Lou wasn't a kid anymore, and he hadn't missed a game in 14 years. He figured to slow up. Then he came back for spring training in 1939."

The Yankee Clipper shook his head and clucked his tongue. "Poor Lou," he said. "He couldn't hit a loud foul. He stood up there once in batting practice and missed 19 straight swings—all on good fastballs that he ordinarily would have smacked into the next county. Still, we didn't really suspect anything. His timing was way off, but the older you are, the longer it takes to get that back in the spring.

"Then we noticed he was having trouble catching thrown balls at first base," DiMaggio said. "Lou had never been a great fielder, but he was good enough to get by. But now he sometimes didn't move his hands up fast enough to protect himself. A ball would go right through them and bounce off his chest. Then one day in Houston, while we were barnstorming north, he fell down the dugout steps."

DiMaggio shook his head again. "Say," he said, "what was the name of that disease he had?"

"Technically, it is called amyotrophic sclerosis," I said. "But I guess almost everybody, including medical men, calls it Gehrig's disease now."

"Funny," DiMaggio said. "Here was the most powerful hitter I ever saw—and one of the greatest ballplayers of all time—and he's more famous for what killed him than for what he did when he was alive. I wonder if they're working on it; it's so rare. Lou was the only one I ever knew who had it."

"Amyotrophic lateral sclerosis, sometimes called Gehrig's disease, or motor-system disease, has characteristics all its own," says a Boston medical specialist. "It is a progressive, degenerative disease of the nerve cells in the spinal cord, and it is not related to anything else. But while we can't yet prevent or cure it, at least we now know what goes on.

"When it hits, it usually affects people in their 40s," the doctor added. "The nerve cells of the spine harden and thicken, the muscles begin to atrophy, and there is increasing inability of various parts of the body to function. The earliest symptoms are failure to coordinate properly, and this becomes more serious as time goes on. Death comes in two to three years."

Gehrig was apparently a bit younger than the average victim of the disease. He was a few weeks short of his 36th birthday in June, 1939, when his case was first diagnosed at the Mayo Clinic in Rochester, Minnesota. Gehrig died on June 2, 1941, two years later almost to the day. He would have been 38 on June 19.

While, as Joe DiMaggio pointed out, Gehrig's fame today seems to rest more on the manner of his death than on the achievements of his life, he ranks among the greatest sluggers that baseball has ever known. Because of his illness and imminent death, Gehrig was voted into the game's Hall of Fame by special election in 1939. Ordinarily, players have to wait until five years after their retirement. If Gehrig had lived, he would have walked in the moment he became eligible for the honor.

His fantastic streak of consecutive games, a record that probably will never be broken, was just one of his claims to immortality. Only Babe Ruth drove in more runs than Gehrig, and only Ruth and Ty Cobb scored more. Gehrig was fourth in lifetime total bases—behind Cobb, Ruth, and Tris Speaker—and fifth in home runs—with only Ruth, Jimmie Foxx, Ted Williams, and Mel Ott ahead of him.

For years Gehrig was the American League's undisputed leader in runs batted in. He led the league five times, and his record of 184 RBI in 1931 has never been matched. Only one man, National Leaguer Hack Wilson, ever knocked in more runs than Gehrig did in a single season. Wilson, on the Chicago Cubs, drove in 190 runs in 1930.

Although he lived in the shadow of Babe Ruth for nearly 10 years, Gehrig was one of baseball's greatest home-run hitters. He was the first man in modern times to hit four in one game, and he was one of the few to hit three in a game three different times. He was baseball's home-run king twice, its

leading batter once, and he was voted the American League's Most Valuable Player in 1936.

Roger Maris and Mickey Mantle notwithstanding, Gehrig formed with Ruth the most fearsome one-two punch in the history of baseball. These two left-handed sluggers, with Ruth batting third and Gehrig fourth, ripped apart both American and National League pitching staffs. Their peak year was 1927, when Ruth hit 60 homers and Gehrig hit 47. A year later they led the Yankees to a murderous four-straight World Series victory over the St. Louis Cardinals. Ruth batted .625 and Gehrig batted .545 in that Series; four of Gehrig's six hits were home runs.

The two were close friends until the winter of 1934, when they got into a bitter argument during an exhibition trip to the Orient. From that time until 1939—after Gehrig's disease became apparent—they rarely spoke to each other.

Gehrig's illness and premature death, although a crushing blow to his many fans, was particularly tragic for his parents—who had already lost their other children. One of four youngsters, Henry Louis Gehrig was born in the Yorkville section of New York City, June 19, 1903. He was educated in the city's public schools and entered Columbia University in 1921, but stayed only through his sophomore year. He signed with the Yankees after his father, a skilled mechanic, lost his job.

Gehrig reported to the ball club in June, 1923, but spent most of that season at Hartford, where he hit 24 home runs in 59 games. After he had another great year in the Eastern League in 1924, the Yankees brought the 22-year-old up permanently for the 1925 season.

Gehrig sat on the bench for about six weeks. On June 1, Wally Pipp, the regular first baseman, reported with a headache, and manager Miller Huggins sent Lou in to replace him. Pipp never got his job back.

For the next 14 years—despite a broken thumb, a broken rib, a broken toe, a twisted back, innumerable colds, and frequent attacks of lumbago—Gehrig didn't miss a ball game.

This was a fantastic achievement even in those years, when there was little or no night baseball, far less traveling than today, and a shorter schedule—154 games instead of 162 that are played now. In Gehrig's time, only seven or eight men played in every game of the season, and few did it two seasons in a row, much less 14.

Eventually, Gehrig broke Everett Scott's record of 1,307 consecutive games and then went on to put his own record out of reach of everyone. The only time the streak was really in danger came after Gehrig suffered a painful head injury. But Joe McCar-

Lou Gehrig weeps unashamedly during ceremonies honoring him at Yankee Stadium on July 4, 1939. "I'm the luckiest man on the face of the earth," Gehrig told the crowd of 61,808 fans. Less than two years later, he was dead at age 37.

thy, the Yankees' manager, sent him up in the lead-off spot, then ordered him back to his hotel. The next day Lou was back to normal again.

A quiet, shy man, Gehrig disliked the spotlight into which he was constantly thrown. He and his roommate, catcher Bill Dickey, were inseparable on the road, and they and their wives were always together when the team was at home. Both men were bridge enthusiasts. On trains and in hotels, they played for years as partners against George Selkirk and Johnny Murphy.

"I first met Gehrig in 1932," says Selkirk, now the Washington Senators' general manager. "But it wasn't until a couple of years later that I really got friendly with him. Although sometimes moody, he was a great guy who would do anything for people he liked. And he was a marvelous bridge player—a real student of the game."

Frank Crosetti, first the shortstop and later the Yankees' third-base coach, remembers Gehrig with deep affection. "He did something for me I'll never forget," says Crosetti. "When I first broke in, I was so scared I didn't dare open my mouth. One day just before the season started, we went to New Haven for an exhibition game with Yale. I had such a cold I could hardly breathe, and Lou was having trouble with his back. McCarthy let us both off early, so I sat in the locker room, waiting to go back to New York with the ball club.

" 'Don't sit around here all afternoon,' Lou said. 'You'll get pneumonia. Come on back to my house.' So one of the greatest hitters in the business drove a scared rookie back to his home in Westchester for the night and made a friend for life."

Although Gehrig wasn't quite up to par during the 1938 season, there seemed nothing wrong with him physically. He spent the winter at his home in New Rochelle, ice skating with his wife, Eleanor, almost every day. When he reported to the club for spring training in 1939, Gehrig appeared to be in excellent shape.

His clumsiness at the plate and first base was obvious to everyone, but not until he fell down the dugout steps in Houston was there any real concern for his health. Even then, McCarthy refrained from broaching the subject. Lou's streak was still going, and the Yankees' manager had decided to let him continue to play until he requested relief himself.

One day, just before the season opened, Eleanor noticed that Lou stepped off a curb feeling his way like a blind man, then she recalled that during the winter he had often fallen on the ice, although he was an excellent skater. She begged him to have a physical checkup, but he insisted that there was nothing wrong.

When the Yankees opened the 1939 season at Washington, Gehrig was still at first base. But in the first eight games of the year, he had only four singles and one run batted in, and the Yankees lost two games because easy grounders went right through his legs. Everyone but Lou himself seemed to realize something was terribly wrong, but he kept going.

Then one day, with Johnny Murphy pitching, somebody hit a routine grounder right at him. Picking the ball up, he flipped it to Murphy, who came over to cover first, and the runner was out. Murphy, Dickey, and the Yanks' second baseman, Joe Gordon, all slapped Gehrig on the back and told him what a great play he had made. But Lou wasn't fooled. He knew his mates were congratulating him for a simple maneuver that he had performed hundreds of times before.

The next day, May 2, he went to McCarthy and said, "Better put Babe Dahlgren on first. I'm not doing the club any good out there."

He went to the Mayo Clinic a few weeks later, then phoned his wife and cheerfully told her that he had a 50-50 chance to live. Eleanor wasn't fooled, either. She had already been given the medical report and knew her husband was doomed.

Gehrig rejoined the ball club and traveled as long as he could. As team captain, he took the lineups out to the plate umpire before each game, but his step was slower, and he had more trouble holding the card in his hand with each passing day.

July 4, 1939, was designated Lou Gehrig Day, and more than 62,000 fans went to Yankee Stadium to honor him. It was there that Babe Ruth came out to the plate, threw his arms around his old friend, and tearfully broke a silence of five years. And it was there that Gehrig, dying and almost surely aware of it, murmured over the microphone his heartfelt thanks and added a sentence remembered from that day to this as a classic of simple courage: "Today, I consider myself the luckiest man on the face of the earth."

Gehrig's physical deterioration was rapid after that, and soon he could not walk without help.

In late May, 1941, Selkirk, accompanied by Tommy Henrich, went to see Gehrig at his Riverdale apartment. Lou, once a powerful 205-pounder, was down to 90 pounds and had trouble speaking, but he grinned a greeting.

"I'll be all right," he said cheerfully. "The doctor told me this thing has to run its course before I'll start building up again."

In recalling it, Selkirk said recently, "But he knew. He just didn't want to worry Eleanor. A week later one of the greatest men baseball has ever known was gone."

Did Babe Herman Triple into a Triple Play?

by Jim Murray
Los Angeles Times

Babe Herman

January, 1973

History, Henry Ford said, is bunk. Or did he?

Did George Washington really throw a dollar across the Rappahannock? Was that midnight rider really Paul Revere? Or two guys from Springfield?

It's the same in sports. Did Babe Ruth really call his shot in the World Series? Did Willie Keeler really say, "Hit 'em where they ain't"?

Men usually become legends posthumously. Nothing promotes the growth of a legend like the demise of anyone who might contradict it.

Which is why I sought out Babe Herman at the Dodgers' Old-Timers' luncheon one day last season. Mention Babe Herman in any gathering of baseball fans, and the smiles immediately come to the corners of the mouth. The old joke is revived: The guy hollers down from the grandstand to the street, "The Dodgers have three men on base!" And the question comes up from the pedestrian below, "Which base?"

Babe Herman's life was a series of flyballs bouncing off his cap, sliding into occupied bases, passing base runners with his head down, starting to trot in from the outfield with only the *second* out and the bases loaded. The Daffy of the Daffy Dodgers. The guy who came into the league a big-eared rookie in 1926 and left it a big-eared rookie 19 years later.

One of the most famous paragraphs in baseball literature was the one the late John Lardner wrote: "Floyd Caves Herman never tripled into a triple play, but he once doubled into a double play, which is the next best thing." Or, "Floyd Caves Herman did not always catch flyballs on the top of his head, but he could do it in a pinch."

"Now, I'll tell you the truth of that," the Babe said doggedly, when I mentioned this. "In the first place, they said I 'tripled into a triple play,' but there was one out so how could I do that? Also, they forget I hit in the winning run in that game. Now, here is what happened: DeBerry [Brooklyn catcher] was on third, Dazzy Vance [Brooklyn pitcher] was on second, and Chick Fewster [second baseman] was on first. We were playing the Braves and George Mogridge hung a curve, and I hit it four feet from the top of the wall in right. DeBerry scores to put us ahead 3-2, which we stayed in the top of the ninth.

Vance runs halfway to third, then he runs around third, then he starts to run back. Fewster is on third, so he starts back to second.

"Now, I got the throw beat, and I slide into second. Safe. Right? So, now, somebody hollers to Jimmy Cooney, the shortstop, and he throws home. Al Spohrer chases Vance back to third. Now, I go to third on the rundown and, naturally, I slide into third. Safe. Right. Now, I was called out for passing Fewster, but Vance is on third and it's his bag by the rules. Spohrer begins tagging everybody—but I am already out. It's like sentencing a dead man. Now, there are only two out, but Fewster wanders out to right field to get his glove and Doc Gautreau, the Braves' second baseman, chases him and tags him out.

"You see, there never were three men on third exactly. See how everything gets mixed up?

"Now, the fielding was another thing they got all mixed up. Here I was playing first base all those years, and one day, Bizzy Bissonette gets sick and can't play right field. So I say, 'Hell, I'll play it.' You see, it was this awful sun field out there, the toughest sun field in the league, and, the sunset, which came through the opening of the roof there, made it worse. So, we didn't have flip glasses in those days, and when it got dark enough, the sky was murder, and when the ball was hit up, there was this black spot you had to pick out of the sun. What? Oh, the black spot was the ball and you can see sometimes how you could camp under the wrong spot." And while waiting he would feel this thunk on the back of his head.

As you can see from the foregoing, covering Babe Herman wasn't the simple historical endeavor the Thirty Years' War was. After all, not many guys come up with the bases loaded and one out and drive home one run and three runners to third base. Somebody probably should have said simply "Herman then doubled to right to load the base."

Frenchy Bordagaray: The Mod Player of the 1930s

by Jack Murphy
Boston Globe

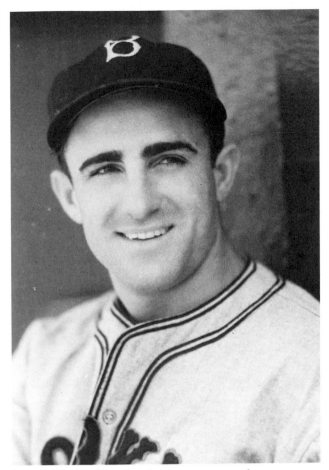

Stanley George (Frenchy) Bordagaray was a fun-loving player who enlivened the National League scene in the 1930s. He once was fined for spitting in the eye of an umpire. "Maybe I did wrong," said Frenchy, "but the penalty was a little more than I expectorated." Bordagaray never reached stardom, but he can claim credit for being in two World Series—as a pinch-runner both times, for Ernie Lombardi in 1939 and for Bill Dickey in 1941. He spent six of his 11 years in the majors with the Brooklyn Dodgers.

April, 1970

He is remembered as a pinch-hitter and a guy who wore a mustache and goatee right out of the gaslight era of baseball. But Frenchy Bordagaray's genius was his ability to irritate Casey Stengel.

The teenyboppers of today are barely aware of Stengel, much less Bordagaray. But it wasn't ever thus. Bordagaray's mustache was an object of curiosity long before the performing arts discovered the Beatles and Joe W. Namath.

Now Frenchy is 58, and his name seldom is heard unless he walks into a room. Then, with gentle persuasion, he'll describe the time he slid into all four bases after hitting a home run against the Giants in the Polo Grounds.

The year was 1935, and Bordagaray was an infielder with the Dodgers. They were the Brooklyn Dodgers then, and he was perfectly cast with this zany team.

He grew the beard and a mustache as a stunt during spring training. "The newspapermen were complaining they had nothing to write about," Frenchy recalls, "so I decided to liven things up a bit. The hair on my face gave them a dandy topic."

In pleasing the journalists, Bordagaray succeeded in annoying Stengel. The manager ordered him to get busy with a razor. "If we're going to have any clowns on this team, it will be me," grumped Stengel.

Bordagaray was clean-shaven when the season began, but his spirit was hairy. This came to Stengel's attention that day in the Polo Grounds when the manager waved Frenchy home from second base on a ball hit to left field.

The throw from outfielder Jo Jo Moore was so quick and accurate that Bordagaray saw he had no chance as he rounded third and headed home. He was out by 15 feet, and he permitted catcher Gus Mancuso to tag him without resistance.

Stengel was furious. "That will cost you $50 for not sliding," he said. Frenchy, in turn, was outraged by this injustice. "You should be fined for such a lousy coaching job," he told Casey.

Later in the day Bordagaray saw a fine opportunity for revenge. He hit his only home run of the season, and a plan formed in his mind as he trotted to first base.

"Casey isn't going to fine me again for not sliding," he vowed.

Then he made a nifty slide into first base, dusted himself off, and slid into second. Stengel instantly recognized the ploy and was waiting for Frenchy at third.

"He was giving me those terrible eyes," Bordagaray remembers.

His language wasn't so nice either. Here was the strange spectacle of a manager running beside a ballplayer as he completed his tour of the bases after a home run. Frenchy slid into third and then gave a highly theatrical performance—"a swan dive"—at home plate.

Stengel was waiting, but not to congratulate him.

"That will cost you a hundred," roared Casey, "for showing me up."

"Nice Guys Are in Last Place," Says Leo

by Frank Graham

Condensed from the *New York Journal-American*

September, 1946

It was twilight at the Polo Grounds. In the Dodgers' dugout, Red Barber, the announcer, was needling Leo Durocher about the home runs the Giants had hit the day before.

"Home runs!" Leo said. "Some home runs! Line drives and pop flies that would have been caught on a bigger field! That's what they were!"

"Why don't you admit they were real home runs?" Red asked, sticking the needle in a little deeper. "Why don't you be a nice guy for a change?"

Leo had been reclining on the bench, watching the Dodgers at batting practice. Now he leaped to his feet.

"A nice guy!" he yelled. "A nice guy! I been around in baseball for a long time, and I've known a lot of nice guys. But I never saw a nice guy who was any good when you needed him. Go up to one of those nice guys sometime when you need a hundred to get you out of a jam, and he'll always give you that:

" 'Sorry, pal. I'd like to help you, but things aren't going so good at the ranch.' "

He screwed up his face and clamped a hand across his hip pocket.

"That's what they'll give you, those nice guys. I'll take the guys who ain't nice. The guys who would put you in a cement mixer if they felt like it. But you get in a jam and you don't have to go to them. They'll come looking for you and say:

" 'How much do you need?'

"They don't ask you what you want it for. Just: 'How much do you need?'

"I got it now. I don't need it from anybody. But I know the time when I didn't have it—and I never got it from a nice guy."

A reporter winked at the others in the dugout.

"You a nice guy?" he asked.

"No," Leo said. "Nobody ever called me that."

"All right," the reporter said. "I'm going to the races tomorrow and when I see you in Boston, I'll probably need about $800. How about it?"

A memorable tit-for-tat kicking duel took place in 1961 between Durocher, then a coach for the Los Angeles Dodgers, and veteran umpire Jocko Conlan. Durocher was protesting a call by Conlan, who ruled a high pop-up hit by Norm Larker of the Dodgers was a foul ball. Leo objected and was thrown out of the game. He had kicked Conlan (top) and the umpire retaliated. The catcher is Hal Smith of the Pirates.

"You'll get it," Leo said.

"The funny part of it is," the reporter said, "I know that if I went to you I would get it."

"Darned right you would," Leo said.

He walked up and down the dugout for a moment, then whirled suddenly and pointed toward the Giants' dugout.

"Nice guys!" he said. "Look over there. Do you know a nicer guy than Mel Ott? Or any of the other Giants? Why, they're the nicest guys in the world! And where are they? Buried in the second division!"

He walked up and down again, beating himself on the chest. Suddenly he stopped, turned, and said:

"Nice guys! I'm not a nice guy—and I'm in first place. Nobody helped me to get there, either, except the guys on this ball club, and they ain't nice guys. There wasn't anybody in this league helped me to get up there. They saw me coming up and they—"

He stamped heavily on the floor of the dugout.

"That's what they gave me!" he yelled. "Nobody said to me: 'You're in third place now, Leo. We want to see you get up to second.'"

He picked up a towel from the bench and held it up high and patted it and said:

"Nobody said: 'You're in second place now, Leo. We'd like to see you in first place.'"

He threw the towel back on the bench.

"No, sir! Nobody wanted to see me up there. All the nice guys in the league wanted to knock me down, which is the way it should be. But in spite of them I got up there. I'm in first place now and . . ."

He waved a hand toward the Giants' dugout.

"The nice guys over there are in last place. Well, let them come and get me!"

The Dodgers were winding up their batting practice, and Eddie Stanky was at the plate.

"Look at that little———!" Leo said. "Think he's a nice guy? The hell he is! He'll knock you down to make a play, if he has to. Yeah, he'll knock you down and pick you up and dust you off and say: 'I'm sorry.'

"That's the kind of guys I want on my club."

He spoke warmly now.

"Look at him," he said. "The little———. He can't run, he can't hit, he can't throw, he can't do nothing. But what a ballplayer! I wouldn't give him for any second baseman in the league. Or for any two second basemen."

The bell rang, and the Dodgers were streaming into the dugout. A reporter who had been sitting on the bench got up.

"All up, boys," he said. "Make room for some nice guys."

"Not in this dugout," Leo said.

He waved toward the Giants' dugout again.

"The nice guys are all over there," he said. "In the second division!"

Durocher gives some of his notorious "lip" to umpires during his tenure as a coach for the Dodgers and later as manager of the Cubs. Branch Rickey once said, "Leo has the most fertile talent in the world for making a bad situation infinitely worse." That talent was generally apparent in his rhubarbs with umpires. He delighted in antagonizing them. His hostility, however, did not prevent him from once doing a television commercial with umpire Tom Gorman, seen arguing with Durocher (left) when Leo was a Dodger coach. Stan Landes, the umpire in the bottom photo, is about to give Leo the heave-ho.

How an .095 Hitter
Won the 1924 World Series

by Herold (Muddy) Ruel
as told to Lloyd Lewis

Condensed from the *Chicago Daily News*

Muddy Ruel

February, 1944

I have either been playing ball or coaching big league clubs since 1915, but in that time, which will soon be a third of a century, I never saw a day in baseball like that of October 10, 1924, in Griffith Stadium, Washington.

It was the seventh game of the World Series between the Senators and the Giants and my 156th game of the year. I had caught 149 games for Washington in the pennant fight, and although we only had a mediocre ball club, we had won it by keeping the team together, that way, day after day, same lineup—Goose Goslin and Sam Rice playing 154 games in the outfield, Joe Judge 140 on first, Roger Peckinpaugh 155 at short, and Bucky Harris 143 at second. It was a tough, determined ball club, paced by the boy-manager, Harris, who would get hit by pitched balls to get to first and who would knock fielders out of his way to get to second.

The Series had started on high, with the Senators' immortal Walter Johnson smothered by telegrams, letters, handshakes, sentimental publicity because this was his first pennant—his first World Series. The great man had never been on a flag winner before, and the whole country seemed to be whooping for him but betting on the Giants.

Even the Giants, looking at us with tolerance and amused confidence, spoke well of the great Walter. They could afford to. They figured the Series was in the bag. In the outfield, they had the really terrific Ross Youngs, a .355 hitter, and Meusel, another .300 man; Hack Wilson, a murderous freshman hitter, and George (Highpockets) Kelly with an average of .323 and 21 home runs to his credit that season. When southpaws worked against the Giants, Kelly went back to first, his old post. But against right-handers, McGraw used a kid named Bill Terry on the bag, a pitcher whom he was converting into a slugger. Great kids the Giants had, an 18-year-older, name of Freddie Lindstrom, on third; a sophomore, aged 20, name of Travis Jackson, on short, and nobody but Frankie Frisch, aged 24, on second.

The whole club had hit .300 for the season, had pulled a pitching staff of Nehf, Bentley, McQuillan, Ryan, Virgil Barnes, and Jonnard through to a flag. They had Hughie Jennings, the "ee-yah" coach, on third, and McGraw scowling from the bench—an awesome club, but not to us. We Senators were tough, too.

The pressure should have been terrific, on us, for the city of Washington was wild with its first flag. Even President Coolidge came out to the first game to root, in his own restrained way, for Walter Johnson. Walter was in the evening of his career, 37 years old, and getting so he'd tire in the late innings, and I'd seen that fast one coming in a shade slower than in other years. The Giants had licked him the first game, 4-3 in 12 innings, tagging him for 14 hits.

The big swarthy kid, Bill Terry, got 3-for-5 off Walter that day, and Art Nehf, Ross Youngs, and Kelly had hammered out two runs in the 12th inning to win. It was a heart-breaker, and the Giants and baseball writers said the Series was as good as over.

But old Tom Zachary—he wasn't old, just looked so sage and crafty and cunning that he'd been called Old Tom from his second year—he stepped out and beat the Giants, 4-3, in the second game. He didn't have anything but a one-fingered knuckleball and a determination to win. He wouldn't give those Giant sluggers anything good. He'd toy around with them, throwing soft curves and funny stuff till they got tired, then he'd throw one right where their strength was and they'd frozzle it in surprise.

The third game we lost, 6-4, but Mogridge had pulled us back in the fourth game by holding New York to six hits and four runs while we got seven runs across. Johnson tried again in the fifth game and lost. The kid Terry was still hammering him—had four hits in seven times up off Walter in two games. And Lindstrom hit Walter that day as if he owned him—4-for-5. He acted as if he didn't know whom he was hitting against.

It looked like curtains for us, but Old Tom

Zachary didn't think so. Pitching slow and tormentingly, he beat the Giants in the sixth game, 2-1, to square it at three all. That brought us up to the pay-off, October 10—and Washington was wilder than ever. President Coolidge was back in his box.

We talked before the game and figured we had to get Terry out of there, so Harris announced Curley Ogden, a second-string right-hander, to start. That meant McGraw would start Terry, who was a left-handed hitter, on first and use Long George Kelly in the outfield.

It worked, and after Ogden had pitched to two batters, Harris took him out and sent in Mogridge, a southpaw, who held them till the sixth, when they tired him out by waiting for walks. With two on and Terry up, McGraw jerked his young first baseman and sent in Meusel.

We had done it! We had got Terry out of the game, and Kelly would now go to first. But we were still in trouble, and Harris sent Mogridge off the hill and brought in Fred Marberry, the greatest relief pitcher I ever saw.

He was a second-year man, 24 years old, and a character. On the mound, he'd snatch-grab at the ball, kick up dirt, paw the ground with his spikes, fume, fret, then rear back, wave his big shoes in the batter's face, and blaze a fast one through. But the Giants weren't bothered by his big feet that inning, and helped by errors by Judge and Oscar Bluege, they scored three. It looked like the game, for we had scored only one off Virgil Barnes.

In the eighth, Leibold doubled for us and I was up. I hadn't made a hit in the whole Series, and I could feel the crowd sigh as I came to the plate. I singled. Then with two out, Harris bounced a sharp one a little to Lindstrom's left. It hopped over Freddie's head, and coming in behind Leibold, I scored the tying run.

The yell from the crowd wasn't any louder or longer, however, than a few minutes later when Walter Johnson came out to pitch the ninth. Washington was crazy for him to get even for the two lacings the Giants had given him.

He had to face the top of the Giants' batting order, with Lindstrom, his kid nemesis, leading off. He got Freddie, but that dad-gummed Frisch hit a triple to center. The ball seemed never to stop rolling, and I was crazy for fear Frisch would come clear home. With him on third, Ross Youngs came up. He'd crouch at the plate and poise himself like lightning about to strike, his eyes boring in on a pitcher, tense as a violin string. I'll never forget that big white bat of his hanging over my head as I crouched behind the plate.

We walked him.

Kelly up, with everybody thinking about those 21 homers of his. Walter threw. Strike one. Youngs went with the pitch for second and Frisch was ready to break for home if I threw. I bluffed it, hoping to trap Frankie. That one run on third was important, for it could win for them. Two runs were no worse, so I let Youngs steal. But Frisch was thinking right along with me and wouldn't be betrayed. He knew, too, that if I did throw to second Harris would run in and cut it off and throw home, and nobody in the history of baseball ever could make that play better than Bucky. So Frisch stuck to the bag, and we went back to work on Kelly.

Walter threw twice more, and I can still see that ball streaking in through Kelly's swing for strike three.

That left Meusel up, with two down. Johnson got him to ground out, but I've always wondered what would have happened if Bill Terry had been kept in the game. It would have been his spot, and he would have loved it! We got Barnes out of there in our half of the eighth. He was followed by Nehf, Mc-Quillan, and Bentley, and they and Johnson kept the plate free till the last of the 12th.

Miller started our 12th going out at first. I hit a high foul over the plate and everybody said, "Two outs," but Hank Gowdy, the Giants' catcher, stepped on his mask, stumbled, and dropped the ball, and on the next pitch, like a sinner forgiven, a lifer pardoned, I doubled—my second hit of the whole Series.

Walter hit sharp to Jackson's right, and I made as if to run past Travis, then turned and scuttled back to second. Jackson fumbled the ball. Two on, one out. The fans were really giving tongue now. They couldn't believe things like this happened.

McNeely up. He bounced one sharply but straight to Lindstrom, who was about 12 feet from third. Running hard, I figured all I could do on a sure out like that would be to throw myself to the left, into the diamond in front of Freddie, and try to get him to try and tag me instead of throwing to first. I saw Freddie hold his hands ready at his chest for the ball, then I saw him jump up. The ball had hit a pebble and bounced away over his head. I swerved back into the baseline, tagged third, and came home with the winning run. Meusel had no chance to get me. It was over. We were in!

I had only hit .095 for the Series, but I had scored the tying and winning runs, and I didn't mind it when Clark Griffith said I'd taken longer to get home in the 12th than any runner he'd ever seen. As a matter of fact, I, like President Coolidge, was thinking how great everything had turned out in the end for Walter Johnson.

Luis Aparicio—
The Game I'll Never Forget

as told to George Vass

September, 1972

I've been in the major leagues since 1956, when I came up to the Chicago White Sox, and in the years since then there have been two games I'll never forget. One was when I was with the Baltimore Orioles in 1966 and I was out there on the field watching Paul Blair catch the fly that ended the World Series. No one could believe that we had beaten the Los Angeles Dodgers four games in a row.

The other game was in 1959, and I was with the White Sox, and Chicago won the American League pennant for the first time in 40 years.

Nobody expected us to win the pennant because we did not have the power of some other teams, like the New York Yankees and Cleveland Indians. The Yankees, like always, were supposed to have the edge. They had won the pennant four years in a row and nine of the past 10 seasons.

We didn't have the kind of players the Yankees had—Mickey Mantle, Yogi Berra, Hank Bauer, Elston Howard, and guys like that—but we had a good team. We had Nellie Fox at second base, Sherm Lollar catching, Jim Rivera, Jim Landis, and Al Smith in the outfield.

We had good speed and some fine pitchers, like Billy Pierce, Dick Donovan, Bob Shaw, Early Wynn, and guys like Gerry Staley and Turk Lown in the bullpen.

We got off to a good start, won our first four games, and surprised everybody by staying in first place almost all the way. We'd steal a game here, squeeze another one out there, and play just good enough to win almost every day.

Maybe it should have been a tipoff when we won the opener at Detroit on a home run in the 14th inning by Nellie Fox. Nellie wasn't a player to hit many home runs but he could beat you a lot of other ways, and he earned the American League's Most Valuable Player Award that year.

As I said, we were never hot—never winning 10, 12 games in a row, or anything like that. We just kept winning, getting by by a run. Won three games here, lost one, won four more, lost two. Real steady. We won 35 games by the margin of one run.

I think the most important series we won was in late August. We went into Cleveland 1½ games ahead of them, with four games to play in the series. We won all four games, and we left Cleveland 5½ games ahead of the Indians, and they were the closest club to us.

After that we were pretty confident we would win the pennant, but you're never sure of that until it says in the standings that you've done it.

Our chance to clinch the pennant came on Tuesday, September 22, 1959. We played the Indians again in Cleveland. We were 3½ games ahead of them. We had four games left to play and they had five, so they still had a mathematical chance. If we won, it was all over.

Early Wynn started for us and Jim Perry, a rookie that year, for the Indians. The Indians got the first chance to score in the second inning when they got Minnie Minoso to third base and Russ Nixon on first with Rocky Colavito at bat and just one out.

Colavito hit a flyball to left field along the line. Al Smith made the catch at a bad angle, but he threw a strike to the plate and Minoso was out trying to score. It might have been a different game if Smitty hadn't made that good throw. But he'd been making it all season.

We got to Perry in the second inning. Bubba Phillips got a single to center, and I hit a double off the right-field wall to score him. Then Billy Goodman got me across with another double.

The Indians got a run in the fifth inning off Wynn on a walk and singles by Gordie Coleman and Jim Piersall to make it 2-1.

The Indians took out Perry for a pinch-hitter in the fifth, so Mudcat Grant started the sixth inning for them. Smitty hit Grant's first pitch over the fence in left. The next batter, Rivera, also hit a homer and we were ahead, 4-1.

Wynn had thrown a lot of pitches by the sixth inning, and when the Indians got another run off him, to make it 4-2, Al Lopez (Sox manager) replaced him with Bob Shaw. Bob got out of trouble that inning and in the seventh and eighth.

But the Indians kept coming. With one out in the ninth, they loaded the bases on Shaw. The third guy to get on was Piersall, who got a single off Fox' glove. A single would tie the game and the next batter was Vic Power, a real good hitter.

Lopez brought in Gerry Staley to pitch to Power. Staley had a great sinker, and he was as effective that year as any relief pitcher I've ever seen.

Staley threw just one pitch. It was a sinker and Power hit it on the ground right to me at shortstop.

Manager Al Lopez bounds out of the dugout and dashes on the field at Cleveland's Municipal Stadium after White Sox clinched the pennant in 1959 by beating the Indians, 4-2. Shortstop Luis Aparicio launched a double play to end the game.

Aparicio (left) with second baseman Nellie Fox, his infield partner in 1959 when the White Sox won their last American League flag. Their defensive play was a big factor in the club's title run that year, with Fox being named the league's Most Valuable Player and Aparicio finishing close behind him in the voting.

The ball was hit real hard and I saw there was plenty of time, so I ran over to second, touched the bag, and threw to first to Ted Kluszewski for the double play.

I don't remember exactly what happened after that. Everybody was hollering and slapping each other on the back. We'd won the pennant and were on our way to the World Series.

The trip back to Chicago after the game was one wild party. There was a big mob of fans at Midway Airport to welcome us, and it's a good thing we didn't have a game the next day.

Everybody wasn't happy. A lot of people were mad that somebody had ordered the air-raid sirens in Chicago set off a few minutes after we won the pennant. I guess a lot of people thought there really was an air raid.

But I didn't learn about that till later. All I know is that when I stepped on second base and threw to first we won the pennant.

Baseball in the Marianas, 1944

by Shirley Povich

Condensed from the *Washington Post*

John Rigney   Mace Brown

May, 1945

In July, 1944, the Japs were playing baseball on the Mariana islands when the word went out: Game called on account of Americans. That was the month the Marines landed on the beaches, chased the Nips into the hills, and proceeded to take over generally.

Recently I saw two teams of big-leaguers play a ball game on the same diamond the Japs had carved out of the jungle. It was the Navy's idea of entertaining the servicemen in these parts, and it was popular. Six thousand sailors rimmed the field and whooped it up for the boys they used to see in big league uniforms.

This was no USO troupe of baseball entertainers. The men on the field were former big-leaguers who are in the Navy now. They don't have any soft berths. When they're not playing ball, they have all the duties of Joe Blow in the Navy. They're sticking their necks out on long over-water flights in land planes to get to the island fields. And the outfielders could, conceivably, have their backs to Jap snipers in the woods.

Mace Brown, the old Pittsburgh pitcher, who is a lieutenant and the only officer with the outfit, manages the Fifth Fleet team that played the Third Fleet team skippered by George Dickey. The players are off 12 of the 16 big league clubs. They like the whole business of this baseball tour. They get taken around. The other day they went for a joyride with a B-29 crew that had seven missions over Tokyo to its credit.

On its next Tokyo flight, incidentally, that crew is going to let the Japs know what it feels like to get conked with a baseball from 35,000 feet. The boys left a dozen autographed balls, "To Tojo with love —" with the crew who said they'd heave 'em through the bomb-bay doors on the target run.

There are baseball fields all over the islands, thanks mostly to the Seabees. What was an impossible gulch replete with a creek last week is a nicely graded diamond this week. Johnny Rigney, the White Sox pitcher, says there's only one complaint.

"There weren't any pitchers with those Seabees when they laid out the fields," says Rigney. "They must all have been hitters. The outfield distances are too short. What the Navy needs is some pitchers in their Seabee battalions to think of these things when they go to work on a ball field."

Mace Brown is having a wonderful time, he says. As an officer and manager of the Fifth Fleet team, he nominates himself as a starting pitcher. "For 10 years in the majors I was a relief pitcher," he says. "I always wanted to know what it felt like to start a game. Now I know, and I'm satisfied. I'll take relief pitching."

There's not much doubt that the two teams out there could pool their talent and win the pennant in either big league. Besides Rigney and Brown, there are Johnny Vander Meer, Hal White, Virgil Trucks, and Tom Ferrick to do the pitching. They have three pretty fair first basemen in Mickey Vernon, Johnny Mize, and Elbie Fletcher. Billy Herman is playing second base, and Pee Wee Reese, shortstop. Merrill May is a third baseman. Outfielders include Barney McCosky.

Mickey Vernon of Washington is the slugging star of the troupe. They're using him as an outfielder, and he hit eight home runs in the first seven games on the islands. He rather likes the idea of playing in the outfield and is ready to kiss off his first-basing career.

Baseball is not exactly a virgin sport on Guam. The native Chamorro kids are playing it every day. They learned it after the American occupation in 1898.

(Editor's Note: Shirley Povich was in the Pacific theater as a war correspondent for the *Washington Post* during World War II. Between war dispatches, he filed this article from the Marianas.)

Jim Gilliam
Recalls Tough Times
in the Negro Leagues

by John Wiebusch
Los Angeles Times

June, 1969

The bus was old and orange and dirty, and the driver would hit a hole in the road and all the seats would shake. A voice would come from somewhere in the darkness saying, "Hey, man, take it easy," and the driver would look up in the mirror and see nothing and say, "Ain't me built these roads."

The bus would move on through New Jersey, and the driver would turn to the kid who sat by the front door with his back to the window and he would yawn and say, "Son, Newark sure has some mighty fine women. Mighty fine indeed." The kid would nod and listen.

The driver would hum and sing softly and the only other sound was the turning of the wheels. The kid fought to stay awake and he would look out the front window. "Ain't no fun, really," the driver would say. "You got the fun playing ball and I got to drive the bus." The kid would nod and the driver would continue. "You're a lucky boy, know that? You in the big time now."

"Big time," the kid would repeat, and the driver would grin and say, "You say hello to Josh next time you see him. Tell him Amos from 78th Street says hello."

And then they would be in Newark, and the kid would be the first one off the bus and the first one in his room in the dollar-a-day hotel. He would look at the New York papers and read about the Giants and the Dodgers and the Yankees.

James Malcomb Gilliam, Jr., would fall asleep and think that he would never be there in that white world where the black man swept the locker room and said, "Yes, sir," when he was spoken to.

It is 23 years away, the bus ride through New Jersey from Baltimore to Newark, and the kid is a man with kids of his own. There is James Malcomb Gilliam III in college, and there is his father, talking about how he left high school after the 10th grade. There is a rookie outfielder who bats left-handed saying, "Hey Junior, teach me how to hit the ball to left field," and there is the patient coach sighing and

saying, "That's what I've been trying to teach you all spring." There is a boy in a Cardinals' T-shirt, holding out an autograph book and a pencil and saying, "You a player?" And there is the lean man of 40, bending down and saying, "Nowadays I just watch, son."

Later he sits in the chill of the lobby with the jukebox roaring and Ray Charles singing about "All the lonely people," and you know what it must have been like. No, you THINK you know what it must have been like. Only the man they call Junior and Jim really knows.

"I'm one of the lucky ones," he says. "I was born at the right time."

It is Stevie Wonder in the background now.

Junior looks up and his soft brown eyes gaze across the table. "I'm lucky," he says, "because I got a chance. Ever hear of Josh Gibson? If they came to Josh Gibson today and he were 17 years old, they would have a blank spot on the contract and they'd say, 'fill the amount in.' That's how good Josh Gibson was."

You have heard of Josh Gibson. As strong as Babe Ruth, they said, and the greatest catcher who ever lived, and probably the greatest slugger of them all. Only he was black.

"How about Tommy Butts and Willie Wells? Tommy played for our team, the Baltimore Elite [he pronounces it, E-light] Giants, and Willie played for the Newark Eagles. They would be playing shortstop for any team around now. And Jonas Gaines, a left-handed pitcher who threw smoke. A great one. There were a hundred others that I know of."

It is Aretha Franklin's turn now, and Junior taps his fingers.

"See why I'm lucky? Most of them are dead.

Most of them never got a chance. They were making $275 a month like me. And you know what? They never thought it would happen. They never thought a black man would play in the white leagues. Most of them were happy doing what they were doing—playing baseball and making a buck."

He was 15 when he quit school to play baseball. The man from the Nashville team in the Southern League—the Southern Negro League—liked the way he handled himself around second base and gave him a job. He made $125 a month for two years.

He was 17 when they sent him to the National League—the National Negro League—and he watched the men—black men—he had heard about while he sat on the bench with the Elite Giants of Baltimore.

He was 18 when he became a regular, and since he was the youngest they called him Junior. He played with the team for five seasons. There were a thousand bus rides and a thousand ghetto hotels and ball parks where the black man could sit right behind the first-base dugout and not have to go to the bleachers.

He was 21 when a scout from the Brooklyn Dodgers saw him play. He was back in Nashville that winter when he heard that the Dodgers had purchased him and pitcher Joe Black from the Elite Giants for $11,500.

He played two years at Montreal, where Jackie Robinson had been, and he went to Brooklyn, where Jackie Robinson was, in 1953. He has been a Dodger ever since.

"I think of the old days often," he says. "I think of the games we played at Bugle Field in Baltimore and how rough it was then. I think of the guys who made it—the Roy Campanellas, the Monte Irvins, the Larry Dobys, the Willie Mayses . . . the Junior Gilliams.

"Then I think of Josh Gibson and the others. And Satchel Paige and the barnstorming days and the guys who played for the New York Black Yankees and the Washington Homestead Grays."

Someone has played Ray Charles again, and Junior Gilliam talks about what it is like, the satisfaction of being a coach, and about how he thinks all the time about becoming a manager someday. He talks about his four children and his wife and about playing golf and shooting pool. He talks about what the good life is like.

And you know that Amos from 78th Street would be prouder than hell of the kid who only nodded and listened.

Jim Gilliam is tagged out at the plate in an attempt to steal home for the Dodgers as batter Roy Campanella falls away from the action. Gilliam was called Junior by his teammates on the Baltimore Elite Giants because he was the youngest player on the club. In 1975 he was completing his 11th season as a coach for the Dodgers, a team he joined in 1953 as a second baseman and remained active with as a player through the 1966 season. A switch-hitter, Gilliam played on seven Dodger pennant winners.

How To Watch a Ball Game

by Red Barber

Condensed from *This Week*

October, 1942

Remember Charlie Keller's ninth-inning triple in the World Series' first game a couple of Octobers ago? Had you watched the ball soar up, up, and away out yonder into right-center—you might have missed the real play. Veteran baseball men are still debating in strong language who should have caught that long fly.

In that play, Cincinnati's Harry Craft, ordinarily a fine fielder, didn't get a quick enough start for the ball. He was a step or two late in going back and over from his post in center field. Ival Goodman, in right field, had a long way to go to make a catch. As the ball started to come down, Goodman was running dangerously close to the stands. Had you focused on the ball instead of the fielders, you wouldn't have seen Ival take a fleeting look to see, first, where the stands were and, second, where Craft was. The nearby fans were yelling so loudly the two outfielders couldn't hear each other calling precious information. That glance, quick as it was, cost Goodman a half-step and also cost him the catch. His glove barely touched the ball, which fell for a triple. It was not only the game's upsetting factor but one of the Series' upsetting factors, too.

The first rule for sports announcers might well hold true for the patrons in the park: follow the ball. But this rule should be broken, or modified, to suit the occasion. You'll see, for example, much more that's important if on a flyball—like Keller's triple—you watch the outfielders. They will lead you to the ball in time anyway—and you'll observe the outfield in action.

A ball game is a very real combat. There is a wealth of strategy based on percentage, human ability, surprise, and, certainly, chance. Full enjoyment of this struggle means more than merely watching the execution of plays.

Tipoffs come to light that hint what's in the minds of the managers. Watching the relief pitchers in the bullpens often provides a clue to an impending change. Sometimes the first sign we can get that the present pitcher is tiring comes from such activity. Nine times out of ten, when a relief pitcher starts throwing in the bullpen, it means something. It may indicate that soon the pitcher will be taken out for a pinch-hitter. It may mean that with certain batters coming up, the relief hurler is figured the better man to pitch to them. Or it may tell you the present pitcher is barely getting by, and the first jam he gets into will see him starting for the showers. I've seen a bullpen pitcher begin warming up just before game time and keep at it as the starting pitcher went to work on the mound. This meant the manager was uncertain of his starter, either due to the man's in-and-out ability or because he was hurt or sick. The starter was getting a chance, but if he didn't show up well, he was to come out at once.

Managers, taking into consideration the percentages, like to have their left-handed pitchers working against left-handed batters, and they want their left-handed hitters to face right-handed hurlers. However, percentages are far from infallible even in this simple matter, as Charlie Dressen discovered one day in 1935 when he was managing the Cincinnati Reds.

Charlie's boys were facing the Pittsburgh Pirates that afternoon, and the Pirates boasted a crew of left-handed hitters who could really tee off against a right-handed pitcher. Charlie had a plan to trick the Pittsburgh team into making frantic last-minute substitutions. Si Johnson, Redleg right-hander, made a great show of warming up before the game and stepped in the pitcher's box to face the first Pirate batter. He walked him—and retired unexpectedly to the showers. In came Tiny Tony Freitas, a *left-*hander, who had been warming up in secret beneath the stands.

Here was a situation that promised the fans not only a ball game to watch but also a subtle turn of strategy. Everyone settled back to observe the Dressen genius in all its glory.

And the Pirates proceeded to pound Tony Freitas for five runs and victory!

One of the surest indications of a team's strategy is the alignment of infield and outfield. The fielders place themselves where the percentage favors the ball to be batted. For a right-handed pull-hitter the defense is shifted toward left field. The reverse is true for a left-handed batter, who pulls most of his shots into right field. All through the game the defense is trying to make the batters hit where they are playing. Needless to say, the batters are trying to hit the other way.

Not all teams handle the same play in the same way. Take the problem of the bunt with runners on first and second and nobody out. Most managers instruct their pitchers to try to get two strikes on the batter without letting him bunt, thus forcing the batter to hit into a hoped-for double play or pop up an infield fly. But not William Terry when he managed the Giants. He wanted his pitcher to get the ball over, usually high, with something on it, but so that the batter could bunt it. Bill had his men ready to field the bunt and wanted his pitcher to get over against the third-base line, his third sacker to fall back, and his first baseman to cover the right side of a short infield. If the batter wasn't careful, Bill's pitcher picked up the bunt, whipping it to third for a force-out; and although there were still men on first and second, there was one out, and the bunt trick had gone up the creek. The percentage is against bunting a high, hard pitch successfully; the ball is either hit too hard or else is popped up. In this situation, where most clubs try to keep the batter from bunting at all, the Giants let him bunt and then play to beat their opponents over the head with their own weapons.

Before digging any deeper, let me advise that plenty does go on in a game that nobody, except the players on the team, is likely to see, no matter how hard he watches. By this I mean signs. The manager makes his will known to his men on the field by signals, or signs. Some managers flash a lot of signs, others just a few. It depends on the manager, the way the game is going, and the players themselves. When a batter steps into the box, he gets his orders what to do. He gets a sign from either the third- or first-base coach or even from the bench. This prearranged sign may tell the batter to do as he pleases or to take the pitch or to bunt it or to hit it. Base-runners are given signs to steal. Batters and runners have signs between them for the hit-and-run. The defense has its signs, such as the signals between catcher and pitcher. Right before our unseeing eyes the players relay information and orders back and forth, and—perish the thought, but 'tis true—sometimes miss signs.

I once asked Bill McKechnie if he worried much about the other team's getting his signs. "Hell, no!" he growled. "I worry about my own fellows getting 'em."

Watching a control pitcher bear down is one of baseball's most fascinating sights. He doesn't get by with sheer stuff alone. He works with his head as much as with his arm. He pitches to spots. He watches hitters between swings. He uses a change of pace to get their timing off. He throws all his stuff with the same motion. He cuts this corner, then that one. He isn't often behind on the ball-and-strike count, so he doesn't have to come right over the plate with a fast one.

When you see a control pitcher having a good day, among other things to watch for carefully is the one fatal pitch that he might make a little too good for the batter. Wham!—eight innings of neat work go down the drain. In connection with control, we might bear in mind that wildness isn't purely a matter of bases on balls. A pitcher may give no walks at all but still be wild enough to get himself in tight spots. Then he has to come right down the groove to avoid walking the batters, and he's licked.

It's always a duel between pitchers and batters.

Walter (Red) Barber was one of the nation's best-known baseball broadcasters for more than three decades, working on both radio and television. He is seen here interviewing Brooklyn manager Leo Durocher during a telecast of a doubleheader between the Dodgers and Cincinnati Reds in 1939. It was the first time TV cameras were focused on major league action. "I started broadcasting baseball in Cincinnati in 1934," recalls Barber. "I spent five years there, 15 years at Ebbets Field, and 13 years at Yankee Stadium." Barber retired from the baseball scene in 1966. How many major league games did he see during his career, which included coverage of 23 World Series? "I can't even begin to count them," he says. In the photo with Barber and Durocher are (left to right) Whitlow Wyatt, Cincinnati manager Bill McKechnie, Dixie Walker, and Dolph Camilli.

Pitching away from batting strength and to batting weakness is a real science. Major league moundsmen can do this most of the time. They have to, or they will get one-way train tickets home. Major league pitching control may explain largely the case of the minor league fence-buster who doesn't make the grade under the big top. The young batter may not care particularly for fastballs under his chin, so all he ever gets in the major leagues is one close shave after another.

Pitchers make it their bread-and-butter business to study batters until they know what each hitter likes—more especially what he doesn't like. Managers hold clubhouse meetings before games and go over methods of pitching to and playing for everybody on the other side. The defense is arranged on law-of-average chances that a certain hitter will drive a certain pitch in a certain direction. You'll have to watch closely to see where good pitchers serve their stuff, but the effort will pay big dividends in baseball enjoyment.

I remember a game at Brooklyn a few summers ago when the Dodgers and Cubs were deadlocked in a tie in the 14th inning. In the last of the 14th, with one out and nobody on, Gene Moore of the Dodgers hit a triple off relief hurler Charlie Root of the Cubs. With the winning run on third, Root had no choice but to load the bases with passes so that he could work for a force-out at home or a double play.

Suppose we figure a little . . . bases full, one out, last of the 14th. The winning run is at third. Manager Durocher is coming to bat. Root is hot—his control is perfect—he's been threading the eye of the needle at 60 feet 6 inches. Durocher is not a long-distance hitter, so he probably won't try a long scoring fly. The Dodgers are afraid of a double play more than anything else. Moore, the runner at third, can run and slide. Durocher is cunning and will take chances. But Root is a wise old bird. The Dodgers have three choices—to hit away, to put on the squeeze, to hope for wildness on Root's part. The third choice is bad—Root's control is too good. The Cubs have moved the infield in, ready for a force-out at home, whether Leo swings or bunts. Root doesn't want to throw too close to Leo, for Durocher won't mind getting hit to force in Moore and win this game before a packed house. Leo is an adept bunter. Root is probably thinking, "I'll throw that Durocher something he can't hit or bunt, and maybe I'll find out from his actions what he's gonna do."

Then Root's right arm swung plate-ward, and all the suspense was over, for as Root made his motion,

Moore started racing for home. The squeeze play was on! Moore was coming, all or nothing, and it was up to his manager at the plate to do something and to keep him from getting put out. But Root had done his job well. The pitch was too good. Durocher missed it. Moore was running to his doom.

But catcher Bob Garbark failed to hold the ball, and it rolled away. Garbark recovered it quickly and dived back toward the plate just as Moore began his slide. Garbark reached for him with the ball—a split second too late. Plate umpire Ziggy Sears flashed the safe sign. As players from both teams swarmed around the plate and thousands of fans howled gleefully, I wondered how many of these fans had enjoyed the full excitement of that play—how many of them had figured out the problems that faced both pitcher and batter and watched to see how each dealt with those problems.

Up to now I've said a lot about the pitcher and batter. But there are nine defensive positions and nine men in the batting order. Let me suggest that to increase your baseball insight, as well as pleasure, you make a practice of watching one position, and one only, for several innings at a stretch. Set your sights, say, on the third baseman, and watch nothing but the way he handles himself. Watch what he does on plays he isn't even in. Watch how he varies his fielding position to meet different situations. See the entire play of the game as the third baseman participates in it or is prepared to even though nothing comes his way. Then switch over to the first baseman, or the left fielder, and keep at it until you've studied each position.

On each play each man has an assignment, one he may not be called on to execute twice a season, yet should he miss it the oversight might cost a ball game. Fate has a way of making these mistakes count in pennant battles. We've all seen throws from right field get past the third baseman and allow a runner to race home for a precious score. Probably we put the blame either on the throw or on the third baseman for failing to handle it. The official scorer would have to charge the error in one of these two ways, for errors are given against acts of commission, not of omission. But maybe the pitcher didn't get over behind third base to back up the play. The chances are that had he done so, he would have recovered the ball, and the runner would either have stuck to third base or been thrown out at the plate.

How to watch a ball game? The best way, of course, is to get to the park in time to hear the magic cry, "Play ball" . . . But there will always be more to a ball game than will ever meet the eye.

Why Kiki Cuyler Was Benched

by Fred Russell
Nashville Banner

May, 1968

The election of Kiki Cuyler to the Hall of Fame prompted a lot of fans to ask: "Why was Cuyler benched the last weeks of the hot 1927 pennant race? Why did manager Donie Bush of Pittsburgh continue to ignore him during the 1927 World Series, refusing to use him even as a pinch-hitter as the Pirates lost four straight to the Yankees?"

Cuyler never cleared it up, never would talk about it, before his death in 1950.

Bush had buried it, too, resisting all inquiries until I approached him in the spring of 1958 at Hollywood, Florida, where his Indianapolis club was training, and found him willing to talk.

First, Bush took pains to try to explain that he was a newcomer to the National League when he succeeded Bill McKechnie as Pittsburgh manager after the 1926 season.

The Pirates had finished third in 1926, only four and one-half games back of the champion St. Louis Cardinals, after having won the pennant and the world championship in 1925. Bush inherited many fine players, including shortstop Glenn Wright, third baseman Pie Traynor, and two of the top-hitting outfielders of the National League, Paul Waner and Cuyler.

In 1925, Cuyler hit .357; in 1926, .321. In the two seasons, he stole 78 bases and was established as a particular Pittsburgh hero for having driven across the runs that beat Washington in the deciding game of the 1925 World Series.

"Cuyler had played center field and batted third in 1926," Bush said. "He wanted to do the same thing in 1927, and we started out that way. But a short time later, I decided he should play left field and hit second. He fretted about this constantly."

Bush was asked why he made this shift when Cuyler was such an outstanding center fielder, with a great arm.

"My reason was that Lloyd Waner, Paul's younger brother, had joined the club, and I regarded him as a better center fielder than Cuyler," he replied.

"Lloyd was as good a hitter. He wound up hitting .355 against Cuyler's .309 that year. [Their lifetime averages were only five points apart: Cuyler, .321; Waner, .316.] And Waner was faster.

"I admit Cuyler did have a great arm. But he was inclined to throw the ball in from the outfield so high that the infielders couldn't cut off the throw and prevent runners from advancing from first or second base. I had spoken to him about it several times.

"One day in early August, in a close game, the opposing club had runners on first and third, with one out. The batter flied to Cuyler. He threw toward the plate, too high for a cutoff, and the runner on first advanced to second. From there he scored on a single. That run beat us.

"When Cuyler came in to the bench, I said to him: 'Won't you ever learn to throw the ball low?'

"He said: 'If you don't like the way I play, get somebody else.'

"I said: 'I will.' And I did."

Cuyler never played for Bush after that. Bush put Clyde Barnhart in left field the rest of the season and on through the World Series.

"It had to be that way," Bush insisted. "I had to maintain discipline.

"One time I had fined Cuyler $50 for not sliding to try to break up a double play in a game against the Giants. But the real reason I benched him was for what he said to me after that high throw.

"I had great respect for Cuyler as a player. He always was in top shape physically. His only trouble was his bullheadedness. If he had apologized to me, I would have put him back in the lineup."

Cuyler's roommate, catcher Johnny Gooch, with other players, got up a petition asking Bush to use Cuyler. But Bush refused.

I've never understood fully why Barney Dreyfuss, owner of the Pittsburgh club, didn't try to heal the breach between Bush and Cuyler. Perhaps the reason was that the Pirates in 1927 continued to win without Cuyler in the lineup.

Dreyfuss traded Kiki to Chicago in November, 1927, for infielder Sparky Adams and outfielder Floyd Scott. It was a poor deal he made. Cuyler went on to eight great seasons with the Cubs, helping them to two pennants and reaching his highest major league batting average, .360, in 1929.

Pittsburgh finished fourth in 1928, and during the 1929 season Bush was replaced as manager by one of his coaches, Jewel Ens.

"If I had to do it all over," Donie told me, "I would handle it the same way."

Hank Bauer Recalls
the Yankees' Glory Years

by Joe McGuff
Kansas City Star

May, 1973

The owner of Hank Bauer's Liquors rang up a sale while his customer, a woman, looked at him quizzically. "Are you the Hank Bauer that played baseball?" she asked. "That's me," the proprietor said, his raspy voice filling the store. "You've just made my whole day for me," she said smiling.

A few minutes later, seated among bottles and beer cases in a back room of his store in Prairie Village, Kansas, Bauer talked about making the transition from baseball to the liquor business and the realization that for the first time in 26 years he would be at home when spring training opened.

"I honestly can't tell you right now how I'm going to feel," Bauer said. "I talked with Joe Collins and Gil McDougald about it, and they both said they missed it. Collins told me that it took him about two years to make the adjustment. You miss the people you've gotten to know in the business. You go to spring training, and you spend 15 hours a day talking about baseball. When you've been doing this as long as I have, you know you're going to miss it."

Bauer, who managed the Athletics and Orioles after retiring as a player, worked in the minors the last two years managing the Mets' Tidewater farm club. He had hoped that a major league managerial or coaching job might turn up. When it didn't, he reluctantly made the decision to bring his baseball career to a close.

"Let's face it, my phone didn't ring," Bauer said in his blunt, honest manner. "I thought I did a pretty good job at Tidewater. We finished third my first year and lost in the final game of the playoffs against Rochester, which had an outstanding team that year. We finished third again last season and won the playoffs.

"I could have gone back to Tidewater but the travel is difficult, and I couldn't see that I had much more to prove in the minors. I never felt I was too good to manage in the minors. I went back hoping something would open up. When it didn't I decided

Hank Bauer (right) with Mickey Mantle (left) and Whitey Ford after they joined in beating the White Sox, 3-0, in a game at Yankee Stadium in 1958.

the time had come to quit. I'm 50 now. In the 23 years I've been married, I've spent one summer at home, and that was the year I got fired at Baltimore.

"I've taken my pension and with what I can make out of this business, I'll be all right. This place will keep me busy and I imagine I'll be at the ball park a few times."

Bauer's career spanned 12 seasons with the Yankees. He appeared in nine World Series and three All-Star games. These were the glory years of the Yankees, who failed to win the pennant only once in a period from 1949 through 1958. The '59 season was Bauer's last with the Yankees. They finished third that year but then won five more pennants in succession before the dynasty collapsed.

"I'm not really sure what made the Yankees so great," Bauer said reflectively. "We had great players and Casey was a good manager, but there was more to it than that. We had a lot of harmony on the team and a lot of pride. If the player wasn't putting out, the other guys would tell him, 'Hey! Quit screwing around with our money.'

"People hear Casey talk at banquets and they think no one understood him, but that's an act. When he had those clubhouse meetings he could make everything pretty clear. He used to say, 'If some of you fellas here don't like it, we can find another place for you.' When you're walking to the bank with that World Series check every November you don't want to leave. There were no Yankees saying play me or trade me.

"Casey was good at handling men. He kept Woodling and me so mad all the time that when we got in there we wanted to prove how good we could play.

"If you remember, Casey had me leading off most of the time. One day I asked him why, because I sure wasn't any base-on-balls man. He said, 'Waal, you can hit the ball out, you can hit a double or a triple, you can score from first on a double, and you can break up a double play pretty good. I like to get a run in the first. It changes the whole game around.'

"I got to thinking about that and what he said makes sense. If you can get a run in the first you can do a lot of things, especially if you're the home team.

"Managers today have all kinds of statistic sheets, but I never saw the old man with any figures on paper. That didn't mean, though, that he didn't know what was going on. He knew if you hit good against certain pitchers and had trouble with the others. One time we're in Cleveland and the old man mentioned that I didn't hit Bob Lemon too good. I told him Lem should be getting me out because Cleveland was paying him more than I was making."

In his years with the Yankees, Hank was a dangerous clutch-hitter. He had a lifetime average of .277, 164 homers, and 703 runs batted in.

Bauer managed three and a half years at Baltimore and worked twice for Charles O. Finley, once in Kansas City and once in Oakland. Bauer found the second time around with Charles O. no easier than the first.

"When you work for Charlie, one of his theories is that you should never lose communication," Bauer said. "Before I was fired in Oakland, almost a month went by and Charlie never called me. I knew then I was gone. We flew into Anaheim, and I told the road secretary he had better get me a plane ticket home.

"Sure enough, a little later Charlie's secretary called and said he was coming to see me and wanted me to stay in my suite. When he came in, I asked him if he wanted some coffee. He said no. Then I asked if he wanted a drink, and he said no, he didn't think so. He must have sat there for five minutes without saying anything. Finally I said, 'What's the matter? Don't you have guts enough to tell me I'm fired?' He looked at me and said, 'How did you know?'

"I told him about the communication. Tears kind of came to his eyes, and he said, 'You so-and-so, I like you but I've got to make a change.' "

In his role as player, manager, and now an elder statesman, Bauer views the American League's designated pinch-hitter rule with largely negative feelings. He especially argues against the claim of proponents that it will keep older stars in the game.

"I was 39 when I quit playing," Bauer said. "I couldn't have gone on any longer even if they had had the pinch-hitter rule. I quit because my bat slowed up. I was a dead fastball hitter when I came to the majors. The last three or four years I was a breaking-ball hitter. That was because I saw so many breaking balls, and I didn't get around on the fastball anymore.

"Why do you think Mantle quit when he did? He wasn't all that old but he just couldn't get the bat around anymore. I don't know whether DiMaggio could have played another year or not, but he was too proud to stay around as a pinch-hitter."

A buzzer rang, and Bauer left to wait on a customer who wanted to know if he had any Montrachet.

"We have some French wine but we don't have shelf room for all of them," the proprietor replied.

136

Reggie Jackson — The Game I'll Never Forget

as told to George Vass

January, 1974

There's my greatest day in any sport and then there's that fifth game of the American League playoffs with the Detroit Tigers in 1972.

That game with Detroit is the one most people remember because we won the pennant for Oakland when we beat the Tigers, 2-1, and I got hurt so I couldn't play in the World Series against the Cincinnati Reds. I had to watch our guys beat the Reds on crutches.

I can still feel my left leg coming apart. What happened was that we were losing, 1-0, in the second inning when Woody Fryman walked me. I stole second base and got to third on an out. With Mike Epstein on first base, we pulled off a delayed double steal.

I went for the plate, and I was about 30 feet away when I hurt myself. I pulled a muscle. If I stopped I'd be out, if I kept going I'd tear up my leg. We needed the run to tie so I kept going.

I could feel everything tear loose when I went into Tiger catcher Bill Freehan at the plate. I ruptured my hamstring, pulled it away from the bone, stretched the ligaments in my knee. But I was safe, and we went on to win the game, 2-1, and the American League pennant.

The leg was so badly torn up that even after surgery I wasn't really sure how I'd be for the 1973 season. But, thank God, the leg came around.

So there's one game I'll never forget.

The other one? Well, it's funny, not too many people remind me of that. But when you have a game like that in any sport—baseball, football, whatever—you feel like everything has come together for just that day.

As a hitter, when you get hot like that you just don't feel like the pitchers can ever get you out.

The game I'm talking about was on June 14, 1969, in Boston. That was the year I hit 47 home runs, 37 by the All-Star game in July, and people were talking about me breaking Roger Maris' record of 61 home runs and comparing me with Babe Ruth.

It was my second full year with the A's, and I was just 23. But even though I was hitting all those

Jackson signs autographs for young admirers. A left-handed batter and thrower, he is the key player around whom owner Charlie Finley built his championship teams. Jackson won the Most Valuable Player Award in the American League in 1973.

home runs I didn't feel like another Babe Ruth. There'll never be another Ruth. I just didn't feel like a 60-home-run-hitter. I was just hot and in the groove and the home runs were coming.

Hank Bauer was managing the A's that year, and Joe DiMaggio was one of our coaches. Both helped me a great deal.

DiMaggio helped me by always talking to me about hitting. He was very encouraging and he gave me specific pointers. Bauer helped my confidence by just telling me to go up there and swing.

We went into Boston for a three-game series on Friday, June 14, to start the greatest weekend I've ever had—or could hope to have. I hit a home run in the first inning Friday off Jim Lonborg with nobody on, and we went on to win the game, 4-1.

It was the next day, Saturday, that I had my greatest day in sports.

I remember the first Red Sox pitcher, Ray Jarvis, but I don't know who came in after that. There were

Jackson zeroes in on one of Wilbur Wood's knuckleballs in a game against the White Sox. Like many other power hitters, Reggie strikes out frequently, but when he connects solidly, the ball is liable to travel record distances. Fans still talk about the stupendous homer he hit in the 1971 All-Star game at Detroit where the ball bounced off a transformer on top of the Tiger Stadium roof in right center.

Jackson heads into the bag on a close play, typical of many he has been involved in during his major league career that began in 1967. During a 1972 playoff game against Detroit, he suffered a severe leg injury in stealing home with a crucial run. His daring gamble helped the A's win the pennant, but the injury sidelined him for the World Series.

plenty of relief pitchers because we won the game, 21-7, and we got 25 hits. I was 5-for-6, but that wasn't what made it the great game it was for me.

In the first inning, I drove in a run with a double. In the third inning, I hit a home run with a man on and did the same in the fifth.

That was five runs batted in and when I came to bat in the sixth the bases were loaded. I figured if I could get a couple of more ribbies I'd really have some kind of day. But I struck out.

That didn't bother me too much because by that time we were ahead, 10-1, and I'd had about as good a day as you could expect.

But, like I say, when you're hot nothing can stop you and everything keeps breaking your way. We loaded the bases again in the seventh, and I banged a single to right to drive in two more runs. Seven ribbies!

It didn't even enter my mind I'd get any more. But we kept on banging away at the Red Sox, and when I came to bat the next time, in the eighth, the bases were loaded again.

This time I hit one into the gap in right-center, and three runs scored. I made the turn at first but decided not to try for a double.

So there it was. I'd gone 5-for-6, with two home runs, two doubles, and a single that should have been a third double. I'd driven in 10 runs in a game, which they told me later was one short of Tony Lazzeri's record.

The funny thing is that I got more hell from Bauer that day than when I struck out five times in a game. I caught it for making a useless throw to the plate to let a couple of runners move up, for throwing on the fly, and for not making a double on the three-run single in the eighth.

The way Bauer talked I was lucky I wasn't fined.

The next day, Sunday, was like a continuation of Saturday's game. I hit my 23rd home run of the season, had a double and triple, and drove in four more runs to give me 15 ribbies for the three games.

I didn't get the last RBI with my bat, though. I came up with the bases loaded again in the eighth inning Sunday, and Bill Landis hit me with a pitch. I don't think he was throwing at me—but you can't always be sure.

Now that I think about it, there was something else that happened that last time at bat. Russ Nixon, the Boston catcher, asked the umpire to look at my bat.

He told the ump, "There's a flat spot in it."

There might have been at that. I sure wore it out that series, and especially that 10-RBI game, the one you know I'll never forget.

Reggie Jackson earlier in his career...

And as a bearded veteran.

Ted Williams' Last At-Bat

by Emil Rothe

April, 1973

On Sunday, September 25, 1960, owner Tom Yawkey of the Boston Red Sox announced that his superstar, Ted Williams, would retire as an active player at the end of that season. Already 42 years of age, Theodore Samuel Williams had accumulated 19 seasons of major league play, all with the Red Sox.

A hastily organized ceremony was arranged to honor one of the greatest baseball players in Boston history on the occasion of his last appearance before the hometown fans in Fenway Park on September 28, 1960.

The day was a foggy, murky one which threatened rain, but still over 10,000 fans turned out to honor their hero. Curt Gowdy, the Red Sox announcer, presided at the pre-game program and introduced the Splendid Splinter as "the greatest hitter who ever lived," and concluded, ". . . he was controversial but colorful."

In response, Ted said, "If I had it to do over again I would want to play for Boston, for the greatest owner in baseball and the greatest fans in America."

The enthusiastic home crowd made up in noise what it may have lacked in numbers, cheering every move that Ted made.

The Baltimore Orioles provided the opposition that day, with Steve Barber on the mound. The Oriole rookie did not stay long. With one out in the bottom of the first, he walked Willie Tasby and, on four straight bad pitches, put Ted Williams on first as the Boston fans, who had come to see Ted hit, gave vent to their displeasure with loud boos.

Jim Pagliaroni was hit by a pitch to fill the bases, and when Barber also walked Frank Malzone to force Tasby across the plate, it was obvious that Barber needed help.

Baltimore manager Paul Richards summoned Jack Fisher from the bullpen to face Lou Clinton, who greeted him with a line drive to center. Jackie Brandt caught the ball and made a good one-hop throw to Gus Triandos at the plate, but Williams was able to slide in safely for the second run of the inning.

Leading off the third inning, Ted smashed Fisher's one-and-one pitch to deep center field, but Brandt was able to make the play. As he returned to the bench, Williams was given a tremendous ovation. They were Ted Williams fans rather than Red Sox fans that day.

With the Red Sox trailing, 3-2, in the fifth, Ted came to bat for the third time, with two men already out. He hit a long drive to center. As the Oriole right fielder, Al Pilarcik, retreated toward the bullpen fence, a rising crescendo of happy anticipation in the stands was suddenly supplanted by a loud groan as Pilarcik, his back brushing the wall, made the catch almost 400 feet from the plate.

While there was no wind to affect flyballs, it was evident that the "heavy" atmosphere had kept the ball in the field of play.

When the Splendid Splinter returned to the bench for the last half of the sixth, he remarked to his teammates, "I hit the living hell out of that one. If that one didn't go out, nothing is going out today."

Tasby came to bat to start the eighth for Boston, now trailing 4-2. He was followed out of the dugout by Ted, who sauntered toward the on-deck circle. As soon as his lanky form emerged from the seclusion of the bench, the cheering started. It increased in volume as Tasby was thrown out on an easy tap to short, and when Ted stepped into the box he was accorded a long, standing ovation.

Everyone sensed that this might be the last at-bat before the home crowd for the Splendid Splinter, concluding 19 seasons of stellar service for the Boston Red Sox.

Play was suspended as the salute to one of baseball's superstars continued unabated. After several minutes, plate umpire Ed Hurley signaled Fisher to resume pitching.

With the first pitch—a ball, low—Fenway Park suddenly fell strangely quiet. On the next pitch, a high slider, Ted uncoiled his home-run swing but missed as the crowd broke into noisy appreciation of his effort. Fisher's next pitch was apparently intended to be a fastball low and away, but it came in waist high over the outside corner where Ted could reach it.

Ted was ready, and from the moment of impact there was no doubt that Williams had his 29th homer of the season and the 521st of his career.

Jackie Brandt raced back to the bullpen fence but watched helplessly as the ball hit the canopy above the bullpen bench and bounced against the wire screen rising in front of the bleachers.

After circling the bases at a faster pace than usual, Ted ducked quickly into the shadows of the Boston bench. Despite wild elation and the fans chanting, "We want Ted" and even after the urgings of the first-base umpire, John Rice, and that of his manager, Pinky Higgins, and his teammates, Ted refused to acknowledge the accolades.

At the end of the eighth inning, he trotted out to left field but before the inning could get under way, Higgins sent Carrol Hardy to replace Ted.

Thus, Williams was given one last solitary excursion from his position as guardian of that immense green expanse, the left-field wall in Fenway Park, to the Boston dugout behind first. But, loping in with those long strides, head down, he again disappeared into the dugout without responding to the plaudits of the crowd.

Only Ted can tell why he failed to signal any recognition of the vocal acclaim from the Red Sox fans on this day that Mayor John Collins of Boston had proclaimed Ted Williams Day.

Only Ted can explain his sudden announcement immediately following the conclusion of the game that he had made his last appearance as a player.

Boston still had a three-game series scheduled in New York to close the season, but Ted chose September 28, 1960, as his finale.

One can only conjecture that Ted felt the tremendous 420-foot home run in his last at-bat before a hometown crowd was a piece of drama befitting the final curtain of his career and one that he could not hope to emulate or surpass in any additional appearances on a baseball field of play.

Perhaps Ted remembered, too, how Babe Ruth had continued to play, pitifully, after his one last moment of glory and had decided that he write "finis" to *his* career with that last dramatic homer in the only major league home field he had ever known.

The actual outcome of the game was decidedly a secondary issue. For the record, Boston won, 5-4. Ted's homer had closed the gap to one run and a two-run ninth salvaged the victory, only the sixth Boston win in the 22 games played with the Orioles that season.

The retirement of Ted Williams was not unexpected. In fact, many fans and baseball authorities felt that he would not even start the 1960 season after a dismal 1959 season, the only year he failed to hit over .300. Ted is the last major-leaguer to hit over .400 (.406 in 1941), and his lifetime batting average of .344 places him in a tie for 10th in that category.

Two terms of military service cost Williams almost four full seasons, seasons in which he undoubtedly would have accumulated enough additional home runs to challenge Ruth's career record and seasons in which he logically might have been expected to augment his lifetime batting average.

Of passing interest is the fact that the Baltimore pitcher, Steve Barber, who started against Boston in Ted's last game, was less than one year old when Ted completed his first full season in Boston.

Some of Ted Williams' early homers were hit off Thornton Lee of the Chicago White Sox, and one of his 29 home runs of 1960 was hit off Don Lee of the Washington Senators, the *son* of Thornton Lee.

One last item of note: his first 1960 home run was hit in the opening game of the season at Washington off Camilo Pascual and was one of the longest he ever hit—a better than 500-foot drive.

His last, however, had to be one of his most dramatic.

Ted Williams hangs up his uniform for the last time after finishing his major league career with a home run in his final at-bat on September 28, 1960.

Amos Rusie: Daddy of the Fire-Ballers

by Burt Hawkins

Condensed from the *Washington Evening Star*

March, 1943

"How good was Amos Rusie?" repeated Clark Griffith. "Well, Walter Johnson is my top pitcher of all time because he was great over a longer stretch, but Rusie was the closest thing to him that baseball's ever seen.

"Rusie was around only nine years—they overworked him—but while he was around he was the best. Only Johnson had more steam on his fastball. I suppose if I had to pick four pitchers from all I've seen I'd take Johnson, Rusie, Christy Mathewson, and Lefty Grove in that order."

Griffith recalls Rusie, who died in December, 1942, at the age of 71, as a pitcher who cost him considerable coin over a span of years.

"I doubt if Rusie ever made $3,000 a year when he was pitching," said Griffith. "Gosh, most any rookie makes that now, but in those days the National League had a salary limit of $2,400, and we'd pick up maybe $500 as a bonus if we won two-thirds of the games we started.

"That was the way Rusie beat me out of money. When I was pitching for Pop Anson's Colts, I had a contract that called for a $500 bonus if I won two-thirds of my games. Well practically every time we met the New York Giants I pitched against Rusie. Golly, I don't know how many times I pitched against that fellow—dozens of games—but I only beat him once. He cost me several bonuses.

"I'm not exaggerating when I say he was the National League—the whole works. He was to baseball then what Babe Ruth was to baseball later. When anybody talked baseball they just naturally talked about Rusie. In addition to that terrific fastball he had a great curve, a simply marvelous curve, and he could control it.

"Just look at that fellow's record," demanded Griffith. "He won 252 games in nine years—that's an average of 28 a season. He started 427 games—that's an average of over 47 a season—and I don't believe he ever started a game that he didn't finish. He was so good he never needed relief.

"Get that—he started and finished an average of 47 games a year. Nowadays a pitcher who comes up with 25 full games a season has a whale of a year.

"He had awfully short arms and was wild as the devil when he was with Indianapolis. When Indianapolis busted up and he came with the Giants though, he developed control. He had that remarkable curve controlled so well that he'd throw it with the count three-and-two.

"I'll never forget one time I had a pretty good chance of beating him. I was pitching against him and we were trailing 2-1 in the ninth. We loaded the bases on him in the ninth, and Anson was due to bat. It looked good for us because Anson was one of the greatest hitters that ever lived.

"Anson, who was our manager, was so good, in fact, that he was arrogant about it. He'd always take two strikes just to defy the pitchers, then get his hit. He was a tough baby though, and he didn't like any advice.

"When he went up to the plate, I said, 'Pop, hit that first pitch,' because I knew it would be right down the middle. He turned to me and said, 'Young man'—he always said that when he was mad—'I'll do the hitting.'

"Sure enough, he took two strikes down the middle, then set himself to hit. Rusie broke off a curve and struck him out, and we lost that game, 2-1. Some of our players tried to get me to say something to Anson, but I never opened my mouth. He would have broken a bat over my head.

"Yes, they moved back the pitcher's box while he was in his prime, but it didn't affect Rusie any. In fact, he pitched the Giants to the world championship that year. Rusie isn't in the Hall of Fame, but he belongs there."

Illegal Hit
That Won
the 1933 World Series

by Bob Stevens
San Francisco Chronicle

Lefty O'Doul

July, 1950

It took him a good many years to get to confessing, but Francis J. (Lefty) O'Doul now admits he could have been the prize umbay of the 1933 World Series between the New York Giants and the Washington Senators instead of a gilt-edged hero.

Francis fudged, but he picked up all the marbles in a riotous second game of a roaring Series that swept through five pulsating phases before the Giants, then under fiery Bill Terry, were coronated kings of the baseball empire.

The Polo Grounders from Coogan's Bluff had won the opener, 4-2, in Big Town but were trailing 1-0 in the sixth inning of the second game when the man in the green suit got into the act. Alvin Crowder, Washington's 24-15 right-hander, had become involved in a spectacular duel with Prince Hal Schumacher, Terry's 19-12 marvel of the mound, and 35,461 nail-gnawers were loving it.

Then the Giants exploded. Joe Moore singled the first pitch thrown at him to open the sixth, and the coin was in the nickelodeon for sure. Hugh Critz forced Moore at second for the first out on an unsuccessful bunt, but Terrible Terry, one of the great "money" players in the business, doubled, and Crowder was crowding catastrophe. Master Melvin Ott, later to manage the Giants, was deliberately walked to load the bases, and . . . but let the *Spalding Official Baseball Guide of 1934* take over from here:

"At this juncture, Terry halted the game to substitute O'Doul as a pinch-hitter for Davis (George, cf), also a strategical maneuver, but one which carried the crowd into a series of cheers, as vigorous as the boos which had greeted Ott's premeditated pass. It was O'Doul's first and only appearance of the Series. . . . The crowd went wild with enthusiastic hope as it recognized the National League batting champion (.368, Brooklyn) of the previous year.

"His time at bat was the turning point of the game, and, as it turned out, of the Series as well. O'Doul began inauspiciously, for he fouled and had a strike called on him by the umpire. He let the next one go by, just outside the plate, after apparently wanting to strike at it, but he let it pass. The next was another foul, the ball striking Sewell (Luke) on the arm. Still with two strikes against him, he swung hard and cracked the next pitch like a shot over Crowder's head into center field for a clean single. Critz and Terry scored and the crowd rose to the occasion vocally."

Six runs resulted from the rally, and O'Doul represented one of them, completing the cycle from third on a perfectly executed squeeze bunt by the lumbering Gus Mancuso.

From here, Francis, the fudger, takes over:

"I wasn't going to let Crowder throw a ball past me, you can bet on that. So with each pitch, I crowded the plate a little closer, a little closer. Finally, I was darn near standing on the thing, and when Crowder threw the pitch I wanted I went out after it as though it was the pot of gold at the end of the rainbow. It was on the outside corner, and I know, now, that in my anxiety to hit it, I stepped across the plate, which was illegal to such an extent that I put myself in jeopardy of being called out by umpire George Moriarty.

"However, George didn't see it, nor did anybody else, and I certainly wasn't going to call his attention to it," said Francis J., looking dreamily across the room as though he could still see that line drive soaring majestically over Crowder's head.

The Giants muscled to victory on the strength of Skipper Lefty's wallop, 6-1, although it was not to completely wipe Washington out of contention. The next afternoon, October 5, with the scene changed to the nation's capital, Earl Whitehill blanked the Giants, 4-0.

But the Polo Grounders prevailed in the next two starts. King Carl Hubbell worked an eight-hitter for 2-1. Schumacher and Crowder opposed each other in the fifth game, but both gave way to relief hurlers before the Giants won, 4-3, this time without the help of Francis the Fudger.

The Jackie Robinson I Knew

by Wendell Smith
Chicago Sun-Times

January, 1973

The Jackie Robinson I knew was a man around whom the winds of controversy swirled and blew during most of his spectacular lifetime.

From his boyhood days in Pasadena, California, throughout his adulthood, he was a constant source of worry and agitation to those who resented his black aggressiveness. They declared he was "too pushy, wanted too much too soon."

But nobody could tell him that and smother his quest for racial equality in American life.

I first met Jackie Robinson in 1945. He was playing shortstop for the Kansas City Monarchs of the Negro American League. He believed then that he was a player of major league quality and was determined to break the barrier which had been erected to keep black players out.

That determination was easily discernable that season, two years before he reached his goal. As sports editor of the *Pittsburgh Courier,* I was taking Jackie and two other black players, Sam Jethroe of the Cleveland Buckeyes and Marvin Williams of the Philadelphia Stars, to Boston for what ostensibly was a tryout with the Boston Red Sox.

We got to talking about this tryout—which turned out to be nothing more than a gesture—and Jackie said grimly: "I don't know what's going to come of this but if it means that the Negro player is a step closer to the major leagues then I'm all for it. I'll do my best to help make this project a success."

We were on a train going from New York, where the players had met me, to Boston.

The following day we went to Fenway Park. The Red Sox had not returned from spring training camp. Instead, they went directly to New York where they were to open the season against the Yankees.

Duffy Lewis, the old-time Boston star, was looking over a group of sandlot and high school prospects. Robinson and the two other black players joined them. Jackie and his two colleagues were impressive, to say the least.

Afterward, Duffy Lewis said good-bye and assured the players that "You'll hear from us."

On the way back to New York, Robinson said, "We probably won't hear from him, but it may have put a crack in the dike."

It did. I stopped off in Brooklyn while Robinson and the other two players returned to their respective teams in Negro baseball. Branch Rickey of the Dodgers expressed an interest immediately and from that point on had scouts tailing Robinson, Jethroe, and Williams.

Jackie didn't know it but he was on his way to the majors then. Instead of Boston, however, he was to end up in Brooklyn.

In the spring of 1946 I accompanied Robinson and a pitcher, John Wright, to Sanford, Florida, the training site of the Montreal Royals and No. 1 Brooklyn farm club.

This event, which Rickey called "the great experiment," was the big training camp story that year. With Robinson and Wright in camp, Montreal, a minor league club, received more publicity than most big league teams.

The press paid more attention to Robinson because he was better known than Wright. Jackie had been an all-around star at UCLA. When World War II came he went into the service and became a first lieutenant.

Controversy followed him there. He became embroiled with some MP's because, according to Robinson, they had roughed up a Negro woman passenger on a bus trip while trying to force her to sit in the back.

Jackie was almost court-martialed for that incident. Only the intervention of Joe Louis, then stationed at Fort Riley, Kansas, saved Jackie from a long sentence. Louis appealed to Washington in Jackie's behalf and the matter was dropped.

During those spring training days in Florida the townspeople in Sanford resented Jackie's presence in the camp. Controversy flared again when a spokesman for the chamber of commerce came to

With the Dodgers trailing, 6-4, in the eighth inning of the opening game of the 1955 World Series against the Yankees, Jackie Robinson (No. 42) broke from third base and stole home, catcher Yogi Berra protesting the umpire's call in vain. Robinson's daring dash for the plate, which was made in a losing cause—the Dodgers lost the game, 6-5—typified his style of play.

me and advised us to get out of town immediately.

When I told Jackie, he balked, saying he wasn't going to leave. Controversy again. I called Branch Rickey at his hotel and told him the problem. "Get Robinson out of this town immediately," he said. "We can't have any racial trouble now." We left with Robinson grumbling and protesting.

Robinson was making his Montreal bid as a shortstop. The regular shortstop was a French-Canadian and popular in the northland. When that was pointed out, Jackie said, "I don't care what he is, I intend to beat him out of the job because I believe I am better than he is." Controversy again. The French press fired its guns at Jackie for his "cockiness."

Wherever he went Jackie was in the midst of a racial controversy. After his first year at Montreal, where he was a sensation, and it became apparent that he was a cinch to play with the Dodgers, Dixie Walker asked to be traded. Even before that, during spring training in 1947, some Dodger players signed a petition against his eventual presence on the team.

And after the season started, the St. Louis Cardinals threatened to strike rather than play against him.

He had a feud with manager Leo Durocher and never hesitated to shower an opposing pitcher he thought was throwing at him with a volley of ob-

scenities. He slid into Roy Smalley of the Cubs at Wrigley Field, and they almost came to blows.

But through all this Jackie Robinson was always himself. He never backed down from a fight, never quit agitating for equality. He demanded respect, too. Those who tangled with him always admitted afterward that he was a man's man, a person who would not compromise his convictions.

In fact, in his last public appearance with death just around the corner, he was still fighting for his people and equality. During the 1972 World Series, he threw out the first ball and thanked baseball for all it had done for him.

His final words were controversial. "I won't be satisfied," he told the capacity crowd and millions on television, "until I look over at the coach's box at third base and see a black manager there."

As I sat there and listened and watched, I just knew that Jackie Robinson was going to say something like that.

(Editor's Note: Former baseball writer Wendell Smith, who died November 26, 1972, before this article was reprinted in *Baseball Digest,* was instrumental in helping Jackie Robinson get his start in the majors.)

Goslin vs. Manush—
Face to Face
for the Bat Title

by Heinie Manush
as told to John P. Carmichael
Condensed from the *Chicago Daily News*

November, 1946

I suppose I should remember the day I won the American League batting championship, the last day of the season in 1926, and I do. I beat out Babe Ruth and that was a great afternoon but, after all, he was playing in St. Louis and I was in Detroit. We weren't on the same field like that closing day two years later when Goose Goslin and I went down to the final game to see who won. Yeah, he won, but that isn't all of it.

I was with the Browns then, hitting third, and Goose was with Washington, also hitting third. We were playing each other in St. Louis, and going into the game he was hitting .379 and I had .377 and a fraction. At least that's what the newspapermen told me before the "kickoff." He'd only made about 170 hits all season to 239 for me, but he hadn't played as many games. And he was up there most of the year, and I had to hit over .400 the last three weeks to even get close. But there we were. Sam Jones started for them, and George Blaeholder was our pitcher.

Before the series opened, Dan Howley, our manager, asked me if I wanted him to throw left-handers at them, because Goose, like myself, was a southpaw hitter. I told him no. "But I wish you'd do one thing," I asked him. "Play Oscar Melillo at second."

We'd been playing a kid named Brannon . . . a fair hitter but not much of a fielder, and I figured I'd like Oscar out there to play Goose back on the grass. I'll say one thing . . . that Melillo made a couple of plays in the first two games that cut at least two hits off Goslin's total.

You see, Goose was a dead pull-hitter, while I hit more or less straightaway, and I recall in that series Lu Blue, our first baseman, played way back even when they had a man on the bag if Goslin was up. Later on, when Goose and I both were with Washington, I followed him in the batting order, and I used to get a lot of hits because sometimes

the other outfield, which would swing way around when he was up, would forget to move back again when I got to the plate, and I'd level one into left. Used to drive Al Simmons crazy with those pokes.

But anyway this particular day Washington was up first, and Goose lifted one into short right field. Earl McNeely, Frank McGowan, and Melillo all went after it, but the ball fell among 'em for a double. McGowan was playing right, and he roomed with me all season and he felt terrible. He came into the bench moaning: "Should have had it, 'Hein' . . . it was my ball."

Well Goslin was batting 1.000 then and, if I'm not wrong, I got out my first trip, so he had the jump on me, especially with two points to start. One of the Washington players told me afterward that Goslin, after that hit, had suggested to Jones that he keep walking me and that Sam refused. "No sir," he told Goose, the way I got it. "I'm going to stop him if I can, but he's entitled to a chance to hit under the circumstances." Anyway, that's what I was told. The game went on and, of course, I was out in left field. I was watching for Goslin to come up the second time.

All of a sudden I looked up and saw Sam Rice starting out from the dugout with a bat in his hand, and it was Goose's turn. For a second I just stood still, and then I let out a yell and began running in. I don't know what might have happened, because I was mad, thinkin' what they were gonna do to protect his average. I was going to stop the game, I know that, and raise a fuss with the umpires and maybe Goslin, and I would have wound up in a fight. But before I got there, Rice had gone back and Goose came out swinging two bats. Somebody—maybe Bucky Harris—must have decided to make him play it out. I know he didn't hit, and the next time I got to the dish I singled, and we were all even so far.

Ol' Sam Jones was pretty good that day, and the hit I got was a "slicer" over short. As it turned out he licked us, 9-1, and gave up only seven hits. They got a one-run lead on us, but Blaeholder was doing all right himself and got the Goose out a second time, so I picked up a little on him. Then came the fifth or sixth inning, whichever it was, and Goslin poled one right onto that ol' roof and they got four runs all told. He had nicked a foul off the end of his bat the previous pitch, and the ball had glanced off the roof of our dugout, barely away from our third baseman's hands. I thought to myself out there by the left-field stands: "He'll probably blast one now," and he did. The boys said later he must have guessed another outside pitch because he stepped

Goose Goslin

Heinie Manush

right into it, and he could get his bat around fast.

Howley sent in a left-hander named Wiltse to get things under control again, and he did, but Goose was 2-for-4 by this time and the Senators were slapping him on the back when he hit the bench. I knew that nothin' but a big rally by our side, which would let me get an extra turn or two at bat, could help. Maybe if we would have had Wiltse in there the whole game, he would have stopped Goslin cold, because he got him out in the seventh or eighth to make him stand 2-for-5 for the nine innings. But that's second-guessing, and besides, I popped up myself on a soft, side-arm curve in the sixth, so I had nothing to kick about. I still can see Harris, at third that day, circling under it, and I thought: "Even if he drops the ball, it doesn't mean a thing."

I got a triple in the ninth to make me batting .500 for the day while Goslin had hit .400, so as things turned out, I gained a point on him but that was just enough to lose. Howley and the boys tried to cheer me up by saying the official records wouldn't be out until December, and maybe I was tied or something, but I found out Eddie Eynon, the Washington secre-

tary, had the figures all tabbed before game time and knew that Goose had made it, .379 to my .378.

When we got in the clubhouse McGowan came over, and he was feeling pretty bad because if he'd caught that one in the first inning Goslin would have had 1-for-5 and I'd a won, .378 to .377, but I didn't let him say anything. What the heck, you do or you don't in baseball, and I've missed a few myself in my days and that's part of the game. But at least it was the closest finish in American League history, as far as I know, and there was something about the two of us, in the same park on the same day, battling it out, that made it a great afternoon, even if I had to lose.

Goose and I played on a pennant team for Washington five years later, but neither of us ever mentioned that game in St. Louis.

(Editor's Note: Heinie Manush spent 16 years in the major leagues, 14 of them in the American with Detroit, St. Louis, Washington, and Boston; the last two in the National with Brooklyn and Pittsburgh. He had a lifetime batting average of .330.)

Johnny Bench:
Baseball's Best Catcher

by Bud Furillo
Los Angeles Herald-Examiner

November, 1970

It is written that the good teams beat you with their bench.

Perhaps this is the literal explanation of why Cincinnati this season was such a superb team. The Reds have baseball's best bench, the only bench, Johnny Lee Bench of Potential Unlimited.

He set the Reds on the right track in the opening series of the 1970 season when he helped Cincinnati sweep three games from the Dodgers.

The final game of that April set was won on a two-hit shutout by rookie Wayne Simpson and a seventh-inning home run by Bench.

Reading a Los Angeles story which played up his role in the victory over Simpson's, the Cincinnati catcher gave script approval. In the presence of Bill Bruns, a journalist, he allowed as how "Simpson could have pitched a shutout for 26 innings and it wouldn't have done any good if we hadn't scored the runs."

Bench, 22, is aware of his worth. Reportedly, he once said:

"I'd be worth $3 million in five years if I played in New York."

On a team which includes Pete Rose, Tony Perez, and Bobby Tolan, Bench has scored a ton of runs. It wouldn't matter if Frank Howard, Roberto Clemente, Harmon Killebrew, and Hank Aaron rounded out the lineup; Bench would produce the most runs.

By season's end, he had hit 45 homers and driven in 148 runs, tops in the majors.

"Bench will be baseball's first $200,000 player," says Rube Walker, the old Dodger catcher who coaches for the Mets.

It takes a catcher to know one, and Walker sees in Bench what everyone else has seen. This young man is going to make everyone who caught before him look like a broken-down rocking chair.

You have to remember that he just completed his third season. He has a right to improve.

He may be the happiest fellow playing the game. Anytime a ballplayer works a night game in San Diego, flies to San Francisco, and returns a tele-

phone call before 10 in the morning, you know he is enthusiastic about his profession.

"I am enjoying this season as I have never enjoyed anything in my life," he said at the time.

"We have an attitude that beats everything. We've had it since spring when the new manager [Sparky Anderson] took over. Not that there was anything wrong with Dave Bristol. We wanted to play for him, too.

"But something happened this spring. Anderson did it. I call him John, as in John McGraw."

"How would you know about John McGraw?" I asked. The great manager of the Giants was dead before Bench was born.

"Everybody knows who John McGraw was," said Bench. "If you don't, you don't know anything about baseball.

"John [Anderson] and our coaches are beautiful people.

"Our pitching improved because of Larry Shepard. He's the pitching coach, and John gives him all the credit for what the pitchers have done.

"When a man believes in you as much as John does in me, you have to feel respected. He has brought me out from behind the plate to play other positions to give me a rest from catching. I almost played short one day."

Baseball's best catcher has played four spots other than the backstop. He can recall his achievements elsewhere.

"I've hit five home runs playing left field, one in

right, one at first base and none at third," he said. "It's great when I can take off from catching and still get my four at-bats every night."

Bench was asked if he is thinking ahead to playing regularly in the field.

"Catching got me here," he said. "I have no complaints. But if you catch 125 games, that's enough. Now I can play the rest, too."

Johnny's father was a catcher in the Army. He told his boy when he was able to understand that catching is what they needed in the major leagues. There was never any doubt in his father's mind that Johnny was going to be a major league catcher, dating back to the boy's play with Fort Cobb Little League in Cement, Oklahoma.

However, the old man never had any visions of grandeur, just the kid.

"I was four years old when I saw Mickey Mantle on television," Johnny said. "I idolized him because he was from Oklahoma like me.

"I grew up on dreams. I dreamed of being this guy or that guy, breaking this record or that one."

In no time at all, Johnny saw a dream come true.

As a rookie for the Reds in 1968, he led the league in passed balls.

He also was named Rookie of the Year because of a .275 batting average, 15 homers, and 82 RBI. He also ran three experienced regular catchers—Johnny Edwards, Jim Coker, and Don Pavletich—off the team with his gun.

"Every time Bench throws, everybody in baseball drools," says Baltimore executive Harry Dalton.

The Dodgers tested him the first time they met the Reds in 1968. They were sorry. Bench threw three of them out in one inning.

"I can throw out any runner alive," he has said.

Bench has this thing he calls inner conceit.

"Inner conceit," said John, "is a self-confidence kind of thing. It's knowing that you can do a certain thing, knowing within yourself you can meet any situation. A lot of young players lack that. It's really an air of confidence.

"It's inner conceit that tells me, 'this guy can't steal off me if he doesn't get too big of a jump. And if he gets too far off base, I'll pick him off.' I feel that a man taking a real big lead is trying to show me up, in a sense. It's the same with hitting. You have to feel that the pitcher can't get you out."

Johnny is from Binger, Oklahoma, population 650.

His dad sold fuel for farming equipment there.

"Binger is the agricultural center of the world," Bench said, proudly. "It produces peanuts, cotton, wheat, alfalfa, and sweet potatoes."

I asked Bench: "What does the sign say on the way into town, 'Welcome to Binger, the Agricultural Center of the World'?"

"As a matter of fact," said the catcher, "it reads, 'Welcome to Binger, The Home of Johnny Bench.'"

He is proud of his hometown because of another instance.

"They gave me a day in Binger after my first season with Cincinnati. And they had a banner that read: 'Our Rookie of the Year.' That was before I was actually voted Rookie of the Year. Binger has faith in me."

There was no need for half-day sessions at Binger High where Johnny played basketball as well as baseball. There were 22 in his graduating class—and he almost missed commencement.

It nearly ended for Johnny when the high school team bus lost its brakes on a turn, hit a guard rail, and flipped several times.

Bench grabbed his nearest teammate, threw him to the floor and fell on top of him. When ambulances reached the scene after the crash, two boys were dead and six were badly injured. Johnny was found unconscious, his foot sticking out the rear emergency door, but neither he nor the boy he fell upon was badly hurt.

There was another occasion when he was driving a car down home after his first year of baseball in the Instructional League. He was hit head-on by another car.

"I didn't know how badly I was hurt and I was terrified about winding up a cripple," Bench remembers. "I guess I was lucky because there was a doctor in the car behind me.

"He treated me until an ambulance arrived. They took 16 stitches in my head and 14 in my shoulder. One of the doctors said I would have had a broken hip for sure if I wasn't big-boned."

Bench is big everything, starting with cheekbones from being one-eighth Choctaw. He is also English, Irish, and Dutch.

"Look at his head," says Rose. "Did you ever see such a big head? On him a cap looks like a beanie. Puts glue in the lining to keep it from poppin' off."

He has big eyes, big hands. His high school nickname was Hands.

"On him a catcher's mitt looks like a golf glove," somebody said. It might have been Leo Durocher, who said: "Bench makes the tag at home like an infielder."

There have been other tributes, but one beats all for Johnny. He has this autographed ball from Ted Williams, and it says: "To Johnny Bench, a Hall of Famer for sure."

They'll Never Forget Dizzy Dean

by John P. Carmichael
Chicago Daily News

October, 1974

You took Dizzy Dean on faith. You had to, because he made a believer of you. Like when he was asked, more than 30 years ago, what was his greatest day in baseball, he replied: "Every time I had a ball in my hand and that suit on, it was my biggest day!"

But they all crystallized into the last game of the 1934 World Series between the St. Louis Cardinals and Detroit when ol' Diz had the Tigers beaten 11-0 with one out in the ninth and Hank Greenberg, whom he had fanned twice before, at bat. As Hank walked to the plate, Dean called time and took a few steps toward the Detroit dugout. "Hey," he called over there, "Ain't you got no pinch-hitter?"

Frank Frisch, the Cardinal manager, ran to the mound. "What are you doing?" he raged. "We got a lot at stake." Leo Durocher, the St. Louis shortstop, joined the conference. "Aw, come on, Frank," laughed Leo, "let Diz have a little fun." Dean chimed in: "Yeah, Frank, you're a great guy, but you worry too much."

When play was resumed, Dean struck out Greenberg, one of the game's greatest sluggers, on four pitched balls. Minutes later, the Cards were the champions of the world. Back in the clubhouse, where the din reached one crescendo after another, Dean went over to where Frisch was slumped in feigned exhaustion on a chair. "You know, Frank," said Diz, "you should take things more easier or, first thing you know, you'll have a heart attack."

Thirty years later, Frisch did suffer a seizure, and although he recovered at the time, he always blamed Dean. Now it is Dean who, at 63, has had all his great days numbered.

(Editor's Note: Dean died July 17, 1974, in St. Mary's hospital in Reno, Nevada, two days after suffering a heart attack.)

But his lifetime of accomplishments still lives. He made the most out of a relatively short career, and his record of 30 victories in 1934 stood for more than three decades after he had hung up his spikes.

Dean was only in his second full major league season in 1933 when the Cubs went to St. Louis for a series. It was Dean versus Guy Bush, the Cub right-hander, and at the end of the first inning, Dean was losing, 1-0. Frisch stormed at Diz as he came back to the bench. "If you don't get better, I'm sending you to the bullpen next inning." Diz grinned back and replied: "I didn't warm up good . . . you just start worryin' about getting me a couple of runs."

The game went on and Diz kept firing. He was oblivious to the number of strike-outs he was piling up, just kept pouring the ball in there. But Jimmy Wilson, his catcher, knew that, with two out in the Cub ninth, Diz had fanned 16 men, tying the National League mark for a single game held by Dazzy Vance, the old Dodger.

Charlie Grimm, the Cub manager, sent up rookie Jim Mosolf to pinch-hit. By this time, Dean had Grimm beside himself. "He kept makin' faces at me from the dugout," said Diz, "and callin' me a big, dumb busher and I never forget what he said: 'You look like you live in one of those Oklahoma penthouses', and I knew what he meant . . . a pigpen with venetian blinds . . . and I just stood there and laughed."

As Mosolf stepped into the batter's box, Wilson spoke up. "This is a helluva place to send a kid like you up," the Card catcher told Mosolf. "You better be loose because that Dizzy moron out there might stick one in your ear. He hates pinch-hitters." Then Wilson would give the sign and pound his big mitt right behind Mosolf's head. Dean put three pitches over the center of the plate, and Mosolf never took the bat off his shoulder. Dean fanned his 17th man for a new record.

Dizzy Dean (left) and his brother Paul, sitting next to him, each won a pair of games to lead the St. Louis Cardinals to a world championship over the Detroit Tigers in 1934. The photo was taken after Paul had turned back the Tigers, 4-3, in the sixth game on October 8. On the following day, Dizzy wrapped it up with an 11-0 decision over the Tigers. Also pictured are manager Frank Frisch, congratulating Paul, and catcher Bill DeLancey. During the 1934 season, Dizzy and Paul won 30 and 19 games respectively for the Cardinals.

The big guy with the high, hard one was a lovable braggart. The fans laughed with him, not at him, and they rejoiced when it turned out that he was kidding on the square. One day in Boston he got into an argument with his catcher, Bruce Ogrodowski, about the comparative values of a pitcher and a catcher. "All you have to do is catch the ball," Diz told him. "I'll throw it." Ogrodowski muttered something about giving the signs and directing the strategy of the game.

"That's a lot of bleep," said Dean. "I don't need no signs. I'll run my own game. You just hang onto the ball." Then he went out against the Braves, beat 'em, 13-0, and never took a sign from Ogrodowski. Moreover, he told each hitter who stepped to the plate: "You ain't gonna get nothin' but fastballs, so don't look for anything else, and be ready."

Dean had his troubles on occasions, most of them self-made. One of the most publicized was his run-in with Ford Frick, then president of the National League. Carl Hubbell, the great Giant southpaw, had beaten Dean 4-1 down in St. Louis. Dean was ahead in the seventh when umpire George Barr called a balk. Before Diz could recover his aplomb, the Giants had scored three runs to win.

Dean went to a banquet in Belleville, Illinois, that night and was quoted as saying that Barr was a crook and so was Frick, for that matter. By the time

Diz had rejoined the club in Brooklyn, he had been suspended without pay and ordered to apologize.

"I told Frick I never said he was a crook and I refused to apologize," Dean told newsmen. "Frisch was so mad he had me laughin', and I wouldn't have signed anything even if I'd been wrong.

"Then I thought of something else. I told Frisch I thought I'd sue Frick and the National League for slander, and he almost fainted. All he wanted was for me to get back in uniform and, after a couple of days night-clubbing around, ol' Frick saw the error of his ways and reinstated me, but I never signed nothin'. By then we were in the Polo Grounds to play the Giants and this time I beat Hubbell, 8-1, and would have had a shutout if Durocher hadn't booted one, and I let him know about it too."

Dean's career began to fade in 1937 when, during the All-Star game in Washington, he was hit on the foot by a line drive off Earl Averill's bat and suffered a broken toe. In typical Dean fashion, he tried to take his next mound turn for the Cards with a splint on the toe, wearing a spiked shoe with the toe plate cut out. But he couldn't bear down enough on that toe to make his overhand effective, so he began dropping down to a three-quarters sidearm delivery and he hurt his arm.

It never came back to its old resiliency, and in 1938 Diz was traded to the Cubs for two players and $185,000 in cash. He helped the Cubs win the flag that year.

In 1938 he had nothing left but control and a big heart. But he spaced his starts and beat clubs such as Cincinnati and Pittsburgh in crucial games.

Then came the World Series with the Yankees in which Diz reached back into his glorious past for one more effort to recapture the wizardry with which he mesmerized so many hitters for upwards of 10 years.

He was leading the American League champions 3-2 into the eighth with Lou Gehrig on first base. Then came disaster. Stan Hack, at third, and Bill Jurges, at short, raced after a bounding ball in the hole and collided. Both fell down. The ball rolled into left field. Carl Reynolds, the Cub outfielder, was backed against the wall and couldn't get to it in time, so Dean had to race out and recover.

Gehrig scored from first with the tying run, and moments later Frank Crosetti, the Yankee shortstop, homered over the left-field wall for ultimate victory. Dean had to leave the game, a dejected figure walking into oblivion.

"I didn't have nothin'," he said. "I had no license to beat anybody. But they coulda cut off my arm in that clubhouse if I'd won that one."

Lou Brock:
1974 Player of the Year

by John Kuenster

December, 1974

It has been a long time since major league baseball has enjoyed such a season as 1974, when historic individual achievements seemed to be the order of the day.

Hank Aaron broke Babe Ruth's record by belting his 715th career homer. John Hiller won 17 games in relief for the Tigers. Bob Gibson fanned his 3,000th batter. Mike Marshall appeared in 106 games for the Dodgers. Nolan Ryan pitched his third no-hitter. Al Kaline collected his 3,000th hit. Gaylord Perry won 15 straight games.

And Louis Clark Brock of the Cardinals stole 118 bases!

Brock not only stole bases in record proportions, but he also played a crisp defensive game in left field, scored a total of 105 runs, and batted a respectable .306 as he became the single most important motivator in the Cardinals' thwarted drive to win the National League's Eastern Division title.

"He's a one-man offense," said teammate Joe Torre during the thick of the division race. "He's the greatest single offensive force I've seen," said Cardinal pitcher John Curtis.

Baseball Digest doesn't quibble with the description and happily nominates Lou Brock as its Player of the Year for 1974.

Before he hangs 'em up, Brock will probably go down as the greatest base-stealer in the history of the game.

No question he set a one-season mark in 1974 that most likely will stand for a long time. And his career thefts (753) are second only to Ty Cobb's 892 among modern players.

When Brock erased Maury Wills' standard of 104 stolen bases in one season (1962), he received the plaudits of the man whose record he wiped out of the books.

"Brock is the youngest 35-year-old I've ever seen," said Wills. "He's as young at 35 as I was at 30. Lou always takes care of himself and he's in great condition."

Despite the constant slides into second base—and sometimes third—Brock escaped the terrible punish-ment that Wills absorbed in his record run more than a decade ago. That year, Wills' legs and thighs were bruised something terrible. Not so with Brock, and the reason can be found in the way he slides into the bag.

"I slide different than Maury," Brock admitted. "I was never able to perfect the hook slide. I didn't know which side I wanted to slide on, the left or the right. And I didn't want to have any indecisiveness about sliding. So I stayed with a very simple slide—a straight-in slide, a pop-up slide."

The technique has played an important role in his awesome base-stealing feats. One, it saves wear and tear on the legs, thighs, and hips, and two, it gives him maximum speed right into the bag.

"My theory," he said, "is to stay up as long as I can. Some of those hook slides you start from 15 feet out."

The other technique—well, maybe it isn't as much technique as natural ability—involves Brock's jump on the pitcher.

Sometimes, but not always, certain moves by the pitcher give Lou the key as to when he should go. From that point on, Brock's talent takes over. He has tremendous acceleration. He goes wham with the left foot, wham with the right foot, and he's driving at full speed for the next base in sight.

There may be faster runners in baseball than Brock, but none excel him in the exquisite timing of his break or in his explosive acceleration.

Brock is an instinctive runner. "When Lou speaks of a sixth sense," says Wills, "I know exactly what he means—knowing when the pick-off throw is com-ing and when it's not, knowing when a pitch-out is coming and when it's not. You have a feeling. From the count, the score, the mere fact that you're on base, that everybody knows you're going. And you know that the pitcher will rely on the catcher's judgment in calling the pitches, or calling for a pitch-out. Even the experienced pitchers. They all get flustered."

Merely by reaching first, Brock provided the Cardinals with an intangible plus on offense. And, he was on base 257 times in 1974.

In upsetting opposing pitchers, Brock reminds fans that the game is more than the roar of the home run, because the stolen base is the essence of base-ball at its best, an intricate blend of timing, instinct, and speed.

Since he joined the Cardinals from the Cubs in that unbelievable trade for a sore-armed pitcher (Ernie Broglio) in June, 1964, Brock has been instrumental in three National League pennant drives —1964, 1967, and 1968. After moving over to St.

Louis, Brock blossomed. He hit .348 and stole 33 bases for the Cardinals that year.

Stan Musial had retired in 1963, and the Cardinals in 1964 found Brock tailored to their needs.

"The Cardinals couldn't have won it with me in left field," Musial said at the time. "And with this kid [Brock was only 25 then], we're going to win a few more."

It was a prophetic observation.

Brock has since become an identity to be appreciated by the St. Louis fans and feared by Cardinal opponents. But he's a low key, unassuming sort and doesn't let fame distort his perspective.

He doesn't even think his base-stealing record is all that monumental.

"I look for someone to steal 150 bases before too long," he said rather casually.

Brock thinks the Dodgers' Dave Lopes some day may obliterate the mark.

"He has everything it takes," says Brock. "And that includes the one big ingredient, the guts to challenge the pitchers, catchers, and infielders. He picks his spots remarkably well, and he has a lot of pride."

Almost sounds like Lou Brock describing Lou Brock.

Tremendous acceleration and raw speed have made Lou Brock (left) the most productive base-stealer in the majors since Ty Cobb. In 1974, he set the baseball world agog by stealing 118 bases, a single-season major league record. Disappointed that the feat failed to earn him the National League's Most Valuable Player Award—which went to Steve Garvey of the Dodgers—Brock entered the 1975 season with hopes of eventually surpassing Cobb's lifetime record of 892 stolen bases. His career total stood at 753 thefts at the start of the season.

The Most Demanding Job in the Majors

by John Kuenster

July, 1971

In the not-so-long-ago, Pedro Ramos was on the mound for the Minnesota Twins and Earl Battey behind the plate in a game against an unremembered foe. Ramos momentarily lost his concentration after making a pitch, and before he knew it, zing, Battey rifled the return throw and it struck Pedro on the jaw. The force of the blow shocked Ramos out of his reverie.

"Dammit, Ramos!" Battey shouted. "Pay attention to me!"

When Ramos recounted the incident some years ago, he automatically rubbed his chin.

"Hit me right here," he said. "That Battey, he throws hard!"

The story is retrieved from memory because it illustrates one method (admittedly extreme) a dedicated catcher can use to keep his pitcher alert, on top of his game. Fire the ball back at him with some zip on it. Don't let the pitcher get lackadaisical. Make him work with you.

No question that Battey was a dedicated catcher —and a valuable one—during his tenure with the Twins. We always remember the day during a spring exhibition tour when Battey looked like the saddest man on earth. That was the day in the airport at San Juan, Puerto Rico, when a reporter interviewed him after he had just been traded from the White Sox to the original and lowly Washington Senators.

Cal Griffith had perpetrated grand theft when he inveigled Bill Veeck to trade him Battey (and Don Mincher and cash) for an aging, injury-plagued Roy Sievers.

For years, the Senators, with such receivers as Lou Berberet, Hal Naragon, and Clint Courtney, were patsies for the rest of the American League. Teams like the White Sox used to steal them dizzy.

But when Battey came on the scene, the fortunes of his new club improved rapidly. He had such a strong throwing arm that few runners challenged him. He, more than any other player, helped turn the Senators around, and in time, as the Minnesota Twins they became contenders and finally pennant winners in 1965.

At the time of the trade (1960), Battey was ready to take over the regular White Sox catching chores from veteran Sherman Lollar, whose legs were starting to go. Veeck knew this, but he had some mysterious yen to have Sievers (an old St. Louis Brownie) on his club, so he succumbed to Griffith's demands for Battey.

It was one of Veeck's worst deals. You don't trade away strong young catchers with the ability to handle pitchers, throw well, and hit for reasonable average.

In any event, and with due apologies to pitchers and shortstops, catching ranks as the most challenging and demanding defensive job in baseball. And the most important part of the catcher's job revolves

Montreal catcher John Boccabella is a study in concentration as he awaits the throw from a cutoff man. In confrontations with charging runners, protective gear may be a comfort to the catcher but it won't always protect him from injury.

Earl Battey of the Twins goes down on one knee as he blocks the plate against an onrushing runner. Violent collisions between catcher and runner at home plate are common in baseball and are a risk receivers have to take. In the 1970 All-Star game, catcher Ray Fosse injured his shoulder when Pete Rose barreled into him to score the winning run. In 1932, Carl Reynolds crashed into Yankee catcher Bill Dickey and sent him sprawling. Dickey got up, punched Reynolds, and broke his jaw. It cost him a $1,000 fine and a 30-day suspension.

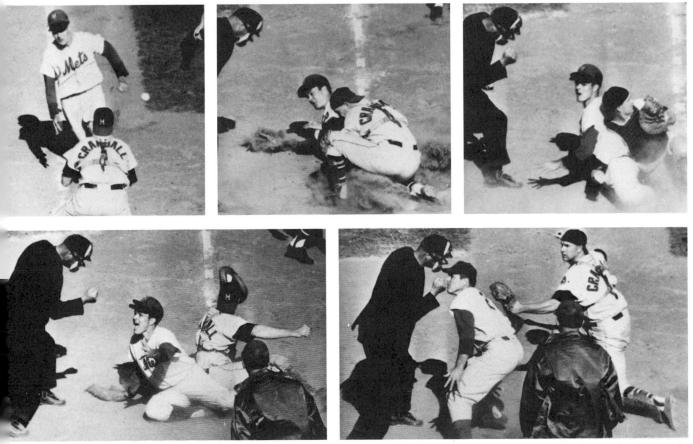

Ball and runner arriving at the plate almost simultaneously, catcher Del Crandall of the Milwaukee Braves deftly puts the tag on Joe Hicks of the New York Mets in a 1963 game at the Polo Grounds. Umpire Tony Venzon signals the runner out, and Hicks protests the call.

155

Mangled fingers are often the price catchers pay for trying to grab foul tips or pitches that bounce in the dirt. Cincinnati's Johnny Bench reacts defensively as an errant pitch skips past him while the Chicago Cubs' Ernie Banks looks on.

around his ability to take charge of the pitchers and get the most out of them, to run the game, and to set up the hitters.

The good catchers seldom call for a wrong pitch. They know the batter's strengths and weaknesses. If there's a runner on first and a left-handed hitter at the plate, they're going to call for hard stuff on the outside to keep the batter from pulling the ball. If the batter does go with the pitch and hits it on the ground, it's likely to go to the shortstop, and there's a good chance there will be a force on the lead runner at second and maybe even an outside shot at a double play. These are the little things that help win games and are often unnoticed by the fans.

Too bad. Smart catchers are invaluable. One of the smartest years ago was Bill Dickey of the Yankees. He had incredible insight into the habits of every man who came to the plate. Yankee pitchers always credited him for much of their effectiveness. Once he spotted a batter's weakness, he never forgot it. They tell the story of an old-time ballplayer, years out of the majors, running into Dickey one day in a hotel elevator.

"Hey, Bill, remember me?" he asked.

Dickey looked him over and said, "I don't remember your name, but you were a sucker for a high inside fastball."

Yogi Berra, who followed Dickey, was like a second manager for the Yankees, not that Casey Stengel needed an alter ego. Berra was a pretty shrewd operator when he squatted behind the plate. Yogi talked to everybody, and a batter could never tell whether Berra was being sociable because that was his nature or because he was trying to create a distraction.

"He just liked to talk," recalls J. C. Martin, a receiver with the Cubs and the 1969 Mets and who also spent time in the American League.

"I remember the first day I went to the plate against the Yankees, Yogi starts talking about the glare coming off the ball, so of course I start looking for the glare, and the first thing I know I've got two strikes on me."

Most good hitters will avoid repartee with the catcher while they are in the batter's box. They don't want anything disturbing their concentration. But some catchers try just the same.

"If I talk to Willie Mays when he's in the batter's box, all he'll usually do is grunt," says Martin. "One time he did say something though. He said, 'I just wish you'd quit talkin' to me.'

"Aaron's the same way. He won't say a word."

Catchers can be wily in their stratagems to throw the opposition off guard. Mickey Cochrane was a crafty one. In the 1929 World Series against the Cubs, he caught Howard Ehmke of the Philadelphia A's in the first game when Ehmke fanned 13 batters.

In the ninth inning, with the A's leading, 3-1, the tying runs were on base and there were two out when Chick Tolson came up to pinch-hit for the Cubs. The count went to two-and-two. Cochrane went out to the mound and formed his strategy with Ehmke. Cochrane went back behind the plate and gave a sign which Ehmke shook off. He gave another sign. There was another shake-off. Tolson didn't know it was all a come-on, designed to upset him. Finally, Ehmke nodded and delivered the ball. As he let go of the pitch, Cochrane shouted, "Hit it!" Tolson reacted abruptly to the command, swung, and missed. That was the ball game.

156

Memories of Connie Mack Stadium

by Jim Barniak
Philadelphia Bulletin

December, 1971

What do you say about an old ball park that's just been cremated?

That you couldn't get enough of it as a kid. Your father would sit you down in the upper deck in left-center and point to the number 5 on the back of the Yankee center fielder and tell you, "Now DiMag is the greatest of them all." And not being very impressed, you would respond, "You mean he's better than Barney McCosky?"

You became more indifferent as you grew older. You learned about other things. Baseball was no longer life and death any more and the trips to the ball park became less frequent. Later, your work as a sportswriter would take you there often, and many nights you hated the place. Nothing much thrilled you, except maybe one of those mammoth home runs by Rich Allen. And something awful was always happening, like the time you caught your new sport coat on a nail.

In a super piece of irony, Connie Mack Stadium was burning down one day last summer when many of the men who made its history were coming to town for an Old-Timers' Night promotion by the Phillies. Slaughter, Musial, and Feller. DiMaggio, Ennis, and Joost. And the Dodgers were in town with Rich Allen, who would surely be blamed for the fire by some.

In the reports in the newspapers, they called the place the Old Lady. Nonsense. Connie Mack Stadium was masculine, an old man who wore a blue collar and carried a lunch pail, a hardened cynic filled with prejudices, a hard-hat in a T-shirt who drank beer on the front stoop, straight from the can. Connie Mack Stadium was a tough old gaffer, and there were many who treated his demise with irreverence. They were glad to see him go.

Rich Allen shrugged his shoulders indifferently when he heard the news. "That place," he said, "has been dead for a long time anyway."

Oh? You couldn't tell by listening to the old-timers.

"It was a crummy place and all that," Rich Ashburn was saying, "but it had an atmosphere all its own. And it had something these new ball parks don't have yet. It had memories. I saw that picture of the fire in the paper and you want to know something? Tears came to my eyes."

There was the game in 1949 the Phillies forfeited to the Dodgers. Ashburn caught a ball knee-high in center field, but the umpire, George Barr, ruled that the ball bounced first.

"What an argument!" said Ashburn. "That was when fans could bring anything they wanted into the park. Beer, soda bottles, picnic coolers. Well, they started throwing everything. Finally, somebody hit Barr on the head with a tomato, and he called the game off."

Somebody once threw a sandwich at Del Ennis. He picked it up and ate it.

"Ham and cheese," said Del. "But what really bugged me was I was having a good day."

"I got my 1,000th hit in that old ball park," said Stan Musial.

Satchel Paige rubbed his chin and furrowed his brow when a guy asked him for a Connie Mack Stadium memory.

"Well, I remember they wouldn't let me and my boys play there," said Satch, recalling his barnstorming days. "We had to go out to 48th and Spruce. About the only way they'd let us play there was if Dizzy Dean was pitching for the other guys."

"My last year when I was with the Giants," Joe Garagiola was saying, "and Murray Dickson is pitching for the Phillies. He's got this underhanded, change-up curveball which I call an American Legion roundhouse. He strikes me out, and I swear I'll kill that pitch the next time.

"Darn if the bases aren't loaded next time, and I'm looking for the pitch so bad my mouth is watering. Here it comes and I smash it. Right back to Dickson. He throws to first for a double play, and I go back to the dugout fuming. Durocher says to me, 'Why the bleep don't you strike out and help the team?'

"Another time I hit a ball to the first baseman. It looks like a close play, so I slide into first. What I didn't know was that the ball went through his legs and was down in the right-field bullpen."

Eddie Stanky was telling about the time he used to jump up and down at second base to disturb the Phillies hitters. Finally, the umps tossed him out. But Andy Seminick was so mad he barreled into Stanky's replacement, Bill Rigney, and started a free-for-all.

"I was listening in the clubhouse," said Stanky. "I locked the door."

Connie Mack Stadium as it appeared in the days when it was known as Shibe Park, named in honor of one of the early owners of the Philadelphia A's, Benjamin F. Shibe. When the park first opened in 1909, it had a larger seating capacity than most of the other parks of the time. After the Athletics moved to Kansas City in 1954, the name of the park was changed to honor Connie Mack, manager of the A's for half a century. Later, the Phillies became tenants and remained until they moved into Veterans Stadium in 1971.

Seminick and Jim Konstanty remember the World Series in 1950. John Quinn remembers the ecstasy and agony of 1964, when the Phils crammed a million-four fans into the old ball park but ended up by blowing the pennant. And Bill Giles remembers futilely yelling, "Get off the field, get off the field" on closing night.

"I've been around here a hundred years," said Jimmy Dykes, "but there was nothing like the World Series game in 1929. We got 10 runs in one inning and tied the game, 8-8.

"I mean when we got the eighth run to tie the game, I pounded the guy next to me and yelled, 'We're tied, we're tied.' I pounded the guy so hard he goes right into the bats. His two legs are sticking up out of the bats. I say, 'Oh my God, it's Mr. Mack.'

"I ran over and pulled him up, and very apologetically I say, 'Gosh, Mr. Mack, I'm awfully sorry.' He says, 'Don't worry, Jimmy. Right now, anything goes.' "

Can't agree with you about the old place, Rich Allen. Sounds to me like the old boy was burned alive.

158

Rogers Hornsby's Five Fabulous Years

by Tom Meany

Condensed from the book
Baseball's Greatest Hitters

March, 1963

An earnest man, Al Spohrer attempted the impossible in the summer of 1929. He tried to talk Rogers Hornsby out of a base hit. Catching for the last-place Boston Braves against the first-place Chicago Cubs at Wrigley Field, Spohrer reached a decision which had been reached in advance of him by many another, and older, head. The decision was that Hornsby couldn't be kept from hitting by ordinary means.

Spohrer, who had been a teammate of Hornsby the year before at Boston, knew of the Rajah's fanatic devotion to steaks. Rogers was the original beef eater and in whatever town he landed, and he landed in several before he was through, he was always on the prowl for a place which served steaks better than any other place in that particular town.

The thought struck Al that if he could get Hornsby talking about his hobby it might take his mind off his hitting. Or, rather, off the Boston pitching which Hornsby was finding as appetizing as any steak.

"Say, Rog," began Spohrer conversationally when Hornsby came to bat for the third time, "my wife has discovered a butcher in Boston who sells the finest steaks anyone ever ate."

"That so?" said Hornsby with polite interest.

"Strike one!" bawled the umpire.

"Not only that, Rog," continued Al, really warming to his task, "but my wife can cook steaks better than anybody I know. Grace really has a knack of broiling 'em."

"That sounds good," commented Rogers.

"Strike two!" was the umpire's contribution to the conversation.

"What Grace and I thought," enthused Spohrer, "was that maybe on the next trip up to Boston, you'd come over to the house for dinner some night and try one."

"Crack!" That wasn't the umpire but the bat. The ball disappeared over the left-field wall of Wrigley Field and Hornsby began a slow trot around the bases. Then as he completed the circuit and put his spikes into the rubber of home plate, he turned to face the chagrined Spohrer.

"What night shall we make it, Al?" Hornsby asked.

The story of Spohrer and Hornsby had been told so often that it has attained the status of a baseball legend and, like so many legends, it may be apocryphal. The chances are, however, it is true; but true or not, it serves as a perfect example of the fierce concentration Hornsby was able to put in his task of hitting a baseball. Nothing, not even conversation about a succulent steak, could cause any deviation from the course he plotted.

To Hornsby, who died early in 1963 at the age of 66, there was only one way to play baseball and that was by giving it one's full and undivided attention. It was the begin-all and end-all of his existence. Many years after the dinner invitation extended to him by Spohrer, Hornsby was sipping a Coke at the bar of the old Auditorium Hotel in Chicago, talking with Bill McCullough, a New York sportswriter who was doing publicity in Chicago that fall.

It was a Saturday evening and the abstemious Hornsby was idly turning the pages of the final sports extra of the *Chicago Daily News*. The date was November 13, 1937, and the front page was filled with reports of the Army-Notre Dame game in New York. There were stories on Wisconsin-Purdue, Northwestern-Minnesota, Illinois-Ohio State, Michigan-Pennsylvania, Pitt-Nebraska—even one on Chicago and Beloit. There were photos and charts, color stories, and play-by-play.

The sports section ran eight pages and was a truly magnificent compilation of the day's doings on the gridiron. As Hornsby looked up one column and down another for some item about baseball without success, he finally put the paper aside.

"Lord, Bill," said Rog to McCullough, "there's *nothing* in the sports pages these days, is there?"

There was always an air of mystery to Hornsby, an air of mystery to his personal comings-and-goings, and an air of mystery to his departure from one club to another.

When Hornsby joined the Giants in the spring of 1927, after being traded from the Cardinals when he had brought St. Louis the first of many pennants, Ferdie Schupp, who had been with Rogers on the Cardinals, was questioned as to what manner of man Hornsby might be.

"Nobody knows," answered Schupp honestly. "He never talks to anybody. He just goes out and plays second base, and when the game is over he comes into the clubhouse, takes off his uniform, takes a shower, and gets dressed without saying a word.

Then he leaves the clubhouse, and nobody knows where he goes."

Hornsby didn't deliberately cultivate this air of mystery. He wasn't precisely antisocial. It might be more accurate to regard him in the light of a self-sufficient man. He needed nobody to lean on, any more than he needed anybody to help him up at the plate. It was this trait which led directly to his many tactless remarks. Rog always spoke his mind —and his mind wasn't always complimentary to his vis-à-vis.

There was no off-the-record stuff with Rog. If you asked his opinion he gave it, and he didn't care whether you printed it or not. It was all one with Hornsby.

When Hornsby reported to the Giants in the spring of 1927, McGraw was absent frequently from the Sarasota camp. He left the club in charge of Rogers. Fred Lindstrom, the third baseman, and Hornsby had an argument over the proper way to make the double play.

Hornsby wanted Lindy to fire the ball to him at second as quickly as possible. (Some said this was to save his own arm, so he wouldn't have to hurry to complete the relay to first base.) Lindstrom said that McGraw always instructed his players to make sure of getting the "head man" on double plays. In other words, McGraw wanted the force-out at second to be certain, preferring to get only one rather than to miss both because the throw to second base was hurried.

"If that's the way the Old Man wants it," snapped Hornsby, "do it that way when he's in charge. When I'm in charge, do it my way."

Lindy, like Hornsby, also could be outspoken. He told Hornsby that once he laid his bat down he was no bargain and not to get all puffed up with his own importance.

"I'm not arguing with you. I'm telling you," declared Hornsby. "You'll do as I say. And keep your mouth shut."

Hornsby paused for a moment to look at the other Giants. "And that goes for the rest of you," he barked. It did, too. Whenever McGraw left Hornsby in charge, and he did it several times, not only that spring but during the summer when the club was fighting for the pennant, Hornsby always took charge literally.

Awkward as was his position with the Giants, it was even more so the following season when he was traded to Boston. McGraw fled to Cuba when the trade was made and never did answer any questions about it. With the Braves, Hornsby joined a slap-happy club with a thoroughly confused front office

Rogers Hornsby

and a manager named Jack Slattery who had been a college baseball coach the year before.

Visiting newspapermen came to Hornsby for interviews in the spring. They knew Hornsby and they didn't know Slattery. There were rumors that Slattery wouldn't even last long enough as manager to get the club home from spring training. As a matter of fact, Jack mightn't have opened the season had the Boston papers not lined up solidly behind him.

At Miami, a writer traveling with the Dodgers accosted Hornsby in the hotel dining room.

"They tell me," opened the writer, "that this club has a chance for the first division."

"These humpty-dumpties," snorted Hornsby in honest disgust. "The first division? With what?"

When Slattery finally was let out, Hornsby at first refused to take over the managership. He felt that baseball would feel he had undermined Slattery. In fact, Slattery was doomed from the start because he never had a ball club. Judge Fuchs argued sufficiently to make Rogers assume the managership, and the Braves played the last two-thirds of the season under Hornsby, no better or no worse than they had played under Slattery.

Hornsby felt a genuine fondness for Fuchs, and he advised Fuchs to sell him that winter for what he would bring on the open market. It was then that he went to the Cubs, back to the playing ranks again under Joe McCarthy. Hornsby helped McCarthy win his first pennant in 1929 and at the end of the following season succeeded McCarthy as manager.

Once again Rogers was on the spot, but he had no more to do with McCarthy leaving the Cubs than he had to do with Slattery leaving the Braves. After the dismal showing of the Cubs in the 1929 World Series, the club was receiving second-guesses in carload lots. And McCarthy, one of the greatest managers the game ever knew, was not one to take second-guessing from the front office.

Hornsby lasted a season and one-half as Cub manager and was released outright, August 2, 1932. He left behind him a club which won the pennant under Charlie Grimm. There was no logical reason for Rog being let out by the Cubs. He was riding the players hard, but he felt that they needed it, that they had the best club and weren't putting out. His contention was borne out when the club won for Grimm. Maybe he should have used sugar instead of vinegar, but nobody had ever sugared up Hornsby. In fact, nobody ever had to.

In view of Hornsby's magnificent achievements as a batter, it may come as a surprise to learn that he was purchased by the Cardinals because that astute scout, Bob Connery, saw fielding greatness in the skinny kid who was playing shortstop for Denison, Texas, in the Class D Western Association.

Hornsby was a perfectly coordinated athlete. He had long, loose arms and sure hands and was a strong thrower. He always maintained that his fielding would have been good enough to keep him in the major leagues even if he had been only an ordinary hitter. Rog's batting was so sensational that his fielding skill, which he maintained even when shifted from short to second, was overlooked. Hornsby had only one fault as a fielder—he had trouble with pop flies. He had one of the great double-play arms of any second baseman in history, throwing straight across his chest with no perceptible shifting of his feet.

Another generally forgotten item about Hornsby is that he came up to the Cardinals as a choke-hitter who batted from a crouch, which may explain his .277 average with Denison. It was Connery and Miller Huggins who got him to adopt the stance he later made famous, standing well back in the box, farther from the plate than any ranking hitter ever did.

Hornsby stood with his feet close together and took a tremendous stride, stepping up to meet the ball. "It was impossible to hit me with a pitched ball," said Rogers, "because I always was moving with the pitch."

Because of this stance Hornsby could, and did, hit to all fields. Hornsby's stance had a lot of imitators, most of them unsuccessful. It is believed by batting theorists that only a batter who takes a stance with his feet close together, and thus is in a position to hit into the opposite field, can ever achieve the magic .400 figure. The only exception to the rule was Ted Williams, who batted over .400 in 1941 without hitting to the opposite field very often. Hornsby hit over .400 in three different years.

Probably Hornsby was the most devastating hitter baseball ever has seen through the five seasons of 1921, 1922, 1923, 1924, and 1925. Rog's averages for those seasons, respectively and respectfully, were .397, .401, .384, .424, and .403. In those five consecutive seasons, the Rajah went to bat 2,679 times and rapped out no fewer than 1,078 base hits. His overall batting average for the five-year period was .402, and his RBI average a more than respectable 140.

There is no question that the lively ball helped Hornsby. His average jumped from .318 in 1919 to .370 in 1920. And once his average went up, it stayed up until he was through. The fact that Rogers was aided by the lively ball is no reflection upon his hitting skill. The other batters of his time were hitting at the same rabbit ball, but Hornsby was outhitting them by so far that he led the National League for six consecutive seasons.

Hornsby had been gone from Boston a decade before Casey Stengel went there to manage, but the magic of Hornsby's name lived on. Braves Field had the reputation of being one of the most difficult parks in the National League for hitters. The prevailing wind was always from the east and swept from the mound to the plate.

One of Stengel's players, in a woeful slump, came back to the dugout, flung his bat from him in disgust, and started to revile the ball park, its architecture, and its prevailing wind.

"How the hell can they expect anybody to hit up there?" he wanted to know. "The wind is always with the pitcher. Nobody can hit up here."

"All I know," answered Stengel mildly, "is that Hornsby played here one whole season and batted .387."

The Day Fred Merkle Returned to the Polo Grounds

by Herbert Bursky

Fred Merkle

December, 1970

The pages of baseball history are rich with tales and anecdotes concerning the fabled events of September 23, 1908. It was on that day that a 19-year-old substitute first baseman of the New York Giants, Frederick Charles Merkle, did not touch second base in a key game against the Chicago Cubs, a contest that would be known ever after as the "Merkle game" and engrave his name indelibly on the folklore of baseball.

The Giants, Cubs, and Pirates were taut rivals for the 1908 National League pennant, and New York and Chicago were playing each other for the last time that season at the Polo Grounds.

It seemed as though the Giants had won when Al Bridwell drove in Moose McCormick with the apparent winning run in the home ninth inning. But Merkle, the runner at first, failed to touch second, a practice not uncommon in that situation among players of the time. Believing the game was over, he ran directly to the center-field clubhouse. Johnny Evers, the alert Cub second baseman, noted Merkle's actions and shouted for the ball. His purpose, of course, was to make a force play on Merkle at second and nullify the run. (The fans were streaming on to the field, and it has never been established clearly if the ball thrown to Evers by a teammate was the same ball that Bridwell hit.)

Merkle was ruled out by umpire Hank O'Day, a decision subsequently upheld by Harry Pulliam, National League president, and the National Commission, then the governing body of baseball. Despite strenuous protests by Giant manager John J. McGraw, the New York victory was disallowed and the game entered the records as a 1-1 tie. In a postseason replay of this famous disputed contest, the Giants lost both the game and the pennant to the Cubs.

September 23, 1908—on that day a young second-year player committed a spur-of-the-moment mistake which followed him unrelentingly to the last day of his life. There was, however, another day, a bright sunlit afternoon at the very same ball park 42 years later, a day I remember well—July 30, 1950. It was the day Fred Merkle came back to the Polo Grounds.

On the last Sunday of July in the summer of 1950, an Old-Timers' game was played at the Polo Grounds between the St. Louis Cardinals' Gashouse Gang champions of 1934 and the 1933 and 1936–37 Giant pennant winners. As an added nostalgic attraction, the Giant management invited Fred Merkle and Larry Doyle, members of McGraw's swashbuckling teams of the first two decades of the century.

Fred Merkle was 61 years old in 1950, and behind him were his 10 years as a Giant, four with the Cubs, a brief span with Brooklyn, and a period as a coach and part-time player with the Yankees of the Murderers' Row era. ("If I didn't think Merkle was a smart ballplayer I wouldn't hire him," snapped Yankee manager Miller Huggins.) Always, wherever he went and whatever he did, the cry of "bonehead" trailed after Merkle in much the same way as the passed ball of the 1941 World Series haunted Mickey Owen and the Bobby Thomson home run in 1951 cast a shadow on Ralph Branca.

The mocking cries, the slurs and the insults, the

bad jokes. They came from raucous fans outside the clubhouse before the game, from the stands and rival dugouts during the game, and then outside the clubhouse again after the game. They came from vaudeville comedians and unthinking acquaintances.

Fred Merkle heard the taunts in 1908, in 1909, in 1910 . . . and on and on through the years, but he continued to play and he played well. In 1927, through as an active player, he left baseball permanently. For 23 years he did not see a major league game.

Then, in 1950, he returned, with misgivings, to the scene of his anguish. New York had changed in many ways, but the Polo Grounds was almost as it was when he was a strapping young first baseman cracking line drives and playing on that lively 1911–13 championship infield with Larry Doyle, Art Fletcher, and Buck Herzog, and Christy Mathewson in the pitcher's box, and McGraw calling out to them from the dugout.

I was a teen-aged copy boy for the International News Service that summer, and I was scheduled to work on Sunday, July 30, but I wanted desperately to go to the Polo Grounds and see the old-timers. I had read voluminously about the players and teams of the past, and from my father I had heard much about the storied Giants who played for McGraw.

Luckily, a change in assignments was effected for just that one Sunday, making it possible for me to be one of the 35,000 fans who went through the Polo Grounds turnstiles on the afternoon of July 30.

There were cheers for the Giants and Cardinals of the 1930s when they were introduced individually—Mel Ott, Joe Medwick, Carl Hubbell, Leo Durocher, Blondy Ryan, Pepper Martin, Joe Moore, Rip Collins, and the others. Many of the fans remembered them. "Look at Lindstrom's feet," one shouted as the "boy hero" of the 1924 World Series assumed his batting position in the Old-Timers' game. "Just like the old days . . . same old Lindy."

Only the older fans remembered Merkle. To the younger ones he was just a name, a name inexorably connected with a celebrated incident in a game played in a far-off time when Theodore Roosevelt was President of the United States and no one knew about places called Belleau Wood and Tarawa and the Mekong River.

After all of the uniformed Giants and Cardinals of the 1930s had been brought on to the field, two graying men in street clothes appeared on the top step of the dugout. Larry Doyle was introduced first, the spirited second baseman, the one called Laughing Larry, who had said almost 40 years before, "It's great to be young and a Giant."

Then it was time for Fred Merkle . . . in the evening of his life, tall and heavy set, tanned from the Florida sun. Once again he was on his way from the bench to the plate, and a cheer went up from the stands which grew to a great roar. There were no catcalls on this day, no cries of "bonehead," only cheers, and I joined with the thousands and clapped my hands. Fred Merkle had played his last game years before I was born, and this would be my only chance to applaud him. After all, I was a Giant rooter, and Merkle, of all the Giants, had been most cruelly treated.

The fans were trying to tell Merkle something. I believe it went like this: "Yes, you made a mistake, not really such a great mistake when you stop and think about it, and you were roasted for it. But you kept on playing regardless of what they called you, so we are tipping our caps to you today. We can't make up for the hurt you suffered but we can give you our hearts today."

Later, Merkle said: "I didn't want to come back here. Now I sort of hate to go home. It makes a man feel good to hear such cheers after all those years. I don't think I'll forget. I expected so much worse.

"I spent close to 10 years in New York with the Giants, and believe me they were not all happy ones for me. I thought I never wanted to get back. I guess I was wrong.

"The fact of the matter is what I did was common practice in those days. The same thing probably had been done half a dozen times during the season, but nobody was ever called on it. The umpires decided to be technical just when I did it."

On East Forty-Fifth Street, in the city room of the International News Service, the boy who took my place made a clerical error for which I was later blamed. I didn't feel bad about it. My day had been a rewarding one.

Many summers have passed since July 30, 1950. The International News Service merged with the United Press. The Polo Grounds was torn down, and the Giants, whom I loved as only a boy can love a baseball team, moved to San Francisco without bothering to send me a short note of farewell. (My name was on their ticket mailing list.)

Fred Merkle died in 1956, joining in death Johnny Evers and Hank O'Day, the other principal figures of the 1908 game.

But the memory of July 30, 1950—a golden midsummer day when the sun was warm and the hearts of all around me were light with laughter and reminiscence—is still vivid in my mind. It was the day Fred Merkle came back to the Polo Grounds.

Big Klu: Muscles but No Malice

by Bob Hertzel
Cincinnati Enquirer

In his playing days, Kluszewski made a practice of trimming off the sleeves of his uniform, a not-so-subtle way of intimidating foes.

July, 1974

Big, Bad Leroy Brown may be the baddest man in the whole damn town, but even ol' Leroy wouldn't have messed with Klu.

Ever since that day so early in his career when he got mad at the company making the Cincinnati Reds' uniforms for not giving him shorter sleeves and he cut the uncomfortable things off, Ted Kluszewski has been a legend in his own time.

So large, so strong, so muscular, he was the gentle giant. He was the man who could tear you apart while licking an ice cream cone but he was also gentle as a baby fawn.

"Never really had a fight in my life," says Klu, now a coach for the Reds. "No one ever wanted to challenge me."

That isn't exactly a truism. There was that one day in Milwaukee, the only day anyone can remember Ted Kluszewski ever getting really mad.

Ernie Johnson, a string-bean relief pitcher, had just come in to pitch for the Braves, and, as Klu recalls the incident, "I hit his first pitch 900 feet but foul."

"That," remembers Johnson, now a broadcaster with the Atlanta Braves, "made me mad."

Ted Kluszewski couldn't hit the next pitch. It was behind him, a pitch carrying a dangerous message. Klu got the message and didn't like it. He decided he was going to get even. He dragged a bunt, and all 245 pounds of him roared down the line. Ernie Johnson went to cover first base, and Klu came down hard, trying to spike the pitcher.

Johnson went wild and started after Klu. Suddenly, common sense prevailed.

"I looked at him standing there, just waiting for me, and said to myself, 'You're smarter than this,'" Johnson recalls.

End of incident. Ernie Johnson lived to pitch another day. Klu's moment of madness ended.

Alvin Dark, once a shortstop and today manager of the Oakland A's, learned the hard way about the strength of the man. Dark was retreating to first on a tag play. Klu got the ball in plenty of time to make the tag. So Dark got tricky.

"He gave me an outside move and I fell for it," says Klu. "Then he came back to the inside. I reached out for him and buried my glove in his back about up to my wrist."

The result? Two fractured ribs for Dark.

Klu, though, wasn't looking to hurt anyone. He doesn't like to see anyone hurt. Solly Hemus, a former Cincinnati infielder, knows this well.

Hemus got mad at Rocky Bridges one day and went after him.

"I'm gonna kill him. I'm gonna kill him," shouted Hemus.

"You're not killing anyone," countered Klu softly.

Hemus had to oblige. He was, you see, a foot in the air, Kluszewski holding him by the scruff of the neck in one giant hand. Klu's strength didn't always manifest itself in such a physical manner. Sometimes he displayed it artistically, with the bat.

Ted Kluszewski played 1,481 major league games at first base from 1947 to 1961 and hit 279 career homers, including a season's high of 49 for the Reds

164

in 1954. And the power behind his swing was awesome.

"I remember Johnny Podres started for the Dodgers at Crosley Field," related Joe Nuxhall, a teammate of Kluszewski's and now a Reds' announcer. "You know the Dodgers have that white button on the top of their caps.

"Well, Klu hit one back through the middle. I swear, it hit the button on Johnny's cap. Podres wrenched his knee trying to get out of the way of the ball and had to leave the game.

"And Bubba Church. Klu almost knocked his head off. Hit him with a line drive right in the left cheek. They had to wire his jaws together and every other thing."

The fame of Ted Kluszewski grew from more than just having the most massive arms ever to be seen on a baseball diamond. It grew, too, because they were seen bare under those cut-off sleeves.

"I never wore any shirt under my uniform and that became a symbol," recalls Klu. "It had to get awfully cold before I'd put a shirt on, 30 degrees or so. When I was playing, the cold just didn't affect me.

"Then, four years ago we were in San Francisco and man, it was cold. I just had to put a shirt on. Everyone got on me real good about it.

"But I told them I didn't care. Even legends get cold."

Legends can get cold, just so long as they don't get old.

Big Klu follows the course of the ball as he unleashes his home-run swing in the first game of the 1959 World Series against the Dodgers at Comiskey Park. Kluszewski played first base for the White Sox. His drive landed in the upper right-field deck for his second homer in the game, won by the White Sox, 11-0. The catcher is John Roseboro.

Ted Kluszewski hefts some bats for the amusement of the Phillies' Richie Ashburn in a 1956 spring training photo taken in Clearwater, Florida. The year before, Klu had hit 47 homers and Ashburn had won the National League batting title with a .338 average.

Rollie Hemsley:
Bad Boy of Baseball

by Hal Lebovitz
Cleveland Plain Dealer

November, 1972

It was just a short few paragraphs on the wire one day last summer . . . Ralston (Rollie) Hemsley died at age 65, of a heart attack in Silver Springs, Maryland.

The story said he had been a major league catcher with seven clubs over a period of 18 years—and not much more.

His passing can't be written off that simply. In his playing days Rollie Hemsley received headlines—not so much for his performance on the field, but for what he did away from it. Particularly when he was a member of the Cleveland Indians.

In those days they called him Rollicking Rollie Hemsley and the One Bad Boy of Baseball. Each day reporters were fearful of waking up and seeing a headline about Rollie in a rival paper. Some writers waited in the lobby until the early hours of the morning—until they saw Rollie totter into the lobby and presumably go to bed. Even then they couldn't safely go to sleep. Rollie . . . well he was a story unto himself. He was colorful copy, a better yarn than the team itself.

Rollie once was hit on the head by a thrown ball as he tried to steal second base. He was woozy and the trainer, Lefty Weiseman, suggested he retire from the game.

"No," howled Rollie, "I've started games dizzier than this."

It was the simple truth. Rollie was a drinker, a rollicking one who couldn't pass a cup and who was unpredictable after his sips.

While a member of the St. Louis Browns, he once squirted a bottle of seltzer on a row of prim ladies who refused an offer to join him in a taste of the grape.

When the manager of the Browns, Rogers Hornsby, sought to clamp down on his players, mainly Rollie, he put a ban on almost everything: no reading papers in the clubhouse, no before-or-after dinner drinks on trains or anywhere else. Even movie going was taboo.

Rollie responded by getting needles and balls of yarn and knitting whenever he was in Hornsby's presence, infuriating the manager to no small degree.

This, of course, spelled the end for Rollie with the Browns, who a few years earlier had turned down sizable cash offers for him.

The Indians wanted Rollie—and got him.

Bob Feller was the reason. After the 1937 season, young Bob, the fire-thrower, went on an exhibition tour with an All-Star team. Hemsley was his catcher. Rollie, who never looked like an athlete, had no difficulty handling the wild Feller's fastball. The youngster was deeply impressed and advised his mentor, Cleveland general manager Cy Slapnicka, to get the catcher. The Indians gave up Roy Hughes, Billy Sullivan, and a minor league pitcher for Rollie, who reported to the Tribe's training camp in New Orleans in the spring of 1938.

The Indians had a new manager, Oscar Vitt, who quickly discovered Rollie had left his knitting behind—but not his thirst.

Within 10 days Hemsley had broken training three times. The third peccadillo belongs in a Mack Sennett comedy.

166

On the night of March 7, some old pals from St. Louis showed up. Reportedly, they had a connection with a brewery, and by the time the night was over Hemsley had staggered into one or more of his pal's fists, accidentally of course, and came out with a beaut of a black eye. Naturally he didn't show up for practice the next day, and photographers kept calling his room to set up picture appointments. Hemsley told them what to do with their cameras.

One intrepid photographer, Jimmy Laughead of the Associated Press, decided to outsmart Hemsley. He went to the hotel where the Indians stayed, tiptoed to Hemsley's room, got his camera and flash equipment ready, and then knocked on the door.

As Hemsley opened it, Laughead snapped his shutter. Unhappily, the flash failed.

Hemsley roared. Laughead turned and ran, with Hemsley, clad only in his pajamas, in full pursuit. Down the hall they went and down the stairs. But as they reached the lobby, Hemsley, realizing he wasn't dressed for a social function, stopped and Laughead dashed away.

But Laughead wasn't going to return to his office without a picture. Thirty minutes later he tiptoed to Hemsley's door again, got his camera and flash all set, and knocked.

This time, to his surprise the door swung wide open, but Hemsley wasn't in sight. The photographer stepped in. Too late, he saw Hemsley, who was standing on a chair alongside the door.

Bang, down on Laughead's head crashed a dresser drawer, knocking him to the floor, his face framed perfectly inside the broken drawer.

"There," said Hemsley, "take a picture of that."

By then Laughead concluded that Rollie didn't want his picture taken, and he left.

Hemsley departed, too. The next morning, Vitt suspended the catcher, ordered him to leave camp, and sent the traveling secretary with Rollie to the railroad station to make sure he used the ticket back to his home in Dixon, Missouri.

Hemsley returned within a week, promising to be good—and he was for short periods. Fines and lectures never had stopped him with other clubs, and Vitt's efforts proved just as fruitless. Rollie, in an effort to help himself, at his own instigation had a "good conduct" bonus clause put in his contract, but he couldn't allow himself to cash in on it.

Nevertheless he always could catch—"he was a better catcher drunk than many catchers were sober," says Feller—and he virtually became Feller's private receiver, causing some friction among the other pitchers and catchers. Johnny Allen, for example, decided he wanted his own catcher, too, and refused to pitch unless Frankie Pytlak was behind the plate.

Around Rollie, somehow, things always happened.

"In those days," Feller recalls, "whenever anything was wrong with a player it was blamed on his teeth, so Slapnicka decided everybody had to go to a dentist during spring training and get his teeth in perfect shape.

"Everybody went but Rollie, so the dentist came to the clubhouse to set up an appointment. Rollie put his hand in his mouth, took out his uppers and lowers, and gave them to the doctor. 'I'm too busy,' he said. 'Take these to your office and examine them.' "

Hemsley, only 31 then, didn't have a tooth in his mouth, and Bob still chuckles at the recollection.

Then there was the wild train ride in the spring of 1939. Hemsley had been on reasonably good behavior most of the spring. After breaking camp, the Indians began their annual spring exhibition tour with the New York Giants, both teams traveling from stop to stop in the same sleeping cars. The clubs were on their way to New York for a game in the Polo Grounds. Somewhere between Richmond, Virginia, and Washington, Hemsley decided 3 o'clock in the morning was a good time for everybody to get up.

Jim Dawson, *New York Times* baseball writer who also preferred something stronger than water, agreed with him. Dawson's prize possession was a trumpet, which he carried on trips. Hemsley picked up a couple of spittoons and together they paraded through the cars, Dawson blowing and Hemsley banging the brass spittoons like cymbals.

As the players awoke complainingly, Hemsley, deciding things were too quiet, struck matches and threw them into the upper berths. Mattresses caught on fire, the alarm was sounded, the train was stopped, and everybody had to run outside wearing whatever they were wearing.

Again Rollie was suspended, and baseball fans were provided with most unusual copy. The Indians sent him to a clinic for a special cure, but he flunked.

During the first week of the 1939 season, he was suspended again. After catching a Feller victory in Detroit, he decided to celebrate, and Vitt ordered him to return to Cleveland.

Now comes a story never before told. Feller revealed it.

"Rollie had a daughter he was crazy about. She later became Miss Missouri, a beautiful girl, and she died of cancer while she was in her early 30s. But at that time she was just a child, and Rollie always talked about her.

"Slapnicka gave Rollie a $1,500 diamond ring and told him it was for his daughter. Rollie was overwhelmed. He said in repayment he would quit drinking on the spot. But Slap knew Rollie needed some extra help, and without telling him, Slap provided it. He asked some members of Alcoholics Anonymous to meet with Rollie."

That part of the story came out a year later.

On opening day, 1940, in Chicago, Feller pitched a no-hitter against the White Sox. His catcher was Hemsley. The Indians won, 1-0, as the result of a triple by Rollie.

That night the catcher, thrilled by the game and pleased with the way his life was going, called a news conference.

He revealed how, the year before, two men met him as he got off a train. They asked him to attend one of their meetings, and from then on Hemsley became a firm member of Alcoholics Anonymous.

"I waited this long before saying anything," Hemsley told reporters, "because I wanted to be sure of myself. I haven't had a drink in a year and I want others to know the reason why, so they can be helped."

During the entire remainder of his life, no one ever saw Hemsley other than cold sober. His closest friends say he never took another drink.

Bob English, head of the R. L. English Co. of Cleveland, for whom Hemsley worked as a salesman in the late 1950s, says, "I've seen him have good reason to get drunk many times, but he would order a soft drink and nothing stronger, no matter what everybody else was drinking."

It was Hemsley who helped give AA its greatest publicity boost, and he worked tirelessly from then on to help others.

But even sober, baseball life never was tranquil for Rollie. He was a maverick. He was one of the ringleaders of the Vitt Rebellion of 1940, in which most of the veteran players went to the owner, Alva Bradley, and asked that the manager be fired. Among their many complaints was that he managed too conservatively.

Bradley stood by the manager, and the Indians became known that year as the Cleveland Crybabies. They lost the pennant in the final weekend of the season.

Vitt was soon fired, and the first to apply for the job was Hemsley. He didn't get it, and when Lou Boudreau became the Boy Manager in 1942, one of his initial moves was to trade Hemsley.

Rollie went to several other clubs, and eventually age ended his active career. Always he had one ambition—to become a major league manager. He nearly got the job with the Phillies while he was catching there, but, headstrong and outspoken, he refused to be quietly patient, and he lost the opportunity that almost certainly would have been his.

Later he managed in the minors with great success. Surprisingly, as a manager he was even more conservative than Vitt, rarely calling for the bunt. In the Cardinals' chain, he led the Columbus Redbirds and other minor league clubs to pennants, and he was being spoken of as the next Cards' manager. But they passed him up because they feared he wouldn't listen to the front office.

Rollicking Rollie Hemsley left his imprint on baseball history in Cleveland. Not as a hero, but as a human . . . very, very human, and his passing simply couldn't be shrugged off in a scant few paragraphs.

Josh Gibson: Greatest Slugger of Them All

by John Holway
Reprinted from the *Chicago Sun-Times*

March, 1970

His name was Josh Gibson. He may have been the hardest hitter in the history of professional baseball. Yet Josh Gibson, who used to wear the pinstripes of the Homestead Grays, doesn't even receive a mention in the *Encyclopedia of Baseball*. (Editor's Note: Gibson was elected to Baseball's Hall of Fame in 1972 by the Special Committee on Negro Leagues.)

His home runs have become legends. They exploded in Yankee Stadium, the Polo Grounds, Griffith Stadium, Cleveland, Philadelphia, and Pittsburgh. He and Babe Ruth were the first to put the ball into the trees beyond Griffith Stadium's centerfield fence. And in the Polo Grounds, Josh once hit one out of the park *between* the upper deck and the roof. It went out like a mortar round.

I saw Josh toward the end of his career, which spanned the last 17 years of the days when there were separate white and black baseball leagues. He died in January, 1947, just three months before the first Negro stepped onto the field in a major league uniform. Josh would have been 36 then, and, says his old teammate Ted Page, "they couldn't have kept him out of the majors."

Gibson was a catcher, as was Roy Campanella. Campanella worshiped Gibson and played against him nine years. "I couldn't carry Josh's glove," says Campanella. "Anything I could do, he could do better."

The Negro teams played 175 to 200 games a summer, and most players put in another three or four months each winter playing in the Caribbean. During the regular season they'd play seven days a week, sometimes up to three games a day. Often the opposition was a semipro club, like the famous Brooklyn Bushwicks, who sent many a player to the majors. The rest of the games were against other Negro teams. Gibson played in the eight-club Negro National, or eastern, League. Eight other teams made up the Negro American, or western, League.

Gibson was born in 1911 in the little town of Buena Vista, Georgia, 100 miles southwest of Atlanta, but moved as a youngster to Pittsburgh. He played sandlot ball in his teens and attracted the attention of the great William (Judy) Johnson, then manager of the Homestead Grays and perhaps the greatest third baseman ever to play the game. Johnson, now a Phillies scout and father-in-law of former Brave Bill Bruton, remembers Josh with gentle affection as "my boy."

"The first game Josh ever played, he played for me," Johnson says. "We were playing a night game in Pittsburgh in 1930, the first night game ever played in Forbes Field." A bus in the outfield contained the generator, and the lights were on huge extension ladders. "The park was jammed—they had to turn people away—and our catcher got mixed up with a ball and split his hand wide open. I'd seen Josh playing around with a playground team and he was in the stands. I asked him if he wanted to catch, and he said 'Yes sir,' and we held the game up while he put on a suit. Well, our regular catcher never did get back in the lineup."

Josh was only 19, but he was a sensation from the start. That's the year he hit the only fair ball ever hit over the Yankee Stadium roof.

"It went up over the roof of the third deck," says Grays shortstop Paul (Pee Wee) Stevens, "and came down just to the right of where the grandstand ends and hit the back of the left-field bullpen," which cuts deeply back into the bleachers. If Gibson had pulled it just a shade, it would have gone out. Says Stevens: "It was the highest, longest ball I've ever seen anyone hit." No one before—not Ruth or Gehrig—had ever hit one that far, and only two men since then have approached that gargantuan smash: Jimmie

169

Foxx put one into the upper left-field stands just below Gibson's blast, and Mickey Mantle lined one against the facing of the roof in right.

Campanella says Gibson hit 75 home runs that year and 67 the next. Teammate James (Cool Papa) Bell counted 72 in 1933. (Of course Gibson was playing 200 games a year, both league games and semipro games.)

In addition to Gibson and Judy Johnson, that Grays team had the great Oscar Charleston at first base.

George Scales and Stevens were the double-play combination, and the outfield included Ted Page, Vic Harris, and Jud Wilson, better known as Boojum because of the sound his line drives used to make rattling against the right-field wall. The pitching staff included Smokey Joe Williams, who is usually linked with Satchel Paige as one of the best right-handers in the Negro leagues, Bill Foster, Lefty Williams, and Ted (Double Duty) Radcliff, who could pitch one day, catch the next, and threw a wicked emery ball, which he gripped with the gnarled fingers of a catcher's battle-scarred hand.

Gibson, meanwhile, was filling out into a six-foot 200-pounder, a right-handed hitter who stood flat-footed in the box, taking hardly any stride. He was one of the first of the modern wrist-hitters. When Ruth or Foxx swung and missed, they often ended up sitting on the ground or with their legs twisted into corkscrews from the force of their swings. Gibson always kept his balance. Gibson hit hard and consistently.

He led the league with .457 in 1936 and .440 two years later. J. Royal (Skink) Browning of Washington, former catcher with the Indianapolis Clowns, says Gibson was more consistent even than Ted Williams. "I saw Ted hit three home runs in one game in Fenway Park," he says. "I've seen Josh do that many times."

And Gibson was fast. "He could steal bases for a big man," says Walter (Buck) Leonard, who joined the club a few years later and went on to win a reputation as the Negro Lou Gehrig. Old-timers agree that Gibson was neither the Negro Leagues' best hitter nor best catcher. They unanimously agree, however, that he was the hardest hitter.

At first, Gibson "couldn't catch a sack of balls," remembers Ted Page. "On foul balls he was terrible. We called him Boxer because he'd catch like he was wearing a boxing glove." It was Judy Johnson, the old third baseman, who began to make a catcher out of the muscular but awkward young man. He taught Josh how to get under foul balls and how to handle bad pitches.

Gibson worked hard learning. He even caught batting practice to sharpen his skills. Says Johnson: "He'd come to me and say, 'Jing (another Johnson nickname), what did I do wrong today?' and I'd say, 'Josh, you caught a real nice game.' That boy was game. I've seen the time Josh had his finger split and tied a piece of tape around it and played just as though nothing had happened. You think these kids now would do that? Never happen."

Gibson learned how to handle every pitch they threw at him, and in the Negro leagues that meant everything: spitters, screwballs, mud balls, and "shine balls" so laden with Vaseline, says Bell, "it made you blink your eyes in the sun."

Johnson didn't have to teach Gibson to throw. "Nobody," says Page, "threw better, more accurately, or quicker." Bell agrees that Campanella was a better defensive catcher than Gibson. "Josh dropped a lot of balls," Bell says. "He didn't have the sure hands Campanella did. But Gibson was a smart catcher. He was smart and he was fast. Sometimes he just dropped the ball on purpose to get some guy to run. And he threw a light ball; you could catch it without a glove. Campanella threw a brick."

Bell says Gibson had his own system for signaling pitches to the outfielders. If he stood up with his glove across his chest, it meant a fastball was coming; if he held it down at his side, it meant a curve. It was an era of shameless sign-stealing. One manager kept his eyes glued to Gibson's muscular right forearm. If the muscles twitched twice, he knew Gibson had just flashed two fingers for a curve.

In 1934 practically the whole Grays team jumped to Pittsburgh, where it became known as the Crawfords, and Monte Irvin calls that the best team of all time because, in addition to the other stars, it included Satchel Paige. The Crawfords soon began advertising that Josh would hit at least one homer and Satch would strike out the first nine men he faced.

That October the Negro All-Stars hooked up in a barnstorming tour with Dizzy and Paul Dean, fresh from their World Series victory over Detroit. Paige recalls that they played nine games, and the Negro All-Stars won seven. Dean won the only two for the big leaguers, but in York, Pennsylvania, Bell says, "in the first inning, I hit, Jerry Benjamin hit, Leonard walked, and Josh hit it over the fence. Next time up, Gibson hit another four-run homer. The people started booing and Diz went into the outfield for a while; he hated to just take himself out of the game." At game's end, Diz trotted past the All-Stars' dugout, mopped his face, and puffed, "Josh, I wish you and Satchel played with me on the Cardinals. Hell, we'd win the pennant by July 4 and go fishin' until World Series time."

Later, in New York, Gibson hit one of Dizzy's pitches so deep to center field that Bell tagged up and scored all the way from second before the relay reached the plate.

In 1936 the Crawfords broke up. Paige moved out west to the Kansas City Monarchs, and Gibson returned to the Homestead Grays.

After that winter season, Gibson and Paige were adversaries, facing each other in the Negro World Series and the annual East-West, or All-Star, games. Gibson was elected to every All-Star team from 1933 to 1945, with the exception of 1941, when he jumped to Mexico and Campanella won the vote of the fans. In 12 games Josh hit an even .500.

Satchel Paige maintains that Gibson and Ted Williams were the two toughest hitters he ever faced, adding that Gibson hit more homers than Ted. He still winces at the memory of one Gibsonian clout against the center-field clock in Comiskey Park. Yet Satchel had a reputation for getting Gibson out. He once reportedly walked two men just to pitch to Gibson, then struck him out.

Radcliff scoffs at the story. "Josh hit three homers one day off Satchel in Wrigley Field, Chicago," he says, "then tripled off the top of the right center-field fence. Josh would hit anybody."

He hit the big-leaguers just as freely. In 1937 he joined a barnstorming tour against a National League All-Star squad.

According to Campanella, one impish young shortstop with the semipro Brooklyn Bushwicks finally figured out how to stop Gibson. The kid's name was Phil Rizzuto, and he froze the balls in a freezer overnight to be sure they'd be dead as rocks by game time.

The balls were already dead enough. The Negro League usually couldn't afford regulation Reach or Spalding balls. It's a good thing, says Radcliff with a grim shake of the head. "If the balls had been lively, Josh would have killed somebody."

That team wrote the most impressive record in modern baseball: between 1937 and 1945 it won nine straight pennants. (The Yankees, in the same span, won six.) In 1946 Gibson again hit more homers (27) into the Griffith Stadium bleachers than the entire American League (13). Papers began referring to him as the Brown Bambino.

But it was a hard life and they played for the love of the game. Gibson's biggest payday came in 1942, when he and Brick Leonard staged a double hold-out, for $1,000 a month plus a dollar a day eating money. (The Grays were outdrawing the Senators at the gate.)

Gibson accepted the rules of Jim Crow philosophically. "He loved life," Ted Page says, "and when others would start to complain about things they didn't have, I remember him making the remark that one of the greatest things his dad ever did for him was to bring him out of Georgia to the North.

"Josh was one of the happiest persons in the world until about the late 1940s. Then he began to realize that he was perhaps the greatest hitter in the world and yet he was deprived of a chance to make $20,000-$30,000-$40,000 while Babe Ruth had pulled down $80,000. He realized that he was just as good as Ruth."

In 1945 Josh led the Negro National League at bat with .393. Campanella finished fourth at .365, and over in the Negro American League, Sam Jethroe was making a name for himself with a league-leading .398. Baseball Commissioner Kenesaw M. Landis had died, and rumors bubbled up again that at last a Negro would be given a chance in the majors. By the following year the rumor was fact: a youngster named Jackie Robinson would get the big chance that every black hitter had been seeking for decades.

That year Josh's average dropped to .331, though he still led the league in homers and was only a few points below another bright young prospect, second baseman Larry Doby of Newark, who hit .339. Monte Irvin, also of Newark, led the league with .389 and won a contract with the Giants. But there was no contract offer for Josh Gibson, who was by then 35 years old and who had ballooned to 230 pounds.

He began to drink and had to be sent to St. Elizabeth's Hospital for two weeks to dry out. Some old friends think he was worried because he and his wife had separated, but Bill Yancey thinks differently. When Campanella got a Dodger contract, he says, Gibson didn't know what to do. "He was a frustrated man."

On a cold Saturday night in January, 1947, Josh bumped into his old friend Ted Page on a Pittsburgh street corner. "He was like always, full of play and kidding around," Page recalls. Gibson returned to his mother's home half drunk and with a headache. In the morning he still complained, a doctor was called, gave him a shot, and put him to sleep. Gibson never woke up. His old friends, Page and Judy Johnson, heard the news by radio and were stunned. "People say Josh Gibson died of a brain hemorrhage," Page says, "but I say he died of a broken heart."

Hank Aaron's Major League Debut

by Bob Hertzel
Cincinnati Enquirer

Hank Aaron joined the Milwaukee Braves in 1954 as a wiry, 20-year-old second baseman but was converted into an outfielder in his first major league season. His rookie year was marred by a broken right ankle suffered on September 5, but he still managed 13 homers as his long pursuit of Babe Ruth's record began. This photo of him was taken on March 3, 1954.

December, 1974

A little more than 20 years ago a skinny and, in his own words, "terrified" rookie made his major league debut. The city was Cincinnati and the ball park was old Crosley Field.

That player is Henry Aaron, the all-time home-run champion, who says Cincinnati is "one city I hold dear."

The ties between Aaron and Cincinnati are deep, going back to that moment in 1954 when he played in his first major league game and went "0-for-4 or 0-for-5, I forget which."

That day, according to Aaron, was the most memorable of a career that is filled with memories covering some exciting moments in the majors.

"You read about the other guys and you play against them in spring training," remembers Aaron. "But this was getting down to the nitty-gritty. Then you find out everything's the same as in spring training."

Aaron's first game, which Joe Nuxhall pitched, was a 9-8 Cincinnati victory. Jim Greengrass, a Reds outfielder, set a record with four doubles, three of them into the sun deck in right.

And, Nuxhall recalls, he hit outfielder Andy Pafko in the head with a pitch.

Aaron thought back to that day 20 years ago, and his memories are hard to fathom today, 733 home runs later.

"I didn't know what might happen," he said. "Like any other rookie I kept my bags packed. I didn't know whether I was going back to the minor leagues or not. It was a terrifying question, especially for a young kid with a family."

The start Henry Aaron got off to was something less than spectacular.

"A typical rookie start," was the way he described it. "I was just fortunate to be playing for Charlie Grimm, who gave me a chance and stuck with me."

That same year, 1954, provided Aaron with another memory of Cincinnati, a broken ankle.

"Yeah, I had my first operation in Cincinnati," he smiled. "I've had two since then."

He also got a chance to have a friendship blossom. Pete Titus then was a postal employee whom Aaron had met. The friendship grew while Aaron was in the hospital.

"He'd come visit and his wife would prepare food for me," Aaron remembered.

Today he calls his friendship with Titus and his wife as good as any he's made in baseball.

"We'd go out after games, have a couple of drinks, talk baseball, and share our problems," said Aaron.

Cincinnati and Aaron continued to go hand-in-hand, becoming closer as the legend of the man grew.

In 1970, with Wayne Simpson pitching in Crosley Field, Aaron beat out an infield grounder behind second base. It was the 3,000th hit of his career.

Did that mean more than the 714th home run he was to hit opening day 1974 in Cincinnati's Riverfront Stadium off Jack Billingham?

"I'd have to say yes," Aaron answered, surprisingly. "I'd been chasing it so long."

The record books will state that Aaron is the all-time home-run champion. But really he looks not the part, and his record is not like that of Babe Ruth with 60 in one spectacular season and 59 in another.

"What people forget," said Aaron, "is that I've played a lot of baseball games. I've gone to the plate a lot of times and that's the secret. The only other thing different in my case from a lot of players is that I have been more consistent."

For 20 years Henry Aaron has been as consistent as the sunrise.

172

The Day a Midget Batted As a Major-Leaguer

by Bob Broeg
St. Louis Post-Dispatch

Eddie Gaedel

March, 1972

Bud Blattner, the former big league infielder now broadcasting for the Kansas City Royals, remembers how puckish Bill Veeck first got the notion to use a midget in a major league ball game.

This was in 1951, when Veeck, who worked wonders at Cleveland, was finding that even Merlin the magician couldn't bestir the Browns out of last place or their fans out of their atrophy and apathy.

"If only we could just get the first man on base in an inning," moaned Veeck to the Browns' broadcaster Blattner.

Back there on August 19, 1951, celebrating the American League's golden anniversary season, Veeck pulled out all the stops to please a crowd of 20,299, which was mighty good for a ball club that was in last place, 37 games behind co-leaders Cleveland and New York.

Fans were given birthday cake, ice cream, and souvenirs when they entered the park. Between games of a doubleheader with Detroit—sure, the Browns lost the first one—an eight-piece band paraded in Gay '90s attire. Antique cars and cycles circled the running track at Sportsman's Park.

A juggler juggled at first base. Trampolinists somersaulted at second. Hand-balancers pyramided at third.

A four-piece Brownie band paraded onto the diamond, with Satchel Paige on the drums, Al Widmar playing the bull fiddle, Ed Redys playing an accordion, and Johnny Berardino, now the movie actor, manipulating the maracas.

Aerial bombs exploded, sending miniature flags floating onto the field. Then popping out of a papier-mâché cake and wielding a miniature bat came a cute little fellow dressed in a Browns' uniform.

The midget, of course. Blattner knew that Veeck had seen a three-foot-seven, 65-pound Chicago stunt man in his office. His name was Eddie Gaedel.

The crowd laughed then but gasped in surprise a half-inning into the second game when field announcer Bernie Ebert intoned over the P.A.:

"For the Browns, No. 1/8, Eddie Gaedel, now batting for Frank Saucier."

Umpire Ed Hurley insisted on seeing the contract manager Zack Taylor brandished when beckoned from the dugout, but the red-necked Irish umpire took it calmly. So did the Detroit battery—pitcher Bob Cain and catcher Bob Swift.

Veeck, the P. T. Barnum of baseball, had admonished the midget, "If you so much as swing that bat at the plate, I'll kill you. No, I won't, but I can get the job done cut-rate because you wouldn't be hard to hide."

Swift couldn't make up his mind whether to try to take the pitches sitting down, but finally decided he'd kneel. Cain wanted to pitch underhanded but, no, the catcher said he'd have to do it correctly. And with Gaedel crouching as coached by Veeck, the pitcher walked the smallest baseball batter ever on four pitches.

Cain actually laughed as Gaedel trotted down to first base. The pitcher could afford to be charitable. The Browns loaded the bases. But, as usual, they didn't score and, also as usual, lost.

Gaedel, replaced by Jim Delsing, reached up to give his pinch-runner an encouraging pat on the rump and retired amid cheers.

Later, after showering, the midget was in the press box. I propped him on the ledge, so I could watch the game and interview him, too.

"For a minute," he said, "I felt like Babe Ruth."

I told him that he was now what I wished I'd become.

"What's that?" he asked.

A former big-leaguer.

Eddie Gaedel's chest suddenly puffed with pride. Two nights later, filled to his half-pint gills just about the time stuff-shirted, high-collared American League president Will Harridge was expunging Edwin F. Gaedel's name from the official records, the little man was arrested—for abusing a cop!

Bill Veeck —
The Game I'll Never Forget

as told to George Vass

March, 1972

There are two games that are very close in importance to me among the many I saw in my years in baseball, and yet it's not hard to choose between them as to which was the most important.

One of those games would be the one in which our Cleveland Indians defeated the Boston Red Sox in the playoff for the American League pennant in 1948. That's the one in which Lou Boudreau hit the two home runs.

The other one also was a game in 1948, and that would really have to be the big one in my memory, the game I'll truly never forget. That's the one Leroy Paige pitched at Comiskey Park against the Chicago White Sox after he joined the Indians in 1948.

How could I ever forget that game! According to the records Satch drew 51,013 fans, the largest ever to see a night game at Comiskey Park. But in point of fact there were probably 70,000 people there.

The people just surrounded the park and threatened to break the gates down. I asked Mrs. Grace Comiskey, owner of the White Sox, "Why don't you just let them in before they break the fences down?" It was an incredible sight. People were coming around the gates, over them, under them, milling all over the place.

The crowd was so great that they simply burst through the police lines like a tidal wave and swamped the turnstiles. They were jammed together so tightly underneath the stands that it was impossible for them to leave, even if they had wanted to. And nobody wanted to, that's for sure.

I didn't even have a seat, it was so crowded. I got tickets for Sidney Schiff, one of my partners, who came with a group. It took them three-quarters of an hour to fight their way in from the cab that brought them to the park from the hotel.

Not having a place to sit, I was pushing my way through the crowd when I noticed Schiff and his group crouched against the railings far from the seats they were supposed to have. I asked, "What are you doing here? Why aren't you in your seats?"

Schiff said, "Joe Louis and a group of his friends are in our seats and I'm not about to fight him for them."

It was just an incredible sight, and it was a vindication to me after the furor that had been aroused when I signed Paige. People were accusing me of making a travesty of the game, of creating a cheap publicity stunt by signing Satchel, who was supposed to be between 42 and 55 years of age.

Taylor Spink of the *Sporting News* wrote a ferocious, long editorial in which he ripped me up and down. He was my most vocal opponent. Every time Paige pitched, I'd send Spink a wire about the results: five hits, seven strike-outs, no runs. Finally, Spink wrote another editorial apologizing to me.

My vindication was complete the first full game Satch pitched for the Indians, that night of August 13, 1948, when it seemed as if all Chicago turned out to see what he could do against the White Sox.

He did all that could be expected right from the start. He was in control all the way in that game with his assortment of fastballs, hesitation pitches, and "bat dodgers." He threw overhanded and three-quarters. He kept the Sox popping up, and he didn't walk a man all night. All the Sox could get off him were five singles.

Satch always could rise to the occasion like that. For Satch, it was the big ones that counted, and this was a big game for us when you consider we had to go all the way to a playoff for the pennant and were never ahead by much all season.

So all he did that night was beat the White Sox, 5-0, in a game that was all-important in several respects—for the Indians, for myself, and for him, in that it proved he could go nine innings without trouble. It certainly showed our detractors that this wasn't just a cheap publicity stunt, that we got Paige because we thought he could help us win a pennant.

After the game, naturally, I went to the locker room to see Satch. He gave me that funny little grin he always had after a game.

"I kept 'em from running us both out of town," he said, referring to the fuss that went up when we signed him. He was soaking his arm in hot water, as he always did for an hour after a game, and he added, "Never in doubt, burrhead." He always called me burrhead.

Last summer, when I went up to Cooperstown to see him inducted into the Hall of Fame, he again made reference to the fact we were both on the spot in that game in Chicago in 1948. "Never in doubt, burrhead."

I can still see him, leaning over, looking at the catcher, giving Luke Appling of the Sox that triple windup, the hesitations, the slow, slow, and slower treatment until Luke was ready to pounce on the ball and beat it to death.

Of course, that was the big one, but he pitched just about like that the rest of the season for us. A week after that game in Comiskey Park he again beat the White Sox, this time, 1-0, in Cleveland in a game that drew 78,342—at that time the largest crowd ever to see a night game.

He was a tremendous help to us the last two months of that season. I don't believe we could have won the pennant without him in 1948. He had a 6-1 record, he saved two or three other games, and he came up with the big ones when we needed them.

You wouldn't believe some of the criticism that was directed against us when we signed him in July.

A lot of people said I was just trying to hypo attendance and that I could possibly hurt the Indians' chances for a pennant. They charged that as great a pitcher as Satch might have been in the Negro leagues he was washed up, and it was too late for him to pitch in the majors.

They also said a lot of other things which weren't as nice.

But it all stopped after that game he pitched against the White Sox in Comiskey Park. That was complete vindication for both of us and it was one of the major steps we took that season in winning the pennant for Cleveland for the first time since 1920.

As Satch said, he kept 'em from running us both out of town.

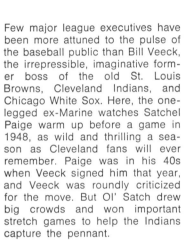

Few major league executives have been more attuned to the pulse of the baseball public than Bill Veeck, the irrepressible, imaginative former boss of the old St. Louis Browns, Cleveland Indians, and Chicago White Sox. Here, the one-legged ex-Marine watches Satchel Paige warm up before a game in 1948, as wild and thrilling a season as Cleveland fans will ever remember. Paige was in his 40s when Veeck signed him that year, and Veeck was roundly criticized for the move. But Ol' Satch drew big crowds and won important stretch games to help the Indians capture the pennant.

How Old Alex Clinched the 1926 World Series

by Dwight Chapin
Los Angeles Times

October, 1971

On the day that Jesse (Pop) Haines, the ex-St. Louis Cardinal pitcher, was inducted into the Hall of Fame last summer, memories were revived of Grover Cleveland Alexander. And a moment more than four decades ago.

It was one of baseball's most enduring memories.

St. Louis had never won a World Series but now, in 1926, they were one game from victory.

Alexander—Ol' Pete, one of the best right-handed pitchers who ever threw a baseball—had put the Cardinals where they were, by beating the New York Yankees of Ruth and Gehrig and Pennock 6-2 in the second game and 10-2 in the sixth.

In the clubhouse after the sixth game, Cardinal manager Rogers Hornsby is supposed to have told Ol' Pete, "Alex, if you want to celebrate tonight, I wouldn't blame you. But go easy, for I may need you tomorrow."

Years later, Alexander insisted that his reply to Hornsby was: "OK, Rog. I'll ride back to the hotel with you, get some sleep, and then meet you tomorrow morning and ride out to the park with you."

But there's the story that Alexander was as familiar with booze as with baseball and never needed an excuse—like a World Series victory—to celebrate. That version says Alex's personal victory party lasted all night and well into the next day, the day of the deciding game.

The St. Louis starter was Pop Haines, a knuckleballer. He'd blanked Murderers' Row in the third game, 4-0, and led the Yanks, 3-2, with two out in the seventh now.

But a blister that had formed on the knuckle of his pitching hand broke, and the hand was so sore he couldn't hold the ball.

Early in the game, Hornsby had sent Alexander down to the bullpen with instructions only to keep an eye on two relief pitchers, Wee Willie Sherdel and Herman Bell. "Keep 'em warmed up, and if I need help I'll depend on you to tell me which one looks best," the manager said.

Hornsby needed help now but he didn't want Sherdel or Bell. He wanted Alexander, the 39-year-old pitcher the Cards had picked up after the Cubs released him.

Ol' Pete strode to the mound. Or, if legend is correct, he tottered unsteadily.

Shadows had begun to fall in Yankee Stadium as Alex completed his journey. The bases were loaded. Tony Lazzeri stood in the batter's box.

Alexander thought, he said later, "Tony is up there all alone and everyone in that Sunday crowd is watching him. I just said to myself, 'Take your time, Lazzeri isn't feeling any too good up there, so let him stew.'"

Alexander had held Lazzeri hitless in four tries the day before.

His first pitch to Lazzeri was a ball, outside. His next was a low fastball for a called strike. Then Alexander gave him a fastball under his chin. Lazzeri whacked it hard down the line but it fell 10 feet foul in the left-field stands. On the next pitch Lazzeri swung and missed.

"It was as if someone had thrown a blanket over that crowd of 69,000," Alex said. "Then they broke the silence and you couldn't hear anything."

Alex stayed to retire the Yankees in order in the eighth and got the first two batters in the ninth. Then, he walked Babe Ruth. But the Babe, on an apparent hit-and-run play, ran on the first pitch to Bob Meusel. Cardinal catcher Bob O'Farrell cut down Ruth easily.

"That was the Series and my second big thrill of the day," said Alexander. "The third came when Judge Landis mailed out the winners' checks for $5,584.51."

His was a familiar if tragic journey—from the heights to the depths. By the late 1930s, the man who won 374 games (only Christy Mathewson, with 367, came close in the National League), pitched 17 1-0 victories and 90 shutouts, the man with the smooth delivery and beautiful control, was reduced to performing as the headliner with a flea circus.

Cardinal owner Sam Breadon, Ford Frick, and others tried to help with jobs and lodging and such, but the man and the means often didn't meet.

In late 1949, Alexander blacked out on the way to watch a telecast of a football game, then was found unconscious in an alley behind his apartment.

Troubled by a hearing loss and his health continuing to deteriorate—among other problems he suffered from epilepsy—he went home to St. Paul, Nebraska, in 1950. That October, Alex returned to Philadelphia to watch the Whiz Kids play the Yankees in the Series.

A month later, he was dead.

Tony Lazzeri

Grover Cleveland Alexander

The 1926 Cardinals brought St. Louis its first major league pennant, going on to beat the Yankees in the World Series. At the far right of the first row, sitting next to catcher Bob O'Farrell, is pitcher Grover Alexander. Manager Rogers Hornsby is seated in the middle of the second row. Alexander won two games in the World Series that year and saved the final and seventh game. Jesse Haines, sitting third from the left in the second row, also won two games.

The Babe Ruth His Teammates Knew

by Waite Hoyt

In his glory years, "Babe Ruth used to pick his own 'All-Star' team," recalls Waite Hoyt (left). In this 1928 photo, Ruth presents certificates to two of his selections, Hoyt and Lou Gehrig. Hoyt followed Ruth to the Yankees from the Boston Red Sox, and there was a long-standing friendship between the two. "Some of the stories about Babe's exploits are exaggerated," insists Hoyt, "but there's no question he was great with kids, he loved the game, and he enjoyed life to the hilt."

August, 1961

I first met Babe Ruth late in July, 1919, when as a rookie I reported to the Boston Red Sox at Fenway Park. Ruth at that time was just a moon-faced, rather homely, but good-natured young fellow of 25.

Babe had a lot on his mind. He was doubling in brass. Mostly he played left field. When he was needed, he pitched. When I arrived on the scene, the fellow who was to become baseball's biggest attraction had clouted 16 home runs. His name was hitting the headlines every day. His world—his oyster—was opening, and the pearls inside dazzled him beyond expression. Ruth was the new sensation, and the world paid him homage.

The first big league game I pitched was against Detroit. It went 13 innings. I beat Detroit, 2-1. Ruth made four hits, including two doubles. He was a comfort, that man.

But this is not a résumé of his exploits. Those are too well known. I prefer this to be a short study of the Gigge the ballplayers knew. (Gigge is the ballplayers' contraction of his first name, George. Ruth was seldom called Babe by his teammates.)

I played with Gigge 10 years and against him four. I saw him hit some 500 home runs. Two of them he hit off me—but those he struck on my behalf far outweighed the loss I suffered from those two.

One of them—the second—was one of his longest. He had been at bat twice with no hits. The third time I had two strikes on him. He knew I was pitching high and outside. He kept leaning toward the plate. I thought I'd cross him with an inside pitch. Now behind the right-field fence in Philadelphia is a street. Beyond that street in Philadelphia is a row of houses. Ruth hit my clever pitch, not only over the fence but over the street and over the houses to a second street beyond. I had seen him do that too many times, so I wasn't exactly amazed—although, as I stood in the pitcher's box, I suddenly realized how opposing pitchers had felt all those years I had played with Ruth.

If you have a young son who is in the first stages of discovery, a youngster who barely knows the name of the president of the United States, whose days are crowded with riotous romping, pleasure, and glory, stupendous plans and projects, and filled with the joy of living—then you have a small edition of Babe Ruth. The guy just never grew up. The world was his, and its trials and tribulations were too minor for Gigge to worry about. His love was baseball— the fans his friends—the world his playground.

To play on the same club with Ruth was not only a pleasure, it was a privilege—an experience which comes once in a lifetime. Babe was no ordinary man. He was not alone the idol of his fans, he was superman to the ballplayers. He was their man, their guy. He was especially that to those in close association.

Ballplayers who had played against him and who eventually joined the Yankees used to say, "I knew how great he was when I played against him, but I never thought I'd see anything like this."

Ruth possessed a magnetism that was positively infectious. When he entered a clubhouse or a room, or when he appeared on a field—it was as if he was a whole parade. There seemed to be flags waving, bands playing constantly. If atomic formulas could be applied to personality, Ruth's measurements were definitely atomic.

To me, there was one, and will always be but one, Babe Ruth—the Gigge.

(Editor's Note: Waite Hoyt won 237 games and lost 182 during his 21 years as a major league pitcher. He was one of Babe Ruth's teammates on the Yankees from 1921 to 1930.)

Allie Reynolds
Talks About
the Art of Pitching

by John Wilson
Houston Chronicle

November, 1971

When Allie Reynolds pitched for the New York Yankees, people thought about him as a big, hard-throwing Indian from Oklahoma who simply intimidated batters. Allie now is president of the American Association. The image of Allie as a pitcher is about as accurate as the picture of him as an Indian. He is three-sixteenth Indian. "I tell people I'm a quarter Indian because I got tired of explaining that three-sixteenth thing," Reynolds explained.

Reynolds could throw hard. But there is a lot more to pitching than that, as he related.

"When Bob Porterfield came to the Yankees he asked me if I would tell him all I knew about pitching," Reynolds said. "I told him that what I knew about pitching might not do him any good at all. That what I knew about pitching was what pitching was to me." Reynolds was making the point that there is some mystery to pitching, that each pitcher is different.

Some days pitching seems to be one of the most complicated things in sports. Other days it seems to be one of the simplest—some pitchers can throw a ball 60 feet 6 inches across a 17-inch plate and the batters can't hit it, and other pitchers can't.

After a two-hour session with Reynolds, I was left with a revived respect for control as one of the keys to the mystery of pitching.

There are the exceptions. Control wasn't why Sandy Koufax and Bob Feller were two of the greatest pitchers who ever lived. But how about Warren Spahn, Robin Roberts, Whitey Ford? "Spahn got all there was out of his ability," Reynolds said. "Ford, too. Whitey came to the Yankees one spring the same year another young left-hander did. They would have taken Ford as the better prospect of the two. The other kid could throw, had simply a great arm. He never pitched in the majors."

And Eddie Lopat, one of the starters for the Yankees when Vic Raschi, Reynolds, and Lopat formed a tremendous Big Three. They always said Lopat couldn't throw hard enough to break an egg.

But he got them out. "He changed speeds, he had control of several pitches, he knew what he was doing," Allie said.

"I always felt I could throw at a four-inch square and hit it 40 out of 50 times," Reynolds said. That reminded me of something Jim Bouton said in his book. He said he had always heard about the pinpoint control of big league pitchers, and he suffered an inferiority complex because he knew he didn't have it. And then he got to the big leagues and discovered that major league pitchers don't have that kind of control.

I think Bouton was basically right. I see coaches having much more trouble getting pitchers to throw the ball over the plate than trying to get them to throw it to spots.

I have seen a lot of pitchers lose their jobs on the Astros because they tried to "nibble" at the corners of the plate, stayed continually behind the batters, and then had to come in with fat pitches. "Don't nibble—throw the ball over the plate," they were told, but maybe they knew they had to "nibble" to have a chance.

But listen to Reynolds: "I never threw a batter a strike if I didn't have to. If he'll hit a bad pitch, I'd rather him do that." But apparently Reynolds' bad pitch was just slightly bad. And when he had to throw it over the plate, he not only could throw it over the plate but over that part of the plate he

179

wanted to. Bouton won 20 games just once—was never a winner again. But Spahn won more than 300 and Roberts nearly 300. Ford was as tough a pitcher for the clutch game as anyone in baseball over a number of years.

In what ways did Reynolds use his control? "I tried not to throw to power," Allie said. "Each hitter has an area where his power is, and I tried not to throw the ball there." To some, he didn't throw the ball over the plate at all. "It was a joke how often I walked Ted Williams," Reynolds said. "I pitched around Williams." Even with Junior Stephens batting behind Ted, Reynolds wasn't afraid. He dropped down and threw side-arm to Stephens. "Stephens would murder your mistakes," Allie said. But apparently Reynolds was confident he didn't make too many mistakes.

"There were a lot of power hitters in the league, guys who pulled the ball to left field," Allie said. "I'd just as soon start with them at two balls and no strikes. I'd deliberately throw two balls to them and then I would throw them a fastball over the outside third of the plate.

"They would be ready and anxious on the two-and-0 count. But they'd try to pull that outside pitch and would hit a flyball to center field. I was lucky to always have good outfielders with the Yankees, so even if they hit it deep, it was just an out. I don't know how many times one of them would say to me, 'You lucky-so-and-so, I just missed getting that one.' They didn't have any idea what had happened."

They used to say that Reynolds was a "mean" pitcher, that he backed them off from the plate with that hard one. "I didn't throw at batters," Allie said. "But when I had two strikes on the batter, I thought of the plate as an L. I was going to throw somewhere along that line of the L and if I missed, it was going to be on the inside rather than in the middle. So sometimes they had to move back."

Reynolds could make his fastball run in on a right-handed hitter by placing the first two fingers slightly to the right or make it a "rise" ball by placing them on top. He laughed at the idea that some pitchers say they don't know what their ball is going to do, and yet I've had pitchers tell me just that.

There have to be some answers as to why some pitchers can get them out, and can do it year in and year out, and others, who can match them in velocity and in "curving" the ball, can't. And I'm convinced Allie Reynolds has a good many of those answers.

Allie Reynolds bears down on Ted Williams, the last batter to face him, as the Yankee right-hander nears completion of his second no-hitter of the season on September 28, 1951. With two strikes on him, Williams hit a twisting foul high behind home plate. Catcher Yogi Berra was unable to make the play, the ball popping out of his mitt. On the next pitch, Williams hit another foul, this time caught by Berra, and Reynolds had his no-hitter. The Chief, as Reynolds was called, was noted as a "clutch" pitcher with the Yankees.

Tom Seaver—
The Game I'll Never Forget

as told to George Vass

November, 1974

I still get needled about Jimmy Qualls. Even now. Even after the years that have gone by. People still say, "Imagine that, Qualls!" They don't let me forget it. But do I have regrets? Lord, no! When you pitch a one-hit shutout in the middle of a pennant race that in itself is a very memorable game.

That's the one, of course, the one-hit game I pitched against the Chicago Cubs in Shea Stadium in 1969. No other game sticks out for me quite like that one. How could it?

You have to remember the situation in July, 1969. The Cubs came into New York on July 8, 1969, five games in front of us (the New York Mets). We were in second place but the Cubs weren't taking us seriously as contenders. Not too many people were.

Just before the first game of the series Ron Santo, the Cub third baseman, made a comparison of their lineup with ours, pointing out how in almost every case Chicago had an established star at a position while we had young, relatively little-known players.

The Cubs did have a good team—Santo, Ernie Banks, Glenn Beckert, Randy Hundley, Don Kessinger, Billy Williams—and maybe our guys weren't as well known.

But Santo totally underrated our ball club. He underrated our defense, and he wasn't aware of the kind of pitching we had. We had very strong, very good pitching. Our pitching staff was young, none of us—Jerry Koosman, Gary Gentry, Nolan Ryan, Tug McGraw, and myself—having been around more than two or three years. I guess maybe there was room for speculation.

Players will frequently do what Santo did, compare lineups and overlook the importance of pitching. If they do that they're going to be wide open to make a mistake. You know, pitching is the most significant factor on any team. Strong pitching can outweigh other major flaws.

I don't have to remind anyone of how important pitching proved for the Mets that season. That's on record.

We beat the Cubs in the first game of the series on July 8, pulling out the game with three runs in the ninth inning after going in trailing, 3-1. After the game, Santo blasted Don Young, the Cub center fielder, for not having caught two flyballs that fell for hits in the ninth. Leo Durocher, the Cub manager, also blasted Young.

The next night, Wednesday, July 9, Qualls was in center field for the Cubs instead of Young. Qualls was a rookie who had been in just a few games and was hitting around .230.

Nobody on our ball club knew anything about Qualls except Bobby Pfiel, who had played against him in the minors. "He usually gets wood on the ball and sprays it around," Pfiel told me. "Throw him hard stuff."

There'd never been a crowd like that to see us in Shea Stadium before. There were 60,000 people packed in there that night when I walked out to the mound. My wife Nancy was in the stands and so was my father. He'd come in from the West Coast and came to the ball park directly from the airport.

I could feel the tension, the excitement, the expectation of the crowd more than I had ever sensed it before. It was stimulating but it also put pressure on me. You couldn't help but feel it.

I was a little concerned when I warmed up because my shoulder felt tight. It took a couple of innings before it loosened up, before the adrenalin started to flow and eased up the shoulder.

Ken Holtzman pitched for the Cubs and we got to him right away. Tommie Agee hit the first pitch for a triple and Pfiel doubled him in. We were ahead, 1-0, after Holtzman had thrown just two pitches.

We scored two more runs in the second inning. I drove in one of them with a double. We got another run in the seventh when Cleon Jones hit a home run to make it 4-0.

Meanwhile I was retiring the Cubs in order, inning after inning. The shoulder that had felt stiff when the game started felt just great. I was throwing harder than I'd ever thrown. I struck out five of the first six Cubs I faced, and when they hit the ball they hit it at somebody.

You try to isolate yourself from the crowd noise during a ball game, to retain your concentration, but as the game continued it got harder and harder to do. By the seventh inning the crowd was cheering every pitch. With every out they were standing up and giving me an ovation.

When Williams went out to end the Cub seventh he was the 21st Cub batter I'd retired in order. I hadn't walked a man. I had a perfect game going. Everybody in the ball park knew it. Nobody on our bench said a word to me but I knew what was going on. How could I help not knowing?

Santo. Banks. Al Spangler. They all went out in the eighth. With every out the crowd roared, 60,000 people yelling, cheering me, pulling for me to pitch a perfect game. Three outs to go. I felt I could do it.

The hitters in the ninth were Hundley, Qualls, then a pinch-hitter for the pitcher. When I went out to the mound, I heard a roar greater than the ones before. Everybody was standing up, cheering.

Hundley squared away to bunt. He laid it down but I got off the mound quickly and threw him out. Just two outs to go!

Qualls stepped in, a left-handed hitter. The first time up he'd hit a fastball to the warning track in right field. The next time he'd hit a curveball very sharply to first base. I was trying different pitches on him, but he seemed to get a piece of everything.

This time I tried to pitch him away, with a fast-ball. The ball didn't sink. It stayed up and Qualls got the bat on it. He hit a line drive to the gap between Tommie Agee in center and Jones in left. It fell for a single.

Disappointed? Of course I was, at the moment. I'd like to have pitched a perfect game. Anybody would.

But I got the next two batters out. Smith then Kessinger and the game was over, a one-hitter. We'd won, 4-0.

When I walked from the dugout through the tunnel toward the locker room I saw Nancy. She had tears in her eyes. "What are you crying for?" I said. "We won, 4-0."

I still feel the same way. Regrets? How can you have regrets about a one-hitter you pitched in the middle of a pennant race?

Seaver towers over interrogators during a 1969 World Series post-game interview. Although he lost the opener in Baltimore, Seaver came back to defeat the Orioles, 2-1, in 10 innings in the fourth game to nudge the Mets closer to their first world championship.

Tom Seaver being congratulated by New York Met teammates after posting another victory in the 1969 pennant race. Pictured are Wayne Garrett (No. 11), catcher Jerry Grote, Bud Harrelson (No. 3), Ed Kranepool (No. 7), and Al Weis (behind Harrelson). In 1969, Seaver won 25 games, lost only seven, and registered a 2.21 ERA, earning him the Cy Young Award in the National League.

The Day Jimmie Foxx Tried To Hang a Curtain

by Francis Stann
Washington Star

January, 1962

"The record those fellows should have been trying to beat this past season ought to have been Jimmie Foxx', not Babe Ruth's," mused Ira Smith. "And it would have been more like 65 home runs."

Ira Smith is an incurable fancier of baseball lore. He writes books on the game, like *Three Men on Third, Baseball's Greatest Outfielders,* and *Baseball's Greatest Pitchers.* He lives in an authentic post-Revolutionary house on Lee Street in Alexandria, Virginia, and probably owns the most complete baseball file in the world.

Ira pushes buttons and moves switches and out of his cabinets pour facts and legends. Recently he was constrained to refresh his memory on Foxx' challenge in 1932 to Ruth's mark. That's when he decided that Roger Maris and Mickey Mantle should be aiming at a record set by Jimmie.

"People don't realize to what extent players' performances on the field are affected by events in their private lives," Ira was saying. He held up a reference to Foxx. "I'll show you what I mean," he promised.

It was August, 1932, Smith began. Foxx' wife was confined to a hospital in Philadelphia. The Athletics were playing on their home grounds most of that month.

"Jimmie was able to visit his wife each evening," Ira said. "He brought her little unusual things to eat and flowers and magazines. Jimmie was a great guy, loyal and cheerful. But when they talked in the hospital, Foxx never mentioned anything about his home-run output, and it worried the missus.

"She finally brought up the subject. The fact is that Jimmie had hit only three home runs in 28 days. He was determined to do something about it for the sake of her morale. He hit seven homers in the next 11 days to bring his total to 51 and put him well ahead of Ruth's pace in 1927.

"Now it's September," Ira Smith continued. "Jimmie has a whale of a chance to set a new record. But then he climbed on a stepladder at home and almost fell off. He saved himself a fall but sprained his wrist doing so."

The result, according to Ira's records, was that Jimmie couldn't swing hard. "In the next 17 games

he picked up only two homers," Smith related. "You hear a lot about the pressure on the hitters who challenge Ruth—the pressure on Mantle, Maris, Greenberg, Wilson, Kiner, and the others. I doubt if Foxx was affected. The season was nearing its end when Jimmie's wrist was strong again, and he hit five home runs in the last five games for his total of 58."

The historian is far from anti-Ruth. "I loved the Babe," Ira tells, "but for sheer power I think Foxx had an edge. A baseball never came off anybody's bat like it did off Jimmie's. The Babe hit a lot of high, looping flies that went for home runs. Foxx put 'em into the seats like they'd been shot out of a cannon."

Foxx' closing surge—five homers in the final five days—was in contrast to Hank Greenberg's abortive bid in 1938, when he also hit 58. On September 27, Hank hit his 57th and 58th and had five games to play, two against the St. Louis Browns. Greenberg never came very close to hitting another home run.

Foxx was destined to run second to Ruth in every department of long-ball hitting, which isn't bad at all. His major league total of 534 homers is topped only by the Babe's incredible 714. Jimmie hit 30 or more homers in each of 12 consecutive seasons. Ruth hit 30 or more in 13 seasons, but not in a row.

Ira Smith's files contain play-by-play records which show that in 1932 Foxx hit at least nine balls against screens in St. Louis and Cleveland. These were not in place to cut down the home runs in Ruth's biggest year. "But Jimmie never complained," Ira said. "This is not from the files but from personal questioning."

Foxx and others beat a path to Smith's home to enjoy an evening, reminiscing over an occasional nip of the grape. "Jimmie never became bitter," Ira said. "He relived and laughed at things that happened."

Smith was asked if Foxx had ever told him exactly what he was doing on that stepladder back in September, 1932, when he ostensibly ruined his chances of beating Ruth's mark.

"Yes," Ira replied. "I believe Jimmie told me he was trying to hang a curtain in a window."

Connie Mack:
First Citizen
of Philadelphia

by John R. Tunis

Condensed from the *Atlantic Monthly*

February, 1943

By his looks he might be a retired manufacturer and former Sunday school superintendent. The sort of man who sits on a sidewalk in the morning sunshine, enjoys his daily game of shuffleboard, and hears Dr. William Lyon Phelps at the weekly meeting of the Iowa Club. After all, at 80 a man has a right to take things easy.

But at 80 Mr. Cornelius McGillicuddy is still in the thick of life—in the thick of a young man's game. Back in 1900, when the American League was starting, he hustled over to Philadelphia, interested a rich man named Benjamin F. Shibe in founding a club in the new organization, and set forth to collect a team. He's been in Philadelphia ever since.

In 1902, before the majority of modern baseball fans were born, he won his first pennant. In 1905 he lost his first World Series to the Giants. In the 1910 Series, he defeated Chance and the Cubs; in the 1911 and 1913 Series, McGraw and the Giants. Unexpectedly he lost to Stallings and the Braves in 1914. He beat Joe McCarthy and the Cubs in the 1929 Series, conquered Gabby Street and the Cards in 1930, and lost to them in the 1931 Series. Nine pennants and five Series triumphs are his record in four decades of baseball.

Most of his contemporaries are no more. Stallings is gone, McGraw is gone. Of the men he helped in founding the American League, Ban Johnson, the first president, is gone; Shibe, the owner of the Athletics, is gone; Comiskey of Chicago is gone. Only Connie Mack remains, still sitting on the bench each afternoon in summer and looking almost the same as that tall, gaunt figure of 1900. But he isn't merely the manager of a baseball team. The fans say, "Let's go watch Connie this afternoon." He's an institution.

It was as a mittless catcher that he caught for East Brookfield in the Central Massachusetts League in 1884, the year he was first able to vote. Later that summer he signed with Meriden for the astounding sum of $90 a month, payable whenever he could collect. Then to Hartford, and in 1886 he was sent with four other players to Washington in the National League for the total sum of $3,500. Connie was still catching them on the first bounce, still catching them meat-handed.

In 1894 he first became a manager, of the Pittsburgh Nationals; in 1897 he went as catcher-manager to Milwaukee, where he stayed until the American League was formed. At 80, he's the greatest living example of the fact that a man is as old as his arteries or that anyone who has a consuming interest in some phase of existence stays young.

Watch him at work in the morning behind the long glass-topped table in the Athletics' office in Shibe Park. He looks—well, 65 at the most. With a quick gesture he snatches a letter from the table or jumps up with the reflexes of a young man, stalking rapidly across to the door. He's tall—six-feet-one—straight, with blue eyes, lots of gray hair parted in the middle, and a kind, mobile face. Catcher's hands, all right—long, strong fingers. Even today his handshake is firm and warm. That's really the amazing thing about this amazing man; not his youthfulness, but his warmth. You feel it in his handshake, see it in his smile—a wonderful smile that lights up his clear blue eyes.

By what magic has this gentle, warmhearted individual taken nine clubs to the top? How has he kept discipline for over 40 years among those wild-eyed individualists, professional ballplayers? Because even in his younger days he was never tough or hard-boiled. How did he do it? Not by force, but by commanding the respect of his players. Not by being hard-boiled, but by being human.

By giving players his confidence he, in turn, wins their respect. That's why he can handle those temperamental prima donnas. The hardest of the lot to manage? "Oh . . . there wasn't any of 'em really hard. You could always talk with 'em and reason with 'em. Even Rube Waddell. Yes sir, even though most of my gray hairs can be traced to wondering where he was when his bed was empty. But when he was right, we've never had another who could touch him."

The easiest to manage in 40 years? "All my players, every one." He speaks with emphasis. "Eddie Collins, especially."

His 1910 team, with the famous $100,000 infield of Baker, Barry, Collins, and Davis, is his favorite. He doesn't say so, but you can see he thinks so. What was his greatest infield? "That 1910 bunch. You see they could rise to heights in critical moments of a Series. You just couldn't improve on those lads. My greatest outfield? Well, I guess that 1929 bunch with Haas, Miller, and Simmons. They had power—they were hitters, those boys."

No manager has had more great pitchers than Connie Mack, with Waddell, Coakley, Bender, Jack Coombs, Eddie Plank, Bush, George Earnshaw, and Lefty Grove among the standouts.

To Mack's annoyance, people still ask him what happened to his 1910 and 1932 teams. Why did he break them up? No mystery, for Connie never sells players unless he needs cash. The story runs round Philadelphia that he has invariably made money with tail-enders and lost with pennant winners. He almost admits the truth of this.

"Yes, I've made money coming up and lost with world champions," he says. "When your club is fighting to the top, the fans take an interest and come to the park. Philadelphia's a right good ball town; folks now are loyal and turn out when we are in last place, but pennant winners get to be an old story. When the club is behind, salaries are low; so are expenses. Champions cost money. In boxing, a manager has one champion; in baseball, 25. We had almost the highest-priced club in history in 1932, not barring the Yanks with Babe Ruth's $80,000 salary. I had five men who drew more than $100,000. Yet attendance fell away that year."

Yet the fans in Philadelphia say there's a reason he sold those men which Connie won't ever mention. They believe that when the A's were winning one man connected with the club took out large profits for other business ventures. The rumor also persists that Connie, in common with several others, got pretty well clipped in the market in 1929 and 1930.

Does he ever make mistakes?

"Yep, I've made hundreds. Make 'em almost daily. Every manager does. The worst mistake of all? Let me see . . . well, to my way of thinking the worst mistake I ever made was back in 1907 when we were running nip and tuck with Detroit. I had a pitcher, name of Jimmy Dygert, who could beat any-one for seven innings. Then he was finished. I could have pitched him seven innings any day in the week. If I'd found this out in time I could have won that pennant. Instead, I didn't realize it until after the season. We finished second, and Detroit won the championship.

"Another time we were playing the Yanks, and Ruth came to bat. I waved my outfield round, and they moved where I motioned, but still I wasn't satisfied and finally had to climb out of the dugout to place them and direct the defense. Meanwhile the pitcher was waiting in the box, and Babe was standing at the plate. After about three minutes' wigwagging, I got everyone set. You can guess what happened. Babe hit the first pitch over the fence.

"Fortunately for a manager, it doesn't always work out that way. I'll never forget the first game Ty Cobb played for us after 22 years with Detroit. He'd been manager six years with the Tigers and knew the weak and strong points of all players in every club. One of the first batters was a man I knew would hit the ball I signaled my pitcher to feed him, to Ty's left. I stood up in the dugout and waved him over with my scorecard. Even the pitcher turned in the box to look. What'd Ty do? He saluted, like the good sport he was, and trotted over to the new position. Believe me, I felt relieved a few seconds later when the batter lined a drive so close he hardly had to move a step to grab it."

He believes the great difference between baseball today and baseball 40 years ago lies in two things:

"First, the improvement in the equipment used. Second, the change in batting and pitching. In the old days we used to throw in four or five balls a game. Nowadays they use a couple of dozen. The pitcher has been handicapped, and the hitter has a great advantage. That's the chief change in baseball to my way of thinking."

Three times Connie Mack (right) met his counterpart, the equally illustrious John McGraw, manager of the New York Giants, in the World Series. McGraw won the 1905 World Series when their two teams met for the championship, but Mack and the Philadelphia A's won in 1911 and 1913.

Farewell, Forbes—
You Won't Be Forgotten

by Byron Rosen
Washington Post

October, 1970

"Those who have seen this stadium, including our own ballplayers, say it is the finest ball park they have ever seen," said Dan Galbreath, president of the Pittsburgh Pirates, in announcing that the club would bow into Three Rivers Stadium last July.

Finest ball park anywhere? Or the second best in Pittsburgh?

The sentimentalist vote says it is second to the one they shut down with a last hurrah at the Pirates-Chicago Cubs doubleheader; the oldest park in the majors, the one that opened 61 years ago last June 30; the one with the far-out dimensions, with tradition that the new super saucer may develop if it lasts 61 years, and with the individuality, the character, the soul Three Rivers will never have . . . Forbes Field.

Forbes Field, the one that opened the year Lincoln's profile supplanted the Indian head on the penny, going on 5,000 Pittsburgh home games ago, none of them a no-hit game, as a-facts-and-figures buff would point out.

It is the place where Danny Nirella's band used to play every opening day and on holidays. The one in the city's cultural center, Oakland, where a kid headed for the ball game could make a big day of it taking in the museum, the University of Pittsburgh's skyscraping Cathedral of Learning, Carnegie Tech on up the way, stroll Schenley Park beyond the outfield walls with its Honus Wagner statue, catch the visiting players on the nearby Schenley Hotel porch in the morning.

It is where a youth, a 40-mile train ride and a wide dollar gap away, always made sure it was a Sunday doubleheader and hoped against hope he would see two full games instead of the second one being suspended by that dratted Pennsylvania blue-law curfew. But as often as not the second game wound up in a tie, such as the one created when Pirate catcher Spud Davis circled the bases behind two teammates while his drive stayed lodged in the right-field screen. It was a homer in the absence of any ground rule, which from the next day forward was on the books as a two-base hit.

It is where you went to hear the old-timers tell about Wagner, Pie Traynor, Max Carey, Casey Stengel, and Fred Clarke.

The place where you could see the real-life versions of the cornball re-creations of Rosey Rowswell, Bob Prince's pioneer broadcasting predecessor whose radio play-by-play had introduced you to the game—like the "doozie-marooney" (Pirate extra-base hit), "dipsy-doodle" (strike-out by a Pirate pitcher), "put 'em on and take 'em off" (Pirate double play). And savor seeing a Pirate home run sail out of the park secure in the knowledge that Rowswell was hollering out to radioland, "Get upstairs there, Aunt Minnie, and raise the window! (pause) Nope, she never made it."

It was a call that Rowswell got to make precious few times at home games in Forbes Field, the park where homers were the scarcest in the majors—until the vastness of left field was curtailed by that aberrant temporary fence that created Greenberg Gardens. Built when the Pirates acquired the great Detroit slugger in his twilight year, it was appropriated by Ralph Kiner throughout its existence (1947–53), and it left when he did. Then, ignoring 1902, Pittsburgh had its only home-run king—seven consecutive years' worth, and they tried to tag it Kiner's Korner but the Greenberg Gardens label stuck.

Three Rivers' home-run territory, over an inner fence forming a 340-410-340 curved perimeter, will look like permanent Greenberg Gardens Northside by comparison with Forbes' regular dimensions.

A home run was a home run of heroic dimension just about anywhere in Forbes Field, making even more memorable Babe Ruth's parting shot, on May 25, 1935, when he became the first man to clear the roof of the right-field stands (built in 1925). It was his third home run of the game for the Boston Braves, the 714th and last of his career, and that roof wasn't cleared again until 1950. Willie Stargell did it seven times since 1967. And the other homer they still shake their heads over, the titanic smash over left field deep into Schenley Park? Young fellow then with the Dodgers delivered that one: Frank Howard.

But mainly Forbes Field was where singles and doubles skipped through that notoriously hard infield—the "alabaster plaster" in Bob Prince's idiom. Where that plentiful acreage of real grass outfield invited bloopers to fall safely and for those beautiful triples and doubles to be stroked into the gaps and roll to places like "the old iron gates." Where with the Pirates' perennial good hitting and perennial mediocre pitching, no wonder there was never a no-hitter there.

It is where only 13 of those nearly 5,000 games were World Series games, their significance and melodrama quotient heightened by their scarcity:

—Three of them that first year, 1909, that Forbes opened and accommodated baseball's first attendances of 30,000, to watch Pittsburgh's Wagner and Detroit's Ty Cobb in the match-up of the game's first superstars, Wagner hitting .333 to Cobb's .231 as the Pirates won in seven. . . .

—Four in 1925, when the Washington Senators, 1924 world champions, lost their best chance from then until now to win another Series. It came down to game seven with the Senators' great Walter Johnson striving, struggling to get a foothold on the muddy mound and his stuff on the soggy ball as rain pelted down. Roger Peckinpaugh, Washington shortstop and the American League's Most Valuable Player, whose seventh error of the Series had let Pittsburgh catch up at 6-6, homered in the top of the eighth for a 7-6 lead. But he committed another error in the home half that opened the gates, and finally Kiki Cuyler laced a Johnson pitch into the soaked outfield for a bases-full, tie-breaking double. Pittsburgh was the winner, 9-7, and world champion. . . .

—Two in 1927, the Ruth-Gehrig-Combs-Koenig-Meusel New York Yankees starting their four-game sweep over the Traynor-Waner-Waner Pirates by taking the first two at Forbes. . . .

—Four in 1960, when after a 33-year National League pennant drought, the Pirates absorbed 16-3, 10-0, and 12-0 bombings from the Mantle-Maris-Berra Yankees, yet carried the Series to a seventh game, at home. Pittsburgh trailed, 7-4, in the eighth inning when Bill Virdon's double-play grounder took a weird hop and hit shortstop Tony Kubek in the throat, a hit that keyed a five-run inning capped by reserve catcher Hal Smith's three-run shot over the wall in left. Another 9-7 victory to match the one over Johnson 35 years earlier? No, the Yankees scored their 54th and 55th runs of the Series in the ninth. And left it to Bill Mazeroski, the all-time great glove man at second base, to give Forbes its most hysterical moment with his home run in the ninth that won it, 10-9. Mazeroski's blast cleared the 406-foot marker, and they gave Three Rivers a touch of tradition by hauling that section of wall over to its Stadium Club. . . .

Well, today, good old Forbes Field has given up all those ghosts and has gone the way of good old Ebbets Field, the Polo Grounds, Griffith Stadium, the old St. Louis and Boston parks, and the Johnny-come-lately (1912) Crosley Field in Cincinnati that the Pittsburgh landmark outlasted by four days.

Take it away, punch-out pattern stadiums. Take it away, Riverfront Stadium and AstroTurf. Take it away, Three Rivers Stadium and Tartan Turf. Take it away.

A cement-hard infield and an extremely long distance to the center-field fence—435 to 457 feet—were features of Forbes Field, home of the Pirates from 1909 to 1970, when the club moved to Three Rivers Stadium. When it opened, the park seated 25,000 fans, and owner Barney Dreyfuss was criticized for overestimating the fans' appetite for the game. But Forbes Field spurred a building boom in the majors which culminated in 1923 with the opening of the 74,000-seat Yankee Stadium.

Pie Traynor:
Greatest of the
Third Basemen

by Harold Kaese
Boston Globe

Harold (Pie) Traynor played his entire major league career with the Pittsburgh Pirates (1920-37), finished with a .320 lifetime batting mark, and although he broke in as a shortstop, was considered the best third baseman of his day. Authorities who saw both play rate Traynor with Brooks Robinson as the game's outstanding fielding third basemen. Traynor was elected to the Hall of Fame in 1948.

June, 1972

The Boston Red Sox have a good record for trading, but don't go back too many years. You will find some blemishes.

Don't go back to Babe Ruth. They sold the greatest of ballplayers before he reached his prime.

They let Jackie Robinson work out at Fenway Park, then did not have the nerve to sign the first of the modern black players.

Before he had played a game in their uniform, they sold Pee Wee Reese to the Dodgers, who won seven pennants with him at shortstop.

In 1920 they did not know enough to sign Pie Traynor, a local boy from Somerville, Massachusetts, who escaped to the Pittsburgh Pirates.

Traynor is the only player in the Hall of Fame named Harold. He was called Pie so much, hardly anyone knew he had a first name.

Earlier this year during spring training, he was in Winter Haven, Florida, walking across the field alone before a Red Sox-Pirates game—in uniform.

"Could he play? How good was he?" a Red Sox player asked.

"Only about 98 percent better than anybody on this team," said a writer. "And here we are talking to you guys and he's out there all alone."

Now Pie is in the Valhalla of Fame. Passed away, gone, a few days after Zack Wheat and Dizzy Trout.

Traynor was in Boston last fall, and Frank Frisch asked him, "Are you living in the past?"

"Sure I am," he said. Traynor was a good-natured pessimist, a genuine old-timer pretty sure the good old days for baseball and the country were gone forever.

Not many of us saw Traynor play third. Old-timers say he was the best, but a few wavered: "Maybe Brooks Robinson is as good."

Writing about him last year, I tried to evaluate him for newcomers by saying he was the Brooks Robinson of his generation. Several days later—when I was out—a woman called me from Pittsburgh.

She wanted to know how I dared put Robinson in Traynor's class: "Robinson couldn't carry his glove."

She identified herself as Pie Traynor's wife.

When Traynor talked of himself, he said things like this:

"I used a small, thin glove, with a felt pad that cushioned the ball. I'd still use it today, despite these baskets they have."

"When young, I liked to play on hard infields, so I could start fast. When old, I preferred soft infields."

"I weighed about 170, but swung a 42-ounce bat with a thick handle. I got a lot of hits off that handle. When I found I couldn't pull anymore, I used to try to hit the pitcher."

"In the first All-Star game [in 1933], I got a double off Lefty Grove that sent the tying run to third. Then he struck out Wally Berger and Gabby Hartnett on six pitches."

"Only two pitchers could win with nothing but fastballs—Walter Johnson and Grove. Koufax has the best left-handed curve, but Grove was faster."

"In my day, we were farmers. All we wanted to do was play."

Instead of backhanding medium-speed balls over the bag, Traynor often grabbed them barehanded. He was noted for getting his throws off quickly. A man two steps from the plate might find himself called out at first. His arm was super-accurate.

In 1929 John McGraw called him—grudgingly—"the best team player in baseball today."

"I've never seen anything like him. I'll bet he ruined more base hits for my club than any other two infielders in the game," McGraw said.

"I wish I knew how many times one of my boys hit a sure two-base hit down the third-base line—sure, that is, with anybody else but him out there. He could come up with the ball and throw a runner out before he had a chance to drop his bat and start running."

Although many observers rated Traynor as the finest fielding third baseman the game has ever known, he was no less impressive at the plate.

In 1,961 games, from 1920 until 1937, Traynor compiled a lifetime batting average of .320. Included were back-to-back seasons of .356 and .366 in 1929

and 1930. He helped the Pirates to a National League pennant and a World Series win over Washington in 1925. He batted .346 in 1927, when the Bucs again won the pennant but lost the Series to the Yankees.

Traynor cost the Pittsburgh club $10,000, which was like buying the Kohinoor diamond at a basement bargain counter.

In 1948 Pie was admitted to the Hall of Fame, enshrined along with pitchers Charlie (Kid) Nichols, Mordecai Brown, and Herb Pennock, and second baseman Charlie Gehringer.

In 1969 Traynor was named the greatest third baseman of all time by the baseball writers. He also was named to the all-time major league all-star team.

Traynor acquired his nickname as a youngster in Somerville, Massachusetts. He frequented a grocery store each day, always asking for pie. The owner called him Pieface, which was later shortened to Pie.

The name stuck with him, although in later years he lost his taste for pie.

Certainly Traynor's career was well laced with thrills, but none more memorable than his first major one. In September of 1924, he scored from first base on Rabbit Maranville's 11th-inning single to beat the Brooklyn Dodgers and fabled Dazzy Vance at Ebbets Field.

"I wasn't so much a veteran then, accustomed to thrills," he once said. "And believe me that score from first base on a single gave me the biggest thrill I ever got in a ball game."

Who was the first Pirate to make 200 hits a season, bat over .300, drive in over 100 runs, score over 100 runs? Not Honus Wagner. Pie Traynor in 1923.

He hit a home run his first time up against Walter Johnson in the 1925 World Series. He broke up Herb Pennock's bid for a no-hitter with an eighth-inning single in the 1927 Series.

He managed the Pirates in 1938, when the club had its World Series press buttons ready, only to have Gabby Hartnett of the Cubs hit his home run shot in the dark and spoil it all.

"In baseball," he used to say, "you've got to be ready for anything."

How a Fan Added Six Big Years to Ted Williams' Career

by Sandy Grady
Philadelphia Bulletin

Ted Williams

May, 1966

When they voted Ted Williams into the Hall of Fame recently, Ed Mifflin was holding the door open. More precisely, Mifflin has been behind Williams for years, huffing and puffing and shoving.

And in his Swarthmore, Pennsylvania, den Ed Mifflin gives a contented sigh. Now he knows how any pop feels when junior gets the diploma in hand.

"If Ted hadn't made it, they should have closed up Cooperstown," Mifflin said. "Nobody deserves it more."

When they nail up Williams' plaque, Mifflin should wield the hammer. Ed Mifflin never got closer to a ball field than a box seat. A sandy-haired man in his 40s, he's a sales manager for a textile firm and a Republican in the Pennsylvania State Legislature. Without him, Williams might still be lingering outside the Hall of Fame gates.

"If it hadn't been for Ed, I would have quit baseball long before I did," Williams says. "In fact, he wouldn't let me quit."

The story goes back to a morning late in the 1954 season. Williams was in the Baltimore train station, hiding behind a newspaper. On the newsstand was a magazine with a piece by Ted proclaiming this to be his last year. Out of the station mobs barged a stocky man with an intense frown.

"Excuse me, Ted," he said, "but what's all this talk about you quitting baseball? You're kidding, aren't you?"

Williams peered over his paper. "Why would I kid about a thing like that?"

"Look, Ted, you'd be crazy," said the stranger.

"That's my business," Williams snapped. "Not yours."

"It's more than just your business," insisted the man. "You've got certain milestones to reach. You owe it to your fans. Do you know how close you are to 400 homers, 1,500 runs batted in, 2,000 hits? You're one of the finest hitters in history, but if you stop now, the record books will never show it."

"Listen, you little—," began Williams, because this pest waving a briefcase, lecturing him like a kid, was a foot shorter.

"What do you know about your own records, Ted?" the stranger asked. "How many hits have you racked up?"

"Er—"

"Just as I thought. You've got 1,930, including yesterday. And in homers, you're not even in the first ten for lifetime totals yet. Why, you should be up there with Gehrig and Ott and Foxx."

Suddenly, Williams was intrigued. "Hey, who are you?"

"A heckuva fan of yours," said the man, as Williams swung aboard a train.

"Call me up," said Williams above the engine's roar. "I want to talk to you."

The brash, baseball cashew, Ed Mifflin, made the

call later. Over a steak, he outlined what Williams could accomplish. "He set up goals that made sense," said Williams. "He kept me going. Ed gave me a blueprint for my career."

For the next six years, Mifflin was the gadfly that stung Williams' flanks. From his Swarthmore statistics lab, he sent Williams such telegrams as: "Get hot. Two singles today puts you 300 total bases short of DiMaggio. Ed." The pair, Williams and his No. 1 cheerleader, met often on the road, becoming such friends that Williams invited the Mifflins to Florida for two weeks.

"When Ted did quit, I think we were both satisfied with his achievements," says Mifflin. "Ranking third in homers I consider the most important. (Ruth, 714; Foxx, 534; Williams, 521.) When I finally charted the 20 great hitters for all departments, only Ruth stands above Ted."

Unlike some literary lions who were clawed by Williams, Mifflin describes him as "a warm, generous man, probably because he knew I had no ax to grind." He last heard from Ted on New Year's Day at 9 a.m., an hour Williams chose to wake up the bleary world.

"How about this Hall of Fame thing, Ted?" said Mifflin, anxious as a jockey on the last furlong.

"Aw, we'll make it," said Williams. "We better."

And he did. Ed Mifflin and his magic file cabinet spurred Williams halfway to immortality. You take it from here, Cooperstown.

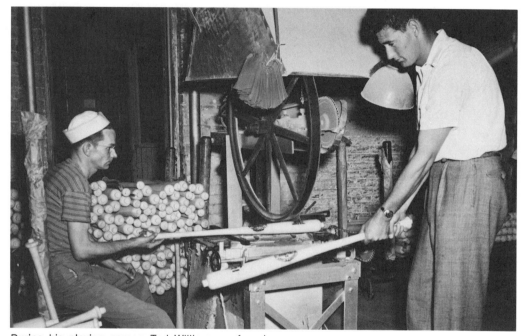

During his playing career, Ted Williams preferred a light bat, generally weighing about 32 ounces. He treated his bats with special care, keeping them usable as long as possible. In this 1946 photo, he tests a model at the Hillerich & Bradsby Company plant in Louisville, Kentucky.

For the Umps,
It's a Long, Long Season

by Todd E. Fandell
Wall Street Journal

Hank Soar

January, 1970

Fifty-five-year-old Albert Henry Soar of Pawtucket, Rhode Island, had the best spot in the Baltimore stadium for the opening game of the 1969 World Series between the Mets and the Orioles. But he didn't care who won. "It was just another ball game," he says.

It's a good thing Hank Soar takes that attitude, for playing favorites is frowned on in his line of work. He's a senior umpire in the American League, and he called the balls and strikes in the Series opener. He worked the bases or the foul lines in the other games.

Hank Soar loves baseball. "If I wasn't doing this for a living, I'd be paying my way into the ball park to watch the games," he says. But he is a realist about his role in the sport, and he doesn't look upon the World Series as the climax to an exciting season. Rather, he and most of the 47 other umpires in the major leagues view the Series as the end to a grueling season of hard work, travel, loneliness, obscurity, and abuse.

An umpire's job is a hard one. In seven months, Soar and his three-man crew logged some 45,000 miles of air travel on more than 40 flights, visiting all 12 American League cities, most of them three or four times. During one six-week stretch, they made seven transcontinental trips. Soar made it home to Pawtucket only four times in the seven months—once was when he took a 10-day leave to attend the college graduation and marriage of his elder daughter—and he was regularly booed in every city he visited (except Pawtucket).

On the field, he and his colleagues claim to work harder than any of the players, some of whom make several times the $22,000 a year that Soar earns. (He received another $6,500 for working the Series.) The umpire's job is taxing mentally and physically. Decisions must be quick—and, of course, correct—and, unlike players, umpires can't escape to the dugout every 20 minutes or so. A six-hour doubleheader on a hot afternoon in Washington or Kansas City would kill men in poorer condition than the rugged, six-foot two-inch 215-pound Hank Soar.

"I've developed an infinitely greater respect for the work fellows like Hank Soar do, under tremendous pressure from everyone, than I had as a player," says Ted Williams, the Boston slugger who had just completed his first season as manager of the Washington Senators.

(Soar has long had great respect for Ted Williams. "Williams is easily the best hitter I've seen," Hank says. Both tell of the inconsequential game in Cleveland when Soar, to test the slugger's claim to know the strike zone better than an umpire knows it, deliberately called as a strike a pitch that was six inches outside. The Red Sox star said nothing. But the next time he came to bat, he turned to the umpire and said, "You know, that strike you called on me was six inches outside." Replied Soar, "You're absolutely right.")

Because the work is so hard and because the demand for umps is increasing as the major leagues expand, the big leagues are having trouble coming up with top-quality umpires like Soar.

Hank Soar worked the minors in 1947, 1948, and 1949 before being called up to the American League. When he was called up in 1950, he achieved the distinction of being the only man in history to reach the major leagues of the three big American sports—football, basketball, and baseball.

Though he was a captain, star, and all-state selection in all three sports at Pawtucket High, football was his favorite. He dropped out of Providence College after three years in 1936 to play pro football for the Boston Shamrocks because he loved the game and because "I couldn't pass up the money they offered—$100 a game." The next year he was with the New York Giants (at $200 a game), and he stayed with them as an offensive halfback and defensive safety through 1946. He says his greatest moment in sports came in 1938 when he caught the winning pass in a championship game against the Green Bay Packers.

During World War II, he was a staff sergeant in the Army for three years, but for two of those years he got weekends off to play with the Giants. After the war, he took a job as player-coach with Providence in the predecessor league to the current National Basketball Association. His career was brief.

"We had a 2-17 record when I was fired in mid-season in 1948," he says. "But my successor was 4-25, so I think the problem might have been the players and not the coaching."

Soar umpired his first baseball game in 1937, as an emergency fill-in in a high school contest. "I didn't know the rules very well, so I checked with both coaches," he recalls. "They admitted they didn't know them either, so I simply announced we would play by my rules. It worked out just fine, and we've been playing by my rules ever since."

That, of course, is a bit of an exaggeration. But baseball people say that if Soar doesn't make up his own rules nowadays, he definitely makes it clear that he—and only he—interprets the rules he is given. Soar's strongest quality, say baseball players and managers, is his take-charge ability.

"When an argument develops," says Ted Williams, "Soar will come right out and tell you exactly what happened. He lets you know where he stands and in no time has it straightened out. He takes no nonsense of any kind and very firmly sets you straight, but in a decent way—he doesn't make the manager or player mad at him."

Hank developed his take-charge ability in the early 1940s, when he umpired in a rough and tough semipro league whose teams were owned by mills in the New England towns they represented.

"There was no discipline. An umpire had to be tough," he says. "We had at least half a dozen big fights a season—and I never lost one. Once, I picked up a guy and threw him back into his dugout to end a brawl."

Everyone agrees Hank runs a tight game, but there is disagreement about his other abilities as an umpire. A former big league catcher says, "Soar's idea of the strike zone isn't the best around—a lot of other umpires are better at calling balls and strikes." Ted Williams disagrees. "He's absolutely consistent, and that's the most important thing in calling a pitch," he says.

Soar admits he may have blown a few calls, but never on balls and strikes. "The most difficult part of umpiring is learning to anticipate a play and getting into the best position to see it," he says. "Once in a while you don't make it, and you blow one." One of the hardest plays to see correctly, he says, is when the first baseman tries to tag the runner instead of touch the bag.

"I've called that one on the basis of the first baseman's facial expression," he says. "A player's face never lies."

Good positioning to make the right call is a cardinal precept for major league umpires, and Augie Donatelli has it as he rules Bud Harrelson (left) out at home on a play in the 10th inning of the second game of the 1973 World Series between the Mets and A's. Harrelson had attempted to score on a fly to Joe Rudi, and Rudi's throw to catcher Ray Fosse (extreme right) was in time to get the runner. Willie Mays charges in to protest Donatelli's call.

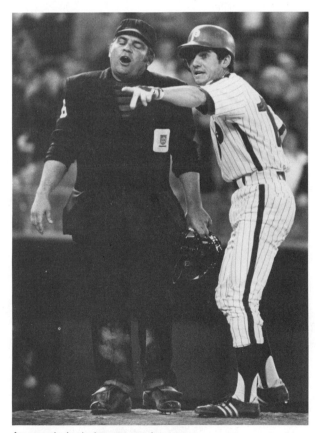

An umpire's judgment undergoes constant attack from players on the field whose version of what actually happened is often at odds with the way the arbiter saw it, as seems to be the case here with the Phils' Larry Bowa.

One play he admits he might have blown was an 11th inning, game-winning homer by Baltimore's Frank Robinson against Washington one night in 1969. It might not have been a homer at all, he concedes. He says he lost sight of the ball and he didn't spot it again until it had landed at the base of the foul pole. "I ruled it fair on the basis of what I'd seen, presuming it had hit the foul pole and dropped down. But to this day I don't really know what happened." The Senators protested the call so vigorously that Hank reported four of them to league headquarters, which presumably fined the players.

Umpire Soar doesn't like to argue with players and does all he can to discourage big scenes. Not all umpires feel that way at all times, however. Tellers of baseball tales say that some years back when Tommy Henrich was picked off second base by several feet in a World Series game, umpire Beans Reardon told the player, "Go on, kick the bag. Raise hell. You looked awful on that play."

Criticism from players does concern Hank Soar. "When an umpire is consistently in trouble with players, it means he must be doing something wrong," he says. But abuse from fans just rolls off his back. He considers it part of his profession, though he hates to become the center of attention at a game.

"I've always worked under the theory that the greatest compliment an umpire can be paid is obscurity," he says. "When the fans leave the park, I want them to have no idea who the umpire was. Some of the best umpires in baseball today are almost unknown to the fans, even if they've been in the big leagues for 10 years or more."

Being obscure is one thing, but being thought of as a ball-and-strike machine is something else, he says ruefully. Many umpires complain that they aren't thought of as normal human beings, and Hank admits he has that feeling, too, at times.

Reprinted by permission from the Christian Science Monitor, © 1973. The Christian Science Publishing Society. All rights reserved.

Umpires must learn to maintain their "cool," despite the wild protests that are lodged against them, often with accompanying acrobatics. Here, Yankee catcher Thurman Munson is expressing his displeasure with arbiter Jim Evans. Munson was irate over a ball-four call by Evans which forced in a run during a game against the White Sox in 1975.

Tim McCarver argues vehemently with umpire Billy Evans on a close call at first base as Cardinal manager Red Schoendienst attempts to ease in between the two to keep McCarver from being ejected from the game. Coach Johnny Lewis (No. 30) looks on. Umpires usually let an aggrieved player have his say but will give him the thumb if his attack gets personal.

Dave Bristol, Cincinnati manager, makes his point as does umpire Augie Donatelli during an argument over an interference call in a 1969 game between the Reds and Astros. Bristol was not ejected from the game despite his difference with Donatelli, but he told the umpire the Reds were playing the game under protest. Umpires learn to live with such challenges to their authority.

Billy Martin—
The Game I'll Never Forget

as told to George Vass

Billy Martin as a Yankee rookie.

August, 1972

When you start to think about which game really sticks out in your mind as the one you'll never forget, it's only natural that the World Series would be the first thing to pop into your head.

Maybe it could be one of the many World Series games I played in with the New York Yankees. Luckily, I never had a bad World Series, and I played in five of them with the Yankees.

In the 1953 Series, I had 12 hits, which still stands as a record for a batter in a six-game series.

I suppose I could have picked out the sixth game, in which we beat the Brooklyn Dodgers, 4-3, to win the Series, as the game that sticks out. That's the game in which the Dodgers scored two runs in the ninth, when Carl Furillo hit a home run to tie up the game 3-3.

I came to bat with two on and one out in the bottom half of the ninth and hit a pitch off Clem Labine to drive in the Series-winning run. You can be sure I'll never forget that.

In thinking about the big game, something else came to mind, too. You know, the first four home runs I ever hit in pro ball were all with the bases loaded. I had 174 runs batted in that year (1947) at Phoenix and hit .392.

But that was in the minor leagues, so I'd have to say, after giving it some thought, that the game I'll never forget would have to be the first one I ever played in the majors, on opening day of the 1950 season.

I was lucky in that a lot of good baseball men helped me when I started playing in the minors after I graduated from high school in 1946. Augie Galan, an ex-National Leaguer, encouraged me at the start.

In 1948 Casey Stengel was my manager at Oakland, where we won the pennant in 1948. After Casey left to manage the Yankees, Charlie Dressen, as smart a baseball man as ever lived, took his job.

I had a good season at Oakland, playing second base and shortstop in 1949, and went to spring training with the Yankees in 1950.

I remember one night during that spring training I was having a beer with Jerry Coleman, the Yankees' regular second baseman. "You're going to get my job," Coleman told me. "I know what you can do and what you can't do."

I knew I wasn't going to get his job, but Jerry didn't let the thought that I was bother him. He helped me every way he could about playing second base. That's the kind of guy he was.

It was a real good spring training for me. I hit .360, but I knew I wasn't going to make the lineup. Coleman was a tremendous second baseman, and no one figured to take his job that year.

But I was still with the team when the season opened, although I was on the bench for the first game. We opened in Boston (April 18) with Mel Parnell pitching for the Red Sox.

Allie Reynolds started for the Yankees, and the Red Sox got three runs off him in the first inning. They scored another run in the second and five more in the fourth.

We got four runs in the sixth inning, when Stengel sent in Dick Wakefield to bat for Coleman. I went in to play second base in Coleman's place.

The Red Sox picked up another run in the seventh and had a 10-4 lead when I came to bat for the first time in the majors in the eighth.

I guess Stengel figured the game was over because he let me bat, although there were two men on when I came up. Parnell was still pitching, and I hit a double off the top of the left-field wall to drive in a run.

We just kept going from there, and I got to bat again the same inning with the bases loaded. This time I hit a single to left and drove in two more runs off Walt Masterson, who had relieved for Parnell.

It was an unbelievable inning. We hit everything in sight, and the Red Sox used five pitchers. We

195

As manager of the Texas Rangers, Martin watches warily during a game in Cleveland in 1974 when the fans became unruly and swarmed onto the playing field. Chief umpire Nestor Chylak had to forfeit the game to the Rangers because the boisterous action of the fans was endangering the players. Note that the players on the Texas bench are holding bats in their hands for possible use in self-defense.

sent 14 guys to the plate and eight of them got base hits. I remember Joe DiMaggio getting a big double.

We scored nine runs that inning to take a 13-10 lead and got a couple of more runs in the ninth to win, 15-10.

It's hard to believe with all that hitting and all those great hitters, like DiMaggio, Ted Williams, Bobby Doerr, and Yogi Berra, but only one home run was hit in the game. That was hit by Billy Goodman, who never hit too many.

After the game, I remember all the reporters gathering around DiMaggio, talking to him about the unbelievable rally. Joe said to 'em, "Think I'm doing good—how about that little Dago," and pointed to me. That's the kind of guy DiMaggio was.

Those two hits didn't earn me a job. The next day Coleman was back at second base and it wasn't long before the Yankees sent me to Kansas City (then a farm team). But I came back before the season ended.

That's the game I'll never forget, the first game I ever played in the majors and in which I'd had two hits in the same inning. That's in the record book: most hits in one inning in first major league game.

Billy Martin was an agile fielder with the Yankees as indicated in this sequence of photos showing him gloving a grounder near second base and throwing to first in a 1956 World Series game against the Brooklyn Dodgers. The ball was hit by Jim Gilliam. It was Martin's final Series with the Yankees. The club traded him to Kansas City the following year.

Ed Cicotte—
"I Did Wrong,
but I Paid for It"

by Joe Falls
Detroit Free Press

February, 1966

The yellow-brick house sets in maybe 300 feet from the road, concealed in front by a dozen tall pines. They left the porch light on, but it didn't help much.

The dirt road in off Seven Mile was dark, and it was impossible to read the name on the mailbox.

He's hiding. He's still hiding from the world.

Frankly, I didn't know what to expect. I'd heard about Ed Cicotte, read about the infamous Black Sox scandal, but I'd never met the man, and a sudden feeling of apprehension came over me as I drove up the dark, narrow road.

I'd looked up his birthdate . . . it was June 19, 1884. That made him 81. I also looked up his record: 210 wins, 147 losses.

He was a 29-game winner in 1919 and a 21-game winner in 1920. After that, nothing. Not even an asterisk. He'd been banned from baseball for his part in the scandal.

What if he won't talk to me? What will I say? What will he say? How can I ask him?

Ed Cicotte was 35 years old when the Chicago White Sox were charged with throwing the 1919 World Series to the Cincinnati Reds. He was one of eight players banished from the game by Commissioner Kenesaw Mountain Landis.

They'd been acquitted of criminal charges by a Cook County jury in 1921, yet Landis made the ban stick. He said: "Regardless of the verdict, no player who throws a ball game, no player who entertains proposals or promises to throw a game, no player who sits in a conference with a bunch of crooked players and gamblers where the ways and means of throwing games are discussed, and does not promptly tell his club about it, will ever again play professional baseball."

Ed Cicotte had lost the first and fourth games of the Series. Frederick G. Lieb, in his book *The Story of the World Series,* wrote:

"Even the most rabid fans could scarcely believe their eyes when Cincinnati won the opener in a 9-1

breeze. Cicotte, the 29-game winner, was belted out in a five-run Red fourth, and reports drifted out of some hot words between Cicotte and Cracker Schalk in which the Chicago catcher accused Cicotte of repeatedly crossing his signals. Reporters also remembered how gamblers had made the Reds strong favorites before the game . . .

"According to other reports, the conspiring players realized that a defeat such as Cicotte's first one looked bad, and Eddie allegedly said, 'We've got to be smarter and think of our next year's contract.'

"Cicotte gave a much better account of himself in the fourth game, yet he lost, 2-0, and managed to bungle things when Cincinnati scored its two runs in the fifth . . .

"With one out, Duncan tapped to the pitcher's box for what should have been an easy out. But Cicotte threw without steadying himself, and his wild throw hit the grandstand as Duncan pulled up at second. Larry Kopf then hit a short single to left, on which Duncan reached third. Jackson fielded the ball cleanly and threw to the plate as Duncan had rounded the base by some 15 feet.

"But instead of letting the ball go through, Cicotte stabbed his glove at it and deflected it from its course. Duncan scored standing up; Kopf reached second, from where he came home on Neale's single . . ."

I pressed the doorbell and caught my breath.

What if he can't talk? Or can't remember?

The door opened.

"Mr. Cicotte?" I said hesitantly.

"Yes," he said.

"I'm Joe Falls of the *Free Press.*"

"Oh, yes," he said brightly. "Won't you come in?"

He gripped my hand . . . gripped it like a vise . . . and in that precise instant I relaxed.

He was dressed in a plaid shirt, blue denims, and tan shoes. His hair was white, and his eyes seemed to twinkle behind his spectacles.

He introduced me to his daughter and to his granddaughter—a redheaded doll of three—and for five minutes we chatted about nothing.

I asked him about the Tigers and, yes, he said he still followed the game, although he didn't think much "of this rubber ball they're playing with nowadays."

We talked of Ty Cobb. They were roommates in Augusta, and he told me how he came to recommend him to the Tigers.

We talked about Babe Ruth. He told me how the Babe never hit a home run off him.

"I used to talk him out of it," he chuckled. "I'd say to Schalk, 'Who's that big bum up there?' and

Ed Cicotte

my, you should have heard the Babe. 'Why, you pea-souper,' he used to say . . . He'd get so mad he couldn't swing."

It went on like this for maybe a half hour. I began to feel a little ashamed. I knew why I was there and he did, too.

Finally, I said: "Ed, does anyone ever come around and ask about the Black Sox thing?"

He smiled. "Yes, they come around," he said. "From time to time they come around."

"What do you tell them?"

He sat forward on the edge of his chair. The smile was gone. He looked straight at me.

"I admit I did wrong, but I've paid for it," he said in a soft, even voice. "I've paid for it for the past 46 years.

"Sure, they asked me about being a crooked ball-player. But I've become calloused to it. I figure if I was crooked in baseball, they were crooked in something else.

"I don't know of anyone who ever went through life without making a mistake. Everybody who has ever lived has committed sins of his own.

"I've tried to make up for it by living as clean a life as I could. I'm proud of the way I've lived, and I think my family is, too.

"That's all I think about, my family. I think they're proud of me—I know they are. I know they look up to me. And my friends, they feel the same way . . ."

His daughter came into the room with a small bronzed trophy and handed it to him.

"Here," he said, "look at this. The Old-Timers' association gave it to me."

It was a plain trophy, showing a batter and catcher. The inscription read: "To Ed Cicotte. Old-Time Baseball Players' Association."

Those were the only words. It didn't say what the trophy meant, what it stood for. It didn't have to.

"They've invited me to every gathering," said Cicotte.

Cicotte spends these twilight years raising strawberries on the five-and-a-half-acre farm behind his house. He's not as active as he used to be, but he still runs his tractor the year round, tilling the soil in summer and clearing his neighbors' driveways in the winter.

He spends much of his spare time answering letters from youngsters all over the country.

"I still get two or three letters a week," he said, his face lighting up in delight. "I answer every one of them—every one."

"Do they ask you about the Black Sox?"

"Some of them do," he said.

"What do you tell them?"

"I tell them I made a mistake, and I'm sorry for it. I try to tell them not to let anyone push them the wrong way."

He is proudest of the letter he got from a lad in Germany. "All he wanted was my autograph," he said. "Imagine that, all the way from Germany."

The hour was growing late, and Ed Cicotte was on his feet again calling for his daughter.

"Virginia, give Mr. Falls some strawberries for his youngsters. He's got five kids, and they like straw-berries."

We shook hands again as we reached the door.

"Listen, now," he said, "if you need more straw-berries or more news, you know where to come. This door is always open."

As I went down the steps, I waved good-bye to the man in the plaid shirt, the blue denim pants, and the tan shoes, but what I noticed for the first time were his socks.

They were white.

Confessions of a Major League Superscout

by Si Burick
Dayton Daily News

October, 1971

When early risers among the Cincinnati Reds straggled into the Marriott hotel lobby in Atlanta one morning last summer, they found, as they usually do on the first day of a new series, the large, smiling, and friendly figure of Ray Shore, the club's superscout, awaiting them.

Snacks Shore—so-called because of the ravenous eating habits displayed when he was a Cincinnati coach—has a unique assignment. Living on the road most of the time, he is given routine scouting chores on occasion—appraising the general strengths and weaknesses of rival players who might suddenly turn up on the market. In such cases, his yea or nay vote would be given serious consideration.

But Shore's basic job is to scout immediate future rivals of the Reds in the fine-tooth-comb manner of a football scout.

Shore watches each player at bat, in the field, and on the pitching mound. He ferrets out the little habits of individual athletes in certain situations. Some are so subtle that only the highly developed senses of a trained baseball sleuth could discern them with the naked eye.

"What I've been doing for the last four years," Snacks says, "isn't altogether original with us, but we've tried to exploit it more than any other club. Far as I know, I'm the only one who's doing this kind of job regularly."

The fact that in the immediate wake of his findings the Reds lost a doubleheader to Atlanta is not necessarily embarrassing to Shore. Human frailty and human unpredictability must be considered. His computer-mind findings, while generally accurate, are not necessarily infallible.

"What you are trying to get is a small percentage edge," he explains. "Like sometimes a guy you have tagged as an absolute pull-hitter will fool you by going the opposite way. Or a guy whose batting weakness is a change-of-pace will climb on an off-speed delivery and knock it out of the park. These things happen. My job is to get as close to the basic facts as possible."

Shore does not like to name names in discussing the weaknesses he has discovered in certain hitters.

"I think that would be unfair to the guy and also to us. If I've spotted something on this hitter, why should I run around the country telling everybody else, so they can take advantage? My job is to help us; not to hurt him."

The purpose of Shore's continuing assignment as a private baseball eye is to be absolutely current on each player. To illustrate this point, he was willing to be specific.

"Take Billy Williams of the Cubs. Certain times of the year, he pulls everything. You pitch to the outside of the plate when he's doing this. Then suddenly, you find he has adjusted. Pitch him outside, he'll hit to left or left-center going with the pitch. (Williams is a left-handed hitter.)

"In that case, I may tell Johnny Bench at one period that Billy's pulling everything. Later I tell the catcher to move the ball around on him. Williams happens to be a smart batter, who changes, who adjusts. There aren't too many hitters who follow this pattern.

"There's always the danger, too, that a pitcher's control isn't fine enough. Suppose he goes for the outside edge but throws the ball six inches in on the plate. The batter'll kill you. Essentially, when you talk of inside and outside, you're not dealing, though, in inches; you're talking about the inside half or the outside half of the plate.

"The better and smarter the hitter, the smaller the pitcher's margin for error is."

No matter how great a hitter is, Shore has discovered that there are certain spots which, if found consistently by the pitcher, will get the man out regularly.

"A lot of things we know are pretty basic," Shore adds. "I mean everybody knows them. But you still have to check for changes."

When a club is going poorly, how important is this intelligence?

"Knowing these things can give you a chance to shave a run off the other guy's total. That can win a game for you. When we were hitting and scoring so well in 1970, we could afford more mistakes than we can now."

Shore's first responsibility is to check the defenses against hitters, comparing them with what the Reds have been doing, and observing how successful they are, if they differ.

"In some cases, you reconfirm an old opinion; sometimes you recommend a change. You'll find that maybe a veteran no longer gets around on a fastball the way he used to. And you find that hitters, some of them, adjust during the season. Maybe early in his career he can't hit a breaking ball or an off-speed pitch. Now after being around a while, he learns how, and you'd better know it if a weakness becomes a strength.

"Then there are the players who chase bad balls. A pitcher has the advantage of a large strike zone with that kind. But you have to be aware of it when the batter reduces his own strike zone by laying off the bad pitch."

When he is scouting the San Francisco Giants, Shore says that watching Willie Mays play center field provides definite defensive keys.

"Mays' judgment is uncanny. If Willie positions himself in center field expecting the batter to pull, you can almost take it for granted he'll pull."

Tony Cloninger, the Cincinnati pitcher, happened to overhear the reference to Mays.

"When I pitched in Milwaukee," Tony said, "our bullpen was in center field, where you could watch Willie work. It was amazing to see the kind of jump he'd get on a flyball, compared to other center fielders."

Shore agrees. "Willie plays center field from what he knows the Giants' pitcher will do in every situation. With certain pitches, when the count reaches three-and-two, he'll move over a couple of steps. He senses that this pitcher unconsciously will release with a little less velocity because he doesn't want to walk the hitter. This gives the batter a better chance to get around on the fastball, so Willie adjusts."

Among other little keys on defense that Shore tries to spot is temporary physical incapacity.

"Sometimes, a guy who normally has a fine arm has a slight muscular problem. He won't show this in pre-game practice. But when the game begins, you can see that he's not throwing as hard, as far, or as accurately as usual. That's when you know he's hurting.

(Several years ago, the Reds got this kind of intelligence on Curt Flood, then with the Cardinals, and had a picnic taking the extra base on the center fielder.)

"You can spot a small muscle pull on an ordinarily fast base-runner, too, and use this to your advantage."

Are all of Shore's tips positive ones?

"No, I try to be basic, not technical. The understanding is that whatever I say is on a 'generally speaking' basis. Generally speaking, this guy hits the low fastball. Generally speaking, you can crowd this hitter. Basically, you can do better throwing this guy off-speed stuff."

The reason for not being specific with the usual

exceptions is that some pitchers could be hurt mentally if they attempted to be too fine with their deliveries.

"If guys like this concentrate too much on your information, they'll get behind the hitter and run into trouble. The pitcher has to rely on his general defense as much as his own control. You'd be specific, though, in the case of a man you refer to as a 'notorious' first-ball hitter. Your pitcher knows he'd better not lay one in there for him."

Sometimes Ray discovers that a hitter prefers a pitch on the inside, or at his knees, or above the belt, and that he can't lay off a delivery in one of these general areas. In these cases, he recommends that the pitchers throw the inside pitch several inches away from the plate, the low ball at the ankles, and the high one at the shoulders or above.

Why would a big league hitter chase a bad ball?

"Because he likes it high, or low, or inside and can't resist it. But you'd better not throw him a strike."

Another of Shore's responsibilities is to make comparisons between enemy pitchers he observes and those on the Reds' staff who have similar qualities.

"Take a fellow like Gary Nolan, whose stuff I know so well. I know his velocity, his curves, and change. Now if I see a pitcher who throws like Nolan but whose stuff is more effective against certain hitters, I suggest it might be smart to try a change of pattern—especially on a day when Gary's fastball is a little off or his curve isn't as sharp. Then the catcher should know what a comparable guy does in the same situation."

Shore admits it is possible after a while for a scout to discover he has had a false impression. "You'd better let the club know this in a hurry."

In judging pitchers, Shore discounts ground balls as a measuring stick. "The only hits that are important are the ones lined or one-bounced past an infielder. A hitter might get five little ground hits in one day, but I wouldn't change my thinking on him as a batter, or on the pitcher.

"What counts is power; how hard is the ball hit? How could you criticize Jim McGlothlin's pitching against the Phils because they loaded the bases on him with two seeing-eye singles and a bunt that couldn't be fielded?" This also goes for the two little grounders that beat Jim, 1-0, in Atlanta last June.

Shore believes this kind of percentage spying can give a team a special edge in modern parks with artificial grass.

"That's when defensive positioning in the outfield is important. Four or five feet can mean the difference between a single and a triple."

The Humor of Casey Stengel

by Maury Allen
New York Post

October, 1970

The stories on Casey Stengel are endless—and priceless. Here are some of them:

Tony Kubek was married while he was in service. Stengel sent him a $50 check and told him to take his wife out for dinner.

"I was stuck without any cash one day in Tacoma, Washington," said Kubek, "and I cashed Stengel's check in a drugstore."

When the check cleared, Stengel sent Kubek a letter.

"I told you to take your wife out to dinner," wrote Casey, "not buy a sandwich in a drugstore. What did you do with the rest of the money?"

"I was getting bombed," said Tug McGraw, "and Casey came out to get me. I didn't want to leave the game, so I begged him to let me pitch to one more man."

"I struck this guy out the last time I faced him," said McGraw.

"Yeah," said Stengel, "but it was in this same inning."

Yogi Berra says Casey once got a letter from a soldier in Korea in 1950 second-guessing Stengel's choice of Raschi over Reynolds in a big game in which Raschi was beaten.

"Casey sent him a telegram," said Yogi. "It said, 'If you are so smart, how come you are still in the Army?'"

Tom Gorman was umpiring in the Polo Grounds. Stengel motioned to the bullpen for a pitcher. In came Alvin Jackson. Stengel looked up just as Jackson reached the mound.

"I didn't want him," Stengel told Gorman, "I wanted the right-hander, Big Ben."

Big Ben—Larry Bearnath—stayed in the bullpen as Gorman ordered Jackson to stay in. "The crowd has seen Jackson come in here, and I'm not letting you change."

Casey reenacts a madcap moment that occurred during his playing career when he doffed his cap while a game was in progress and watched as a bird flew off his head.

Jackson went on to win the game. The next day Stengel presented his lineup card to Gorman without a pitcher.

"Who's pitching?" Gorman asked.

"You done so splendid picking one yesterday," said Stengel, "I'll let you pick him again today."

Casey was trying to teach Ed Kranepool how to play the outfield in 1963.

"He held the ball over his head," said Kranepool, "and he was showing me how to throw the ball down, across the seams, and how to hit the cutoff man. Then he throws it down at a sharp angle, and the ball goes off his own foot."

"Now," said Stengel, "that's how you keep the ball down."

Mark Freeman was pitching for the Yankees in 1960 with his career on the line. He loaded the bases in a spring game against the Tigers. He had two balls and no strikes on Steve Bilko. He went into his stretch, stopped, and suddenly staggered off the mound holding his eye. A balk was called.

"I couldn't help it, Casey," Freeman explained. "A bug flew in my eye."

"Dammit," shouted Stengel, "if you are going to pitch in the major leagues, you're gonna hafta learn to catch them in your mouth."

Yogi Berra was catching a game in Chicago in temperatures reaching over 100 degrees. Berra called a pitch, and Stengel didn't like it. The batter got a clutch hit.

Stengel yelled to John Blanchard: "Get your equipment on. You're going out there."

Blanchard dressed in all the catching gear. Two hours later Berra caught a foul pop, the final out of the game. Blanchard, still sitting in the corner of the dugout with all his equipment on, picked up a full bucket of ice water and poured it on his own head.

Photographers loved Casey Stengel for his knack of striking most any pose they desired, including this one of obvious bewilderment as he delights Duke Snider with his interpretation of a Mexican identification form required of the Mets for a spring training visit to Mexico City.

Stengel uses a bemused Gil Hodges as a model during a lecture on the new strike zone imposed in 1963. "Far as the plate is concerned," the Mets manager explained in simple Stengelese, "it's not any longer. It's just vertically." Confused listeners decided to let the umpires do the worrying. Others in the spring training photo are (left to right) pitcher Roger Craig, shortstop Bruce Fitzpatrick, and Bob Catton.

Roy Campanella
Recalls Branch Rickey
and the Dodgers

by Milton Gross
New York Post

Roy Campanella

November, 1969

It was an October night in 1945, Ruppert Stadium in Newark, and the start of the eighth inning of an exhibition game between an All-Star major league team and one from the Negro National and American leagues.

Charlie Dressen managed the whites. "I want to see you after the game," he said to Roy Campanella. "I'll meet you in front of the park."

Campanella had almost forgotten by the time he dressed afterward, and he was waiting under a street lamp for a bus when he heard a whistle and a voice call, "Hey, Campanella."

It was Dressen. "Where you staying?" Charlie asked.

"Up in Harlem, the Woodside Hotel," Campy said. "Why?"

"Mr. Rickey wants to see you." Dressen took an envelope from his pocket and wrote: "Take the A train, Independent line. Off at Jay St., Borough Hall. Montague Street, No. 215."

"Be there tomorrow at 10 sharp," Charlie said.

Roy made it to the old Dodger offices at 9:55. All the way downtown he speculated about the appointment. He had heard that Branch Rickey was going to form a team called the Brown Dodgers in something called the United States League. But at 24, Roy was one of the best and highest paid players in the Negro leagues. He was making $6,000 a year, including winter ball in Puerto Rico, Venezuela, and Cuba.

Campanella was struck by two things about Rickey: those overgrown eyebrows and a little book from which he read to Roy. It contained almost as much about Campanella as he knew about himself —personal qualities, family background, his baseball record going back to when the catcher was 15.

"Would you like to play for me?" Rickey said.

"Mr. Rickey," said Roy, "I'm doing all right where I am."

"Make me a promise you won't sign a contract with anyone else until you've talked to me again," Rickey said. "I'll be in touch with you."

A week later, Campanella and other black players were at the Woodside before leaving for Caracas. Among them was Jackie Robinson of the Kansas City Monarchs of the Negro American League. They went up to Campy's room for a gin game.

"I hear you went over to see Mr. Rickey last week," said Jackie.

"How'd you know?" Campy asked.

"I was over there myself," said Robinson. "Did you sign?"

"What do I want with the Brown Dodgers?" Campy said.

"Did Mr. Rickey tell you he wanted you for the Brown Dodgers?" Jackie asked.

"No," said Roy, "come to think of it."

"Look," said Jackie, "I signed, but it's a secret. You got to keep it that way—at least until tomorrow."

Jackie looked squarely at Roy. "I didn't sign with the Brown Dodgers," he said. "I'm going to play for Montreal."

The cigar in Campy's mouth went out as the significance of what Jackie had told him penetrated. Robinson was going to be the first black in organized baseball.

"In a year or two," said Jackie, "Mr. Rickey assured me I'd be with the Dodgers."

It wasn't until the following March that Campy heard again from Rickey. A cable advised him to report to Montague St. Campy caught the first plane out of Venezuela, but Rickey was in Sanford, Flor-

A smart catcher with leadership qualities, Campanella might have become the first black manager in the majors if it had not been for his tragic auto accident in 1958. He played 10 years with the Dodgers, led National League catchers four times in fielding percentage, hit 242 lifetime homers, and played in five World Series.

ida, where Robinson was in his first minor league training base. Bob Finch, Rickey's assistant, talked to Campy and then talked by phone to Rickey. Branch said there was trouble in Sanford, and Campy couldn't join the Montreal team. He suggested Danville of the Three-I League, which didn't want him either. "Mr. Rickey told me," said Finch, "to try Nashua, Class B."

Nashua wanted Campy. Buzzi Bavasi was the team's young general manager. Its manager was Walter Alston. A young black pitcher named Don Newcombe would make the trip to New Hampshire with Campy.

It all seems so long ago now. Nashua in 1946. Montreal in 1947. St. Paul in 1948, after Rickey told Campy: "I know you can make the Dodgers as a catcher, but I want you to do something bigger. I want you to become the first colored ballplayer in the American Association. Do you want to do this?"

"Mr. Rickey," said Roy, "I'm a ballplayer, not a pioneer. If you want me at St. Paul that's where I'll play. Because it's my contract. For no other reason."

He went. He came back to the Dodgers after 35 games. He stayed with the Dodgers until that horrible car accident on January 28, 1958, which left him a quadraplegic. Three times Campy was the National League's Most Valuable Player, and this summer in Cooperstown he was inducted into the Hall of Fame.

Rickey is gone and Dressen is gone, and Jackie and Roy were the beginning. Mays and Aaron and Frank Robinson and Gibson would soon follow, and there will be no end.

Branch Rickey shakes hands with manager Burt Shotton (left) after announcing that Shotton would be retained as manager of the Brooklyn Dodgers for the 1950 season. Shotton was Roy Campanella's first manager in the majors, Campanella having broken in with the Dodgers during the 1948 season.

The Death of Ebbets Field

by Murray Robinson
New York Journal-American

March, 1960

Until the very end of the Los Angeles Dodgers' lease on Ebbets Field, which expired with 1959, yearning Brooklyn fans hoped somebody—perhaps the backers of the New York entry in the Continental League—would come along and give the old park a reprieve, if only for a year.

Plans announced recently killed that hope for all time. Before summer Ebbets Field will be torn down to make way for a big apartment project to be built in the shape of an "H." The least they could do, it would seem to me, is to build it in the shape of an "E." Or maybe the "H" stands for Hebbets, as the late Eddie Bettan, the Dodgers' No. 1 fan, used to pronounce it.

I wonder how long it will take Brooklyn to forget the Bedford Avenue ball park. Not too long, if things run true to form. It isn't hard to imagine a scene in one of the 1,317 apartments in the new project on a summer's evening in say, 1985. The young host and a couple of pals are watching a Continental League game on pay-TV on a flat screen the size of the wall.

"Listen to those fans," the broadcaster, a chap called Gray Barber, chortles. "Sounds like a crowd at old Ebbets Field, yes indeedy . . ."

"Just where WAS Ebbets Field?" one of the "yoots" watching the game asks.

"Search me," the host replies, yawning. "The old man says it was right where this building is, but you know how they put it on. It could have been where that heliport is around the corner . . ."

"Naw," the other kid says. "That used to be Prospect Park; it had a zoo and a merry-go-round, stuff for real-square earthlings, my mater says."

I couldn't fault the 1985 teen-ager for doubting that he was sitting on the site of a legend, because the same thing once happened to me. This was in a speakeasy called Jimmy's away out in Brooklyn, and an old-timer was boozily recalling the glories that once were the Gravesend Race Track's.

"I've heard a lot about Gravesend Track," I cut in. "Just where was it?"

A hush fell over the joint. The old gent took off his cap and held it over his heart. "It so happens," he said with overwhelming reverence, "that you are standing right smack on the turn for home of the old Gravesend Track this very moment."

I still don't believe it. It's hard to believe that an apartment house, or a speakeasy, was once a fabled sports arena. Ghosts—except in English castles—are notoriously silent and invisible. Do they ever come out to cavort and wail under a watery moon on the site of old Madison Square Garden? (And ask the next guy you meet where it stood.)

But until the house-wreckers' lethal ball swings against Ebbets Field a few months hence, its physical presence will keep alive memories unmatched in any other ball park.

Charlie Ebbets, a rugged individualist with curly gray hair and a high, hard collar, opened it in 1913 on a droll note which was to become its trademark. There was a parade of dignitaries to the gaudy "rotunder" of which he was so proud—and then it was discovered that the key which was to open the gates with a flourish was missing.

The ball park was built on grassy ground favored by flocks of goats, chief fauna of the wild terrain, and it seemed that the god Pan, half-man, half-goat, played his pipes for the Dodgers to dance to ever after. They ran the bases like he was coaching at first.

Ebbets Field was craftily planned for verbal exchanges at close range. To reach the clubhouses, players and managers had to walk a grim last mile under the stand, separated from the vociferous customers by an iron picket fence. Hundreds of fans denounced their pet targets here, after every game, secure in the knowledge that the purpling performers couldn't get at them.

It was, indeed, a ball park to remember: Casey Stengel letting a sparrow, caught by the late Leon (26-inning) Cadore, out from under his cap while at bat. Manager Wilbert Robinson platooning 40 years ago, with Jimmy Johnston playing every position but the battery; Hy Myers playing second base, short, and center, and Clarence Mitchell, a left-handed spit-baller, doubling at first base.

Two of the club directors battling at a meeting; one was in the scavenging business and the other in the hat game. One screamed at the other: "Straw hats, derbies! Straw hats, derbies!" The other mounted a table and roared, "Dead horses, dead cats! Dead horses, dead cats!"

Uncle Robbie fighting in the clubhouse with pitcher "Boily" Grimes. A promising young outfielder named Bert Griffith ending his career after two years by injuring his heel—aboard a ship en route to Japan. Unforgettable fans: Big Abe Bettan, brother of Eddie of whistle-and-helmet fame; Shorty Laurice and the Dodgers Sym-Phony Band; Hilda Chester and her cowbell; and Mrs. Dorothy J. Killam, one of the angels of the New York team in the Continental League, who did the Lady Bountiful bit daily in her Ebbets Field box.

Zack Wheat, Dazzy Vance, Babe Herman, Lefty O'Doul, Dixie Walker, Pee Wee Reese, Roy Campanella, and Jackie Robinson—but don't forget Senator Griffin and Babe Hamberger, clubhouse clowns. Or the daffiest event in Ebbets Field history —Musical Depreciation Night, admission being any musical instrument. Two guys brought a piano.

Part of the zany setting at Ebbets Field was the Dodgers Sym-Phony Band. When a batter struck out at the plate, the band would provide him with musical accompaniment as he headed back to the dugout and give him a drumroll as he sat down. The fans were so alive and so many offbeat things happened at Ebbets Field that baseball's Commissioner Judge Kenesaw M. Landis once commented: "This doggone park is like a pinball machine."

Most famous of Dodger fans before the club pulled up its roots in Brooklyn's Ebbets Field was Hilda Chester, whose voice, Joe Garagiola once said, "sounded like the 10-second buzzer at Madison Square Garden. When she let out, you heard every word." But just in case, she also brought along a cowbell.

The Making of a Baseball Fanatic

by Sister Mary Barbara Browne, C.S.C.

January, 1973

Where does that special species known as the "baseball nut" grow? Recently I strolled past a beautifully grassed school lot where some Little Leaguers—Giants and Dodgers, decked out in appropriate uniforms—were playing. An announcer blared each player's name, the crowd roared, and the future star stepped to the plate. This is how the "nut" gets his start in an affluent society today; but the real ones flourished in the city streets and sandlots 40 years ago.

I first became aware of the "national pastime" when we lived behind old Recreation Park in San Francisco. In its place today stands a used-car lot, but in 1929 the park housed the now defunct San Francisco Seals. We lived in a lower flat right behind the wooden structure. In the vacant lot between the flats and the park, many of the kids of the neighborhood gathered, especially on game days. We delighted in knocking out knotholes in the wooden wall of the park in order to get a one-eyed view of home plate. Even the young Joe DiMaggio had his knothole so that he could watch his brother Vince—whom he was later to replace and go on to eclipse in fame—play for the San Francisco Seals.

At one time you'd have thought a machine gun had peppered the wall. Then the management decided to fill up the holes with cement. But never underestimate the power of the baseball nut, no matter what his age. Suffice it to say, we were at our holes the next day. How did we dissolve the cement? Let's just say it's a secret held sacred by all kids who run the streets of the asphalt jungle and play the game by their own rules.

Many a future major-leaguer stood at home plate and hit balls to their loyal fans outside the hallowed walls of the Old Rec. When Frankie Crosetti or Gussie Suhr were at the plate, we yelled and screamed for a trophy—and many times they obliged.

We weren't always satisfied to be banished to a vacant lot, however. Sans money or tickets, we devised a way to get into the park. After the seventh inning, the ticket windows closed, but a wary gatekeeper guarded the entrance.

Now for a gang of boys and girls who wanted to get into the ball park, he was fair game. Since kids can scamper like rabbits, more often than not we got past the watchman. Naturally, he made a show of trying to stop us, but once we got past him, he paid little heed. His resistance was only token, for he loved the neighborhood gang who lived by their wits and no pennies jingling in their pockets.

After the game we lined up outside the locker room doors, waiting for our favorites to emerge. Those ballplayers were kind to the kids—maybe because they remembered when they were in our position, or maybe they just understood our love of baseball. I can't recall any one of them refusing to sign our grubby little notebooks. If only I could find that tablet that had the scrawls of such Seal greats as Frankie Crosetti, Vince DiMaggio, and Gussie Suhr, but it has long since been lost along with other childhood treasures. What a collector's item it would be today.

Then one day the awful news came—they were going to tear down Recreation Park and build Seals' Stadium at Sixteenth and Bryant Streets. For the neighborhood gang, something else was torn down with the park. Our favorites were moving away—we'd never be so close again. There would be no knotholes in the concrete walls of Seals' Stadium; no locker room door would open on to the street. Oh, yes, we could get to the new park by streetcar, or more likely by hiking 15 blocks uphill. But it was never the same.

Loving the Seals the way we did, we followed them to their new home, which yielded its share of memories. During the summers of my high school years, I spent several afternoons a week at the ball park when the Seals played, for each week day was Ladies' Day. For awhile my sister went with me, but she gave that up because she said I disgraced her with my yelling and screaming for the home team. But what else does a baseball nut do?

I recall one night when our whole family went to a rather crucial game. As far as I know, this was the first and last time my mother ever attended a baseball game. I don't remember whom the Seals were playing, but I vividly recall the bottom of the ninth when the Seals came from behind to win the game. We screamed, yelled, and hollered and did everything else sports fans do when the home team wins. What makes this game so memorable is that in the excitement my father threw his new Panama straw hat in the air—and it never came back. I don't think Mom ever forgave him for that. The lost hat is still a favorite family anecdote.

Then there was Lefty O'Doul, the peppery man-

The DiMaggio brothers Dom, Joe, and Vince (left to right) were idolized by San Francisco baseball fans of another generation.

ager of the Seals. Now, there isn't a manager or fan in baseball who agrees with the decision of the umpire, unless, of course, the judgment is in favor of the home team. After a particularly exasperating call that irritated Lefty beyond endurance, he took out a large white handkerchief and waved it. Naturally that was the signal for the fans. The stands looked like Mrs. Murphy's backyard on laundry day. I don't know for sure, but I assume the umpire banished Lefty to the locker room for the remainder of the contest; however, after that, a waving mass of white handkerchiefs greeted every unpopular decision by an umpire—one of Lefty's legacies to the lore of the game. I guess that's strictly minor league stuff because I don't see such manifestation of emotions today.

As for the players I remember, Joe DiMaggio has to be the greatest. My most treasured memory is his throw from center field to get the runner out at the plate. I know you don't believe it, but I saw it. Of course, he was one of the greatest batters of all time. Long before he went to the Yankees, we dubbed him Deadpan because no matter whether he struck out or hit a homer, his expression never changed. Joe DiMaggio belongs to San Francisco as much as the cable car, Fisherman's Wharf, or Coit Tower. His name is as synonomous with San Francisco as St. Francis. To most of us who grew up in the late 1920s and early 1930s, he symbolizes the "local boy makes good" in the big city of New York.

Perhaps I remember DiMaggio so vividly because

the year I became a nun—1936—he went to the Yankees. I amused all my friends in the Novitiate by dating my entrance with DiMaggio's departure from Baghdad by the Bay. When a person enters religious life, he talks of things and persons given up. When I said the hardest thing for me to leave behind was baseball games, I was eyed as a nut of some kind. I'm not sure that anyone understood, but when you have baseballs for red corpuscles, you don't give up the game without a constriction of the blood vessels.

Years later I returned to California and the Bay Area only to find that my favorite team, the Seals, had been ousted by some team known as the New York Giants, who played in Seals' Stadium. I didn't even get interested in the now San Francisco Giants until they moved into Candlestick Park—and then, not because they were a baseball team but because the name of the park intrigued me. I think it's the most imaginative name for any ball park in the majors.

Then the baseball nut that had lain dormant for years began to respond to the names of Willie Mays, Juan Marichal, Willie McCovey, et al. When I visited my family in San Francisco, the talk revolved around the Giants. The fever started, mounted, and has never abated. My poor Mom still hates the game because during the season, a game is on TV and every member of the family has a radio plug in his ear, or else both TV and radio blare at the same time.

After so many years of not attending ball games, I looked forward with keen interest to my first visit to Candlestick Park. I'll never forget the first view—it was like coming home. I don't expect anyone but a baseball nut to understand how I felt, how I yelled, how I enjoyed the game. As the game progressed and we talked—a baseball crowd is just one big happy family—one young man (I always seem to sit beside a man who can't resist "the brotherhood" and after half a six-pack becomes talkative) asked, "How do you know so much about baseball?"

I looked at him, young and enthusiastic. He probably knew his baseball via the Little League route. I said, "I grew up behind old Recreation Park in San Francisco." Right there the generation gap became a chasm. Certainly he'd heard of Seals' Stadium, but the Old Rec meant nothing to him.

His noncommittal "Oh" demonstrated how young he was and how old I am.

However, an old-timer heard my answer, and I had found a kindred spirit. Between pitches we swapped stories that could only have been known by knothole watchers, and we bemoaned the fact that baseball would never be the same.

Carl Yastrzemski— The Game I'll Never Forget

as told to George Vass

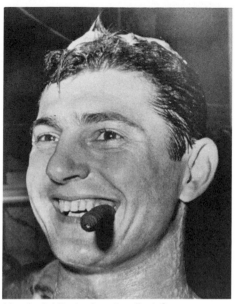

Yaz is jubilant after the Red Sox learned they had clinched the 1967 pennant. The players had to wait until the Tigers were eliminated by the Angels before being assured of the American League championship.

July, 1974

The game that I'll never forget was played the last day of the 1967 season, the one in which the Red Sox won the pennant to bring to life what they later called the Impossible Dream.

It has to be the game that day not only because we won the pennant but because it capped my finest year.

Everything seemed to fall into place for me that season and finishing on top made it perfect. The only disappointment we had was not winning the World Series from the St. Louis Cardinals, but it was an achievement to get into it.

Nobody really figured us to win that year. It was still a 10-club league in 1967, and until July it looked like Chicago, Detroit, and Minnesota would fight it out for the pennant to the end.

We started coming on in July, though, and people began taking us seriously after we went to Chicago for a weekend series of five games and won three from the White Sox in late August. We were in the middle of things.

We stayed right there through September as first one, then the other of the four clubs going for the pennant put on a surge only to fade back. For a while it looked like the White Sox would win it, but then the last week of the season the Kansas City A's took two from them in one day.

That put Detroit in good position. The Tigers went into the final weekend with four single games against the California Angels at Detroit. If they won all four they'd have the pennant.

But it rained the first two days in Detroit, and the Tigers were forced to play doubleheaders on Saturday and Sunday, the last two days of the season, which figured to put a strain on their pitching.

Our last two games were against the Twins, Saturday, September 30, and Sunday, October 1, at Fenway Park in Boston. The Twins were a game ahead of us in first place, with a 91-69 record. The Tigers were a game back with an 89-69 record and we were 90-70, also a game out.

To win the pennant we had to beat the Twins twice and the Angels had to beat the Tigers at least two of the four games they had left.

We won the game from the Twins, 6-4, on Saturday to pull into a first-place tie with them, while the Tigers were splitting with the Angels at Detroit.

There was something else at stake, too, in that Saturday game. Both Harmon Killebrew of the Twins and I went into the game with 43 home runs. I wanted to beat him out bad because I was leading the league in batting and in runs batted in, and if I won the home-run title, too, I'd get the Triple Crown.

I had a good day. I had three hits and drove in four runs, three with my 44th home run off Jim Merritt, who was the third Minnesota pitcher. But Killebrew hit a home run, too, so that added even more excitement and pressure—if possible—to the final day of the season.

Everything was on the line for us Sunday. If we beat the Twins and the Angels could beat the Tigers at least one of their two games in Detroit the pennant was ours. Even if the Tigers won both their games we could force them into a playoff by winning.

The home-run title was on the line, too, and the Triple Crown with it. If Killebrew hit his 45th and I didn't get one, I'd lose the Triple Crown, something few men ever have won.

I can tell you I didn't get much sleep Saturday night, thinking about what was at stake and worrying about whether I'd be able to hit Dean Chance, a real good right-hander who was pitching for the Twins Sunday. Chance already had won 20 games.

Manager Dick Williams had saved Jim Lonborg, our top pitcher who already had won 21 games, to throw against the Twins.

Right: Yastrzemski put it all together in 1967 to ignite the Red Sox in their pennant drive, winning the Triple Crown in batting and being voted the Most Valuable Player in the American League. In addition to 1967 when he hit .326, Yaz won league batting titles in 1963 (.321) and 1968 (.301), barely missing a fourth in 1970 with a mark of .3286 to Alex Johnson's .3289. Above: Yastrzemski (right) and pitcher Jim Lonborg after Yaz helped spark the Red Sox to a 5-3 victory over the Twins in the final game of the 1967 season.

The Twins got in front, 1-0, in the first inning, which was something to worry about with a guy like Chance pitching. They got another run in the third when, with Cesar Tovar on first, I played a single by Killebrew into an error, permitting Tovar to score.

You can imagine how that made me feel, though I'd gotten a single off Chance my first time up. I felt a little better when I got another single in the third inning. But we didn't score and we were still behind, 2-0, when our turn came in the fifth.

Lonborg beat out a bunt to start it out, Jerry Adair singled and then Dalton Jones got another single to load the bases. I was up, thinking we had Chance on the spot. We couldn't afford to let him off the hook.

I waited for my pitch. I figured Chance would come in with a sinker low and away sooner or later. I let the first pitch, a fastball inside, go by for ball one. Now I was ready for the sinker. All I had to do was to meet the ball, not try to kill it.

I guessed right. He threw the sinker, low and outside. I got the bat on it and lined the ball over the second baseman's head to drive in Lonborg and Adair with the tying runs.

Before the inning was over, we got three more runs and had a 5-2 lead. We had all the runs we needed. Lonnie gave up another run in the eighth but hung on.

The moment the game was over I sprinted for the dugout. The fans were pouring onto the field, and if they'd caught me they'd have torn my uniform into shreds for souvenirs. As it was I got pawed all over.

I'd gone 4-for-4 in the last game and got six hits in my last six trips to finish the season. Lonnie had kept Killebrew from hitting another home run, and we shared that title with 44. I'd won the Triple Crown with a batting average of .326 and 121 ribbies to go with the 44 homers.

But when the game was over we still hadn't won the pennant clear. The Tigers beat the Angels in their first game and the second one was still being played. If they won that too they'd tie us with a 92-70 record. We didn't want a playoff. You could never tell what might happen.

We all gathered around the radio near my locker listening to the game in Detroit. The Tigers led early but the Angels took a 4-3 lead in the third inning. That brought a big cheer from all the guys.

We still didn't feel too confident. That's a small ball park in Detroit, and it didn't take much to score a lot of runs. The Tigers could do it. We'd had it happen to us.

The Angels added to their lead and pretty soon they were ahead, 7-3. But the Tigers kept hacking away, and it was 8-5 when they came up for their last turn in the ninth.

It was deathly quiet in our locker room when the Tigers got two men on in the ninth with nobody out. The beer and sandwiches were untouched. But the third batter went out, and when Dick McAuliffe hit into a double play to end the game we went wild.

We tore the place apart and it was champagne instead of beer. We'd won the pennant.

210

The Funny Side of Baseball Brawls

by Wayne Lockwood
San Diego Union

August, 1973

Baseball brawls, even major ones, are over quickly. But the stories go on for days . . .

There was Joe Pepitone, explaining his role in the skirmish that broke out between the Giants and the Cubs in a game last spring.

"I assumed my defensive position," explained Joe Pep, demonstrating.

It seems that his defensive position involves placing one hand squarely atop his cap (and thus his toupee) and, with the other, clutching a bat at the trademark in limp-wristed fashion.

"I stood like that for awhile," he remembers, "and then some guy comes up and taps me on the back.

"I turn around, and it's Willie Mac [McCovey]. I say, 'Hey, Willie Mac, I'm on your side. I like more guys on your team than I do on mine.' "

Showing more heroism, perhaps, but less sense is Jose Cardenal.

Showing more courage than sense, Jose Cardenal (5-foot-10, 150 pounds) once challenged Willie McCovey (6-foot-4, 225 pounds) during a scuffle between the Cubs and Giants. "I want you, beeg man," said Jose (bottom). McCovey (left) said nothing. He laughed.

When the scuffle broke out, Cardenal bolted directly toward McCovey.

"I want you, beeg man," the five-foot-ten, 150-pounder said while leaping in the air to launch a swing at the six-foot-four McCovey.

It was still a foot short. Even McCovey had to laugh . . .

Brawls, of course, are nothing new to the Cubs.

There was, for instance, the moment last summer in a game between the Cubs and the San Diego Padres when Rick Monday and Pat Corrales suddenly became don't-invitems at home plate.

That one caught Ken Rudolph in the clubhouse, where he had snuck from the bullpen to shave.

Such things being against club rules during the game, Rudolph hurried to finish—nicking himself a couple of times in the process—and joined his teammates just as the scuffle came to an end.

Some players, observing his bleeding face, treated him as a wounded hero.

Those in the bullpen who knew better were laughing too hard to say anything.

Then there was the game in Wrigley Field last year, one in which Milt Pappas posted his 200th career major league victory.

It also was one in which Cardenal, knocked down by a pitch, directed some choice language at Expo manager Gene Mauch.

As the game ended, Mauch and some 20 of his players strode toward the Chicago clubhouse to express their displeasure at Jose's indelicacy.

"Look at that!" marveled Chicago broadcaster Jack Brickhouse. "That's the most sportsman-like thing I've ever seen. Gene Mauch is leading his entire team over to congratulate Milt Pappas on his 200th victory."

The last word on matters of this kind was audible during spring training when the Giants and Angels got into it.

As the hostilities flourished, one voice could be heard above the rest.

"Get Fox, get that [censored]!" it suggested.

Charlie Fox is the San Francisco manager. The voice belonged to Al Gallagher, then the San Francisco third baseman.

It was not exactly a shock that Al was later traded to the Angels. . . .

In 1957, when the White Sox and Yankees engaged in a wild fight at Comiskey Park, Bob Keegan watched the start of the battle from the safety of the center-field bullpen. Unable to restrain himself any longer, Keegan shouted, "Whitey Ford is my man!" He then jumped the fence to join the fray and fell unceremoniously into a puddle of water. He never did get to Ford.

Carl Mays Recalls That Tragic Pitch

by Jack Murphy
San Diego Union

May, 1971

He is best remembered as the man who threw the pitch that killed Ray Chapman 50 years ago. His name is Carl W. Mays. He will be 80 on his next birthday, and he deserves better from history than he has received.

The death of Chapman gave him the kind of notoriety that tends to eclipse his accomplishments during the period of 1915–29. He was a 20-game winner in both the American and National leagues, he is one of 62 pitchers in a century of baseball with 200 or more victories, and his earned run average (2.92) places him 14th among his peers.

Mays, you might conclude, is a fellow who belongs in the Baseball Hall of Fame. Yet when the veterans committee of the Baseball Writers Association of America recently voted to enshrine six old-timers, including Rube Marquard and Chick Hafey, Mays was not among them.

That was another disappointment for the old submarine pitcher in his twilight years, and he doesn't try to conceal it.

"I think I belong," he says, "I know I earned it. They took in Marquard this year, and that's fine with me. He was a great pitcher. But I deserve it, too. I won seven more games than Rube, and I lost 51 less than he did. What's wrong with me?"

A good question. There are some who believe that Mays not only belongs in the Hall of Fame but deserves a citation for courage. It is not easy to go through life with the memory of killing a man, and Mays has borne it well. Further, he had the strength to prevent the accident from destroying his career.

It was August 16, 1920, when Ray Chapman crumpled after being struck by one of Mays' submarine fastballs. He died the next morning in a hospital, and there was speculation the tragedy would shatter Mays. Ban Johnson, the league president, predicted Mays would never throw another pitch.

He did, though. He pitched in turn and did his job so effectively he won 26 games for the New York Yankees that year. The following season, 1921, his record was 27-9.

A half century later, Mays freely discusses his role in the death of Chapman because he feels no guilt or remorse. Mays is a young 79. He looks 60, and his only concessions to age are a cane for his arthritic-ridden legs and a tendency to shout.

He doesn't hear very well. "If I don't talk loud I can't hear myself."

But he's spry enough to go bird and deer hunting in the country around his home in Dayville, Oregon, population 174, and he goes south each winter to San Diego to assist his nephew, Jerry Bartow, the baseball coach at Hoover High School. Three afternoons each week he does the thing he loves best—teach baseball to young people who are eager to listen and learn.

If they ask, he'll tell them about Ty Cobb ("the greatest and the meanest ballplayer who ever lived"), Babe Ruth (his roommate for 13 years), and Ray Chapman, the only ballplayer ever killed by a pitch.

"I don't mind discussing it," he says, "it's not on my conscience. It wasn't my fault."

He reconstructs the scene. "Chapman was the fastest base-runner in the league; he could fly. He liked to push the ball toward second or down the first-base line and run. I had to guard against this, of course.

"I knew that Chapman had to shift his feet in order to get into position to push the ball. I saw him doing this—I was looking up at him because I was an underhand pitcher, my hand almost scraped the ground—and I threw my fastball high and tight so he would pop up.

"Chapman ran into the ball. If he had stayed in the batter's box, it would have missed him by a foot."

Mays summoned strength to continue his career. "I fooled them. I went out and pitched the rest of the year. Why should I let it ruin the rest of my life? I had a wife and two children, and they had to eat. I had to make a living. I had to provide for them."

The tragedy of Ray Chapman aside, Carl William Mays was a pitcher to remember. Five times he won 20 or more games, and when he quit after the 1929 season he had a career total of 208 victories and 126 defeats.

Later, Duffy Lewis was to say of him: "Carl Mays wasn't very popular, but when nobody else could win Carl could. He was a great stopper."

He became a submarine pitcher because of a sore arm, and his competitiveness was legend. In 1918 he pitched and won both games of a doubleheader against Philadelphia to clinch the pennant for the Boston Red Sox. He pitched in a way calculated to inspire respect, even fear, among the hitters.

"I had a good sinking fastball—what they call a slider now—and it broke in on either right- or left-handers. I pitched inside to everybody."

Harry Hooper, voted into the Hall of Fame this year, remembers Carl Mays: "Carl had an odd disposition but he was a great pitcher, and I have a warm regard for him."

When Mays retired as an active player, he served for 20 years as a scout with the Cleveland and Milwaukee clubs, and that part of his life gave him great pleasure. He likes young people, and he enjoys their company. His son, Carl Jr., is senior vice-president of the National Bank of Oregon, and you can see the pride in the face of the elder Mays when he shows you the clipping.

He'll also roll up a trouser leg and show you a long, ugly scar—a souvenir from the spikes of Ty Cobb. He got it while covering first. Cobb laughed at the bloody wound.

"The next time you cover the bag," he told Mays, "I'll take the skin off the other leg."

That was baseball in the time of Carl Mays. They didn't hit one of his pitches out of the ball park until August of his third season in the big leagues. A pitcher, Reb Russell, was the first. Mays was humiliated.

"I couldn't eat that night. I thought I was through. A pitcher had done that to me. It was awful."

That was 1917. Poor Carl. He only lasted 12 more seasons.

Carl Mays

Ray Chapman

They Pinch-Hit for the Greats!

by Herbert Simons

February, 1962

The situation was desperate. The manager turned to Walter Mitty, placed a hand on his knee, and said, "Mitt, I can't even depend on the Babe in a spot as tough as this. Only you can be counted upon. Go up there, Mitt, and give us that winning hit." A roar of approval went up from the stands as Mitty grabbed a bat and strode confidently. . .

That's the way James Thurber's famed daydreamer would have envisioned it. But a handful of big-leaguers had it all over Mitty. He only daydreamed the miracle. Sid Gordon, Ben Paschal, Fred Payne, Carroll Hardy, and several others actually lived such an unforgettable moment.

They pinch-hit for the greats!

Some of the game's greatest stars—Hall-of-Famers such as Babe Ruth, Ty Cobb, and Lou Gehrig—have sat on the bench while someone was swinging for them, Babe Ruth at least five times!

According to one of the cherished anecdotes about Cobb, the Georgia Peach, then in the twilight of his career, supposedly said to Connie Mack, his manager, one afternoon: "No one ever pinch-hits for Cobb." The story goes further, adding that Cobb then strode to the plate and came through with a base hit.

Even if Cobb did make the remark, what he said wasn't true, for there were times when pinch-hitters were used for Cobb. Four times, to be exact.

The first time was April 24, 1906, when the Tigers were at St. Louis. This was in Cobb's first full major league season. Manager William Armour sent Sam Crawford to the plate to swing for Cobb against Barney Pelty in the ninth inning. Crawford singled, but the Tigers lost anyway, 2-0.

A pinch-hitter was also used for Cobb later in the same season, on September 18, 1906, when Boston was at Detroit. This time a pitcher, George Mullin, swung for Cobb.

Legend persists that Cobb was substituted for under the most unusual circumstances. The Tigers, supposedly, were six runs behind starting the ninth inning and so Cobb, who had been the last batter retired in the eighth, headed for the clubhouse, figuring he wouldn't get to bat again. But the Tigers then rallied and had scored four runs and had the bases loaded when it was Cobb's turn to bat.

"Where's Cobb?" asked manager Hughey Jennings.

"Under the showers," he was told.

A pretty story, of course, but not quite true.

First, Armour and not Jennings was the Tiger manager at the time. Second, the Tigers never did score as many as four runs in the game and lost,

Duffy Lewis: He singled for Babe Ruth.

Sid Gordon: He singled for Mel Ott.

7-2. Third, newspaper accounts of the incident indicate that Cobb was withdrawn because of a batting slump. Here is an account from the files of the *Detroit Free Press:*

"In the ninth Armour derricked Cobb, and Mullin, who subbed, hit center field with a triple. It was a run, Payne coming right along with his third safe drive of the day."

The report also makes mention of the fact that Cobb was hitting .323 at the time and was fourth in the American League race. However, he had gone 0-for-4 against Nick Altrock of the Chicago White Sox the day before and was 0-for-3 in the Boston game against Jesse Tannehill, fanning twice on slow curves.

"On two days left-handers put a dent in Cobb's batting average," the *Free Press* said.

Fred Payne, who had a .215 lifetime average and never played a full season during his six years in the majors, is distinguished by the fact that he batted for Cobb in the eighth inning May 30, 1906, and singled.

"Cobb struck out three times in a row and in the eighth Armour sent catcher Payne in to bat for him," the next morning's papers chronicled.

Thus three men batted for Cobb during his first season in the majors—and none in the next 15 years. In fact, it wasn't until May 5, 1922, that a fourth man achieved the distinction. The honor went to Bob Fothergill, a noted pinch-hitter.

The Browns were playing at Detroit that day, and, the press reported at the time, "Manager Cobb

benched himself for a pinch-hitter in the ninth, sending in Fothergill, who flied out to Ken Williams in left field." The Tygers, as the fancy writers spelled the team name in those days, lost, 6-1.

Duffy Lewis has the distinction of serving as the first of several substitute batters for Babe Ruth. This was in 1914, the day the Babe made his major league debut. The date was July 11, a Saturday, and the Babe, just purchased by the Red Sox from Baltimore as an outstanding pitching prospect, started against Cleveland at Boston.

Through six innings the Babe held the Indians to five scattered hits, all singles, while his mates gave him a 3-1 lead. But in the seventh, three singles and a sacrifice netted two runs for Cleveland and tied the score.

It was in the home half of the seventh, then, that Lewis, who with Harry Hooper and Tris Speaker formed one of the greatest outfields of all time, batted for the Babe and singled in second baseman Steve Yerkes with the run that won the game, 4-3.

Dutch Leonard finished on the mound for the Red Sox, striking out four of the six Indians who faced him and preserving the victory for Ruth, who thus made his first big league appearance a winning one, if not a complete one.

"I was out with a bad ankle at the time," Duffy recalled recently. "The Babe could hit the long ball, but he struck out a lot of the time. Our manager, Bill Carrigan, asked me if I could hit. I told him I thought I could and, as it turned out, I did."

At least three other players batted for Ruth dur-

Carroll Hardy: He popped up in batting for Ted Williams.

Bobby Veach: He singled as Ruth's substitute.

ing the era in which he was primarily a great left-handed pitcher prior to his becoming the greatest homer-hitter the game has ever known. They were Forrest (Hick) Cady, April 24, 1915, against the Philadelphia Athletics; Delos (Sheriff) Gainor, June 29, 1915, against the Yankees, and Olaf Henriksen, July 7, 1916, against Cleveland. Cady and Gainor failed to get a hit, but Henriksen drew a pass.

In every instance that a pinch-hitter was used for pitcher Ruth, the Babe had hurled good ball. Once the pinch-hitter won the game for him, and another time the pinch-hitter saved him a defeat.

Ruth, sent in to replace Dutch Leonard in the fourth inning, had pitched three and one-third hitless innings when Cady batted for him in the seventh inning of the 1915 game against the A's, but the game already had been lost, 6-3, when Ruth went to the mound.

It was in the 10th inning of the June 29, 1915, game that Gainor batted for Ruth. The Babe had pitched eight-hit ball but could only get a 2-2 tie against Ray Caldwell in regulation time.

The Yanks went ahead, 3-2, against Ruth in the 10th. Henriksen, batting for the catcher, then opened the home half with a walk. Gainor, sent in to hit for Ruth, tried to sacrifice and popped a little fly to Caldwell. But the Red Sox did get another man on, and Tris Speaker's fifth consecutive single off Caldwell capped a two-run rally that gave Ruth the win.

When Henriksen batted for Ruth, the walk he drew figured in the run that tied the score at 1-1, after Ruth had allowed only four hits in seven innings. The Red Sox scored again in the eighth, and the 2-1 victory went to reliever Carl Mays.

After Ruth became a full-time outfielder, a pinch-hitter was used for him only once. That was on August 9, 1925, when Ruth was with the Yankees. The pinch-hitter was Bobby Veach.

This was in the eighth inning of a 12-inning game with the White Sox at Yankee Stadium, which the Chicagoans won, 4-3. One account of the game noted: "Babe Ruth was replaced in the eighth inning by Bob Veach, who was announced as pinch-hitter for the home-run king. Ruth had not been feeling well and was willing to retire."

The *Chicago Tribune* didn't phrase it so gently. "The fans were treated to the unusual spectacle of His Royal Highness being yanked for a pinch-hitter," bluntly reported their correspondent.

Veach singled when he batted for the Babe and then went to center field with Earle Combs moving over from center to fill the Babe's role of right fielder.

Just seven days before Veach batted for Ruth, a pinch-hitter was used for Lou Gehrig. Imagine!

Pinch-hitters for both Ruth and Gehrig within a week!

It was on August 2, 1925, that Ben Paschal went up to the plate for Larruping Lou. Cleveland, playing at Yankee Stadium, had gone ahead by one run in the eighth. With Southpaw Walter Miller on the mound for the Indians, manager Miller Huggins sent the right-handed Paschal up to bat for his yearling No. 5 hitter, the left-handed Gehrig. Paschal was retired, and the Yanks lost, 3-2.

A pinch-hitter was used for Stan Musial quite a few times during his first season, 1942. At that time he was being platooned with Coaker Triplett and it happened more or less frequently, he says.

The only time a pinch-hitter was used for Ted Williams, as far as available evidence reveals, was during the last few days of his illustrious career—and then only because he'd injured himself by fouling a ball onto his foot.

So Carroll Hardy gained immortality of a sort by rushing in from the Red Sox bench to pinch-hit for him. On the next pitch Hardy bunted a pop fly to pitcher Skinny Brown, who threw to first to double up Willie Tasby. End of Big Moment.

When a pinch-hitter was used for Mel Ott, it was his own doing. It was Labor Day, 1946 (September 2), in Boston and the Giants had lost the first game of the holiday doubleheader to Mort Cooper, 6-2. The Giants were trailing, 3-0, going into the seventh inning of the nightcap when Walker Cooper, Mort's brother, tied the score with a three-run homer off right-hander Ed Wright.

After a pair of singles and a double error followed the homer, putting another run in and leaving two on, Ernie White, a lefty, was sent in to replace Wright. Ott, a lefty, too, immediately pulled himself and designated Sid Gordon to hit for him. Gordon singled Willard Marshall home to continue a rally that wasn't stopped until it amassed eight runs for an 8-3 triumph.

From time to time reports have been printed that Honus Wagner, the Pittsburgh immortal, had a pinch-hitter once, too. Fellow by the name of Bill Wagner, who supposedly did the Walter Mitty bit for Honus in 1916. Intensive research, however, has failed to substantiate this.

To the best of everyone's knowledge, including Yankee officialdom, no one ever pinch-hit for Joe DiMaggio, either.

But if no one pinch-hit for DiMaggio or Wagner, there certainly were pinch-hitters for Cobb, Ruth, Gehrig, Musial, Ott, and other greats.

If nothing else this should prove that pinch-hitters aren't just aiming at the stars. Some of them have swung for them, too.

216

When Hank Greenberg Chased Babe Ruth's Mark

by John F. Steadman
Baltimore News-American

Hank Greenberg

May, 1965

He made the scene in the greatest era of home-run hitters baseball ever knew. Babe Ruth was at the end of his storied career but there were names like Lou Gehrig, Jimmie Foxx, Joe DiMaggio, Hal Trosky, Zeke Bonura, Ted Williams, Mel Ott, Johnny Mize, Chuck Klein and, yes, Hank Greenberg.

Greenberg, the kid who had once worshiped Babe Ruth from his seat in the bleachers, was an awesome and destructive giant with a bat in his hand.

The Detroit Tigers signed Greenberg away from the New York Giants and the Yankees, and he went on to establish himself as one of the most respected long-ball hitters in all history.

Four of what would have been Greenberg's most productive years were spent in military service. He enlisted in the Army in 1941, seven months before the Japanese pulled the hidden ball trick at Pearl Harbor, and didn't get out until just before the atom bomb knocked down the fences at Hiroshima in 1945.

Greenberg had some highly productive seasons. He helped the Tigers to four pennants—in 1934, 1935, 1940, and 1945—the latter season when as a tired old soldier mustered out of the service he hit a grand-slam homer on the final day of the schedule to give his club the championship.

It was 25 years ago that Hank produced an average of .340, drove in 150 runs, and thundered 41 home runs out of the park.

In 1938 Greenberg had chased after and failed to match the Babe's record of 60 home runs in a single season. He hit 58 and had five games remaining to get two more, but he never found them.

The 1938 pursuit of Ruth found Greenberg in Cleveland on the final day, playing a doubleheader. In the opening game Bob Feller set a record of 18 strike-outs, two by Greenberg. Time ran out before the second game, with Johnny Humphries pitching, could be completed.

The umpire was George Moriarty, an Irishman who never backed off from a fight and who was fond of the popular Greenberg. There was no night ball yet in the American League, and so at the end of seven innings, Moriarty said, "I'm sorry, Hank,

I'll have to call the game. This is as far as I can go."

"That's all right," answered Greenberg, "This is as far as I can go, too."

That 58 home-run year was the closest approach to Ruth's mighty mark until Roger Maris slugged 61 in 1961 in 161 games. In a way, it was a shame that Greenberg didn't get to Ruth's mark first.

Greenberg never openly complained that he came so close but missed in his quest of 60 home runs. "I never compared myself to Ruth," he said. "Nobody could."

Hank was extremely articulate, kind and considerate, highly admired by his teammates and opponents. When he was a boy in the Bronx, going to James Monroe High School, Hank had watched Ruth and lived in awe of his ponderous home-run swing.

Greenberg was six-foot-four and 215 pounds and didn't exactly have the moves of a ballet dancer. But by dint of hard work he more than made the grade. In fact, he improved himself by application and perspiration to earn a place in the Hall of Fame.

He would arrive at the ball park early, even as a major-leaguer, to work on his fielding and hitting. The curveball, the bane of so many hitters, once gave Greenberg trouble but he learned to handle it as his lifetime total of 331 home runs and an average of .313 attest.

"When I was a kid, I practiced eight hours a day for nothing," said Hank, "so why wouldn't I do the same thing when I got to be a pro?"

With the Tigers, Greenberg once used a first baseman's mitt that was as long as a cestus. He had an immense reach as it was, but the oversized mitt gave him the impression of almost being able to reach halfway across the infield.

A measurement was made of Hank's trapper model, with a long net on it, and he was told it was so large that it violated the rules governing a first baseman's mitt. He tailored it down and everybody was happy.

Greenberg played with those fiery Detroit Tiger teams of the 1930s, which included the likes of Mickey Cochrane, Charlie Gehringer, Schoolboy Rowe, Tommy Bridges, JoJo White, and Flea Clifton.

It may not have any personal meaning for Greenberg to know it, but there's a sportswriter in Baltimore who once pursued him for an autograph in Washington when the Tigers were playing there. He had already disappeared down the tunnel of the dugout toward the clubhouse, but he heard the cry of a small boy hollering almost pitifully, "Hank . . . Hank . . . come back."

Hank Greenberg did turn around. He walked out to meet his No. 1 fan. He smiled, took the book and the pencil. We still have Hank Greenberg's autograph.

Rudy York (left) was the Tigers' catcher and Hank Greenberg the first baseman in 1938 when Greenberg made his assault on Ruth's one-season home-run mark. Hank hit 58, two short of the Babe's record. York hit 33 home runs himself that year.

A big (6-foot-3½) right-handed hitter, Hank Greenberg takes his cut in a game during the height of his career. He played for the Detroit Tigers from 1933 through 1946 and finished with the Pittsburgh Pirates in 1947, amassing 331 lifetime homers. Greenberg was elected to the Hall of Fame in 1956.

Hack Wilson:
The Tragic End
of a Great Hitter

by Al Drooz
Cincinnati Enquirer

October, 1974

In 1974, the year of the momentous home run, when a new king has been crowned and the old one resurrected, the memory of the man who still holds the National League season record for homers, as well as the major league RBI mark, continues to gather dust.

In fact, Hack Wilson has been forgotten so long, from the Hall of Fame on down, one is almost tempted these days to suspect a cover-up.

You see, Hack Wilson batted right-handed and threw right-handed, but he drank equally well from either side. He played as hard off the field as on, and toward the end of his career it showed in his play.

There are those who still remember the day Brooklyn pitcher Boom Boom Beck, disgusted with being lifted, turned and heaved the ball off the outfield wall, waking up Hack, who ran the ball down and pegged it home.

But for half a dozen years, Hack was the premier power hitter in the league, the highest-paid player in the game except for Babe Ruth, and the man who put National League sluggers on a par with the American when he slammed 56 homers in 1930, shattering the NL record by 13. His major league record 190 runs batted in (the same year) hasn't been approached in 37 years.

Few ballplayers ever looked less the part than Lewis Robert Wilson, who packed close to 200 pounds on a five-foot-six frame. Perhaps because of his stature he became an instant favorite with the fans when John McGraw brought him up to the Giants in 1924.

"There was something comic about Wilson," wrote long-time Hall of Fame historian Lee Allen. "He looked like a sawed-off Babe Ruth." He took a lot of ribbing from opposing bench jockeys, and writers called him the Pudgy One. But there was no denying his talent, and fans took to him immediately.

He became so popular, in fact, that a New York paper held a contest to give him a nickname. The winning entry was "Hackenschmidt," for the legendary wrestler of the day, George Hackenschmidt. So Lewis Robert Wilson became Hack.

Through a clerical error, he became eligible for drafting, so 1925 saw the amiable Hack packing his 40-ounce bat for Chicago.

The next five years were Hack's glory years; he led the league in homers four of the five years, and over the period the only men in the game who drove more runs across the plate were Babe Ruth and Lou Gehrig. His lowest average was .313. And he took Chicago by storm, meeting much of the population personally after hours.

In 1929 Hack led the Cubs to the World Series with a banner year in which he collected 39 homers, 156 RBI, and a .345 average. Wilson, who rarely let razzing get to him ("Let 'em yowl"), provided Fourth of July fireworks one day when he left first base for the Reds' dugout and proceeded to punch out pitcher Ray Kolp. When he got the thumb, it was duly reported, "He departed with a smile on his face."

But the whole season came crashing down in the Series against the Athletics. In the fourth game, the Cubs cruising along 8-0, Hack lost a fly that started the most productive inning in Series history: the A's went on to score 10, three of which came when Hack lost another fly that went for a homer for Mule Haas.

The performance not only earned Hack a pair of goat horns, but an undeserved tag as a butcher in the field. "He never lived down the Series," says Waite Hoyt, his teammate briefly in 1931. "He wasn't a DiMaggio . . . but not too bad an outfielder."

Perhaps it was the bitter Series, perhaps the wild nights weren't taking their toll yet, or perhaps Hack was simply hitting his peak, but in 1930 it all came together and he had what may be the greatest season in league history.

Statistically, his season record was incredible: 56 homers, 190 RBI, .356 on 208 hits (while collecting 105 walks), 423 total bases. Under the circumstances, the stats are even more impressive.

Hack went into August with 36 homers, seven shy of Chuck Klein's league record. He went on to pound out 10 in both August and September. All the while, the rest of the Cubs were going into early hibernation, blowing a comfortable lead to the Cardinals in the stretch.

When he hit the record-breaker, No. 44, the story goes, he called his shot, promising his pitcher "a legit

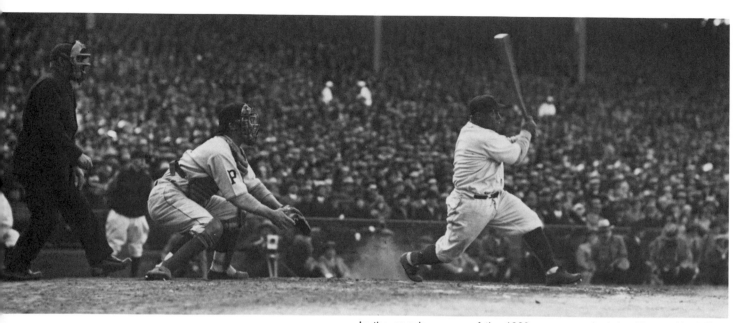

In the opening game of the 1929 season against the Pirates, Hack Wilson smacks one out in the first inning before a capacity crowd at Wrigley Field. The stocky, five-foot-six, 195-pound right-hander went on to hit 39 homers that season, and the following year slammed 56 to set a National League record which still stands. His playing skills deteriorated rapidly in 1931, and the Cubs traded him to the Dodgers after the season.

homer—and in this very inning" for losing a flyball in the field.

Of such stuff are legends normally made, but when remembered at all, Hack is usually associated with his off-the-field antics. "He managed to thrust himself on the public consciousness as a guy who didn't take care of himself," says Hoyt.

Hoyt admits the impression was an accurate one. "He was a very irresponsible type of fellow, especially in the later days. He would have been better off if he knew his limitations." Instead, the simple Wilson depended on home remedies like a quart of milk before a game to offset a quart of whiskey the night before. Mostly, gin was his tonic. In his own defense, Wilson said, "I guess a lot of people think I was half stiff all the time I was playing. That's not true. I played 11 years in the big league, and I never took a drink before a game. Sure, afterwards. And sometimes I'd play with a bad hangover. But I never took a drink before a game."

Two years after he commanded a Depression-time salary of $33,000, Hack was washed up in the majors. After a year in Albany, he was out of the game and in for hard times.

Hack turned up in 1938 playing the buffoon in Flynn's Tavern near Brooklyn's Ebbets Field, belting out "Take Me Out To the Ball Game" ("I don't sing so hot. But it's good and loud") and talking with the crowd. He was broke, the result of a costly divorce and a bad investment in a sporting goods store.

The next year, he tried his hand at his own club, the Hack Wilson Home Run Club in suburban Chicago. That, too, flopped.

He didn't surface again until 1942, when he showed up in Baltimore looking for a wartime defense job, which folded. He then begged for "any kind of a job" and was given a job as a laborer. He later was made manager of a park swimming pool when his identity was learned.

Hack became ill late in 1948, suffered a bad "fall out of bed," and succumbed to pneumonia at the age of 48, just a few months after Ruth's death. Only a $350 grant from the National League saved him from a pauper's grave, paying for his transportation to his Martinsville, West Virginia home.

It was a tragic ending for one of the greatest hitters in the long history of the National League.

Baseball's Best Years: The 1950s?

by Paul Borden

Condensed from the *Louisville Courier-Journal and Times Magazine*

January, 1975

Major league baseball was at its best in the 1950s. I know there are those of you who will take issue with me for such a presumption and berate me for my arrogance, but it was in the 1950s that I grew up into baseball. It was then that I learned how to pronounce Kluszewski, that it was the Cleveland Indians, not the Cleveland Browns, in the American League, and that it was 127 feet, 3⅜ inches from home plate to second base. And so I won't argue about it, not even for a "Let's clean house with Ike & Dick" campaign button. Baseball was at its best in the 1950s, and that's that.

It was easier to get acquainted with, for one thing. Eight teams in two leagues, American and National. No East-West split, no division playoffs. Only 400 players on 16 teams, and you knew every lineup. Even the batting orders. You could even hope to get a complete set of baseball cards, although nobody I knew ever did.

And the names. Not just Mantle and Musial and Mays, or Robinson and Campanella, or Williams and Berra. Not just Roberts and Simmons, or Raschi and Lopat and Reynolds, or Wynn and Garcia and Lemon. But the magical ones, like Bobby Del Greco and Sibby Sisti and the immortal Wayne Terwilliger. Who is there today? Wayne Twitchell? He's close.

Baseball was grilled hot dogs and mustard on your shirt, peanuts in the shell, four-hour car rides, and five-hour doubleheaders. It was listening to Harry Caray on static-filled radios on muggy summer nights or sitting in cramped upper-deck seats in crusty old arenas called Crosley Field and Sportsman's Park. Maybe you only got one trip there a year, but it didn't matter. After all, how many times could you go to heaven?

But what really made baseball, what put the major leagues at their best in the 1950s, was the World Series. Baseball ran the Series then, not television.

Baseball scheduled the Series, and it decreed the Series would start on a Wednesday, be played during the day, and if you wanted to listen to the game or watch it, you fit *your* schedule to theirs, not the other way around.

It meant that you rushed home from school at noon to get the first pitch, and you stayed until five minutes to one, though that meant you would be late since it was a 10-minute ride to school. You listened to the game in fourth period study hall, and in class, too, if you were lucky. No teacher gave tests in Series week.

It was that way every October, an autumn madness that transcended all of football. But it was especially so when the Dodgers challenged the Yankees. The Yankees—the team of Ruth and Gehrig and home runs, perennial champions. The Dodgers, famous for once having three men on third at one time, challenged them with ordinary weapons—bats and gloves and pitching arms. The Yankees had those, plus image and tradition. They won by reputation. They won because they were *supposed* to win.

You can ask Pee Wee Reese.

"I had always been a DiMaggio fan as a kid," Reese said, relaxing in his Louisville home. "Then to be in a World Series in 1941, just two years after I got my start in the old American Association, to be playing against Joe DiMaggio and Bill Dickey, well, it was just awesome. To walk into Yankee Stadium was an awesome thing."

Reese was a World Series fixture by the 1950s. He had played on Dodger teams in 1941, 1947, and 1949, all losing efforts to the Yankees. Thus Brooklyn begat its rallying cry, "Wait till next year!"

They thought it would be "next year" in 1952. The Dodgers had blown the pennant to the Giants the year before, but behind the bats of Robinson, Campanella, Snider, Hodges, and Reese, the glove of Billy Cox and the arm of Carl Furillo, the pitching of Preacher Roe, Carl Erskine, and especially Joe Black, they had swept to the National League pennant by four and a half games and were primed for the Yankees.

They beat the Yanks in the first, third, and fifth games despite the horrendous slump of Gil Hodges, who was to go hitless in 21 times at bat. "They tell the story about the priest in Brooklyn who said, 'It's too hot for a sermon today. Just say a prayer for Gil,' " Reese said.

But the Lord, that year at least, was a Yankee fan. The Yankees won the seventh game, 4-2, snuffing out a Dodger rally in the seventh on Billy Martin's running, knee-high catch of Robinson's pop-up with the bases loaded.

"Joe Collins was playing first base and he lost the ball in the sun," Reese said. "It was a fairly high pop-up, and everyone sort of stood around and

221

Dejected Dodger catcher Roy Campanella walks away from the plate after Hank Bauer (No. 9) scored the winning run for the Yankees in the sixth and final game of the 1953 World Series. Yankee coach Frank Crosetti (No. 2) and third baseman Gil McDougald, with bats in hand, are among the jubilant Yankees in the background. It was the fifth straight world championship for the Yankees.

watched it for a while. Then Billy took off. I had been on first at the time and was around to third when he made the catch. It was a helluva play."

The next year, the Yankees wiped out the Dodgers in six games. It was the fifth straight world championship for New York, a record yet unmatched. But at least one chronicle of Series history says that these Yankee teams, with Berra, Collins, Martin, Rizzuto, McDougald, Woodling, Mantle, and Bauer, did not rank with the truly great Yankee teams.

"That writer must have been thinking of the 1927 team with Ruth and Gehrig," Reese said, somewhat surprised. "This Yankee team was tough enough for us, and we had a good ball club. Not that they rolled over us.

"The thing about the Yankees, and you've probably heard this before, was that they could take a mediocre ballplayer or one like Johnny Hopp, Johnny Mize, Enos Slaughter, and Johnny Sain, someone in the twilight of his career, put a Yankee uniform on him and it would do something for him. He'd have a great year or make a big play for them."

In 1954, neither the Dodgers nor the Yankees made the Series. But they were back in 1955, and "next year" finally came for Brooklyn.

The Series began much like the others. The Yankees won the first two games before the teams switched to Ebbets Field, where "you could look up into the upper deck and recognize your mother, the stands were so close to the field," Reese said, and the Dodgers won the next three. The Yankees won the sixth game back in Yankee Stadium, and then came Game No. 7.

It was 2-0 Dodgers going into the bottom of the sixth inning with a left-hander named Johnny Pod-

res baffling the Yankees with his assortment of curveballs. Then the Yankees put two men on and Yogi Berra was up. He hit a pop fly down the left-field line, and Sandy Amoros, who had been put into the game that inning for defensive purposes, started his run to glory. He may have been the only one in the park who thought he had a chance to catch it. Certainly Gil McDougald, the runner on first, didn't think he could reach it.

"As I went out to get the relay, I saw McDougald out of the corner of my eye rounding second," Reese said, warming to the memory. "When Sandy caught the ball and threw to me, I didn't hesitate at all. I knew we had a chance to double up McDougald at first and I just whirled and threw it."

Reese's relay to first beat McDougald back, the threat was over, and Amoros had made the play that saved the Series for the Dodgers.

"The funny thing is, if I had noticed where Sandy was playing Yogi I would have moved him over closer to the line," Reese said. "Yogi used to hit a lot to left off of left-handed pitches. I thought Sandy was too far to the right."

While Amoros saved the Dodgers' 2-0 victory, Reese ended it. He scooped up Elston Howard's grounder and made a perfect peg to Hodges at first for the final out. Perfect peg?

"A few years ago, Don Hoak and I were in Cincinnati sitting around a hotel room having a couple of drinks, and he asked me about that play. He said the throw was in the dirt.

"I said, 'What do you mean the ball was in the dirt? You're crazy. I'll bet you $20 it was a good throw.' We kept talking about it, and I knew it was a good throw because I have some films of that Se-

Pee Wee Reese soars over a sliding base-runner in a double-play action that was typical of the Dodger shortstop in the 1950s. Reese and second baseman Jackie Robinson formed one of the memorable keystone combinations in the game and helped drive the Dodgers to National League pennants in 1952, 1953, 1955, and 1956. Reese was named the all-time Dodger shortstop by fans in 1969.

ries and have watched them several times. What Gil did was catch the ball a couple of feet above the ground and then sort of slap it down in the dirt.

"Anyway, Hoak insisted it was in the dirt and so I said, 'Let's call Gil.' It was about midnight then, and Gil was managing the Mets and was in another town somewhere, so we called him and got him out of bed. I said, 'How about that last throw to you to get Howard. Hoak says the ball was in the dirt.' Gil said, 'Pee Wee, it was in the dirt.'

"I said, 'Why you lying s.o.b., you know it was a good throw.' Then Gil started laughing and finally he said, 'Tell Hoak I said the throw was at least a foot off the ground.' So I got Hoak's $20 but I still don't think he believed us."

With the Reese-to-Hodges putout, the Dodgers, in their sixth shot at the Yankees and eighth at a world title, had finally won it all.

"I was beginning to think I never would play on a World Series championship team," Reese said. "I was kind of stunned when it was over. I just sat there in the locker room like I could hardly believe it. I was the only one on that ball club who had been there when we started all those things back in '41."

The following fall, Brooklyn got back to normal. The Yankees beat the Dodgers in the Series again, and Don Larsen threw a perfect game at the Dodgers to boot. It is the only no-hitter in World Series history.

Then baseball changed. The Dodgers tried to trade Jackie Robinson to the Giants, and he quit instead of going. In 1958, the Dodgers packed up and went to Los Angeles and the Giants went to San Francisco. The rivalry flamed between the Dodgers and the Giants for a while but as the old veterans, like Reese, began to retire, it flickered and nearly died.

The Yankees? They kept on winning, pennants at least. The Series was a 50-50 proposition. They split with the Braves in '57 and '58, lost to the Pirates in '60 and beat the Reds and Giants in '61 and '62. Finally, in 1963, the Los Angeles Dodgers whipped them in four straight. The Cardinals won in seven games over the Yankees in 1964, and the Yankees were never the same again. The veterans would put on their pinstripes, and the only thing the uniform did was make them itch. The Yankees haven't been in the Series in 10 years.

The leagues ballooned to 12 teams apiece and suddenly, it seemed, every hundred miles or so a big league stadium sprang up. They divided up the leagues into divisions, meaning a team that had survived a 162-game schedule had to fight its way through a five-game playoff to get into the Series.

"Maybe baseball, the game itself, would be stronger if they had just eight teams," Reese said. "But it's pretty hard to say, 'Well, Houston, you can't have major league baseball.' If they can support it, there's no way you can say they can't have it."

And what about the game itself? Has expansion diluted the product? Nope, Reese said.

"You take a ball club like Cincinnati with Bench and Rose and Morgan and Perez. There you've got speed and power and a very exciting team to watch. If someone doesn't like to watch a team like that play, then they just don't like to watch baseball."

Perhaps, then, in another 20 or so years, someone will sit down and write, "Baseball was at its best in the '70s." But I doubt it.

...And Their Catchers Weren't Too Good, Either!

by Harold Rosenthal

April, 1975

In their first undistinguished year of origin (1962), the New York Mets lost 120 games and used seven catchers. You could get rich betting the most ardent fan he couldn't name half this number.

The first man drafted by the Mets in the expansion was Hobie Landrith, made available by the San Francisco Giants. The Mets' idea was get a good catcher before anything else because that's what you need more than anything else. Hobie was little but durable—that is, he was durable until he came to the Mets. And Hobie, pronounced with a long "o," was his real name.

Once in an exhibition game in St. Petersburg, Florida, at Al Lang Field, there suddenly was a commotion around home plate which shivered the crowd back to awareness. Landrith was on the ground, and they were trying to slip his mask off. It developed that a backswing had nailed him on the side of the head . . . a rare occurrence.

Catchers know instinctively how close they can get without being hit. After 10 years of playing, Landrith had to become a Met to learn that his micromeasurements could be off by that vital fraction.

A couple of weeks later, when the Mets went over to Orlando to play the Senators, Landrith was back in business behind the plate. He didn't stay there long. Another backswing got him. "God," he exclaimed, "10 years without being hit and now twice in a month."

Landrith lasted until mid-summer, when he went to the Baltimore Orioles in part payment for first baseman Marv Throneberry. Throneberry was another story which won't be gone into here.

Then there was Clarence (Choo-Choo) Coleman, and I forget where the Mets got him. Casey Stengel liked him because of his low stance. "He catches them on his belly like a snake," said the old man. Couldn't hit, though, and there was a certain spareness in his vocabulary. Someone made the mistake of interviewing him on TV between games of a doubleheader and nothing happened. Finally in desperation, the announcer asked, "Choo-Choo, what sport do you like best?" "Tennis," said Choo-Choo. "Tennis? Where would you have played tennis?"

"High school," said Choo-Choo. End of interview.

At the end of that first lamentable season, and to get ready for another equally as inept, the players were asked to provide the club with their home phone numbers. Choo-Choo gave his Daytona Beach number to the road secretary.

During the winter there was occasion to get in touch with him. The face of the secretary placing the call was something to see. "This is the number of the Daytona Beach city hall," she said in a semiquaver while trying to contact Coleman.

And then there was Chris Cannizzaro, a tense young man drafted out of the Cards' organization. Stengel, never much on names, called him Canzoneri. There had been a lightweight champion, Tony Canzoneri, about 30 years earlier.

Cannizzaro was a graceful performer behind the plate although you had to bat him seventh or eighth because of his threadbare hitting. Came that inevitable afternoon when Cannizzaro let a low pitch get past him, and it cost the Mets a ball game against the Giants they thought had been won.

It seemed to shock Stengel well beyond its importance in the general aura of ineptitude surrounding the Mets. Someone asked him why he was taking it so badly.

"Jeez," rasped Stengel, "they told me he couldn't hit but they forget to tell me he couldn't catch neither."

But there were other catchers that incredible first year, people like Joe Pignatano, the ex-Dodger, who was to stay on as a coach for Gil Hodges and pick up a World Series check seven years later; Joe Ginsberg, acquired as a possible attraction for Jewish fans (Jewish fans or not, he was cut after appearing in only two games).

And there was Harry Chiti, who came from Detroit. He was a big, slow-moving right-handed hitter, and someone told George Weiss, who had brought his talent-sniffing abilities with him when he came from the Yankees, that Chiti would hit, given the chance. And with a 16-foot wall only 279 feet away in the old Polo Grounds, man, get that Chiti. He got his chance to hit. His .195 effort indicated that you can't win 'em all.

The best hitter the Mets had that first year was Frank Thomas, a third baseman-outfielder acquired from Milwaukee in a big deal. Thomas hit 34 homers. A dozen years later it's still a Met record.

Thomas, like the Chiti trade, was funny; but not as in hah-hah. Someone had tagged him with the

Choo-Choo Coleman   Harry Chiti   Hobie Landrith

nickname Big Donkey. Sometimes he gloried in it, laughing it up; sometimes he resented it. You just had to be sure you picked the right day.

Thomas' biggest moment was not seen by roaring thousands in the Polo Grounds or by millions on TV. It came during a pre-game warm-up before a game with the San Francisco Giants at that aging ball park, which was to become a housing development only a few years later.

Thomas was standing around the batting cage hooting down some of the Giants' pitchers, who were throwing batting practice. "Can't you throw any harder than THAT?" he'd demand. "I could catch you barehanded."

Willie Mays, jumping to the defense of his lesser-salaried teammates, came through with a brilliant retort. "Shut up, Thomas," he exclaimed.

"And you, too, Mays," Thomas retorted. "I can catch anything *you* throw barehanded."

"For how much?" demanded Mays. "For anything you wanna bet," responded Thomas.

"For 10 bucks," said Mays. "You got it," said Thomas.

So while the field crew wheeled away the batting cage, Mays strode to the mound, ball clenched in his right fist. Thomas took up his position behind home plate, wearing an owlish look and nothing on his hands.

"Y'still wanna do it?" shouted Mays, trying to figure out why someone would want to get himself crippled.

Thomas answered in the affirmative.

Mays wound up. The arm whipped back, and the few newspapermen who were in on the whole thing from the first exchange cringed. The ball would go right through Thomas approximately in the vicinity of his belt buckle.

Mays let go. In whizzed the throw. Thomas put his two hands in front of him to meet the throw just over the plate. On contact, he whipped his hands *with the ball,* to his left. The force of the throw took his clenched hands and the ball back somewhere behind his shoulder blade, but he held on.

Still unsmiling, he called out, "Okay, Mays, pay me."

Mays' eyes bugged. Then he glared at Thomas. He made a derogatory comment at Thomas, turned on his heel, and made for the dugout.

That's how it was with the Mets and their catchers in 1962.

How Pete Gray
Defied the Odds

by Robert Hendrickson

May, 1971

No one ever penned a panegyric on Pete Gray; in fact, he is not listed in any *Who's Who,* or even *Who Was Who In Sports.* His name is confined in print to old news columns, a few baseball encyclopedias, and less than a line in various histories of the game. Nothing more about one of the most fascinating players ever to throw a ball or swing a bat, and who was as great a hero, in his own way, as Babe Ruth.

Gray, who was born right-handed, is listed in the record books as Throws Left, Bats Left; but no asterisk explains that the outfielder *had* to throw left and bat left . . . that he was one-armed. Though he came on the scene in the early 1940s, it was not World War II that took his arm, for he was barely six years old at the time of his tragic accident. While in his hometown of Nanticoke, Pennsylvania, he jumped out of a grocer's moving truck. His right arm was crushed against the curb and was so badly mangled that it had to be amputated at the elbow.

Pete Gray was born that same day, six years after Pete Wyshner was born on March 6, 1917, although he did not take his pseudonym until he began his playing career. By the time he had chosen baseball he was about 13. Despite the odds against him, he made the Nanticoke High team, but he quit school in his first year, though a good student, to devote himself to the game. The pattern was already clear.

When he was only 15, he hitchhiked from Nanticoke to Chicago to see the 1932 World Series at Wrigley Field, an important turning point in his life. "That was when Ruth, with two strikes on him, hit Charlie Root's next pitch into the bleachers for a home run," he recalled later. "I said to myself, 'Pete, the whole trick is confidence in yourself. If you are sure you can do it, you *will* do it.' " Ruth's homer —after the Babe had held up one finger, indicating he had one more swing—convinced him that he would play major league ball.

Back in Nanticoke, Gray became the mascot of the local team. For the next 10 years he found out that time assuages little. He didn't marry, but de-voted himself entirely to baseball; he kept to himself, didn't drink, and his outside interests were few.

A lean, mean green kid, earning little and learning much, he battled his way through the bushes with top semipro teams like the Brooklyn Bushwicks until his first break came in 1942 when he made the Three Rivers Club in the American-Canadian League. There manager Mickey O'Neil, a former major league catcher, taught him more than anyone before about the game's fine points. That short season, in 42 games, Gray had 61 hits in 160 times at bat, batted .381 to lead the league, and scored 31 runs. He struck out only three times, and that pitchers respected him was evidenced by the 14 walks he gathered. By season's end, he was already being called Wonder Boy and the One-Armed Wonder.

When Pete Gray played for Three Rivers, baseball was fast becoming the modern game it is today. The fans liked Gray—what he lacked in power he made up with perfect place-hitting, superb fielding, and daring base-running.

In 1943, he signed with Toronto, but differences with manager Burleigh Grimes led to his dismissal before spring training was over. Gray, an excellent pool player, hadn't been able to find a game one night and joined a group of ballplayers in the hotel lobby discussing Grimes' managerial abilities, which Pete did not hold in high regard. Perhaps fortunately, Grimes happened to be eavesdropping from behind a potted palm, and the next morning the one-armed outfielder found himself a member of the Memphis Chicks of the Southern Association, a Class A-1 league.

At Memphis, Gray became the biggest box-office attraction in minor league baseball history. For two years he batted over .300 and fielded 1,000. He didn't depend on scratch hits to maintain his batting average, either, and could hit the long ball.

"Gray is a sharp line-drive hitter and slams them between outfielders for extra bases," Doc Protho, the Chicks' manager, commented. "He's very fast on the bases and is an expert at bunt and drag. The boy is at his best when the chips are down. It is actually uncanny how sure of a catch he is with one hand."

Other observers remarked on Gray's amazing sense of balance. "Imagine strapping your right arm to your side and running at top speed—and then winding up with a hook slide into a base!" one writer exclaimed. Pete hurt his hand early in the 1943 season, but this did not keep him from cracking eight hits in nine times at bat during the time he was injured.

Oddly enough, his favorite pitch was an inside fastball across his knees, which he could usually pull into right field. His longest drive was a 417-foot home run he hit while playing semipro ball in Canada, but he got his share of homers with Memphis, too.

In 1944, he smashed five home runs, including one 330-foot drive, in addition to batting .333 and stealing 68 bases to tie the league record. But these figures tell only part of the story. Gray was a colorful player who drew capacity crowds at parks from Memphis to New Orleans. An example of his unerring place-hitting was seen in a game against the Nashville Vols. In the fourth inning, he beat out a bunt. In the sixth, he lined a single to left. Then in the ninth, with the bases loaded, the Nashville outfield shifted to left when he came to bat, and he promptly lined to right, scoring two runners.

Though he was a flashy dresser off the field, Gray was basically a shy person. On the diamond he was a spirited player, and went out of his way to bait rival players and push umpires, regarding the men in blue as square heads in round masks. The fans idolized him. Every game he'd chase one that another outfielder wouldn't take a chance with, and he often came up with breathtaking catches, throwing runners out at the plate a number of times.

Gray was voted the Southern Association's Most Valuable Player in 1944. "If there is one guy who could pack them in in the big leagues, to beat Babe Ruth as a drawing card," a United Press newsman wrote, "his name is Pete Gray. He can hit the ball where they ain't—and there isn't a better outfielder in any league." It was on the strength of predictions like this that the St. Louis Browns bought Gray from Memphis for $20,000 in 1945.

The Browns had won the first pennant in their history the year before and were looking forward to another war victory in 1945. It was probably the war that gave Gray his big chance, though he would never have admitted it. Pete did get his break because of the manpower shortage that began when the first major-leaguer, Philadelphia's Hugh Mulcahy, was drafted in 1941.

During the war years, baseball was far from its best, but was close and exciting, a combination custom-made for a one-armed outfielder. Unusual characters breathed life into the game. There was the Dodgers' Frenchy Bordagaray, who has the honor of being the first major-leaguer to wear a goatee. In 1944, Cincinnati left-hander Joe Nuxhall started a major league game when he was only 15 years old, though he was shipped back to the minors

One-armed Pete Gray played 77 games in the outfield for the St. Louis Browns in 1945 when the major league rosters were filled with youngsters and ancient veterans because of the World War II manpower shortage. Gray lost his right arm as a young boy, but he didn't let the handicap keep him from developing into a skillful fielder. He caught the ball with his gloved left hand, quickly slipped the glove under the stump of his right arm, and let the ball roll down into his left hand so he could make his throw. At the plate, he anchored the base of the bat against his body and was able to make reasonably firm contact by powering the bat with his strong left arm.

for eight years soon after his debut. Bert Shepard, a former Air Force officer who lost his right leg in a crash, took the mound for the Washington Senators on a wooden limb.

The 1945 season began with great expectations for Gray. He wasn't upset by the imminent return of former big league stars. "Do you think you'll be able to hit the pitching of Bob Feller," one reporter asked him. "No, I suppose not," he countered, "but who can?"

On the first turn of the circuit, Gray and the Browns drew huge crowds wherever they played. At the start of the season, American League president Will Harridge announced a special ruling on catches by the one-armed outfielder. As was the case in the Southern Association, Harridge instructed umpires to give Gray credit for momentary catches, but not to rule any catch an out if he dropped the ball in the process of removing his glove.

Fans jammed the ball parks just to see the one-armed outfielder catch a ball; his style was imitated by sandlot players across the country, though usually inaccurately. Gray could catch and then throw the ball many ways, but over the years he had evolved a technique that was both quick and natural to him. In order to make his glove loose, light, and flexible, he had removed practically all the padding from it. He did not toss the ball into the air, drop his glove, and then snatch the ball and fling it back to the infield after he made a catch.

His actual performance was so quick that he had to demonstrate it to newsmen in slow motion. After making a catch, he would raise his glove to his right armpit, let the ball roll down his wrist against his chest, clamp his glove between his arm stump and body, withdraw his hand from the glove tucked under the arm stub, lower his hand, and then let the ball roll into his palm. "In this motion," in the words of one admirer, "the ball rolled out of his glove and up his wrist as if it were a ball bearing between the arm and body."

Gray was just as interesting to watch at the plate. Surprisingly, he used a 38-ounce bat, heavier than the average 36-ouncer used at the time, claiming that it helped his balance and timing as well as giving him extra power. He swung with a full follow-through. Hitting from the first-base side of the batter's box, he held the bat just one hand up from the handle, allowing exactly enough room for the right hand he didn't have, and batted from a perfect classic stance, his bat about a foot behind and level with his head. The only time Gray choked up was when he bunted, and he had such perfect control of the bat that he could invariably apply the backspin needed to drag a bunt down the line.

On the day he played his first major league game for the Browns, the one-armed outfielder was finally king, but there was no happy ending that season. Gray did not become a major league star his first and last year in the majors, no more than the Browns won the pennant again in 1945. He proved a trifle too slow for even wartime major league ball. He couldn't handle fast controlled pitching and in the field, despite his amazing speed, the split second he lost in transferring the ball to his hand often meant an extra base for a clever runner. After a 77-game season, during which he hit .218, the Browns traded him to Toledo, and aside from some barnstorming later, his playing days were over.

But Gray had had his moment of glory. Just by making it to the majors, the one-armed outfielder had become a baseball legend.

The Most Dramatic Moment in Baseball

by Harold Kaese
Boston Globe

September, 1970

Andy Pafko stood helplessly at the base of the left-field fence, at the 315-foot mark near the foul line, and saw the ball sail into the seats not far above his head.

Bobby Thomson's home run ended the third game of the 1951 National League playoffs by giving the Giants a 5-4 victory over the neighboring Dodgers and put them in the World Series against the Yankees.

It was the most timely, most important, most dramatic home run ever hit.

And for me, it has been the most memorable event covered as a sportswriter.

The home run not only turned the game around, it turned the whole season around. It put most of those present, including 34,320 fans, in a state of shock, notably Ralph Branca, Brooklyn right-hander off whom the blow was struck.

When the ball disappeared, it felt to me as though my hair—and I had more of it 19 years ago—was standing on end. My skin was crawling with excitement.

Before Thomson swung, the Dodgers had game and pennant won. After he swung, the Giants owned them.

It was a sensational denouement to a plot superbly developed. The Giants had trailed the Dodgers by 13½ games in mid-August. To finish in a tie over the regulation 154 games, they had won 10 of their last 11 games.

And now they had won two out of three in the head-to-head showdown for 39 victories in their last 47 games.

Over that stretch, Thomson, the 27-year-old Glasgow-born Scot, had batted .383.

The Dodgers went into the last of the ninth inning leading 4-1, having scored three runs off Sal Maglie in the eighth. Don Newcombe, their starter, was still pitching.

Alvin Dark, Giant shortstop, opened their ninth with a single off the mitt of first baseman Gil Hodges. Don Mueller then sent Dark to third with a single past Hodges. If Hodges had not been holding Dark close to first, he would have fielded Mueller's grounder, second-guessers later pointed out.

The Giants had something going. The crowd stirred. But when Monte Irvin fouled out to Hodges, an announcement was made in the press box.

"Attention, press: World Series credentials for Ebbets Field can be picked up at 6 o'clock tonight at the Biltmore Hotel."

Ebbets Field was in Brooklyn. The whammy was on the Dodgers.

I started down through the stands to be among the first in the clubhouse to greet the victorious Dodgers when they pranced into their locker room.

But Whitey Lockman then slapped a double to left, scoring Dark and sending Mueller to third, where he sprained an ankle stopping. There was a 10-minute delay while he was lugged off on a stretcher.

I found myself in the right-field stands when Thomson came to bat. Charlie Dressen, Brooklyn manager, changed pitchers. He brought in Branca, leaving Carl Erskine in the bullpen.

Thomson had knocked in the tying run in the seventh on a fly, which then was not recognized as a sacrifice as it would have been today.

But in other ways, he had been a goat. He had singled after Lockman in the second but had over-run first base and been tagged out. When the Dodgers scored three runs in the eighth, two hits got away from him that Billy Cox, Brooklyn third baseman, would have gobbled up.

A few fans booed Thomson, but most—being Giants rooters—encouraged him.

"A home run wins it," a fan near me said, as though he had made a great discovery.

"First is open. They may walk him."

"That puts the winning run on first."

"But it sets up a double play."

"Willie Mays is next. He's done nothing in the playoffs."

"But he's dangerous and due."

"But he's a rookie and Thomson's red hot. He's murdered the Dodgers—and Branca—all season."

The fans kicked it around pretty good. So did others. In a seat nearer the plate, Bill Terry, ex-Giants manager, nudged Bob Coleman, ex-Braves manager, and said, "Bob, this is one fellow I wouldn't use in a spot like this."

Most observers waited to second-guess Charlie Dressen until after Thomson's home run.

The crowd tensed as Dressen elected to pitch to Thomson.

Cookie Lavagetto sits glumly on the clubhouse stairs and pitcher Ralph Branca, lying on the steps, buries his head following the Dodgers' loss to the Giants in the decisive 1951 playoff game.

Bobby Thomson (center) celebrates in the Giants' clubhouse with owner Horace Stoneham (left) and manager Leo Durocher after Thomson had hit his dramatic playoff homer in 1951.

Branca's first pitch was a called strike. The fans relaxed just a little. After all, weren't the odds just too great?

Branca's next pitch was fast, a little high, a little inside. Thomson's bat met the ball solidly. It went on a line to left. A park nearly full of people stopped breathing.

Everyone who knew the Polo Grounds with its grotesquely short foul lines knew it was long enough to reach the fence, but was it high enough to go over?

It was. The ball was in the seats. The game was over. The season was over. Game, set, and match. Presto! A wave of Thomson's wand, and the Giants had been transformed from losers into champions. A bum one minute, a hero the next.

The reaction was an upheaval. A woman beside me stood with clenched fists, trembling and trying to scream from a throat that could not produce a sound.

"Good God almighty," the man with her said over and over.

Another woman was so stunned she did not realize what had happened. Her escort shouted in her ear, "It's over, Alice! It's over! The Giants win it!"

On the field, the Giants were antic in their acrobatics. The Dodgers had shrunk to ghosts.

Eddie Stanky ran from the Giants' dugout and for some reason hopped on the back of Leo Durocher, the manager who was coaching at third.

Most of the Giants waited for Thomson to jump jubilantly on the plate, caught him before he landed, and carried him shoulder-high up the field to the clubhouse in center field.

The drooping Dodgers, walking like men paralyzed, had preceded them. I hurried after them.

The celebrating of the Giants, of course, was maximum—the 1969 Mets, the 1967 Red Sox could not enlarge upon it.

But what was different about this triumph was the sense of wonder it aroused in those who were there.

"It was like catching lightning in a bottle," said the beaten manager, Dressen.

"Nothing compares with this," yelled Freddie Fitzsimmons, a Giants coach.

"You can't even tie it," yelled Frank Shellenback, tutor of the pitchers.

Carl Hubbell never yelled, but he said, "We won't live long enough to see anything like it again."

In his office, Leo Durocher saluted Thomson by pointing to the outer room and saying, "The biggest man in the world, he's out there."

The biggest man was saying, "If I'd been a good hitter, I'd a taken the damn ball. It was almost head-high."

One of the saddest sights I've ever seen in sports greeted me in the Dodgers' room, which had an upper level and a lower level, joined by a broad set of steps. Ralph Branca lay on these steps face down, his feet on the floor, his head buried in his arms on the top step.

A New York photographer (Barney Stein) got a knockout picture of an athlete who had been seriously wounded in action.

Dressen, red of face as usual, was telling why he let Branca pitch to Thomson:

"I thought of it. Five times this year I walked the winning run and got away with it every time. But Thomson? The guy behind him—Mays—could have hit a home run, too."

Then he was telling why he plucked Branca from the bullpen, vindicating himself, it seemed, at the expense of Clyde Sukeforth, the bullpen coach:

"I talked to the bullpen. Sukeforth said Erskine had nothing and Branca had a good fastball. I go on what they tell me."

Jackie Robinson, Dodgers second baseman, went into the Giants' room where they were destroying the six cases of champagne they had carried with them all the way from Boston, the scene of their last regular-season game.

"It's all over," said Robinson, shaking Maglie's hand. "No hard feelings."

Thomson had made the last of his "curtain calls," waving from a clubhouse window to the hundreds of fans still on the field.

"I'm going home and try to get a good night's sleep," Thomson said. "The World Series starts tomorrow."

Because the World Series followed so quickly, Thomson's pennant-winning home run did not get the full treatment then that it deserved. But for a few hours it set New York ablaze and put out the lights in Brooklyn.

Downtown, Tallulah Bankhead said, "I'm so happy I don't make sense. What I've been through with this team. I wish I could care so much for my own career."

A lot of people were temporarily deranged when Thomson hit his homer. I was one of them. That's why, I guess, other rousing events I've covered are a shade less memorable for me than Bobby Thomson's win-it-all homer in 1951.

Lou Boudreau—
My Most Memorable Game

as told to Irv Haag

October, 1973

My old boss, Bill Veeck, wrote in his book, *Veeck —As in Wreck,* there was absolutely no doubt in his mind that Cleveland would beat Boston in our sudden-death playoff for the 1948 American League pennant.

I sure wish he'd told me that before the game.

I was far from bursting with confidence, let me tell you. And I didn't have more than a few hours' sleep—reporters were everywhere trying to outscoop each other.

For one thing, I refused to tell anybody who would be my starting pitcher. Our ball club knew it would be Gene Bearden, but they, too, kept it a secret, thank heavens.

So many thoughts kept racing through my mind, I wished the game would get started so at least I could concentrate on playing ball and managing. I'd got to Fenway Park early as usual—it was my habit to tape my ankles before every game.

I can't even remember doing it that day, maybe because I was second-guessing myself a thousand times. Even thinking about the money to be won or lost—up to $7,000 for the World Series winners— made me edgy.

Finally, out on the field, I saw Bearden. He looked well rested anyway. Our plan had worked out okay. Instead of the press pestering him, they hounded Bob Feller, Bob Lemon, Satchel Paige, and my other pitchers, never dreaming my knuckle-baller would start.

After all, Bearden had been spectacular on Saturday, beating the Tigers 8-0 for his 19th win of the year. That clinched at least a tie for the pennant. We could have been "in" on Sunday before our home fans except for those fired-up Tigers. Over 75,000 turned out to see us wrap up the pennant. But instead, Hal Newhouser had a great day and caught Feller on an off day, and they whipped us, 7-1.

While we were disappointing our rooters, Boston was knocking off the Yankees, 10-5. The Red Sox and Indians both finished with 96 wins, 58 losses.

So here we were in Boston. Forcing myself to appear unworried, I had told the press we just came to Boston a day early, meaning, of course, to face

the Braves, the National League champs, in the Series. I wondered if I'd have to eat my words.

Across the way, I spotted Joe McCarthy, Red Sox manager. I knew how badly he wanted this game—it was his first year with Boston. And you know the kind of record he had with the Yankees, six pennants in seven years (1937 through 1943).

He had a surprise up his sleeve, too. Instead of going with lefty Mel Parnell (15-8) as most of us figured, he named right-hander Denny Galehouse. Joe's strategy made sense. Galehouse had held us to only two hits in eight and two-thirds innings about mid-summer.

The sight of Ted Williams didn't do much to calm me down, either. He was leading the league in hitting at about .365 and had 25 homers, 44 doubles, and 127 RBI. What worried me most was —he was hot. He'd gone 6-for-8 to lead the Sox in three straight wins over the Yanks to force this playoff.

Then I looked out at the Green Monster, Fenway's giant 37-foot left-field wall that, with its screen on top, rises about 60 feet. How inviting to a visiting team. It looks as if you could pop one out as easy as pie. It fools a lot of hitters into going for the wall, only to pop up or hit into the dirt.

Still, my strategy was based on the hope we could pepper that wall and get a few runs on the board. That's why I wanted as many right-handed batters in our lineup as possible. I even put Allie Clark at first base instead of my regular first baseman, left-handed swinger Eddie Robinson.

To put it mildly, both Veeck and Hank Greenberg strongly disagreed with my move. I must admit they had a point. Eddie had belted 16 homers and had 83 RBI. (In fact, counting the playoff game, our infield alone accounted for 432 runs. Second baseman Joe Gordon had 32 homers and 124 RBI, third baseman Ken Keltner had 31 homers and 119 RBI. I chipped in 18 homers and 106 RBI.)

I wasn't kidding myself, McCarthy's team was loaded with power, too. Besides Williams, he could send up guys like Vern Stephens, with 29 home runs; Dom DiMaggio, with 185 hits, including 40 doubles; Billy Goodman hitting .310, and Bobby Doerr, with 27 homers.

Knowing how Veeck and Greenberg felt about my substituting for Robinson, I would have only myself to blame if we blew it. If only the American League did what the National League had done—make it a three-game playoff!

Maybe that would have been just as nerve-racking, I don't know. One thing's for sure. Some great competitors got us to the playoff, and I certainly didn't want to let them down. Feller, for example.

Manager-player Lou Boudreau (center) poses happily with pitcher Gene Bearden (left) and third baseman Ken Keltner after Cleveland defeated Boston in a one-game playoff for the American League pennant in 1948. Boudreau hit two homers and Keltner one to spark the Indians.

He started off with a rocky year, but in the stretch, he was just great and wound up winning 19 games for us. Satchel Paige with six wins out of seven. What a help *he* was! Bob Lemon, 20-14, Sam Zoldak, picked up by Veeck during the season for relief insurance, 11 wins.

Then there was our other great rookie, Larry Doby, who not only hit .301 but also contributed 14 homers. And Jim Hegan behind the plate. He had his greatest season ever. Despite his .248 batting average, he had 14 homers, and he was valuable in handling our pitchers.

I thought the game would never start, but when it did, about the only thing that eased my mind was the fact I was also playing. If I'd been a bench manager, I would've been climbing the dugout walls.

A crowd of 33,957 fans had elbowed into Fenway, and the game started out tamely enough. Galehouse retired our slugging left fielder, Dale Mitchell (.336), and Clark, our utility man.

I was up next. All I had on my mind was to do what I told my ballplayers to do—aim for that wall. Luckily, I got pretty good wood on the two-and-one pitch and just cleared the left-field screen. It wasn't a booming homer by any means, but I was mighty happy to accept it!

The way the Sox started off in their half of the first didn't chase any of the butterflies in my stomach. We got Dom DiMaggio, but then Johnny Pesky came up. I had a hunch and signaled my right fielder, Bob Kennedy, to move over and play Pesky to pull. Johnny ripped one down the right-field line, but Kennedy was in a position to hold him to a double.

Williams stepped in, and something told me to look for one up the middle. Fortunately, that's where Ted put it and I robbed him of a hit. We couldn't stop Stephens, though. He singled to drive in Pesky with the tying run. It remained 1-1 until the fourth.

Leading off, I singled. Gordon also singled and I stopped at second. As Keltner was stepping into the batter's box, I had my first big decision of the day to make. Even though Ken was a power hitter, should I have him lay one down, hopefully to surprise the Sox? Or, should I have him swing away? Doby was on deck. If we got the runners to second and third, a hit by Larry meant one run for sure, and probably two.

Anyway, I gambled, signaling for Keltner to hit away. Ken made me look like a genius. He parked the ball over the left-field wall, and we were out front, 4-1. After that, McCarthy wasted no time. He pulled Galehouse and brought in Ellis Kinder.

Doby greeted him with a double, I had Kennedy sacrifice Larry to third, and he scored as Stephens was throwing out Hegan, making it 5-1.

Sure, I felt a lot more secure with that lead, but I also remembered how many other times I'd seen big leads disappear like magic at Fenway.

That's why I was especially happy to add another run in the fifth. Actually, Kinder had me fooled on the pitch, but I recovered in time to put another one over the wall—I was pulling everything that day. It wasn't much of a blast, either, but it counted.

Meanwhile, Bearden was holding the Sox in check. At the finish, he'd yielded only six hits and no more than one to each hitter. Doerr hit a two-run homer in the sixth to end Boston's scoring for the day. We added a run in the eighth and ninth, one when Williams dropped Bearden's high fly, allowing Hegan to score from second; another on singles by Kennedy, myself, a wild pitch, and a double play.

What a performance by Bearden! He allowed only two hits in the last seven innings. Making it even more outstanding, the two runs he gave up in the sixth were unearned, when Gordon couldn't handle Williams' high fly. Gene struck out the dangerous Stephens for what should have been the third out.

Then came the greatest moment of the most memorable game in my career. My last time up, the fans gave me a standing ovation. I'd never experienced anything quite like it. Here they'd seen their beloved Red Sox almost certain to lose, barring a miracle, and they give *me* a standing ovation! I've never felt so gratified in my life. I'm sure it lasted only a few seconds, but to me, it was like hours of sweet, sweet music.

That pennant playoff game on October 4, 1948, was the most unforgettable and satisfying moment of my baseball career.

The Night Tommie Agee Ruined the Cubs' Pennant Hopes

by Larry Merchant
New York Post

December, 1969

"I come to kill you," Leo Durocher once said, among other things he once said. Trouble is, that's a good way to get killed yourself. One night last September, on the sweet killing ground of Shea Stadium, it happened.

Leo Durocher came with the first-place Cubs to kill the second-place Mets. For a professional baseball killer like Leo Durocher, it had to be a demeaning contract, like Machine Gun Kelly going out to do in a Little League team. Durocher didn't believe the Mets in July, and here it was September and they had to be believed.

Well, Leo Durocher got killed. You can't trust Little Leaguers these days.

It was going to be done with a bullet, right in front of 49,000 people, with enough lights on to make it broad daylight. The first pitch to the Mets was aimed at the Mets. Bill Hands sent Tommie Agee into the dirt. It was a pitch designed to send him and the Mets to their maker.

"They were trying to run us out of the ball park," said Tommie Agee.

Agee raised himself from the neatly chalked grave, his white uniform now his brown uniform. Before the game would be over, the uniform would get browner and the patch on his left shoulder would be torn off, proving how alive he was.

"Sometimes a team comes to town and reads in the paper that you've hit a home run leading off," Tommie Agee said, the would-be victim trying to explain the motive of the would-be assassin. "I hit one on the next pitch after Champion [Billy, of the Phillies] knocked me down Sunday. I think they came in and said let's knock him down and see what he can do."

The Cubs might have made up their minds about that after those six games in July. Agee led off three of them with extra-base hits—double, triple, homer. This infuriated the Cubs because not only are the Mets supposed to be unbelievable but the only slugger on the damned team leads off, which is ridiculous except that it works.

"I don't mind being knocked down," Agee said. "If you're hitting, they're going to knock you down. The only thing I don't like is if we don't retaliate."

Funny, Jerry Koosman doesn't like the same thing, and he was pitching for the Mets against the Cubs. The first pitch in the second inning hit Ron Santo on the arm. As they say in the dugouts, an arm-for-an-arm, a Ron-for-a-Tommie.

"It's a matter of survival," Jerry Koosman said. "Agee doesn't have a chance to get even in center field. His way of getting even is through the pitcher."

Koosman had a good teacher, a fellow who used to play for Leo Durocher. "Eddie Stanky told us in the minors that if they hit your man hit three of theirs," he said.

Tommie Agee said he wasn't rooting for Koosman to hit Santo, but it did not exactly make him break down and cry. "I'm not going to stick my neck out for a pitcher who won't protect me," he said. "When he protects me, it gives me great incentive to win for this pitcher."

So Tommie Agee won for Jerry Koosman.

He grounded to third after the knockdown in the first inning. "A lot of times when I'm knocked down I get so mad I try to hit the ball too hard. But I'm not as emotional as I used to be. A game like this is supposed to bring out the best in a professional. Maybe if you're playing Montreal you figure you'll win anyway, but I've been thinking about this game all day long and what I have to do."

In the third inning, what Agee had to do was hit his 26th home run with a man on. He did.

In the sixth inning, right after the Cubs tied the score, Agee faked a bunt. Santo crept in at third. What Agee had to do then was drive a ground ball past Santo, which he did. The ball lagged to a stop in the tall grass, and so Agee had to hustle it into a belly-sliding double. Which he did, too. Wayne Garrett followed with a single to right field. Agee hesitated, then went. When he got to third, it seemed like a good idea to wait there for someone else to deliver him: there were none out. But Eddie Yost, the third-base coach, waved him in, and all Agee had to do then was beat the quick and true throw by Jim Hickman. Naturally he did, sliding in and scoring the winning run on a close call at the plate, because if he didn't they might still be playing.

Neither Agee nor Durocher was quite through yet. Agee led off the eighth inning with a walk, then broke up a double play with a killing slide. In the bottom half Hands remembered what Koosman had done to Santo and knocked Koosman down.

That was just a ritual gesture though, a reflex action from a dead assassin. Leo Durocher had nothing to say when it was all over. He had been killed at his own game.

(Editor's Note: Outfielder Tommie Agee was a prime mover in the New York Mets' stunning pennant rush in 1969. His performance in the opener of a crucial two-game series with the Cubs in September, 1969, will long be remembered by those fans who saw it at Shea Stadium. The Cubs had held an eight and a half game first-place lead as late as August 14, but by the time they arrived in New York for their final showdown series with the Mets in early September, the margin had dwindled to two and a half games. After Agee destroyed the Cubs in the opener, there was no stopping the Mets. They beat the Cubs the next night behind Tom Seaver, 7-1, and moved into first place to stay on September 10 by sweeping a twi-nighter from Montreal. Agee was traded by the Mets after the 1972 season and finished his major league career with Houston and St. Louis in 1973.)

Tommie Agee slides past catcher Randy Hundley with the decisive run in the New York Mets' 3-2 victory over the Cubs in a crucial game at Shea Stadium on September 8, 1969. Agee had doubled and scored on Wayne Garrett's hit to right. Earlier in the game, Agee had slammed a two-run homer.

Tony Lazzeri: Player of the Years

by Red Smith
Condensed from the *New York Herald-Tribune*

October, 1946

When the iceman cometh, it doesn't make a great deal of difference which route he takes, for the ultimate result is the same in any case. Nevertheless, there was something especially tragic in the way death came to Tony Lazzeri, finding him and leaving him all alone in a dark and silent house—a house which must, in that last moment, have seemed frighteningly silent to a man whose ears remembered the roar of the crowd as Tony's did.

A man who knew the roar of the crowd? Shucks, Tony Lazzeri was the man who made the crowds and who made them roar. Frank Graham, in his absorbing history of the Yankees, tells about the coming of Lazzeri and about the crowds that trooped into the stadium to see him, the noisily jubilant Italian-American crowds with their rallying cry of "Poosh 'em up, Tony!"

"And now," Frank wrote in effect, "a new type of fan was coming to the stadium. A fan who didn't know where first base was. He came, and what he saw brought him back again and again until he not only knew where first base was, but second base as well."

It was a shock to read, in the reports of Lazzeri's death, that he was only 42 years old. There are at least a few right around that age still playing in the major leagues. One would have guessed Lazzeri's age a good deal higher because his name and fame are inextricably associated with an era which already has become a legend—the era that is always referred to as the time of "the old Yankees."

You can't think of Tony without thinking also of Babe Ruth and Bob Meusel and Herb Pennock and Waite Hoyt and Lou Gehrig and Mark Koenig and Benny Bengough and Wilcy Moore, all of whom have been gone from the playing fields for what seems a long time.

And you think of Grover Cleveland Alexander, too, for it was Lazzeri's misfortune that although he was as great a ballplayer as ever lived, the most vivid memory he left in most minds concerned the day he failed.

That was, of course, in the seventh game of the 1926 World Series when the Yankees filled the bases against the leading Cardinals, drove Jess Haines from the hill, and sent Rogers Hornsby out toward the Cardinals' bullpen where Alexander drowsed in the dusk.

Everyone knows that story, how the St. Louis manager walked out to take a look at Alexander's eyes, how he found them as clear as could be expected, and sent Old Pete in there to save the world championship by striking out Lazzeri. Come to think of it, Alex wasn't a lot younger at that time than Lazzeri was when he died.

It was after that game that someone asked Alexander how he felt when Lazzeri struck out.

"How did I feel?" he snorted. "Go ask Lazzeri how he felt."

Tony never told how he felt. Not that it was necessary, anyway, but he wasn't one to be telling much, ever. He was a rookie when a baseball writer first used a line that has been worn to tatters since. "Interviewing that guy," the reporter grumbled, "is like mining coal with a nail file."

Silent and unsmiling though he was, Lazzeri wasn't entirely devoid of a taste for dugout humor. Babe Ruth, dressing in haste after one tardy arrival in the stadium, tried to pull a shoe out of his locker and found it wouldn't move. He didn't have to be told who had nailed it to the floor.

When other players found cigarette butts in their footgear or discovered their shirts tied in water-soaked knots or were unable to locate their shoelaces, they blamed only one man.

Lefty Gomez used to tell of the day, long after Lazzeri's experience in the 1926 World Series, when he lost control and filled the bases. Lazzeri trotted in from second base to talk to him. Lazzeri always was the man who took charge when trouble threatened the Yankees. Even in his first season, when he was a rookie who'd never seen a big league game until he played in one, he was the steadying influence, the balance wheel. So after this incident, Gomez was asked what words Lazzeri had used to reassure him in the clutch.

"He said," replied Lefty, who didn't necessarily expect to be believed, " 'You put those runners on there. Now you get out of the jam yourself.' "

They chose Lazzeri Player of the Year after one of his closing seasons. They could just as well have made it Player of the Years, for in all his time with the Yankees there was no one whose hitting and fielding and hustle and fire and brilliantly swift thinking meant more to any team.

Other clubs tried to profit by those qualities of his

Second baseman Tony Lazzeri, second from left, with other members of the 1937 Yankees infield, including first baseman Lou Gehrig, shortstop Frank Crosetti, and third baseman Red Rolfe. That year the Yankees ran away with the American League pennant, finishing 13 games ahead of the Tigers. Lazzeri was a star in the Pacific Coast League, where he hit 60 homers in 1925 before joining the Yankees.

before he was through. He went to the Cubs and the Dodgers and the Giants. None of these experiments was particularly happy; none endured for long. He managed Toronto for a while, and then just before the war he went back home to San Francisco. That was the last stop.

(Editor's Note: Tony Lazzeri, who suffered from epilepsy, died in San Francisco on August 6, 1946.

It is believed a seizure caused him to fall and suffer a fatal injury at the relatively young age of 42. He played in six World Series with the New York Yankees and one with the Chicago Cubs and had a .292 lifetime batting average when his major league career ended in 1939.

Ironically, Grover Cleveland Alexander, the pitcher Lazzeri faced in their 1926 World Series showdown, also suffered from epilepsy.)

Dusty Rhodes and "His" Biggest Hit

by Dave Distel
Los Angeles Times

Dusty Rhodes

December, 1972

Each World Series belongs to someone, maybe a Don Larsen or a Bill Mazeroski or a Mickey Lolich.

In 1954, when the New York Giants swept the Cleveland Indians, the Series belonged to Dusty Rhodes.

Willie Mays, indeed, made a remarkable catch in center field of New York's Polo Grounds. But Dusty Rhodes had a career that week, hitting .667 and driving in seven runs.

"My most memorable hit," Rhodes said, "wasn't during the World Series. It was during the regular season."

Today James Lamar Rhodes, 45, is nearly bald, but he looks very much like the Dusty Rhodes of many summers ago.

He was talking about the hit *he* remembers most. He talked with an inflection which was part Alabama, where he was raised, and part New York, where he lives.

Dusty Rhodes' most memorable hit came at a time in 1954 when Brooklyn had closed to within one game of the first-place Giants. The Dodgers were within one out of gaining a tie for the lead.

"We had the bases loaded," Rhodes recalled, "with two out in the 13th inning. They were ahead by a run, and Leo Durocher sent me in to hit for Monte Irvin."

Clem Labine, the Dodger pitcher, slipped two strikes past Rhodes on the inside. Rhodes suggested to the umpire that they were too far inside, and he smashed his bat on the plate. Durocher leaped from the dugout.

"I sent you up there to hit," the Lion roared, "not to take."

Labine's next pitch was a fastball away. Rhodes lined it into left field, and the Giants won.

America's baseball fans are more likely to remember the Rhodes of the fall of 1954, the man who hit a three-run pinch-hit homer off Bob Lemon to give the Giants a 5-2 win in the 10-inning World Series opener.

"My intention was to take the first pitch," Rhodes recalled, "because I'd never hit Lemon good in spring training. But Bob hung a curveball—and I changed my mind.

"And what I remember most about that hit is that Lemon's glove went farther than the ball."

Rhodes pulled his drive down the right-field line, a cozy 260 feet away in the Polo Grounds. He swears the disgusted Lemon threw his glove 290 feet into the air.

"In the Polo Grounds," Rhodes mused, "you either pulled the ball 260 feet and got a home run or you hit it 490 feet straightaway for an out."

In the second game, Rhodes lined a pinch-single to tie the game and later homered over the right-field roof. He hit another pinch-single, this one driving home two runs, in the third game.

"The fourth game I sat it out," he said.

In that Series, Rhodes was 3-for-3 as a pinch-hitter—batting each time for Monte Irvin.

"It seemed," Rhodes said, "like I used to bear down a little more with men on base. In the regular season that year, I had 56 hits and 50 runs batted in."

Dusty Rhodes spent most of his major league career in residence on the Giants' bench, pinch-hitting or, occasionally, starting against a right-hander.

"Deep down inside," he shrugged, "I didn't want to play every day. I just liked to hang around and come up with men on base."

The First Baseman
Who Outpitched
Walter Johnson

by George Sisler
as told to Lyall Smith

Condensed from the *Chicago Daily News*

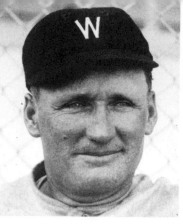

Walter Johnson

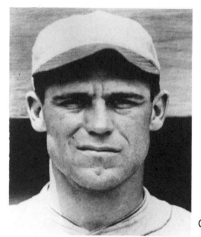

George Sisler

September, 1965

Every American kid has a baseball idol. Mine was Walter Johnson, the Big Train. Come to think about it, Walter still is my idea of the real ballplayer. He was graceful. He had rhythm. And when he heaved that ball in to the plate, he threw with his whole body just so easylike that you'd think the ball was flowing off his arm and hand.

I was just a husky kid in Akron (Ohio) High School back around 1910–11 when Johnson began making a name for himself with the Senators, and I was so crazy about the man that I'd read every line and keep every picture of him I could get my hands on.

Naturally, admiring Johnson as I did, I decided to be a pitcher. Even though I wound up as a first baseman, my biggest day in baseball was a hot muggy afternoon in St. Louis when I pitched against him and beat him. Never knew that, did you? Most fans don't. But it's right. Me, a kid just out of the University of Michigan beat the great Walter Johnson. It was on August 29, 1915, my first year as a ballplayer, the first time I ever was in a game against the man who I thought was the greatest pitcher in the world.

I guess I was a pretty fair pitcher myself at Central High in Akron. I had a strong left arm, and I could throw them in there all day long and never have an ache or pain.

I pitched three years of varsity ball at the University of Michigan, and while I was at Ann Arbor, I signed up with Branch Rickey, who at that time was manager of the St. Louis Browns. When I was graduated on June 10, 1915, Rickey wired me to join the Browns in Chicago.

Now all this time I was up at school, I still had my sights set on Walter Johnson. When he pitched his 56 consecutive scoreless innings in 1913, I was as proud as though I'd done it myself. After all, I felt as though I had adopted him. He was my hero.

He won 36 games and lost only seven in 1913, and he came back the next season to win 28 more and lose 18. He was really getting the headlines in those days, and I was keeping all of them in my scrapbook.

Well, then I left Michigan in 1915 and came down to Chicago, where I officially became a professional ballplayer. I hit town one morning, and that same day we were getting beat pretty bad so Rickey called me over to the dugout.

"George," he said, "I know you just got in town and that you don't know any of the players and you're probably tired and nervous. But I want to see what you have in that left arm of yours. Let's see you pitch these last three innings."

I gulped hard a couple of times, muttered something that sounded like "thanks," and went out and pitched those last three innings. Did pretty good, too. I gave up one hit, but the White Sox didn't get any runs so I figured that I was all right.

Next day, though, I was out warming up and meeting more of the Browns when Rickey came over to me. He was carrying a first baseman's glove. "Here," he said. "Put this on and get over there on first base."

Well, nothing much happened between the time I joined the club in June until long about the last part of August. Rickey would pitch me one day, stick me in the outfield the next, and then put me over on first the next three or four. I was hitting pretty good, and by the time we got back to St. Louis the sportswriters were saying some nice things about me.

They were saying it chiefly because of my hitting. I'd only won two-three games pitching up to then. I still remember the first one. I beat Cleveland and struck out nine men. Some clothing store gave me a pair of white flannels for winning, and I was right proud of them. Didn't even wear them for a long time, figured they were too fancy.

As I was saying, we got back to St. Louis late in August. Early one week I picked up a paper and saw that a St. Louis writer, Billy Murphy, had written a story about Washington coming to town the following Sunday and that Walter Johnson was going to pitch.

I was still a Johnson fan and I guess Murphy knew it, for about halfway through the story he had me pitching against Johnson on the big day, Sunday, August 29.

That was the first I knew about it, and I figured it was the first Rickey knew about it. Here it was only Tuesday, and Murphy had the pitchers all lined up for the following Sunday.

Well, he knew what he was talking about, because after the Saturday game Rickey stuck his head in the locker room and told me I was going to pitch against Johnson the next day. I went back to my hotel that night but I couldn't eat. I was really nervous. I went to bed but I couldn't sleep. At four in the morning, I was still tossing and rolling around. Finally, I got up and just sat there, waiting for daylight and the big game.

I managed to get some breakfast in me and was out at Sportsman's Park before the gates opened. It was one of those typical August days in St. Louis, and when game time finally rolled around it was so hot that the sweat ran down your face even when you were standing in the shadow of the stands.

All the time I was warming up I'd steal a look over at Johnson in the Washington bullpen. When he'd stretch way out and throw in a fastball, I'd try to do the same.

Well, the game finally started and I tried to be calm. First man to face me was Dan Moeller, Washington's left fielder. I didn't waste any time and threw three fast ones in there to strike him out. Eddie Foster was up next, and he singled to right field. Clyde Milan singled to right-center, and I was really scared. I could see Mr. Rickey leaning out of the dugout watching me real close, so I kept them high to Hank Shanks and got him to fly out to Tilly Walker in center field. He hit it back pretty far though, and Foster, a fast man, started out for third

base. Walker made a perfect peg into the infield, but Johnny Lavan, our shortstop, fumbled the relay and Foster kept right on going to score. That was all they got in the inning, but I wasn't feeling too sure when I came in to the bench. I figured we weren't going to get many runs off Johnson, and I knew I couldn't be giving up many myself.

Then Johnson went out to face us, and I really got a thrill out of watching him pitch. He struck out the first two Brownies and made Del Pratt fly to short-center. Then I had to go out again and got by all right. In the second inning, Walker led off with a single to center field, and Baby Doll Jacobson dumped a bunt in front of the plate. Rip Williams, Washington catcher, scooped it up and threw it 10 feet over the first baseman's head. Walker already was around second, and he came in and scored while Baby Doll reached third.

I think I actually felt sorry for Johnson. I knew just how he felt because after all, the same thing had happened to me in the first inning. Del Howard was up next for us, and he singled Jacobson home to give us two runs and me a 2-1 lead.

Well, that was all the scoring for the day, although I gave up five more hits over the route. Johnson got one in the first of the fifth, a blooper over second. I was up in the last of the same inning, and I'll be darned if I didn't get the same kind. So he and I were even up anyway. We each hit one man, too.

There wasn't much more to the game. Only one man reached third on me after the first inning, and only two got that far on Johnson.

When I got the last man out in the first of the ninth and went off the field, I looked down at the Washington bench hoping to get another look at Johnson. But he already had ducked down to the locker room.

I don't know what I expected to do if I had seen him. For a minute I thought maybe I'd go over and shake his hand and tell him that I was sorry I beat him, but I guess that was just the silly idea of a kid who had just come face to face with his idol and beaten him.

(Editor's Note: When George Sisler was elected to the Hall of Fame in 1939, it was as a first baseman, who led the American League in hitting with .407 in 1920 and .420 in 1922, and who had a lifetime .340 batting average for 2,055 games. But during his stardom with the St. Louis Browns (1915–27) one of his biggest moments came through his arm, not his bat, as he himself relates here. He also pitched in 21 other games through his career, winning five in all.)

When Willie Mays Said Good-bye

by Frank Dolson
Philadelphia Inquirer

Tears course down Willie Mays' face as he thanks the fans during farewell ceremonies at Shea Stadium in 1973. "You don't know what's going on inside me tonight," he told the crowd.

August, 1974

New York was always his town. Even during those 14 years in San Francisco it remained his town. And now the town was saying good-bye.

"Ladies and gentlemen, Willie Mays . . ."

The cheers on that September night in 1973 rolled across Shea Stadium, louder and louder, longer and longer. Thirty seconds . . . a minute. Willie Mays had received three cars, a trip around the world for two, a diamond watch, and a white mink coat for his wife on this night. But those long, loud, lingering cheers must have been the sweetest gift of all.

"This is a sad day for me," he said when the noise had finally subsided. "I may not look sad, but in my heart it is sad to hear you cheer for me and not be able to do anything about it . . ."

And then, surely the most touching moment of all, the 42-year-old Willie Mays—no more than a spectator as his New York Mets teammates fought for the pennant in the closing days of the 1973 National League season—apologized for quitting his final pennant race and said: "I look at the kids over here, the way they're playing, the way they're fighting for themselves, and it tells me one thing: 'Willie, say good-bye to America.' "

Beautiful, poignant words, nearly as heart-tugging in their way as Lou Gehrig's in his Yankee Stadium farewell. "Today, I consider myself the luckiest man on the face of the earth."

This was Willie Mays' turn to feel lucky . . . and sad . . . and grateful. He had enjoyed better years than 1973. Much better years. But this may have been his most beautiful moment, and the people responded. Perhaps the sign hanging from the left-field stands expressed it best: "We Who Are About to Cry Salute You."

"He was the greatest ballplayer I ever saw in most departments," Expo manager Gene Mauch said. "I don't know how many people have driven in 150 runs in a year, hit 50 home runs in a year, batted .350 in a year, stolen 50 bases in a year, and played their position peerlessly."

Okay, he was exaggerating slightly. Mays' top RBI total was "only" 141. His greatest number of steals "only" 40. His top batting average "only" .347.

No matter. This was a night for memories that transcended statistics. Numbers alone could never do justice to a Willie Mays.

"All I can say," said Duke Snider, who played center field for the Brooklyn Dodgers when Mays played it for the New York Giants, "I hated to see him come to bat; I hated to see him get on base, and it was a tragedy when we hit one to him."

The kids couldn't really appreciate what Snider meant. But Mauch could. He had seen Willie Mays when he WAS Willie Mays.

"I saw him get his first hit [a 1951 Polo Grounds home run off Warren Spahn]," Gene reminisced. "I saw him get his 3,000th hit. And it seems to me I saw him get half the hits in between."

And then there were the catches. Like the one Willie made on Ruben Amaro at Connie Mack Stadium when Mauch's Phillies had the tying run on second and the go-ahead run on first.

"The chances of him making that play were almost as remote as Ruben hitting the ball that far."

Amaro hit the ball so far that it was about to carom off the scoreboard in right-center. "Willie ran and jumped," Mauch recalled. "He sank both spikes in the scoreboard this high [pointing to his chest]; he caught the ball, and he came down on his neck . . ."

And then there were the base-running feats. Like the time Mays was hopelessly out at the plate against the Phillies. Or so it seemed . . .

"Willie Mays was never out," Mauch said. "Pat Corrales had the ball and Willie came in . . ."

POW! Mays' left foot flew through the air and hit the catcher in the jaw, knocking him woozy. His right foot hit the plate.

"If I'm lying, I'm dying," Mauch said, seeing the disbelieving looks on the Expo bench.

"That's the truth," trainer Joe Liscio confirmed. "I had to take Corrales to the doctor that night."

"He would have been in the Hall of Fame if he'd played 10 years, let alone 20," Mauch said.

But somehow, he lasted 22. "I never felt I would ever quit baseball," Willie said in his emotional farewell. "But as you know, there is always a time for someone to get out."

For Willie Mays, it was a time to remember.

Mays holds the bat and ball he used to record his 600th home run in 1969. Mays' blast gave the San Francisco Giants a 4-2 victory over the San Diego Padres. Willie finished his career with 660 home runs.

Mays reaches high over the fence at Candlestick Park to rob Cincinnati's Bob Tolan of a home run. Teammate Bobby Bonds (No. 25) made a run for the ball and collided with Mays. Mays had the wind knocked out of him, but he held on to the ball and continued in the game.

Fighting Words

by John Kuenster

January, 1961

What really triggers a baseball player's temper? The knockdown pitch . . . the thrown bat . . . the high slide. These light the fuse. But in the end, it's words . . . usually unprintable words . . . that cause the explosion.

Take the celebrated case of Jim Brewer vs. Billy Martin last summer. Their fight resulted in an unprecedented $1,040,000 suit by the Chicago Cubs and Brewer against Martin.

What ignited the brawl?

Martin, batting leadoff for the Cincinnati Reds, came to the plate in the second inning of a game that didn't mean a great deal to either side. There were two out.

Brewer's first pitch was over Martin's head and nicked his bat for strike one. Martin moved around aimlessly for a few seconds before stepping back into the batter's box. It appeared as though he had some course of action in mind but wasn't quite ready to go through with it.

The second pitch came over for a strike, and as Martin swung at the ball, he let his bat fly in the direction of the mound. He then walked out toward the mound, apparently to retrieve the bat.

"I just asked him what he was trying to do," said Brewer later.

"He said he was just coming out to pick up his bat. I wasn't looking for a fight . . . I was relaxed. I took my eyes off him. That's when he nailed me."

Martin threw a right-hand punch that landed near Brewer's right eye. It was alleged that the punch fractured Brewer's orbit bone, pushing it in about half an inch.

Brewer, up to the majors for the first time, was placed on the disabled list for the rest of the season. He was hospitalized for 17 days, requiring three operations to repair the damage.

His recitation of what transpired between him and Martin near the mound before the fight was not complete, according to Martin.

"Nothing would've happened," said Billy, "but he started saying some things to me when I got out there and giving me a lot of mouth, so I hit him.

"If he hadn't said anything, I would've picked up my bat and gone back to the plate."

What were the words that caused Martin to explode? According to the Cincinnati infielder, they were:

"You come out here again and I'll really knock you on your - - -!"

Brewer never commented on what Martin said to him.

The punch cost Martin a $500 fine and a five-day suspension. It also made front-page news in Chicago.

While it is often difficult to tell who is guilty and who is innocent in warfare that erupts on the field, it can be said in most cases—as in the instance of Brewer vs. Martin—that words have a very significant bearing on the proceedings.

Eddie Mathews of the Braves got into an altercation with Cincinnati's Frank Robinson last season, following a hard slide by Robinson into third base.

"He took a swipe at me with his arm," Mathews recalled. "We exchanged words in a moment of passion."

It was then that Mathews decked Robinson and swarmed all over him. According to a dispassionate observer, Mathews called Robinson a name and Robby gave it right back to him.

Mathews remembers another near incident he had with a Cincinnati player the same season. It was Martin again.

"I cut the hell out of Martin in a slide into second . . . accidentally," Mathews remarked. "I told him, 'Damn, I'm sorry, Billy,' and that was all there was to it. Nothing came of it."

In 1957, Art Ditmar of the Yankees threw a pitch over Larry Doby's head at Comiskey Park. The throw got away from the catcher, and Ditmar came in to cover the plate in the event Minnie Minoso, who had raced to third from second, tried to score.

"Watch where you're throwing that ball," growled Doby, give or take a few words.

Ditmar responded with something that might be scribbled on the wall of a railroad underpass.

"What'd you say?" Doby asked menacingly.

"I said - - - - - - - - - - - - -!" snapped Ditmar, and with that he was knocked on the seat of his pants by Doby's left hook.

The ensuing melee between the Yankees and White Sox resulted in $150 fines for Doby, Enos Slaughter, and Martin and $100 fines for Walt Dropo and Ditmar.

The same day Johnny Logan of the Braves and Don Drysdale of the Dodgers went at it in a game at Ebbets Field.

"I was batting behind Billy Bruton then," Logan said. "The first time up, he hit a home run. Drysdale then hit me on the thigh with a pitch. Next time up,

A furious Juan Marichal (No. 27) attacks Dodger catcher John Roseboro with a bat during a 1965 game at Candlestick Park. The Giants' pitcher became enraged when Roseboro threw close to his head as he waited at the plate. Roseboro was returning the ball to pitcher Sandy Koufax (No. 32), who jumps in to stop Marichal. When Roseboro's toss whizzed past Marichal's right ear, Juan angrily demanded of the catcher, "Why did you do that?" and the fight was on.

Roseboro is being pushed by the Giants' shortstop, Tito Fuentes (No. 26), who was due to bat next. Koufax tries to pull Roseboro away while umpire Shag Crawford and Giants' coach Charlie Fox try to restore peace. But before it was over, the fracas turned into a general melee as both dugouts emptied, the players spoiling for a fight. Roseboro said Marichal clubbed him three times on the head with the bat. Marichal, who claimed he hit the Dodger catcher only once, was suspended for eight days and fined $1,750.

Bruton hits another homer, and then I got it in the ribs. It really stung."

As Logan trotted to first, he and Drysdale traded words.

"In case you get to first and go into second on a double play," yelled Logan, "you better duck."

"If you've got anything on your mind," bristled Drysdale, "come out and get me."

The subsequent free-for-all lasted 10 minutes. Drysdale swung and missed a wild right, and Logan appeared to get in several good punches at a rate of about $33 per punch. Logan was fined $100; Drysdale, $40.

"Words can lead to fights," concedes lumbering Joe Adcock, who has a sweet disposition most of the time.

"But," adds the Milwaukee first baseman with heavy humor, "I don't think you can quote any of them."

In 1956, Ruben Gomez of the then New York Giants unleashed a few choice epithets at Adcock and there followed one of the daffiest episodes on record.

Gomez had just clipped Adcock's right wrist with an inside pitch, and as Joe walked toward first base, the pair exchanged adjectives and nouns not found even in the unabridged dictionary.

"I said something to him," Adcock was pressed to admit recently but couldn't bring himself to reveal it precisely. Gomez, of course, wasn't speechless.

Suddenly, Adcock turned and rushed toward the mound. Gomez, who had a new ball by this time, flung it at the charging Adcock, hitting him flush on the left thigh.

Later, the Puerto Rican pitcher, who ran for his life with a furious Adcock in hot pursuit, claimed he didn't hear what Adcock had said to him.

"I turned around and I saw him charge at me. I ran from him. I didn't want him to break my ribs!" confessed Gomez.

Adcock, nursing an inflamed wrist and bruised thigh, said, "He called me a name and I chased him.

While the Braves' Eddie Mathews and the Reds' Jim O'Toole (both obscured) are combating each other on the ground, other Milwaukee and Cincinnati players mill around the action during a game at Milwaukee's County Stadium in 1961. The fight started when O'Toole, the Cincinnati pitcher, punched the ball from third baseman Mathews' hand during a squeeze play. O'Toole was ruled out, and Mathews was ejected. Cincinnati manager Fred Hutchinson (capless) hovers directly over the combatants. Among the Braves who can be identified are Joe Adcock (No. 9), manager Charlie Dressen (No. 7), Lew Burdette (No. 33), Hank Aaron (No. 44, in front of Burdette), and Warren Spahn, bareheaded and to Aaron's right.

Cubs' first baseman Frank Thomas (No. 25) hangs over scuffling Chicago pitcher Jim Brewer and Cincinnati's Billy Martin (center) in 1960 game at Wrigley Field. Martin had gone to the area of the mound to retrieve his bat which had flown out of his hands. He accused Brewer of throwing at his head. The two exchanged insults, and Martin punched Brewer. Umpire Chris Pelekoudas rushes in from first base to halt the fight. Brewer later sued Martin for an injury he sustained in the fracas.

I was never so mad in my life! It's a good thing I didn't catch him."

In his playing days, Billy Jurges was a quick-handed shortstop with a quick temper. Once he had a run-in with teammate Wally Stephenson, a Southerner and substitute catcher for the Cubs.

It happened in the Cubs' dugout before game time. Brooklyn-born Jurges taunted Stephenson about the Civil War.

"My grandpappy," he chortled, "chased your grandpappy out of Carolina with a cornstalk."

That touched off a battle royal, and manager Charlie Grimm had to stop it for fear Jurges would break a hand and ruin the Cubs' flag chances.

Ill-advised words can lead to fights between players and spectators.

Duke Snider was once involved in a fracas with a fan after a night game at Crosley Field.

When Snider was leaving the field, the fan screamed, "What's the matter, Duke? Ain't you got no guts?"

The remark cost the spectator two false teeth which he said broke when Snider hit him.

Some words, of course, carry a sting but serve as a deterrent also. The late Bill Klem, one of the game's famous umpires, had a knack of curbing enraged players.

He would often stifle angry displays by shouting: "Are you a fighter, too? I thought you were a ballplayer!"

And there are words that fray a player's temper, but not enough to make him start swinging.

When Jimmie Foxx was in his prime with the old Philadelphia A's and clouting homers all over the place, he once hit a tremendous round-tripper off Lloyd Brown to beat him in a close game.

Later, Brown and Foxx bumped into each other en route to the clubhouse.

"You'll never hit another one off me, you fathead!" exclaimed Brown.

"Why not?" answered Foxx casually. "You quitting baseball or something?"

Roberto Clemente: A Sensitive Superstar

by Milton Richman
United Press International

March, 1973

Roberto Clemente was like most baseball players, a little boy inside.

Sometimes he was moody . . . petulant . . . complaining . . . and openly antagonistic.

But other times he was the warmest, softest, most compassionate human being you could ever hope to meet.

You had to be around him awhile to see both sides. I've seen him when he'd rail up at a newsman's perfectly innocent question, and as a guest at his home in Rio Piedras, Puerto Rico, as well as on other occasions, I've seen him when he was one of the most hospitable, helpful, and cooperative individuals ever to wear a major league uniform.

Roberto Clemente was a superstar, and he knew it, but that still didn't keep him from being extremely self-conscious about the fact. Particularly outside the environs he knew best—baseball parks.

He didn't go for public celebrations. Maybe it was because he didn't want to show too much of the real Roberto Clemente to the general public. In that way, he was a private person.

When all the rest of the Pittsburgh Pirates were dousing themselves with champagne after knocking over the Baltimore Orioles in the final game of the 1971 World Series, Clemente purposely passed up most of the high jinks, much the same way he had after the Pirates had clinched the National League pennant two weeks earlier.

"That's OK for some of the younger fellows," said Clemente, when they asked him why he wasn't participating.

But on the plane back to Pittsburgh from Baltimore, an episode took place which never got into any newspaper.

"My wife, Karen, and I were on the plane, and Roberto suddenly came over and embraced me," remembers pitcher Steve Blass, who beat the Orioles in the deciding contest.

"That was a very personal thing with me," says Blass. "I could feel the true warmth of the man."

Dave Giusti, the Pirates' reliever, remembers something else.

"I recall a game in Houston," he says. "I hadn't gone six innings in three years, and I finally went six in this one. Bobby made a point of coming over to me. It was the way he approached me, and the way he said what he did. You could tell he was sincere."

Roberto Clemente was paid very well by the Pirates, his salary climbing above the $135,000 level, but he wanted one thing even more than he wanted money, and that was recognition.

I remember him showing me a particular bat at his home in Rio Piedras.

"See this," he said, picking up the thick-handled bat. "This is the bat I used when we won the world championship in 1960. I think I should've won the MVP that year, but I didn't get it. Not because I didn't deserve it, but because of 'political' reasons."

Despite this tremendous desire for the recognition he felt was due him, Clemente wasn't that serious he couldn't laugh at himself.

He was sensitive about repeated charges he wouldn't play at times because he said he was ailing, yet he sat in a corner of the Pirates' clubhouse and laughed heartily one day when one of the club doctors came in and made a ritual of examining a life-sized statue of him some of his teammates had obtained and placed on the training table.

Roberto Clemente later complained that there weren't enough writers following him around as he was approaching his 3,000-hit milestone, yet he laughed louder than anybody else when some of the Pirate players dug up a picture of all major-leaguers ever to achieve 3,000 hits, Clemente included, and pasted it in their lavatory.

Clemente's 3,000th hit was his last in regular Na-

A sensational defensive player in right field, Roberto Clemente makes a leaping, backhanded catch of a long drive and desperately tries to keep on his feet as he lunges straight ahead. The Pirate center fielder in the background is Bill Virdon. Roberto made his catch on a ball hit by Bobby Thomson, then with the Chicago Cubs, in a game at Wrigley Field in 1958. Clemente played 18 years with the Pirates (1955-72), finishing with an even 3,000 hits in regular-season play. After his death, he was voted into the Hall of Fame in a special election held in 1973.

Clemente is shown with his family in 1971 when he was honored at Shea Stadium in New York during "Roberto Clemente Night" ceremonies. With him are his wife, Vera, and three sons, from left: Enrique, Roberto, and Luis.

tional League play in 1972. After the accomplishment, he announced he would not play in the last three regular season games.

"I'm glad it's over," he said at the time. "Now I can get some rest."

Clemente rested for the National League playoffs against the Cincinnati Reds, which Pittsburgh lost in five games. He had four hits in 17 at-bats for a .235 average.

Asked if he was glad the 3,000th hit was a line drive, he said, "I was just glad to get the hit, period. I give this hit to the fans of Pittsburgh and to the people of Puerto Rico."

He said that he had been embarrassed by the standing ovation.

"I feel bashful when I get a big ovation. I am really shy and so is my family. I never was a big shot and I never will be a big shot."

Clemente was asked if the hit was his most satisfying moment in 18 years in the majors.

"The World Series was more satisfying, because we won," he said.

The Pirates won the World Series in both 1960 against the New York Yankees and in 1971 against the Baltimore Orioles, both in seven games. He hit .310 in the 1960 Series and was the outstanding player in the 1971 Series, with a .414 average. Clemente hit safely in all 14 Series games in which he played.

Clemente had compiled a .318 lifetime batting average while winning four National League batting titles. He batted over .300 in 13 seasons. His highest average was .357 in 1967. In 1972, he hit .312 in 102 games.

He won the National League's Most Valuable Player Award in 1966 and was selected for the All-Star game 12 times.

Perhaps because of his all-out play, Clemente missed many games during his career because of a myriad of injuries which went beyond conventional bumps and bruises.

In his last season, he was stricken with tendonitis of the ankles shortly after recovering from an intestinal virus, which took more than 10 pounds off his 5-foot-11, 182-pound frame. In previous seasons he had had everything from malaria and bone chips to food poisoning and insomnia.

This all led to an image of Clemente as baseball's leading hypochondriac, an image he claimed had been fostered by baseball writers.

Clemente criticized writers for allegedly refusing to accept top Latin players as the equals of other stars. Yet he was nearly always patient and pleasant with writers, just as he was with autograph seekers —even those who interrupted him in restaurants.

Following his tragic death on December 31, 1972, at age 38, the Baseball Writers of America in 1973 voted Clemente into the Hall of Fame in a special election.

Roberto Clemente gave much to baseball. He will be missed by all who knew him—as a man and as an extremely gifted player.

Joe Jackson
Belongs in the
Hall of Fame

by Furman Bisher
Atlanta Journal

Before the fall: Joe Jackson (left) poses in 1915 with White Sox teammate Charlie Jackson, a fringe player who had only one at-bat with the White Sox that year. Joe Jackson, still in his prime at 28, had been traded to the White Sox from the Cleveland Indians in 1915. Note the size of Jackson's hand holding the ball.

July, 1973

Everybody who knows Chuck Tanner recognizes him as effervescent, energetic, ambitious, enthusiastic, diplomatic, though not much on history. The White Sox manager is all these things, but he's also weak on history.

Historians never made good baseball managers anyway. And history isn't one of the requirements for a manager, along with making out lineups, keeping pitchers in rotation, enforcing curfew, arguing with umpires, allowing the players time for union meetings, owners' sons to be bat boys, never missing a plane, and winning games.

One day not long ago, though, Tanner did get involved with those who regard themselves as keepers of the archives. He said, quite innocently enough—as well as diplomatically, for there's nothing like praise to raise a batting average 10 points—that Richie Allen is the greatest player in Chicago White Sox history.

Here's a guy who has a lifetime record of .308, 113 runs batted in, 37 home runs, and 19 stolen bases as a White Sox and he's the greatest. Tanner didn't mean to start a war. He just meant to jack up the spirit around this fellow who can hit the ball out of sight.

Immediately the Old Guard started throwing names of the old greats at Tanner—Luke Appling, Eddie Collins, Ted Lyons, Red Faber, and Ed Walsh, for a few.

I won't scold Tanner for his psych job on Allen. But I will scold the others who left their bias showing and passed over Shoeless Joe Jackson, as great a White Sox as there ever was, Richie Allen to the contrary.

Jackson's name is brought up here for a reason. In baseball, he's a wipe-out. His memory is declared illegal. Baseball trampled it in the dust and said don't ever bring it up again. He's revived sporadically only for that line, "Say it ain't so, Joe," which was bogus. He's the only .356 lifetime hitter not in the Hall of Fame.

In 1919, Jackson and seven other White Sox players, some of whom confessed, some of whom took it on the lam for good, and some who pleaded innocence, were accused of accepting money to "adjust" the outcome of the World Series with Cincinnati. Those who confessed later repudiated their confessions. All were indicted, and all were acquitted in a jury trial. But in 1921, the eight players were banned from baseball by the new commissioner, Judge Kenesaw Mountain Landis.

The fact that Jackson batted .375 and fielded like a jewel in the Series, the fact that he was cleared by a federal court jury, the fact that he maintained his innocence down to his death in 1951 were dismissed by baseball as legal balderdash and whining.

I feel a little more authoritative on the subject than most, for a few years before his death, I spent a few days with Jackson in his mill village home near Greenville, South Carolina, and he talked about the "fix." There was no question in my mind but that he listened to the proposition. There was no question in my mind but that he was tempted, for he made no more than $3,000 a year.

There was also no question in my mind but that he went ahead playing his game. He was an uneducated man and not the most intelligent. He'd had no opportunities other than those available in the almost medieval mill village he grew up in. But he'd been brought up to know sin when he saw it, and this was sin in capital letters.

I always remember one thing he said, because I still have the notes, if for no other reason: "I'm not what you call a Christian, but I believe in the Good Book. What you sow, so shall you reap.

"I asked the Lord for guidance and I'm sure he gave it to me."

Okay, so Shoeless Joe Jackson was tempted. For his indulgence he was cast out of baseball at the age of 32.

But after 50 years, hasn't anybody given some thought to forgiving Joe Jackson for something he probably didn't even do? And say, "Come on, Joe, we got a resting place in Cooperstown for you. You've paid more than twice your price."

Did you ever check Joe Jackson's record? He had a lifetime batting average of .356 in 4,981 at-bats. Babe Ruth called him the greatest natural hitter he ever saw. Their styles were similar. During his 11 seasons in the major leagues he batted .354, .387, .408, .395, .373. . . You don't need the rest. After his final season, in 1920, he left the game with a .382 beside his name, 121 runs batted in, and 12 home runs just as the lively ball was coming in.

The year he batted .408 he didn't lead the American League, but only because Ty Cobb batted .420.

Cobb once described Jackson as "the perfect hitter. Joe's swing was purely natural."

Times have changed, and changed a lot since 1921. They forgive now, apply lenience on the basis of no chance, poverty, ignorance, and neglect. Joe Jackson knew them all. Society is paying a lot of old debts these days. Baseball has one to pay here.

I don't mean take it carte blanche. Look into a case that reeks of injustice. Though all that's left is a headstone in a cemetery somewhere and a name vague in a lot of memories, there's a debt here that can only be paid off in Cooperstown. Then when they speak of great White Sox ballplayers, they can mention Joe Jackson's name without using code.

Indicted for conspiring to defraud the public by fixing the outcome of the 1919 World Series against Cincinnati, six White Sox players are seen here with their attorneys during the jury trial in Chicago in 1921. Seated (left to right) are attorney Thomas Nash, Joe Jackson, Buck Weaver, Ed Cicotte, Swede Risberg, Lefty Williams, and Chick Gandil. The two attorneys standing on the left are unidentified. Next to them are attorneys Max Luster and Joseph O'Brien. Eight players were indicted, including Happy Felsch (not pictured), and although all were acquitted they were banned from ever again playing professional baseball by Commissioner Kenesaw M. Landis. After their expulsion, the Black Sox gradually drifted from public notice. The low pay of the players involved, including Jackson—one of the best players of the era—reportedly set the stage for the scandal.

The Day Andy Seminick
Wiped Out
the Giants' Infield

by Rich Ashburn
Philadelphia Bulletin

August, 1974

Baseball players as fighters are usually pretty good baseball players. I haven't seen any good fighters in baseball. I've seen a lot of tough guys who could be good fighters but they never got involved in fights for a simple reason: Who wants to fight a guy who knows how to fight?

I've seen guys who thought they were fighters. The late Don Hoak was one of those. He got into a lot of fights but to my knowledge never won one. In fact, his fight record was so bad, the players used to call him Canvasback and accused him of having "Eat at Joe's" written on the bottom of his shoes.

Billy Martin is supposed to be a tough bird, and maybe he is. I only saw him in one fight. When I played with the Cubs, we had a fight with Cincinnati. Martin was an infielder with the Reds, and he and pitcher Jim Brewer of the Cubs had some words between the mound and home plate. It appeared that words would be the extent of the action, and Brewer turned to walk away. Martin hit him hard then. Brewer, who suffered a severe facial injury requiring a long hospital stay, always claimed Martin hit him with a sneak punch.

I played with one guy who I know was tough, and I know he could fight. I'm referring to a tough Russian, former Phils catcher Andy Seminick. By nature he was easy-going, and I can't think of anyone who didn't get along with him. But you never wanted to get him riled up. I saw that happen one day, and it was frightening. It happened in the early 1950s.

The New York Giants were in town. They came into Philadelphia with a pretty good ball club—after Andy got through with them they were a shambles. The Giant second baseman, Eddie Stanky, started the whole thing.

The first time Andy came to bat in the game, Stanky got directly behind the pitcher and started jumping up and down and waving his arms. He did this in order to distract Andy when the pitcher threw the ball, and this obviously can be very dangerous to the hitter when you can't concentrate on seeing the

ball. (Incidentally, Stanky's antics caused a rule change that now prohibits such gesturing.)

Andy got on base anyway, and a ground ball later, Stanky was taken out of action by a crunching football block at second base. The Giants' first mistake in the game was having Stanky jump up and down. Their second mistake was letting Seminick get on base for the second time in the game.

Andy's second slide into second base knocked Giant shortstop Bill Rigney almost into left field. Rigney took offense at this and took a swing at Andy. One more swing later, this one by Seminick, Bill Rigney was taken off the field on a stretcher. Now the Giants had lost their second baseman and their shortstop. However Andy wasn't through yet.

Somebody hit a long flyball to the outfield, and Seminick tagged at second, then made a dash for third base. It looked like it would be a close play. The Giant third baseman, Henry Thompson, was standing at third waiting for the ball to come to him. The ball did come to him but unfortunately for Henry, Andy got there at the same time.

I was never a Giant fan but I felt just a pang of remorse for Henry Thompson. Andy turned him every way but loose—all you could see were arms and legs and a few teeth (they were Henry's). And sure enough, Henry left the game on a stretcher.

Giant manager Leo Durocher was beside himself. Andy had just wiped out three-fourths of a very fine infield, and he was still on third base, kinda pawing the ground and snorting like a wounded bull. Leo appealed to the umpires to take Andy out of the game —the Giants were fighting for a pennant and Leo didn't want to blow the whole season because of Andy Seminick.

I've never seen the umpires do too many favors for Leo Durocher, but I think even they felt sorry for him this day. They didn't throw Andy out of the game—they gently asked him to leave. As I said, Andy, by nature, was a gentle man. He didn't have a beef against the umpires, so he left peacefully.

251

Mental Blunders
Are Part of the Game

by Edward Prell

August, 1971

Baseball lore is bulging with thrilling incidents, mostly on the plus side. But the boo-boos also add to the game's excitement. Who can forget the New York Giants' Fred Merkle neglecting to touch second base on a teammate's single which brought the Cubs a pennant in 1908 when the game was replayed because of his boner. . . . And there's Mickey Owen's passed ball that cost the Brooklyn Dodgers their 1941 World Series with the New York Yankees. . . . A few flubs like that.

The game has also been marked by many tactical blunders committed by managers and players alike. These blunders form an interesting litany of human frailty and have shook up such experienced baseball people as Leo Durocher and Paul Richards at least once or twice in their careers.

Durocher unabashedly recites his devastating goof.

"This was in Pittsburgh's old Forbes Field and my Giants were tied with the Pirates, who had the bases loaded with two out in the ninth inning," Leo began with a grimace.

"I called in Hoyt Wilhelm from the bullpen. His first pitch sailed behind the batter, but my catcher made a great save. The second one was way off the target. And after Wilhelm's next pitch was almost a wild one, I jumped up and yelled to Freddy Fitzsimmons, my pitching coach, 'Get him out of there!'

"I don't recall the name of the pitcher we called in from the bullpen as Wilhelm started that slow walk off the field. My new man started tossing practice pitches.

"So here came toward our dugout the plate umpire, my old pal, Jocko Conlan.

" 'You can't do that!' Jocko yelled in his high-pitched voice.

" 'Yeah, I know it now,' I said, peeking out from the towel I'd thrown over my head to hide my shame.

"I had completely forgotten that a pitcher, starter or reliever, must face at least one batter. Wilhelm had gone only three-fourths of the way. I sent a bench-warmer on the double to the clubhouse, where Hoyt already was stripped to his shorts. So he put on his baseball clothes and returned to the mound.

"His first pitch missed the strike zone, and a Pirate walked home with the winning run. It wasn't any comfort to me that the Pirates also had been unaware a pitching change couldn't be made. And I've always thought, too, that Jocko was a trifle slower on the trigger than usual!"

In 1942, Lou Boudreau, later to become a Hall-of-Famer, was the 24-year-old shortstop-manager of the Cleveland Indians. One day he was sniffling from a cold but still felt strong enough to flash signals from the bench.

"Our sign for the double steal was putting a towel to the face," recalls Lou. "Pat Seerey, sometimes called Fat Pat and who couldn't beat his sister in a footrace, was on second base. Our guy on first, whose name I can't recall, never set any speed records, either.

"Well, my nose was dripping, and I picked up a towel and blew my nose. First thing I saw, Seerey was huffing and puffing toward third base and his other accomplice was resolutely plodding toward second base. Both were thrown out for a double play.

"I turned to one of my coaches, Oscar [Spinach] Melillo, and barked, 'What ever made you put on a deal like that with those truck horses on the bases?' He reminded me I had been the guilty party.

"After the game, Bill Veeck, then the Indians' owner, asked me to explain my strategy and I 'fessed up.

" 'Next time you have to blow your nose, go into the runway, out of sight,' Bill suggested.

"Incidentally, we also blew the game!"

Joe Cronin, president of the American League, confesses his biggest mistake in baseball stemmed from a violation of the manager's code of strategy.

"When I was managing the Boston Red Sox we were playing the Chicago White Sox in Comiskey Park," recounts Cronin. "We went into the ninth inning with a two-run lead. The White Sox put the tying runs on third and second with two out. Their next hitter was Luke Appling, who had won two American League batting championships. Following Luke in the batting order was Oris Hockett.

"Now, to whom would you rather pitch—Luke Appling or Oris Hockett?

"Even though I knew it was a cardinal sin for a manager to deliberately put the winning run on base, I ordered Appling walked.

"A few seconds later, I was a raving maniac. Oris Hockett had cleared the bases with a triple!"

It was the second game of the 1917 World Series between John McGraw's Giants and Pants Rowland's White Sox in Comiskey Park—October 7, a Sunday. Urban [Red] Faber, who was to win three times as the Sox won in six games for their last World Series triumph, was making his debut in the big show.

This is the record book's account of Chicago's fifth inning in that second game:

> With one out, the Giants' Art Fletcher booted Buck Weaver's grounder. Buck took second on Ray Schalk's infield out. Faber singled to right, Weaver holding third, but Faber slid into second base on the throw to the plate. Faber tried to steal third with Weaver occupying the bag, Heinie Zimmerman tagging him after taking the throw from catcher Bill Rariden.

"Well," recites Faber, "I can't argue with that play-by-play, but I can fill you in on some details.

"When I went into second base, I figured Weaver had scored. I dusted off my pants, and when I saw the Giants' pitcher, Pol Perritt, winding up, I took off for third base.

"Gosh blame [Red's pet expression], was I surprised as I came down the baseline to see Weaver scooting back to third. 'Where do you think you're going?' Buck growled.

" 'Back to pitch,' I told him."

The White Sox won, 7-2. Faber lost to Ferdie Schupp in the fourth game, won the fifth in relief, and the sixth to complete the conquest with a route-going job.

Fred Lindstrom, a boy wonder third baseman with the New York Giants and star with the champion Cubs of 1935, was back in the old Polo Grounds in 1936, but as a left fielder for the Brooklyn Dodgers. Here's his account of how he turned a win into a loss for Brooklyn in a game against his original team:

"The Giants and Dodgers had a tremendous rivalry in New York, just as they now have in California," said Lindstrom. "Van Lingle Mungo, the fire-balling and pugnacious right-hander, was our pitcher, and we led in a freewheeling battle, 8-6, when the Giants came up in the ninth. Our manager was Casey Stengel.

"Eventually, the inning reached the point where the bases were filled and two were out. Travis Jackson hit a high pop fly into left field—remember, it was only 280 feet from the plate to the wall. The sun came right over the top of Coogan's Bluff in the late afternoon, hitting you smack in the eyes, making left field indeed hazardous.

Joe Cronin, shown here in his playing days with Boston, recalls his biggest mistake as a manager was ordering Luke Appling intentionally walked in a 1945 game so his Red Sox pitcher could work on Oris Hockett, a nondistinguished hitter with the White Sox. Hockett tripled to clear the bases.

"When Jackson connected, I flipped down my sunglasses and charged in. I didn't notice that our shortstop, James [Lord] Jordan—he had elevated the prestige of sweaty ballplayers by marrying a Romanian countess—also was zeroing in on the ball. I think I had yelled that I'd take it. But maybe not.

"Anyway, just as the ball settled into his glove I crashed into him. The ball popped out and rolled away. We both sprawled and my sunglasses were knocked off. By the time our second baseman, or maybe the center fielder, retrieved the ball, it was too late. All three base-runners had scored. In that split second, I had turned an 8-6 victory into a 9-8 defeat!

"Not a word was said in the clubhouse. For once, even Stengel was speechless. I had never felt so badly in my baseball life. I think we all sensed—even the hot-tempered Mungo—that this was the time for not only a moment of silence but to forget it into eternity!"

Did Paul Richards ever get mixed up in his thinking and do a mental flip-flop? Richards, as manager of the White Sox and Baltimore Orioles, was rated one of the sharpest tacticians ever, though his teams never won a pennant.

"My biggest goof," Paul acknowledges, "came in 1950 when I was managing Seattle in the Pacific Coast League. Remember Jim Wilson, who later pitched for the White Sox? Now this season he was our man against Fred Haney's Hollywood Stars on their field.

"Jim had won 16 straight games. After this game with the Stars, his next start would be in Seattle. And if that winning streak was still alive, we'd draw at least 12,000 when he went after No. 18.

"So now it's the seventh inning against Haney's team. Wilson is leading, 2-1. My thought then was that he would not lose this game if I could help it. I was thinking about that return to Seattle with the record intact. I told Skinny Brown, my star reliever, to get ready; if the Stars got that tying run on base he was coming in. That way Wilson couldn't possibly lose.

"Wilson cut down the Stars until two were out in the ninth. Then our shortstop, John Albright, kicked an easy ground ball. Now the tying run was on base, and it was time for me to act to make it certain Wilson would arrive in Seattle with the streak alive.

"Here came Skinny Brown from the bullpen. Then I made the mistake of trying to think. Heck, I told myself, Wilson has pitched a great game and was in trouble through no fault of his. I must say I had the thought, too, that I might be criticized for yanking him. So I waved Skinny back to the bullpen.

"So . . . Frank Kelleher smashed Wilson's first pitch for a game-winning homer. End of streak and also the glorious homecoming to Seattle.

"Moral to all managers: When you make up your mind, go through with it no matter if it 'hair-lips' all of Ellis County, of which my hometown Waxahachie, Texas, is the county seat!"

Mayo Smith, manager of the 1968 world champion Detroit Tigers, also admits to a mistake or two along the way.

"I've pulled more than my share of rocks," he concedes. "I can't think of a more shocking boo-boo to my ego than what happened when I was playing in 1941 for Buffalo in the International League.

"Steve O'Neill was our manager, and we were playing the old Montreal Royals in Buffalo. It was the eighth inning, and I hit a triple to drive in the tying run. I felt great—you might say exhilarated—as I slid into third.

"Don Ross, the Montreal third baseman, told me, 'Hey, get off the bag and let me dust it off.'

"I obligingly stepped off—and bingo! He tagged me in the ribs with the ball. And did those home fans start hooting!

"What did manager O'Neill say? Nothing. I don't think he knew, either, that Ross had possessed the ball in this unusual version of the old hidden-ball trick.

"Yes, we lost in extra innings. But the bitter lesson served me well. After that, I always knew where the ball was, even though sometimes as a batter I couldn't hit it!"

Pete Reiser, more than one smart man has testified, would have landed among the greatest except for a flaming competitive spirit which compelled him to crash into outfield walls to the detriment of his career as a Dodger.

Pete's moment of embarrassment on the playing field came in 1940, his rookie season in Brooklyn's cozy Ebbets Field. The cast of characters:

Hilda, the notorious cowbell-wielding fan of the Dodgers; Reiser, the kid center fielder; Leo Durocher, the Dodgers' manager; Larry MacPhail, the Dodgers' president; pitchers Whitlow Wyatt and Hugh Casey.

"We were pretty far out in front," says Reiser, "when Hilda yelled down to me while we were in the field. She tossed me a wadded-up piece of paper. 'Give this to Leo,' she commanded.

"When the inning was over and as I came toward our dugout, I spoke to MacPhail, who was sitting in a nearby box. Leo was within earshot, and I told him, 'Here's a note for you.'

"I noticed that Durocher had a puzzled look. Next inning, when Wyatt got into mild trouble, Durocher hastily called in Casey, our star reliever. Casey didn't have it that day, but because of a wide lead we held on to win.

"After it was all over, Leo shouted to me, 'Don't you, or anyone else, ever bring me a note from MacPhail.'

" 'But, Mr. Durocher,' I protested, 'that wasn't from Mr. MacPhail.'

" 'Then who in hell gave it to you?' he inquired.

" 'Hilda,' I answered.

"I hadn't read her crumpled message. Long afterward, when I'd made it with Leo and the Dodgers, I asked him about that note.

" 'It said that Wyatt was losing his stuff and to get Casey ready,' Durocher laughed. 'I've heard of front office interference, but how about me listening to that crazy dame with the cowbell!' "

Ernie Banks, seen backing up Gene Baker on a play at second base, remembers a game early in his career when with no runner on first base he fielded a ground ball at short and flipped it to a startled Baker near second. Baker recovered from his surprise in time to flip the relay to first for a putout on the batter-runner. Banks went on to win the National League's Most Valuable Player Award in 1958 and 1959.

In 1954, the first full season for Ernie Banks with the Cubs, the team one day was playing the Pittsburgh Pirates and the score was tied in the seventh inning.

"The Pirates had a runner on third base, and our infield was drawn in for a play at the plate," is the way Banks sketches the scene. "Jim Greengrass was the batter. I was playing shortstop. Gene Baker was our second baseman and over at first base was Dee Fondy.

"Greengrass grounded the ball sharply to me. I threw it to Baker, who recovered from surprise just in time to stab the ball and flip it to Fondy at first base to nick Greengrass. The Pittsburgh runner on third also was so surprised that he failed to break for the plate.

"Baker, my roomie, had kidded me before when I made the wrong play, just to keep me loose. But this time he really scolded me because I hadn't thrown the ball to Fondy for the automatic out.

" 'Ernie, you gotta do a little thinking out there on the field,' he said. 'That was the dumbest play I ever saw, even if it didn't cost us a run. Why did you do it?'

" 'I just knew you'd have a better idea than me on what to do,' was my weak answer."

Don Gutteridge, one-time manager of the White Sox as successor to Al Lopez, was a speed boy in his playing days, most of them with the Cardinals. Don also had played with the Red Sox before they traded him to the Pirates just before the 1948 race started.

"On this day early in the season, we were playing Cincinnati," Gutteridge recounts. "Clyde Kluttz, our slow-footed catcher, doubled in the late innings and Billy Meyer, the manager, told me to run for him.

"As I jumped out of the dugout, I heard Billy tell the other players: 'Watch this fellow. You'll learn something. He's one of the best base-runners in the business.'

"Lanky Ewell Blackwell was pitching for the Reds. With Meyer's praise still ringing in my ears, I took a couple of extra steps off the bag. First thing I knew, Blackwell had whirled and Bobby Adams, the second baseman, was tagging me out."

Joe DiMaggio was known as the perfect player, but he didn't have to ponder long to come up with his most painful *faux pas.*

"We were playing the Tigers in Yankee Stadium," says the Hall-of-Famer. "Hank Greenberg was at the plate, and Rudy York was on first base. Hank blasted one a country mile, and I brushed against the Colonel Jake Ruppert monument in deep center as I leaped for a one-handed catch.

"Sixty thousand fans were cheering like mad and the 'Great DiMag' stood there taking bows. Next thing I knew, Frankie Crosetti, our shortstop, was racing toward me, frantically waving his arms. Then I came to my senses. Frankie wanted the ball. By this time York, sometimes accused of running in the same place and who had rounded second base, was digging back toward first.

"I fired the ball to Crosetti. His hurried throw hit Rudy. The ball bounced away, Rudy wound up on second base, and Frankie was charged with an error on what should have been a simple double play! It was my most red-faced moment in baseball—a thrill gone completely sour."

255

Ty Cobb—Riled Up, He'd Annihilate You

by Bob French

Condensed from the *Toledo Blade*

November, 1942

Ty Cobb has been out of baseball so long it is difficult to get the right slant on the achievements of this remarkable athlete. In some instances, the legendary feature is at work and exaggeration creeps in until one is inclined to doubt the testimony. On the other hand, fierce opponents of Cobb in his playing days still come up from time to time with some criticism of his efforts and refuse to give him credit for what he really did. Cobb was no sweet tempered pal of other players back in his halcyon days, and some of them haven't yet forgiven him.

Fred Haney, manager of the Toledo Mud Hens, is one of the best sources of unprejudiced Cobb history. Fred was closely associated with Cobb for six years and studied without prejudice the amazing career of the Georgian both as player and manager at Detroit. Haney appreciated Cobb's outstanding ability as a player and his tremendous mental qualifications, but at the same time he wasn't blind to his eccentricities.

"Cobb was the first man who really put psychology into baseball," said Haney the other day. "He knew how to spur himself and his players to a mental pitch which would help his side; he also knew how to worry the opposition until it lost some of its efficiency. He worked along entirely original lines.

"There probably have been players in the game who had as much natural ability and as good a physique as Cobb; there may also have been some—although I doubt it—who could think as fast. But there certainly never was another athlete who combined Cobb's ability and his smartness—or even came close."

Cobb was the perfect example of an athlete who thrived on the fiercest sort of opposition. The tougher the other fellows were the better Cobb played baseball. But merely the taunts of spectators and the attacks of opposing players weren't enough to suit him. He actually would battle with himself, Haney says, in order to fan the flames of competition in his own breast.

"It was a study watching Cobb on the bench as his turn to bat approached," Haney went on. "It could easily be seen from his facial expression that he was lashing himself into that fighting mood which made him feel that nobody on earth, and especially no pitcher, could stop him. In his baseball he instinctively centered on the fellows who gave him the most trouble, gradually found out how to circumvent them, and finally had them utterly licked and pushed into the background so far as he was concerned.

"When he first broke into the American League, Doc White, the great southpaw pitcher of the Chicago White Sox, had Cobb completely stymied. Tyrus could hardly get a foul ball off White, and many believed that as soon as other pitchers learned White's knack of fooling Cobb, the fiery young man would be chased out of the league.

"Exactly the opposite happened. Cobb centered on White. He studied him as he studied no other player. Pretty soon Cobb was hitting White, and soon after that he was murdering the Chicago star. Baseball history will show that when Cobb really reached his stride, White was his easiest victim.

"The same thing with his many fistfights. Cobb was no great battler in his early days as a player. But he was willing to fight anybody, and he took one beating after another. The climax came when he got into a wordy war with a well-known and husky umpire. Cobb invited the umpire to meet him under the stands after the game. The umpire was more than willing. The two got together, and Cobb just about got his head knocked off.

"That winter Cobb hired a boxing instructor and took him to his winter home in Georgia. Ty worked all winter with the gloves. When the next season rolled around, he could hardly wait until that umpire appeared in a Detroit series. The big day came at last. Cobb rushed up to the umpire after the first game of the series. 'I still think you're all the things I called you last fall,' shouted Cobb, 'and I dare you to meet me under the stands again.' The umpire gladly complied, and this time Cobb just about murdered the umpire."

The place where they really went after Cobb was in New York. The instant he came on the field there the crowd would be on him, and thus encouraged, the Yankees would center on him with terrific energy and venom.

"And if Cobb had played all his games in New York," Haney said, "he would have had a lifetime batting average of .750 and would have stolen about 200 bases a season. The instant Ty came on the field and the abuse started, he began to boil and steam, and by the time the game started he was sim-

Ty Cobb slides into third base against Frank (Home Run) Baker of the Philadelphia A's during a game early in his career. Baker was spiked on the play, precipitating a famous fight between the two future Hall-of-Famers. Cobb was probably the most hated player of his time, disliked even by some of his Detroit teammates. He gave no quarter in his play, and expected none. He would often go from first to third on an infield out, forcing the opposition to hurry their throws, throw poorly, or drop the ball because of fear of his sharp spikes. But Cobb was also respected as the best all-round player of his time. And when the first selections for the Hall of Fame were made (in 1936), Cobb was one of only five chosen; the others were Walter Johnson, Christy Mathewson, Babe Ruth, and Hans Wagner.

ply invincible. The Tigers loved to play in New York; the rest of them could take it easy, and Cobb would win the games all by himself."

It is a fact that Connie Mack, who had great ball clubs in Philadelphia when Cobb was tearing things apart, used to caution his players to let Cobb strictly alone. Connie believed that if Cobb were not antagonized he would be easier to handle.

"Let him sleep, if he will," said the wise old Connie. "If you get him riled up, he'll annihilate us."

Once when Haney was battling for a job with the Tigers, he discovered he could read the signs of Steve O'Neill, catching for Cleveland. Haney at once went to Cobb and suggested that he be allowed to work on the coaching lines and flash information to Detroit hitters on curveballs and fast ones. But Cobb was not enthusiastic.

"You probably could do it all right, Fred," said Cobb, "but it won't help much. I know just about every ball a pitcher is going to throw to us without looking for the signs. I've tried to wise up our fellows, but they don't seem to profit by it."

Haney must have indicated that he didn't believe Cobb was clairvoyant, so Tyrus said: "Come over to the bench when the game starts; I'll show you something."

As the game began, Cobb sat on the edge of the dugout and made no effort to get the catcher's signs. He admitted he couldn't call the first pitch, but after it was made—a fastball and a strike—he used that for his first information and correctly told in advance what the pitcher was going to throw for *26 consecutive* pitches. He missed on the *27th*.

"It's not so hard," Ty explained, "when you know these catchers like I know Steve O'Neill. I know what he's going to call for when I know the count, the score, the inning, the hitter, and such details. You can learn these things if you watch for 'em."

(Editor's Note: Ty Cobb's major league career spanned 24 seasons—1905–28. In 23 of these, he hit over .300; in three, over .400; in 12 he led the American League. His lifetime batting average was .367.)

Pitchers Hate
Tape-Measure Homers

by John Kuenster

September, 1971

Since Willie Stargell has been splintering the furniture at Three Rivers Stadium in Pittsburgh and other National League parks this season, it seems appropriate at the moment to delve into the subject of mammoth home runs.

There have been countless gigantic blasts in major league history that have been propelled by longball hitters like Stargell, Mickey Mantle, Frank Howard, Harmon Killebrew, Norm Cash, and, of course, Babe Ruth.

And also by such lesser-known performers as Ron Jackson and Dave Nicholson. You remember Ron Jackson and Dave Nicholson, don't you?

Neither was too successful in the majors, but both unloaded drives that rank way up there with the game's more famous tape-measure productions. One year during the spring exhibition season—this would be about 1958—Jackson, a six-foot-seven first baseman trying to make it with the White Sox, hit a home run against the Cardinals that traveled about 510 feet in a game at Denver.

With tape in hand, White Sox publicitor Ed Short measured the distance of the prodigious clout. "Don't you think the thin air had something to do with the distance the ball traveled?" a cynical scribe inquired. Short feigned insult. He never did believe in the negative approach.

Jackson's homer was something to see, but so was the one Nicholson (oddly enough he also was with the White Sox at the time) hit at Comiskey Park one night against Moe Drabowsky of the then Kansas City A's. That one cleared the roof over the left-field stands and landed outside the park.

After Nicholson's drive, a spoilsport reporter ventured out to the upper left-field stands and awoke a couple of fans dozing there to inquire if they heard the ball bounce on the roof.

None of them seemed sure they heard the ball bounce, but it didn't matter. It still landed outside the park and resulted in a fleeting moment of fame for Nicholson, a powerfully built right-handed hitter.

About the only other notoriety Nicholson gained in the American League, outside of his frequent

Dave Nicholson holds the ball he drove completely out of Comiskey Park in a game against the Kansas City A's on May 6, 1964. That's Jimmy Dykes, the A's coach, on the right. The young fan, who retrieved the ball behind the left-field grandstand, received an autographed ball in return. The homer landed in a nearby playground.

Willie Stargell of the Pirates on occasion has used a sledgehammer for a few warm-up swings before stepping into the batter's box, a rather awesome sight for opposing pitchers. Stargell has hit home runs with such force they have splintered the backs of seats more than 350 feet away.

strike-outs, was the time when he was with the Orioles, he turned the shower faucets off so tightly, teammate Joe Ginsberg couldn't turn them back on after coming into the clubhouse following a workout.

Jimmie Foxx and Hank Greenberg reached the left-field roof at Comiskey Park, and going back earlier in history, Ruth cleared the right-field stands before the upper deck was built. "I saw that one," recalls Bill Downes, who was the home-team bat boy that day. "It was a line-drive shot that kept rising. After clearing the park, it landed in a soccer field behind the right-field stands and kept rolling until it came to rest near the old Armory on what was then Wentworth Avenue." Without stretching the truth, that would put the ball about 800 feet away from home plate. On the bounce, of course.

In the old days, home runs were measured as the crow flies or computed by rubber imaginations. One time, long after his playing days had ended, Ruth pointed to a hotel beyond the right-field fence at Al Lang Field in St. Petersburg, Florida. "I hit that hotel once," said the Babe.

"That doesn't look like much of a drive," said his listener.

"Hell, man, the ball park was over there then," retorted Ruth, pointing to a spot about 200 feet in the opposite direction.

The distances of some of Ruth's homers were estimated at anywhere from 520 to 1,000 feet. Today, tape-measure historians figure in precise footage.

The longest measured home run ever hit in Baltimore's Memorial Stadium, for instance, was a 471-foot drive by Killebrew on May 24, 1964, off Milt Pappas, a pitcher with a "gopher ball" tendency. The ball cleared the hedge in left center field.

Frank Robinson is the only player who has hit a ball completely out of Memorial Stadium. In the second game of a doubleheader with Cleveland on May 8, 1966, Robinson hit a Luis Tiant pitch over the left-field stands and into the parking lot beyond —a drive that measured 451 feet on the fly. The ball rolled to a stop 540 feet away from home plate.

Since Detroit's Tiger Stadium was renovated along its present lines in 1938, eight players have hit a total of 13 baseballs out of the park.

In 1939, Ted Williams sent a shot winging some 527 feet over the triple-decked right-field stands on a three-and-0 pitch by the Tigers' Bob Harris.

Norm Cash has belted four homers over the right-field deck in Detroit—once in 1961 and three times in 1962. Mantle cleared the park three times. Killebrew, Don Mincher, Frank Howard, Boog Powell, and Jim Northrup have all done it once. Killebrew and Howard have cleared the left-field roof at Tiger Stadium.

Mantle hit long ones in every American League park, including Yankee Stadium, where on at least three separate occasions, he almost cleared the roof high over the right-field stands. Once, in Washington's old Griffith Stadium, he drilled a 565-foot homer.

These mighty cannon shots not only dent stadium woodwork, they also shatter a pitcher's ego. A few years ago, a left-handed pitcher named Frank Baumann was recalling with dismay what Roger Maris had done to his most effective delivery—a pitch low and away. Baumann had a glazed look in his eyes as he recounted the disaster. "He pulled that pitch," he said in disbelief. "I don't know how, but he pulled it and hit a line drive into the upper deck in right field. It was my best pitch!"

Baumann needn't have been chagrined. It wasn't the first time a pitcher had suffered a rude awakening at the hands of a power hitter, nor would it be the last. Happens all the time, especially in the National League, where batters seem more adept at actually golfing those low pitches into the stands.

The harder a pitcher throws sometimes, the farther the heavy hitters slam the ball.

Stargell's towering homers this year, of course, rightfully give the Pirates a feeling of grandeur while making opposing pitchers duly respectful.

The long, long ball drives in runs, but it's also a potent psychological weapon. What pitcher wants to get into the record book as being the victim of a tape-measure homer?

When somebody once asked Willie McCovey how he'd pitch to himself if he could, the Giants' power man had a quick and appropriate response.

"I'd walk me," said Willie.

Remember Rip Sewell and the "Ephus Ball"?

by Joe Falls
Detroit Free Press

July, 1975

Who remembers the Ephus Pitch?

Ah, yes, the old blooper ball. The one that floated in like a balloon. Rip Sewell, the square-jawed pitcher of the Pittsburgh Pirates, would lob it 25 feet into the air, higher than they do in a slow-pitch softball game, and it would float down to the batters looking bigger than a beach ball.

Oh my, what they wanted to do to the Ephus Pitch. They wanted to hit it over the roof. Out of the ball park. Out of sight. They wanted to hit it downtown.

They'd watch it come floatin' down, and they'd start cranking up. They'd move up in the batter's box, cock their bats, crank up again, and again—even again—and squish!

"They'd hit it about as high as the ceiling in this room," giggled the old man sitting there in his easy chair, slapping his two artificial legs in great glee. "Or they'd miss it by two feet. Why, if I pitched today," said Rip Sewell, "I'd make Catfish Hunter seem like a pauper."

He might just do that, too. Nobody in all the history of baseball ever threw a pitch the way Truett (Rip) Sewell did. Not Cy Young, Walter Johnson, Christy Mathewson, Bob Feller, Sandy Koufax, or even the celebrated James (Catfish) Hunter. Not any of them.

Just as there was only one Babe, one Georgia Peach, one Joe D., one Ducky Wucky, and one Yogi, there was only one Ephus Pitch and only Rip Sewell could throw it.

He is 65 now and lives in retirement in Plant City, Florida. He hobbles around on two wooden limbs, and his pension from baseball is only $215 a month. But spare your sympathy. This is one of the richest men in the world, a man so vibrant that the air itself seems to crackle when he speaks.

"I remember once we were playing the Boston Braves," smiled Sewell. "Eddie Miller, their shortstop, used to go crazy when I'd give him the old Ephus.

"He'd stand there and scream at me, 'I'm going to get you! I'm going to knock your head off.'

"Poor Eddie. He couldn't take it anymore, and this one day he just reached out and caught the ball as it came over the plate. He threw it up into the air and lined it right back at me. I caught it right here, in front of my face.

"The umpire called it a strike on him." Sewell was beaming as he spoke. He is a proud man, very proud. And well he should be.

Sewell lost his legs to a circulatory condition in 1972. But that's nothing. Let him show you the shotgun wounds in his thighs and stomach and hips. He was hit in a hunting accident, took two full barrels from 30 feet, and they said then he would never walk again.

The date of the mishap was December 7, 1941.

"I was hit with 12 of the 18 pellets—nine in each barrel," he said, "and six of them went right through my legs. I've still got three of them in my abdomen. But I'll tell you, I was back pitching that next season."

No mere shotgun was going to keep Rip Sewell from doing the thing that he loved most in life. He spent 13 seasons in the major leagues, all but one with the Pirates. He was with them from 1938 through 1949. His other season was when he broke in with the Tigers in 1932.

It was against the Tigers, ironically, that he unveiled the strangest pitch in the history of baseball.

"It was in an exhibition game in Muncie, Indiana," said Sewell. "I'd been fooling around with the pitch in the bullpen, and Al Lopez, our catcher, kept egging me on to try it in a game.

"I was working three innings this day. I had two out in my last inning, and Dick Wakefield was the batter. I decided, well, what the heck—I'll give it a try."

Sewell reared back as if to give Wakefield a fastball and, oof, the pitch went almost straight up into the air like a kid losing his balloon at a circus.

"Wakefield looked at it, started to swing, held up, started to swing again—and missed it by two feet. I think everybody in the ball park fell off their chairs," Sewell chuckled.

Nobody had ever seen such a—well, what was it?—and the writers all scrambled down to the Pittsburgh dugout. They didn't even wait until the game had ended.

"What the hell was that?" one of the writers asked Sewell, who was sitting there drying himself off with a towel.

"I don't have a name for it, I just throw it," grinned Sewell.

Down the bench, an outfielder named Maurice

Van Robays piped up with, "It's an Ephus Pitch, that's what."

"What's that?" the writers wondered.

"It ain't nothin'," said Van Robays, "and that's what that pitch is—nothin'."

Thus, history was born in a small Indiana town in 1943. Sewell went on to throw the Ephus Pitch, which was to become known as the blooper ball, for the rest of his career. He threw it for the first time in a big league ball park when the Pirates visited Detroit for an exhibition after the game in Muncie.

"They had so many people turn out for the game, the Detroit management couldn't believe it," said Sewell.

Dizzy Trout, a character in his own right, tried to strike back at his team's tormentor and threw Sewell a blooper ball of his own. Sewell ripped a double down the left-field line.

What made Sewell's pitch so effective, so utterly baffling, is that he threw it in the same motion as his fastball. He merely put three fingers on the ball instead of four, and it would come off his fingertips with a tremendous backspin.

The batters cursed it. They fumed at their inability to hit it. Whitey Kurowski of the Cardinals spit at it every time it came across the plate. Ernie Lombardi, the hulking Cincinnati catcher, once pleaded with the umpire to give him one more strike after Sewell had fanned him with three straight Ephus pitches.

Sewell threw the pitch up to 15 times a game. He won 21 games in 1943 and again in 1944. Even when the stars came back after the war, he was 13-3 with his maddening pitch in 1948.

Stan Musial was the only National League player ever to get an extra-base hit off Sewell's blooper. He tripled off the right-field screen in Pittsburgh.

The blooper's most famous moment came in the 1946 All-Star game when Ted Williams caught hold of it and sent it screaming some 20 rows up in the right-field bleachers in Fenway Park.

Everybody talks about that moment, but few remember that Sewell threw another to the next batter, Charlie (King Kong) Keller of the Yankees, and he popped it up like a yo-yo. Sewell was given a standing ovation as he walked off the mound.

Rip Sewell demonstrates his blooper pitch for the photographer during spring training in 1947. Sewell was nearing the end of his career at the time. Batters were confident they could knock the pitch out of the park, but they seldom did.

What They Thought When the Pressure Was the Greatest!

by John Kuenster

June, 1961

What does a ballplayer think of when he's under pressure . . . when his hit will clinch a pennant or win a World Series . . . when his pitch will wreck or save a perfect no-hitter?

In covering the American and National league beats the last few years, we've had a chance to talk to players involved in some rather dramatic situations that put a high premium on their skill, courage, and determination.

We selected six particularly exciting games over the last decade and used them as a focal point to find out what the star performers actually **DID** think of when destiny beckoned.

Their admissions—some of them revealed here for the first time—provide an interesting insight into human behavior in time of stress.

October 1, 1950—Robin Roberts retires two Dodger hitters with bases filled in ninth inning as Philadelphia Phillies clinch pennant on final day of National League season.

"I was scared. The score was tied, 1-1, in the bottom of the ninth at Ebbets Field, and the Dodgers had the bases filled, with only one out. If they scored, a playoff would have been necessary to settle the championship.

"Carl Furillo and Gil Hodges, two tough hitters, were coming up. I was scared because *I was thinking of all the things that could go wrong*—a freak hop of the ball, an error, a bad pitch.

"I was determined, but on edge, tense. At one time we held a seven-game lead on the Dodgers and now they were breathing down our necks. I was going to fire away with the best I had.

"Furillo hit the first pitch, a high fastball. He popped up. I got behind on Hodges, and then got him to fly out, also on a fastball.

"That took the pressure off, and we went on to win the game on Dick Sisler's three-run homer in the 10th inning.

"When I think back about that game, it seems more dramatic than when I was going through it. Maybe, at the time, if I thought too much about what the game meant to us, I might not have done so well."

October 3, 1951—Bobby Thomson slams three-run ninth-inning homer at the Polo Grounds to provide Giants with 5-4 comeback victory over Dodgers in final game of pennant playoff series.

"We were trailing the Dodgers, 4-2, with one out and two runners on base in the last of the ninth. *I was never more thankful* that I had a chance to get up and hit.

"In the eighth inning, Don Newcombe had blown us down so easily, it didn't look like we'd have a chance. But now, as Ralph Branca emerged from the bullpen in center field to replace Newcombe, it dawned on me we might win it after all.

"Before I got in the batter's box, all I thought about was hitting the ball. *I got mad at myself.* I said to myself, 'Get in there, you so-and-so, and bear down. Watch the ball, wait for it. Don't swing at a bad pitch.'

"I guess my anger was a way of disciplining my anxiety, forcing me to concentrate on the pitch, making me be selective.

"I let Branca's first pitch go by, then swung at the second, a high fastball. It was up where I could see it, and I pulled it into the left-field stands, about 30 feet fair. I wasn't mad anymore. I was floating on a cloud."

October 9, 1956—Don Larsen of New York Yankees pitches first perfect, as well as first no-hit, no-run, game in World Series history, retiring 27 Dodgers in a row to post 2-0 triumph.

"I knew I had a no-hitter going for me in the seventh inning, but I didn't think too much about it until then. When the Dodgers came to bat in the ninth inning, I was so weak in the knees, I thought I was going to faint.

"*I had been nervous* since the seventh inning. Before we went out on the field in the ninth, Yogi Berra hit me on the seat of the pants and said, 'Go out there and let's get the first batter.'

"When Furillo came up to lead off, the thing I wanted to do more than anything else in my life was to get out of the ninth inning. *I mumbled a little prayer.* I said, 'Please help me get through this.'

"I got Furillo on a mild fly, Roy Campanella on a slow roller to Billy Martin, and pinch-hitter Dale Mitchell on a called third strike.

"Just before I threw the last pitch to Mitchell, I said to myself, *'Well, here goes nothing.'*

Dick Sisler is greeted at home plate after hitting a three-run homer in the 10th inning of the final game of the 1950 season to clinch the National League pennant for the Phillies. The game, played against the Dodgers at Ebbets Field, was won by the Phils, 4-1. Sisler's blast came after Philadelphia's Robin Roberts had pitched out of a jam in the ninth inning. With the game tied, 1-1, the bases loaded, and only one out in the bottom of the inning, Roberts had retired the last two Dodger hitters.

Don Larsen is hugged by catcher Yogi Berra (No. 8) after he had pitched the first no-hit, no-run game in World Series history, against the Dodgers at Yankee Stadium in 1956. But more remarkable, he pitched a perfect game—no batter reaching first base.

"Looking back on that ninth inning, I can say every one of those three batters looked like Ted Williams to me."

June 27, 1958—Billy Pierce of Chicago White Sox comes within one out of pitching perfect no-hitter against Washington Senators, his bid ruined by an opposite-field double.

"It was a warm, muggy night at Comiskey Park. My curveball was breaking real good, and I was getting my fastball where I wanted it.

"For eight and two-thirds innings I didn't allow a Washington runner to reach first. From the fifth inning on, I had thrown exactly nine pitches in each inning, so I wasn't tired.

"Now I had one more batter to go. Ed Fitz Gerald, a right-handed pinch-hitter, was up. We had a 3-0 lead, so there wasn't much at stake except that no-hitter.

"I knew I had a perfect game going from the third inning on. When I saw Fitz Gerald in the box, there was only one thought on my mind: keep the ball down and away from him.

"I figured he was a good fastball hitter, so I threw him a curve—about where I wanted—but he got the end of his bat on it and slammed the ball down the first-base line, fair by two feet. I struck

Bill Mazeroski rounds third base after hitting his decisive ninth-inning homer in the seventh game of the 1960 World Series against the Yankees. Jubilant Pirate fans are already beginning to swarm onto the playing field.

out the next batter, Albie Pearson, on three pitches, and that was the game.

"Since then, I've thought more about that game than when I actually pitched it. *I was concentrating so hard* on keeping the ball down and away from Fitz Gerald, I can't say I had any emotion one way or another."

May 26, 1959—Harvey Haddix of Pittsburgh Pirates pitches perfect ball for 12 innings, only to lose to Milwaukee Braves, 1-0, in 13th inning.

"I reached a peak in the ninth inning. I wanted that no-hitter. It had always been my ambition to do something like that.

"After the ninth inning, I was concentrating on trying to keep the Braves from scoring, but I felt more pressure on me in the ninth than at any other time.

"I think *I got a little bit angry.* I don't know exactly what I got mad at . . . maybe just at myself in trying to finish something that is very difficult.

"After I struck out Lew Burdette, the 27th batter to face me, the thing uppermost in my mind was the hope our guys would get me a run or two.

"I knew I had a no-hitter all the time, but I didn't know I had a perfect game. I thought I might have walked a man somewhere along the line.

"In the 13th inning, an error, a walk, and Joe Adcock's double scoring Felix Mantilla turned the game into just another loss. But *it hurt a little more.*"

October 13, 1960—Bill Mazeroski blasts Ralph Terry's fastball over left-field wall at Forbes Field in deciding game of World Series to give Pirates title, 10-9.

"When we trotted off the field for our turn at bat in the ninth, I was thinking, 'I'd like to hit a home run and win it all.'

"The time before, in the seventh inning, I had gone for the long ball and I overswung. I grounded into a double play. This time, I kept saying to myself, 'Don't overswing. Just meet the ball.'

"I thought I'd be more nervous this time, but I wasn't a bit. I wanted a homer, but I didn't want to overswing. *I was guessing* all the way. As Terry wound up, I was saying to myself, 'Fastball! Fastball!' That's what I wanted.

"The first one was a high slider. The next one was down a little, but still high—a fastball right into my power.

"A moment after I hit that ball, *a shiver ran down my back.* We always felt we could pull it out—even after the Yankees tied it up in the ninth—but I didn't think I'd be the guy to do it."

Bob Feller's Fame Still Trails Him

by Dwight Chapin
Los Angeles Times

October, 1969

The road led south, out of Calgary and Lethbridge, Alberta, and into Montana. Bob Feller, driving along the lonely highway, stopped for lunch at Shelby.

"There was this guy in the kitchen, slinging hash," Feller said, "and a couple of minutes after I sat down he came out and asked me if I weren't Bob Feller.

"It surprised me so much I asked him if he hadn't lived in Cleveland or maybe one of the other Eastern states when I was pitching. He told me he'd never been out of Shelby in his life."

Feller paused, to let what he had said rest a minute with his listener, and then he continued:

"I don't know a lot about football, but in the little towns of this country, the podunk towns, base-ball is still the sport that's a part of the people. Baseball."

Feller is familiar with "podunk" towns. He came out of one—Van Meter, Iowa—33 years ago as a 17-year-old rookie to blaze a baseball as few men have. And since his retirement as a pitcher in 1957, he has spent a lot of his time traveling the country's back roads—promoting baseball and making a buck in the process.

At 50, he hasn't changed much. His words are still as outspoken as his fastball was rapid.

As he moves around the United States, he sees a lot of kids, and Feller doesn't like what he sees in a lot of them.

"Things were a little hungry when I grew up, in the 1930s," he says. "It's hard to forget all those dust storms blowing through Iowa. When you're chewing dust all day long, you don't have time to think about much of anything but getting away from the dust, away to something better.

"Today, it's changed. For the first time, kids in their 20s have no economic insecurity. They have an education; you can't take that away from them. They have a car and material things; you can't take those away from them. They can tell people off without any fear at all.

"And meanwhile, there are the politicians, prom-

Bob Feller as he appeared early in his career with the Cleveland Indians and later (right), after he had established himself as one of the game's all-time great right-handers. Although he lost more than three prime years due to service in the Navy during World War II, Feller compiled 266 lifetime victories, pitching three no-hitters and 12 one-hitters from 1936 through 1956. He spent his entire career with the Indians.

ising 'If you vote for me, then I'll get things for you. I'll give them to you.' There are so many deadbeats around now, and that's the reason."

Feller's athletic career was marked by working for what he got. And so is his life-style.

He was blessed with a magnificent right arm. But his 266 major league victories with Cleveland, his 18 strike-outs in a game, his 348 strike-outs in a season, his three no-hitters, his 12 one-hitters, didn't come on his arm alone. He kept in shape. Even in his last years in the game, he outran the rookies in practice every day.

Feller does not believe baseball has changed much since the days when he was active.

"The pitchers," he says, "are more hep on different pitches but as far as being able to throw any harder or with any better stuff, I don't think so.

"But the kids do get less hitting practice now. And they swing hard on all three swings. That's different, and it hurts them."

Feller says that if he or Ted Williams came along again, "We'd probably do about the same."

But there can only be speculation about how either man would have done if World War II had not interfered. Feller missed nearly four full seasons, when he was at the pinnacle. He had won 25 games the year (1941) before he entered the Navy. In his first full season after the war, 1946, he had his finest year, winning 26 and striking out 348 batters.

"Most of the top athletes had to serve," Feller said. "Actually, I was lucky. All I suffered in four years was a broken finger, and that was when I came out of the hatch late and the cover slammed on me. No Purple Heart."

But there was the Hall of Fame, the first year he was eligible, in 1962. And everywhere he goes, the name Bob Feller still has a special magic. It is true in the small towns where business takes him, or where he appears for a speaking engagement.

Over the years, Feller has sometimes been critical of baseball, particularly its owners.

But he is a salesman of the sport now. Any ills that need solving, he feels, will require no basic changes in the game. Proper promotion, he thinks, is the only medication baseball needs.

His recall of the events of 18 years in the majors is brilliantly clear. He can remember hitters, such as Tommy Henrich, the Yankees' Old Reliable ("toughest I ever faced—a real money hitter"). He can remember pitchers, such as Satchel Paige. ("We toured all over the country in the winters. His curve wasn't that good but he had to be one of the best ever. Very consistent. Never a bad game.")

As for himself, he says that people sometimes downgraded his curveball, because his fastball was so good.

"My curve," he says, "was darned good, too."

If it were 1936 again and he had just come out of the cornfields, Feller would alter one thing.

"I'd concentrate much more on control," he said, "on trying to make every pitch a strike. For a long time, I just threw hard. I was careless; I walked too many batters. I made it so much tougher on myself than I should have."

An Iowa farm boy who broke into the majors at age 17, Bob Feller (third from the left) reached the apex of his baseball career in 1962, when he was admitted to the Hall of Fame with Edd Roush (left), Jackie Robinson, and Bill McKechnie.

1945 — Baseball's Most Chaotic Year

by William G. Nicholson

August, 1971

John J. McGraw always maintained that errors were as important as key hits and brilliant plays in the field, and he used to say that without errors baseball would perish within a month. Perhaps that is why major league baseball in 1945, the last of the World War II years, thrived as it did.

From 1942 on, when bona fide major-leaguers were being inducted into the armed services in large numbers, positions on big league teams had increasingly been filled by graybeards and second-rate journeyman ballplayers. By 1945, the standard of play had hit an all-time low, and the result was chaotic baseball, marked by tactical errors and outstanding reversals of form. Teams would go hot and cold, soar and then plummet. It is commonplace to say that the only certain thing about the game was its uncertainty.

Clearly it was bad baseball; nevertheless, it was interesting and entertaining. There were few stars, but there were a number of colorful or extremely incompetent or truly unique ballplayers moving around on big league diamonds. Perhaps this was what enabled the majors to draw the biggest crowds in years. At any rate, the first few games of the 1945 season set the pattern for the rest of the year.

George (Catfish) Metkovich opened the season at first base for the Red Sox against the Yankees and quickly established the American League record with three errors in the seventh inning. A few days later Johnny Lindell of the Yankees spiked his teammate, Herschel Martin, *in the nose,* as the two outfielders took a tumble chasing a flyball.

In the National League's opening week, the Pirates' Jim Russell hit what should have been a two-run homer but which was nullified when it was discovered that teammate Frankie Zak had asked the umpire for an official time-out to tie a shoelace at first base. Frankie, who was to reach first base only seven times all season, was undoubtedly savoring the experience. But the Braves' Elmer (Butch) Nieman, a rawboned outfielder from Herkimer, Kansas, hit three home runs in his team's first four games, all in the ninth inning, to cheer the Boston fans.

Dropped flyballs, slow base-running, inability to hit in the clutch, and missed signals plagued major league managers. One afternoon, Luke Sewell, manager of the Browns, and Lou Boudreau, youthful skipper of the Indians, found themselves in conversation after the Indians had thoroughly beaten the Browns. "You know, Luke," said Boudreau, perhaps hoping to soften the embarrassment his rival was feeling, "I think my players have your team's signs." Sewell hesitated a moment, and then retorted, "In that case, Lou, I wish you'd hang around a few days and teach them to *my* players. They haven't learned them yet."

Four former big league stars who all made their debuts in the mid-1920s—Jimmie Foxx, Joe Cronin, Red Ruffing, and Mel Ott—played in 1945. There were numerous others whose major league careers began in the late 1920s or early 1930s who were active on a more or less regular basis. Among this group were Rick Ferrell, Joe (Ducky) Medwick, Frank Crosetti, Louis (Bobo) Newsom, and both of the Waner brothers—Paul (Big Poison) and Lloyd (Little Poison). Many of the oldsters had been recalled from the minors, others had been prevailed upon to postpone overdue retirements.

Mel Ott, player-manager of the Giants, was clearly the most successful practitioner of all the veterans in 1945. He played in 135 games, hit 21 home runs, and batted .308 in his 20th year with the Giants. He even hit the 500th homer of his career on August 1! Eschewing eyeglasses, Ott maintained, "I've tried them and I know they don't help."

Another aged athlete in the 1940s who would not give testimonials to opticians was outfielder Paul Waner, even though he admitted to his manager that he could not see well enough to read advertisements on the outfield walls. "Well how do you hit the ball?" the manager asked. "Oh, that's different," replied Waner. "The pitcher's so near that the ball looks as big as a grapefruit." "Then what about flyballs? How do you see them?" persisted his boss. The unruffled Waner paused for a moment, and then blandly replied, "I *don't* see 'em at *first.* But I can tell by the sound as they hit the bat which way they're going, and then I pick 'em up when they get out aways!"

Geriatric wonders were also performed by Jimmie Foxx, who made his first big league pitching start at the age of 38 with the 1945 Phillies. Old Double X registered a 4-2 win over Cincinnati, giving up only four hits in nearly seven innings before being relieved. The next day the hard-living Foxx played first base, hitting a home run and a bases-loaded ninth-inning single to beat the Reds again, 4-3.

George (Catfish) Metkovich   Louis (Bobo) Newsom

It was also the year in which only the second one-armed man in history played major league baseball. Pete Gray was bought from the Memphis Chicks for $20,000 by the Browns before the 1945 season. Having lost most of his right arm in a childhood accident, the rangy 28-year-old outfielder hit .218 in 77 games in 1945. In a doubleheader against the Indians on June 10, he had five hits, all singles. The day before the doubleheader he had hit a triple, his first major league extra-base hit; the day after, he lashed a double. He fielded .959, not a high average for an outfielder, but remarkable enough for a man who had to both catch and throw a baseball with his left hand.

There were a number of fast-living, hard-drinking ballplayers who wore major league uniforms in 1945. Nate Andrews, a Braves pitcher who had been straightened out by Alcoholics Anonymous, had had a good 1944 season, but he fell off the wagon with a thud a year later. The burly Andrews jumped the club in Chicago and went home to Rowland, North Carolina. He later rejoined the team but failed to show up at the park on a day he was to pitch. The Braves, in disgust, traded him to the Reds, a team which needed pitching even more desperately.

Al (Bear Tracks) Javery had combined with teammate Nate in 1943 and 1944 to lose 70 games between them! But alternating in the Braves' start-ing rotation was not all they did together. Bear Tracks was fined $300 by the Braves' management for missing a train; later in the season the rangy right-hander was suspended. The fact that the two bad boys of the stumbling Braves together pitched over 586 innings in one season alone probably had something to do with their seeking solace in bar rooms of towns throughout the league.

On the same Braves' pitching staff was Jim Tobin, possessor of one of the slowest knuckleballs in major league history. While most of his fellow pitchers worried about sore arms, Big Jim worried about hangnails. He used to warm up by having the team's trainer rub his knuckles rigorously for two minutes.

But the aging Tobin had performed some remarkable feats during the war years. In 1943, he had hit three home runs in one game, and he needed every one of them to defeat the Cubs, 6-5. A year later he threw two no-hitters, the first against the Dodgers, the second against the Phillies. The closest the Dodgers came to a base hit was a bunt that was foul by two inches. Leo Durocher nearly went berserk that afternoon watching the Bums swing feebly at Big Jim's powder-puff delivery.

Bobo Newsom, the loquacious South Carolinian who was to throw 257 innings and lose 20 games for Connie Mack's Athletics, tried the iron man bit by starting *both* games of a doubleheader against

268

Elisha (Bitsy) Mott

George (Snuffy) Stirnweiss

the Tigers in August at the age of 38. He left in the seventh inning of the first game to rest for the second with a 6-3 lead, but he was knocked out in the ninth inning of the nightcap, when the Tigers rallied to win. Earlier in his career, the colorful pitcher had once arrived for spring training in a flamboyant car with BOBO in neon lights on one door and a horn that played the first four notes of *Tiger Rag!*

The Senators had four knuckleball pitchers who won a total of 60 of Washington's 87 victories in 1945. Dutch Leonard, Johnny Niggeling, Roger Wolff, and Mickey Haefner averaged 36 years in age, something of a record for a starting pitcher quartet. Rick Ferrell, 40-year-old veteran Washington catcher, aged perceptively as he chased the majority of the 40 passed balls the Senator catchers allowed that year. The Senators' catching staff dreamed of fluttering knucklers that plagued them day after cruel day.

Even William (Whitey) Wietelmann, the Braves' switch-hitting (and light-hitting) shortstop, decided to give pitching a try late in the season. One of the greatest letter writers in the history of the game, Wietelmann answered every fan letter he received. But the unfortunate shortstop had had a finger shattered by a line drive in spring training, which necessitated nearly complete amputation. The gutsy Brave gave up six hits, two walks, and six runs after one inning of hurling and quietly returned to his shortstop position, where he had been somewhat more successful.

Anton Karl, the Phillies pitcher, set a mark of working 167 innings in relief in 1945. The hapless Phillies, doormat of the National League that year, won 46 and lost 108 for the season. And there were two Phillies above all the others who helped Karl set his record.

One was among the league's outstanding rookies of the year, Elisha Matthew (Bitsy) Mott. The diminutive, 27-year-old Bitsy parlayed a .221 batting average and a .944 fielding mark to take his place in baseball history. The other was pitcher Dick (Kewpie) Barrett, who had to be relieved in nearly all of his games as he staggered to a 7-20 mark, losing 10 in a row at one point. The 39-year-old Kewpie had been out of major league baseball from 1934 to 1943, and he, like most of the '45 Phillies, was once again out of the majors in 1946.

The Athletics' Russ Christopher mirrored the "streak" quality of pitchers as well as teams in 1945. On July 1, he had an 11-3 record; at the end of the season it was 13-13. His ninth victory was only the Athletics' 16th at the time. With fellow pitcher Bobo Newsom losing 12 straight at one time, Connie Mack's minions eventually finished dead last, 34½ games out of the lead.

The Braves, after winning nine games in a row, bowed to the Phillies, who broke a 16-game losing streak by winning, 5-4, in 15 innings on June 13! The Phils did not do it by themselves, however; it took *eight* errors by the Braves to break both streaks.

Even Joe McCarthy's Yankees were having their problems with losing streaks in 1945. When the Yanks lost their ninth game in a row at St. Louis on August 18, it was the longest losing streak ever suffered by McCarthy in his 16 years at the New York helm.

The pennant-winning Cubs set one unusual team record and tied another in 1945. They won 20 doubleheaders during the season. And by beating the Reds 21 out of 22 games, they tied a National League mark.

The most remarkable record might have been the one that was set by the Red Sox, who managed to complete 198 double plays, a major league all-time high at that point. The Sox lacked pitching and finished fifth in club fielding. If anything, 1945 proved that a steady keystone combination was *not* the way to establish records. Five players were used at second base, two at shortstop, six at third, and four at first base. One of the reasons for the Red Sox success had to be the dearth of speed in the league that year.

With few exceptions, there was a paucity of offensive power in the majors in 1945. No player in the American League achieved a slugging percentage of .500 or better, and only one American Leaguer batted in over 100 runs.

George (Snuffy) Stirnweiss, Yankee second baseman, won the American League batting championship in 1945 with a .309 average, the lowest in the majors up to that time since Elmer Flick's .306 in 1905. But 37-year-old Tony Cuccinello of the White Sox, who had been recalled from the minors and had had a .227 average in the majors from 1940 to 1944, had led most of the season. Stirnweiss' average was actually .30854430; Cuccinello's was .30845771.

On the morning of the last day, the White Sox third baseman was still ahead; but Stirnweiss collected three hits in his last game, the final one a drag bunt between first and second, which he beat out for the scratchiest of singles. Meanwhile, the veteran Cuccinello was watching his team's final doubleheader being rained out and finally canceled.

Cuccinello, the league's near batting leader, was released three months after the season ended, never to play in another major league game. His teammate and the American League's third leading batter at .302, Johnny Dickshot, was also released at the end of 1945. The tenacious Snuffy, however, staggered

through seven postwar seasons with a cumulative .246 mark. It took him all seven seasons to equal his 1945 home-run mark—10!

Injuries in 1945 were frequent and often spectacular—a reflection of the ages or the general condition of the players. Joe Cronin, 39-year-old shortstop-manager of the Red Sox, severely fractured his ankle while sliding into second base at Yankee Stadium and vowed he would never play again. He did not. Al Benton, Detroit pitcher back from the wars, had his ankle fractured by a line drive off the bat of the A's Bobby Estalella. Joe Haynes, another pitcher, broke his leg sliding into third base for the White Sox in Briggs Stadium a few weeks later. Late in the season, yet another American League shortstop-manager, Lou Boudreau of the Indians, broke his ankle in a collision at second base in a game with Boston.

Another oddity of the year occurred when, undaunted by his 12-14 mark and his league-leading number of bases on balls in 1944, Rufe Gentry of the Tigers became one of the few players who ever made good on their threats to hold out. When the Tiger management adamantly refused to grant him a $1,000 raise, he spent the entire season at his Daisy Station, North Carolina, home.

Big league umpires, perhaps more acutely aware than any other group of the depths to which baseball had fallen, found their tempers flaring and nerves snapping as the war years drew to a close. When Bill Klem, the aged umpire, was accused by a batter of calling a wrong pitch, he haughtily retorted, "I wouldn't have missed it if I'd had a bat in *my* hand." And when Bill McGowan, who had spent 22 years in the American League, called a 1945 .300 hitter out on strikes, the latter defiantly notified him, "I can't be called out on that." McGowan raised an eyebrow and said, "No? Well, buddy, you read tomorrow's newspapers, and you'll find out that I can."

On the other hand, George Magerkurth reacted physically to a long and hot summer afternoon by reaching into a field box in Cincinnati and punching a spectator who, along with inept and complaining athletes, had provided him with a miserable day behind the plate. But the two-fisted George quickly apologized and handed his tormentor $100.

That's the way it was in the major leagues in 1945, baseball's most chaotic year.

(Editor's Note: In 1945, even the quality of the two pennant winners—the Tigers in the American League and the Cubs in the National League—was far below par. When a wire-service writer asked columnist Warren Brown which of the two teams he thought would win the World Series, Brown replied, "I don't think either of them can win.")

How To Stay Alive on Second Base

by Nelson Fox
as told to Milton Richman
Reprinted from *This Week*

November, 1956

Have you ever been hit by a car just as you stepped off the curb? I know exactly how it feels because it happens to me practically every day during the summer. Not that I'm ever hit by an auto, but I get knocked over time after time by some of the burliest base-runners in the American League, and take it from me, there can't be much difference.

My job is playing second base for the White Sox, and even though I wouldn't trade it for a seat in the Senate, it's as risky as directing traffic at State and Madison Streets in downtown Chicago.

The runners who fly into me trying to break up a double play aren't dropping around for pink tea. Those steel spikes can cut like a butcher slicing a side of beef.

My future as a big league second baseman depends on my ability to avoid the 101 different hazards at my position. When I first broke into the majors nine years ago, I was only 19 and green as grass. I remember asking a veteran the best way to stay in one piece out there at second base.

"Kid," he said, "it's simple. All you need is the nerve of a tightrope walker, the guts of a burglar, and the grace of an adagio dancer."

Since then I've found that a little luck doesn't hurt, either, but there are days when nothing helps.

Take that day last year when Hank Bauer of the Yankees crashed into me. Bauer hit me so hard coming into second that the newspapers built it up as an all-out feud between the White Sox and Yankees. Actually, Bauer was merely insisting that as a runner he was entitled to the base path. Me? My teeth were loosened up a bit, but I considered it all in a day's work.

If you've ever seen me play you know darn well I don't get by on my brawn. Standing on my toes I'm only 5 feet 8½ inches, and the last time I got on a scale I weighed 157 pounds. Minnie Minoso, one of my teammates, calls me Li'l Bit. But don't get me wrong, I'm not looking for any sympathy.

When I pick up my glove and head out for sec-ond base, I know what I'm getting into. I can show you spike scars on my legs where runners left their calling cards. You come to expect that.

But playing second base has its rewards, too. It gives you the satisfying feeling of being right in the middle of the action. People always ask me what it feels like to click off one of those real quick double plays. Well, picture this if you can:

There are a couple of men on base, and the ball is hit to either third or short. You race for second base, and the ball and the runner both come at you from different directions. That's the time I like to get my business over with fast and get out of the runner's way in a hurry. Moving on instinct and generally without looking, I brush second base with my right foot—that leaves me in a better position to throw. Then I pivot—sometimes leap-frogging over the runner at the same time—and fire the ball to the first baseman.

There's no use worrying about the onrushing runner or his spikes, because if a second baseman does this, he's a dead duck. What's more, he gets the reputation for being "gun shy," and it spreads around the league quicker than a prairie fire.

Naturally, there are ways for a second baseman to protect himself. On the throw to first base, for example, we generally aim the ball right at the runner. It's the only way to make the runner duck and slide into the bag instead of having him come into you full tilt. What happens when the runner doesn't duck? Dizzy Dean didn't in the fourth game of the 1934 World Series between the Cardinals and Tigers. He was hit on the head with the ball and had to be carried off the field.

That leap-frog stunt is another handy maneuver. It's the best way of avoiding the runner's spikes and getting rid of the ball at the same time.

Then there's a trick called "cheating." That takes some finesse. To cheat on a double play, you catch the ball from the third baseman or shortstop with your foot off the bag instead of on it, as the rules specify. Then you make your throw to first just as if everything is according to Hoyle. Several second basemen in the majors cheat. Frankly, so did I. But Bill McKinley, the umpire, caught me twice against the Red Sox, so I can't get away with it anymore.

Don't get the idea, though, that the double play is the only thing I have on my mind. There are plenty of other problems. When the other team has a man on first, for instance, and we know they're going to bunt, our first baseman charges the plate, and I have to run over and cover his position. It can become confusing.

A play exactly like that helped shorten the career of second baseman Davey Williams of the Giants two years ago. Jackie Robinson of the Dodgers bunted and Williams hustled over to cover first base. Williams had to reach in toward the infield for the throw and Robinson barreled into him on his "blind" side. Davey was out of action 11 days, and his back bothered him so much after the collision that he finally quit as an active player last year even though he was only 26 years old.

Pop flies look as if they're a cinch, too—from a seat in the grandstand. The average fan gets the idea that my seven-year-old daughter, Bonnie Ray, could catch any pop-up. But some of those cloud-scrapers have a habit of getting caught in the wind and blowing near the stands. Texas Leaguers can drive a second baseman crazy, too. They're the balls which somehow manage to fall safely between the infield and the outfield.

Jim Busby, who used to play center field for the White Sox but is now with Cleveland, came tearing in on a pop fly one day while I was dashing out trying for the same ball. I thought the roof caved in on me when we rammed together. My ribs hurt me for two weeks. Busby was luckier; he only sprained his thumb. And with all that, the ball dropped between us for a hit.

Maybe it's pure coincidence, but I always seem to get some lumps from the Yankees. Bob Cerv flattened me just a few weeks ago. And it was a Yankee player, Johnny Lindell, who hit me so hard in 1949 that repercussions were heard in the American League office.

At that time I was playing for the Philadelphia Athletics. Lindell was on first, and Joe DiMaggio on second. We had a chance to make a double play but Lindell took care of that and me at the same time. When I came to, I was lying out in left field. Di-Maggio scored from second, and Lindell rambled on to third.

Soon afterward, there was an official announcement from the American League office that henceforth a runner coming from first base would have to slide at second base, not at the second baseman! But when a runner is charging down my way, I don't have time to get out the rule book and read it to him.

Actually, they call third base the "hot corner" in baseball. That's because so many hot grounders are hit in that vicinity. But there isn't a third baseman in the big leagues who wouldn't tell you that more action takes place at second.

Maybe my Dad knew all that in 1944 when he took me from our home in St. Thomas, Pennsylvania, to meet Connie Mack, manager of the A's.

"Mr. Mack," Dad said, "my boy can play second base."

Pop must have been a convincing talker because I was only 16 years old and weighed 140 pounds. Anyway, I was given a tryout and sent to Lancaster, Pennsylvania, in the Class B Inter-State League. My contract called for only $125 a month but I was tickled to death.

Matter of fact, I still am because I think I have the best job in the world. Dangerous? Sure! But that just adds to the excitement.

Whenever I leave my house for the ball park, my wife, Joanne, always says, "Good luck." There are days when I need it.

Little Nellie Fox (5-foot-9 and 160 pounds) is upended in action at second base by big Bob Allison (6-foot-4, 212 pounds) in a 1961 game between the White Sox and the Twins at Chicago. Allison had tried to stretch a single into a double, while Fox was taking a throw from center fielder Jim Landis. An aggressive, scrappy player, Fox was one of the premier second basemen in the American League in the 1950s. He finished his playing career in 1965 in the National League at Houston, where he helped tutor Joe Morgan, who became a star second baseman with the Cincinnati Reds.

Bob O'Farrell Talks About the "Good Old Days"

by Arthur R. Ahrens

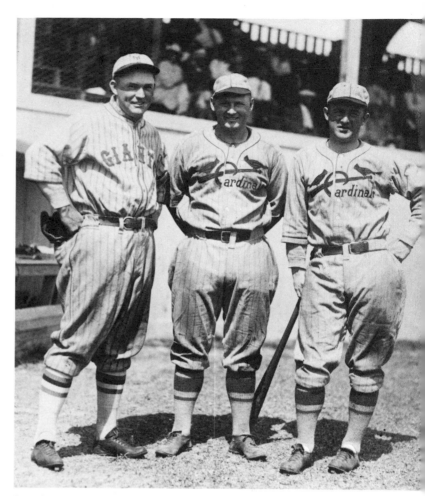

In this rare 1927 photo, Bob O'Farrell (center) poses with Rogers Hornsby (left) and Frankie Frisch. O'Farrell was manager of the St. Louis Cardinals at the time, having succeeded Hornsby, who had been traded to the New York Giants before the season started in exchange for Frisch. In 1927, however, Hornsby and Frisch were players only. Both of them became members of the Hall of Fame. Under O'Farrell, the 1927 Cardinals finished second, a game and a half behind the pennant-winning Pirates.

April, 1975

The time was October 10, 1926. The scene was the seventh game of the Yankee-Cardinal World Series at Yankee Stadium. With two out in the bottom of the seventh and the bags loaded for the Yanks, the Cardinals nursed a 3-2 lead. On the mound for St. Louis in relief of Jesse Haines was Grover Cleveland Alexander. With a one-and-two count on the Yankee batter, Tony Lazzeri, the great Alex breathed a sigh of relief. Moments earlier, his second "strike" had twisted foul by inches down the left-field line, robbing Lazzeri of a grand-slam home run.

The Cardinal catcher trotted out to the hill and called for a low curve on the outside. Alex obeyed and Lazzeri fanned, to end both the rally and the inning. Two innings later, with two out in the ninth, Babe Ruth walked and—to everyone's surprise—attempted to steal second. The catcher promptly cut him down with a perfect peg to Rogers Hornsby to gain the world's championship for the Cardinals.

The St. Louis receiver that historic afternoon was Bob O'Farrell. Now 78 and retired, he lives with his wife in an immaculately kept apartment in his hometown of Waukegan, Illinois. Still an avid baseball fan, Bob retains many mementos from his playing days, as well as scores of stories.

"Throwing out Ruth to end the '26 Series is still my greatest thrill," he said, smiling nostalgically.

O'Farrell's first big break came in 1915 when he was playing for a semipro team in Waukegan, shortly after graduating from high school. "We were playing an exhibition game with the Cubs," Bob recalled. "I tossed out two Cub runners at second base, and they signed me on the spot. I played my first major league game on September 7, 1915, at the Cubs' West Side Park."

Although he did not become a regular until 1920, O'Farrell was a Cub for the next 10 years and a big-leaguer until the end of 1935. He was traded to the Cardinals in 1925, to the Giants in 1928, back to the Cards in 1933, to the Reds in 1934, back to the Cubs the same year, and finally back to the Cards in 1935. He posted a career batting average of .273, with 1,120 hits in 1,492 games. Three times he led all National League receivers in putouts and twice in assists. The apex of his career came after the 1926 World Series when he was voted the National League's Most Valuable Player.

During his 21 seasons in the majors (still the all-time record for catchers), Bob played with two pennant winners—the 1918 Cubs and the aforementioned 1926 Cardinals. In comparing the two teams, he remarked that "between the two, I think the '26 Cardinals were better. We played together as a team better than the 1918 Cubs. It wasn't that the '18 Cubs didn't hustle, but the '26 Cards hustled more.

Rogers Hornsby was the glue that held the team together, just as Charlie Hollocher was the spark plug on the '18 Cubs.

"The Cardinals' big pitchers in those days were Flint Rhem, Jesse Haines, and Bill Sherdel. Jesse was best on the fastball, but he had a good knuckler, too. They threw the knuckler faster in those days, and it didn't break as much as the knucklers do now.

"With the Cubs in 1918, our best asset was our pitching. We had a great staff—Hippo Vaughn, Lefty Tyler, Claude Hendrix, and Phil Douglas. In the early part of the year we had Alexander, too, but then he went into the Army and was away for the rest of the year.

"Jim Vaughn was our ace and he won 22 games. Jim was a lefty and had a blinding fastball—I mean really fast. But sometimes his control wasn't as good as it could have been.

"George Tyler was another good lefty. He used to fire birdshot from between his teeth by curling up his tongue and shooting a toothpick through it. He peppered a lot of our opponents that way, and a lot of umpires, too. Occasionally, he'd do it to our wives when they were sitting in a hotel lobby, and the girls never could figure out where all that birdshot was coming from.

"We played the Red Sox in the 1918 World Series. The funny part about it was that we outscored them, 10 runs to nine, but they won the Series, four games to two. Babe Ruth was a great pitcher for Boston at that time and one of the best I ever faced. I batted against him twice, and each time I got good wood on the ball and thought I had a hit. But the Red Sox had a great shortstop, Everett Scott. He covered a lot of ground and threw me out both times."

In 1918, the spitball was still legal, and Bob recalls it well. "I didn't have much trouble catching the spitter," he related, "because I put dirt in my glove whenever I caught a spit-baller. But I did have trouble throwing the wet ball to second base. And we were always afraid that the second baseman wouldn't be able to hold onto it.

"The best spit-baller on the Cubs was Phil Douglas. He put slippery elm on the ball, and that was what made it effective. He looked like a big octopus, the way he used to stand on the mound and wave his arms all over the place, to distract the batter. And Phil wasn't an alcoholic, like a lot of people said he was. He drank a lot, but it was just to have a good time.

"Claude Hendrix sometimes threw a spitter, too, but it was not as good as Phil's."

O'Farrell had his best years at the plate in 1922 and 1923, when he batted .324 and .319, respectively. The latter average was tied by Arnold Statz for the best among Cub regulars in 1923. Bob was particularly adept at punching singles to right-center. "I guess I hit Al Demaree, Dick Rudolph, and Slim Salee the best," he recollected with a grin. "I used to call them 'my cousins.' "

Although almost half a century has elapsed, Bob recalls his teammates of that era with vividness and accuracy:

"The Cubs didn't have an outstanding team in the early '20s, but we had a colorful bunch. One guy I'll never forget was Charlie Hollocher, our shortstop. He was one of the greatest hustlers I ever saw. It seemed like he was always on base. He was a great fielding shortstop and just as good a hitter—and a hard man to strike out. But he had a very nervous stomach, which shortened his career and ruined his health.

"Our third baseman then was Barney Friberg. He was a good third baseman and a ballplayer's ballplayer.

"We had another fine infielder in Sparky Adams. He was extremely hard to pitch to, and he became one of the best leadoff men in the game.

"Our top home-run hitter in those days was Hack Miller, who grew up in Chicago. He was a great hitter but was just adequate as an outfielder. Hack was so strong that he probably could have lifted up an automobile by the bumper just to change a tire. I remember seeing him pound an iron spike into the back gate at Cubs' park with his bare fist.

"Our other top hitter was Ray Grimes, the first baseman whom everybody called Bummer. He was a big rawboned guy who could always hit in the clutch.

"In center field we had Arnold Statz. He was a native of Waukegan, and his father played on the local team here. I nicknamed him Jigger because he was a very animated fellow and was always jiggling around.

"We had a second baseman on the Cubs named George Grantham. He was a good hitter and a good base-runner, but he made a lot of bad throws. I remember one incident back in 1923 or '24 when we were playing the White Sox in a city series game at Comiskey Park. George asked Tony Kaufmann, one of our pitchers, if he could borrow his glove. Tony agreed to it but told George to be careful with it since it was his favorite glove. So at the end of the game, George decided to make a grandstand play for the fans by throwing them a baseball from his gloved hand. Well, he threw the ball, all right—and the glove flew along with it, into the crowd. And that was the last we ever saw of Tony Kaufmann's favorite glove."

During his long career, O'Farrell saw hundreds of players perform. When asked what players impressed him the most, he replied without hesitation, "Frank Frisch was the best all-around player I ever saw. He could do anything. But Rogers Hornsby was the best hitter."

Bob caught many a pitcher, too, during his two decades in the big time. To a similar inquiry as to the best pitchers he ever caught, he replied, "Grover Alexander, Carl Hubbell, and Dizzy Dean were the best I ever caught, and of those, Alex was probably the best. His best pitch during his later days was his slider, although they didn't call it a slider back then. He alternated between the slider and the sinker, and often threw side-arm. He still had a fine fastball, too. But his greatest asset was his control. He hardly ever walked a batter."

Bob's most splendid memory from his days with the Giants is when he caught Carl Hubbell's no-hitter against the Pirates on May 8, 1929. He recalled that "Carl had a great screwball that day. Our wives were sitting in a box seat at the Polo Grounds, and as the game progressed they became so nervous that they went up to the grandstand to be further away from the action.

"In the ninth inning the Pirates got a man on base on an error. Then the next batter hit a bouncer to the mound. Now Carl always had trouble throwing to second on a double-play ball, but this time he executed it perfectly, and that ended the game.

"But the thing I like most about Hubbell was his disposition. Some pitchers got sore if a player made an error while they were pitching, but not Carl. He never got sore at anyone. Nothing ever rattled him.

"When the Giants traded me back to the Cardinals in 1933, I caught Dizzy Dean several times. His fastball was even better than Vaughn's. But the incident I remember most is when his brother Paul pitched a one-hit game in 1935. Diz was the happiest guy in the park that day and ran all over the place telling everybody about his brother's accomplishment."

Still as husky as he was in his playing days, Bob O'Farrell is now a living symbol of a bygone era. As the survivors of those days dwindle with the passing of each day, his recollections become increasingly precious, if not priceless.

Thanks for the memories, Bob.

Bob O'Farrell (far right) with other members of the 1922 Chicago Cubs, who finished fifth in the league. His teammates (left to right) are Charlie Hollocher, shortstop; Hack Miller, outfielder; Ray Grimes, first baseman; Barney Friberg, outfielder-third baseman; and Jigger Statz, outfielder. O'Farrell caught 125 games that year and batted .324, his best one-season performance in 21 years in the majors.

The Day a Relief Pitcher Started in the Series

by Jim Ferguson
Dayton Daily News

Robin Roberts, a 20-game winner, normally would have been the starter for the Phillies in the first game of the 1950 World Series, but he had pitched in three games during the final five days of the torrid National League flag race and needed a rest. Manager Eddie Sawyer instead chose to open with reliever Jim Konstanty. Roberts pitched nine innings of the second game, losing 2-1.

October, 1971

It has been more than 20 years since Jim Konstanty was involved in one of the most unusual and dramatic stories in World Series history.

I've always had a special affinity for Konstanty, a fellow who wore glasses when he was pitching some 20 to 25 years ago, a time when not too many major league players wore them. It was easy for me, burdened with glasses as a kid, to have a feeling of rapport with a man who could stop in the middle of a baseball game, step off the mound, and wipe off his lenses before resuming pitching.

But it is not for his wearing glasses that Konstanty will be remembered. It was the strange circumstances of the opening game of the 1950 World Series, which matched Konstanty's Philadelphia Phils against the ever-present New York Yankees.

Jim was named by manager Eddie Sawyer to start for the Phils in the opening game, a move which startled the baseball world. It was not that the stocky right-hander didn't have the record for it. He won 16 games for the Whiz Kids that season.

But Konstanty did it all as a relief pitcher. He had been in 74 games that season, a league record, but had not started even once. Now here he was in the first game of baseball's biggest show as the starting pitcher.

It was as if Sparky Anderson had picked Wayne Granger to work the first game against Baltimore last October. Come to think of it, Sparky wasn't too far from having to do that very thing with Wayne Simpson, Jim McGlothlin, and Jim Merritt on the injured list.

Much the same situation confronted Sawyer as he directed the Phils into their first World Series in 35 years.

It wasn't easy. The Phils didn't win the title until the 10th inning of the last game of the season, when Dick Sisler, later to manage the Reds, came through with a home run to beat the Dodgers.

Robin Roberts, ace of the Phils' pitching staff, won the game that put an end to a tailspin which almost took the Phils right out of the championship.

They had been seven games in front with nine to play.

"We lost almost every game after that," recalled Sisler. "We even lost two doubleheaders in a row. We were fighting for our lives right to the end, but Roberts won the game we had to win.

"Actually, our pitching was so pressed at the time that Sawyer was almost forced to use Konstanty as a starter. He had to give Roberts another day of rest. Curt Simmons had been called into the Army a few weeks before and never got back. Bubba Church and Bob Miller were hurt. If we had lost that last game and had to go into a playoff, we'd have been dead."

"I hadn't started a game for three years," Konstanty said, "but when Sawyer asked me if I wanted to start I told him yes. I had pitched nine innings in relief, and I figured I could do it as starter, too.

276

Jim Konstanty being tossed the ball by catcher Andy Seminick as the Phillies' top reliever makes another appearance in the 1950 World Series against the Yankees. To everyone's surprise, Konstanty, who pitched 74 games in relief during the pennant drive, had started in the opener of the World Series, losing 1-0. He made two appearances in relief as the Phillies were swept aside by the Yankees in four games.

"It had been such a frantic month and everybody was so 'down' from the way we finished that I don't think anybody felt badly about missing a start themselves. About that time, everybody felt I was the only hope. After all, I had won 16 games and saved 22."

"Jim had such a fantastic year, we didn't think he'd have any trouble," agreed Richie Ashburn, who was the center fielder for the Phils that season. "He had so much confidence in his ability he didn't think anybody was ever going to get a hit off him."

"Konstanty had as fine a year as I've ever seen by a relief pitcher," Sisler said. "He had one of those years where you could bring him into a tie game with the bases loaded and no outs, and he'd get out of it. It was almost indescribable. Jim won the Most Valuable Player Award that year and he sure deserved it."

So that was the situation in the opening game of the World Series. It couldn't have been created any better by a Hollywood scenario writer. But there was one slight flaw.

Konstanty didn't win the game. He pitched a great game, allowing the mighty Yankees only four hits in his eight innings on the mound. Unfortunately, New York's Vic Raschi gave up just two, and the Yankees won, 1-0, to start a four-game sweep.

"Everybody I talked to about it remembers that Joe DiMaggio hit a homer to beat me," said Konstanty, with a smile, "but actually that happened in the second game. Joe beat Robin in the 10th inning.

"Actually, I threw a pitch right in on the fists of Bobby Brown, the fellow who was studying to be a doctor, but the ball sailed just out of reach down the line for a double. Two flyballs moved him around to score and that was it. It was tough, but one of those things. We lost the next three games to make it a sweep, although two of them were pretty close. I wasn't going to start again, no matter what, so I got into the last two games in relief."

Konstanty was not in the bullpen to stay, however. "No, a couple of years later Steve O'Neill became our manager. He thought starters were more important than relief pitchers, so he made me a starter. I had a 10-4 record at the All-Star break in 1953, but I didn't get picked for the team."

Casey Stengel —
My Greatest Thrill
as a Player

as told to John P. Carmichael
Condensed from the *Chicago Daily News*

April, 1950

I joined the Brooklyn Dodgers for my first crack at the big leagues in 1912, and the things that happened to me in that first game on September 17 that year make it the greatest of 'em all for me as a player.

I'd gone two and a half years to dental school and saved up $150 for another year's tuition plus instruments. I was playing in Montgomery (Alabama) when I got the offer to join Brooklyn.

The fabulous Kid Elberfield, just back from the majors, told me, "Forget about being a dentist . . . you're good enough so you'll never come back. Get yourself a decent grip and forget about the money."

So I laid out 18 dollars for the bag, and there I was in New York. A cab driver showed me a cheap hotel on Forty-Seventh Street, and I spent that first evening walking a block or two and then hustling back to the lobby for fear I'd get lost.

By midnight I'd made it as far as Forty-Second Street, and back, and I went to bed. Next morning I started for the park. Brooklyn played at Fifth Avenue and Third then, and I reported to the gateman there. He waved me toward the clubhouse and called after me, "You better be good."

I'll never forget walking into the locker room. There was a crap game going on in one corner. The only fellow who paid any attention to me was Zack Wheat. He introduced me around. Nobody shook hands. Some grunted. A few said hello.

I walked over to the game and decided maybe I ought to get in good with the boys by participating in the sport, so I fished out 20 dollars and asked if I could shoot.

Somebody said, "Sure." And somebody handed me the dice. I rolled 'em out. A hand reached for my 20 and a voice said, "Craps, busher." And I never even got the bones back. I was about to reach for more money, when I felt a tap on my shoulder. I looked around and there was manager Bill Dahlen.

"Are you a crapshooter or a ballplayer, kid?" he

Casey Stengel was born in Kansas City, Missouri, and that's how he got his nickname. "I came from K.C., so they started callin' me Casey," he once explained. "My real name is Charles Dillon Stengel, and in case you're wondering, Dillon was my mother's name."

asked. I told him I was a player, and he said, "Well, get into a suit and on that field while you still have carfare."

I hustled, believe me, and I've never touched dice since, either. I got to the bench and just sat there. I knew better than to pick up a bat and go to the plate.

Elberfield told me what happened to rookies who tried that. Finally, Dahlen came over and said, "Let's see you chase a few," and I ran like the devil for the outfield.

Behind the fence was a big building with fire escapes all down one side, and guys in shirt sleeves were parked on the steps, passing around pails of beer and getting set for the game.

I never expected to play, but just as the umpires came out Dahlen told me to "get in center." Hub Northen, the regular center fielder, had been sick, and I guess they decided they might as well get me over with quick.

My first time at bat we had a man on first, and Dahlen gave me the bunt sign. The pitch wasn't good and I let it go by.

Claude Hendrix, the league's leading pitcher, was working for Pittsburgh, and George Gibson was catching.

Hendrix threw another, and I singled to right center. When I got back to the bench after the inning, Dahlen stopped me. "Didn't you see the bunt sign?" he asked.

A left-handed batter and thrower, Stengel was 31 when the Phillies traded him to the New York Giants in 1921. He played with the Giants through the 1922 and 1923 seasons, when they won pennants. His performance in the 1923 World Series against the Yankees, which the Giants lost in six games, was spectacular. Stengel played flawlessly in center field, batted a cool .417, and hit two homers—both of which won a game for the Giants. His ninth-inning inside-the-park homer won the first game, 5-4, and his blast into the right-field bleachers decided the third game, 1-0. Casey finished his playing career with the Boston Braves in 1925.

I told him yes, but that down South we had the privilege of switching on the next pitch if we wanted to.

"I don't want you to carry too much responsibility, kid," he said, "so I'll run the team, and that way all you'll have to worry about is fielding and hitting." My ears were red when I got to center field.

Up on the fire escape the boys were having drinks on my hit, and I could hear them speaking real favorably of me. I heard somebody holler, and it was Wheat telling me to move back.

Hans Wagner was at the plate. He larruped one, and I went way back and grabbed it. In the dugout Wheat said, "Play deeper for him."

I thought of the catch I'd made and said to myself, "I can grab anything he can hit."

Two innings later he came up again, and Wheat waved me back, but I wouldn't go. And wham! Old Hans peeled one off.

The ball went by me like a BB shot, and he was roosting on third when I caught up with it. Wheat just looked at me as much as to say, "You'll learn."

I got three more hits (all singles) right in a row. The first time Hendrix had fed me a fastball, figurin' why waste his best pitch, a spitter, on a busher.

He was pretty mad by the time I combed two blows off his spitter and another off his hook. Once when I was on first, Dahlen gave me the steal sign, and away I went.

I beat Gibson's throw, and Wagner just stood there, looking down at me. Never said a word.

I stole two bases, and when I came up the fifth time we'd knocked Hendrix out and a left-hander was pitching for the Bucs.

Pittsburgh manager Fred Clarke hollered at me, "All right, phenom, let's see you cross over." I was cocky enough to do it.

I stepped across the plate and stood hitting right-handed, and darned if I didn't get a base on balls.

"You hit fourth tomorrow," said Dahlen after the game. Those words were like music to my ears. Why, the big leagues were no different than any place else!

(Editor's Note: Stengel spent his entire major league playing career in the National League as an outfielder for Brooklyn, Pittsburgh, Philadelphia, New York, and Boston from 1912 to 1925. He was in three World Series, 1916 with the Dodgers, and in 1922 and 1923 with the New York Giants. In the 1923 Series, he hit two homers—one, inside the park—to win as many games, on October 10 and 12, against the Yankees, a team he later piloted to 10 American League pennants. Stengel posted a .284 lifetime batting average in the majors.)

Rube Marquard
Really Won
20 Games in a Row

by John Steadman
Baltimore News American

November, 1971

It took Richard Marquard—he wasn't known as Rube then—five days and nights of riding freight trains, sleeping in open fields, and dodging railroad detectives to make it to Waterloo, Iowa, from his home in Cleveland.

The year was 1906, and he was 16 years old. He wanted a tryout with the Waterloo team of the Iowa State League.

They pitched him the day he arrived, and he won, 6-1, but the manager told him he had beaten the last-place club and his opening performance wasn't that significant.

Waterloo wanted young Marquard to wait around, without a contract and none of his expenses paid, to prove himself over again—against a rival team that was in second place.

But Rube hopped another train back home. The next year, 1907, he had a contract with Canton of the Central League and won 23 games.

The following season, he pitched at Indianapolis, where he won 28, and then was bought up by the New York Giants for the then record sum of $11,000.

From 1908 to 1925, Marquard was with the Giants, Brooklyn Dodgers, and Boston Braves, winning 201 games and losing 177. In three consecutive years—1911, 1912, and 1913—his season records were 24-7, 26-11, and 23-10.

During the period from April 11 to July 3, in the year 1912, Marquard won 19 straight games without losing—still a record and a near impossible one to beat.

Marquard should have been credited with 20 straight wins in 1912 and not a mere 19. Scoring rules were different then.

Rube had entered in the eighth inning, after the game was tied 3-3, looked at three men on base, and prevented further scoring. He put down Brooklyn's Zack Wheat, Jake Daubert, and George Cutshaw in order, and then the Giants scored a run to beat the Dodgers in the bottom of the ninth inning.

The decision, based on scoring regulations then in vogue, meant the victory was awarded to the starter, Jeff Tesreau. The triumph, by today's standards, belonged to Marquard. But Rube has never gone around asking for a recount. Nineteen in a row ain't bad.

Marquard has a fund of great stories, dating back to the glorious days of John McGraw and Christy Mathewson, which is better than a half century ago.

Rube likes to tell of the time in 1914 when he pitched against the Pittsburgh Pirates and went 21 innings to win 3-1. His pitching rival, Babe Adams, went all the way, too.

The Giants won pennants in 1911, 1912, and 1913. The next year Boston's Miracle Braves came from last place on July 4 to first, won the pennant, and then knocked off the Philadelphia A's four straight in the World Series.

McGraw, the Giants' manager, was so sure his team—which then boasted a seven-game lead—was going to win when his club went to play Boston that he took a vacation at the Empire City racetrack.

He outlined the pitching rotation. Marquard, Mathewson, and Tesreau pitched brilliantly but still lost, and the Giants watched their lead vanish.

In the summer of 1970, with all the dignity any man would ever want, Marquard was entered into the Baseball Hall of Fame at Cooperstown, New York—the place where he has long hoped to be enshrined.

Now 81 years old and pencil-straight, Marquard said it was the crowning moment of his life. The Hall of Fame distinction is the highest honor that can come to a ballplayer, and now he owns it.

Marquard, who ran away from home for a baseball tryout in 1906, was so elated that he literally jumped for joy and ran into the Hall of Fame when they opened the door for his induction ceremony.

It's been a great life for Rube Marquard.

Frank Crosetti's 17 Years in the Third-Base Box

by Til Ferdenzi
New York Journal-American

From the late 1940s until the close of the 1968 season, Frank Crosetti was a familiar figure in the third-base coaching box for the New York Yankees. He figures he must have waved home more than 16,000 base-runners during that span of time. The Crow, as he was called, was a shortstop for most of the 17 years he played for the Yankees. As coach and player, he cashed in 23 World Series checks.

May, 1964

The third-base coach is usually fat, anonymous, and a close friend of somebody in the organization—usually the manager. The man who holds the job at Yankee Stadium is thin, ascetic-looking, and bald. He's held the job for 17 years, which proves he is not anonymous, nor is he gainfully employed because he happens to be on cordial terms with Ralph Houk or Yogi Berra, the general manager and the field manager of the Yankees, respectively.

Frank Crosetti is, in fact, no part of a clubhouse politician. That strain runs deep among the fraternity of third-base coaches, major league branch. But the Crow, at 53 years of age, has mellowed a bit in an aging process which covers 33 years as player and coach for the pinstriped gentry. Still, Frank Peter Joseph Crosetti could never qualify as a striped-trousered diplomat at the United Nations. He is crusty and sometimes blunt, but no one ever had to guess just where he stood with the former shortstop.

Crosetti is unique in other ways. He refuses to treat his job like some traffic cop at a busy intersection. To the Crow, directing traffic at third base is an exact science, and he spends just as much time trying to improve his technique at this job as he did during the 17 years he played with the Yankees, most of them as a shortstop.

"You get these new outfielders coming into the league all the time," he said. "You can't do a good job at coaching if you don't know what their arms are like."

In the Crow's book—and he keeps it all up there between his ears—you've got to have ready access to baseball's grapevine. There are, of course, lots of secrets in baseball, but none a fellow can't ferret out if his antenna is hoisted high enough.

That's answer enough to explain why Crosetti is so hep on the minor league comings and goings of everybody on the Yankee roster.

"A kid comes up with some club, and I begin to think who around here maybe played in the same league with him," he said.

Crosetti says he usually finds the fellow. And he usually learns what he needs to learn about the new boy in the enemy's outfield.

"I remember that there are some kids you have to know more about than what other ballplayers can tell you," Crosetti said. "The first time I saw Rocky Colavito throw I didn't think I was seeing right. I had to see him throw two-three times in practice before the game to convince myself he was real. I'll tell you something, that first time I saw him throw I knew I'd never seen an arm that strong before."

Even so, the Crow wanted it made clear this necessarily didn't mean the Rock's arm was the best in the league. The coach says a strong arm doesn't make up the whole package.

"Outfielders are different," he said. "Sure they got to have strong arms in the first place, but then there are other things a coach has to take into consideration. How does the guy charge the ball? How long does it take him to get it away? How accurate is he? When you can catalog them that way, you've got a good start on figuring your chances on sending a guy in on a hit or holding him up."

Crosetti says every now and then an outfielder comes along who makes a believer out of a coach "very, very fast."

"That guy Al Kaline makes a third-base coach's job tough," the Crow said. "He drives me nuts. He can charge a ball like an infielder and get rid of the ball all in one motion, it seems."

Crosetti laughed. He said the joke was on him.

The coach was plucking new baseballs out of the boxes. The memory of that day five years ago was too much. When he stopped laughing, he took a kick at one of the empty boxes.

"I should have known better," he said, "but about five or six years ago we're in a tight ball game in Detroit. Two times in one inning," he stopped, shaking his head. "Just think. Two times in one inning that Kaline threw guys out at the plate. And that was no accident."

According to Crosetti, there is one thing a third-base coach ought to do whenever a runner is on second base and the ball is hit to right field against the Tigers.

"Just keep your fingers crossed the ball is not right at Kaline," the coach said. "Just hope it's to his right or over to his left enough so's he can't charge the ball. If the ball is at him hard enough you better forget sending the man home. You're gambling if you do."

The Crow does a lot of his homework before the game starts. He gets a good seat in the dugout and watches the opposing outfielders heave the ball to the plate in the pre-game practice.

"I got one rule of thumb that always works," he said. "I watch the outfielder pick up the ball, then I switch my eyes to the pitcher's mound. It's the way the ball carries in that area that really tells you how much the guy's got on his throw. If a throw is going to die, it usually starts to die around the pitcher's box. It's those throws that still have plenty of life there that are going to hurt you."

It was becoming more and more evident that the old canard about how a law ought to be passed for base-line coaches to pay their way into ball parks was just that—a bare-faced canard.

"You've got to know the speed of the man at bat," he said, ticking off his litany for survival. "You've got to know the speed of the men on the bases. Then you've got to be a good judge of the way the ball is hit. Is it on the glove side of the fielder? Is he getting it on a big hop, on a short hop? Is the outfielder the kind of guy who charges the ball? Is he the kind of fielder who will boot the ball now and then? Is he the conservative, play-it-safe type of guy? You know, you could almost write a book about this stuff."

The Crow was reminded this was no book, but would he mind furnishing more material. He didn't need much urging. Crosetti is a quiet man who keeps pretty much to himself. When the subject is baseball, though, he is real chatty.

The coach readily admitted there was a calculated risk attached to his job. He also admitted there was the risk of being second-guessed.

"It's your judgment against the crowd's," he said with a grin. "When they think you're wrong, they let you know."

Crosetti says, and with hardly any reservation at all, that it's much easier to direct traffic at third base when you've got what he calls "instinctive base-runners." He adds the Yanks have had their share of them.

It also came as hardly a surprise that Joe Di-Maggio was Crosetti's favorite example of what he meant by being an instinctive base-runner.

"Joe didn't need any help from me or any other coach," the Crow said. "It is a fact that real base-runners could do all right without a coach in the coach's box at all."

The way Crosetti sees it—and he's been seeing things as the top man among the league's third-base coaches—there are many situations where the coach might just as well be up in the stands for all the good he can do down on the field.

Crosetti, understandably enough, knows the fine difference between a good base-runner and a poor one. He says the instinct to try for the extra base is a gift. Mickey Mantle has it. Roger Maris ditto. Bobby Richardson and Tony Kubek are good ones. Not so long ago, Gil McDougald ranked high among the game's quality base-runners.

But when it comes to the newcomers, Crosetti says they don't come any better than Tom Tresh.

"Tresh is great," Crosetti said. "He's been in the league only two years, but infielders on the other clubs know he's going to run like the devil to first base no matter what kind of ball he hits. He figures that once out of every 50 times maybe the infielder will bobble the ball or muff an easy pop."

In rating professionals in the coaching boxes of the major leagues, you've got to put Frank Crosetti right up there with the best.

"I try never to leave anything to chance," he says.

Al Gionfriddo's Famous Catch

by Dave Distel
Los Angeles Times

Al Gionfriddo

February, 1973

Al's Dugout is on a sidestreet of Goleta, California, a Santa Barbara suburb. It has only a modest reputation as a restaurant, but the proprietor is a man of renown. Baseball fans still talk about the catch he made for Brooklyn in the 1947 World Series.

"I think it's fantastic that people still remember," said the man who went to the fence at Yankee Stadium to rob Joe DiMaggio of a three-run homer. "I don't believe it."

Just as no one believed the catch itself.

"Swung on," cried Red Barber, the man behind the microphone that afternoon, "and belted. It's a long one, deep to left-center. Back goes Gionfriddo. Back, back, back, back. He makes a one-handed catch against the bullpen! OHHhhhh doctor!!!"

Baseball pictures hang from virtually every wall of Al's Dugout. The one most prominently displayed is that of a hatless Al Gionfriddo, leaning precariously against the fence in front of the 415-foot sign with the ball white in his glove.

"The fans couldn't believe it," the 50-year-old Gionfriddo said with a smile. "They were Yankee fans and they booed me. I heard someone holler, 'Oh, no!' One of the pictures shows a fan holding his head."

That catch was not merely the highlight of Al Gionfriddo's major league career. It *was* his career.

He did not know it at the time, but that game was his last in the majors. Fortunately for him, the World Series is the big show and he made the big play.

Until Al Gionfriddo made that catch, he had spent his life in obscurity. After that catch, he lived and played in some obscure places—but never in obscurity.

"Aren't you the guy . . ." he was asked so many times. "Are you *the* Al Gionfriddo?"

Albert Francis Gionfriddo is a good-natured man, whose main concession to age is a diminishing hairline. His weight today is 165, same as in 1947.

"To this day," he said, "I get letters asking me to autograph pictures cut out of magazines. I get 'em from kids and older people both."

"The catch" has made Gionfriddo's life more memorable, but not necessarily more affluent. Al's Dugout is on Orange Street, not Easy Street.

Robbing DiMag of that home run was not even enough to assure Gionfriddo of a job with the Dodgers in 1948.

"Branch Rickey told me if I went to Montreal and had a good year he'd bring me back," he recalled. "I hit .310 with 25 home runs and close to 100 runs batted in, and I didn't come back."

Gionfriddo played with Montreal for four years and ended his playing career in the California League. He spent three years as general manager of the Dodgers' Santa Barbara farm club and then retired to the restaurant business 10 years ago.

Al's Dugout is a modest establishment, running more to cafe than to restaurant.

"Working people eat here," he said. "The same people who are the backbone of sports. The people who have to save their dollars to go to a game."

Gionfriddo comes from a family of working people. He was raised in Dysart, Pennsylvania, one of seven boys in a family of 13. The family worked in the coal mines to put food on the table.

"I worked in the coal mines," Gionfriddo said, "and I didn't like that."

Gionfriddo played well enough on a neighborhood baseball team to attract the eye of a scout or two.

He signed with Pittsburgh, mainly because it happened to be the city closest to home.

"I signed for $65 a month and the love of baseball," he said. "I just wanted to get into baseball."

And out of the coal mines. Gionfriddo worked at a number of jobs during the baseball off-seasons but never again in the mines.

Gionfriddo made it to the major leagues with Pittsburgh in 1944, playing four games at the end of the season. He played 122 games and batted .284 in 1945, his most productive season in the majors.

By the end of the regular season in 1947, he had played in 228 games and had a lifetime average of .266. His major league career was only a few games from ending, but his fame was only a few games from being born.

Gionfriddo, owner and cook, sat at one of the tables with the red-and-white checked tablecloths and reflected upon "the catch" and the fame which has ensued.

"Red Barber told me after the game," he said, "that there are a lot of good catches, but mine was an impossible catch."

What's the greatest catch Gionfriddo has seen?

"Willie Mays' catch was the best I ever sat and watched," observed Gionfriddo. "I think *that* was an impossible catch."

Mays' catch was made against Cleveland's Vic Wertz in the 1954 World Series.

Joe Rudi made an outstanding catch in the 1972 World Series, jumping against the left-field wall in Cincinnati to deprive Denis Menke of extra bases.

"I've seen a lot of guys climb walls," shrugged Gionfriddo. "I don't want to take anything away from Rudi, because he made a good catch. But it wasn't impossible."

Gionfriddo's catch gave Brooklyn an extra day of life in that Series. (Editor's Note: Gionfriddo had gone into the game in the sixth inning as a defensive replacement with the Dodgers leading, 8-5. His catch with two Yankees on base was the third out in the inning, and Brooklyn went on to win, 8-6.) The Yankees won the next day, however, so the only beneficiary was management, which pocketed another day of gate receipts.

"Branch Rickey Jr. told me that catch made them over $100,000," Gionfriddo sighed, "but I never saw any of it."

Al's Dugout is far from the beaten path. Former teammates rarely come his way.

"I go to a few Dodger and Angel games every year," he said. "A group of guys will get together and hire a bus, and we'll go as a group."

Walter Alston once managed Gionfriddo at Montreal, but the man who made "the catch" is not one to go through the hassle it takes to get to the clubhouse to visit his former boss.

"I just go down and watch the game," he said. "I have fun while I'm there, and when it's over I leave."

Twenty-five years after his moment in the limelight, Al Gionfriddo is one of those working men who saves his dollars to go to the games. Maybe not a typical fan, but a fan nevertheless. After all, how many Walter Mittys really *did* rob DiMaggio?

After making his celebrated catch in the 1947 World Series, Gionfriddo is bussed on the cheek by Pee Wee Reese. Other admiring teammates joining in the frivolity are (left to right) Dixie Walker, Bobby Bragan, and Eddie Stanky.

Catfish Hunter:
A "Money" Pitcher
from the Start

by Joe Gergen
Condensed from *Newsday*

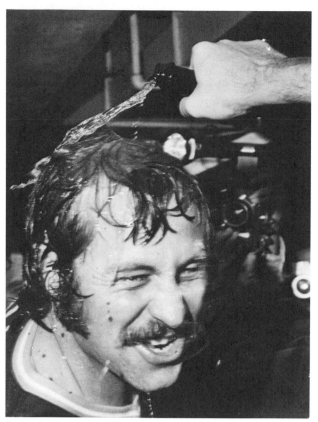

A dousing with champagne is Hunter's reward after the A's won the 1973 World Series from the Mets. In three World Series with Oakland (1972 to 1974), Hunter posted a 4-0 record.

June, 1975

The self-image of Jim (Catfish) Hunter, baseball pitcher, is as clear and tranquil as the streams of Perquimans County, North Carolina, where he earned his nickname with a fishing pole. In stability there is success as well as strength.

The accuracy of the image, that subtle blend of control and self-control which has made Hunter a rich man, was evident as far back as 1968, when he was 22 and still learning his craft. It was the ninth inning of a game against the Minnesota Twins in Oakland on May 8, and Hunter was one batter away from the American League's first regular-season perfect game in 46 years.

The count went to two balls, two strikes on Rich Reese, a pinch-hitter for the Twins' pitcher. Reese then fouled off five pitches in a row, and Hunter's wife, Helen, seated in the stands, began to cry aloud from the tension. "I thought I had Reese struck out on the next pitch, a slider," Hunter recalled. "The umpire called it a ball."

Considering the nature of the moment, it would not have been unreasonable behavior for Hunter to stomp around the mound, lose his concentration and throw the next pitch over the backstop. Hunter simply wound up and threw again.

"I don't argue with umpires," he explained. "I just thought, I'll get him with the next pitch." And that's just what he did, blowing a fastball by the swinging Reese. Not only had he pitched a perfect game but he'd also driven in all of the A's four runs.

It's what baseball people call the perfect temperament for the job. "As we say in the trade," said Clyde Kluttz, the scout who signed Hunter for the A's—then in Kansas City—11 years ago and who delivered him to the Yankees on New Year's Eve, 1974, "you can't cut them open and see what they're made of. But he had all the intangibles."

All of Hunter's considerable assets, the tangible as well as the intangible, are expected to pay for the Yankees. With an overall investment of more than $3,000,000 in Hunter's future, the Yankees are expecting a lot.

That, according to former teammate Dick Green, is what they will get. "Catfish is it," Green said. "He's the No. 1 pitcher in baseball now. He doesn't like to talk about it. He just goes out and does it."

Over the last four seasons, Hunter has amassed 88 victories and one Cy Young Award. Consistency has always been one of his greatest assets. "He pitches the same way all the time," said Thurman Munson, the Yankees' catcher. "He's got that easy delivery, and besides, he pitches every fourth day. He never has arm trouble. That's a big consideration."

It was a consideration to Kluttz when he advised Charles O. Finley to spend $50,000 of his money for the purpose of signing Hunter in 1964. Remember, Catfish still was hobbling at the time from the shotgun pellets fired into his right foot by his brother, Pete, in a hunting accident.

"As I look at a pitcher," said Kluttz, presently the Yankees' director of player procurement and scouting, "the fastball is the most important thing and delivery is the second most important. If he doesn't have a good delivery, he's liable to injure his arm before reaching his peak.

"In his senior year of high school, he wasn't able

to push off the rubber because of the injury, but he still had the smooth delivery. That delivery hasn't changed. Bill Posedel was the pitching coach when we signed him and he told him, 'If anyone tries to change that delivery, you have my permission to punch him in the nose.' "

Hunter can't remember pitching any differently than he does now. The delivery, like the control which is his trademark, was assimilated through years of playing the game and watching his brothers do the same. "I always had a baseball in my hand growing up," he said. "I watched my brother, Pete, pitch and I watched baseball on television.

"I've always had real good control, although it's been better the last three or four years. Even in high school I tried to hit the corners."

"I don't think Jim was ever an overpowering pitcher," Kluttz said. "Even at 18 he had the ability to spot the ball well. In high school, you don't have to do that. But you could see him trying. Although he was an old country boy and you had to drag things out of him, he had a very impressive knowledge of baseball. He knew instinctively how to pitch. There was no way you can give that to him. Those kind of guys just are born, and not very often. Gaylord Perry was the same type. I scouted him in high school."

Hunter underwent a second operation after signing with the A's and spent the last two months of the 1964 season with the team, throwing batting practice and learning to be a major-leaguer at the age of 18.

"He always impressed me as a kid who had it all together," recalled Ed Charles, then the A's third baseman and currently a Mets' scout. "He was a wholesome character to have on the team. He was always in control of himself. Cat was one of those guys always listening and trying to learn. I think one of the greatest assets he had at the time was his ability to receive instructions."

Hunter is the first to say he had a lot to learn. Green is the second. "I didn't think he was worth the bonus he got," said Green, the A's slick second baseman. "He didn't have the real good control then and his velocity was not especially impressive. His ball was so straight, so true."

But the A's were a last-place team, so Hunter, without a single game of minor league experience, became a starting pitcher for the A's in 1965. "I gave up a lot of home runs then," he said. "I still do because of my control, being around the plate all the time. At first, I thought you weren't supposed to give up homers. Then I found out it happened to everyone."

He said he acquired the nickname Boom Boom after yielding three home runs in the first two innings of his first start at Cleveland. "They had fireworks after home runs like I never saw in North Carolina. The next time there, the Cleveland manager, Birdie Tebbetts, comes over to Haywood Sullivan, our manager, and says he'd rather I didn't pitch there. Tebbetts says it cost $500 for fireworks every time they hit a home run, and it was too expensive to have me pitch."

Green laughed hysterically at the memory. "All our pitchers had the nickname, Boom Boom," he said. "The guys who played on our Kansas City teams felt we should have gotten paid more just because we were out on the field so long."

In time, the A's shucked their circus image, which had been promoted by Finley (a mule on the field, a zoo behind the right-field fence, and a mechanical rabbit popping out of the ground with baseballs). In time, the A's bolted from Kansas City to Oakland. In time, the A's grew up, and opponents stopped laughing at the uniforms, the funny nicknames, and the owner.

Despite that perfect game in 1968, despite his run of four consecutive 20-game seasons, and despite his phenomenal 7-1 record in post-season games, Hunter never has been accorded the respect of a Jim Palmer or a Tom Seaver. In the World Series last fall, Hunter saved the first game by striking out the Dodgers' Joe Ferguson in the ninth inning, then yielded only one run in seven and one-third innings in the third game. Yet there was Bill Buckner mouthing off afterwards: "I thought I should have hit the ball hard every time."

"You don't hear a veteran ballplayer say that," Green said. "His stuff is a lot better than everyone thinks it is. Sure, he can pinpoint the ball, but he can throw pretty hard."

Hunter said he just ignores the talk. "It doesn't bother me when I hear that," he said. And then he went on to prove it by retelling, with obvious relish, a story about the time he shut out the Milwaukee Brewers and manager Dave Bristol reacted by calling a clubhouse meeting after the game. "For 10 minutes he just repeated my name," Hunter said. "Then he said, 'Catfish Hunter, my ear. If you can't hit him you can't hit anybody.' "

Munson, for one, can vouch that it's harder than it looks. "He throws a ball where he wants to," said Munson. "And he's got a lot of guts. He challenges the hitter. He doesn't have an overpowering fastball but it sneaks up on you. The most important thing about a pitch is the last 10-to-15 feet. His ball moves enough so it's hard to pick up.

"There's a lot of comfortable 0-for-4 pitchers in this league. He doesn't scare you out there but he's tough. I always had trouble with him. He gets you out."

Which is, of course, the idea. "Nothing mysterious about him," says Baltimore manager Earl Weaver. "He just throws strikes." In one game a few years ago, it has been reliably reported, Hunter went four and one-third innings without throwing one pitch which was called a ball.

"I try to get a guy to hit the first pitch," he said. "Some guys are nibbling all the time. A lot of guys like to strike out everybody. I can't stand to get out there and mess around."

He has been at his best in big games. Baseball people called him a money pitcher even before the Yankees got around to making it official. "He doesn't feel that much pressure out there," Green said. "He just doesn't."

Hunter acknowledged as much. "A lot of players sit around and think about those games," he said. "A night before a game I like to go out and have a good time. I like to swing a bat and shoot the bull before a game. I can't sit in a corner and worry about what I'm going to throw this guy or that guy. When I get on the mound, that's when I think about it."

All the pre-season talk assumed that Hunter, the millionaire, would be the same pitcher he was while he slaved for Finley. "I don't think anything's going to change this boy's thinking or his desire for the game," Kluttz said. "Some people get the idea he got the money and now the hell with it. He's not going to have that attitude.

"In the negotiations, he told me one club offered him a $300,000 salary. He told me, 'I don't want to be paid $300,000 a year. I don't want to sit on a pedestal. I don't think any ballplayer deserves $300,000 a year.' That's Jimmy Hunter. At that New Year's Eve press conference, someone asked him what would happen if he shot off another toe while hunting. He said, 'Then I'll pitch with eight.' And he would, too. That's the determination he has."

"He's a beautiful person to know," Ed Charles said. "His head is not going to leave his shoulders. His attitude? He'll blend right in. He's a good man to have on any team."

"I like to get out there and win," Hunter said. "I win with control. I used to listen to Frankie Frisch say, 'Control, control, control, that's the name of the game.' I used to think, 'Now what does that man know about it.' I found out he knew a lot."

Control, control, control . . .

Catfish Hunter began his baseball life anew in 1975 as a member of the Yankees, who came up with a lucrative contract to sign him up after he had been declared a free agent. Hunter spent 10 seasons with the A's, first in Kansas City and then in Oakland, winning 161 games for them. In 1968, he pitched a perfect game, a 4-0 no-hitter, against the Minnesota Twins.